BEFORE THE STORM

THEODOR FONTANE (1819–98) was born in Neuruppin, Brandenburg, of a Huguenot family, but spent most of his long life in Berlin. His father was a pharmacist and until he was thirty Fontane pursued the same career; but in 1850, the year of his marriage, he abandoned this and all other regular employment to devote himself entirely to writing. During the following half-century he published an enormous quantity of journalism and miscellaneous writing, the best-known of which is the four-volume *Wanderungen durch die Mark Brandenburg* (1862–82). From 1855 to 1859 he lived in London, supporting himself and his family as a correspondent for German magazines and newspapers, and visited Scotland, which he described in *Jenseit des Tweed*. During the 1860s he reported the wars of the Bismarck era and employed the material he gathered in many 'war books': this period came to a climax and conclusion with the Franco-Prussian War of 1870, in which he was for three months a prisoner of the French. Between 1870 and 1890 he was a theatre critic for the *Vossische Zeitung*. Throughout his life he never ceased to publish poetry, the first collected edition of which appeared in 1851 and the fifth in the year of his death. But it was not until 1878, when he was fifty-nine, that he found his true vocation with the publication of his first novel, *Vor dem Sturm*; and this and the sixteen further novels that followed at the rate of one a year established him as one of the foremost German writers of his time and one of the great realist novelists of the late nineteenth century.

R. J. HOLLINGDALE has published eleven volumes of translations of Nietzsche and two books about him, and the article on Nietzsche to ... also published translations ... Schopenhauer and E. T. ... *Guardian* in London.

THE WORLD'S CLASSICS

THEODOR FONTANE
Before the Storm
A Novel of the Winter of 1812–13

Translated and edited with an Introduction by
R. J. HOLLINGDALE

Oxford   New York
OXFORD UNIVERSITY PRESS
1985

Oxford University Press, Walton Street, Oxford OX2 6DP

London New York Toronto
Delhi Bombay Calcutta Madras Karachi
Kuala Lumpur Singapore Hong Kong Tokyo
Nairobi Dar es Salaam Cape Town
Melbourne Auckland

and associated companies in
Beirut Berlin Ibadan Mexico City Nicosia

Oxford is a trade mark of Oxford University Press

Before the Storm first published 1878
This translation first published 1985
Introduction, Further reading, Translation, Chronology, list of Principal characters and Notes
© R. J. Hollingdale 1985

British Library Cataloguing in Publication Data

Fontane, Theodor
Before the storm.—(The World's classics)
I. Title   II. Vor dem Sturm, English
833'.8[F]   PT1863.V6
ISBN 0-19-281649-7

Set by Wyvern Typesetting Ltd.
Printed in Great Britain by
Hazell Watson & Viney Limited
Aylesbury, Bucks

CONTENTS

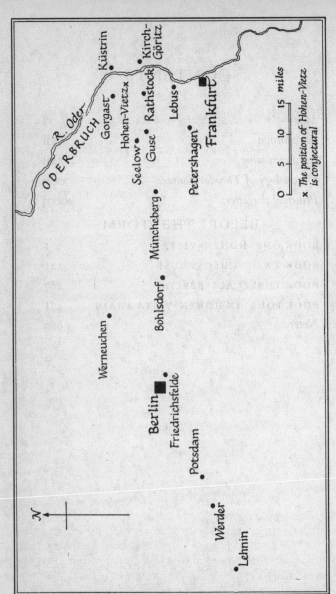

PART OF BRANDENBURG

The position of Hohen-Vietz is conjectural

0   5   10   15 miles

INTRODUCTION

AIDED as we are by the development the art of the novel has undergone during the century and more that has passed since *Before the Storm* was first published, we are in a better position to read it with ease and understanding than its first readers seem to have been. By the year 1878 Fontane was in possession of a large reputation—as a poet, as a travel writer, as a reviewer and, most recently, as an author of 'war books'—but he had not yet appeared before the public in the role that was subsequently to supersede all others, that of novelist; and when the first chapters of *Vor dem Sturm* began to appear in the pages of the magazine *Daheim* it seemed to many well-wishers that it was no accident that he had attained to the age of fifty-nine without publishing a novel, for it seemed to be a form for which he had little aptitude. The appearance of the completed work in book form later the same year seemed to confirm rather than confound the initial criticisms.

On the face of it, *Before the Storm* was a historical novel modelled, in a general sense, on the historical novels of Walter Scott, and more immediately on those of the still popular novelist Willibald Alexis, who had between 1832 and 1856 produced a series of eight novels dealing with episodes in the history of Prussia and, in particular, Brandenburg, one of which, *Isegrimm* (1854), treated in fictional form the same events as those treated in *Before the Storm*: where the two novels differed, however, they seemed to differ to the disadvantage of Fontane, inasmuch as, though Alexis had not been a notably concise writer, he was concision itself compared with Fontane, who had employed some 700 pages to narrate a story reducible in its essence to a couple of paragraphs. The technique by which this feat had been achieved was to all appearance that which had characterized his most popular publication, the *Travels through the March of Brandenburg*, the first volume of which had appeared in 1862 and the third and most recent in 1873 (a fourth and final volume was to appear in 1882); and that technique was the singular one of relinquishing all ambition for shape or directionality and allowing the course of the text to be determined entirely by what reflection, story, piece of history or topographical or architectural description happened to enter the author's mind (or even, indeed, to be lying on his desk) at any particular moment. So far as the *Travels* itself is concerned, the effect produced by this manner of presentation is that of an endlessly knowledgeable and eloquent *raconteur* who is willing to go on talking for as long as you are willing to listen to him; and the book is designed for, and made its essential appeal to, an age in which reading for entertainment occupied a larger part of civilized life than it does now; whether such informality and prolixity could be applied successfully to a 'historical novel' supposedly telling a story was, however, something that *Before the Storm* seemed to call into question. To many the book was, simply, a failure.

The objective facts about the novel do indeed seem to second that judgement. It is very long, yet the time-span covered by the events it depicts is, especially for a 'historical novel', very short: it commences on 24 December 1812 and the last ascertainable date is 7 February 1813, a period of just over six weeks. The action contained in this six-week period is divided into no fewer than eighty-one chapters (with an eighty-second chapter as an epilogue), which suggests an uncommonly large amount of action: yet, until the final quarter of the book, there is hardly any action at all—so little, indeed, that when so relatively trivial an incident as the nocturnal break-in at the manor house at Hohen-Vietz occurs in the thirty-first chapter the author entitles the chapter 'Something Happens'. Again, the novel neglects, as though on purpose, every kind of event which might of itself have caught the interest of the reader of a historical novel: Napoleon haunts its edges but, except in the context of brief recollections, never steps on to its stage; the surrender of York at Tauroggen is reported but not witnessed or described; the centre and possessors of power whose decisions and actions are a vital element of the story are heard of but never seen (the closest we come to the domain of government is the very aged and, by his own admission, wholly ineffectual Prince Ferdinand); the Wars of Liberation start a short time after the novel stops. But if nothing is happening, either of a public or a private nature, what is the author filling all these dozens of chapters with?

Now, Fontane was himself aware what answer his first readers would give to this question. Writing to his wife, Emilie, on 29 August 1877, he reported that he was then engaged in correcting 'my celebrated Borodino chapter', which, he added, 'the critics of my novel, my wife included, will no doubt pronounce superfluous.' The chapter—Book III, Chapter 11—is devoted to a reading by a Captain von Meerheimb of an account of the Battle of Borodino as he experienced it. His audience is composed of the guests a retired cavalry captain, von Jürgass, has invited to lunch; the preceding chapter includes, in addition to a record of the conversation accompanying this lunch, the text of Jürgass's aunt's last will and testament, in which she bequeaths to him the wealth that enables him to live in the style in which he has been depicted as living, and a retelling of a story of a regimental escapade of Jürgass's youth. A large part of the lunchtime conversation is taken up by an excursus on the names of the kings of Denmark. The chapter which follows the Borodino chapter includes a translation, by one of the novel's central figures, Lewin von Vitzewitz, of a 14-line French nursery rhyme, together with his landlady's reaction when he reads it to her. Wherever we look in the novel, in fact, we find page after page that its critics did indeed find 'superfluous': the extended discussion of the merits of the inferior poet Pastor Schmidt of Werneuchen, for example (Book I, Chapter 15); or Aunt Schorlemmer's recollections of her life as a Herrnhut missionary in Greenland (Book II, Chapter 16); or the playbill, reproduced in French, for the New Year's Eve dramatic performance at Schloss Guse (Book II, Chapter 19); or the visit to Lehnin abbey and a second lunch with Jürgass (Book III, Chapter 15); or the story of the Woman in White (Book IV, Chapter 12); or the poems of Novalis, Hölderlin, John Prince and others inserted into the text; or, more generally, the large quantity of apparently gratuitous information to be encountered everywhere and the long stretches of apparently aimless talk (about half the novel's text is talk). When these were not pronounced simple superfluities, they were accounted for as a product of the author's need to pad out a very thin plot, or, more concretely, to fill in the space between Berndt von Vitzewitz's announcement to his son that he intends to act against the supposedly defeated and demoralized Napoleon on his own account if the government does not act against him (Book I, Chapter 4) and the execution of this threat (Book IV, Chapters 17–19): the outcome, on either supposition, being a repetition of the style of the *Travels through the March of Brandenburg* in a place where something a lot more rigorous and purposeful would have been much more in order.

Fontane, however, considered criticism in this direction unjustified; he believed that the purpose of his novel, and therefore its form, had been misunderstood. One critic who seemed to have misunderstood it was the writer and poet Paul Heyse, and to him Fontane wrote a defence of *Before the Storm*. 'Do you not think', he said in a letter of 9 December 1878,

that, beside novels, such as for example 'Copperfield', in which we view a human life from its beginning onwards, there is not also a place for those which bring under the magnifying-glass, not a single individual, but the manifold forms of a whole epoch? In such a case, can a multiplicity not become a unity? The greater dramatic interest will, I concede, always remain with stories 'with *one* hero'; but the multiple novel [*Vielheitsroman*], with all its latitude and delayings, with its mass of portraits and episodes, will be able to stand beside the unitary novel [*Einheitsroman*] as an equal—not in its effect but in its art—provided it does not proceed arbitrarily but introduces only those retardations which, while they seem for the moment to have forgotten the goal and purpose of the work, are actually furthering it. Not you, but others have told me the novel is weak in its construction; I believe quite sincerely that, on the contrary, it is in this direction that its strength lies.

Any suspicion that this miniature manifesto was in reality conceived after the deed it purports to explain had already been done is dispelled when we consider what a *Vielheitsroman* would look like in any concrete case and then examine Fontane's practice in the novels he wrote after *Before the Storm*. The chief respect in which a *Vielheitsroman* would differ from an *Einheitsroman* would clearly lie in the region of everything we summarize in the word 'plot': a novel 'with *one* hero' would naturally tend to be a novel with one 'plot' centred on the 'hero' and, since the hero would, if he was to remain the hero, have to be present on the page for the greater part of the novel, the greater part of the novel would tend to be in some sense concerned with the plot; a novel which sought to 'bring the manifold forms of a whole epoch under the magnifying-glass', on the other hand, would possess either a very large number of plots evolving side by side or a single but very attenuated plot which would often be lost sight of (in an extreme case it would have no plot at all). Now, since Fontane devised the term *Vielheitsroman* for the purpose of characterizing *Before the Storm*, we shall not be precisely surprised to discover that it is one: it does possess a plot, and the kind of plot we would expect to find in a 'historical novel', but its plot is stretched out into an exceedingly thin line which is for long periods all but obliterated by attendant—'superfluous'—material possessing only an indirect, sometimes very indirect, bearing on it; the word 'superfluous' belongs, however, within ironical quotation-marks because this material would be truly superfluous only if the novel were a failed *Einheitsroman*. That this is not the case seems to be proved by an examination of Fontane's subsequent novels. At the opposite end of the scale so far as size is concerned stands his fifth novel, *Schach von Wuthenow*, which compares with *Before the Storm* as Mercury does with Jupiter; yet, despite the vast difference in scale, and also despite the fact that the later novel, unlike the earlier, does have a single central figure or 'hero', the general structure or form is the same in both: in *Schach von Wuthenow*, too, the plot, in itself the briefest of anecdotes, is for three-quarters of the novel all but overwhelmed by 'superfluous' matter and comes through to determine the course of the narrative only in the final quarter. Its diminutive scale notwithstanding, *Schach von Wuthenow* too is a *Vielheitsroman*.

Schach is also a historical novel, but the tendency to suppress plot in favour of a wide-angled view of a whole society is not limited to this particular *genre*. Fontane published four novels having at their centre the theme of adultery and set in the then contemporary world (mostly Berlin): his third novel,

L'Adultera, his eighth, *Cécile*, his twelfth, *Unwiederbringlich*, and his fourteenth, *Effi Briest*; they all possess far less plot than *Madame Bovary*, which was on its appearance regarded as having diminished the element of connected story to an irreducible minimum (a view held perhaps by Flaubert himself), and contain many pages whose relevance to the main theme is tangential—*Cécile* is especially remarkable for the paucity of its action and the apparent 'superfluity' of most of its contents. The sixteenth and last completed novel, *Der Stechlin*, finally —nineteen years after *Before the Storm*—has in the accepted sense of the word no plot at all, unless the fact that the lord of the manor, Dubslav von Stechlin, is growing old and his son, Waldemar, is growing up is to be considered a plot.

What all this goes to show is that the form of Fontane's first novel was the outcome not of a blunder on the part of a writer venturing into a new medium, but of a basic disposition in him. For it is clear from his practice that, of the great realist novelists of the nineteenth century, Fontane is the one most embarrassed by the necessity of articulating a novel by means of a chronological plot; the construction of an original story the telling of which is to be the ostensible purpose of the narrative was not merely something for which he had little liking, it was also something that worked directly against his actual artistic purpose in composing a novel, which had to do with the reproduction, and thus preservation, of the life and real presence of a particular society in a particular epoch—for it hardly needs to be said that 'real life' is not composed of plots, or that the element of plot is the most artificial element in the nineteenth-century realist novel. Thus, while *Before the Storm* tells a story, the purpose of the novel is achieved within the interstices of the story; the immense space between the threat of a popular uprising and its execution is filled not with superfluous matter or padding, but for the most part with the novel itself.

To read *Before the Storm* with understanding requires, therefore, only that we do not confuse *plot* with *theme*. When, in her chapter on *Bleak House* in *Dickens the Novelist* (1970), Q. D. Leavis says of its plot that it is 'not altogether identical with the theme though not, as in *Oliver Twist, Nicholas Nickleby* and *The*

Old Curiosity Shop, simply irrelevant to it and a nuisance', she brings out clearly the distinction between plot and theme in the case of the novelist cited by Fontane himself as being in an important respect his opposite, at any rate as regards the structure of *Before the Storm*. Dickens's plots are, of course, at the other end of the spectrum from Fontane's; but once we distinguish plot from theme, the two novelists are seen to be as similarly inclined with respect to quantity of thematic content as they are different from one another with respect to quantity of plot.

Fontane took a very long time to complete his first novel. There are indications that he already had it in mind as early as 1854—the year of Alexis's *Isegrimm*—and a firm idea as to what it was to be like may well have come to him during the second half of 1860, when he was writing the *Wanderungen* chapters on Schloss Gusow and Schloss Friedersdorf, for the former is the Schloss Guse of the novel and the latter the residence of the Marwitz family (see notes to pp. 123 and 23). He began serious work on the novel in the winter of 1863–4, and on 14 November 1865 signed a contract for its publication. It was then called *Lewin von Vitzewitz*. Work was now interrupted by Fontane's war reporting, and a long period elapsed before it was resumed: the fact is evident from the quite marked improvement in narrative style from Book II onwards as compared with the more immature manner of the first book. When at long last he resolved to complete it he worked reasonably fast: between the late autumn of 1876 and September 1877 he continued it to the end of Book III, and Book IV followed between October 1877 and April 1878, by which time the earlier chapters were already appearing in *Daheim*. The complete novel was published in two volumes in October and November: Fontane oversaw the proofs, and the text of this first edition is thus regarded as authoritative.

The somewhat cool critical reception it initially received, the main thrust of which was, as already indicated, that it exhibited '*Kompositionslosigkeit*'—that it lacked structure—has given way in the present century to a willingness to see it as belonging to the same *genre* as Tostoy's *War and Peace*: not, that is to say, as an overlong and too slackly constructed 'historical novel', but as a novel depicting a whole society at a particularly 'historic' moment of the past.

With the plot of *Before the Storm*, which concerns the inter-linked histories of two families, the von Vitzewitzes of Hohen-Vietz and the von Ladalinskis of Berlin, the reader will experience no difficulty; with its theme, however, which is the coming into being of modern Germany, some assistance may perhaps be welcome. The problem to be faced is that of the very large number of historical and other references contained in the novel, some knowledge of which is both assumed in the reader and necessary for a full understanding of its theme. There are many scores of different names—of people high and low, of cities, towns and villages, of provinces and counties, of streets and squares, of palaces, churches, inns and restaurants, of regiments and battles, of forests and rivers, of nations and races, of plays, books and paintings—in *Before the Storm*; I have included some of them in the annotations at the end of the book, but not all: in general I have offered a note only when knowledge of some particular fact or detail seemed to me relevant to a full understanding of the novel. With a very few exceptions, most of which are noted, all the names are of real people, places and things; some of the chief characters derive some of their characteristics from people who lived in the period in which the novel is set, though in no case is there anything approaching an exact correspondence; and the course of events in the public sphere is approximately historical. Because of the importance of warfare in the novel's scheme I have taken care to date all the battles mentioned and to indicate very briefly who fought them; and I have also annotated other more remote historical events referred to. But there are, in addition, a number of recurring or background themes which I feel the reader could usefully have in the front rather than at the back of the book, so that their significance will already be clear when they are encountered. There are six general topics that fall under this head.

1. *The colonization of the March*. The term 'March' (German *Mark*) is synonymous with the term 'the province of

Brandenburg', which came into existence as the march or borderland of the medieval German empire. The course of German colonization of the territory is indicated by the regional names Altmark (west and east of the Elbe), Mittelmark (between the Elbe and the Oder) and Neumark (east of the Oder). This process of conquest and colonization began in earnest in 1134 under the leadership of Albrecht I, called the Bear; Albrecht's heirs bore the name Ascanians, and they died out in Brandenburg in 1319. The conquests of Albrecht the Bear had, however, been preceded in the tenth century by an unsuccessful attempt to colonize the March which had been defeated by its inhabitants, a nation of Slavic tribes called by the Germans 'the Wends': at first overborne and reduced to a colonial population, the Wends organized a mighty uprising in 983, destroyed the German civilization that had been erected on top of them and drove what remained of the Germans back across the Elbe. After this rout, German colonization of the March did not resume until the twelfth century. Reference to the Wends is frequent in *Before the Storm*, often to assert the Wendishness of many things mistakenly thought to be German; in particular, however, they are the basis of the theme of Pastor Seidentopf's obsession. In Seidentopf, the pastor of Hohen-Vietz, the awakening of national feeling that is the underlying theme of the whole novel has assumed the form of a historical delusion: the theory that the Wends whom the Germans encountered when they invaded the March had themselves invaded it at a much earlier period and displaced a German civilization already in existence there, that of the 'Semnones'; from which supposed fact it would follow that when Brandenburg was taken from the Slavs this was no more than the restitution to the Germans of land originally theirs. This thesis could be established only through archaeology, and Seidentopf has thus become obsessed with the need to discover archaeological evidence of the pre-Wendish existence of a Semnonian civilization in the March. As the Semnones were, in historical fact, no more than a backward Germanic tribe which lingered on after the Wends had moved into the region in about 500 and established in it the first advanced form of civilization it had ever seen, Seidentopf's cranky researches are a rich source of comedy. (A community of 'Wends' still exists as a distinct entity in East Germany, where they are known as Sorbs.)

2. *The reign of Friedrich the Great*. Friedrich II, called the Great and, more familiarly, 'Old Fritz', was King of Prussia from 1740 to 1786. References to his reign permeate *Before the Storm*: in recollection it appears as the 'great age' of Prussian history and, as such, the antithesis to the age of defeat and national humiliation in which everyone is now living. Friedrich himself is evoked dozens of times as a model king and by implication (once directly) contrasted with Napoleon. Of his many battles two are of particular significance: Kunersdorf (12 August 1759), in which he sustained a defeat at the hands of the Russians and Austrians from which it seemed he could not possibly recover (thus a parallel with the Battle of Jena), and Torgau (3 November 1760), in which he won a victory over the Austrians after supposedly having rallied the wavering Prussian grenadiers with the most celebrated of the many remarks attributed to him: 'You rascals, do you want to live for ever, then?' Of his works of peace the one most relevant to the novel, and the one most often recalled, is the draining of the Oderbruch. Sometimes called simply 'the Bruch', the Oderbruch is the fenland and marsh area to both sides of the Oder where it passes through Brandenburg; during the period of reconstruction that followed the Seven Years War (1756–63) large areas of the Bruch were drained and made suitable for agriculture. It was an improvement which led to a considerable influx of 'foreigners', such as the inn-keeping family the Scharwenkas, who cultivated the former fenlands, previously ownerless, and enriched themselves in doing so. The immigration was so considerable that by 1786 the number of new settlers had more or less compensated for the losses of the war (usually put at 300,000). Hohen-Vietz is in the Oderbruch, as are Hohen-Ziesar and Schloss Guse. The owner of this last, Aunt Amelie, is representative of another side of the reign of Friedrich the Great of relevance to the novel: its overestimation of French culture to the detriment of German. This effect proceeded from Friedrich himself, to whom the language, literature and life of France were superior in almost every way

to those of Prussia, and whose court at Potsdam evolved accordingly. The influence it exercised involved two distinct elements: on the one hand, it encouraged an appreciation of that in which France at that time clearly was superior to Prussia and an ability to profit from it without the intrusion of 'nationalist' feelings of resentment; on the other, however, it led to an unintelligent overvaluation of all things French merely because they were French. It is this latter element that is most strongly marked in Aunt Amelie. We learn immediately on being introduced to her that, although her native language is German, she is ignorant of Klopstock's *Messias* though she has passages of Voltaire's *Henriade* by heart. Later she is shown preferring Lemierre's dramatization of the life of William Tell to Schiller's, and this for a performance before a German audience at the end of 1812. In both cases the worse is elevated above the better for no other reason than that it is French. Above all, she is quite unable to enter into, or even understand, the mood of patriotic revival that is beginning to animate the country, since she is quite unable to feel anti-French. This bias has been powerfully reinforced by her years of residence at Rheinsberg, the court of Friedrich's disaffected younger brother, Prince Heinrich of Prussia (1726–1802), where French was spoken habitually (Heinrich himself is always represented as speaking it). A direct link with the Friedrician age is provided in the figure of Friedrich's youngest brother, Prince Ferdinand (1730–1813), of whom Fontane paints a very sympathetic portrait (Book III, Chapter 1).

3. *The Revolutionary and Napoleonic Wars*. Of the incidents of the Revolutionary and Napoleonic Wars that occurred before the novel opens and are referred to in it the following are of special thematic significance. At the *Peace of Basel* (5 April 1795), concluded between Prussia and France, Prussia agreed to desert the anti-French coalition. In the same year Prussia participated with Russia in the so-called *Third Partition of Poland* which temporarily erased Poland from the map; Warsaw became a Prussian city and the population of Prussia was increased to 7.5 million by the addition of 3.5 million Poles. These two actions, both of which proved to have been exceedingly ill-judged, are part of the background of the disapproval

of Prussian behaviour voiced by some of the leading characters of the novel. The *double battle of Jena and Auerstädt* (14 October 1806) ended in the total defeat of the combined forces of Prussia and Saxony by the French under Napoleon; the defeat was succeeded by headlong flight, armies and fortresses surrendered without resistance, and Berlin was evacuated by the government and left undefended; Napoleon rode into it unimpeded on 27 October: recollection of these events is part of the common consciousness of the whole population of *Before the Storm* and they are repeatedly recalled; to some they constitute a punishment for the policies pursued from 1795 onwards. The *retreat from Moscow* in the autumn of 1812 is the event from which the action of the novel takes its start: it began with the conflagration of Moscow, ignited by the Russians themselves on 14 to 16 September, which deprived Napoleon of any means of sustaining himself in the heart of Russia, and by Christmas the remnants of the Grande Armée were approaching Brandenburg (how far they are away is a subject of much confident but ill-informed debate); the 29th communiqué that is the cause of so much agitation is the bulletin from Napoleon's headquarters, dated 3 December 1812 and published in Paris on the 16th, which more or less admits the failure of the Russian campaign.

4. *Three acts of rebellion*. The failure of the *coup* of 20 July 1944 is ultimately attributable to the extreme difficulty experienced by members of the German officer corps in acting against their commander-in-chief, even if he is Adolf Hitler: rebellion is something against which their instincts rebel and for which they have no training or aptitude. When Berndt von Vitzewitz, a major in the Prussian Army, none the less resolves to lead a popular rebellion against the French without the sanction of the government—an act which, as he freely admits, could be construed as high treason—his resolution is in need of support. It is provided by three acts of rebellion against the constituted authority in Prussia—two in the immediate past, one during the course of the novel—that are alluded to with a *leitmotiv*-like brevity that makes it certain Fontane expected his reader to grasp their significance without the need for explanation. The earliest is that associated with the name *Schill*. Ferdinand von

Schill (1776–1809), a major in the Prussian Army, was so incensed by the policy pursued by the government following the defeat at Jena in October 1806, and by the humiliations heaped upon the head of Prussia at the Peace of Tilsit in June 1807, that later during the latter year he formed an irregular cavalry unit of his own with the intention of continuing the war against Napoleon on a freelance basis. In May 1809, in what became a celebrated gesture of rebellion, he led this force, numbering about a hundred men, directly from the parade-ground at Berlin northwards towards Mecklenburg with the stated objective of joining the English army installed there; on the 31st he arrived in the Baltic port of Stralsund, where he was encountered by Dutch and Danish troops and fell fighting in the streets. This action at once made of Schill a national hero—as witness the presence of his portrait at the inn at Hohen-Vietz—but also gave actuality to the question whether behaviour of this kind was or was not under all circumstances reprehensible. The second act of rebellion was the *resignation of the three hundred officers*: a famous act of independence and insubordination on the part of members of the Prussian officer corps. It occurred in March 1812 as a protest against the agreement signed with Napoleon under which Prussia was to furnish 20,000 troops—about half the number it was allowed to possess under the terms of the Peace of Tilsit—to Napoleon's projected campaign against Russia. Other provisions of the agreement included the restoration in Prussia of full French military occupation (designed, of course, to protect the rear of the Grande Armée, but felt as a new and gratuitous humiliation). Clausewitz, Boyen and Gneisenau were among those who resigned; Scharnhorst wanted to retire from service and, when refused permission to do so, relinquished the post of chief of the general staff. Altogether about a quarter of the officer corps was involved in the mutiny; and many compounded their offence by enlisting in the Russian service and taking to the field in defence of Russia—an act which, since the invading army included 20,000 Prussians, could be looked upon as waging a species of civil war. The third act of rebellion is that summarized in the novel by Ladalinski's announcement '*York has capitulated*.' Ludwig Count York von Wartenburg

(1759–1830), a field marshal in the Prussian Army, was in command of the Prussian auxiliary force furnished to Napoleon's Russian campaign; in December 1812 this force was engaged in covering the retreat out of Russia of the northern French army corps under Macdonald when, without having been ordered to do so and without warning anyone first, he withdrew it from the war and, at a convention signed with the Russians at Tauroggen on 30 December, declared the troops serving under him to be neutral. This was the most signal act of insubordination in Prussian history and, in the context of the moment, next door to a *coup d'état*, inasmuch as it virtually compelled the government in Berlin to take the logical next step and declare war on France (which it did on 16 March 1813).

5. *The Proclamation*. From the way in which it is discussed in the novel, the 'Proclamation' on which so many hopes are pinned must surely be the King's address headed 'To my People' ('*An mein Volk*'), the first official appeal to popular patriotism in the history of Prussia; if so, however, it has been displaced chronologically, for when it is promulgated we are still at the beginning of February 1813 and the 'Proclamation' was not issued until 17 March, the day after Prussia had declared war on France. There was a series of earlier proclamations, beginning on 3 February, but these were of far more limited import and do not seem to be what the characters in *Before the Storm* have been reading and listening to; certainly the address '*An mein Volk*' is what Fontane's first readers would have understood by 'the Proclamation'.

6. *Berlin*. At the beginning of the nineteenth century it possessed a population of about 170,000. The kingdom of Prussia came into existence in 1701, and Berlin, the capital of Brandenburg, became the capital of the new kingdom in 1709. The somewhat austere but on the whole clean and spacious appearance it presented at the date of *Before the Storm* was acquired largely during the reign of the second Prussian king, the years 1713 to 1740. The third king, Friedrich the Great, had the medieval walls removed, though the gates remained. Expansion failed to follow, however, and the villages around the city, now merely the names of suburbs, remained intact;

Brandenburg as a whole remained overwhelmingly rural. Of the great grey architecture which the name Berlin probably brings before the reader's eye there was as yet no trace: 'Alt-Berlin', Old Berlin, was a city of medieval survivals, Gothic churches and, in its newest portions, a species of baroque, contained in an area not very much larger than that occupied by Brighton.

FURTHER READING

THE text of *Vor dem Sturm* that served as the basis of the present translation is that contained in Fontane's *Werke, Schriften und Briefe*, edited by Walter Keitel and Helmuth Nürnberger and published by Hanser Verlag, Munich (2nd edn, 1971). Together with Keitel and Nürnberger's extensive and informative apparatus and annotations it is reprinted in pocket-size format and soft covers by the Deutscher Taschenbuch Verlag, Munich (1980). For anyone who wished to attempt the novel in German I cannot think any edition could be preferred to this one.

Readers who, having enjoyed *Before the Storm*, would like to read other of Fontane's novels in English might try the following modern translations:

Beyond Recall (Unwiederbringlich): translated with an introduction by Douglas Parmée (Oxford University Press, 1964)

A Man of Honour (Schach von Wuthenow): translated with an introduction and notes by E. M. Valk (Unger, 1975)

Jenny Treibel: translated with an introduction and notes by Ulf Zimmermann (Unger, 1976)

Effi Briest: translated with an introduction by Douglas Parmée (Penguin, 1976)

The Woman Taken in Adultery (L'Adultera) and *The Poggenpuhl Family (Die Poggenpuhls)*: translated by Gabriele Annan, with an introduction by Erich Heller (Chicago University Press, 1979)

No selection of Fontane's letters exists in English, so far as I know; for the reader who can attempt German the most rewarding selection would be the two volumes devoted to Fontane in Heimeran's series *Dichter über ihre Dichtungen* (edited by Richard Brinkmann, Munich, 1973), which contain letters and extracts from letters relating to the author's works. The most recent biographical study in English is A. R. Robinson: *Theodor Fontane: an Introduction to the Man and his Work* (University of Wales Press, Cardiff, 1978).

Recent studies in English of Fontane's work are contained in the following:

J. P. Stern: *Reinterpretations* (London, 1964) and *Idylls and Realities* (London, 1971)

Henry C. Hatfield: *Crisis and Continuity in Modern German Fiction* (Cornell University Press, 1966)

Gertrude Michielsen: *The Preparation of the Future: Techniques of Anticipation in the Novels of Theodor Fontane and Thomas Mann* (Lang, Berne, 1978)

R. Geoffrey Leckey: *Some Aspects of Balladesque Art and their Relevance for the Novels of Theodor Fontane* (Lang, Berne, 1979)

Helen Elizabeth Chambers: *Supernatural and Irrational Elements in the Works of Theodor Fontane* (Heinz, Stuttgart, 1980)

Henry Garland: *The Berlin Novels of Theodor Fontane* (Oxford, Clarendon Press, 1980)

By far the greater part of the scholarly and critical work on Fontane is of course in German: a comprehensive bibliography of it will be found in Charlotte Jolles: *Theodor Fontane* (Stuttgart, 1976)

CHRONOLOGY OF THEODOR FONTANE

1819   Henri Theodor Fontane born in Neuruppin, Brandenburg (30 December). Ancestors on both sides are Huguenots. His father is a pharmacist. (The name was originally Fontaine; the 'i' was dropped, and the accent placed on the first syllable, to make it more German, but the final 'e' remained silent: *Font*aan.)

1827   The family—including four children, Theo, Rudolf, Jenny and Max—move to Swinemünde, on the Baltic coast.

1832   Fontane returns to Neuruppin to attend school.

1833   He goes for the first time to Berlin, where he is to spend much of his life, to attend technical college with the object of following his father's trade.

1836   He enters a Berlin pharmacy as an apprentice pharmacist.

1839   He begins his literary career with the publication in the *Berliner Figaro* of a story, 'Geschwisterliebe'; he also begins to associate with Berlin literary clubs, the best-known of which, the Tunnel über der Spree (the Kastalia of *Before the Storm*), he joins in 1843.

1840–3   He works in a succession of pharmacies in Burg, near Magdeburg, Leipzig, Dresden and again in Berlin; his earliest poems, many of them political, are written and published in magazines; and he commences to work as a journalist, producing a stream of political and occasional articles, dramatic and literary reviews and critiques of art exhibitions, for the rest of his life.

1844–5   He does a year's military service. From 25 May to 10 June 1844 he pays his first visit to London.

1848   He participates in the Berlin revolution of 18 March as a fighter on the barricades; the failure of the revolution greatly diminishes his interest in conventional politics.

1849 Fontane deserts the pharmacy, and all other regular employment, to attempt to support himself as a freelance journalist, reviewer and poet.

1850 *Von der schönen Rosamunde* and *Männer und Helden*, collections of poems, published. Fontane marries Emilie Fouanet-Kummer, to whom he has been engaged for five years. They will have three sons and a daughter.

1851 *Gedichte*, his first collected edition of poems, published (five editions will be published during his lifetime).

1852 He visits London again (23 April–25 September).

1854 *Ein Sommer in London* published.

1855–9 Fontane lives in England, chiefly London, and supports himself and his family by writing. He also visits Scotland.

1860 *Aus England* and *Jenseit des Tweed* published.

1861 *Balladen* published.

1862 The first volume of *Wanderungen durch die Mark Brandenburg* published. Three more appear between 1863 and 1882.

1864 Fontane travels to Schleswig-Holstein and Denmark in pursuit of his new career as war correspondent.

1866 *Der Schleswig-Holsteinische Krieg im Jahre 1864* published. He visits the battlefields of the German War of 1866 in Bohemia and south Germany.

1870 *Der deutsche Krieg von 1866* I published. On a visit to the front (the Franco-Prussian War of 1870–1) he is taken prisoner at Domrémy and interned for three months.

1871 *Der deutsche Krieg* II published; also *Kriegsgefangen*, and *Aus den Tagen der Okkupation*.

1873 *Der Krieg gegen Frankreich 1870–71* I published.

PRINCIPAL CHARACTERS

IN HOHEN-VIETZ

BERNDT VON VITZEWITZ, lord of the manor of Hohen-Vietz; LEWIN, his son; and RENATE, his daughter.

AUNT SCHORLEMMER, KRIST, JEETZE and PACHALY: members of the Vitzewitz household.

KNIEHASE, the village mayor, and his foster-daughter, MARIE.

SEIDENTOPF, the village pastor.

KUBALKE, the sexton, and his daughters, EVE and MALINE.

SCHARWENKA, the innkeeper, and his son.

KÜMMERITZ (KÜMMRITZ), KALLIES, REETZKE, KRULL and MIEKLEY: farmers and residents of the village.

HOPPENMARIEKEN.

IN BERLIN

ALEXANDER VON LADALINSKI, privy councillor; TUBAL, his son; and KATHINKA, his daughter.

JÜRGASS, BUMMCKE, HANSEN-GRELL, HIMMERLICH, RABATZKI, DR SASSNITZ, HIRSCHFELDT and MEERHEIMB: friends of LEWIN in Berlin.

FRAU HULEN, Lewin's landlady; FRAU ZUNZ, FRÄULEIN LAACKE, HERR and FRAU ZIEBOLD, HERR SCHIMMELPENNING, and HERR GRÜNEBERG and his daughter, ULRIKE, friends of FRAU HULEN.

RABE, STEPPENBECK, NIEDLICH, SCHNÖKEL and KLEMM: citizens of Berlin.

COUNT BNINSKI.

AT SCHLOSS GUSE

AMELIE, COUNTESS VON PUDAGLA (Aunt Amelie), sister of BERNDT VON VITZEWITZ and sister-in-law of ALEXANDER VON LADALINSKI.

COUNT DROSSELSTEIN, MEDEWITZ, KRACH, MAJOR-GENERAL VON BAMME, RUTZE and BARON PEHLEMANN: friends of AUNT AMELIE and guests at Schloss Guse.

OTHERS

JUSTIZRAT TURGANY, of Frankfurt-on-Oder.
OTHEGRAVEN, schoolmaster, of Frankfurt.
DR FAULSTICH, of Kirch-Göritz.

BEFORE THE STORM

BOOK ONE

★

HOHEN-VIETZ

I

Christmas Eve

IT was Christmas Eve in the year 1812. A few flakes of snow were falling on to the white blanket which had for many days lain in the streets of the capital. The lamps suspended from their long chains gave only a meagre light, but inside the houses it was growing brighter minute by minute and the 'spirit of Christmas', which was here and there already putting in an appearance, also cast its glow into the darkness outside.

So it was too in the Klosterstrasse. The 'musical clock' of the parish church* was just preparing to play the first bars of its tune as a sleigh drove out of the Green Tree inn and straight-away halted on the other side of the street before a two-storey house whose tall mansard roof contained an attic room. The driver leaned forward and looked up at the topmost windows; but when he perceived that all remained quiet he descended from his seat, unharnessed the horses, walked up to the house and disappeared through the half-open door into the dark entrance hall. Anyone following him would have heard how, cautious and awkward, he stamped and stumbled his way up the three steps.

The sleigh, a simple sledge with a basket-carriage on it, stood all this while quietly in the roadway close beside the opening in a wall of snow heaped up at the roadside. The back of the basket-carriage itself was, presumably to enhance its warmth and comfort, filled to the top with straw; forward of it lay a sack of straw just wide enough to accommodate two people. Everything was as simple and primitive as it could be. And the horses too were sufficiently unpretentious: little ponies which, since they were now wearing their rough winter coats, looked unbrushed and thus to some extent neglected. Be that as it may, however, the Russian harness, and the sleigh-bells that hung across their backs on broad, red-bordered leather girdles, left it in no doubt that the vehicle came from a good house.

Five or more minutes passed before a light appeared in the entrance hall. An old woman in a white nightcap stuck her head into the street inquisitively, shielding the lamp with her hand as she did so; then the coachman emerged carrying a portmanteau and a cardboard box; and last, behind him, a tall and erect young man of a free and noble bearing. He wore a hunting-cap and a jacket and so far as his upper half was concerned was clad in a manner not at all suited to winter. On his feet, however, he wore tall felt boots. 'A merry Christmas, Frau Hulen,' he said, extending a hand to the old woman; then he mounted the sleigh and took his seat beside the coachman. 'Off we go, Krist; by midnight we shall be in Hohen-Vietz.* Papa did right to send the ponies.'

The ponies moved off and, in obedience to their nature, attempted to fall into a gentle trot; but only when they had the Königsstrasse, with its Christmas crowds and humming of *Waldteufels*,* behind them did they pick up more speed along the Landsbergerstrasse and, their bells jingling more and more merrily, finally emerge through the Frankfurter Tor.

Outside the city, night and silence embraced them; the sky cleared and the first stars came out. A light but keen east wind blew across the expanse of snow, and the hero of our story, Lewin von Vitzewitz,* who was driving to his family estate Hohen-Vietz to spend the Christmas holiday there, now turned to the companion sitting beside him and said, with a trace of the dialect of the March: 'Well, Krist, how about it? Shouldn't we light up?' He placed his thumb and forefinger against his chin and puffed with his mouth. The 'we' was only a piece of friendly familiarity: Lewin himself did not smoke. Krist, however, who had no doubt been waiting for this invitation ever since they had put the city behind them, without more ado laid the reins into his young master's hands, plunged into his coat pocket and drew from it, first a short pipe with a lead bowl, then a new packet of tobacco. He took both between his knees, opened the gum-sealed packet, filled his pipe, and then with the same slow punctiliousness began to search for match and tinder. At length the pipe was alight; retrieving the reins he began to draw on it, and as little sparks began to spit forth from beneath its lid they drove on towards

Friedrichsfeld, whose lights they could see shining from across the snow-white land.

The village soon lay behind them. Lewin, who in the meantime had made himself comfortable and by pressing a number of straw-bundles more firmly together had created something to lean on, now seemed in the mood to start a conversation—in any event it would not have been a good idea to do so before the coachman's pipe was alight.

'Has anything been happening, Krist?' Lewin began, leaning more firmly against the straw bolster. 'What has my godson, Willem, been up to?'

'He's up and about again now, young sir, thank you very much.'

'Why, what happened to him?'

'He had a nasty shock. And it was on his birthday, too. It was three weeks ago now; yes, three weeks to the day. But old Dr Leist from Lebus made him better again.'

'He had a nasty shock?'

'Yes, young sir, that's what we all think. It was about five o'clock when my wife said: "Willem, go and fetch a couple of apples, the rennets in the straw near by the beanstalks." And our Willem went and I heard him whistling and singing and the clattering of his clogs over the flagstones. But then I heard nothing more, and when he got to the old rickety door and was going to go into the big room where the apples are laid out and which people say is haunted by old Matthias something must have happened to him. He didn't come back and didn't come back; and when I went to see where he had got to, he was lying there just over the threshold, as lifeless as a stone.'

'The poor child! And your wife . . .'

'She came too, and we carried him back indoors. My wife always has a little rheumatic spirits in the house. And when he came round again his whole little body was shaking and he said over and over "I saw him." '

Lewin had pulled himself up. 'So he is better again,' he said, not knowing what else to say; and as if to dispel the thoughts and images the coachman's story had aroused in him started to inquire about all kinds of things, to which questions Krist replied in as much detail as the rapidity with which they followed one another permitted. The village mayor, Kniehase, had lost one of his bays; Hoppenmarieken had had a chimney fire; Pachaly the nightwatchman had seen a middle-sized coffin with a wreath on it standing outside Widow Gräbschen's door, 'and because it was a *middle-sized* coffin they had thought it was for the youngest, Hanna Gräbschen.'

More and more stars were coming out. Lewin lifted his cap to let the fresh winter air waft over his brow, and gazed up into the sparkling sky in amazement and reverence. He felt as though the whole dark destiny that was the inheritance of his house was falling from him and his soul was drawing light and brightness down from above. He fetched a deep breath of relief. Two or three sleighs flew past them, waving at them and singing: clearly they were guests hurrying to the festivities at the nearby village; then, not five minutes later, our friends glided beneath the gables of the inn at Bohlsdorf.

Bohlsdorf was a third of the way to Hohen-Vietz. No one came to meet them. There was no light in the windows; the innkeeper and his family must be in the back and have failed to hear the arrival of the sleigh despite the jingling of its bells. Krist paid little heed to this; he dismounted, fetched one of the troughs that stood covered in snow along the fence surrounding the yard, and shook out into it the oats for the horses.

Lewin too had dismounted. He stamped once or twice in the snow as though to set his blood circulating, and then went into the guest-room to warm himself and find something to eat. Inside all was dark and empty; but behind the counter, where three steps led to an alcove higher up, a Christmas tree glittered with lights and golden chains. In a Christmas tableau contained in the narrow space of the room there stood the innkeeper's wife in a bodice and flannel skirt with a little blond-headed child on her arm reaching out for the lights on the tree; the innkeeper himself stood beside her and gazed upon the happiness that life and this day had bestowed upon him.

Lewin was deeply moved at the sight of this tableau: it was almost as though the scene were an apparition. He retreated again more quietly than he had come in and stepped out into the village street. Opposite the inn and surrounded by a stone wall lay the church, an old Cistercian building from the days of the first colonization.★ From the church there came a sound as though someone was playing the organ, and as he stood and listened Lewin noticed that one of the little Romanesque windows that ran round the building halfway up its wall was dully illumined. Curious to know whether or not he had been deceiving himself, he climbed over the low wall and walked between the graves up to the church. In the side of the church, about halfway along its longer side, he noticed a door: it was not shut but only on the latch. He opened it softly and went in. It was as he had supposed. An old man with a velvet cap and scanty white hair was sitting before the organ, while a stump of candle beside him provided him with a meagre light. Sunk in his playing, he failed to notice that someone had come in, and the Christmas hymns continued to resound through the church, solemnly but in subdued tones, as before.

Was the old man practising for the morrow or was he celebrating his own Christmas here by himself with psalms and chorales? Lewin had hardly asked himself the question before he noticed another glimmer of light: on the bottom step of the altar stood a little house-lantern. As he approached closer he saw that a woman's hand must have recently been busy here. A hand-brush lay beside a short stepladder whose top was wound round with cloths. The light from the lamp fell on to two tombstones embedded in the paving tiles in front of the altar; the one to the left contained only a name and a date, but the one to the right had a picture and an inscription engraved in it. Two lime-trees bent their tops towards one another, and underneath them were inscribed some verses, ten or twelve lines. Only the lines of the second stanza were still clearly legible:

> She now beholds the light
> Of angels' faces bright
> Who at her service stand;
> In Heaven she raises high
> The banner of victory,
> And she can walk on stars.★

Lewin read them two or three times until he knew the stanza by heart; the last line especially had made a deep impression on him, of a kind for which he could not account. Then he looked again about the strangely illumined church, with its shadowy pillars and choir-stalls, and, softly closing the door on the latch again, he returned first to the churchyard, then, with a quick leap over the wall, to the village street.

In the meantime, the aspect of the inn had changed. There was light in the guest-room; Krist was standing beside the counter in eager conversation with the innkeeper, while the wife, emerging from the kitchen, was setting down a glass of Kirsch-punch. They carried on chatting for a while longer, among other things about the old sacristan over in the church, who since he had become a widower was accustomed to celebrate his Christmas Eve by playing the organ; then they all shook hands and wished one another a merry Christmas, and our friends departed and drove off past the silent dwellings of the village again into the night.

Lewin talked of the innkeeper and his family; Krist commended them very highly. But he thought less of the Bohlsdorf administrator, and least of all of the miller of Petershagen, past whose burned-down mill they were just driving. From all this it emerged that Krist, who travelled this road every week, preserved a faithful recollection of the chatter of all the tap rooms between Berlin and Hohen-Vietz. He knew about everything, and he ceased talking only when Lewin began to fall increasingly silent. Thereafter only brief admonitions to the horses enlivened the journey. The regular recurrence of these commands, and the monotonous jingling of the bells, which soon seemed to be sounding as though from far away, induced an increasing somnolence in our hero. Forms and figures of all kinds passed before his half-closed eyes; but one of them, the most resplendent, he took with him into his dreams. He sat before her on a low stool; she laughed at him, and when he sought for her hand to kiss it she struck him gently with her fan. A hundred candles reflected in tall mirrors burned around her, and before her there lay a great carpet upon which the goddess Venus flew through the air drawn by her doves. Then it seemed as though all these candles were suddenly extinguished; only two candle-stumps continued to burn; it was like a church full of flittering shadows, and where the carpet had lain there now lay a tombstone, and upon it the words:

In Heaven she raises high
The banner of victory,
And she can walk on stars.

The sweetness and pain these words had shortly before moved him to in reality they now again moved him to in dreams. He awoke.

'Another half mile, young sir,' said Krist.

'Then we shall be in Dolgelin?'

'No, in Hohen-Vietz.'

'Then I've had a long sleep.'

'An hour and a half.'

The first thing Lewin was aware of was the care with which the old coachman had been tending to him while he had been asleep. The sack with the horses' fodder had been pushed beneath his feet, both their blankets lay spread across his knees.

It was not long before the tower of the church at Hohen-Vietz became visible. On the highest point of a range of hills that enclosed the landscape to the east its grey mass stood like a shadow in the starry night sky.

The son of the house always felt his heart beat higher when he caught sight of this token and landmark of his home. But today he had little time in which to take pleasure in the singular qualities of this picture: the snow-laden trees of the park interposed themselves between him and the church, and a few minutes afterwards the dogs began to bark and the sleigh described a curve between a pair of gateposts and halted before the portal-like glass doors to which two broad sandstone steps led up.

Lewin, who had already risen, sprang out and strode to the steps. He was received by an old servant in gaiters and a dress-coat whose big polished buttons were the only sign that it was supposed to be livery. 'Good evening, young sir,' the servant said.

'Good evening, Jeetze. How are you?'

But Lewin did not get beyond this greeting, for at that moment a splendid Newfoundlander leaped up before him and, laying its forepaws on his shoulders, overwhelmed him with passionate embraces.

'Leave off, Hector, you'll kill me.' With these words our hero entered the hall of his ancestral house. A couple of logs still glowing in the hearth cast a gleam upon the ancient pictures on the wall opposite. Lewin gazed around him, not without a tinge of joyful pride to be standing in the home of his fathers.

Then the old servant lighted his way up the steep double staircase, while Hector followed behind.

2

Hohen-Vietz

THERE are still a few logs smouldering in the hall; let us throw some pine-cones on to them and, drawing a couple of chairs to the hearth, talk about Hohen-Vietz.

Hohen-Vietz was originally an ancient castle from the days of the last Ascanians, with walls and a moat and an open view eastwards upon the Oder. It lay on the same range of hills as the church whose shadowy image we encountered at the end of the previous chapter, and dominated the broad river as it did no less the road that leads along the left bank from Frankfurt to Küstrin. It was regarded as being very strong, and for centuries there was a rhyme which ran:

> As firm upon its seat it sits
> As Vitzewitz on Hohen-Vietz.

The Pomeranians* twice invested it; the Hussites* attacked it when they burned and ravaged the land around Lebus and Barnim,* but the Holy Virgin on the ecclesiastical banner protected the castle and when the Vitzewitz of the time, as to whose forenames differing sources fail to agree, hurled Greek fire* into the Hussites' camp they withdrew, though not before devastating all the villages in the region. The lord of the castle had brought the art of making Greek fire home with him from Rhodes, where he had participated in two campaigns against the Turks.

This was in 1432. There came more peaceful times. The high fame of Hohen-Vietz lived on, though now there was no longer any opportunity of confirming it anew. It was only with the Thirty Years War* that it was subjected to new trials, and this time to much sterner ones.

On 29 March 1631, almost exactly two hundred years after the Hussite invasion, six companies of the Imperial Army at Frankfurt* appeared before Hohen-Vietz, which had the previous day and in face of protest by the lord of the castle, Rochus von Vitzewitz, been occupied by Swedish troops advancing from Stettin and Garz. Colonel Maradas, who commanded the Imperial force, demanded that the castle surrender. When this demand was refused, the Imperial force, which was composed of two companies of the Butler Regiment, two of the Lichtenstein Regiment and two of the Maradas Regiment, set up ladders, stormed the castle, burned it down to the bare walls and put the Swedish garrison to the sword.

For a moment Rochus von Vitzewitz was in danger of sharing the garrison's fate; his two young sons, however —they were perhaps sixteen and seventeen years old—threw themselves in front of their father and rescued him through their presence of mind. Looking favourably on the young men, Colonel Maradas offered them a place in the Imperial Army, an offer which the younger of the two, Matthias, accepted with little hesitation and without opposition from his father. These were no times for brooding long over injustices, which the fortunes of war inflicted on friend and foe alike. Matthias joined the Lichtenstein Regiment as a cornet; but the elder son, Anselm, declared his intention of remaining with their father and standing by him in the rebuilding of the castle.

This rebuilding was, however, much delayed. When, after the withdrawal of the warring armies, who had now chosen south Germany for their battleground, it was supposed to begin, the unremitting depredations of war had reduced the land to such a state that the materials for building a castle simply did not exist. Rochus therefore resolved to descend from the hill of Hohen-Vietz from which his family had gazed out upon the land for three hundred years or more; and at its foot, on the northern edge of the ancient village that lay at this spot, to erect a simple manor house. This was in 1634.

Anselm assisted him in every way, and by the Sunday after Ascension, eleven months after building began, the new home of the Vitzewitzes was ready for occupation.

It was a framework house, long, low, with a tall roof. An inscription had been carved in the balcony running above the door:

> This is the Vitzewitzes' house,
> Their ancient house they had to leave;
> If God's blessing enters in
> A sure defence shall it receive.

And it almost seemed as though this inscription would be fulfilled and that in the midst of all the troubles of war that lay upon the land a new happiness could blossom in this new-established home. Of Matthias—who had transferred from the Lichtenstein to the Tiefenbach Regiment, been wounded at Nördlingen,* and six months later, barely twenty years old, had risen to the rank of captain of the Imperial Army—there arrived news which, although old Rochus was inclined to the Swedes, filled his heart with joy and pride. Without his having sought it Anselm found himself drawn to the court and joined the corps of gentlemen-at-arms in which all the Vitzewitzes had for a century served their lord, the Elector; but what inspired hope and gratitude above all else was the two wonderfully fruitful years Heaven bestowed upon the fields of Hohen-Vietz, truly magnificent harvests out of the produce of which they could now acquire the means to construct a stately addition to the house. This annexe, a single large room furnished with galleries, coats-of-arms and mounted antlers, and set at a right-angle to the dwelling-house, again revived the spirits of old Rochus, who had an exalted idea of the duties and responsibilities of his line, and reminded him of the hospitable days of old. On the first occasion he entertained the neighbouring nobility in this 'banqueting hall', as he liked to hear the annexe called, he made them a speech in which he expressed the conviction that the house of Vitzewitz would one day go 'up the hill' again and not stand for ever 'bowed before the wind'. All things, he said, had their time, even war and the ravages of war, and the day would come when his dear friends and neighbours would again be his guests up on the *heights* and with him again gaze upon the prospect to the east.

All agreed with these sentiments. But if ever words were unprophetic, these were. War returned, and hunger and pestilence with it, and destroyed either the health and well-being of the villagers or the villages themselves. Entire districts were transformed into a wilderness and half the stalls in the farm at Hohen-Vietz stood empty because their occupants had either died or fled. In the midst of this misery, before the first glimmerings of better times had dawned, Rochus closed his weary eyes, and they carried him up the hill to the crypt beneath the altar and placed the copper coffin, with its embellishments and armorial shield and a silver crucifix soldered to it, in the long row of the ancestors who had gone before him. Nothing was omitted, for the exigencies of the time were not to be allowed to curtail the obsequies due to the father. Thus the elder son would have it; the younger, who was with his regiment on the Saale in Franconia, was unable to be present at the funeral.

Anselm was now the master at Hohen-Vietz.

It was with a sad heart that he cast the first seed on to the ill-ploughed land; but behold, the corn sprang up before friend or foe—for there had long been no difference between them—had trampled on the young ears; it seemed that the war had burned itself out like a fire that has exhausted its fuel, and before the decade was over the rumour ran from mouth to mouth that there was now peace.

And there *was* peace. What everyone had abandoned hope of ever seeing again had returned. And after another two years had passed across the land without Swedish or Imperial troops having camped and plundered in the Lebus region, and even the most sceptical were obliged to relinquish their doubts that peace really had come, there arrived at the Hohen-Vietz manor house a letter addressed 'To the Worshipful, High and Noble Anselm von Vitzewitz, domiciled at Hohen-Vietz, in the district of Lebus'. The letter itself read:

My especially well beloved brother!
Two weeks from today, if God gives his blessing to my plans, I shall be with you in Hohen-Vietz. I am only awaiting permission from

Vienna, which his Imperial Majesty will not refuse me. Perhaps *tempora futura* will again bring us together as we were together in our days of childhood and *adolescentia*. We Lutherans—despite the fact that at Münster and Osnabrügge★ they proclaimed peace between the religions as loudly as they could—are suffered very little in the Imperial Army, and no day passes without its being made clear to us that we are no longer needed. I hear that our most gracious Herr Elector,★ whom I have never failed to regard as my lord and sovereign, is recruiting a Brandenburg army, on which account he is taking over considerable numbers of officers and generals from the Swedish and Imperial armies. It would be a truly great joy to me if I should make one of them; for, to admit the truth, I long to be home again in my dear Lebus. Our cousins and neighbours the Burgsdorffs,★ who *post mortem Schwarzenbergii*★ are the alpha and omega of the court, will surely want to do something for an old war-horse who knows the service as well as he knows the *Catechismus Lutheri. Interim bene vale.*★

I, your brother Matthias von Vitzewitz, Colonel of the Imperial Army.

And Matthias really did come when he said he would. A feast was arranged to celebrate his arrival home. Three tables were laid in the grand annexe; two of them stood beside one another lengthwise along the floor of the hall, the third table stood obliquely in a gallery which was hung with banners and coats-of-arms and could be reached by a flight of three steps. Their whole circle of friends from Barnim and Lebus was invited; the brothers sat opposite one another; beside them at the gallery table there sat Adam and Beteve Pfuel from Jahnsfelde, Peter Ihlow from Ringenwalde, Balthasar Walffen from Tempelberg, Hans and Nikolaus Barfus from Upper- and Lower-Predikow, and with them Tamme Stranz, Achim von Kracht, two Schapelows, two Beerfeldes and five of the Burgsdorffs. If only on account of their confession they were all more inclined towards the Swedish than the Imperial side, and this was especially true of Peter Ihlow, who, a nephew of Field Marshal Ihlow, had a grudge against the court at Vienna, accusing it of having treacherously murdered his uncle at Schloss Eger.★ He repeated the accusation on this occasion too, though it must remain uncertain whether in doing so he momentarily forgot who was present or whether he forgot it on purpose.

When he heard his commander-in-chief the Emperor inveighed against in so challenging a fashion, Matthias von Vitzewitz rose and cried: 'Peter Ihlow, watch what you say. I am an officer of the Imperial Army.'

'You are one,' Anselm then shouted across the table—it was the voice of the wine but even more that of his Protestant heart—'you are one, but it would be better if you never had been.'

'Better or not, I *am* one. The Emperor's honour is my honour.'

'It is a good thing you have had enough of that honour. We foreigners are suffered very little in the Imperial Army.'

Matthias, who had hitherto been maintaining his composure only with difficulty, lost all control of himself when he saw how he had been trapped and overborne by his own words in so mean a fashion. His eyes started from his head and, laying his hand on his sword, he cried: 'He who says it lies.'

'He who denies it lies.'

At this moment both drew their swords. Those sitting immediately beside them leaped up, but before anyone had time to spring between them the younger brother's sword had pierced the chest of the elder. Anselm had been struck a mortal blow.

Beside himself at what had happened, Matthias wanted to surrender himself to the Elector; it was only with reluctance that he acquiesced to the promptings of those who urged him to flee. He returned to his garrison town of Böhmisch-Grätz, and made a report of what had happened to Vienna; there the matter ended. To show him what little weight the War Office placed on the affair, which had in any case arisen in the first instance from a defence of the honour of the Emperor, he was promoted to general and given a command in Hungary. But, grateful though he was for this evidence of the favour in which he was held, it failed to restore to him the inner peace for which he thirsted, and from Peterwardein,* where he was encamped, he wrote to the Elector and begged for his mercy 'for the sake of him to whom all men owe their salvation and mercy'.

The Elector hesitated; but after Peter Ihlow, Beteke Pfuel and Ehrenreich von Burgsdorff had deposed an oath that both brothers had drawn at the same time, he agreed to a general pardon 'as though the event had never occurred', and Matthias returned to Hohen-Vietz which, except for that one ill-fated festive day, he had not seen since the day on which Colonel Maradas had stormed the castle.

He returned and brought, as the people of Hohen-Vietz continued to tell long afterwards, 'a barrel of gold with him'; for the donation of estates and acquisitions of land such as were then traditional had made him rich. The Elector received him with marks of exceptional favour and with all the traditional forms confirmed him in full possession of the estate that had fallen vacant. The new lord of the manor immediately set about the erection of a castle-like Renaissance building, richly furnished with a broad staircase and high stuccoed rooms, which, running parallel with the austere framework house, produced a horseshoe-shaped complex in which the 'banqueting hall'—the annexe erected by old Rochus—formed the line uniting the two sides. Mindful of what had taken place there, however, Matthias von Vitzewitz transformed this annexe itself into a chapel. Above the altar he placed a picture whose content was taken from the story of the Prodigal Son; beside it he hung the blade with which he had killed his brother. He entered the chapel only at twilight; he wished no one to know of it, let alone talk of it, but anyone who had anything to do on the paved surround of the dwelling house that abutted it, or was idling about in that region, could hear his voice raised loudly in prayer.

His repentance lasted his whole life long, and he lived for many years. Late in life he married. He departed this temporal world in the autumn of the same year that saw the demise of his lord the Elector, and the people of Hohen-Vietz, with the eighteen-year-old son of the house at their head, carried him up to the ancient church on the hill and laid him in the crypt beside the copper coffin of his father, and in such a way that Anselm stood on the right hand of the father, Matthias on the left.

He died in the conviction that God had accepted his repentance; and those who came after him shared that faith. But this faith, however much it might offer a firm basis for their life, yet it could not restore to them their joy in life. They all wore a serious mien. And this trait began to be inherited. The character of the family, which had in ancient days been one of jovial boisterousness, gave way to a gloomy brooding, and the pleasure they had formerly taken in feasting and revelry was transformed into a tendency to self-castigation and asceticism. And this tendency seemed to them to be nourished and confirmed by many outward events, both real and supernatural. In the annexe, which had been transformed into a chapel and which, grown dirty and derelict, had finally ceased to bear any resemblance to a chapel and had become a store-room, old Matthias walked as he did in life and knelt before the altar he had founded. No one living in the house had any doubt about it. But if anyone had denied the existence of the ghost and, whether out of faith or the lack of it, had repudiated the apparition as an invention of superstition, other signs would have manifested themselves to him. For a century and a half the family was of one accord in seeing in this the finger of God: never again should two brothers take up arms against one another.

It hardly needs to be said that the inhabitants of the village cherished all this like a valuable treasure, and in the spinning-rooms nothing was discussed more eagerly than whether or not old Matthias had been seen. It was a kind of point of honour to have seen him. He was joked about and feared. The farmers themselves were as credulous about it as their maids. On the hill close beside the church there stood an old beech-tree whose trunk had divided itself into two at about half the height of a man and grew in different directions to right and left. This corresponded to the fate of Hohen-Vietz, and the story was that when they were still children the two brothers had planted the tree together: but when Anselm had fallen at the hand of his younger brother the trunk had divided. And others still knew that when Matthias had finished praying in the chapel he would climb the great walnut-tree avenue up to the church and embrace the trunk of the beech-tree at the place it divided and try to press it together. But in vain. Then he would sit at the foot of the tree and wail aloud.

But if the romantic need for the spectral and dreadful liked to express itself in these melancholy images, another trait in the people at Hohen-Vietz preferred just as decidedly to look to an ultimate reconciliation, and young and old were familiar with a rhyme that gave expression to this hope of reconciliation. It was also familiar to the inhabitants of the manor house, and it went as follows:

> And one day the house will receive a princess,
> Then the bloodstain will fade in the heat of a fire,
> The divided stem together will press,
> And again become one, grow whole and entire,
> And once again from its ancient seat
> House Vitzewitz the dawn will greet.

3

Christmas Morning

RESTLESS dreams had in the meantime been passing through Lewin's soul. The journey in the east wind had made him feverish, and it was only towards morning that he went properly to sleep. An hour later the house had already started to come awake; footsteps resounded up and down the long corridor at whose north-east corner Lewin's room lay, heavy baskets of wood were set before the fireplaces and large logs brought in and laid in the stoves. Soon afterwards the door opened and the old servant who had received his young master the evening before entered with a light in his hand. Hector stayed where he was lying on the deerskin rug, stretched himself and only wagged his tail, as though to report: all in order. Jeetze, who had been carefully shielding the flame with his hand, set a lamp-glass over it and began to collect up all the items of clothing that were lying about. He himself was still in his morning costume: with the velvet trousers and gaiters, without which he was scarcely to be conceived, he wore a working-jacket of coarse cotton. When he had got everything together he withdrew as quietly as he had arrived, murmuring incomprehensible words as he did so in the manner of old people. The affirmative nodding of his head, however, made it clear that he was in a good mood and well contented.

The door remained half open and though the room had now

grown silent again the familiar, homely sounds of the awakening life of the house began to penetrate into it more and more
loudly. The great sprucewood logs split asunder with a loud
crack, the water that ran in little rivulets into the fire from the
damp splinters hissed from time to time, and from the niche in
the corridor there could be heard the assured and regular
strokes with which Jeetze's brush sought to master the dust and
hairs that refused to come free.

All this was audible enough, but Lewin did not hear it. At
length Hector decided to put an end to Jeetze's and his own
impatience, raised himself up, laid both his forepaws on the
coverlet, and licked the sleeper's face without worrying over-
much whether his blandishments were welcome or not. Lewin
awoke; initial confusion gave way to a cheerful burst of
laughter. 'Down, Hector,' he cried, and leaped from the bed.
His morning sleep had revived him, and within a few minutes
he was dressed, an accomplishment made possible by his
military training. He paced the room a couple of times,
regarded with a smile a sheet of paper fixed to the table-cover
with four needles on which there stood in large letters:
'Welcome to Hohen-Vietz', let his glance wander over two
silhouettes which he had known from his youth but which it
always gave him the same pleasure to behold, and then stepped
over to one of the frozen corner windows. His breath melted
away the ice-ferns, a sliver no bigger than an eyeglass came free
and he now caught his first sight of the Christmas sun, which
was just rising, a red ball, behind the top of Hohen-Vietz
church-tower. Between him and the church there rose the trees
of the hillside park, outlined fantastically with frost and on one
of them a pair of ravens, gazing into the sun and greeting the
day with hoarse cries.

Lewin was still enjoying this panorama when there came a
knock on the door.

'Do come in!'

A slim young lady entered, and brother and sister embraced
one another with a heartfelt kiss. That they were brother and
sister was clear from the very first sight of them: the same form
and bearing, the same oval heads, above all the same eyes alive
with imagination, sagacity and loyalty.

'How glad I am to have you here again. You'll be staying over the holiday, won't you? And how fine you look, Lewin! They say we resemble one another; it will make me vain if it is so.'

Lewin's sister, who had until then been standing before her brother as though surveying him, now put her arm in his and, beginning to walk up and down on the wide straw mat that lay in the room, continued with their talk.

'You wouldn't believe, Lewin, how empty our days are now. For the past week nothing has come into the house except snowflakes.'

'But you have Papa . . .'

'Yes and no. I have him and don't have him; in any event, he is no longer as he was. The little attentions I used to receive from him I receive no more; he no longer pays any heed to me, or when he does he forces himself and smiles. And for all this the newspapers are to blame, though I admit I too shouldn't like to be without them. As soon as Hoppenmarieken brings in the post he loses all composure. He walks past me without seeing me. Letters are written; the horses are hardly out of their harness; carriage and sleigh fly hither and thither. Often we are left alone all day. It is good I have Aunt Schorlemmer or I would worry myself to death.'

'Aunt Schorlemmer! So there is a season for everything.'

'Oh, she is always in season, no one knows that better than you and I. But one thing has not been granted to our good Aunt Schorlemmer, to be sure, and that is the ability to make an empty day less empty. Would you like to sit snowed up a whole winter long with her and her words of wisdom?'

'Not for all the world. But where is the pastor? And where is Marie? Has everyone vanished?'

'No, no, they are here, and they come and see us and are just as they were, as dear and good as ever. But our days at Hohen-Vietz are long, and longest when in the calendar the days are shortest. Marie is coming this evening, though; she has just inquired if she could do so.'

'And how is our darling?'

'In the three months you have been away she has grown up. She is like a fairy-tale. If a golden coach arrived at the Kniehases' tomorrow to take her away from the mayoral house with two pages to carry her train it would not surprise me. And yet I am anxious about her. But the more I worry, the more I love her.'

The pair had got thus far in their chatter when Jeetze, now clad in full livery, appeared in the doorway to inform his young master and mistress that it was now time.

'Where is Papa?'

'He is getting things ready. Krist and I have had to help.'

'And Aunt Schorlemmer?'

'Is downstairs. The carol-singers have just arrived.'

Lewin and Renate nodded to one another and then, smiling and with jaunty step, each proud of the other, went out into the corridor. At the same moment as they arrived at the head of the stairs they heard the Christmas sound of clear children's voices coming up to them from below. And yet what they were singing was not a true Christmas carol: it was the old hymn 'Now thank we all our God',★ the hymn that comes most readily from the throats of the people of the March and expresses most fluently their souls' feelings. 'How lovely,' said Lewin, and listened to the end of the first stanza.

When brother and sister had descended the stairs as far as the lowest landing they again halted and regarded the scene at their feet. The vaulted entrance hall, large and spacious notwithstanding the oaken cabinets that were ranged around it, was filled with people young and old; a number of old ladies were crouching on the stairway, whose bottom steps jutted well out into the hall. To the left, towards the door leading to the park and garden, there stood the children, some dressed in their Sunday best, the rest in the best they had, and behind them the poor of the village, the infirm and crippled among them; towards the right all who belonged to the house had taken their places: the gamekeeper, the inspector, the steward, Krist and Jeetze, together with the maids, most of them young and pretty and all clad in the picturesque costume of the region, the red flannel skirt, the black silk headscarf and the little flowered velveteen jacket. In front of this colourful group of girls they saw an elderly lady of more than fifty, clad in grey with a white scarf and a little tulle cap, her hands folded, her head bent forward as though to follow the singing of the children with more devout attention. She was Aunt Schorlemmer; and only when brother and sister appeared on the landing did she alter her posture and reply to Lewin's wave with a friendly nod.

Now the second stanza too had been sung, and there commenced the distribution of Christmas gifts to the children and the poor of the village: a custom of the house from ancient times. No one tried to press to the front; each knew he would receive his due. The infirm were given soup, the cripples a sum of money, all received a festive cake, and the maids ran up to the children and shook apples and nuts into the bags and sacks the children had brought with them.

The giving of gifts was hardly over before the big folding doors that led into the great hall of the house were opened from within and bright illumination flooded into the hitherto dimly lighted entrance hall. This was the signal that the house itself was now about to be bestowed. Old Vitzewitz stepped between the doors and the Christmas tree and, catching sight of Lewin, who was heading the festive procession on his sister's arm, called to him: 'Welcome to Hohen-Vietz, Lewin.' Father and son greeted one another warmly; then brother and sister resumed their progress round the table, while out in the entrance hall the children began again to sing:

> 'All praise and thanks to God
> The Father now be given,
> The Son, and Him who reigns
> With them in highest Heaven.'

The procession now dispersed and everyone went to his place and his presents. Everything, the shawls, the waistcoats, the silk kerchiefs, gave delight and satisfaction. No ill-humour or disappointment was visible in any face: everyone knew that times were hard, and that the much afflicted master of Hohen-Vietz had had to deny himself much to maintain the traditions of the house even in evil days.

On each side of the hearth, over whose marble fireplace there hung a more than life-size portrait of old Matthias, the father had spread out on two little tables the presents he had chosen for Lewin and Renate. There were not very many of them, though they included things he knew they wanted. At Lewin's place at the table there lay a rifled double-barrelled carbine, Suhl★ workmanship, clean-lined, light, firm, a joy to the connoisseur.

'That is for you, Lewin. We live in strange times. And now come and let us have a talk.'

They stepped into the neighbouring room, while in the great hall the Christmas lights began to burn down.

4

Berndt von Vitzewitz★

LEWIN'S father was Berndt von Vitzewitz, a man in his late fifties. When he was thirteen★ he had joined the Knobelsdorff Dragoons garrisoned at Landsberg; after serving for almost thirty years he had just assumed command of this famous regiment when, in the spring of 1795, the conclusion of the Peace of Basel induced him to resign his commission. Full of abhorrence for the regime of terror in Paris, he saw in this 'compact with the regicides' not only a debasement of Prussia but also a danger to it. He returned ill-humouredly to Hohen-Vietz; and perhaps it was as an expression of his disgruntlement that, in ordinary social life at least, he preferred to have his military rank ignored and to be addressed merely as Herr von Vitzewitz. The estate itself had devolved upon him seven years previously, almost immediately after his marriage to Madeleine von Dumoulin, the eldest daughter of General von Dumoulin, who as the youngest officer of Captain von Wakenitz's squadron had at Zorndorf★ performed miracles of bravery and, after twice breaking through the Russian square, had received the *Pour le mérite*★ on the battlefield.

Madeleine von Dumoulin, tall, slim, blonde, a typical German beauty as the daughters of the old French nobility so often are, was her husband's idol. And yet she looked up to him: without pretensions, almost without whims or caprices, she submitted to the superiority of his character. The birth of a son while they were still at Landsberg enhanced their happiness, which radiated even more brightly from their eyes when, shortly after they had come into possession of Hohen-Vietz, a daughter too was born to them. It happened in the May of 1795, a light spring rain was falling and the sign of the covenant between God and man, the rainbow, stood over the ancient house like a promise. But this promise, though it might have applied to the child, did not apply to the father. Like so many of his line, he too was not spared a dreadful catastrophe: it was different in kind, but it was no less grievous.

The Battle of Jena had decided the fate of Prussia; eleven days later several French officers whose impending arrival had already been announced appeared at the manor house at Hohen-Vietz, and so as not to occasion any offence the lady of the house too was present to receive them, though she had barely recovered from a fever and was still pale with the effects of it. A table was laid in the hall. Frau von Vitzewitz joined them and seemed to have achieved her aim of producing a reasonable degree of understanding between host and guests when, as the dessert was being brought in, a captain sitting opposite her, a man from the Spanish border region with an olive complexion and a thin, pointed beard, rose and in an act of the most unseemly kind of homage lisped at her words that sent the blood to the fair lady's cheeks. Berndt von Vitzewitz rushed at the wretch, other officers sprang between them as they wrestled and separated them; and, taking the side of the offended wife, they marked out in the park the arena where the affair was to be settled there and then. Berndt, a master of swordsmanship, gave his opponent a severe head wound, and the French, true to their chivalrous disposition, congratulated him on his triumph without showing the slightest sign of ill-feeling. But it was a brief victory, or at least a dearly bought one. The violent excitations inseparable from such events compelled his wife to return to the sickbed, on the third day she was given up for dead, on the ninth they carried her along the ancient walnut-tree avenue up to the church of Hohen-Vietz and, omitting none of the obsequies she herself had stipulated, laid her to rest. Not in the crypt, however, but, as she had so often prayed to be, in 'God's good Brandenburg earth'. The bells tolled out over the land all day long, and when the spring came a stone lay upon the grave bearing no name and no date but only the deeply engraved inscription: 'Here lies my happiness.'*

Under the effect of these blows, the seriousness that had hitherto characterized Berndt's nature deteriorated to unalloyed gloom. The situation of the disintegrated fatherland, which had almost been struck from the roster of nations, was not calculated to elevate his spirits. His own property depreciated, harvests pillaged, half the farm burned down by brigands —thus he gradually declined into a brooding melancholy, and he revived again only when the cares and misfortunes that pressed upon him almost without cease had matured within him an overwhelming sense of hatred. Then he again grew energetic and active, he had aims and objectives, he lived again.

The hatred which he had to thank for this revival was directed at everything that came from beyond the Rhine, and yet there was a distinction between what he felt towards the leader of the French nation and what he felt towards the French nation itself. For the latter, whose courage, spirit and capacity for sacrifice he had so often lauded and represented as a model, he had, like almost all Brandenburgers, in the depths of his heart an inextinguishable predilection, and all the hatred which, in spite of this love, he clearly and honestly demonstrated was much less immediate feeling than calculation and design grown out of the continual and assiduously cherished reflection that—to employ his own words—'the most ungrateful of all nations slaughtered a good king so as to yoke itself to the triumphal car of a tyrant who has murdered liberty.' His hatred for Bonaparte himself was quite different. In no way fabricated or artificial, it sprang from his heart like a hot spring. Even the name revolted him. He was no Frenchman, he was an Italian, a Corsican, grown up in the only spot in Europe where vendetta was still law and custom; and even the greatness it must be admitted he possessed was worthy only of astonishment, not of admiration, because it lacked all sanctification from Heaven. He saw in Bonaparte a demon, nothing more; a scourge, a destroyer, a Genghis Khan of the West. When in the middle of November it became known that the Emperor would be passing through Küstrin on his way to the

Vistula, Bernt took his two growing children—Renate was eleven, Lewin just sixteen—to the ancient fortress on the Oder and stationed himself at the Müncheberg Gate so as to show them 'him whom God has set His mark on'. And when the latter rode into the silent town through the vaulted gateway, and his yellow waxen face appeared like an uncanny luminosity between the horse's shoulder and the hat pulled down deep over the forehead, he thrust the children forward into the front row and cried audibly: 'Look closely, that is the *wickedest man* on earth.'

But he who knows how to hate, provided it is hatred of the right kind, also knows how to love, and the passionate attachment Berndt had for so many years borne in his heart for his too soon departed wife he now transferred to his children, who were growing up the image of their mother. Slim, blond and of a transparent skin, they differed in every respect from the outward appearance of their father, with whose thickset form there was combined the swarthiest complexion and dark, short-cropped hair with as yet only the faintest trace of grey. And their characters differed as widely as did their appearance. Changeable and credulous, always inclined to admire and to forgive, the children possessed the cheerful light of the soul while the father possessed its sombre fire. Humble and full of good will, always ready to make others happy and to be happy themselves, their paths were illumined by all-transfiguring fantasy. Their father rejoiced in them. He dreamed of a transformation that through them would come over his house.

Like all who have set their heart on something, Berndt von Vitzewitz made no great display of it; his love possessed a befitting sense of modesty. But he liked just as little to exhibit a rough exterior. Because he had authority he had no need continually to assert it. In converse with his children he liked to ignore the difference in years, and he ridiculed those parents who, making a virtue of necessity, were accustomed to divide the world of their thoughts and feelings under two headings, one half for their 'intimates' and the other for their offspring. He was open and accommodating towards Lewin, full of attentiveness towards Renate. Only in recent weeks, as the sister had already complained to her brother, a change had taken place; he avoided encountering her, said little, and when he was not out paying calls in the neighbourhood he sat half the night at his desk or paced the floor talking to himself in the one-windowed closet that constituted his study.

This study was as deep as it was narrow, so that its yellow walls, long grown black from the smoke of tobacco and of the lamp, appeared darker than they were in the little light that entered. There was not a trace of luxury: all that had been attended to was comfort, that comfort of having everything close at hand required by men engaged in intellectual work for whom nothing is more unendurable than having to fetch or look for something, let alone wait for it. The two doors of the closet, one of which led to the hall and the other to the ladies' drawing-room, were adjacent to the window, which meant that two wide blank walls were left to accommodate a desk and a leather-covered sofa, both of considerable length. A wooden footstool with the proportions of a piece of garden furniture which stood between them would have blocked the passage from one end of the room to the other completely if the desk-top had not had a piece of corresponding size cut out of it. Over the desk there hung a fine portrait of a woman, a half-length picture in darkened colours, over the sofa a long narrow mirror whose smoke-stained surface left no doubt that where it was hanging it was altogether useless. A key-board, together with two or three mounted antlers with various hats and caps suspended from them, completed the furnishings. Walking-sticks, a duck-shooting gun and a cavalry sword stood in the corners, while to the panels of the window-alcove there had been fastened several maps of areas of Russia with tacks and flags affixed to them. Countless red lines and dots demonstrated that their owner had, with the newspaper in his hand, already accomplished many journeys back and forth between Moscow and Smolensk.

This was the room which, as was told at the end of the previous chapter, father and son entered. Both took their seat on the sofa opposite the portrait, which now looked down on them. Berndt, who was clad in his usual indoor dress—wide trousers of Scotch cloth, a dark velvet coat, a red silk scarf loosely tied around his neck—extended his right foot on to a high floor-cushion. From respect and habit, Lewin sat beside him upright.

'Well, now, Lewin, how are things? What have you got to tell me?'

'Perhaps a piece of news. Tomorrow the papers will carry the communiqué which admits that the army has been destroyed. The Ladalinskis had the French text; Kathinka read us the most important parts. I was shaken by it.'

'So was I, but I was even more exalted.'

'So you know its contents already? Once again I am forestalled.'

'Aunt Amelie received the newspaper cutting yesterday; you know her old connections. Count Drosselstein, who was with her yesterday, offered to bring me the news himself. We talked together for a good hour. And, believe me, the communiqué doesn't tell the half of it. We have had letters from Minsk and Bialystock: they are utterly annihilated.'

'What a judgement!'

'Yes, Lewin, that is the word. The great hand that appeared at the feast of Belshazzar has again written on the wall, and this time what it has written is no riddle. All the world can read it: "Numbered, weighed and finished." Divine judgement has condemned him. And yet I fear, Lewin, that some of our sapient rulers would like to restrain the wrath of the Almighty. They must not be allowed to. If they try to, they are lost, they and we with them.—What is the mood like in Berlin?'

'Good. It seems to me that a change has come over people's spirits. The whole atmosphere is brighter; where gloom and pessimism still reigns it doesn't dare show itself. What is lacking is a guiding will, a resolute word.'

'The word *must* be spoken, in one way or another. If men remain dumb, the very stones will cry it out. God demands that we understand his signs. Lewin, all of us here are resolved. All of us here are waiting for the word; if it is *not* spoken we shall obey the word that speaks loudly within us ourselves. It is easy to get buried in the snow. Only, no cowardly mercy. Now or never. Few will get across the Niemen, *none must get across the Oder.*'

Lewin sat silent for a time; he avoided his father's eyes. Then he said, half to himself: 'We are the Emperor's allies.* We want to break this alliance, and God grant we do so, but—'

'So you disapprove of what we intend.'

'I cannot do otherwise. What you intend, and what thousands of the best of us want, is against my nature. I have no sympathy for what they now admiringly call Spanish warfare. I detest anything that takes its victim from behind. I am for open battle, in the full light of day with trumpets blaring. How often have I wept with delight when I sat on the footstool beside Mama and she told how her father, when he was barely eighteen years old, broke through the Russian square, and how Captain von Wakenitz then kissed him in front of the squadron and cried to him: "Junker von Dumoulin, let us exchange swords." Yes, I want to wage war, but in the German fashion, not the Spanish, nor the Slav. You know, Papa, I am my mother's son.'

'That you are, and it is well that you are. A lucky star stood over your mother's childhood, and I pray God that the blessing of her house may be on you and on Renate.'

Lewin again fell silent. Berndt von Vitzewitz, however, went on: 'I know what it means to be of a certain nature; all that is inherited and inborn, provided it does not conflict with the laws of God, is sacred to me; go your own way, Lewin, I shall not try to compel you. But as for me, in the stillness of many nights I have sworn to myself that I shall go mine!'

A short pause followed during which Berndt paced up and down the narrow room. Then, paying no heed to the silence in which Lewin was still sunk, he resumed: 'You in the towns —and you have become a town-dweller, Lewin—you don't know, you haven't experienced it. Under the eyes of the authorities oppression has been moderated and the unlawful acquired the forms of law. They are even proud of the fact and themselves almost believe they have broken our chains. But we in the country know better, and I tell you, Lewin, that the bloody hand that set fire to the barns, that tore the rings from the fingers of our dead, has not been forgotten hereabouts, and a bloodier hand will one day requite it.'

Lewin was about to reply to his father; but the latter, suddenly moderating the vehemence with which he had been speaking, went on in visible agitation: 'You were still a boy when the enemy of man came into our land; the lustre of his deeds preceded him. What in the arrogance of his good fortune he then had the audacity to say to our Queen*: "How could you dare to take up arms against *me*?"—this question has since been repeated by a thousand helpless and wretched people of our own land as though it were the alpha and omega of all wisdom. And it was with this idea that we are impotent that you grew up, you and Renate. You have seen nothing but our insignificance and you have heard nothing but the greatness of our conqueror. But, Lewin, it was not always so, and we older people who once beheld the eyes of the Great King, we taste bitterly the cup of humiliation that is now set to our lips every day.'

'And I am certain', Lewin now interposed, 'that it will be taken from us. We shall have a joyous, a holy war. But for the present we are our enemy's friend, we have stood side by side with him in arms; he counts on us, he drags himself to our doors as confidently as if it were the threshold of his own house; the light he sees gleaming means to him rescue, life, and it is precisely on the threshold of this house that we shall take him, defenceless as he is, and throttle him.'

At this moment the bells of the ancient tower of Hohen-Vietz began to sound, summoning the people to church. They rang out loud and clear in the winter air. Berndt gave ear to them; then, raising his hand towards the east, from which direction the sound of the bells came, he took up where Lewin had stopped: 'I know that it is written: "vengeance is mine", and he who sees into our hearts knows that in human frailty I have at all times followed his commandments. I do not fear to blaspheme when I say: there is a vengeance that is holy. It was holy vengeance when Samson grasped the pillars of the temple and buried himself and his enemies beneath the ruins. Perhaps our vengeance will likewise be nothing other than a common grave. So be it; I am resolved; I stake upon it my life, and, thanks be to God, I have the *right* to. If I raise this hand, I raise it not to revenge a personal injustice, no, I raise it against the common enemy of all mankind, and because I cannot strike at him himself I destroy his weapons wherever I find them. The great criminal draws many of the innocent with him into his fatal destiny; we cannot discriminate. The net is spread, and the more who are caught in it the better. We shall speak of this further, Lewin. Now it is time for church. Let us not neglect God's word. We have need of it.'

Thus they parted, as the bells began to ring for a second time.

5

In Church

THE humming of the bells was still resounding in the air as Berndt von Vitzewitz, Renate on his arm, turned out of a path swept in the snow into the great walnut-tree avenue which, rising gently, led in a straight line from the entrance of the manor house up to the church on the hill. They were followed by Lewin and Aunt Schorlemmer. All were clad for winter; the hands of the ladies were encased in Greenland muffs; only Lewin, disdaining furs of any kind, wore a light grey cloak with a wide collar.

The oft-mentioned church on the hill towards which they were walking was an ancient stone building dating from the first arrival of Christianity, from the days of colonization by the Cistercians; evidence of this was the cleanly squared stone, the apse, and above all the little high-set Romanesque windows which gave this church, as they did all the pre-Gothic churches of the March, the character of a fortress. The passing centuries had changed it little. A few windows had been widened, a couple of side-doors for the clergy and the family of the manor had been put in; otherwise, with the exception of the tower and a new extension to the crypt at the north wall, everything stood as it had stood in the days of the friars.

But if the exterior of the church had remained as good as unaltered, its interior had undergone all the transformations of half a millennium. From the days when the Ascanians had here fought out their regularly recurring feuds with the Pomeranian dukes, down to the days when the Great King had on this selfsame spot, at Zorndorf and Kunersdorf, engaged in his bloodiest battles, no century had passed over the church of Hohen-Vietz that had not added to or detracted from the appearance of its interior, had not bestowed on it or taken from it one thing or another.

The same, it may be said in passing, applies to the majority of the village churches of the March, which thereby acquire their charm and uniqueness. It is especially striking when compared with the secular buildings of our land. When you survey the latter you soon perceive that they fall into two groups: those with age but no history, and those with history but no age. Castle Soltwedel★ is primevally old but says nothing. The palace of Sanssouci★ speaks but is as young as a parvenu. Only our village churches can be seen to be to a large extent the repositories of our *whole* history and, displaying as they do the changes effected by the centuries one after another, they possess and make manifest the magic of historical continuity.

Hohen-Vietz church had three entrances, the main one for the congregation at its west end. The tower through which this entrance passed was cemented together roughly out of stone; it lacked the clean lines that distinguished the older building. Down from the ceiling there hung a rope with which the prayer-bell was rung. Against the right wall there stood a bier, with strips of fabric lying on it for lowering the coffins. On the wall opposite, worm-eaten wooden figures, the remains of a carved altar of the Catholic period, had been collected together; beside them a heap of wooden logs, probably for heating the sacristy. The actual showpiece of this vestibule, however, was the 'Turkish bell' celebrated for its tone and its size which, having hung in the tower for many years and resounded up and down the Oder, had now been fetched from its former heights, cracked. According to legend, it had been cast from cannon brought home from the Turkish wars by Isaschar von Vitzewitz, the son of old Matthias. Its rim was embellished with inscriptions. One of them read:

> Whenever I call alert thy mind,
> He who serves God reward shall find.

The heavy iron clapper stood in a corner beside it. From the tower one stepped into the central aisle of the church; close beside the entry there stood a granite baptismal font without its foot and supports and split down the middle, likewise a relic of the Cistercian age. Further to the left, in the corner where the tower and the nave met, an alcove had been made in the north wall; from an iron bar there was suspended a Madonna (the Christ-child had fallen from her arm) with at its head the simple date 1431. This was the year of the Hussites. No doubt the Vitzewitzes had established this votive altar after the departure of their enemies. To right and left of the central aisle half the church was filled with pews, all of them dusted clean and shut; only the foremost was half open, its door swinging on its hinges. Since the days immediately following the Battle of Kunersdorf this had been called the 'major's pew'. In flight from the battle, grenadiers of the Itzenplitz Regiment had borne their wounded major to this spot and laid him on this bench, here he had raised himself up and torn off his bandages: 'Children, I want to die.' Since then the bench had been stained with blood and everyone avoided it.

Among the chief ornaments of Hohen-Vietz church were its tombstones. They had once lain on the floor between the altar and the middle of the nave, but since the ancient vault had been filled in and the new crypt we have already mentioned constructed they had stood upright against the north wall of the church. Mostly they were simple stones furnished with brief or lengthy inscriptions, according to the custom of the time, which told of Malplaquet* and Mollwitz,* but also of quieter days begun and ended in Hohen-Vietz.

Legends attached to two of these stones. Beside the alcove with the Madonna there stood one larger than the others and thick with inscriptions: whoever read them would learn that Katharina von Gollmitz, a friend of the house, had once lain beneath this stone. Grete von Vitzewitz, being especially devoted to the deceased, had assigned to her a place of honour in the church when she had been taken ill and died while on a visit to Hohen-Vietz; but her friend in the grave was insensible of this distinction and longed to go home. Whenever Grete von Vitzewitz stepped over the tombstone she heard a voice say: 'Grete, open my grave.' Finally she opened the grave and carried the coffin to Jurgelin, where Katharina von Gollmitz's home was. Thereafter all was quiet. The tombstone, however, she immured in the wall.

Another stone, whose inscription had long since been trampled away, still lay close before the altar. It was the only one which had been left in peace in its old place, perhaps because it was broken. It obstinately refused to stay level with the stones lying beside it, and gradually created a trough. However often its two halves were taken up and sand and gravel were trodden into the depths beneath it the stone continued to sink. The people said: 'Old Matthias is lying under there and keeps going down deeper and deeper.'

This was an error, to be sure, old Matthias lay elsewhere, but the great tomb which, from an artistic point of view, constituted the chief ornament of Hohen-Vietz church, did certainly belong to him. It was a marble monument, overladen and rococo yet of masterly workmanship. In respect of its subject it showed a certain resemblance to the altar picture in the annexe. Matthias von Vitzewitz and his lady were kneeling and gazing up reverently at a Crucifixion of Christ: all was in bas-relief, the couple themselves almost in detached sculpture. Beneath them their names and the dates of their birth and death. A master from the Netherlands performed the work and himself brought it by ship to the Oder.

As the residents of the manor house stepped into the church the singing of the congregation began. A narrow flight of steps commencing at one of the small side-doors led up to their pew. A very simple wooden structure resting on pillars, it had originally been enclosed behind tall sliding-windows, but these had long since been removed and now only two narrow boards rising from the balustrade of the pew right up to the ceiling divided the space into three large frames. On the front of the partition there stood the Vitzewitz coat-of-arms, a cross of St Andrew white on a red ground.

The family noiselessly took its seat to the front of this manorial pew, directly behind the balustrade: first Berndt von Vitzewitz, beside him on his left Renate, then Aunt Schorlemmer. Lewin sat himself in the second row. Neglected though everything was, it possessed a certain charm. Immediately to the right stood altar and pulpit; in front of the altar the baptismal font, a silver basin richly adorned with allegorical figures and indecipherable inscriptions which it had cost great effort to rescue from the hands of the enemy. Beside the wall opposite there was the marble monument of old Matthias and his lady previously referred to. The best thing, however, that belonged to this unpretentious place was the great, almost semicircular window which allowed a view out over the churchyard and further down the hill to a few scattered houses and cottages that stood like outposts of the village. Hard by the church wall beside this window stood a yew-tree, the longest of whose branches reached out and regularly knocked against the window-pane whenever Pastor Seidentopf propounded his three-part sermon to the people of Hohen-Vietz. Lewin always sat so that he would have a clear view of the window. Like all the Vitzewitzes since the reformed doctrine had come to the land,* he firmly adhered to the *Catechismus Lutheri*: yet there was also something else in him that from time to time led him to pay more attention to the yew-tree outside than to the voice from the pulpit, and would have done so even if this voice had been a mightier one than that of the old friend and teacher upon whom the Sunday edification was incumbent.

The sun was shining brightly, and a beam of sunlight falling through the window illumined half of the north wall in sudden splendour, and especially the great memorial tomb opposite the manorial pew. It was as though a breath of roseate life had been wafted upon the life-sized figures. Lewin had never before been so fully aware of the beauty of this sculpture; he read the long inscription—the first time, as he admitted to himself, that he had done so.

The singing came to an end; while the last verses were still being sung Pastor Seidentopf had mounted the pulpit: a man in his sixties with thinning white hair and of a dignified bearing and mild and gentle features. Lewin regarded this beneficent figure, then lowered his eyes and followed the quiet prayer with devout attention. The congregation did likewise, bowed their heads and then, when he had ended the prayer and raised his head again, gazed up at their pastor in longing and expectation. For at that time all minds were open to comfort and exhortation from the pulpit, and they paid no heed to whether the words sounded Lutheran or Calvinist* provided only they proceeded from a *Prussian* heart. Seidentopf, who in normal times had many opponents to stand up against among the strictly orthodox conventiclists* of his village, well understood the new mood of unanimity, and the joy this gave him radiated from his face as, after he had finished reading from the Gospel, he began to expound the text. He spoke of the angel of the Lord who appeared to the shepherds to announce to them the birth of a new salvation. Such angels, he went on, are sent by God in every age, and above all in times when the night of affliction lies upon nations. And a night of affliction was upon the fatherland: but sooner than we thought an angel would appear in the midst of our fear and trepidation and cry to us: 'Fear not: for, behold, I bring you good tidings of great joy.' For the judgement of the Lord had struck down our enemies, and as once before the water had returned and 'covered the chariots, and the horsemen, and all the host of Pharaoh, that there remained not so much as one of them', so would it come to pass again.

At this point, with a brief allusion to the Christmas story, Pastor Seidentopf ought to have stopped; but, under the impress of the idea that a proper sermon must be of a proper length, he now began to extend the comparison between the ancient and the modern Pharaoh to the minutest particulars. And to this task he was not equal: he lacked the requisite exuberance of imagination and vigour of expression. The hosts of Egypt passed by like phantoms. The attentiveness of the congregation lapsed into a mere passive listening, and Lewin, who up till then had not missed a single word, let his eyes wander from the pulpit and began to transfer his attention to the window, outside which a robin redbreast was now sitting on a branch of the snow-covered yew-tree and making it rock gently up and down.

Only Berndt followed his pastor's address with liveliness and pleasure. The energy of his own mind contributed; where contours were unsure and vacillating he sharpened them. To what appeared as a shadow he gave life and form. He beheld the Egyptians. Battalions with golden eagles, squadrons of cavalry, the black horse-tails trailing over their white cloaks, thus they rose in an endless procession before him, and over all their splendour and magnificence there closed the waves of the sea. But over *one* they did *not* close; he gained the bank, a northerly icy shore, and behold, away over the glittering expanse there now speeded a sleigh, and two dark, deep-set eyes stared out into the flying snow. Pastor Seidentopf had no better auditor than the patron of his church, who—and not merely today—knew how to practise the amiable art of filling in the gaps. From the sketch he created a picture, yet believed he had received this picture from without, as a gift from his friend.

Now the sands had run out and the sermon came to an end. Then the pastor again approached the ledge of the pulpit and, in an urgent tone that again engaged the hearts of all who were there, he began:

'With the birth of Christ which we celebrate today there begins the Christian new year. A new year; what will it bring to us? To wish to know were folly; but our heart is permitted to hope. God has given a sign; may we be interpreting it aright when we say that it means he intends to raise us up again, that our repentance has been received, that our prayers have been heard. The scourge which by his will has for six long years been laid upon us he has broken; he has had mercy on our servitude, and the Christmas sun which shines upon us proclaims to us that brighter days again await us. Whether they will come with quiet triumph or with the clashing of swords, who can say? Our hope may well be mingled with a fear that victory will not be won without a final sacrifice of blood and treasure. And so let us then pray, my dear friends, and once more call upon the grace of the Lord, that he may lend us strength in the hour of decision. Let the words of Judas Maccabaeus⋆ be ours: "May thought of flight be far from us. If our time is come, let us die gallantly for our brothers' sake and let our honour not be lost." God desires *no* universal nation, God desires no Tower of Babel reaching to Heaven, and we stand up for his eternal ordinances when we stand up *for ourselves*. Our hearth, our land are holy places in accordance with the will of God. And he will remain true to us if *we* are true even unto death. Let us act when the hour strikes, but till then let us wait in patience.'

Then he bowed his head to repeat in silence the Lord's Prayer; the organ broke in solemnly; the congregation, visibly uplifted by the pastor's closing words, slowly left the church. The farmers and tenants made their way along the various winding paths that led down from the church to their farms in the village, half covered by the snow. The girls and women followed. Seen from the village street below the scene presented a charming picture: the snow, the Wendish costume and over it all the sparkling sunlight.

The family of the manor again made their way along the walnut-tree avenue. When, turning into the side path, they came to the door giving on to the yard, Krist was standing on the bottom step. He tugged at his hat: the silver edging upon it had long ago become black, its cockade bowed and bent. Catching sight of his coachman, Berndt went up to him and said tersely: 'Be ready at five! The small carriage.'

'The bays, your honour?'

'No, the ponies.'

'Very good, sir!' With these words our friends went back into the house.

6

At the Fireside

KRIST was ready punctually at five; Berndt did not like to be kept waiting. He had taken a brief farewell of his children to pay a neighbourly call on his sister at Schloss Guse—Aunt Amelie, as she was called in the house at Hohen-Vietz. It was not to be assumed that he would be returning the same evening; on the contrary, he had intimated that the little excursion could turn into a trip to the capital. It was the restlessness he felt that drove him out. Today, as for many years past, he had insisted on making all the Christmas arrangements himself, but hardly was he free of them before, in the feeling he had now done his duty, he found his thoughts resuming their old accustomed course. He longed for action, or at least for an insight into the affairs of the world—a longing which the narrow confines of his house could not satisfy. Lewin had sensed when they were eating that his father's conversation had been forced and constrained, and this had robbed the young people's talk too of all animation. A certain embarrassment had supervened. And so it was that, all their love for their father notwithstanding, brother and sister felt his absence almost as a liberation; heart and tongue could now venture wherever they wished. It hardly needs to be said that they were no more petty or selfish in their thoughts than others were: only they had no wish to be *compelled* to talk of the 'wickedest of men' over and over again, as though there were nothing else in the world worth talking about.

Together with Aunt Schorlemmer they had made their way to the living-room and were now seated (it might have been about seven o'clock) around the tall, old-fashioned fireplace. With them was Marie, Renate's friend, the dark-eyed daughter of the wealthy Kniehase, whose visit had been announced for this evening. Each of the three ladies was occupied in her own way. Renate, who was sitting closest to the fire, had in her right hand a fan-palm with which she sought alternately to kindle the flames and to protect herself from them; Aunt Schorlemmer was knitting with four large wooden needles a shawl which hung down beside her armchair like a fleece; Marie was leafing inquisitively through an account of a journey in Greenland which Aunt Schorlemmer had given her for Christmas, embellished with a dedicatory verse from Zinzendorf.* Between Marie and Lewin, but in no way constituting a barrier between them, there stood the Christmas tree, which Jeetze had carried in from the hall. The plundering of the tree, which was Lewin's task, had just commenced. He threw each golden nut he plucked from it over the top of the tree in a high arc and Marie on the other side tried to catch it. Throwing and catching were performed with equal dexterity.

Lewin enjoyed this game; and Christmas-tree sweetmeats had, moreover, always put him in the best of moods. Nibbling biscuits was something he normally refrained from, but in face of the gingerbread knights, nuns and fishes he was quite helpless and would assert again and again that 'no matter how thin a gingerbread figure may be there is always a little manna from Heaven in it.'

Lewin's happy mood soon provoked him to tease, and no one had to suffer more than Aunt Schorlemmer. 'Working on a holy day!' he expostulated, indicating as he did so the four wooden knitting-needles, which, it goes without saying, were only stimulated to more vigorous activity by this jocular reprimand. At last it grew too much for her. She flushed red and put an end to it by saying: 'My Greenlanders cannot wait.'

Since we can discover in the whole long course of our story not a single spot that would of itself offer a place for the insertion of a biographical sketch under the title 'Aunt Schorlemmer', we consider that the moment for us to do our duty by that excellent lady has now come. For Aunt Schorlemmer is no subordinate figure in this book, and since, after briefly making her acquaintance in entrance hall and church, we are now already meeting her for a third time, the reader has a right to demand to know who Aunt Schorlemmer actually is.

Aunt Schorlemmer was a Herrnhuter.* One day that now lay thirty years in the past she, then known as Sister Brigitte, was informed that Brother Jonathan Schorlemmer, at that time residing in Greenland, desired a wifely companion prepared to work beside him in the heavy task he was undertaking. She had obeyed this call, marked her name on her linen, and travelled north on the next Danish ship out of Hamburg. On a day that had no night she had landed in Greenland, Brother Schorlemmer had received her and personally consecrated their union. The marriage remained childless, a fact to which both submitted with Christian resignation. Thus there passed ten happy years. At the beginning of the eleventh Jonathan Schorlemmer died of a lung-catarrh and was buried in a coffin lined with sealskin. His widow however, after having given the people everything she possessed and assured each one of them she would never forget him, returned with the Greenland ship, first to Copenhagen and thence to her German homeland.

To her German homeland, but not to Herrnhut. On her circuitous return journey she touched on Berlin, where she had several relatives living, and decided to stay in that circle; she moved into the quarter, a modest one, to which fifty years before the immigrant Bohemian Brethren* and Herrnhuter had been consigned. Among these little houses of the Wilhelmstrasse she would very probably have ended her quiet and devout life had there not floated into the house one day a paper in which she read the following:

An older lady, preferably a widow, is sought to run a household in the country. She would in particular be responsible for looking after a twelve-year-old daughter. The applicant must be of a suitable disposition and a Christian. Applications to: B.v.V., *poste restante*, Küstrin.

Aunt Schorlemmer wrote; transactions were swiftly concluded. She arrived in Hohen-Vietz at the Christmas of 1806; it was a gloomy festive season that was then in progress at the manor house. An attitude of mutual trust prevailed from the first and it was only a few weeks before Aunt Schorlemmer's influence began to make itself felt. It could not bring happiness into the house, but it did bring peace and calm. Renate was inseparable from her, Lewin knew how to value the care she took of them, Berndt von Vitzewitz had a profound respect for her as a Herrnhuter.

And in this, to be sure, he differed from his children. The latter may have respected the sincerity of Aunt Schorlemmer's Christian beliefs, but not their profundity. Her passionless equanimity, which the father found so congenial, seemed to brother and sister merely weakness. Their view was that she employed her Christianity like a medicine-chest, and in this they were not wholly wrong. For all ordinary mishaps she had ready the *sal sedativum** of a pious everyday reflection such as 'Faith that's clear knows no fear' or 'However dark the night, still are we in God's sight'; in more serious cases, however, she reached for the potent and nerve-strengthening *sal volatile* of some more forceful dictum: 'Satan and his power must flee if my Lord Jesus stands by me.' The essential distinction between the mild and the strong medicines was that in the latter the Evil One was always challenged to come forth and assured that all his exertions would avail him nothing. All these sayings, however, whether mild or strong, were enunciated with the same imperturbability and the same firmness of belief in their efficacy. And therein lay the fault, or what the brother and sister saw as a fault. This imperturbability, which in relation to the quantity of sympathetic interest demanded often seemed like indifference, irritated these young people and often tried their patience severely. Berndt had a better understanding of this quiet Christianness and had himself experienced that the comfort to be drawn from the word of God was more than the comforting words of men.

This was Aunt Schorlemmer. The joking about her supposed indifference to the third commandment* had seriously annoyed her for a moment; paying no heed to this, however, Lewin went on with his teasing: 'Our friend seems, moreover, to be in entire ignorance of what an exalted visitor recently drew up at the Herrnhut communal house.'

'Who?' the two girls cried together.

'No less a person than Napoleon himself. On the night of the eleventh and twelfth.* And the Herrnhuter once again forbore to assume a heroic place in world history. They gaped at the Emperor, so far as night and driving snow made this possible, and allowed him to ride on. It happened because Herrnhut courage lives abroad, in China, in Greenland, in Hohen-Vietz. It is everywhere except at home. I am sure that Aunt Schorlemmer would have had him arrested and brought to trial as a disturber of the universal peace.'

Aunt Schorlemmer pointed one of her great knitting-needles threateningly at Lewin, who was in any case soon about to be forced to go over from attack to defence. The Emperor had not been evoked in vain; once drawn into a conversation, whether seriously or in jest, he began to exert his power, and Lewin, forgetting at any rate for the moment the teasing tone he had been using, began to paint a picture of that journey, or flight, which had taken the Emperor, for the first time deserted by his good fortune, from Smolensk back to his capital in the space of a fortnight. He told of things they already knew and things that were news to them, lingering over certain items longer than might perhaps have been strictly necessary.

Aunt Schorlemmer and Marie had listened attentively to this narrative; Renate, however, exclaimed: 'Excellent, and how instructive! A real general report on Russo-German post-stages. Oh, you cultivated city gentlemen, how badly you tell a story, and the cleverer you are the worse you tell it. All narrative and no dialogue!'

'So be it, Renate; I'll not deny it. But if we tell a story badly, you women listen to one even worse. You lack all patience, and when we perceive that we get confused, lose the thread and go straying off in all directions. What you want is pictures from a peep-show: Moscow in flames, Rostopchin,* the Kremlin, the crossing of the Beresina,* all in three minutes. Any story which is to bear you and what you are interested in along has to be as comfortable as an upholstered state-barge but at the same time as light as a canoe. I know well enough where the root of the evil is: context and connection mean nothing to you; you jump like knights on a chessboard.'

Renate laughed. 'Yes, we do; but if we jump too much you jump too little. You are so thorough it is offensive. You always think that we are far behind in our knowledge of the way the world is going, and yet we too know that the Emperor has arrived back in Paris. Oh, I could publish communiqués from Hohen-Vietz. But let us leave off feuding, Lewin. What is it I hear about a red window at the palace at Berlin? There was something about it in the paper; Kathinka wrote about it too, in more detail.'

'What did she write?'

'Oh, how funny you are. Now you're worried about what Kathinka wrote. That I was so foolish as to mention the name.'

Lewin tried to conceal his passing embarrassment. 'You're wrong, I'm not changing the subject; I have been much concerned with the phenomenon you spoke of. It happened three times; on the third day I saw it myself.'

'And what was it?'

'On each of the three days, at about half an hour after sunset, the upper windows of the Old Palace suddenly began to glow. The guard reported it. As the sun had long since gone down they suspected a fire. But nothing was found. The windows of the New Palace remained dark. People say it means war.'

'An easy prophecy,' Aunt Schorlemmer remarked quickly. 'We had war this year and we shall take it with us into the New Year too.'

'I believe that the whole thing would quickly have been

forgotten', Lewin went on, 'if on the second day afterwards
one of our papers, one that doesn't reach here, had not carried a
story which, with all its obscurities, was none the less clearly
intended to bestow on the phenomenon at the palace a profounder significance, to make it appear as signs and wonders.'

'Oh, tell us!'

'Certainly. But you must promise not to become impatient.'

'Would you notice?'

'Very well. It is a tale from Swedish history. The headline the
paper gave it was: "Charles XI* and the Apparition in the
Throne-Room at Stockholm". I don't guarantee that I can
repeat it exactly as the paper gave it, but in the main I've got it
right. What you want to know you retain. "Memory is love,"
Tubal said only yesterday, and even Kathinka agreed.'

At the mention of the name Tubal, Renate blushed red.
Lewin, however, continued as though he had not noticed:
'Charles XI was ill. He lay sleepless late at night in his room and
gazed across at the windows of the throne-room in the other
wing of the palace. No one was with him except Baron Bjelke,
the president of the Regency Council. Suddenly it seemed to
the King that the windows of the throne-room were beginning
to glow, and pointing to them he asked the baron: "What light
is that?" The baron replied: "It is the light of the moon reflected
in the glass." At that moment Count Oxenstierna came in to
ask how the King was, and the King, again pointing to the
glowing windows, asked him: "What light is that? I believe it is
a fire." The count too replied: "No, God be praised, it is not
that; it is the light of the moon reflected in the glass." But the
King grew more and more anxious, and at last he said:
"Gentlemen, all is not well over there; I shall go and see what it
can be." Thereupon they went along a corridor that led past the
Gustav Erichson Chamber until they stood before the great
doors of the throne-room. The King called upon the baron to
open the door, and when the baron begged to be allowed to let
it remain closed he took the key and opened it himself. When he
set foot on the threshold he stepped back hastily and said:
"Gentlemen, if you are willing to follow me we shall see what
is happening here; perhaps God in his grace intends to reveal
something to us." The others replied: "Yes." '

Here Lewin was interrupted. Jeetze entered with a bowl of fruit, cane-apples and Gravensteiners, which grew well at Hohen-Vietz. Aunt Schorlemmer employed the interruption to give a number of domestic instructions, Renate however remarked: 'I do not see how these events are connected; but, of course, the more mysterious the more exciting to the imagination.'

Lewin nodded in agreement: 'That impression will grow stronger as we go on.' Then he continued: 'When the King and his two counsellors went in they became aware of a long table at which a number of venerable men were seated and at the middle a young prince, recognizable as such from the throne which, bedecked with coats-of-arms and red tapestries, had been erected immediately behind him. It was clear that a court was in session. At the lower end of the table there stood an executioner's block, and around the block in a wide semicircle stood the accused, richly clad yet not in the costume at that time worn in Sweden. The men sitting in judgement pointed at the books they were holding in their hands; they were reluctant to let the young prince have his way, but the latter shook his head haughtily and gestured towards the lower end of the table, where head after head was now falling until blood began to stream across the floor. The King and his attendants turned away from this scene in horror; when they again looked back, the throne had crumbled to pieces. The King then seized the hand of Baron Bjelke and cried aloud: "What is this that the voice of the Lord is telling me? God, when shall all this come to pass?"

'And after he had called on God for a third time, the answer came: "This shall not come to pass in your time, but in the time of the sixth ruler after you. There will be a bloodbath such as there has never been before in Sweden. But then there shall come a great king and with him peace and a new age." And when these words had been spoken the apparition vanished. The King had a struggle to contain himself. Then, however, he returned to his sleeping-chamber along the same corridor. The two counsellors followed.'

Lewin fell silent. In the living-room it had grown quiet; the fan was still, even the knitting-needles were still; each was sunk in his own thoughts. After a pause Renate asked: 'Who was the sixth ruler in Sweden?'

'Gustav IV;* he lost his throne.'

'So you regard the whole story as true, as a real vision?'

'I say neither yes nor no. The deposition which records the event lies in the archives at Stockholm. It was written that same night by the King himself; his two companions both signed it as well. That the hands are genuine has been attested. I have neither the right nor the courage to deny the possibility of such apparitions. Allow me to say, Renate, *we* do not have the right.'

Lewin emphasized the 'we'. Then, resuming his former jocular tone, he turned to Aunt Schorlemmer and Marie and urged them to say whether or not they believed in such apparitions.

Marie stood up, and they all now saw for the first time how profound an impression the story had made upon her. She pressed the twigs that, without knowing why, she had been breaking from the fir-tree, together into a knot and threw them on to the dully glowing fire. The sudden flame they made was followed by a billow of smoke, in the midst of which she herself stood for a moment like an apparition; all that could be seen was her outline and the red ribbons that fell over her hair and down her neck. So far as she was concerned no further avowal was needed: she herself was the answer to Lewin's question.

Aunt Schorlemmer, however, took up her needles again and shook her head sadly; then, as though she were warding off a ghost, she rapidly repeated in a voice loud and clear:

> 'While God protects me,
> Guards and directs me,
> Evil must fly me.
> Let Satan haunt me,
> Enemies taunt me,
> Jesus stands by me.'*

7

At the Inn

THE village of Hohen-Vietz proper (there were also outlying fields with occupied dwellings on them) was limited to a single long street which, tracing a path beneath the foot of the hill, ended to the north in the Vitzewitz estate and to the south in a large mill.

The buildings of the estate consisted of two horseshoe-shaped halves, one of which was composed of the three wings of the manor house and the other of the stalls and barns of the manorial farm. The open ends of the horseshoes faced one another, and between them there ran a paved road which also served as a driveway to the house and, extending beyond the estate, mounted the hill to become the walnut-tree avenue we have already referred to.

The mill was even more agreeably situated. It was both an oil-mill and a saw-mill, and a stream that dropped steeply past the village drove the machinery of both. The stream was now frozen: but the snow and ice that hung in fantastic shapes from the great driving-wheels enhanced, if not the idyllic, at any rate the picturesque charm of the houses, sheds and store-rooms which, thrown together in colourful confusion, constituted the mill-yard.

Manorial estate and mill-yard were the extremities; between them ran the street, with its thirty or more houses divided irregularly on either side. The left side of the street, the east side, was the privileged side. Here lay the parsonage, the school, the mayor's house; while the right side, which was inhabited almost exclusively by cottagers and labourers, exhibited but one solitary building of any distinction: the *inn*.

We shall now enter this building. It did not look very much like a village inn, for it lacked the usual gable-awning which, sustained by wooden pillars, served to protect arriving carriages from the weather; instead of this, almost a third of the house-front was filled by a flight of wide brick steps which jutted out before it. The balustrade was of stone. This external appearance, which had more of the town than the village in it, was matched by the furnishings within. Of the two guest-rooms, which were separated by the tile-covered entrance hall, one, with its clean-scrubbed tables and high-backed chairs into which a heart had been carved, certainly still preserved the character of an inn; the other, however, contained muslin curtains and framed copperplate pictures, among them likenes-ses of Schill and Archduke Karl,* and in almost every way resembled a middle-class club-room; it even possessed a read-ing-table with the *Lebuser Amtsblatt*, the *Beobachter an der Spree* and the *Berlinische Nachrichten von Staats- und gelehrten Sachen* spread out upon it. Everything exuded ease and affluence, and well might it do so, for the farmers of Hohen-Vietz who came here to play cards had an abundant command of both. If they had ever existed in a state of servitude it had long since given way to happier circumstances, in this region in which new fruitful acres were continually being won from fen and swamp-land previously without owner, and because he himself felt free Berndt von Vitzewitz did not merely welcome this growing independence but wherever he could encouraged it. An incident in his youth had contributed to this attitude. Shortly before the campaign of '92,* while he was still in garrison, he had paid a visit to the Salzweld district and while he was there one of the Knesebecks of Schloss Tylsen, a former member of his own regiment, had taken him down to the village and had said to him: 'Look, Vitzewitz, here you will see something you have never seen before in your life: *free peasant farmers*.' And these words, together with the peasant farmers themselves, had not failed to make a deep impression upon him. That now lay twenty years in the past, but it had never been forgotten and had more than once been of benefit to the inhabitants of Hohen-Vietz.

And today too, Christmas Day 1812, a number of local worthies, all men in their mid-fifties and older and all peasant farmers, had assembled in the guest-room. There were four of them: Kümmeritz, Kallies, Reetzke and Krull, all from genuine Hohen-Vietz families who, inhabitants of this place from time immemorial, had lived in the old hillside village with the Vitzewitzes and with them had deserted it, and together with them had experienced all the good times and the bad. All were in holiday costume, stiffly upright on the broad wooden seats eight or ten of which stood at a large, russet-coloured round table.

As a fifth they had been joined by the innkeeper himself, Scharwenka: through inheritance from his wife's side he had acquired a very large holding and was the richest man in the village of any kind, but, notwithstanding the six hundred acres of former fenland he had under the plough, he was still not regarded as being a full peer and equal. For that the peasants found two good reasons. One derived from the fact that it was only his grandfather who, during the draining of the Oder-bruch, had arrived in the village with other colonists from Bohemia; the other was more weighty and amounted to the reproach that, despite all attempts at dissuasion, he persisted in pursuing the ill-esteemed trade of innkeeping. Whenever this ticklish point came up, Scharwenka was accustomed to invoke his late grandfather, who had taught him from infancy up: never despise ducats. But the real reason he refused to abandon the pot-house life of 'menial service' had nothing to do with ducats. The wealthy peasant farmer was far less interested in the nice profits to be made from innkeeping than he was in the daily encounter with fresh faces that it afforded; the talk and chatter, but above all listening, and acquiring knowledge of the affairs of others, *that* was what bound him to this trade. It was a matter of pride to him that he would know of some peasant *mésalliance* which circumstances had rendered imperative twenty-four hours before anyone else did. He could foretell bankruptcies as an almanac-maker foretells the weather; his actual speciality, however, was millers suspected of setting fire to their mills. The register he kept of all this encompassed more or less the entire place.

That was the innkeeper Scharwenka.

He had taken his seat directly opposite the door, so that he could see and welcome everyone who came in. Immediately beside him sat Reetzke and Krull, who for the past hour had been smoking in silence, in marked contrast to Kümmeritz and

Kallies, who were of the loquacious breed. A word about these gentlemen too.

Despite his fifty years, Kümmeritz possessed the bearing and authority of an old soldier, and he had a right to both. He had been first a grenadier, then a lance-corporal in the Möllendorf Regiment, had participated in the Rhine campaign★ and twice stormed the Weissenburg lines;★ had then been wounded at Kaiserslautern★ and had been discharged. Together with the mayor, Kniehase, who chanced not to be there that day, he represented within this circle at the inn the traditions of the Prussian Army, plotted the course of the Emperor Napoleon, drew his battles on the table and maintained the view that Jena, 'where we already had victory in our hands', had been lost only by a trick.

Kallies was the exact opposite of Kümmeritz. A tall, narrow-shouldered man, mentally alert but in character weak and yielding, he was obliged to submit to a degree of teasing and banter to which, regardless of anything else, the nickname he had acquired seemed to offer a challenge. For at an age when he could hardly walk he had fallen into a large vat of cream and since then he had been called, very aptly it seemed, 'Creampot'. Something milky had indeed continued to adhere to him all his life.

All five were now smoking their long Dutch pipes and each had a taper beside him. Kallies was speaking, and from what he was saying it was clear that another guest, a traveller, a merchant it would seem, had just left the room.

'Whenever I see him standing there like that,' Kallies said, emphasizing his words, 'I think of his father, old Crucible Schultze; he always used to stand in the same way, with his hands in his trouser pockets, and was just the same kind of merry fellow, with an expression on him as though he had cheated Old Nick at cards. Scharwenka, you must have known old Crucible Schultze.'

Scharwenka nodded; Kümmeritz, however, who had just refilled his pipe and was starting to smoke it, said between puffs: 'Crucible Schultze? The deuce take it if I have ever heard the name in my life. And I too am a Hohen-Vietzer born and bred.'

'It was when you were with the army, Kümmeritz. In the 'eighties or thereabouts. Crucible Schultze was dead after that, if he ever did die.'

Kümmeritz, who had left at any rate part of his Wendish superstitiousness behind him with the army, grinned and then said: 'Don't let's have any foolishness, Creampot. Be sensible. Anyone who is dead is dead. He can come back as a ghost, but he has to die first. Why was he called Crucible Schultze?'

'His name was Schultze. But everyone called him Crucible Schultze. I often used to go and see him when I used to deliver the beets. Always paid in cash. The Schwedter used to say: "*He's* got plenty." He used to be standing behind the table, always with his hands in his pockets, and would look at you in such a confounded way you didn't know where you were. But there was never no haggling. You must remember that, Scharwenka.'

Scharwenka nodded again. Creampot went on: 'The work shop looked like a prison, high, white and iron bars at the window. There was nothing in it except three shelves on the wall, and on the shelves there stood hundreds of crucibles, big ones and small ones, earthenware ones and ones made of clay, that's why he was called Crucible Schultze. A couple of them were black and were made out of charcoal.'

'What was he then, a smelter, an alchemist?'

'That he was, and he smelted out many a bright ingot for the Schwedter Margrave.* But when the Margrave thought he had learned it all by watching Schultze, and could now do it for himself, he wanted to get rid of him, invited him to the palace, picked a quarrel with him and fired off at him both barrels of a Suhler rifle that he had loaded with two golden pins. They were the kind the Polish nobility wear on their coats. But Crucible Schultze only laughed, caught the two pins with his left hand, for he was left-handed, you know, showed them to the Margrave and said: "I shall wear these in remembrance of my gracious lord."'

It was plain that Kallies, who was now well launched, proposed to expatiate further on the race of the Crucible Schultzes, on beets, alchemy and the ingratitude of the

Schwedter Margrave: but before he could do so a new guest entered and gave a new turn to the conversation.

The new arrival was the miller, Miekley, who owned the oil- and saw-mill at the southern end of the village. He was below middle height, wore a light grey coat, and his face bore that peculiar expression found among almost all country people who are involved in religious controversy, who are sectarians or want to be. Where intellectual labour has traced its lin- eaments on the face from the days of youth onward, the lineament of the sectarian is only one among many and it can easily get lost or be overlooked in the totality; with country people, however, it stands out unmistakably, and the fewer its rivals for domination are the more unmistakable it is. This characteristic, a mixture of sensuality and renunciation, of pride and humility, was pronouncedly present in miller Miekley, who was for the rest a conscientious man, maintained his family honour and enjoyed the especial protection of Aunt Schorlemmer. This could happen without anyone's taking offence at it since Miekley had not really deserted the village church: he regular attended the sermons of Pastor Seidentopf, and it was only once a quarter that he drew sustenance from the 'deeper well' of Kandidat Uhlenhorst* when the latter, on circuit through the Oderbruch and the Neumark, assembled around him in Hohen-Sathen all the conventiclists from both sides of the Oder. Then, to be sure, there was a holiday and festivity: all work ceased, the best horses came out of the stable, and even had the ways been bottomless our Old Lutheran miller would have accounted it mortal sin to have missed the distribution of manna.

Miekley sat himself to the left of Kümmeritz. The latter, no doubt realizing that a religious discussion had now become unavoidable, anticipated it by saying: 'Well, Miekley, how did you like the sermon today?'

'I liked it very well, Kümmeritz, even though he said nothing of the fact that on this day salvation was born to us in Bethlehem in Judea. And he spoke even less of the "Son of God become man". Uhlenhorst would have shaken his head. But he spoke like a worthy man. I know him well, he has a Prussian heart.'

'And a Christian one too,' the others cried as though with a single voice.

'He doesn't rant against people or call damnation down on them,' Kallies interposed; 'he is no Pharisee. He has humility, Miekley, and that is the main thing.'

'Creampot is right,' averred Kümmeritz. 'There is no one hereabouts to compare with our Seidentopf. He has only one fault, he is too good and too credulous, and sees everything as he wants to see it. The sea engulfed the host of Egypt, so he said. But King Pharaoh is again sitting in his capital spinning his plots as before. We are still in alliance with him, and Heaven alone knows whether we shall ever get safely free of him. May God grant us an honest war.'

'That you shall have,' exclaimed Miekley, who despite his Lutheranism had retained a strong belief in ghosts and ghostly stories, 'that you shall have and all of us with you. The Alt-Landsberg reapers have been reaping again, and you all know what that signifies. They reaped for seven days before Old Fritz went to war, and the stubble was then as red as if it had rained blood. This last November they were reaping again in a bare field.'

'And from the direction of the sunset,' Scharwenka broke in, 'which means to say that the enemy will come from the west. We shall have the French back again, young, fresh soldiers with the same old tricks and dodges, and whoever has a daughter at home had better watch out. They have an insolent way with them and the women run after them.'

'That they should not,' Miekley protested, 'and if they do, let the shame fall on us. Where wicked lust shoots overnight into the corn, a bad seed lay at its heart from the first; but where there is chastity and good morals and devoutness the Evil One has no power, even when he disguises himself as a wicked Frenchman.'

All nodded in agreement. 'But', Miekley went on, 'the reason they are an abomination is not that they are wanton, no, it is because they are an unholy nation. They have presumed to depose from his dominion and throne the everlasting God of Heaven and earth, and, what can almost be called worse, they have presumed to set him up again. Now they again have a

God, only he is a God of their own; it is not a true Christian God, it is merely a French God, one pulled down and set up. They know only how to worship their Emperor, not how to worship God, and in all these years whenever I have seen a Frenchman in our churches it has been only to cause mischief.'

'They have removed the fringes from the altar-cloth; they have cut out the golden embroidery; they have melted down the candlesticks!' several voices exclaimed.

'Oh, they have done worse things than that, not here but in places not far away. They buried the pastor at Görlsdorf up to the armpits because he had hidden the church property, and thought better of it only when he begged them to kill him instead of torturing him. In Hohen-Finow they drank the communion wine and sang wicked songs; then they carried the altar-table out of the church into the churchyard, threw their Devil's bones into the communion chalice and played dice. They went down into the crypt and ripped the silk dress from a woman who had recently died.'

'They did so,' interposed Creampot, who, like all weak natures, had an inclination for overtrumping, 'but in Haselberg they had to pay for it, at least one of them did. The crypt at Haselberg is what they call a mummy-crypt, there are supposed to be several at Hohen-Barnim. Well, when the French broke open the coffins they saw that the bodies were not decomposed. That made them laugh. Then they carried one of the coffins out of the crypt into the church, took out the body, and when they found they could move its arms they decided to crucify it. They placed it against the altar wall and drove two nails through its hands. But one of the hands came loose again and as it fell gave one of the miscreants a box round the ears. It gave him such a shock he fell dead to the ground.'

'It was the judgement of God upon him,' cried Miekley. 'And they shall all be dealt with likewise, though the dead have to rise from their graves.'

'Before God performs his miracles, however,' Kümmeritz concluded the conversation, 'we must make ourselves worthy of them. Is that not so, Miekley? We must not sit with our arms folded. The Alt-Landsberg reapers have been reaping; when the King calls, those who still have strength to reap, let them join in the reaping. I am resolved. My all for Prussia and the King!'

The farmers rose and went off in different directions along the village street. To the northward a red glow appeared in the sky.

'Is that a fire?' asked Krull.

'No,' said Miekley, 'it is the Northern Lights, Heaven is giving us a sign.'

8

Hoppenmarieken*

HOPPENMARIEKEN lived in the 'woodland acre', on the edge of which a street composed of mere mud-huts had formed itself a century or more before. This street, which the Hohen-Vietzers always regarded as something alien to them, stood at a right-angle to the actual village, commenced a hundred paces behind the mill-yard and ran up the hill parallel to the walnut-tree avenue that was a continuation of the driveway to the manor house. It was the poor quarter of Hohen-Vietz, a place of shelter for the exiled and down-and-out, a kind of stationary gypsy encampment where people came and went without the authorities in the village paying any particular attention. 'That is how the woodland acre has always been.' Thus they let it alone and intervened in its affairs only when some piece of gross misconduct made punitive action altogether unavoidable.

The appearance of the woodland acre matched its moral status. The huts in which its inhabitants dwelt differed from the stalls which stood to front and rear of them only in the hearth-fire smoke that came twisting up through their roofs. The snow that at present covered everything created a complete uniformity.

In the last of the mud-huts, which was situated halfway up the hill, there lived (as we began our chapter by stating) Hoppenmarieken. There were no stalls; in their place a thick hedge surrounded the little house, which possessed a door and a window to the front but no other kind of entrance or aperture. It resembled a die with only two spots. The interior contained but few rooms. The hallway, the far end of which also included facilities for cooking, was as narrow as it was long, and completely dark; in summer, however, it received light through the open door, while in winter the fire burning in the hearth had to help out. Beside the hallway lay the parlour, behind that the alcove.

That was Hoppenmarieken's house. But who was Hoppenmarieken?

Hoppenmarieken was a dwarf. Where she came from no one could say for certain. The older Hohen-Vietzers told how she had arrived in the village some thirty years previously and, appearing to be more or less a tramp, was, like many before her and after her, received with something less than open arms. The then lord of the manor, however, Berndt von Vitzewitz's father, had taken pity on her, and had pacified those who still objected with the half-humorous rejoinder: 'That's what we have the woodland acre for.' Even then, they said, she had looked just the same as she did now, just as old, just as ugly, had worn the same waterproof boots and the same headscarf, and was already recognizable far and wide, just as she was today, by her red flannel skirt, the wicker basket on her back and the tall, crooklike staff in her hand.

Since that time (so much was certain) Hoppenmarieken had been in residence at the woodland acre and had become the best-known person in the entire southern half of the Oderbruch. The cause of her fame was not only her singular appearance but also her trade. She had, indeed, several trades. In the first place she was a postwoman. Three times a week, whatever the weather might be, she departed early in the morning or late in the evening according to when the post left, collected letters, newspapers and parcels, and returned to Hohen-Vietz from Frankfurt or Küstrin* twelve hours later. And as her performance of this office had made her a familiar figure everywhere, so, in spite of all that was now and then urged against her, it in the end also made her popular. Everyone rejoiced to see Hoppenmarieken coming across the yard and, by the peculiar way she carried her staff, which she swung somewhat like a drum-major, announcing: 'I am bringing you some news.' In the country the postman is always popular.

This postal service, however, constituted merely the foundation of her existence; more important to her, or at any rate more profitable, was the commission business she conducted beside it. The trade in eggs in all the villages for a mile and a half around Hohen-Vietz was really in her hands, and in pursuing it she knew how to multiply the commission she received twofold. She achieved this result by conducting the entire business through barter. A farmer's wife in Zechin or Wuschewier who wanted a new headscarf would make sure she encountered Hoppenmarieken when the latter came her way, stow into her wicker basket a cockerel she had kept ready, together with a couple of score of eggs, and then leave it to Hoppenmarieken's genius and discretion to procure the headscarf. It could and did happen that in this or that article Hoppenmarieken controlled the entire market. The profits that fell to her in this way were regarded as honest gain, and so they were. But not all her gains were of so honest a nature. On the woodland acre there lived people who, themselves of ill repute, related evil things of her. Such tales were, however, also told in the village itself. Low and loose women used to slip into her house at night; she was a clairvoyante, she told fortunes with cards. On Sunday she was always in church and in her harsh voice joined in singing the hymns, the best-known of which she knew by heart; but nobody believed that she was really a Christian. She was regarded as a cross between a dwarf and a witch. Even in the manor house—where, partly because she was a village curiosity, but also partly on account of her usefulness, many things about her were overlooked—she was on the whole little better thought of. Only Lewin, inspired by a certain poetical attachment, stood by her. He liked to weave teasing fantasies around her: her age could not be determined, she was a mysterious relic of the ancient world of the Wends, a product of the soil of the region, like the dwarf pine-trees a few of which still stood up on the hills. Again on other occasions, when it was pointed out to him that the Wends had very probably been a handsome race, he would content himself with giving her out as a heathen idol which, when the last of the

Czernebog temples* fell, had suddenly come alive and was now haunting the regions it formerly ruled. He might also add that Hoppenmarieken would never die, for she was not alive: she was no more than a spectre. In this, however, he was quite mistaken: she was not merely alive, she very much enjoyed being alive and lived, moreover, with that sensual pleasure in living which dwarfs always and the avaricious usually possess. And she was both: dwarfish and avaricious.

The farmers had hardly dispersed from their discussion at Scharwenka's inn when Hoppenmarieken came up the village street with the heavy tread imposed by her waterproof boots. As always she was walking quickly, snorting down her nose and talking incomprehensibly to herself; her tall crooked staff moved rhythmically up and down as she went, and her red flannel skirt flashed in the sunlight.

When she had passed the mill-yard she wheeled to the left and walked up the snow-covered street of stalls and mud-huts towards her house. The door was only on the latch, and rightly so, indeed, for everything inside the house was guarded by the uncanny atmosphere that pervaded it. On entering she was met by total darkness; feeling her way with her stick, she groped as far as the middle of the hallway, where she laid aside stick and basket and then felt around with her horny hand in the ashes on the hearth until a couple of glowing coals were disclosed. Then she blew on them, took a sulphur-match and with its aid ignited a tin lamp, without, however, making any immediate use of the modest light it gave out: instead she crawled into the mouth of a large oven standing directly beside the hearth, stirred about here too with a long, half-charred log of wood among the glimmer of fire lying deep in the oven's recesses, and threw up a number of twigs, pine-cones and a couple of pieces of stone-hard peat; only then did she enter the parlour.

The parlour was spacious. Hoppenmarieken cast the light of the lamp around it, examined every corner, glanced into the alcove at the back of the room and, murmuring away continually to herself, at length expressed her satisfaction with the state of things as she had found them. The lamp emitted just enough light to illumine everything present in the parlour. Next to the window, pushed right into the corner, there stood a cupboard with cups and plates in it; the oaken table was scoured clean; on the alcove door there hung a large, round mirror, cracked down the middle, though whether it hung there as an accessory of vanity or of business must be left undecided—for it looked as though it must surely play some role when fortune-telling and reading of cards was under way. For the rest, a certain Christmas festiveness, which Hoppenmarieken herself seemed to have prepared the previous day, was clearly in evidence. The four-poster bed had fresh curtains, the floorboards were strewn with sprigs of fir and from the ceiling-hook there hung a branch of rowan whose berries were still red despite the early arrival of winter. All this must have produced an impression almost of cheerful warmth, had not three other things also been present: first the person of Hoppenmarieken, then her bird-cages, and third and last the alcove. Hoppenmarieken herself we know already; but a word about the other two.

Along all four walls, close beneath the ceiling, ran a row of bird-cages: there must have been about twenty of them. Only where the bed and the stove stood was the row interrupted. What was actually in the cages had not been clearly apparent when Hoppenmarieken had made her inspection with the lamp: all that was visible was a variety of dark bird-eyes staring, large and sleepy, into the light. It was impossible to avoid the thought that these eyes kept watch here when their mistress was absent.

This strange frieze of bird-cages, in which a race dedicated to silence seemed to dwell, was uncanny enough, but the alcove was uncannier still. The mirror hanging on the door already caused misgiving. Within the alcove all was empty: the only thing there was a row of bunches of herbs, which ran around the walls in a fashion similar to that of the bird-cages in the next room. There were herbs both wholesome and harmful: balm-mint, yarrow, and arnica, but also long-rooted garlic, wild rosemary, and juniper. Among them hung bundles of stalks of rye, whose healthful ears had long since fallen out, while those of the poisonous blue ergot still adhered; the odour they produced together was stupefying. What a keen observer would perhaps have been struck by most of all was the fact that, instead of from simple nails, the entire herbarium was suspended from wooden pegs of a thickness in diameter that bore no relation whatever to the tiny weight they were required to carry.

Hoppenmarieken, who had meanwhile made herself comfortable and exchanged her tall waterproof boots for a pair of felt shoes, now fetched the basket in from the hall and from all the activities that followed seemed intent on preparing a feast for herself. She slowly rummaged about in her basket until she had found the objects she was seeking. The first thing to emerge from the depths was a tapering blue paper bag, then came two eggs, which she examined against the light, finally an old printed pocket-handkerchief in which something of greater consequence, however, was enveloped: so it seemed, at least, for she held the bundle up to her ear with both hands and shook it, and the sound it emitted appeared to quieten her mind. Then she laid everything on to the table, one thing beside the other, and fetched from the cupboard an old faience pot with a broken handle, a whisk and a metal spoon. Now everything was assembled. She shook a spoonful of sugar from the blue bag into the pot, broke into it the two eggs, unwound from the handkerchief a bottle of rum, gazed upon it with affection, poured it in, and whisked. Only one thing was still lacking: the boiling water. But that too had been taken care of. She went out into the hall, again crawled into the mouth of the oven and re-emerged with a spouted tea-kettle, the contents of which disappeared, bubbling and hissing, into the great pot.

With that the preparations were to be regarded as complete: the actual feast could begin. She cleared the table again, heaped up before her a large brown pound-cake, and supporting her head on both hands gazed with voluptuous contentment at the meal she had prepared. But even now she was concerned not to hasten too much. Whether she saw in a deferment of gratification a means of enhancing it, or whether she had her own Hoppenmariekenish ideas of how a Christmas Day ought to be celebrated, is all one: the outcome was that she provisionally contented herself with breathing in the rising steam, at the same time opening wide the table-drawer where, separated by a dividing board, there lay on one side a hymn-book and on the other a pack of cards. She took up the hymn-book, opened it at the Christmas carol 'From Heaven on high, thence am I come', read aloud, in a kind of recitative which she herself may well have regarded as singing, the first three and then the last strophes, slammed the book shut again and took a first hearty draught. Immediately thereafter she proceeded to the most energetic possible attack on the pound-cake, which in the space of ten minutes had vanished from the table. She scraped the crumbs together in the flat of her left hand and shook them all carefully into her mouth.

Only now that the faience pot no longer possessed a rival was she in a position to demonstrate to it what it meant to her. Stroking and patting it, she placed her hands around it, sounded with her knuckles all the protuberant places, bent down over it and sipped, quaffed and then resumed full-bodied draughts. After having thus revelled through the whole syllabus of pleasure,* she opened the drawer a second time but now she took out, not the hymn-book, but the pack of cards. They were familiar playing-cards: spades, hearts, clubs; they were pressed together into a trough, though this presented no difficulty to Hoppenmarieken's hands. But when she had dealt, shuffled and dealt them again for some thirty minutes without the cards coming out as they ought to have come out the blood rushed to her head.

The Jack of Spades would not quit her side. That displeased her; she knew quite well who the Jack of Spades was. What? Here he was again beside her. She stood up in disquiet, seized the lamp, looked behind the stove, inspected the alcove two or three times, and then sat herself down again. But the tightening of the heart she felt would not go away: so she unfastened the flowered cotton bodice that she wore, and felt, tore and tugged after a little pocket that hung on her breast fastened with a leather strap. It was there. She brought it forth, counted its contents and found that everything was as it should be.

This restored her composure. She decided to try once more and began to deal out the cards again. This time all went well: the Jack of Spades lay far away. An ugly grin passed across her face; then she finished her drink, bolted the door with a large wooden bolt, and extinguished the light.

When an hour later the moon shone through the window, it

also shone on the weather-worn face of the dwarf Hoppenmarieken: now that the black headscarf had been pushed aside and the strands of white hair came into view it was even uglier than before. The moon passed across: it did not like what it saw. Hoppenmarieken, however, dreamed that the Jack of Spades had seized her by the throat and was tearing at the leather strap so as to wrench away the little pocket. She struggled with him; she sweated with fear; but as she did so she none the less cried out: 'Stop, I say: thief, thief!'

Her cries echoed through the empty house. The birds descended slowly from their perches and stared through their bars at the bed whence the cries proceeded.

9

The Village Mayor*

OPPOSITE the inn there lay the establishment of the village mayor. It consisted of a house with a tiled roof and two long, narrow stable-buildings running directly behind it and joined together at the far end by a barn. A field planted with fruit-trees and raspberry bushes lying behind this barn was extended by two narrow beds of flowers almost to the village street, so that in summer when you looked down from the church on to the mayor's farm it resembled a large garden embracing house and yard as though in two extended arms. And then not even Miekley's mill looked more attractive. The mallows blossomed right up to the roof, the bees hummed about the hive, the grapes hung from the trellis, while from the ancient pear-tree that stood on guard to the right of the courtyard gate the heavy fruit detached itself from time to time and fell with a bump on to the stone threshold. Of the occupants of the house none paid any heed to this sound; only a girl sitting on the stone steps that jutted out before the house under the honeysuckle and elder that grew there would look up for a moment, listen, and then go on with winding her thread or sewing a hem.

Thus it was in late summer. But in winter, too, the home of the village mayor presented an attractive picture; as it did now, indeed, on the second day of Christmas. In the yard the snow had been shovelled together to form a wall; the stable doors stood open and the warm air within them wafted out like a mist. There were sparrows before the house door pecking up single seeds from the ground. Otherwise all was still; even the yard-dog was taking a holiday. His kennel stood in one of the corners formed by the stables and the barn; he had moved some of his straw out in front of the kennel door and now his pointed wolflike head lay on this pillow and gazed contentedly into the morning.

And the stillness and festive air of the world outside was repeated within the house. The steps that led up to it were strewn with sand; young pine-trees stood in the corners of the vestibule and filled the air with their resinous odour; and from a hook in the middle of the hallway there hung a cluster of mistletoe. The living-rooms were nicely warm and the doors of the stoves were closed; only to the right of the hall, where the big drawing-room lay, was a fire still crackling and throwing its flickering light. A cat rubbed herself against the warm corner and, arching her back, purred as a sign of her especial contentment.

In the front living-room three people were sitting around a heavy oak table. Nearest to the window, and with his back turned towards it, there was a broad-shouldered man in his fifties: his face was characterized by strength, resolution and benevolence; his hair was blond and thinning, he was clad in his Sunday best and wore a long, dark-brown coat. The woman to his left was, despite her forty years, still handsome; she was dark of complexion and dressed in the Wendish fashion: a wide collar fell over her black-cloth bodice and her short flannel skirt was folded into a hundred pleats; her gleaming black hair was only half hidden beneath her small net cap. The jewellery she wore was all of silver: around her neck there was wound a thick chain fastened together at the front with a slide; her earrings resembled great silver drops.

This was the mayoral couple, the Kniehases. Opposite the man, in the full light of the window, was the daughter of the house, Marie, sitting just as upright as she had before the fireside of the manor house the previous day. She was wearing the same taffeta dress and the same red ribbon in her hair; and with the same degree of attention with which yesterday she had followed Lewin's narrations she was today following her father's readings: first the Christmas Gospel, then the eighth chapter of the Book of Daniel. Old Kniehase had chosen this chapter with careful deliberation. Maria's hands lay motionless in her lap. And when they reached the passage:

And in the latter time of their kingdom a king of fierce countenance and understanding dark sentences shall stand up. And his power shall be mighty, but not by his own power; and through his policy also he shall cause craft to prosper in his hand: he shall also stand up against the Prince of princes; *but he shall be broken without hand*

—her eyes grew bigger as they had at the story of the fire in the palace at Stockholm, for when her mind was aroused everything she heard of took on a living shape. But except for this all remained as it was. The robin redbreast hopped with a gentle chirp from his perch on to the branch and back from the branch on to the perch; the pendulum of the grandfather-clock continued to beat its measured rhythm. And so, too, did the heart of the village mayor.

Kniehase was a 'Pfälzer', a man from the Palatinate. How did he come to be in this Wendish village? And how did he become its mayor?

At the same time as the Scharwenkas emigrated there from Bohemia with other Czech families, the Kniehases did the same, with other families from the Rhine. This was about 1750, when Friedrich the Great was taking steps to drain the swamplands of the Oderbruch and to colonize them. Because there were only a few of them, the Czech families found accommodation in the old Wendish villages, and thus the Scharwenkas came to Hohen-Vietz. The colonists from the Rhine, however—who, regardless of whether they came from Cleves or Siegen, from Nassau or the Palatinate, were all called 'Pfälzer' (just as in Ireland all new arrivals are called 'Saxons')—founded their own villages, of which Neu-Barnim was the biggest. It was in this village that our Kniehase was born, on the day of the Peace of Hubertusburg.* From this circumstance his father concluded that his son must become a parson, and had him educated to the extent that the modest means available permitted. But the young Kniehase was very far from wanting to become a man of peace; only the world of the soldier held any attraction for him, and as early as the age of twenty, after having overcome his father's resistance without much difficulty, he enlisted in the grenadier company of the Möllendorf Regiment, which was at that time garrisoned in Berlin. Its rigorous austerity notwithstanding, he much enjoyed service in the regiment, and as early as 1792, at the commencement of the Rhine campaign, he had become one of its colour-corporals. He received a decoration at Valmy, and a second at Kaiserslautern. This is how it happened. The Von Thadden Company saw itself compelled to evacuate a hill position it had commanded since the beginning of the battle; enemy artillery came up and now dominated the sloping terrain, some 1,500 feet wide, across which the retreating company, which had in part disintegrated into mere squads of men, was carrying out its withdrawal. Halfway down the slope lay a lance-corporal wounded in the leg who begged his comrades not to leave him behind. A number of them paused; but the fire of grape-shot coming across snapped their resolution; their courage deserted even the bravest. Then Corporal Kniehase leaped up, ran back to the wounded man, loaded him on to his shoulder and bore him out of the line of fire. When the company had reassembled, Staff-Captain von Thadden stepped up to Kniehase and shook him by the hand; the grenadiers themselves broke into a loud cheer, and half an hour later they recaptured the hill position they had lost.

The actions of this day led our Kniehase, if not directly then by an orderly progression of events, to the ancient Wendish village of which he was now the ruling official. For the lance-corporal he had so courageously borne out of the fire of the enemy was none other than our friend of the inn at Hohen-Vietz, Peter Kümmeritz. Become an invalid, he received his discharge; two years later, however, the war ended and the entire Rhine army returned to its garrison, the Möllendorf Regiment with it.

It was after the harvest, in '95. The gossamer was already wafting through the air when, on one of those stainless bright

days that September can bring, a broad-shouldered man dressed in the King's uniform turned past Miekley's mill into the
village street at Hohen-Vietz. A pair of medals gleamed on his
chest, and anyone who could recognize braid and facings
would have seen that he was a non-commissioned officer of the
Möllendorf Regiment. It was, indeed, none other than our
Corporal Kniehase. When, pursued by half the youth of the
village who, timid but eager, were trying to answer his
questions, he was about to enter the home of his former lance-
corporal, he was met on the threshold, not by Peter Kümmeritz in person, but by Trude Kümmeritz, his sister. From
everything that followed it has to be assumed that this deputiz-
ing of sister for brother was not at all unpleasing to our
Kniehase, since before leaving the hospitable Kümmeritz
house a week later to rejoin his regiment he had not only
renewed his wartime comradeship with Peter but was also
engaged to a marital comradeship with Trude. In any event, he
returned to his garrison only for the purpose of turning his
leave into a permanent discharge, and then to purchase a house
at Neu-Barnim and to transport his Trude from her Wendish
into his Pfälzer village. But the reverse was what happened. A
place at Hohen-Vietz unexpectedly fell vacant, the treasuries of
the houses of Kümmeritz and Kniehase came together, and
when in the summer of '96 the rape bloomed and its scent lay
over all the fields a wedding procession went up the hill to the
church, the bells rang out, and the village band played until the
bridal couple were across the threshold. Kniehase wore his
uniform, Trude the colourful costume of the Wends, and
young and old agreed that Hohen-Vietz had not seen such a
bridal couple within living memory. No, not within living
memory had there been a grander or happier couple: nor,
above all, a better. Envy and slander fell silent; and if at first
some were heard to complain that 'a Pfälzer had finally got into
the village', this complaint too was silenced as soon as they got
to know the Pfälzer better. When counsel was needed he was
there, and when action was needed he was there twofold. He
knew how to write and how to draw up petitions, how to keep
accounts and records; and when in 1800 the old mayor,
Wendelin Pyterke, died—he had occupied his office since the

Seven Years War, a full twenty-four years, and after the Battle of Kunersdorf had been the saving of the village when the Russians arrived—they elected Kniehase as their mayor: with but two or three exceptions they paid no heed whatever to his origins. Berndt von Vitzewitz himself said: 'My farmers have always been sensible, but I never before realized they were as sensible as this.'

Kniehase had no enemies; even the people of the woodland acre spoke well of him. At the manor house they said: 'He is a sound man', at the mill they said: 'He is a devout man'; but Peter Kümmeritz, whose respect for his brother-in-law grew with every day that passed, looked up to him as though he had won the battle of Kaiserslautern all by himself. He summed up his feelings in the words: 'I owe to him my life, and my sister owes to him her happiness.'

The Kniehases were a happy couple; but no happiness is perfect: they remained childless. Then it happened that a daughter was given them: no child of their own, yet loved as if she were.

It was at Christmas 1804, two years before Frau von Vitzewitz died, that a 'mighty man' arrived in the village: he was one of those travelling showmen who appear first in red tights and juggle with five big balls, and then put a watch or a handkerchief in a drawer and when they open it again a pair of doves fly out. The mighty man seemed to have seen better days; his whole demeanour suggested that he had not always spent his time travelling from village to village in a covered waggon. He stopped before Scharwenka's inn, led his lean horse into the stable, and in the evening there was a performance. A little girl perhaps ten years old alternated with him: she sang songs and recited recitations; finally she appeared in a short dress of gauze decorated with little stars made of gold paper and performed the shawl-dance. The farmers of Hohen-Vietz, especially the older ones, were as though confused and confounded by all this, and they stroked the head of the child with their great hands. Soon they would have an opportunity of demonstrating their good-heartedness further.

For a long time the 'mighty man' had no longer been a mighty man: he had been sick and ill. He took to his bed and his condition rapidly went downhill. Pastor Seidentopf sat at his bedside and spoke to him words of consolation; but the dying man, who knew quite well he was dying, shook his head, drew the pastor closer to him and said firmly: 'I am glad it is coming to an end.' Then with a gentle sideways motion of his head he gestured towards the little girl, who was sitting at the window, pressed both hands to his heart, and went on in a voice half-choked: 'If only it were not for the child.' And as he said this, losing all control of himself he broke into convulsive sobbing. When she heard the sound of weeping, the little girl came running over and passionately kissed the dying man's hand. The latter stroked her hair, looked at her and smiled. It was as though he had gazed into a brighter future. Thus he died. On the table beside him stood the little magic-box which he made the doves fly out of. Pastor Seidentopf was profoundly moved.

The people of Hohen-Vietz now faced two problems, and it would be hard to say which agitated their minds more. The *first* problem was: 'What shall we do about the deceased?'

The farmers of the old Wendish lands were kind and good-natured, but they none the less took matters of this sort very earnestly. Simply to shovel the mighty man under ground seemed to them a piece of unseemly crudity, but to bury him in their Christian churchyard an even more unseemly piece of profanation. Was he a Christian at all? The majority doubted it. Then Pastor Seidentopf discovered under the dead man's pillow a wallet containing all kinds of papers, among them a certificate of baptism and a marriage-certificate. The letters it contained provided more information. It appeared that he had been an actor, that he had married the daughter of a good house against the will of her parents, and that his wife had died in grief and penury but without reproaching him and without regrets. Her last letters, which showed signs of having been read again and again, were dated from a convent hospital in Silesia. What emerged from all the letters was a life of failure, but not an unhappy life, for what had brought the two together had surmounted distress and death and survived them.

After he had read these letters, Pastor Seidentopf returned to his farmers, who awaited him below in the inn, and two days

later the mighty man received a Christian burial, just as though
he had been a Kümmeritz or a Miekley. Although there was a
heavy snowstorm the children of the school sang him up the
hill, Frau von Vitzewitz, gracious as ever, stood with them at
the graveside and threw the first handful of earth upon the
coffin, and Berndt von Vitzewitz himself had a cross erected
upon which the following couplet, composed by the old sexton
Jeserich Kubalke, was inscribed:

> A Mightier has the mighty man o'ercome,
> God in His mercy receive him home.

Thus the first problem was solved.—The second problem
was: 'What shall we do about the *child*?' Pastor Seidentopf
pondered the question, a hundred solutions occurred to him
but none seemed the right one. The farmers were hesitant and
loath to come forward. Then the village mayor, Kniehase,
stepped into the midst of them and, leading the weeping child
out of the inn and across to his own house, said: 'Mother, God
has given her to us.'

And the next day, because it was near to Christmas he began
to decorate a tree for her and called her his Christmas doll and
his fairy child.

At first the farmers looked on with some anxiety; 'she will
run away from him', some of them said, 'and that would be the
best thing for him', said the others. But she did not run away,
and Pastor Seidentopf said: 'She will bring him blessings and
good fortune, like the martins under the roof.'

10

Marie*

'SHE will bring to the house blessings and good fortune, like
the martins under the roof': thus Pastor Seidentopf had prophesied, and his words were to be fulfilled. The headshaking soon
ceased. What happened was what always happens in cases like
this: as obscure birth and a strange and curious life awaken
suspicion, so they also awaken a feeling of sympathy, and men

are inspired with the desire to compensate the unfortunate for his unmerited destiny. The charm of mystery sustains the sympathetic interest thus awoken.

This is what befell Marie. Before the winter was over she was the darling of the village; no one mocked any more at the dress of gauze with the stars of gold paper in which she had first appeared before them: on the contrary, this mere breath of a dress now seemed to them her natural costume, and when Kniehase, who had loved the child beyond all measure from the very first moment, sat over in the inn and assured them, half in earnest, half in jest: 'She is a fairy child', no one contradicted him, for what he said was no more than what they had all of them long since come to believe. Even so, though, no one still believed she would one day run away—except, that is, for the girls in the spinning-room, who, thirsting as they did for the thrills of the supernatural, always had some new and marvellous tale to tell of her. And not all of it was invention. She had an uncontrollable predilection for the snow. Whenever the snowflakes fell gently from the sky, or danced and whirled about as though a feather-bed were being emptied, she would run out of the house, climb up the long, sloping ladder that led to the very top of the roof of the barn, and stand there aloft enveloped in a vortex of snow. The girls also asserted that at such times she had been heard singing: what fantastic and vast conclusions were drawn from that fact hardly needs spelling out.

Thus it was in winter. When summer came and she could move around more freely, she won everyone over completely. She visited not only the individual farms but also the outlying dwellings that lay farther off in the fenlands, she played with the children and told them stories. The strange and mysterious air which had clung to her from the first still attended her, but nobody was any longer surprised by it—not even the girls of the village. Once she got lost; there was great agitation in the Kniehase household; everyone searched for her, out as far as the Oder. At length she was found, not a quarter of a mile from the village. She was lying asleep in the corn, a couple of poppy-flowers clutched in her hand; a little bird was sitting at her feet. As it flew away and all eyes followed it, no one could recognize what kind of bird it was. 'It was protecting her!' said the people of Hohen-Vietz.

As a rule she played on the slope between the church and the village, and liked most of all to play in the churchyard itself. She read the inscriptions, kissed the grass on her father's grave, clambered upon the high stone wall and gazed down at the sails of the boats gliding past on the Oder in the glow of the setting sun. If the old sexton Kubalke's maid should then come along to ring the evening bells, she would follow her, pull with her once or twice on the bellrope, and then slip away into the already twilit church. Here she would sit herself on the very edge of the front pew on which the major of the Itzenplitz Regiment had bled to death on the day after the Battle of Kunersdorf; would look timidly sidewards at the dark stain, which no amount of scrubbing had been able to remove; and then, to banish the terrors she had deliberately brought upon herself, would gaze across at the great Vitzewitz memorial which bore the inscription: 'If Thou art with me who will be against me?' There she would stay until the sound of the bells had died away. Then she would go out again into the church-yard, gaze after the maid as she descended the winding path to the village, and with trepidation would circle closer and closer around the ancient beech-tree whose divided trunk was, according to legend, a reminder of the fratricidal strife of the Vitzewitzes. If a leaf should then fall, or a bird fly out, she would start back in fear.

They were lovely days, those days of the first summer in Hohen-Vietz; but those lovely days could not last for ever. The Kniehases had both been concerned for some time. All this roaming about had already been going on too long: now the time had come for work, routine, school. But how were these to be introduced? Husband and wife were both far from wanting to turn their foster-child into a little princess, but they were equally certain that the village school was no place for her. She did not belong among the local clog-shod children, quite apart from the fact that, although she had never yet had a single lesson, she could read considerably better than old Jeserich Kubalke could, especially when he had forgotten his spectacles.

In this dilemma the good Frau von Vitzewitz came to their

aid. She had long thought of taking the singular child, of whose fanciful nature she had heard so much, into her own house as a companion for Renate in play and study, but all kinds of considerations which spoke against it had so far prevented it from happening. However winning her ways might be, the Kniehases' foster-child was, after all, still the daughter of a juggler, or at best of an impoverished actor; and though Frau von Vitzewitz herself took no exception to that, she believed that in questions of education she ought to pay heed less to her own free and noble sentiments than to the view of the matter more generally held and founded on experience and a sense of duty. So her idea had come to nothing. Pastor Seidentopf could, to be sure, have taken steps to bring about a different resolution of the problem; but in a matter of such responsibility he did not want to intervene unasked, and preferred to let things sort themselves out in their own way.

And they did sort themselves out, and did so in a very peculiar way. At the edge of the Vitzewitz park, where the ground was already beginning to rise, a statue of Flora* stood facing down a wide gravel path towards the front of the manor house garden. At the foot of the statue lay five triangular flower-beds which together formed a semicircle around it. On her daily excursion round the village Marie had often stopped at this spot and picked a few flowers, balsamine or mignonette, and had never been told not to do so. On the contrary, the gardener, delighted to see the strange pretty child in his park, had nodded his approval, and had once even hung a couple of fuchsia-buds over her left ear. Now it was September, the red verbenas were blooming, and among them there grew out of flowerpots buried in the ground a couple of insignificant looking flowers which Marie, playing about the flower-beds, took to be dark forget-me-nots and plucked them. They were, however, heliotropes, which in those days were still somewhat rare, and Frau von Vitzewitz wanted to know who had taken them and deprived her of the sight of her favourite flowers. When Marie heard of this she made a swift decision: she sat herself on a bench just beside the statue, and when on her walk through the park Frau von Vitzewitz came along the wide gravel path she jumped up, ran towards the approaching figure, kissed her hand and said: 'It was I who took them.' She trembled and blushed bright red as she said this, but there was no weeping. From that moment on they were friends. Frau von Vitzewitz stroked her hair and fixed her with a friendly gaze; then she led her back to the bench, asked her questions and listened to her replies. Everything confirmed the first impression. Thus they parted: that same afternoon, however, Frau von Vitzewitz said to Seidentopf: 'That is a rare child', and before a week was out she was Renate's companion.

At first she was behind; reading and declamation were her only accomplishments. But she had a gift of quick comprehension and this, sustained by memory and a passionate zeal, enabled her to catch up on what she had hitherto neglected with lightning speed, so that before six months had passed she was in most subjects the equal of Renate. And as she fulfilled Frau von Vitzewitz's expectations with regard to her abilities, so she did those with regard to her character. She lacked all obstinacy or capriciousness; a certain impetuosity she possessed was always amenable to a friendly word. The two girls loved one another like sisters.

All had gone well, the intentions of Frau von Vitzewitz had been fulfilled beyond her expectations, yet she was repeatedly plagued by misgivings—not, now, respecting Renate's happiness, but Marie's. There was not only the present to be consulted, but the future too. What would this future be like? Was it right to give a child of the village mayor the upbringing of a noble house? Would Marie not be placed in a contradictory situation which might ruin her life? She communicated these misgivings to her husband, who, having harboured the same thoughts from the beginning, at once resolved to discuss the matter with Kniehase, in whose good sense he had always trusted.

Berndt went to the mayor's house, found Kniehase in the midst of balancing the accounts for the supply of straw and oats to Küstrin, retired with him into the bay window, and told him of everything he and Frau von Vitzewitz had been discussing.

The mayor listened attentively; then, when the lord of the manor had finished, he said that from the time the matter had first been spoken of he too had reflected whether it would not make for a loss of the child's peace of mind, which was after all worth more than all possible knowledge and learning. All his reflecting, however, had led him only to the belief that the best thing would be to let the gracious lady alone to carry on quietly with her good intentions. That was what they had done for six months: to change things now would, he thought, be advisable only if that was the gracious lady's express desire. For several months now he himself had certainly desired nothing of the kind: the misgivings he had had at first had increasingly fallen from him. And he well knew why. The child whom the hand of God had left almost on the threshold of his house was no peasant child; she was not a peasant by birth and she did not look like a peasant. Sometimes he would sit in the twilight and let his imagination wander, as no doubt other people did too, but whatever pictures he might conjure up he could never see his Marie in a tucked-up dress and carrying two milk-pails crossing the yard to the shouts and cat-calls of laughing menials and servants. He loved the child as though it were his own, but he none the less regarded her as a stranger who would one day be demanded of him again: not by men, but by the world of nature. It would be as it was with the ducks in the poultry-yard, who one day go swimming off while the hen is left behind on the bank.

After Kniehase had spoken thus Berndt von Vitzewitz had proffered him his hand, and from that day on all misgivings were silenced in the manor house.

Even the death of Frau von Vitzewitz, painfully though Marie felt it, did nothing to alter her relations with the other members of the family. Aunt Schorlemmer arrived in the house and, far from showing any favouritism towards Renate, regarded both girls as though they were sisters of one another and embraced them in an equal affection.

After they were confirmed the lessons ceased, but the girls were inwardly united far too strongly for the disappearance of this external bond to have any effect at all on the way in which they lived. Renate ignored the differences of birth and rank that divided them, and Marie was quite insensible of them: she looked upon the world as upon a dream, and was herself dreamlike as she moved about in it; and without having ever given any precise consideration to the matter, she instinctively regarded the higher and lower social ranks as mere roles that people played, which might have differing names but were in their essential nature all of equivalent value. It was in accord with this idea that, of all the pictures in the Vitzewitz house, the one that, all the horrors it contained notwithstanding, produced the most sublime impression on her was a reproduction of the 'Lübeck Dance of Death'*: the preaching of the ultimate equality of all earthly things was an expression of something she was already obscurely aware of within her. At the same time she lacked all pretensions and all covetousness: drawn towards everything beautiful, she desired only to participate in it, not to own it. To her the beautiful was like the starry sky: she took pleasure in its brightness, but she did not reach out her hands after it.

This lack of covetousness also showed itself on her sixteenth birthday, when as the great present of the day she was given a room of her own. The Kniehases conducted her with a certain solemnity to the gable-room on the north side which looked directly on to the park with the church visible to the left and said: 'Marie, this is now yours; do here what you will; it is your domain.'

In the first flush of enthusiasm Marie had begun to arrange and rearrange her cupboard and sewing-table, her bookshelf and clothes-chest, but that was the limit of what she did: it did not occur to her to add anything new to these old and familiar possessions. What she had she loved, what she did not have she did not miss.

'She is brave and she is also submissive,' Frau von Vitzewitz had told Pastor Seidentopf after that first encounter in the park. She could have added: 'Above all she is true.' That miracle which God in his mercy so often performs had been accomplished here too: within a world of hypocrisy there had blossomed a human heart over which falsehood had gained no power. And even less had impurity. Aunt Schorlemmer said: 'Our Marie sees only what is good for her; to what is bad for her she is blind.' And so it was. Fantasy and feeling filled her wholly, and thus they also protected her. Because she felt strongly, she also felt purely.

At the manor house at Hohen-Vietz—it was in the winter before our story opened—Renate sang a song the refrain of which went:

> For she was born by the roadside,
> By the road where the roses bloom . . .

She accompanied the words on the piano.

'Do you know who it is I think of whenever I sing this song?' Renate asked Lewin, who was standing behind her chair.

'Yes,' Lewin replied. 'That is not a difficult riddle to solve.'

'Well?'

'Of Marie.'

Renate nodded and closed the piano.

I I

The Village Pastor

IN the middle of the village, next door to the mayor's house, there stood the parsonage: a gabled house over a century old that stood back a little from the street and was far less grand than most of the farmers' establishments. It was the only sizeable house in the village that still had a thatched roof. This thatched roof had somehow seemed to show a lack of proper respect not only for the pastor himself but also for the village community as a whole, and from time to time there had been talk of replacing it with a tiled roof; but our friend Seidentopf,★ who on this point at least possessed a certain sense of style, had always protested against any such modernization. 'It is all right as it is': and in saying that he was completely justified. The house was a perfect rustic dwelling and any alteration to it could only have spoiled it. The gable-ends protruded at the front; close beneath the thatched roof there ran a row of little windows of the friendliest possible appearance, while the outside walls were decked with trelliswork to the very top and covered with vines, syringa and espalier-fruit the whole summer long. Next to the house-door there stood a rose-tree which grew up as far as the coping of the wall and was famed for its age and beauty throughout the entire Oderbruch. In winter, too, the parsonage presented a picture that was not without its charm: a mighty dome of snow sat upon its roof, while the branches of the vines, laid down and wound round with straw, and the sacking spread out over the espalier-fruit to protect it, bestowed on the whole an appearance of solicitous homeliness.

The inside of the house produced a similar impression. As is often the case with the parsonages of the March, the house-door possessed a bell which was not of the large, noisy kind that cries to the occupants 'Look out, someone's coming', but one of the quiet little kind that seems to say to the visitor 'Come in, I have already announced you.' Opposite the door, at the other end of a hallway that ran almost the whole depth of the house, was the kitchen, whose ever-open door vouchsafed a view of polished cooking-pots and a flickering oven-fire. The rooms lay to the right. Against the left hallway wall, which was also the weather-wall of the house, stood all kinds of cup-boards, wide and narrow, old and new, whose shelves were decorated with broken urns; between them, in the numerous corners they created, hollowed-out posts of petrified wood, whale-ribs and tombstones half weathered away had found a place; while from the crossbeams of the hall there hung various stuffed animals, among them a young alligator with a remark-able set of teeth who began to rock uncannily from side to side whenever the wind came through the house-door, as though it were flying through the air: all in all, an array which left it in no doubt that the parsonage of Hohen-Vietz was also the home of a passionate collector.

If the mere hallway produced this impression, it was much enhanced when you entered the nearest room, which looked much more like a cabinet of antiques than the study of a Christian minister. It is true that its occupant had clearly struggled to establish a certain equilibrium between his office and his inclinations, but the effort had been unavailing. Let us dwell on this point for a moment.

The study possessed two windows looking out on to the garden; between them our friend had drawn a dividing wall extending as far as the middle of the room, and had thus created two large window-bays one of which belonged to the pastor Seidentopf and the other to the collector and antiquary of the same name. The system of balances apparent in their external arrangement was likewise preserved within these bays, inasmuch as Bekmann's *History of the Electorate of Brandenburg*★ (Berlin 1751 to 1753) lay open on the desk of the *camera archaeologica*, while on that of the *camera theologica*★ there lay Dr Martin Luther's translation of the Bible (Augsburg 1613). Both were luxuriant volumes such as only a collector would possess, large, thick, bound in leather and with a hundred illustrations. Kandidat Uhlenhorst is supposed to have remarked to a congregation at Hohen-Sathen that 'Pastor Seidentopf sometimes makes a mistake and looks up a passage in Bekmann instead of in the Bible', but it would hardly be fair to pursue that point just now.

It was, of course, merely a typical piece of Uhlenhorst sarcasm, of the kind conventiclists are very prone to; but it had this to be said for it, that not only had the armchair in the archaeological department obviously been sat in far more often, but the whole of this side of the room in fact constituted a pagan museum, a simple continuation of the array of exhibits in the hallway. Only the whale-ribs and the alligator were lacking. Two huge glass display-cases standing on either side of the door and joined above it by another display-case that connected them formed a kind of *arcus triumphalis*★ beneath which you entered the room; and all that the earth of the March had ever yielded in the way of archaeological finds, from the stone knife and the antique funeral urn onwards, could be found assembled here. With this the theological library contained in the room could not endure comparison: quite apart from its extremely dusty condition, it was wholly accommodated in a narrow, two-shelfed bookstand between the projecting wall and the stove.

Our Seidentopf was as great an enthusiast for archaeology as anyone could be, and he was equipped with all those weaknesses that are as inseparable from enthusiasm as jealousy is from love. He let his imagination run away with him, he allowed himself to be taken in; but in one respect he differed from the grand army of his fellow enthusiasts: he collected, not for the sake of collecting, but for the sake of an idea. He was a collector with a purpose.

Within the church he was, as Uhlenhorst said, lukewarm and tolerant, but when it came to sepulchral urns he exhibited the dogmatic severity of a Grand Inquisitor. He brooked no compromises, and the first and last outcome of all his researches was the unalterable conviction that the March of Brandenburg had not only been a German land from the very beginning but throughout all the centuries had *remained* one. The Wendish invasion had been a wave breaking over the country, bringing a few superficial changes and leaving behind a few Slavic names: but nothing more than that. As the sagas of Fricke and Wotan demonstrated, German custom and saga had lived on among the people; and least of all had the Wends, as was so often asserted, penetrated down into the Brandenburg earth. He would concede to them their so-called 'Wendish burial grounds' and their inferior sepulchral urns; but everything else that, with an instinctive avoidance of surface and superficiality, had been sunk and buried, everything that was at once an expression of culture and cult, was Germanic as surely as Teut himself had been a German.* No discussion was of any moment to him unless it revolved around these propositions. He was convinced that in his archaeological museum he possessed incontestable evidence in support of his thesis, but he distinguished between a minor and a major proof. Personally he preferred the minor, as being more refined and subtle; but he was sufficiently familiar with the thick-wittedness of the masses never to offer them anything but a major proof. The pieces that constituted this proof were collected all together in the two large glass display-cases of the *arcus triumphalis*, but were themselves again divided into irrefutable and wholly irrefutable proofs, and it was only the latter which bore the inscription '*Ultima ratio Semnonum*'.* There were ten or twelve exhibits, all numbered and with labels affixed to them each containing a quotation from Tacitus. Exhibit No. 1 was itself one of the principal items: a bronze likeness of a wild boar whose label read: '*Insigne superstitionis formas aprorum gestant*' —'They (the ancient Germans) bestowed on their idols the form of wild boars.' The other numbers exhibited brooches, rings, breast-pins, swords, and concluded with the *sanspareil* and actual clinching proof of the collection, three coins of the

Imperial Era bearing the heads of Nero, Titus and Trajan. The Trajan coin bore around the laurel-wreathed head the legend 'Imp. Caes. Trajano Optimo',* and the label beside it read: 'Found at Torwein, in the province of Lebus, in a sepulchral urn'. The words 'in a sepulchral urn' were thickly under-lined—and from our friend's point of view quite rightly so, for they provided the proof, or at least were supposed to provide it, that not all sepulchral urns had been Wendish but that 'sepulchral urns of a superior kind' were also of Germanic-Semnonic origin.

Resistance to such eloquent witnesses seemed to Seidentopf impossible, yet he had to encounter it; and it turned out, fortunately or unfortunately, that his most vehement assailant and his oldest friend were one and the same person. It said much for both of them that their friendship did not merely not suffer on account of this conflict but actually grew more firmly rooted—though this was, to be sure, due less to our pastor than to his goodnatured antagonist, who, as a man of the world and thus standing above the matter in question, was unwilling to injure a cordial relationship lasting many years through fight-ing out the Semnonian–Lutitian* question to the bitter end. In reality, indeed, these 'urns' truly engaged his interest only when they began to assume the more modern shape of punch-bowls.

This old friend and adversary was Justizrat* Turgany, of Frankfurt-on-Oder, who, firmly opposed to all trial proceed-ings without the benefit of refreshment and especially so in the case of Lutizii contra Semnones, had cracked many a fine bottle in his time, occasionally in the parsonage at Hohen-Vietz but by preference in his own house, on the principle that the wine-cellar on which he was most amply briefed was his own. The two friends encountered one another as long ago as their student days, in the mid-seventies, at Göttingen,* where they had exchanged vows beneath the 'German Oak-tree' and, reciting Klopstock's bardic odes, dedicated themselves to the everlasting service of the fatherland of Hermann and Thusnelda.* Seidentopf had remained true to his oath. As it had in the days of youthful exaltation, so still today the remainder of the world seemed to him no more than raw material for the accomplishment of the Germanic moral mission; Turgany, however, had long since forgotten the oaths he had taken under the influence of Klopstock and punch, laid all the blame for them on the latter, and now took pleasure, or at any rate appeared to take pleasure, in posing as an apostle of Pan-Slavism. The possibility of Europe's regeneration, he maintained, lay between the Don and the Dnieper and even farther to the east. 'Rejuvenation', he had asserted on his last visit to Hohen-Vietz, 'has always come from the banks of the Volga, and once again we stand before a process of renewal of this kind'; paradoxes enunciated half in earnest, half in jest, and characterized by Seidentopf simply as political heresies on the part of his friend.

But this friend was not half as black as he painted himself. The principle on which he entered upon debate at all was that of steel and stone, hardness striking hardness: that was what produced the sparks that were more important to him than the matter itself under debate. The Pan-Slavic magistrate knew, moreover, that conflict and a victory that was constantly called into question had long been a necessity of life to Seidentopf, and he thus relished his role of adversary even more on that account than for the pleasure he himself derived from it.

12

Visitors at the Parsonage

AND it was Justizrat Turgany who was expected that day, the second day of Christmas 1812, at the Hohen-Vietz parsonage; Lewin and Renate had also accepted an invitation, as had Aunt Schorlemmer and Marie.

It was past four o'clock; already it was getting dark, and the visitors might arrive at any minute. Festive preparations had been made; wherever there was still a speck of dust our friend pounced upon it with a feather-duster, then he again took out his handkerchief and polished the glass of his beloved cabinets. He who relies on weapons takes care to keep them clean. Only the theological bookcase, where the dust was too thick, escaped his attentions. Then an incident occurred which made him look up from his labours for a moment. As though she had a whole world to see to, a woman with a red face and a white cap swept imperiously past him into the study, poured a quantity of essence of perfume such as was then fashionable on to a little shovel that she extended before her, waved it in the air a couple of times, and then shot off into the next room to continue her operations, which resembled a cross between fencing with a foil and swinging a censer. Pastor Seidentopf smiled as he looked after her and he seemed about to make some jocular remark, but before he could do so there was a ringing at the house-door, and the sound of the stamping of feet on the steps and the straw-mat outside was a clear indication that a visitor had arrived.

But it was not the Frankfurt magistrate: his friends from the manor house had arrived first. Lewin conducted Aunt Schorlemmer in, Renate and Marie followed. They all greeted one another warmly. Renate removed her shawl and stood for a moment with the brooch-pin in her hand, as though undecided where she should put it. Then she opened the glass cabinet and laid the brooch in one of the broken urns. It was as though she were a child in the house. Everyone laughed, Seidentopf also joining in.

'Look here, dear pastor,' Renate began; 'if what is now falling from the sky were a rain of ash, what ideas it would give the Seidentopfs of the future, this cameo-brooch in a Wendish funeral urn!'

'Not Wendish, absolutely not. But my fair Renate is not going to draw me out,' Seidentopf replied good-humouredly. 'Turgany is still to come and I mustn't spend my forces on minor skirmishes, no matter how enticing they may be. But where shall we take coffee?'

'Here, here in your study and smoking-room,' they all cried together, laying stress on the last word. Seidentopf demurred, but Renate insisted. 'We want no sacrifices,' she said.

'Even if it were one, the greater the sacrifice the greater the joy.'

'Oh how courteous! Quite like the good old days. And our visitor from the capital'—here a roguish glance at Lewin

—'fancies he is going to teach us good breeding: but here is the seat where it is taught, here at the parsonage at Hohen-Vietz.'

Chairs were assembled; they took their places at a round table that had been brought into the *camera archaeologica*, and the woman already referred to appeared to lay the table for coffee. She was immediately greeted by all those present in a fashion that left no doubt as to the importance of her position within the Hohen-Vietz parsonage. By birth and station she ought, of course, still to have been wearing the flannel skirt and the black silk headscarf; but all housekeepers finally grow above their station, and the Hohen-Vietzers were no exception.

She laid claim to all kinds of little acts of homage and expected, for example, to be received by the pastor's guests with every mark of distinction, and afterwards to be invited by the pastor himself to join them at the festive table. But that was sufficient to satisfy her self-respect. She regularly declined and was contented with the fact that the invitation had been accorded.

She now laid the table-napkins, placed a pair of two-branched candlesticks together with a sugar-bowl with lion's-feet in the middle of the table, and flanked this majestic centre-piece with two silver baskets, one of which contained all kinds of small cakes and the other a pyramid of biscuits; last of all came the Dresden coffee-pot itself, on whose lid the god Cupid was leaning roguishly against his bow. The pastor had never taken exception to this figure, but then perhaps he had never noticed it.

Renate played hostess, put the sugar into the cups first (large sugar-blocks were not yet in fashion) and handled the sugar-tongs as she did so with that grace of movement which alone is able to reconcile us to these unmanageable instruments. After the first audacious skirmishes, conversation was very soon restored to its normal course and commenced with the weather. In the year 1812 the weather possessed a quite special significance: you might say that it was patriotic in that year to talk of the weather. Cold and snow were the great confederates and allies of the Russians.

The snow, which had at first been blown about in little feathery flakes, gradually began to whirl more thickly past the windows, and from the security of Pastor Seidentopf's study—doubly snug now that it had also become a coffee-room—host and guests looked out at the eddying dance outside.

There was a pause. 'More and more snow,' began Lewin, who had the place closest to the window; 'it is as though God himself wanted to bury them all. Destruction is coming upon them: it is falling from the sky in gentle flakes. And in the midst of them I hear a voice that calls to us: "Do not get involved, do not seek to do more than I myself am doing: I shall accomplish it alone." I know very well, dear pastor, that the voice I hear is only the voice of the pity I feel. Ought I to close my ears to it? Is this pity a weakness? Ought I to lay it aside?'

'No, Lewin, your heart is, as always, in the right place. If there is anything we should never regret following it is our impulse to pity. Moreover, we are bound to an alliance with our enemies. And so let these present days teach us to be loyal, loyal even to our enemies, just as these past years have taught us to be humble. Let us wait. The time will come when it will seem to us that God himself is placing his sword in our hands. But that day, though it may be near, has not yet come. One thing, however, it behoves us to be, today and always: candid and open in all we do. That is *German*.'

Lewin was about to reply but the sound of a whip cracking and the jingling of bells coming along the road interrupted the conversation, and Seidentopf cried: 'Here they are!'

There were three men; two, dressed in grey cloaks and black cloth caps, occupied the upholstered seat of the sleigh, while the third, in a fur coat and cap, sat on the platform. This last leaped down first from his driving-chair, handed the reins to the servant who came hurrying up, and then assisted his two, much younger but more ponderous companions out of their foot-muffs and safely down to the ground.

Our friends observed all this activity through the window, so far as the falling snow permitted, with that unfeigned lively interest known only to him who has experienced for himself the silence and stillness of a village in winter.

'Who are the two strangers Turgany has saddled himself

with?' Lewin asked; 'our legal friend in his elegant mink coat looks very out of place as a serving-man to those grey-cloaks.'

'They are brother ministers of mine,' replied Seidentopf, paying no heed to the blush which this slight embarrassment caused to suffuse Lewin's features, 'a full colleague and a half colleague. The full colleague, whom you ought to recognize, is our neighbour, the pastor of Dolgelin; the half colleague is still provisionally an assistant schoolmaster, but will soon be succeeding to the parsonage at the Holy Spirit. Konrektor Othegraven*, a particular friend of Turgany's.'

In the meantime the newcomers had extricated themselves from their cloaks and furs, and the voice of the magistrate resounded in the hallway with that note of firmness and clarity which always indicates that its possessor is half at home in the place he has arrived at. Then the door opened and all three came in. Salutations were soon over, and the party then crowded closer together, a second table was set at right-angles to the first, and a lively conversation was soon in progress. As he himself liked proudly to aver, Turgany could not endure empty intervals.

With the skill in leadership that distinguished him in such things, he had secured for himself the best position and was seated not only beneath one of his friend's urn-cases (which he would have forgone if need be) but also between Renate and Marie, a place he had procured through skilfully dispatching Aunt Schorlemmer by whispering to her that his friend Othegraven would very much like to converse with her about missions to Greenland. 'Othegraven wanted to be a missionary himself,' he had said. He had then without further ado proceeded to occupy the site that had fallen to him by this stratagem and was now entertaining the two ladies with the adventures he had just that day experienced. His tale was not marked by any particular attention to discretion (which was in any case not his strong suit) and he did not scruple in the slightest to make the pastor of Dolgelin its comic hero—though the latter's demeanour did, admittedly, seem of itself to qualify him for that role. A gust of wind had, he said, blown his travelling companion's headgear across a field, and the natural consequence had been a kind of hat-chase. He would never forget the sight. Getting itself under the high collar of the pastor's cloak, the wind had borne him on and on as though he were a direct descendant of Doctor Faustus; until the whole fantastic apparition had finally vanished into the depths of an Oderbruch ditch. Yes, the pastor had fallen into it. But when the elect fell it was always a blessing in disguise, and so it was here: for in the ditch which the pastor had fallen into lay his hat.

The pastor of Dolgelin was in the meantime engaged with Lewin in discussing the price of corn; Aunt Schorlemmer and Konrektor Othegraven were indulging in comparisons between missions to the South and those to the North Pole; while Turgany had just begun to describe an improvised children's ball he had taken part in on Christmas Eve, imitating the speech of the little girls and, employing a certain degree of talent he possessed for acting, impersonating the childish gravity of their bearing and demeanour. Thus the conversation ran on, and thus the magistrate's ideal was achieved: no empty intervals.

Turgany—to add a few more strokes to our portrait of him—was a healthy man of fifty and was reasonably well aware of the youthfulness of his appearance. Resistant to all flattery, he yet tolerated the one piece of flattery that would have him born *after* the Seven Years War: it meant for him a pure gain of ten years. He held himself erect, wore a pair of gold spectacles and a toupee of flaxen-blond locks. These locks had once played about another's forehead, and when the mood seized him our friend himself laughed at this blond abundance, which far surpassed the real flaxen locks of his youth; he joked about it, but was not in the last amused when others followed his example. His face, which still preserved its freshness, could have been called correctly proportioned were it not that the left half of his nose, which had been cut off in a fencing bout and badly sewn on again by the doctor in attendance, formed a kind of arch quite large enough to accommodate a normal half-nose under it. The impudence that was part of his nature was enhanced by this feature, as it was confirmed by the wanton high spirits that played about the corners of his mouth.

The two ministers were men of a very different stamp, and they differed from one another as much as they both did from their friend the magistrate. They had nothing in common except their black coats and their white scarves. Konrektor Othegraven was of a persuasion at that time rarely encountered in the lands of the March: strict orthodoxy combined with joyfulness of belief. A stay of several years in Holstein,* where he had come to know the *Wandsbeck Messenger*,* and subsequently Claus Harms,* too, at his Dithmarschen parsonage, had not been without lasting influence on him. He spoke little of Christianity or questions of belief, but the manner in which he dealt with profane things bestowed on them a kind of holiness. He saw all things in their relationship to God; that gave him clarity of mind and peace of heart. When he spoke there was something luminous about him that could reconcile one to his otherwise stiff and pedantic external appearance.

The pastor of Dolgelin lacked many of nature's gifts, but what he most obviously lacked was a passionate and shining faith. The pastoral care he was concerned with was of the practical sort, and he considered that it included conducting legal cases on behalf of the farmers: on account of which he had to submit to hearing Turgany describe him on different occasions as 'colleague', 'the oracle of Dolgelin' or 'the Lebus share index'. He was neither Orthodox nor Rationalist, but confessed simply to the ancient country-parson persuasion of whist *à trois*. And he did not always do so with the necessary circumspection: once, or at least so Turgany said, he had complained to an ageing spinster that he had been unable to find a 'partner' in Dolgelin, which had given rise to the most delicious misunderstandings. For the rest, he was a worthy if limited man, and was popular in the parish: all that was missing was that he was not accorded respect.

Such were the new arrivals. The magistrate was just rising to demonstrate to Renate and Marie how at the Frankfurt children's ball a deformed little amateur musician had played the cello for three hours without a break when Aunt Schorlemmer, seizing one of the candlesticks, signalled that the study was now to be relieved of its social duties. The old lady herself led the way into a neighbouring room and then on to a second room beyond it; all the younger elements of the party followed her, not excluding Othegraven or even Pastor Zabel.

Only the old friends and adversaries Turgany and Seidentopf remained behind in the study.

13

Odin's Chariot

THE hour before dinner—in accordance with an ancient tradition, which Turgany would yet not have been sorry to see waived that day—was devoted to the exchange of scientific ideas: that is to say, to warfare. It was within this brief space of time that those battles were fought to which the magistrate looked forward with cheerful resolution but whose approach, though he too looked forward to them, filled the pastor with a feeling of fear and dread. For however loudly he might proclaim the unshakeability of his doctrine, his firmest assertions concealed the most tormenting doubts. All doctrines hitherto have fallen, he said to himself; and before every new debate he was assailed with the idea: suppose this time my structure should crumble!

This idea came to him today as well, and the feeling of fear and dread that attended it became for a moment more intense as Turgany, who had in the meantime brought a little box in from the hallway, now placed it on the table with a certain air of solemnity and without preamble made the following announcement: 'This is for you, Seidentopf. Unchristian though its contents may be, accept it from me as a Christmas present. Whether you will find a place for it, within you or without, remains of course to be seen. If it can be accommodated to your doctrine, forge weapons against me out of it; it would then be my pride myself to have assisted you to victory. In the opposite case, however, have the courage openly to admit defeat. And now open it.'

Seidentopf unfastened the lid and took out of the box a little bronze chariot: it ran on three wheels and had a short pair of shafts upon which, close to the axle, there sat six birds, likewise of bronze, all made as if poised for flight. The whole was a little larger than a man's hand and revealed technical accomplishment and sense of beautiful form in equal measure.

The pastor was dazzled; for a moment all that was critic or systematizer in him was submerged in the naïve joy of the collector, and grasping the magistrate's hand he said: 'This is unique: it will become the jewel of my collection.'

Then he let the chariot roll across the table with a sensation and an expression on his face that would have been more appropriate had he been fifty years younger.

Turgany was pleased at the happiness he had given; but quickly seized again by his old spirit of opposition, he tore our Seidentopf out of the unaffected delight he was feeling with an abrupt: 'Well then?'

Still immersed in that gentle mood evoked by sensations of joy and gratitude, the pastor at first sought to avoid this inquisitorial 'Well then?' with all kinds of secondary questions as to how the chariot had been acquired and where it had been discovered. But he did so in vain. The latter question itself, indeed, took them over into the realm of contention, and when he replied to it Turgany was therefore careful to accord certain words especial emphasis: 'It is from *beyond* the Oder; road-workers found it between Reppen and Drossen;* it was concealed in the marl; Drossen is *Wendish* and means "town on the road". The Oder has always been a *frontier* river.'

'That means nothing,' Seidentopf replied with composure. 'You know that there was a time when Germans lived on both sides of the river; they were of different tribes, that is all. *Which* tribe was this side and which the other may be a matter of contention; all I assert is that they were both Germanic.'

Turgany smiled. 'So do you really believe that your Semnones, or some other tribe like them, who it can be proved lived outdoors under the trees and dressed in animal skins, were capable of creating works of art like this?' He indicated the chariot. 'To repeat what I have said often before, they have vanished away like the leaves of their trees, like the aurochs that shared their woods with them. It is possible that the world will one day learn of the surprising discovery of a petrified Semnone preserved in rock-salt in some moor or bog; I should be delighted at such a discovery, but it would prove absolutely nothing with regard to the issue in question here. Semnones existed, certainly, but they created nothing. They propagated themselves, that was all. Creation in the sense of art or invention was unknown to them. This chariot is the product of a higher culture. Who brought culture to these regions? That is the question. You know what my answer is.'

Seidentopf remained silent.

'I have told you so often,' Turgany went on, 'and I must now repeat, that it is incomprehensible to me how a man of your seriousness in scientific affairs, distinguished in a hundred other matters by his openness of mind, can continue to dispute the culture of the Slavic forelands. Your doctrine is a heap of sophistries. From our old home in Priegnitz,* where we were born, to this province of Lebus, in which we now live, both the regions of the country and the towns and villages in them bear, as an everlasting sign that they were the product of Wendish hands, good Slavic names; not least this very Hohen-Vietz, whose inhabitants, along with their many other virtues, have a relaxed attitude towards questions of race and origin. I, for my part, cannot follow their example. Things are as they are. The Germans of this region were savages; they practised human sacrifice, they slit open the bellies of their enemies with flints. The others, however, the civilized Wends whose existence you deny, they possessed temples, wore fine cloth, and decorated themselves and their gods with gold brooches. What have your Semnones to show that can approach the legendary splendour of Vineta, the fantastic size of the temples of Rethra and Oregunga?'*

'*Legendary* splendour,' Seidentopf repeated; 'the admission that lies in this adjective could be all I need: I prefer, however, not to employ weapons which, if you will forgive me, the heedlessness of my adversary has placed in my hands. So I do not intend to try to explain away the culture of Rethra and Julin.* But this Wendish culture, which came to surpass itself under the stimulus of our Germanic world, is a culture of the present millennium, while this bronze chariot obviously dates back to the first centuries of our calendar. I would place it in the third century, perhaps even earlier.'

'Good. And what do you take it for? What is it? What does it mean?'

'I would have wished to see this conflict set aside for today, when I feel so greatly indebted to you. As, however, this is not to be, I have no hesitation in describing it with absolute positiveness as a symbol of the ancient Germanic cult. It is nothing other than a representation of Odin's chariot.'

'You are straining rather high,' Turgany retorted, his voice growing sharper. 'As the question, so the answer: and thus I, for my part, have no hesitation in asserting with absolute positiveness that this has about as much right to be called Odin's chariot as a rocking-horse found in some bed of marl would have to be called a representation of the Wendish sun-horse. You must not bend your bow too far. This chariot is simply the child's toy of a Lutitian or Obotritan* prince's son, of some young Pribislav or Mistivoi.'*

Seidentopf made to reply, but Turgany went on: 'A picture of a happy family is unfolding before my eyes. Wooden pillars with richly carved capitals bear the fantastically decorated ceiling, and gaming and drinking at the tables there sit the Wendish swordsmen, at their head the prince. He drinks the health of his only son, to celebrate whose birthday the guests have today appeared in such numbers. Inclining her head to right and left, Pribislava, the princess, advances down the hall, and the golden valances of her white robe glitter with every gesture of greeting. By her right hand she leads her boy, his locks welling forth from beneath his cap of otter's fur, while behind him there rolls and rattles the opulent toy this happy day has brought him. And this toy is *here*.' With that, Turgany took up the supposed chariot of Odin and then set it back on the table.

The pastor smiled. And Turgany, who had grown more lighthearted in viewing the picture he himself had conjured up, again looked more composed and said in a conciliatory tone: 'Seidentopf, I have played trump against trump. You challenged me. If, in imitation of you, I spoke of absolute positiveness, you will realize what I meant by it. We both lack only one little thing: proof.'

'I can furnish proof.'

'Very well, do so.'

'You admit, firstly, that this object is made of bronze?'

The magistrate nodded.

'You admit further that bronze belongs as exclusively to the Germanic era as iron does to the Wendish?'

Turgany nodded again, but now with signs of growing impatience.

'Good. These admissions on your part', Seidentopf went on, 'seem to me to have simplified our contest: I thank you for this act of impartiality and self-command. The chariot is made of bronze and *because* it is made of bronze, it is Germanic. That is the point that matters. What it was *within* the Germanic world is of only secondary significance: yet I must still maintain that here too there can be no real room for doubt. These birds here, on the axle and the shafts, afford the proof. They are Odin's ravens. They fly on ahead before him; if I may avail myself of the expression, they draw the enigmatic vehicle.'

'So you regard these as ravens?'

'Plain appearance makes any further discourse superfluous,' replied the pastor.

'Well then, permit me to say that, so far as my knowledge of ornithology goes—and for the whole range between pheasant and common snipe at any rate it is superior to yours—these so-called ravens of Odin could be no more and no less than *anything* that has ever flown with wings, from the stork and the swan to the hawfinch and the crossbill. And thus *I* cry to you: "Hail to this chariot of Isis and Osiris, for six ibises sit on its shafts! Hail to this chariot of Jupiter, for six eagles fly before it!" '

While this controversy was in progress the housekeeper had been clattering the plates and cups in the neighbouring room, and had screwed in the legs of the extension-table with that inconsiderate noisiness which, convinced of its own importance, the kitchen department has from time immemorial claimed as its privilege. This racket notwithstanding, Turgany's caustic tones had penetrated to the drawing-room lying beyond, where they gave rise to a general decampment that was all the speedier in that the ever-welcome cry 'The table is laid' might in any case be raised at any moment. Renate and

Marie, who led the procession, appeared on the threshold of the study just as the magistrate was playing his last mocking trump.

'Welcome!' Turgany cried. 'Our young lady friends, the representatives of cheerful impartiality in this circle, shall constitute a court and adjudicate between you and me. *Cour d'amour*, minstrels' contest; Seidentopf and Turgany into the lists.'

Seidentopf was content with this proposal. Everyone gathered round the table and Renate, taking the chair, invited the opposing parties to present their case. Turgany spoke first; then Seidentopf concluded: 'And thus the question amounts simply to this: is this chariot a cult object, or is it merely a toy? Was it looked upon with reverence or was it played with? And now, ye ravens of Odin, describe your circle and declare the truth.'

Renate bestowed a glance on the contestants, then she said: 'What blindness, O friends, not to see the wood for the trees! Was there ever a question easier to answer? Why go questing in places obscure and far away? This chariot, which has of course a symbolic significance, is nothing other than a *war-chariot*: the image, found between Drossen and Reppen, of your own eternal feud.'

Everyone cheerfully agreed with this verdict, and the contestants, both condemned, shook hands with one another. Renate, however, finally paying due attention to the signs being made by the old housekeeper occupied in the background, now took Seidentopf's arm and proceeded to the neighbouring room, where on a hospitably laid table the linen was shining and the candles burning.

14

'All That Can Fly, Let It Fly High'

THE neighbouring room was the dining-room, and it exploited to the full the privilege, enjoyed by all rooms where meals are taken, of being bare and undecorated. Only two things disturbed the predominant sobriety: above the door leading out to the corridor there hung a large, badly darkened representation of a bear-baiting done by some unidentified Netherlander of the school of Rubens, while against a pier of the wall opposite there stood a tall walnut *étagère* upon whose topmost ledge was displayed an open-work basket containing painted alabaster oranges, pears and grapes. The 'Bear-baiting' had strayed to the parsonage from the manor house more than fifty years before, when the Vitzewitz dining-hall had been redecorated and the parsonage had been occupied by a jovial predecessor of Seidentopf's in the cure of souls at Hohen-Vietz (in so far, that is, as he had not been engaged in fox-hunting and the coursing of hares).

This impression of bareness and sobriety was transformed into its opposite, however, from the moment Seidentopf's guests began to fill the room and enliven it. The branched candlesticks, the green and plain glasses, above all the tree-cake* occupying the middle of the table which, with its abundance of long, brown branches, constituted a speciality of the Hohen-Vietz parsonage, produced the most festive possible picture, and one that derived advantage rather than otherwise from its strangely assorted frame of bare walls, darkened Rubens and alabaster fruit.

After successfully negotiating a cup of tea down the table, Turgany, who had again managed to secure a place between the two young ladies, whispered a few words into the ear of the aged housekeeper, who was attending on them in person; the latter appeared to understand and responded with a nod of the head.

'Fresh plotting in progress?' asked Renate.

'Perhaps', Turgany replied. 'But only of the kind that will not keep my fair neighbour's curiosity long in suspense. In any event a surprise of greater general interest than "Odin's chariot".'

While this conversation was still going on the housekeeper reappeared at the head of the table and began to hand around a shallow dish, the contents of which—a black granular substance heavily garnished with slices of lemon—could no longer leave the nature of the surprise in any doubt.

'But Turgany,' Seidentopf murmured in friendly mock reproach.

'No precipitate gratitude,' the magistrate interposed. 'You have no suspicion of the hidden knavery that lurks behind these black granules. In despite of all the laws of the table which would have lively discussion of any kind excluded from the pleasures of a repast, I am carrying the ancient Turgany–Seidentopf conflict to this your hospitable board and am borrowing new weapons against you from this surprise dish which, trusting in your indulgence, I have permitted myself to interpolate. Yes, dear friend, here is the salt of the earth, the only kind that has not yet lost its savour. These black granules, what are they but an advanced guard from the East, an *avant-garde* of the great Slavic world. Envoys from the Volga; Astrakhan★ advances into this ancient land of Lebus. A profound symbol of all this! Already the riders of the steppes, who share the same homeland, are following; let us be ready for them, let us prepare our hearts. Long live the salt of the new age; long live great Slava, the first mother of our Wendish world, long live Russia!'

Seidentopf, much too goodnatured not to take such teasing as this in good part, rose immediately. 'I ask you to fill your glasses,' he began; 'the green ones, of course. Our friend has cried long life to the salt of our age, to Russia, to the plains of Astrakhan. I could call attention to the fact that, as travellers for example have reported, optical illusions, gigantic magnifications are among the characteristic phenomena found in these regions of steppe, so that simple clusters of heather might appear like majestic trees; but I desist from remarks that could only stoke the fires of our conflict. I thirst, not for feuding, but for reconciliation. Very well, then, long live the salt of the Volga that refreshes, but at the same time let us imbibe this German wine that cheers and elevates. Let the fiery be joined to the astringent, enthusiasm to strength: thus shall the Germanic and the Slavic worlds be wedded. It is an *old* wine still that sparkles in our glasses, and the ground that bore and ripened it once was ours. It shall be ours again. May the grapes of this coming year lie in wine-presses that are German.'

Everyone resoundingly clashed glasses, including Turgany

and Seidentopf. The adversaries embraced, everyone shook hands with everyone else, and the feeling of patriotic fervour expanded as, taking the 29th communiqué* as its basis, conversation at the table glided over into the region of conjectural politics.

Only when they left the table did conversation come to an end: the ladies, too, had participated and had done so all the more readily in that, in the absence of really reliable information, no one was in any way inhibited from strewing his remarks with '*On dit*'* or from allowing his imagination to take wing, thus filling with his own inventions the gaps left by the shortage of facts. And most people, indeed, are happier with conversations erected on such shaky foundations as this than they are with those whose course is determined by uncomfortable realities.

The company now moved out of the dining-room into the end room, the dressing-room, which was furnished essentially as it had been left by the late Frau Pastor Seidentopf, who had died ten years before almost immediately after the celebration of her silver wedding. Against the wall on the long side of the room there stood a sofa and a Birkenmaser piano, the former high-backed with five hard stuffed cushions decorated with large flowers, the latter standing on narrow, bowed legs of a thinness exceeded only by that of the tone of the instrument itself. Opposite the sofa there stood the 'jubilee cabinet', in which was accommodated everything that had been presented to Seidentopf by way of gift or token of respect on the occasion of the twenty-fifth anniversary of his assuming the incumbency at Hohen-Vietz, which had coincided with his silver wedding. On display here, in addition to the garland and the presentation-cup, were two flower-vases with quaking-grass in them, a mug for pipe-lighters, an album and a writing-case decorated with two large bead-pictures, one depicting the church at Hohen-Vietz, the other the house of correction at Landsberg, where our Seidentopf had for several years officiated. It was in this same era, too, that there originated a little crucifix made of bread paste which, unpretentious in itself, was enclosed in an equally unpretentious frame on the wall just above the back of the sofa. It was the work of a fettered prisoner condemned to lifelong incarceration who, having begun it simply so as to have something to do, had through the work of his hands transformed himself into a believing Christian. Turgany was accustomed to say of this story that it was one more demonstration of how each of us creates for himself his own god and his own beliefs; Seidentopf however, whose innermost being was here involved and who held the opposite view, stuck to his opinion, was firmly convinced that *this* malefactor too had heard spoken the words: 'Today shalt thou be with me in Paradise', and accounted himself fortunate to have received this breadpaste-crucifix from the hands of a dying believer. He regarded it as nothing less than a talisman or, to employ a more Christian expression, a shield and a blessing on his house.

This was the room. Aunt Schorlemmer took her seat on the sofa, the two young ladies sat beside her, while the men seated around the table completed the circle.

'What shall we play?' Renate asked. 'We can choose between spinning-the-plate, passing-the-penny and throwing-the-handkerchief.'

'Does it absolutely have to be a forfeits game?' asked Pastor Zabel, aware perhaps of some slight feeling of trepidation.

'Most certainly,' Turgany replied.

'In that case,' Renate decided, 'all things considered I am for Lewin's favourite: All that can fly, let it fly high! He considers it the greatest of all games.'

'Then I would like to know it,' said Turgany.

'I confess to the opinion Renate has ascribed to me,' Lewin now began. 'All games are good if you view them correctly, but my favourite game is the best of all. It has, in the first place, an element of comedy in it, though this can, to be sure, become apparent only to those who bring to it a modest amount of imagination and imitative ability. He to whom the animals named, great or small, are no more than words, no more than the classifications of natural history; he to whom it occurs only afterwards, so to speak, as an outcome of knowledge and reflection, that leopards do *not* fly; on him the magic of this game will be forever lost. But he who, at the moment when a finger is raised at the wrong time, really sees a Siamese elephant flying in the midst of humming-birds and canaries, will find in the grotesque pictures this game evokes a lasting source of enjoyment.'

'Very good, very good,' said Turgany, clearly excited at this prospect.

'And yet this side of the game', Lewin went on, 'is only a subsidiary one. There is another side to it that is much more important. For it disciplines our mind and teaches us how to keep a swift and strict control over our reactions. In the physical as in the spiritual world there rules the same law of inertia. The ball rolls on through inertia. Here, too, it is just the same. Seven times we have raised our finger, and with increasing speed; it has got into a rotating movement and flies almost of its own accord; then the heaviest and most ponderous thing intrudes itself into our company of weightless fluttering birds and, behold, our finger does what it ought not to do and flies on. This is the point of it! To react to the sudden appearance of an image with an equally sudden act of will by which a movement originating in the law of inertia is halted: that is the spiritual schooling we obtain from this game. I could believe that exercises such as this might be of assistance in building our character.'

Konrektor Othegraven smiled. He seemed to have a somewhat lower opinion of the pedagogic value of the game. Only Turgany reiterated his approval. The game began and assumed its usual course, not failing as it did so to exercise its customary fascination; and the players were not spared the ancient dispute as to whether or not dragons can fly. When it was broken off, a whole heap of forfeits lay in the shallow work-basket Marie had fetched into the room.

'Our friend Lewin', Turgany now resumed, 'has spoken to us of the greatest of all games, and has illuminated his subject from the artistic, the pedagogic and the moral point of view, that is to say from *three* sides, as is only appropriate in a parsonage. I cannot resist the temptation to expatiate with similar expansiveness on a related theme. Would you be prepared to believe, ladies, that the profoundest mysteries of nature are revealed in the pledging of forfeits?'

'Goodness gracious!' exclaimed the pastor of Dolgelin,

whose conscience in this regard may not have been completely clear.

'To choose something of indeterminate value', Turgany went on, 'without lapsing into the really trivial: *that* is the art. A cambric handkerchief, a notebook, a scent-bottle, a brooch, may be regarded as model examples. They can seldom be surpassed. But I once knew a foreign lady, come from the south and beached here on the banks of our Oder, who smilingly removed a pearl-pin from her black hair and handed this pin over. I would have liked to kiss the hand that did it. That was an exception on the splendid side. It is much easier to fall *below* the golden mean of the scent-bottle and the brooch. I recall a professor's wife who had reached the period of middle-aged spread who time and again drew her wedding-ring from her finger as a forfeit. Absolve me from describing to you the condition of that marriage. In the same company there was a gentleman who never wearied of depositing his English pocket-knife, which had ten blades, a corkscrew and a fire-steel, into the laps of the ladies, until, after several silk dresses had been torn by it, the monstrosity finally vanished before the cry of universal indignation.'

The magistrate was able to deliver this lecture without fear of giving offence: for he had been following the pledging of forfeits with particular attentiveness and knew precisely who had pledged what. Even Pastor Zabel had handed over nothing worse than a large cornelian watch-key, which he carried not on the watch but by itself in one of his large side-pockets like a kind of pocket-pistol.

They now proceeded to the redemption of the forfeits.

Lewin, who was indebted the most, had to 'cart rocks', 'build a bridge' and 'make a chain', while it fell to the pastor of Dolgelin to try his luck as a 'Polish beggar'.

Finally they cried: 'What shall he do who owns this forfeit?' 'Slice ham!'

It was a neckscarf belonging to Marie. She rose, stepped into the middle of the room, and began: 'Here I am, slicing ham, and him whom I love I shall point to.'

Whereupon she pointed to the schoolmaster from Frankfurt and with complete unaffectedness offered him her mouth.

Othegraven, who was normally highly self-controlled, felt the blood rush to his temples. He kissed her on the forehead; then they both returned to their places.

Apart from Renate, only Turgany had noticed Othegraven's momentary embarrassment.

15

Schmidt of Werneuchen

THE last forfeit left to be redeemed, a notebook, belonged to Renate, who was now invited to sing a song. She was ready to do so, but as always the question was: what song? Luckily all kinds of sheet music was piled upon the little Birkenmaser and Renate began to search through it. The music comprised songs and vocal compositions which, so far as their texts were concerned, were, with a kind of social diplomacy, taken from *both* schools of poetry which at that time had their birthplaces, or at least their nurseries, almost in the immediate vicinity of Hohen-Vietz. The nearest, from the local point of view, was the school of Nieder-Barnim, the other that of Lebus: the former the solid-realistic school represented by Pastor Schmidt of Werneuchen,★ the latter the aristocratic-romantic school represented by Ludwig Tieck★ and the circle patronized by the Burgsdorffs and their friends at Ziebingen.★ The pastor of Hohen-Vietz, who, the exceptional case of the Semnones apart, was in general incapable of coming down firmly on one side or the other, as far as possible sought to mediate between these two schools, alternately commending Werneuchen and admiring Ziebingen, and gave expression to this characteristic lukewarmness of feeling—which whenever it involved ecclesiastical questions evoked the mockery of Miekley and Uhlenhorst—in the realm of literature too by acquiring Schmidt's *Muses' Almanac* today and Tieck's *Zerbino* or *Phantasus*★ tomorrow. Most of the piano music, however, belonged to the days when the late Frau Seidentopf was still living, and she, having been born in Barnim herself and possessing less of the spirit of conciliation than her husband, had shown a slight preference for the poet of Werneuchen.

After leafing through this music, Renate at length selected, to put an end to the searching, a number of stanzas of Pastor Schmidt's directed to the friend of all unfortunate lovers—'To the Moon'. Subjoined to the title was the bracketed remark: 'At the window, eleven at night'.

> 'So many a night I sorrow here
> In loving's mute regret;
> Then on my pain thy friendly beam
> Through the sad willows casts its gleam,
> And makes my heart forget.
>
> Were but the light of her I love
> So kindly on me bent!
> O moonlight, seek her where she lies
> And sadly look into her eyes,
> And make her heart repent.'★

Renate, who seemed to be familiar with both words and music, sang the song with great self-assurance, but also with that exaggerated expenditure of tone and emotion through which the performer seeks to convey that he looks down on the thing he is performing.

This was not lost on Renate's audience, the majority of whom seemed to approve of her ironical treatment of the song. Only Seidentopf rose, came to the piano, and said: 'Our old friend from Barnim appears to be out of favour with our young friend from Lebus.'

'How should he not be,' Renate replied; 'however unassuming he may make himself out to be, he has pretensions to being a poet, and he isn't one. It is reasonable to imagine a poet mounted upon a winged horse, because the first task of all poetry is to leave prosaic everyday things behind; but I ask you, dear pastor, upon what horse, winged or otherwise, are you able to imagine our Schmidt of Werneuchen mounted? Perhaps upon

> 'the spotless royal palfrey,
> With motley plume a'fluttering in the wind,
> His breast like snow with a blue veil adorned?'★

'No, dear Renate,' answered Seidentopf, 'certainly *not* upon any such spotless royal palfrey. The centuries of the Crusades, which are still almost the only ones that count among the people at Ziebingen, is not the era with which you would associate our simple-hearted Schmidt, who it will not be denied is firmly tied to home and country; he is wholly of the present, wholly devoted to normal life, wholly of the March. He is as unromantic as he could possibly be, but he is *none the less* a poet.'

'That he is,' interposed the pastor of Dolgelin, one of whose little vanities it was to advertise his acquaintanceship with his colleague of Werneuchen; he desired, moreover, at long last to introduce himself into the conversation, and the moment seemed to him to have arrived. 'Our much assaulted friend', he went on, 'is as much of a poet as anyone; but I can well see that our Fräulein Renate has been paying too many visits to Frankfurt and has gone over from the Barmin school, which is so truly a Brandenburg school, to the school of Lebus, where all they read now is Spanish writings★ and make an idol of Herr Tieck, as though there had been no poetry at all before his "enchanted, moon-illumined night",★ and no real moon either. And I find this arrogance provoking and, although Dolgelin is an old Lebus village, in this poetic feud I stand wholly on the side of Nieder-Barnim, and if you want to tell me that

> Yon little golden star,
> From me for ever far,★

which everyone is playing these days, is the most beautiful thing ever written, then I say: no, gentlemen, what is to your taste is not to my taste, and the robust style of our Werneuchen friend appeals to me much more when he begins:

> A summoning call the village bugler sounds,
> The pairs come in and lighter grow all hearts,
> The clerk attends, the peasants cry: Away,
> Remove the tables, now the merry-making starts!

That is what I call language. I can see the bridegroom in his worsted waistcoat and hear them all clicking their heels together as they dance. There is genuine gold in it which the "little golden star" is no match for.'

Turgany laughed heartily. Then there was a little embarrassed pause, which Seidentopf, skilfully circumventing the whole intermezzo formed by the Dolgelin pastor's speech for the defence, at last interrupted by turning to his fair adversary: 'You undervalue him, dear Renate, as so many others do also. Perhaps I fall into the opposite error, because I rediscover the qualities of his heart in his poetry too. But for that you have to know him.'

'Well, let us share in your knowledge, tell us about him.'

'Turgany must do that,' the pastor replied. 'He possesses the gift of forceful description, he knows him and esteems him too, if I recall former conversations correctly.'

Turgany at first made a gesture of refusal, and then explained: 'Dear Seidentopf, you must be confusing me with someone else, perhaps with your colleague Pastor Zabel, whom we have just seen becoming enthusiastic in the grateful memory of a worsted waistcoat. Your call would be in order if directed at *him*.'

But, as could have been foreseen, this refusal was made in vain; everyone urged Turgany to go on, and in the end he was obliged, for good or ill, to accede to this universal demand. Perhaps he did so not altogether unwillingly: for he loved nothing more than to exercise his talent for delicate mockery. 'Well, then,' he began, 'you all know that our friend from Werneuchen is a pastor and poet, but what you perhaps do *not* know, and what constitutes the real key to an understanding of his poetry, is that he is also a husband and father. He is closely connected with the pulpit, but even more closely connected with the cradle. His house is a nursery, or as they say hereabouts: more screeching than preaching. That he is a good and godly man goes without saying. He raises bees and grows flowers and when he invites guests to his house he does so not in prose, but in verse, mainly in sonnets. He is modest and conceited, yielding and obstinate, inoffensive and cunning, in sum a man of the March. Not content with being for his own part Pastor Schmidt of Werneuchen, he must have for his best friend Pastor Schultze of Döbritz.* *Nomen et omen.** He smokes a long pipe and wears a tasselled cap and dressing-gown, and when, exceptionally, he is not wearing the latter, he gives the impression he is wearing two. Of his poems, those which have always made the strongest impression on me is the little collection with the title "Songs for Country Girls, to be sung in the evening while milking": for in a note appended to it he says he has composed them to keep sleepy milkmaids awake while they are milking. I doubt that he achieved his aim.'

Seidentopf was at pains to evince some small displeasure. 'This doesn't take us any further, Turgany; even you yourself will not try to say that your account does him the slightest justice.'

'I don't know about that,' Lewin interposed. 'We are all familiar with the vivid and colourful way in which our legal friend speaks, but, divested of its somewhat excessive form of expression, he has said nothing that I would not subscribe to with all my heart. The ideal of this Werneuchen poetry is in fact nothing other than the tassel-capped *pater familias*, and the rebuke it received from Weimar* was well deserved. Sometimes he succeeds, it is true: this, for instance, is very fine:

> He whose love is faithful,
> He likes to find a lonely place,
> In secrecy and silence
> His joy there to embrace.
> There, far from any witness,
> He dreams alone, he loves alone;
> There his desire, his being,
> He enjoys them as his own.

But beside such well-devised lines as these there lie abysses. He has a pleasing gift of rhyme and an eye for nature: that is all. His descriptions may occasionally count as oases, but his thoughts are the desert they stand in. Sand and more sand. But what does Marie think of him? I seem to recall her reading his songs more than once and talking with Renate about them.'

Marie flushed red to the temples. She could hardly have done otherwise. Lewin, who knew from many evenings of gossip how little she liked the Werneuchen poet, overlooked the fact that the circle before whom he had so suddenly invited her to speak was a larger one than she was used to. But she quickly collected herself and then said, at once firmly and shyly: 'I am of the same view as Renate; he is no poet because he knows only the real world.'

'And his gift of description?' Seidentopf interposed.

'I do not like that either. It is the best thing about him, certainly, but when I read: "the golden stars ascended the endless vault of heaven",* I suddenly feel the infinite difference between *these* stars and our Schmidt's everyday stars. I doubt, though, whether I would be able to say what this difference is.'

'You will be able to: just begin,' Lewin and Renate urged her.

'I shall try. The poet ought to be a mirror of all things. But Schmidt mirrors nothing: he only repeats nature itself.'

'Good, good,' Turgany interrupted; 'I have read more than one analysis of the poet that doesn't get as far as this critical début. Schmidt's mirror is, if I have understood correctly, not a mirror at all but only the frame of one, and the pictures he presents are nothing but pieces of living nature set within it: nature as it appears to us if we stand three paces back from an open window. Very good.'

Seidentopf, who had been growing more and more restless, made to reply; but, as though he had noticed nothing of his friend's ill-humour, Turgany continued in his own manner: 'We have now given our verdict and, notwithstanding the favourable but altogether biased depositions of his colleagues of Hohen-Vietz and Dolgelin, the defendant has been found guilty. Othegraven's approving nod when the "golden stars" of Bürger's Lenore ascended I have, I hope not unjustly, interpreted as placing him within the anti-Schmidt faction. One weighty vote, however, is still outstanding. I herewith pose the clear and precise question: "What is the position of Herrnhut in regard to Werneuchen?"'

Aunt Schorlemmer shook her head back and forth and began to increase the speed of her knitting, which she had picked up again after the redemption of the forfeits. Even now she seemed reluctant to offer any answer.

Turgany, however, continued unabashed in his impersonation of judicial solemnity: 'In that case we must go on to apply the sternest measures available to us. In the name of Zinzendorf . . .'

Thus adjured, Aunt Schorlemmer raised the knitting-needle that had just become free and, pointing it at the magistrate in mock menace, said: 'Renate and Marie are right: he is horrid.'

'He is horrid,' Turgany repeated. 'With this belated testimony, in which by the way I believe I detect a Saxonism, our proceedings enter a new phase. It appears that with the charge relating to the aesthetic sphere there is now to be associated, if but mildly, a moral element.'

'No, not that,' Aunt Schorlemmer now went on in a determined voice: 'but I dislike him altogether. I dislike him because he wears his spiritual dress without spiritual dignity. Justizrat Turgany has got to the heart of it: he is closer to the cradle than he is to the pulpit. To him even the holy feast of Christmas is not a feast dedicated to the child of God, to him it is only a feast for his own children. He does not shrink even from indecencies, and then I am ashamed for his pastor's soul. No, this is not for a Herrnhut heart, in whose ears there still resound the Christmas carols of childhood.'

Turgany fell silent. Renate went up to Aunt Schorlemmer and said: 'Sing us the carol you sang on the first Christmas you were with us. I do love it so. Sing it, and I will sing with you.'

Aunt Schorlemmer vigorously resumed her knitting. Then she said: 'Very well, I will; we are in a Christian parsonage, after all.' Therewith she rose and went and sat at the piano. She began in a tremulous voice, until Renate's lovely contralto joined in like the sound of a bell. The piano accompanied them softly. And thus they sang together:

> 'Shepherd sweet
> At whose feet
> Even lions graze,
> Tend and keep
> Us thy sheep
> Through our childhood days.

> Let us share,
> Shepherd dear,
> In thy childhood joy,
> Let us be
> True as thee,
> Thou who wast man and boy.'*

And thus ended the second day of Christmas at the parsonage at Hohen-Vietz.

16

A Confidential Conversation

IT was about half-past ten when the subdued cracking of a whip and the abrupt jingling of bells whenever the two bays impatiently tossed their heads warned the visitors from Frankfurt that their sleigh had drawn up before the parsonage.

It was not long before the hallway was alive with activity and the laughter of Turgany—who, emerging from the second room, had bumped against the alligator and set the monster swaying uncannily—resounded out into the street, where, stamping up and down, the servant of the parsonage was holding the reins and by breathing and blowing on his half-numb fingers was trying to prevent them from becoming completely rigid. Immediately afterwards the house-door opened, the thin tone of its bell mingling with the jingling of the sleighbells, and Turgany and the schoolmaster quickly entered the waiting sleigh and made themselves comfortable on the low upholstered seat. A final wave in the direction of the hallway, a flick of the reins on the backs of the horses, and off they went along the snow-covered street towards the exit from the village. The pastor of Dolgelin, who still had some business to settle with Seidentopf, remained behind at the parsonage.

Hohen-Vietz was already asleep. All the farms lay in darkness; only Miekley's mill still showed a light, and a bright gleam fell upon a square stone that had been occupying the spot it stood on for a good hundred years and which marked the point from where the footpath branched off up to the woodland acre.

'The miller is still awake,' said Turgany; 'a conventicle, no doubt, with Uhlenhorst in person.'

In the same instant, however, the horses whinnied violently and shied away from the spot, so that it required some exertion to get them to pass it. When they had succeeded in going by, the magistrate looked back inquisitively and only then did he recognize Hoppenmarieken, who had been seated on the stone and, on catching sight of the sleigh, had saluted it with her crooked stick at just the wrong moment.

'Who is the hobgoblin?' asked Othegraven.

'Hoppenmarieken,' Turgany replied; 'by trade Hohen-Vietz's errand-woman, but no doubt a lot of other things as well. There are rumours of this and that, but no evidence to support them. Often she goes off at night and next morning she is back again.'

'A weird creature.'

'That she is. But an original, too, and she finds that an advantage. Old Vitzewitz closes his eyes to a lot that she does. Lewin, however, is her real advocate.'

Turgany's sleigh sped along, raking the snow a foot high every time it swerved or turned. Willow-trees with branches lopped, alternating with tall poplars, enclosed the road and, where they did not have to trust to chance, indicated the direction their journey had to take. Now and then a crow fluttered up, drowsy and silent, only to settle again on the nearest treetop. Above them stood the starry sky, sparkling in all its wintry splendour. The two travellers fell into a dreamlike state: it was as though the jingling of the sleighbells was dying away, while the gentle echo of sounds from far, far off seemed to grow ever louder, ever more passionate. What was close at hand lost its power over the ear; but the distant, the scarcely audible, resounded like bells.

Turgany was the first to shake off this paralysing half-dream.

'A glorious night!' he began.

'The lovely close of a lovely day,' replied Othegraven, who, as though a magic formula had been uttered, was also liberated from the spell. 'What a goodnatured man is your friend Seidentopf! How lively he is, how well he knows how to participate in everything, in the smallest and pettiest things, even a game of forfeits.'

Nothing could have been more welcome to the magistrate than that the conversation should have taken this turn. 'Seidentopf', he said, 'is a man like a child. I have found him tried and true a whole lifetime now. For forty years the same. Unchangingly loyal. But why do you count games of forfeits as among the pettiest things? You are wrong there: games of forfeits are a very important matter.'

So far as the voluminousness of his cloak would allow it, Othegraven looked questioningly at the magistrate. The latter laid his fur-clad left arm on the schoolmaster's shoulder and continued with a degree of warmth and sincerity not normally associated with him: 'I ought not to put this question, or at any rate not in this form. The subject forbids it, and who you are forbids it too. So out with it, Othegraven: you love Marie.'

Othegraven paused for a moment, and then said in a firm voice in which there was not the slightest trace of embarrassment: 'Yes, with all my heart.'

Question and answer had gone thus far when the friends' conversation was interrupted by their entry into the next village. They had advanced no further than the first houses before they could hear the sound of bass and clarinet coming from the inn, and when they reached it they saw that, in spite of the bitter cold, several couples were standing outside under the balcony and out as far as the road, and the girls were even in short sleeves. But this apparent thoughtlessness seemed excusable when you saw the clouds of thick smoke that were billowing through the open windows of the room where the dancing was taking place. 'There's some "merry-making" going on in there,' said Turgany: 'a shame our Dolgelin pastor isn't with us.'

The sleigh had now gone past the inn, the noise died away, and a wide expanse of snow again lay before them. Presuming that Othegraven's thoughts too were still on the subject they had been talking about, Turgany resumed, as though there had been no interruption: 'And how well she spoke. Every word hit home.'

'Whatever she does she will always do well. She will always do the right thing.'

'Hello, schoolmaster, already so sunk in admiration! But do you know this child's history? You realize she is an orphan.'

'I know everything,' the schoolmaster replied. 'I was at the mayor's three weeks ago and the Kniehases told me all about their foster-daughter. I know that she used to dance and recite, and would go round with a plate collecting coins. I am bound to say that I am not scandalized by any of this. It only makes me feel for her the more.'

'As it does me,' said Turgany. 'But, my dear Othegraven, we are very different people. I am a worldling, not much better than a heathen. You are a clergyman: still in the chrysalis stage of an assistant schoolmaster for the present, but the butterfly can come fluttering out at any time.'

Othegraven was silent for a moment. Then he said: 'Let me speak to you frankly, dear friend: I feel the urge to do so, and I find it easy to speak beneath these stars. You call yourself a heathen; I have my doubts about it. But be that as it may, you are wrong if you regard Christianity as being narrow and prejudiced, especially in this area. On the contrary, it is free and open. And that it should exercise this freedom is in accordance with the profoundest part of our faith.'

The magistrate seemed to want to reply, but Othegraven went on: 'We are all born in sin, and what sustains us is not our own strength but a strength that comes to us from without, in plain words the mercy of God. Do you know our wonderful Schildhorn saga?* Well, as it was with the Wendish prince Jaczko, so it is with us all: we should sink under in the heavy armour of our vain ego, of our selfish defiance, if the finger of God did not draw us up.'

Turgany nodded. 'You will not suppose, Othegraven, that I intend to break a lance on behalf of the self-righteousness of men or of the tangle of prejudices that grows out of it. I have long known how little cause we have to take pride in our virtues, and if there is any saying in the Bible that weighs with me it is: "let him first cast a stone at her." I would be the last person with a right to submit the lives of my fellow men to an *examen rigorosum*. Not to speak of the past history of this dear child! All I meant by my question was something like: "it is a piece of good fortune to come of a good house." And the simple truth of this proposition can hardly be gainsaid. Knie-hase's house is a good house. But the house of the "mighty man", who lies beneath a wooden cross up in Hohen-Vietz churchyard, can hardly have been such a house.'

'That is questionable,' said Othegraven. 'I could almost believe the opposite. It was a house of stern trials, of increasing humiliation; but where so much love reigned, and so much effort to spare a young life the consequences of an uncertainty in her birth, of any suspicion of illegitimacy, that house could not have been a house of immorality. I was not unmoved by the life-story of the "mighty man". He was unfortunate, not unholy; afflicted, not accursed.'

'You surprise me,' the magistrate put in. 'I am not as instructed in dogma as you are; but would you, apart from your affection for Marie, always draw so sharp a distinction between misfortune and unholiness as you do at this moment? Would you not be inclined to regard affliction as a consequence of guilt, as a punishment, as rejection and reprobation? Am I wrong in thinking that men of precisely your persuasion lay great weight on the preservation of the simple morals and customs of our forefathers?'

'No, you are not wrong,' Othegraven replied. 'Certainly there is a distinction between the house of Lot and the house of Sodom, and to want to disregard this distinction in the absence of a clear sign would be to rebel against custom and command-ment. But what decides and determines is always the grace of God. And this grace of God, it goes its own way. It is bound by no rules, it is a law to itself. Like the martins, it builds its nest in houses of every kind, in good ones and bad, and when it builds its nest in bad houses they are bad houses no longer. A new life has entered into them. Morality and custom is much, but election is everything.'

'And this you discover in Marie?'

'To you, dearest friend, I do not need to answer this question: for we have the same perceptions, each of us in his own way. And if the past life of this child were even more obscure and confused than it actually is, I should pay no heed to this confusion. For there exist natures over which the impure has no power; the clear flame that burns within them ensures that. I never see Marie without feeling, with a kind of joyful certainty, that she is destined to make others happy and to be happy herself.'

Turgany pressed his friend's hand. 'Othegraven, I have always had a high opinion of you: from today forward I shall not let go of you.'

Thus went their conversation; the sleighbells rang out across the snow; in the villages all was silent; no light but the twinkling stars.

The same stars also shone through a gable-window of the house of Kniehase, the village mayor. Marie was asleep; images from the previous evening that life and poetry had presented to her passed by her in a fantastic procession: at its head the pastor of Dolgelin with Schmidt of Werneuchen's village bugler, who, instead of sounding his bugle, was wearing it over his shoulder; then 'Odin's chariot', enormously enlarged, with Pastor Seidentopf standing on its axle. At the end of the procession, however, came 'the shepherd sweet', and the Christmas carol Aunt Schorlemmer and Renate had sung echoed in her dream.

17

Tubal to Lewin

THE third day of Christmas fell on a Sunday. The morning was bright and clear; the windows looking out on the park were bathed in the golden light of the sun just coming up over the church on the hill, but everywhere, even in places lying in shadow, there glittered the snow newly fallen the previous evening.

It was about nine o'clock. Lewin and Renate were sitting in the large living-room into which we conducted the reader in an earlier chapter, though this time they were not around the fireside as on the evening of Christmas Day but close to the corner-window that formed a deep alcove in the wall. Here they not only had the best light but were able to see, beyond the broad driveway which led to the manor house, the village street, whose comings and goings were always a distraction and often the only matter for conversation in the solitude of country life.

Breakfast seemed to be over; the cups had been pushed away and Lewin was just closing an elegantly bound book and laying it on the table. 'I fear, Renate, that we did him an injustice. But that inept enthusiasm exhibited by the Dolgelin pastor was too much! One loses patience. Yet there is much that is excellent here. So I now have to offer my tardy apology; *amende honorable retardée*,★ or *"moutarde après le dîner"*,★ as Aunt Amelie would prefer to say.'

Renate nodded.

'*Apropos* our aunt,' Lewin went on, 'I have ordered the small sleigh, for two o'clock; we shall be there in an hour, I shall drive myself.—And Marie has never yet been to Guse?' he added after a short pause.

'No,' replied Renate

'But you wrote that she had made a good impression on our aunt. If "Countess Pudagla" condescended to encounter our dear girl in this room, I should have thought the ice must have been broken beforehand.'

'The encounter was unintentional; Marie, who was bringing me a book from Pastor Seidentopf, came in unexpectedly. But in general, Lewin, you must not continually keep forgetting that our aunt is old and belongs to another age than ours. Why will you not make allowances for caste prejudices?'

'I do make allowances for them, perhaps more than I should. But what I will not make allowances for is the superficialities that attend them. Aunt Amelie—if the Vitzewitzes will forgive me for saying so—has through marrying into the Pudagla family in a certain sense grown beyond us, she is a lady of the nobility, and if it were her aristocratic habit to sit fanning herself and cuddling her Bolognese dog and talking about the unavoidable distinctions between man and man, then I would kiss her hand with the utmost respect and the last thing I would do would be to try to contradict her. I repeat, I can respect all that, even if my own inclinations do lie in another direction.

B S.—7

But Aunt Amelie is not one of these countesses of the old school. She considers herself enlightened, a radical. No day, no hour passes without her quoting from Montesquieu or Rousseau,* or talking high-mindedly about the "*vaine fumée*" which "*le vulgaire appelle gloire et grandeur, mais dont le sage connaît le néant*";* but when it comes to applying all this philosophical grandiloquence to any concrete case, it all turns out to be nothing but pompous empty phrases, a mere mask concealing the same old self-conceit.'

His sister made to reply, but Lewin went on: 'No, no, Renate, do not try to make excuses for her; I know them and that is what they are like one and all, these Rheinsberg countesses whose heads have been turned by French books and Prince Henri. Tirades about humanity, and behind them their old innate nature. If you will forgive the pretentious simile, they are like the palimpsests in our libraries: old parchments originally used for writing heathen verses until monks covered them with pious texts. But the amorous sighs of Chloe and Lalage return again and again. In plain terms: prejudices I make allowances for; falsehoods make me angry.'

'To tell the truth,' Renate now interposed, 'I recently had a conversation with our aunt on precisely this subject. She admitted there was something contradictory about her attitude, and she made this admission in so disarming a fashion you too would have been disarmed. I am sure I should not have known you.'

Lewin smiled. 'Where was this, here or over in Guse?'

'Here. It was on the occasion of the meeting I told you about in my letter; only I failed to describe to you the conversation which followed. There were three of us, Papa, our aunt, and I. Our good Schorlemmer was, as usual, absent; as you know, the "two aunts" do not get on well with one another. Marie came in and for a moment was taken aback. She is too bright not to have realized long ago how our aunt felt about her. But she quickly collected herself, bowed, performed the errand the pastor had given her and, apologizing for having disturbed us, departed again.'

'And our aunt?'

'She stayed silent, though her sharp eyes had scrutinized

every movement. Only after Papa had left did she say—without my asking her, which I wouldn't have dared to do: "The girl is *charmante, a beauté* from a fairy-tale, what eyelashes!"—"We love her very much," I ventured to say, whereupon our aunt went on, not unkindly and in her most Frenchified manner, which I will spare you: "I know, I know, and now I have seen her I understand what I previously took for a whim. In Lewin's case I thought it was more. It may be I am mistaken," she added when she noticed I was shaking my head. There followed a short pause, during which the *tabatière* was opened and closed a couple of times; then she said gaily: "I have been considering these past few minutes whether I should invite you to bring the girl over to Guse with you; we lack her kind there, and I love young people as much as I hate old ladies. But Renate, *ma chère*, it wouldn't do. I have come to realize that certain tastes and notions I have are stronger than my principles. It is quite true: *On renonce plus aisément à ses principes qu'à son goût.** I well remember the day Prince Henri surprised us by making a similar admission. The prince and the philosopher were always at odds with one another. Now you see, this girl has great charm: yet I feel that, no matter how amply she was clad, I would be unable to resist the thought that at any moment she might tuck up her dress and start doing the shawl-dance. I have no wish to wrong the girl by such thoughts, so I think it would be best to leave things as they are.' '

Lewin, who had followed all this attentively, was about to respond in the most conciliatory way when the appearance of Hoppenmarieken turning out of the village street into the courtyard interrupted the conversation. Fitted out, in her customary fashion, in flannel skirt and high boots, back-basket and crooked stick, she advanced straight towards the manor house, saluted the youthful couple, whom she recognized through the window, and the next minute letters and newspapers lay spread out on the table.

Weighty though their contents were, the newspapers contained nothing Lewin would not already have known; of the letters, one was from Papa, who had written them a few lines to say he hoped to be in Schloss Guse by that evening, the other from Cousin Ladalinski, Lewin's fellow-student and bosom friend. Lewin beamed as his eyes fell on the two closely written sheets; Renate blushed slightly and said: 'Now read it.'

And Lewin read.

Dear Lewin!

Much pampered as you are, these lines, which in themselves represent an act of homage, will come as no little spur to your vanity. But I am filled with a desire to chatter and am conscious every hour of your absence. For you are one of the few with a talent for listening, a talent doubly rare in those who also know how to speak.

We had a splendid Christmas Eve, and it is this I am writing to you about. You will think when I say this that I am speaking of the joys of the Christmas tree, as indeed I ought to be; but it is not so. In a house where there are no children the Christ-child will always have a difficult time, unless it be that the adults retain some sense of childhood. And Kathinka, who possesses so much (perhaps *because* she possesses so much), does not possess this sense. So far as I myself am concerned, I have been at any rate lightly touched by the hand that bestows this gift: just sufficiently to feel a longing for it.

There were only a very few of us: Papa, Kathinka, a new friend of hers whom you do not yet know, and I. Just as we were going in to see the tree Count Bninski arrived. He had little gifts for us all, too generous to my way of thinking; but Kathinka seemed not to feel it so. The brightly lit room, the sparkling tree, were a delight to the eyes but, as I must say again, they made no deeper impression. It all had the look of a gaudy decoration. Even the lace drapery *à la Reine Hortense** (note for Renate) that Papa had procured from Paris made no difference. The conversation after the first exchanges of thanks was constrained. The count knew the contents of the communiqué; we refrained from discussing it, so as not to wound his feelings.

In these circumstances it came almost as a deliverance when a loosely folded slip of paper was handed to me on which was written, in the usual pithy style of our friend Jürgass: 'Today, Thursday the 24th, *Christmas punch*. Mundt's wine-cellar, Königsbrücke 3, nine o'clock; better late than not at all. Guests welcome. J.' I handed the note to the count, who only the previous day had expressed the wish to visit our club, indicated the last two words, and asked him if it would be agreeable to him to accompany me. He accepted the invitation —somewhat to my surprise, for he appeared not to be in a very sociable mood. In any event, I had no cause later on to regret he had done so.

Soon after nine o'clock we were at our rendezvous, which could not have been better chosen. In such things as this you can rely on Jürgass.

You will recall that the river-banks on both sides of the Königsbrücke form a high quay, on to which project the gables and side-wings of a number of old buildings. That is where Mundt's house stands. We descended from the street down into the cellar, felt our way along a dark passage, and at last emerged into a large but low-ceilinged and wood-panelled salon which, reawakening in me old memories, vividly called to mind the cabins of English warships. Some of our company had already assembled: von Schach, Bummcke, Dr Sassnitz and Rabatzki, the bookseller. Jürgass was still missing. I introduced Bninski; then we took our seats. It was only then that I could see how cosy and comfortable the place really was: well lit, a fire in the stove, a long table covered with a white cloth, and the seating so arranged as to give an unobstructed view of the Spree.*

The windows were almost as tall as the room itself and extended down to the floor, and through them you could watch the colourful Christmas crowd moving past. Skaters carrying stick-lanterns, boys with *Waldteufels*, little girls with angel dolls, all surged along before our windows, now brightly lit, now plunged into darkness, like a magical apparition; and from the direction of the Königsbrücke there came the jingling of sleighbells and the subdued noise of the city.

At last Jürgass arrived; in his hand he held a large blue paper bag. 'Behold, I bring you Christmas,' he said; 'but the main thing I bring my guests—for I ask to be allowed to regard you as such today—is himself a guest. As goes without saying, he is a poet.' With that he indicated a gentleman who had entered with him. Before I had had time to introduce Bninski and Jürgass to one another, the latter continued: 'I have the honour to present to you Herr Grell, or, to give him his full name and title, Herr Detleff Hansen-Grell, student of divinity, a kind of tenant of mine, a bondsman of the Jürgasses at Gantzer. The genealogical facts relating to the Grells, or to the Hansen-Grells, I shall keep in reserve for the time being.' Everyone looked at Jürgass, laughing if a little surprised at his words; the latter, without waiting for any response, went on in the same tone: 'Our Kastalia* is drying up; it lacks new blood. One could suspect the gentlemen of our circle of being afraid to face the rivalry of poets new arisen. Were it not for *me* and Bummke and our friend Rabatzki here, who to fill the last column of his *Sonntagsblatt* now and then ensnares a young lyricist, our fount of the muses would, its high-sounding name notwithstanding, soon cease to gush. Is it not absurd that, to ward off this threatening danger, I have to apply to my father's estate for lyrical succour?'

The entry of a waiter in regulation leather apron interrupted this speech. He bore in a bowl of punch, and the large paper bag Jürgass had brought with him began to go the rounds: together with walnuts from the Rhine it also contained a number of packets of French gingerbread. Jürgass took the chair. 'I bid you welcome,' he resumed. 'With regard to the paper bag I recommend a cautious economy: its contents are for the moment irreplaceable. But the punch-bowl can expect replenishment, if necessary several replenishments.'

Glasses were clashed together. When we had come in I had taken a seat on one of the narrow sides of the table; Bninski sat opposite me. This position permitted me unobtrusively to observe the 'lyrical succour' who was to aid the recovery of our Kastalia. Despite possessing a good profile, he was ugly rather than handsome: his hair was dull, his pale eyes were protuberant, and he had few eyelashes; his eyelids were, moreover, slightly red and he had thin stubbly whiskers. The worst thing about him was his complexion. Overall impression: commonplace.

My glance glided over to Bninski, who I thought might also have been examining him. I divined what he was thinking.

Desultory conversation followed. Bummke loudly regretted your absence; apart from you, Kandidat Himmerlich was most missed—for what reason I could not discover. Perhaps they thought that a theology student such as Grell would find nothing more to his taste than to be presented with one of his own kind: but I doubt that this proposition is likely to be true.

It must have been about eleven o'clock, and the jingling of bells had died away on the bridge and the street outside, when Jürgass began: 'I believe we should improvise a meeting of Kastalia. Herr Hansen-Grell will have the goodness to read something to us.'

This announcement was received with a noticeable, though excusable, coolness. Our guest looked as unpoetical as he possibly could have, and our Jürgass's recommendation was, as you will appreciate, not precisely calculated to enhance him in our eyes. None the less, he drew from his pocket a manuscript of a suspiciously large bulk; I believe the heart sank in everyone present.

But we were soon to change our minds. He unaffectedly asked permission to read to us a ballad whose subject was taken from Norwegian legend: *Hakon Borkenbart*. He lived for a time in Copenhagen, it seems. How he came to do so you will learn, together with much else, at another time. He then began, and read with expression, a firm and well-modulated voice, and increasing fire. There were some twenty stanzas. The first, which was repeated in the discussion that followed, has stayed in my memory:

> The brave King Hakon Borkenbart
> Was famed for deeds in peace and war,
> Had arms and men, and on the sea
> Of stately ships had many a score.
> His barns were rich in stores,
> But he was rich in scars,
> In scars which from the Danes he wore.

In the second stanza Hakon, his fifty years notwithstanding, sets out to woo fair Ingeborg. I struggle in vain to recall the verses, but with the third stanza, which particularly appealed to me, I shall have more success. This, roughly at any event, is how it went:

> Already tower and castle stand
> Before his proud and smiling gaze;
> Then from his mount he says: 'Though I
> Am old, it is but old in days.
> In courting scars and fame
> My spirit, still the same,
> Retains its youthful wonted ways.'

At this point, as you can imagine, old Bummke broke into loud exclamations of delight. I am quite sure he thought he was Hakon Borkenbart at that moment. The poem goes on to tell how fair Ingeborg repulses him and he vows revenge. He disguises himself as a beggar and sits himself before Ingeborg's castle with a golden distaff. She desires to have the distaff; he refuses to give it to her. Her desire for it is so strong she gives herself to the beggar so as to possess it. Then follow the familiar complications: father enraged, daughter thrust out. Finally the beggar unmasks himself as Hakon Borkenbart, and all ends happily.

I found the poem very pleasurable, and I believe we all did. Next to the poet himself, Bninski interested me the most. He grew more and more serious. 'Strange,' his face seemed to say, 'what a prosaic appearance, and behind it what sacred fire!'

Now this fire in fact resided in the spell of the subject of the poem itself and of the way in which it was delivered. Otherwise it was open to criticism on many points. Dr Sassnitz, who on this occasion too led the *avant-garde* of our critique, was the first to speak. He rightly called attention to the fact that our honoured guest had exerted his great poetic capacities upon a subject that would have been better served by a smaller expenditure of effort. As he himself had remarked, the whole thing was a fairy-tale: the simplicity which constituted the charm of such a subject ought not to be disrupted by any unnecessary magnificence in the way it was expressed. Though its merits were undeniable, the poem was too long and, more especially, too weighty.

If our guest could have gained more credit with us than he already possessed, it would have been through the manner in which he accepted this criticism. He nodded in agreement and then said to Sassnitz: 'I am very grateful to you: your censures are entirely to the point. I did not know why it was my own work failed to satisfy me: now I do know.'

Conversation now resumed. Soon afterwards the punch-bowl was emptied and, assured that Bummcke at least would hold out, Jürgass ordered a second. Bninski and I, however, did not await its arrival; in any event it would soon be midnight. When we stepped out into the silent square, starlight lay upon the streets almost as bright as day. I gazed aloft, and it was as though the Christ-child were descending into my poor heart out of this starry splendour. Bninski accompanied me; we remained silent. As we parted, he said in a voice I had hitherto not known in him: 'I am grateful to you for this evening, Tubal; I should be glad to see your friends more often.'

There you have the latest meeting of Kastalia, and an improvised one at that.

And now farewell. I hope Renate is with you. This form of seasonal compliment will, I hope, be worth a thousand greetings to my fair cousin. Your *Tubal*.

Postscript. Your Papa is with mine at the moment. They talk much of politics, perhaps *too* much. He sends his best wishes and, as he has written to you already, hopes to be at Schloss Guse tomorrow evening. He offered me a seat in his carriage, but I declined it. Aunt Amelie has too many 'friends and acquaintances' assembled around her for my taste. But I long for Hohen-Vietz and its quietness. If I can persuade Kathinka to accompany me, you may expect us *very soon*.

Your T.

BOOK TWO

★

SCHLOSS GUSE

Schloss Guse*

THE course of our story now takes us away from Hohen-Vietz and the eastern region of the Oderbruch to its *western hills*, at whose foot there still lie, as there did in former days, the historical villages of this land—estates of the old nobility whose names, mostly of Wendish origin, are already to be found in our earliest records. Here, in the neighbourhood of Wrietzen and Freienwalde, there dwelt the Sparrs and the Uchtenhagens, who are still remembered in song and story; here at the time of the Reformation and the Swedish occupation the Barfus, the Pfuels, the Ihlows had their seats; and here in the days immediately following the Seven Years War Lestwitz and Prittwitz* lived side by side in friendly neighbourliness: Prittwitz who at Kunersdorf had saved the King, Lestwitz who at Torgau had saved the fatherland. Or, as an expression then current at the court (which was given to imitating the French at any rate linguistically) had it: 'Prittwitz a sauvé le roi, Lestwitz a sauvé l'état.'*

Soon after the draining of the Oderbruch—some thirty years before the commencement of our story, that is to say—all these estates began to add to their other merits that of natural beauty. To wander through this region at Whitsuntide, when the fields of rape were in bloom and scattering their gold and odour far and wide, was to fancy yourself transported from the March away to some distant, more opulent land. The fruitfulness of this virgin soil moved the heart to a feeling of joyful gratitude, such as the Patriarchs may have felt when, in regions empty of men, they numbered the God-given yield of their house and their herds. For it is only where the hand of man wrests a few poor blades of corn from the barren earth by dint of hard, unremitting toil that it can occur to him it is *he* who has created this meagre yield; where the earth brings forth fruit a hundred-fold, however, and out of every grain of corn that is scattered creates an abundance, there the human heart feels itself in the immediate presence of the grace of God and renounces all sense of self-sufficiency. It was at this hilly western border of the Oderbruch that the Great King, gazing across the golden fields, spoke the words: 'Here without resort to war I have gained a province.'★

This cry would, to be sure, hardly have been justified by the picture presented by the low-lying countryside on this third day of Christmas in 1812. Everything lay buried in snow. But even on such a day as this the view from the 'Seelower Höhe',★ which dominates the Bruch, was not without its charm: over the numerous farmsteads and hamlets set out across the land there drifted trails of smoke that told of human habitations, while the church-towers of the larger villages, only half covered in snow, could be seen glittering for miles in the bright sunshine.

One of these church-towers, the nearest, appeared not a rifle-shot away from the above-named height, and an avenue of old oak-trees, whose brown foliage was clearly visible where the wind had shaken down the snow, ran in a straight line directly to the church. Beside this avenue there rose high above the weather-cock on the church-tower the tops of mighty trees, some of them strangers to this country and to all appearance belonging to a great park that curved around the left side of the village.

This village was *Guse*.

Although of Wendish origin, as its name proclaims, it entered the history of our land only at the time of the Thirty Years War, when the Schaplows had their seat here. Two years before the conclusion of the Peace of Osnabrück, Georg von Derfflinger,★ then still a general in the service of the Swedes, married Margarethe Tugendreich von Schaplow and took over the estate—not as part of his wife's inheritance but by purchase: the Schaplows, encumbered by debt, were unable to maintain it.

This purchase of the estate by the general was at first little more than a capital investment, perhaps also an attempt to establish himself in Brandenburg, territorially and politically; but already by the sixties, long before the Battle of Fehrbellin★ and the Pomeranian and East Prussian campaign★ had raised

Derfflinger to the height of his fame, we see him engaged not merely in making good the ravages of years of neglect, but in creating through new buildings and installations—in all following the example of his lord the Elector—a model establishment. Drains were dug, dams and pathways through the fens were constructed, the château was erected; the church was enlarged and then provided with a crypt, and a barracks, still recognizable to this day, was occupied by a detachment of dragoons dispatched to Guse from the local garrison for daily service with their commander and general. The undertaking which lay closest to the old man's heart, however, was the park, which soon became a source of greater joy to him than the fame of his deeds. An excellent manager and housekeeper, as are almost all those who exchange the sword for the plough, he was none the less inclined to be profligate when it came to the acquisition of beautiful trees: cypresses and magnolia-trees were procured at great expense, and a cedar-grove in the park still bears the name 'New Lebanon'.

To live in seclusion on this estate increasingly became the field marshal's sole desire; he was now eighty years old and, as he himself put it, had tasted 'much that was sour and sweet' at the court, 'but more of the sour'. The days when he could write in the album of his friend, Count Baudissin:*

> Storm and rain
> Blow again and again;
> *I duck* and let them blow over me,
> For I know the storm must have its way,

these days of almost cheerful resignation now lay far behind him, and he had grown irritable, obstinate and crusty. At length the Elector—who wanted to retain him in service, his advanced years notwithstanding—gave in, and the field marshal had his will and his freedom; he abandoned the city and went to Guse. Here for a little while yet he looked upon all he had created and rejoiced in the yield of his fields and the comforts of his house: but he was weary, weary even of his happiness; and before the century had run out his full life came to an end. As he had decreed, he was buried without ostentation, in the crypt he had himself constructed. The minister too had to confine himself to the simple epitaph: 'God permitted the deceased to rise from the lowest rank in the war service to the highest.' The old man had had sufficient fame in his lifetime to be able to do without the echo of it now he was dead.

His only surviving son, Friedrich von Derfflinger,* acceded to the whole rich inheritance, which in addition to the village and Schloss Guse included five other estates in the Oderbruch. Like his father, he commanded a regiment of dragoons; but there the similarity ended, for he possessed little of the warlike temperament and leadership that had brought his father such high honours.

A difference in the ages in which they lived can hardly have been the cause of this difference between father and son, for, after a brief period of peace, the new century began with one of the most ferocious wars of all time,* and at Turin* and Malplaquet the bodies of Brandenburgers lay heaped among the dead. But if the annals of war fail to speak of him, those of Guse do: here he was concerned from the moment of his accession, not only to continue the work his father had begun, but to honour this same father as well. He extended the park, he embellished the château, but above all he had a monument erected to the late field marshal. The finest talents available in the Berlin of the age of Schlüter* were engaged in the construction of this memorial. Above an open stone sarcophagus, into which the son placed his father's field marshal's baton, there was set up a bust of Georg von Derfflinger, an image of Fame blew into a trumpet, and two blue-silk Derfflinger standards with the inscription 'agere aut pati fortiora'* were crossed to form an armorial trophy. This memorial has been preserved in the church at Guse to the present day.

Three decades after the death of his father, Friedrich von Derfflinger also died, and with him the celebrated name was extinguished: it had glittered for hardly more than half a century, yet brightly enough during this brief period to rescue the name of the village of Guse from obscurity for ever. The former Derfflinger estate passed through various hands until it came into the possession of Count von Pudagla.* The count did not reside there at first but had it administered for him; and it was at this time, when national sentiment was again beginning to stir, that pilgrimages to the Derfflinger crypt began. They were not to the advantage of him who reposed in it: the pilgrims, eager for mementoes and concealing their impiety behind a pretence of historical interest, tore at the dead man's garments, so that before a decade was out he lay in his coffin utterly plundered, clad only in a buckled breastplate and his tall riding-boots.

In the year 1790 Count Pudagla died, and his widow, taking over the estate, put an end to the mischief.

This widow was *Aunt Amelie*.★

2

Aunt Amelie

AUNT Amelie was the elder sister of Berndt von Vitzewitz. Born at the middle of the century—at a time, that is, when the influence of the Friederician court was already beginning to make itself felt in the circles of the aristocracy—she received a French education and knew long passages of the *Henriade* by heart before she was so much as aware of the existence of a *Messiade*★ (the name of whose author, if she had known it, would in any case have prevented her from reading it).

She was a very beautiful child, mature early, the terror of all the ignorant and self-important ladies of the neighbourhood, and when she was twenty realized her parents' hopes that she would make a brilliant marriage: in the autumn of 1770 she became Countess Pudagla.

Count Pudagla, a man in his forties, had participated in the war, distinguished himself at the Battle of Leuthen,★ and at the end of hostilities held the rank of captain in the Anspach and Bayreuth Regiment of Dragoons. He seemed assured of a brilliant military career: at the next regimental review, however, he found himself overwhelmed with harsh reproaches by the King, who believed he had detected some gross error, and as a consequence of this the count took his departure. He withdrew to his ample properties, which occupied half the island of Usedom, toured over several years the capitals of western Europe, and upon his return gave public expression to his dissatisfaction by accepting a title of chamberlain to Prince Heinrich: he *wanted* to be counted among the '*frondeurs*'★ whom, as is well known, the prince was assembling around him. A few weeks later he married the beautiful Amelie von Vitzewitz and, after a brief sojourn at the Pomeranian estates, removed to Rheinsberg.

The advantages which the little court derived from the count's presence were, so far as his own person was concerned, slight. His wife reproached him with having, '*au fond du coeur*',★ an aversion to princes, and she was right; he took offence at the morals, the cult of flattery, and the arrogant criticism of others that had their abode here, and was always glad when, after weeks of summary service, he could return again to his native island, rejoice in his *paterna rura*★ and bury himself in English parliamentary debates: for he loved England and saw in its people, its freedom, its law and justice, the model of the only state system worth emulating.

However much the count might neglect his duty to stimulate and flatter the court, however, the countess more than made up for this neglect. In the briefest possible time she had become the soul of society, and as she came to dominate the court so she did its leading figure, the prince—a phenomenon which could come as a surprise only to those who took a more one-sided and superficial view of the Great King's celebrated brother than they ought to have done. For, while he hated women, he also felt drawn to them. Full of aversion for the sex as such whenever it made uncomfortable demands on him, he possessed sufficient aesthetic understanding and fineness of feeling to appreciate the characteristic good qualities of the feminine mind: directness, wit and good humour, acuteness and aptness of expression. Thus there came about the contradictory state of affairs that a court which denied women as women was dominated by women, and dominated by them indeed without their having to renounce for a moment any of their feminine qualities and failings. The prince required only that he be *personally* spared: for the rest, he was inclined to tolerate all that went on around him, not in spite of the lack of punctiliousness it revealed in regard to morals but precisely because, offering as it did an inexhaustible fund of material for his sarcastic disposition, it provided his favourite subject of entertaining conversation. Love-intrigues were the order of the day; but one of the many things that united him with our young countess was the perception that, though she might rival him in boldness and freedom of thought, she declined to translate this freedom of thought into action and never for a moment gave ground for any suspicion of fashioning her principles to suit her convenience. For, like all who stand outside traditional morality, the prince too in the last resort concealed behind his disbelief in the existence of virtue a profound respect for it. Adhering unshakeably to his general view of things, he saw in the countess 'the exception that confirms the rule', and congratulated himself on being able to entertain, in a way far superior to the commonplace petty liaison, a relationship of the most intimate sort with a woman who, endowed with all the advantages of the feminine nature, was at the same time free of all its weaknesses. The countess afforded him in addition a particular pleasure through the fact that she had for her husband the same cheerful coolness as she had for all other members of the Rheinsberg court, and treated the question of the continuance of the house of Pudagla with imperturbable unconcern.

One of her most prominent characteristics was her frankness. She knew she was free to say more than others could and she availed herself of this privilege. A mixture of raciness and charm of which she had command allowed her to venture on boldnesses that would not have been so readily excused perhaps in any other member of the court; but the real secret of the lasting favour she enjoyed was that she knew precisely how to distinguish differing domains of conversation one from another and to behave accordingly: at all events, she knew where boldness was in place and where it was not. If she was exceedingly frank and open she was, to an even greater degree, also exceedingly sagacious. The domain of philosophy, the Church, morality constituted for her an arena with no fixed boundaries, while in politics there were several areas marked *défendu*★ and, because the vanities of the prince were involved in it, in the military sphere there was a whole host of them. The countess bore this distinction in mind at all times, and while she might perhaps defend Voltaire's conception of Joan of Arc★ to the limit of the possible, when it came to discussing some princely heroic deed of war she immediately altered her tone and intrepid daring gave way to the humblest respect and admiration. In the formulation of such expressions of respect and admiration—whether by chance in conversation or prepared beforehand at formal festivities—she possessed an inexhaustible fund of invention, and if the prince himself enjoyed a well-deserved reputation in this sphere, the countess showed herself to be at the very least his attentive pupil. Her complete indifference to military parades and the exploits of war she was able to conceal behind a pretended interest in them which, because it had to be simulated, appeared all the more lively. She knew that he who desires the end must also desire the means to it, and thus the roster of the prince's battles was soon engraved in her memory more firmly than the feasts of the Christian calendar. The sixth of May, the anniversary of the Battle of Prague,★ never passed without some solemn commemoration of it; ever new surprises were then brought forth: embroidered tapestries showing Hradshin Castle★ and the Moldau Bridge, together with four grenadier's caps in the corners; *tableaux vivants* in which Mars and Minerva, feeling themselves outdone, bowed the knee to the higher divinity of Rheinsberg; dialogues and whole plays with Greek and Roman heroes, myrmidons and legionaries, who were in the end invariably unmasked as Prince Heinrich and the Itzenplitz Regiment storming the heights at Prague.

If all this gave evidence of a capacity for ingenuity, her capacity for keeping silent, for suppressing and disavowing—an art she had constantly to practise—was hardly less formidable. 'Schwerin with the banner'★ was never so much as to be called to mind; any reference to the prince's mighty rival at Prague would have led only to the most violent discord and, desiring to obviate in advance any such unpleasant event, the prince had not scrupled to characterize 'that hero's death celebrated in song at every annual fair' as simply a '*bêtise*'.★

The countess knew how to accommodate herself to all these moods and quirks of the prince, even when they descended to capriciousness and injustice, and the reward of her efforts was that for sixteen years she ruled the court. It was not until the year 1786 that, though this domination itself was left undisturbed, a general realignment took place within the establishment: the Great King died and, as it did elsewhere, his demise had a profound effect on life at Rheinsberg. The little court was as though blown to pieces: all its more independent elements, who had for the most part congregated around the prince less from love of him than out of opposition to the King, again made their peace with the state government and were glad to be able to desert a narrow circle which offered them no prospects and return to the public service. Among them was Count Pudagla. In the same autumn he departed for England: a mission for which, in addition to his familiarity with the politics and language of the country, the friendly relations he enjoyed with several influential families qualified him. On receiving this distinguishing commission, and so that he might prove a more useful envoy, he proposed to the countess that she should accompany him: she, however, declined, partly because she was in fact sincerely attached to the prince, but mainly out of an innate aversion to England.

So she stayed, stayed and continued to pay homage, though without being really happy about doing either. The great days were, after all, in the past: everything had altered, not only the court but the prince as well. His periods of ill-humour grew more frequent; state affairs, neglected and banished for so many years, again stepped into the foreground and he found them troubling and unsettling, especially so from the moment when it became clear that the storm-clouds were gathering in Paris. For his great, now departed brother, though he had had little love for him and had been much given to carping at and criticizing him, he had had at bottom a profound and quite unfeigned respect; but he felt nothing of the sort for the new regime,* not to speak of the personalities that flourished in it. Because it was divested of all that was refined and intellectual, petticoat government* was an abomination to him; and graciously kissing our countess's hand he said, when on one occasion the name of Madame Rietz was spoken in his presence: '*Je la déteste de tout mon cœur; mes attentions, comme vous savez bien, appartiennent aux dames, mais jamais aux femmes.*'[*]

Such confidences showed that she still enjoyed the prince's especial favour: none the less the countess was overcome by the feeling that her days at Rheinsberg were numbered. She did not desire to leave but in her heart she prepared herself for that eventuality: and the moment of its arrival came sooner than she expected. In 1789 the count returned on a brief holiday; in the King's antechamber he was struck down by a stroke, and the following day he was dead. The news affected his widow more than those who knew their marriage had expected it would: she now came to realize that, in her pride and capriciousness, she had underestimated not his love, but the worth of his aristocratic mind and bearing; and though she was by nature incapable of sentimental remorse, his testament, which was one more perfect expression of this aristocratic mind, could only bring home to her more forcefully how unjust she had been. Schloss Guse, which, having been acquired by the count himself, was not regarded as part of the familial estates, was, together with a considerable sum of money, assigned to the countess; and she decided to take possession of her inheritance and to administer the estate herself. She wanted to remain at the Rheinsberg court only until the end of the winter, and when the winter ended she departed; it was not without emotion that she left the prince, who together with other souvenirs had presented her with an acrostic poem he had composed himself.

On the eve of Easter 1790 she arrived at Schloss Guse.

At first sight the château appeared to be completely uninhabitable: the years during which the estate had been left in the hands of an administrator had transformed it, a few of the rooms excepted, into a kind of storehouse for corn and fodder; wheat and rape lay in heaps, and the corridors were choked with hay and straw. The most distressing sight of all was that presented by the left wing, whose crumbling floorboards were everywhere overgrown with fungus. Old paintings from the time of the Derfflingers, torn and spotted with mould and most of them without frames, hung crooked and isolated on the walls, and served only to intensify the impression of decay.

Nevertheless, the countess did not allow herself to be disconcerted by the sight of all this damage and destruction the château had undergone; on the contrary, her energetic nature was stimulated by the prospect of activity it presented. She moved into two small rooms on the first floor which had suffered least from the general ruination and were at the same time well ventilated and had an unimpeded view of the handsome park, and from there she directed the artisans of all the villages roundabout, who were soon joined by artists from the capital she was acquainted with, in the reconstruction and redecoration of the interior of the building, a work that was completed to the extent intended in a relatively short time. Superstitious as she was, and always influenced by significant dates, she took possession of the renovated rooms on 31 December 1790: since, for all kinds of pagan–philosophical reasons in which profundity and nonsense had an equal share, New Year's Eve counted as an exceptionally lucky day.

The renovated rooms all lay on the right side of the building and consisted of a billiard-room, a mirrored- or flower-room, and a drawing-room, to which, in the corresponding side-wing, there were attached the dining-room and the theatre —for persons schooled at the Rheinsberg court could hardly imagine a comfortable life at all in the absence of curtains and coulisses. Apart from ventilation of the rooms and the removal of everything that did not properly belong in them, the left side of the château remained untouched, while the great entrance hall that lay between its two sides was made into an emporium of all the relics of the Derfflingers. Here there were installed two falconets,* two model dragoons with glass eyes, and the best-preserved of the portraits and battle-paintings that had previously been scattered among the rooms of the château; in front of the two dragoons, occupying approximately the centre of the hallway, there stood an imitation of an antique satyr, whose mocking laugh was the best possible comment on all that stood around him.

To consecrate these newly occupied rooms, on the following day, New Year's Day 1791, the countess held her first *soirée*. The nobility of the neighbourhood was invited, and Aunt Amelie did the honours in precisely the way her means, her mind and the habits she had acquired at court would lead you to expect. Everyone was enchanted; both hostess and guests promised themselves a stimulating, perhaps even an intimate acquaintanceship with one another; plans were projected; and the future seemed a long series of musical matinées and *declamatoria*, of *hombre** parties and performances of French comedies.

But things transpired otherwise.

Before even a year was out both parties were obliged to accept the fact that they were unsuited to one another: the countess was too intelligent, the local nobility not intelligent enough. And this was especially true of the women: their French (which was only a little better than their German), their pretended literary interests, their constant chatter about things about which they were as ignorant as they were indifferent, could not but offend the sensibilities of a lady who had hitherto divided her life between the personal friendship of a prince and the intellectual society of some of the leading minds of the age. Only the fleetingness of their first encounters could have concealed all this; and as soon as the countess realized how things really were, she desisted from all traffic with her neighbours and, surrendering herself again to her passion for reading, confined herself for many years to the narrowest possible circle: it comprised her brother Berndt at Hohen-Vietz, Count Drosselstein,* who lived at Hohen-Ziesar,* and the eighty-three-year-old superintendent* at Seelow, who was old enough to have participated as an army chaplain in the Battle of Mollwitz. This purely masculine circle (Berndt's wife was excluded from it) satisfied only very imperfectly the deep need she felt for scandal and gossip, and she sought to make good this deficiency through a chatty correspondence with the prince, who, a connoisseur in the realm of the *chronique scandaleuse*, spared no effort to encourage her in it, for it profited them both equally.

It lasted until 1802, when the prince died. Only then did she feel again an inclination to emerge out of her isolation, which was indeed quite contrary to her true nature and had only been forced upon her by circumstances: and so she did. Women —towards whom she harboured an aversion which with the years had grown almost to a mania—were excluded as before;

but she sought to enlarge the little circle of men which had hitherto constituted her only society. A convenient opportunity for doing so was afforded by a change in the ownership of several of the neighbouring estates; and there began the construction of that social circle which, a decade before the commencement of our story, had already given rise to critical comments of all kinds on the part of her brother Berndt, but also to the countess's defensive conclusion: '*Tous les gens sont bons, hors l'ennuyeux.*'*

'Good,' Berndt had responded; 'but in that case you must fulfil the condition. You wouldn't want to describe Chamberlain von Medewitz as "*hors l'ennuyeux*", would you?'

'Oh yes I would,' his sister had replied, and broken off a conversation in which each was in the right from his own point of view. Selfish in all she did, the countess proceeded, not in accordance with generally accepted principles, but in accordance with her own personal taste; and her circle of acquaintances, which Berndt described somewhat sarcastically as 'friends of various kinds', was selected, not with an eye to pleasing others, but solely with an eye to pleasing *herself*. What she despised most was adherence to tradition: her own pleasure was sovereign. She was entertained just as much by one who extorted a smile from her, or gave her an opportunity for sarcastic humour, as she was by those who brought with them an abundance of wit or a store of anecdotes: the only people who failed to interest her were those who never opened their mouths; while anyone out of the common, regardless of whether he was uncommonly clever or uncommonly stupid, possessed for her a degree of piquancy and charm.

Let us now take a closer look at the nature of these 'friends of various kinds' who congregated at Schloss Guse.

3

Friends of Various Kinds

THE 'friends of various kinds' were ordered into an outer and an inner circle. The inner circle consisted of seven people, namely the following: Count Drosselstein of Hohen-Ziesar, Chairman von Krach★ of Bingenwalde, Major-General von Bamme★ of Quirlsdorf, Baron von Pehlemann of Wusche-wier, Canon von Medewitz of Alt-Medewitz, Captain von Rutze of Protzhagen, and Dr Faulstich of Kirch-Göritz.

It will now be our task to append to this mere roster of these gentlemen, who with the exception of Dr Faulstich had each attained to or passed his sixtieth year, a brief characterization of each of them. If this procedure offends against the rules of good story-telling, perhaps the reader will be good enough to make allowances, and the more so in that the error about to be committed is possibly more apparent than real. For however right it may be to condemn the presentation of single figures wearing their thoughts and actions like labels stuck to their coats, and to laud instead that art which inspires the reader's own imagination to the creative development and completion of what is merely indi-cated and hinted at, this just rule may be waived when, as here, the exhibition of finished figures one beside the other is intended to represent little more than a *portrait gallery* offered to the reader less for the sake of the pictures themselves than for that of the *place* where they are to be found.

The noblest frequenter of Schloss Guse, and the one who had belonged to the circle the longest, was *Count Drosselstein*. Born in Königsberg,★ in whose vicinity the family estates also lay, he was, despite having moved to another province, a perfect representative of the East Prussian aristocracy. Originating far from the court and the 'service', this aristocracy did, to be sure, have to forgo—in those days, at any rate—the fame enjoyed by the Brandenburg and Pomeranian families whose names were inscribed in the annals of our history, which up to that time consisted of little more than a succession of battles; but what it thereby lost in national popularity and historical renown was made up for by an awareness of having preserved its independence. Less involved in and subordinate to the military and bureaucratic machinery of the state, the whole of East Prussia, and especially its aristocracy, had known—in certain individual respects to its disadvantage, on the whole to its profit—how to preserve a strongly marked local quality of its own.

This local quality, which can perhaps best be described as a sometimes austere expression of free-spiritedness, was also possessed by Count Drosselstein; and when at the table of his friend, the countess of Guse, he sat opposite the bow-legged Major-General von Bamme and listened to him telling ambiguous anecdotes or, less out of boastfulness than from arrogance and bad upbringing, expatiating in shrill-voiced jargon about horses, princes and ballerinas, he might with an access of East Prussian pride reflect on the difference between his provincial homeland and that hearth of the nation, the March of Brandenburg. But such accesses of pride vanished as quickly as they came. Of a rare impartiality, a stranger to narrow-mindedness and self-seeking of whatever kind, he had long been aware that, all that was unbearable about it notwithstanding, the March was to be regarded as the kernel and heartland of the monarchy, with or without people like Bamme, indeed partly *on account* of them.

The count had served the state for only a short time. At the age of twenty he had joined the first Guards Battalion, but after no more than a year he had discharged himself on grounds of ill-health and had been happy to be able to exchange the sight of the parade-ground at Potsdam* for that of the promenade at Nice. Restored, he travelled in Italy and, devoting himself entirely to the study of art, lived first in Rome, then in Paris, and concluded his 'grand tour' with an excursion to Holland and England.

He was in his late thirties when, in 1788, family affairs took him to the court at St Petersburg. Here he became acquainted with a Countess Lieven, who with her transparent alabaster beauty made him her captive the moment he saw her. He courted her and was not repulsed; the Empress herself congratulated the handsome couple, and immediately after a wedding celebrated with great splendour and in the presence of the nobility of the Petersburg court they withdrew to the count's estates in East Prussia.

But the quiet happiness of the honeymoon soon seemed *too* quiet to the young countess. She longed for the distractions of 'society', and since neither the political situation nor the sentiments of the count made it seem likely they would again visit the Russian court—which is what the young countess would have most liked to do—it was decided to remove to Hohen-Ziesar, an estate originally belonging to the Brandenburg Drosselsteins that had passed to the East Prussian line only two or three years previously.

From Hohen-Ziesar it was relatively easy to travel to the capital, where the court, whose life had very nearly come to a halt during the Friederician age, was at just that time beginning to revive again. If it was not Petersburg it was at least Berlin. Although she sometimes wore an expression that was half weary and half distracted, as though her soul were seeking for something lost and far away, she none the less gave herself over unreservedly to the pleasures of the capital. She was considered happy, and she certainly seemed to be. But her transparent alabaster complexion had not been a good sign: shortly before a performance at the opera house she was unexpectedly the victim of a violent haemorrhage; a consumption followed, and she died before the winter was out.

The count was crushed. For a long time he avoided everyone; he even stayed away from Schloss Guse, where he was already a regular visitor. When he again appeared in society he was in perfect command of himself; but he had lost that happy, man-of-the-world disposition and affable cheerfulness that had formerly distinguished him. He no longer laughed: he exhibited only the smile of those who have settled accounts with life. Here and there it was said that it was not the death of the young countess alone that had brought about this transformation in his nature. He turned to great construction projects; pleasure parks in particular began to divert him. Hohen-Ziesar offered good materials for such things, and thus there arose, in accordance with the taste of that time, a costly creation which, viewed from the flat roof of the château or, even better, from the church-tower, presented itself as a relief-map of the Alps executed in earth and stone. Blocks of granite were heaped up to form some kind of Rigi,* two passes ran over the ridge of the mountain and led to Altorf or Küssnacht,* while a lake fed from invisible springs sent a mountain stream over many cataracts into the depths. Pasturelands and open country succeeded one another; at the foot of this elaborate piece of artificiality, however, and extending over into the actual Oderbruch, there lay a charming flatland panorama, with fields and meadows, with river, stream and bridges, and a quiet pond surrounded with willows and with swans encircling its Japanese island chalet.

Our countess of Guse, who felt drawn to everything rococo, took the liveliest interest in the construction of this park, visits became more frequent, letters were exchanged, conferences held: and the end result was not only the erection of the 'Switzerland' of Hohen-Ziesar but also the establishment of a friendship which since then had, especially on the part of the countess, grown to a true intimacy that went far beyond the vagaries of moods and the need for diversion.

It could hardly have been otherwise. For, however much the countess might cling to her friends, however little she wished to dispense with the founding figures of her circle, she was very sensible of what the majority of them lacked: polish, cultivation, tone, above all any appreciation of art and beauty. All these the count possessed: he was not merely as elevated as the company at Rheinsberg, he even excelled it in also commanding that lasting esteem that comes only from the possession of selflessness and virtue.

Their friendship, already firm, was cemented even more firmly when the count took the countess into his confidence as to the facts concerning his wife's death and the events immediately preceding it. The tale he told was as follows.

After a violent fit of coughing, the young countess seemed to fall into a deep slumber; and the count, too, wearied by daylong attendance at her bedside, slept in his armchair. It was late and the only light was that of a shaded lamp. When he awoke he noticed that the sick woman had risen from her bed and was making for the doors of a wall-cupboard. A lethargic heaviness, and at the same time an obscure feeling he ought not to disturb the invalid in what she was doing, fixed him firmly to his seat. He then saw how she first took a little box from the cupboard, then from a concealed compartment in the box a number of letters tied together with a red cord. She walked back again past him, convinced herself he was asleep, and then went to the fireplace. She touched the letters with her lips, and then threw them one by one into the half-extinguished fire, taking care as she did so that the flames did not leap up too brightly. When everything was burned and the fire had died down again, she returned to her bed, covered herself with the bedclothes and breathed a profound sigh of relief, as though freed from some dreadful burden. It was the last thing she did. Before morning she had departed. What a day that morning brought for the survivor! He had thought she had loved him: now all was a dream and a delusion! Whose was the hand that had written letters which their recipient had cherished to the end as though they were her dearest possession? He asked the question again and again, but he could find no answer. The secret lay with the dead woman and the ashes in the fireplace.

This was the count's story. That he had told it, however, sealed the friendship which from that day forward existed inextinguishably between the widower count of Hohen-Ziesar and the widowed countess of Schloss Guse.

But Schloss Guse possessed only one Drosselstein: all the other 'friends of various kinds' who assembled there could be considered as more or less the reverse side of the count.

Next to him in rank stood *Chairman von Krach*, a man of gifts and character. He was regarded as one of the leading lawyers of his time, had by obstinately opposing him succeeded in arousing the wrath of the Great King and, in profound ill-humour at the iniquity he had suffered on this occasion, had withdrawn himself to Bingenwalde. He was lean, tall, caustic, short-tempered. His most prominent characteristic was meanness. He contested every bill he received, and paid it only after legal proceedings had been instituted, on the principle 'Time gained is money gained.' Those affected by this practice laughed at him and averred that he was so enamoured of the letter of the law he could not keep away from the courts. Equally celebrated were his grand dinners, which, though they recurred only once a year, were a real horror to the aristocracy of the Oderbruch. Old Bamme—whose tipping and lively equivocal jests had made him the favourite of the coachmen and gardeners who

served as liveried attendants on these occasions—was the only
guest who, through surreptitiously smuggling in his own
bottles, had so far succeeded in enjoying them; so that Baron
Pehlemann for example had asserted with the utmost seriousness: 'Never since Krach's dinners began has the "General"
drunk a drop of wine that did not come from his own cellar.'
Bamme himself, in any case imbued with an almost pathological need to show off as a dashing hussar, was highly delighted
with such expressions of admiration; but on the other hand,
and naturally only so as to add one more malicious gibe against
Krach, he never failed heatedly to contest that he had scored
any victory of cunning over him: Krach, he averred, was much
too astute ever to be deceived in this way; he had thirty years of
practice in inquisitorial and criminal investigation, he saw all,
he knew all; but at the same time he kept silent, for, though he
might feel slightly annoyed at the deception, he perceived at
once how advantageous it was to himself, and the only question that really plagued him was: 'Why aren't they all like
Bamme?'

Though she herself was very liberal, the countess was little
offended by this meanness. She had lived long enough to have
learned that thrift practised with equal severity towards oneself
and others toughened the body and sharpened the mind, but
above all tended to produce original characters, though not the
most pleasant ones to be sure. But she was not worried by this
last consideration. What ultimately decided her in Krach's
favour was that the prince too had had a strong predilection for
economizing.

The third figure of the circle was the aforementioned Major-
General von *Bamme*, or 'the General', as he was called at Schloss
Guse: a small, very ugly man with prominent cheekbones and
legs like a rococo table, in appearance resembling a hussar but
even more a Kalmuck.

He belonged to an ancient Havel-land line, the house of
Bamme near Rathenow, which was extinguished when he
died. Truth to tell, very little was extinguished when that
happened. His own youth was dissipated away, and strange
tales were told of it. A young girl of the nobility, the daughter
of a neighbour, who believed he was in love with her, had been

dishonoured by him; her brother, who demanded he marry her, he hunted out of the court; the girl herself, who remained at her parents' house, became insane.

A year later the elder Bamme died: father and son had been worthy of one another. They placed the old man's coffin over a pit in the church crypt, and the son stationed himself beside it, a flaming torch in his hand; he wore the scarlet uniform of the Zieten Regiment of Hussars, and the little church was hung with black. At the moment when the coffin was lowered the mad woman, who had concealed herself in the organ-loft, cried out: 'Look, now he is going down to Hell!' All were horror-struck; only he at whom she had directed the words was able to smile at them. Besides, he was an excellent soldier, and that sustained him.

The Peace of Basel annoyed him, and after it was concluded he left the regiment and removed from the Havel-land to the Oderbruch, where he settled not far from Schloss Guse. The inhabitants of Gross-Quirlsdorf had little to complain of on his account; he continued in his customary way of life, to be sure, but the people of the Oderbruch, themselves not disposed to be *diffizil*, placed no difficulties in his way by their disapproval. His tastes grew stranger and stranger. If any young person died in the village, boy or girl, he would have a grand funeral arranged, on condition that the mourners allowed the corpse to be rouged and laid on a bier in a brightly illuminated hall. Then he would station himself at the foot of the bier, puff at his meerschaum, and gaze at the corpse for half an hour through eyes half-closed. What then passed through his soul no one knew. He was accounted mischievous and malicious, and worse things than that: at the same time he was a general, a soldier and Brandenburger from head to toe, and of a puckishly audacious courage. His last *rencontre* had taken place only three years previously. A barn burned down on a neighbouring estate; Bamme, who could not endure the owner, said at dinner for all to hear: 'Well-insured barns always burn down.' A retraction was demanded; instead of retracting, Bamme surveyed his opponent and shrilled: 'Every fire insurance says the same.'

The outcome was a duel; Captain von Rutze acted as his

second. The challenger shot off the lobe of Bamme's right ear, together with the little gold earring he wore 'to ward off rheumatism'. Bamme thereupon had a new ring drawn through the half ear still remaining to him, since when he had looked more disreputable than ever.

A certain roguishness, it must be admitted, reconciled many of his adversaries to him; in addition to which, he never pretended to be other than he was, and had no qualms whatever about exposing the facts of his past life in piquant anecdotes. Intellectually, his need was for teasing, ridicule and playing practical jokes: on which account all the collectors and anti-quaries of Barnim and Lebus feared him as they did no other. The better to practise his deceptions he had become a member of the Archaeological Society. He had flint weapons, bronze idols, and fragments of pottery concealed in various places in the way one conceals Easter eggs, and was delighted beyond measure when the 'grown-up children' began to seek them out and determine what period they belonged to. Turgany, as may well be believed, derived all the advantage he could from these practical jests, and whenever Seidentopf had discovered some-thing supposedly primevally Germanic, and was about to deliver the decisive blow against his hard-pressed antagonist, he would throw out the remark, as if it had just then occurred to him: 'Unless, that is, Bamme . . .'—a sentence that was never concluded, since the mere opening words sufficed to reduce the pastor to total confusion.

All in all, the 'General' was a favourite guest at Schloss Guse, though he was also the pike in the fish-pond. The perils and inconveniences that resulted from his presence were balanced by the fresh breath of life he brought with him. That he had his own view of morality was considered beside the point: the countess rebutted every adverse comment on the subject with the remark: 'L'immoralité ouverte, c'est la seule garantie contre l'hypocrisie.'*

Only the Vitzewitzes, old and young, remained unimpres-sed by such arguments; though displaying an outward tolera-tion of the old soldier, they continued in their aversion to him, and Berndt used to say: 'Bamme and Hoppenmarieken, that would make a fine couple!'

Next to Bamme, and at the same time his natural antithesis, stood Baron *Pehlemann*, the fourth figure of the Guse circle. Pehlemann was deficient in courage to the degree that Bamme had an excess of it. That he thereby aroused in the countess an interest hardly less lively than did his braver counterpart scarcely needs to be said; but the circle itself, too, was very far from holding this lack of manliness seriously against him. And especially not its military men. The same thing can still be observed today: all stay-at-homes prate continually of 'sacrifice in the field'; old seasoned soldiers, however, who know from the experience of fifty battles what a strange and uncertain thing courage is, and on the other hand how small a degree of excitation suffices to produce the heroic deed of the ordinary stamp, all these keep a very cool head with regard to acts of bravery and have as a rule long since ceased to see anything especially glorious about them. So it was that Bamme and Pehlemann were the best of friends. Naturally this did not mean that no teasing went on. Only a few weeks before the commencement of our story Pehlemann, who was sometimes seized by sudden fits of self-confidence, had asserted that 'his aversion to firearms was due entirely to the over-sensitivity of his ears'; whereupon Bamme had responded, with as much gravity as he could manage: 'That is quite possible, certainly; in that case let us, as old students, fight a bout with scimitars; that makes no noise at all; your ears will be quite untroubled. At most I should hack them off.' Such provoking and chaffing was the order of the day, but it did not for a moment disrupt good relations, for the 'Baron of Wuschewier', as he was called by all and sundry, though he might differ fundamentally from Bamme in other respects, had at any rate one good quality in common with him: he lacked self-importance. Even as a poet—which, according to his own confession, he had become on account of his gout. He maintained he had observed that whenever his muse appeared his gout disappeared: a confidential communication which the Guse circle employed as the basis of the following verses:

> Cedo majori*
> When the baron's resident gout
> Beheld the baron's muse arrive,

'Alas', cried he, 'beyond a doubt
We two together can never thrive!'
He packed his bags, was quickly gone,
And left the loving pair alone.

It was pretended that Bamme had composed these verses; in reality everyone knew they originated with Dr Faulstich, who was always prepared to have his little pirate boat sail under a foreign flag.

The fifth member of the circle was Chamberlain von *Medewitz*, of Alt-Medewitz, a tedious, pedantic gentleman, very much permeated with the importance of the Medewitzes, even though the pages of the history of the fatherland nowhere recorded their name. His speciality was inventions, in regard to which in the manner of the philosophers he recognized no distinction between great and small: he loved them all equally. Economical heating, airtight windows, the removal of nitre from the walls of stalls and stables, the artificial cultivation of edible fungus: these were some of the questions which engaged his ceaselessly questing mind. He was well known to the military authorities through the written proposals he was repeatedly handing in for the easier wearing of packs and more efficient rolling of cloaks—always with appended illustrations. His actual hobby-horse, however, was ornamental boxes. He was a collector, and one could well say that what Seidentopf was to sepulchral urns, von Medewitz was to *tabatières* and everything related to them. So far as the Frederician age was concerned, his collection was as good as complete: from the Mollwitz box, on which the young King was greeted at the gate at Ohlau with musket-shots, to the Hubertusburg box, on which a courier flew through the world with a fluttering banner with the word 'Peace' on it, he had them all, and some he even had twice.

Up to this point all was well. He was not content, however, with the 'soundless box', he was above all also a passionate devotee of those miniature barrel-organs, finished in gold and tortoiseshell, which stood at that time at the summit of their fame and had gone round the world under the name of musical-boxes. Von Medewitz always carried with him a selection of these music-laden cannon and it was by means of them that he carried out his social *attentats*. Just as there are people of whom you cannot be quite certain what they are going to say even if you are sitting with them in a funeral hearse, so you could never be quite certain of one of Medewitz's musical-boxes. He was aware of possessing this power, and exercised it: sometimes pleasantly and judiciously through filling in anxious pauses in the conversation, but much more often in obedience to inspirations of mere caprice or wounded vanity. Incapable of contributing anything to the company on his own account, he watched jealously over anyone distinguished by great knowledge or a talent for speaking, and when, for instance, a speaker was about to bring a well-constructed sentence to its conclusion you would be sure to hear an aria of Papageno or the 'Battle of Marengo' intruding into it—an act of pure spite. The most depressing thing about it was that, its staleness notwithstanding, when there was even one unfamiliar guest at the table the trick was unfailingly effective. It would have been easy for the countess to have put an end to this vindictive music; but, though she found Medewitz's conduct tasteless, she repeatedly took pleasure in observing the embarrassment and chagrin of whoever had thus been deprived of his oratorical triumph.

The most insignificant member of the Guse circle was *von Rutze*: a passionate huntsman, tall, sinewy, taciturn, a former captain in the Pomeranian Pirch Regiment. He had purchased Protzhagen, which had belonged to the Rutzes in the distant past, only twenty years or so previously: the tale of how he came to do so goes as follows:

At Stargard, where the Pirch Regiment was garrisoned, there turned up a descriptive account of the Oderbruch,* and on page 114, in the chapter 'Buckow and its Environs', it read:

Near to Protzhagen, an estate that for three centuries belonged to the Rutzes, there runs a deep ravine, the 'Junker Hans's Ravine'. It bears this name because it was here that Junker Hans von Rutze fell and perished in an accident; this was in 1693. He was the *last of the Rutzes*.

No sooner had one of his fellow officers discovered this passage than Rutze began to be plagued with the endless repetition of the facetious remark: 'Rutze is a changeling; there are no longer any Rutzes; the last of them has lain for years in the church at Protzhagen.' Our captain, who was no master of repartee, grew dejected; he resigned his commission and purchased Protzhagen, so as to demonstrate on the spot that to speak of the 'last of the Rutzes' had been somewhat premature. But he profited little from this action: the raillery he had been subjected to at Stargard became noised abroad and was now being continued at Schloss Guse. Bamme swore faithfully that one or other of the two 'last Rutzes', the earlier or the later, must necessarily be peculiar: either the dead Hans von Rutze had been nothing but a wraith, a prefiguration of something still to come, or the friend who walked among them, who, he observed, was in any case almost fleshless, was a *revenant*. So far as he (Bamme) was personally concerned, he tended to prefer the first supposition, since it meant that reality still owed them a stag-hunt, a fall into a ravine and a Rutze with his neck broken.

The aged captain listened to this dissertation every time it was pronounced with a sour-sweet expression on his face, but had long since ceased to protest against it. Now and then he himself went over on to the offensive, but the adroit Bamme always got the better of him.

Among his other little weaknesses the most noteworthy was that, since his Protzhagen territory consisted largely of ravines and declivities, he considered himself a kind of mountain-dweller. 'We on the heights' was one of his favourite expressions.

The countess prized him for the exceptional degree of respect he showed her: for, however much she might like to pretend to be above admiration and flattery, she was in the end not wholly indifferent to them.

The seventh and last member of the 'inner circle' was Doctor *Faulstich*. Of him we shall give a more detailed account in a later chapter.

4

Before Dinner

THE whole circle—with the exception of Dr Faulstich, who by ancient tradition was accustomed to spend the third day of Christmas at Ziebingen—had been invited to Schloss Guse. Lewin and Renate, as we know already, had also been invited.

They were the first to arrive. The invitation had been for four o'clock, but it was a good hour earlier that Lewin's sleigh turned into one of the great avenues. This time it was not the covered sleigh with bundles of straw and a stuffed bolster in which we first made our hero's acquaintance; though occasionally slovenly herself, Aunt Amelie insisted on elegance of appearance in others, and the family at Hohen-Vietz accommodated themselves to her as far as they were able. The seat of the sleigh, covered with a bearskin, was in the familiar shape of a conch-shell, snow-blankets edged in blue fluttered like sails on the horses, and in place of the rusty sleighbells that had jingled our Lewin to sleep on Christmas Eve there stood on their backs a set of tubular chimes with two stiff little red and white plumes waving above them. Hundreds of sparrows pecking at corn in the village street flew up as the sleigh made its way to the château; then it crossed the bridge decorated with sphinxes, and came to a halt. Hastily throwing back the coverlet, Lewin extended his hand to Renate, who with the quickness of youth sprang out of the sleigh on to a rush mat spread over the hard snow. Then she hurried to the entrance: she seemed taller than usual, perhaps on account of the long silk cloak, grey with red edging, from whose raised hood her clear-eyed countenance shone out doubly bright today—for the journey had been long and the air keen.

The hallway received her with comforting warmth; in the old-fashioned tall fireplace flanked by the two Derfflinger dragoons a well-banked fire had been burning for several hours.

A servant in huntsman's dress who wore his sword with a

swashbuckling air took their cloaks from them, and reported that the countess requested to be excused for a few minutes: this was the way in which guests were regularly received. Lewin and Renate looked at one another knowingly, and walked through the billiard-room and mirrored-room into the 'salon'. Here left to themselves, they went to a corner window set in a wide and deep alcove in the wall: the bottom half of the window consisted of a single pane of glass—something rare in those days and much admired. The ice-ferns were half melted away and they could see through to the grounds outside. Beyond the little swan-house, whose pointed roof stuck up out of the snow-filled moat of the château, they looked straight down an avenue of bare cherry-trees that ran to the edge of the park. A number of bird-snares with their red bunches of rowan were visible on the branches of the trees nearest to them, while where the avenue came to an end there stood the dark church-tower of Carzow, its gilded dome gleaming in the light of the setting sun. All was still around the brother and sister; the only sound was that of the thawing ice as it fell drop by drop into the metal tank.

This place by the window was sufficiently cosy; any other visitor, however, would none the less have preferred to use the last glimmers of daylight for an inspection of the 'salon' itself. It was a square room whose appointments united tastefulness and comfort. The side opposite the window was occupied by a semicircular divan which, divided in the middle, left open a path to the folding-doors that led to the dining-room. Laurel and oleander bushes stood to left and right in the corners: a spiral staircase ascended beside the corner with the oleanders. A thick carpet in which Turkish red predominated covered the floor; everything else was blue: the walls, the curtains, the furniture fabric. All around, on pillars and console-tables, stood busts and statuettes whose gleaming whiteness was the first impression you received on entering; it was only after-wards that you also noticed the pictures which, much darkened, decorated the room in hardly fewer numbers than the aforementioned works in marble and alabaster. All were memorials of the Rheinsberg days. First there was a portrait of the prince himself, somewhat baroque in conception and execution, with facings of tiger-skin on his coat and his hand leaning on a rock and a battle-plan; opposite him Schloss Rheinsberg, its façade reflected in the water, and gliding across the lake a little boat at whose helm sat a beautiful woman with hair unloosed, blonde as a mermaid. It was supposed to be the countess. On the piers between the windows, in shadow and hardly visible, hung pastel portraits of the prince's round table: Tauentzien, the Wreechs, Knyphausen, Knesebeck; most were presents from the subjects themselves.

Lewin and Renate were still watching the sun go down when they heard from the other end of the room the call: 'Soyez les bien-venus.'* They turned and saw their aunt advancing towards them from the spiral staircase; and they hastened to kiss her hand.

The countess was dressed in black, and was even wearing a widow's cap: it was the garb which, following the example of ruling houses, she had not laid aside since the demise of the count. The cap and frills, however, could have been fresher without necessarily spoiling the effect.

Close to the corner-window there stood a causeuse* covered with the same bleu-de-France as all the rest of the furniture: this was the countess's favourite spot. Renate drew up a floor-cushion, while Lewin sat himself opposite their aunt. Conversation was soon well under way, with a rich admixture of French words and locutions in it (though we shall spare the reader most of them). Aunt Amelie seemed to be in a good mood and asked question after question. Christmas morning at Hohen-Vietz, even Odin's chariot, had to be discussed in detail; the latter caused the most surprise, for in the matter of antiquarianism there was little to choose between the countess of Guse and Bamme. Marie, too, was remembered, but only briefly; then conversation turned to the Ladalinskis. To see the Ladalinskis joined to the house of Vitzewitz through a double marriage was Aunt Amelie's most ardent wish: since she was the wealthy relative whose property they hoped to inherit, it would in any case have been advisable to satisfy this wish of hers as far as one possibly could; as it turned out, however, the familial plans of Guse and the heartfelt desire of the brother and sister of Hohen-Vietz in this case coincided.

'How did you leave Tubal?' asked Aunt Amelie.

'In the best of health,' Lewin replied, 'and a letter that arrived from him this morning permits me to assume that he had not got worse over the holiday.'

'What does he write?'

'A great deal about his literary friends. But he preceded it with a brief account of Christmas Eve, and how the Christmas candles at the Ladalinskis burned somewhat dimly. He also said something about Kathinka. May I read it to you?'

'*Je vous en prie.*'

Lewin unfolded the letter. The room was already growing dark, and he therefore moved closer to the window, which was glowing with the last red of sunset. Then, passing over the introductory lines, he read: 'In a house where there are no children the Christ-child will always have a difficult time, unless it be that the adults retain some sense of childhood. And Kathinka, who possesses so much (perhaps *because* she possesses so much) does not possess this sense.'

Lewin fell silent for a moment, as it seemed to him his aunt was about to speak. Then the latter said: 'It is a correct observation, but I am surprised to hear it from Tubal. It is as though Seidentopf were speaking. Kathinka is a Pole, *ça dit tout*,* and that is why she is dear to me. Sense of childhood! *Bêtise allemande.** However could a Ladalinski have got so sentimental? *C'est étonnant.** I would suppose it must be his German mother if, by a trick of chance, *par un caprice du sort*,* there had not been more Polish blood active in that mother than in half-a-dozen "itzkis" or "inskis". Sense of childhood! *Dieu m'en garde!** I beg you, my dears, close your ears to the vain idea that these German emotional specialities of ours are indispensable to God's everlasting world-order.'

Renate was the first to collect her thoughts, and said: 'I believe I have never entertained the idea you mention, but in something as familiar as the Bible we see a sense of childhood valued as something precious.'

Aunt Amelie smiled. Then, as she was accustomed to do, she took her niece's hand, stroked it, and said: 'You possess this sense, and may God preserve it in you. But do I have to offer explanations to you, who know me so well? *A quoi bon?** There is something lovely about a childlike heart, certainly, as there is about everything that is natural and pure. But continual talking about it, or that assertiveness that always emerges where appearance has taken the place of reality, is German *petit bourgeois, et voilà ce qui me fâche.*★ And that too was what used to annoy the prince. In his ill-humour he would then fail to make any distinction between the genuinely devout and the hypocrites; normally so careful of his words, he would in this instance weigh them hardly at all; and I, too, *je n'aime pas à marchander les mots.*★ If some must go cheap, they must. But let us hear some more, Lewin.'

Lewin read on: 'Just as we were going in to see the tree Count Bninski arrived. He had little gifts for us all, too generous to my way of thinking; but Kathinka seemed not to feel it so.'

'But Kathinka seemed not to feel it so,' the countess repeated slowly, shaking her head. Then she went on: '*Oh cet air bourgeois, ne se perdra-t-il jamais?*★ New cards but still the same old game. *Je ne le comprends pas.*★ For as long as the world has existed youth and beauty have taken pleasure in presents, in the splendour of flowers, in the glitter of jewels. They go together. But Tubal is frightened of them; they put him on his guard, as though he had to defend some grocer's daughter whose virtue was threatened with brooches and pins. And that is called morality! Morality, sense of childhood, *je les respecte, mais j'en déteste la caricature.*★ And of that we have enough and more than enough in this country.'

'I am sure', Lewin interposed, 'that Tubal feels as you do, as we all do. If I understand him aright, the misgivings he expressed applied not to the gifts but to the giver. Count Bninski is making advances to Kathinka, he is courting her hand. Perhaps I am wrong, but I do not believe so.'

Aunt Amelie was visibly startled. Then she asked hurriedly: 'And her father?'

'He is against it; so is Tubal. They hold the count in esteem personally, he is rich and respected. But you know their views, at least you know the father's. And Bninski is a Pole from head to toe.'

'And Kathinka herself?'

The question remained unanswered, since before Lewin

could answer it there came from the mirrored-room the loud sound of voices and, preceded by the huntsman bearing two double candlesticks, there entered in pairs first Krach and Bamme, then Medewitz and Rutze.

After a brief greeting the newcomers took their places on the large sofa and the countess, dividing her attention between her groups of guests, informed them that Baron Pehlemann had had to decline her invitation on account of a new and violent attack of gout, and that Drosselstein, detained by business affairs, would be arriving only at half-past four. 'I think we should wait for him,' she declared. 'Every guest is allowed a quarter of an hour, let us allow him a second quarter.' Everyone acquiesced, though under silent protest.

Such half-hours of waiting are generally not favourable to conversation: the silent are more silent than ever, but the eloquent too, disinclined to see the point of some sparkling anecdote decapitated by the entry of a servant, maintain an anxious reserve. Bamme belonged to this latter group but none the less endeavoured to come to the countess's assistance in the efforts she was visibly making to keep the conversation going. He was the only one to do so, however, and his success was only partial: talk proceeded in fits and starts, many questions were asked but no one waited for an answer. Baron Pehlemann's gout was the subject that proved most productive. 'Why did he have to be present again at the last badger-hunt? Ridden with gout and spends two hours in the snow! Why could he not refrain from the Rauenthaler? But that kind of bravado is just like Pehlemann: a joyful sacrificial death on the altar of *gourmandise*! And by the way, what about "*Cedo majori*"? Why did he not summon his muse?'

'He did,' the countess rejoined, and took from an alabaster vase standing before her a delicately folded *billet*. But the two mantelpiece clocks to whose equal oscillations Aunt Amelie attended with painful conscientiousness at that moment struck the half-hour, the period of grace was up, and the folding doors giving on to the brightly illuminated dining-room opened silently and punctually.

The countess and Krach made their way forward. At the same instant Drosselstein entered and, gesturing across the room with his left hand as though to indicate that he did not wish to interrupt the procession to the table, offered his right arm to Renate. Bamme and Lewin followed, then came Medewitz. Rutze brought up the rear.

This last, a passionate addict of snuff, exploited the opportunity of taking a pinch from the *tabatière* the countess had left behind. He did not do so with impunity: the storm had struck even before he had crossed the threshold of the dining-room. Everyone laughed, and Bamme exclaimed: 'Detected!' Only Krach maintained his usual composure.

5

Le Dîner

IN spite of the presence of an open fire, the temperature in the dining-room was, as was appropriate, fairly low. An oval table had been laid. In accordance with tradition, the countess sat between Krach and Drosselstein, with Renate opposite her. Huntsmen and servants in livery were busy; a chandelier was burning.

As he fastened his napkin, the count surveyed the room: as always, its architectural proportions, aided by simple embellishments, made upon him the most pleasant of impressions. There were four stuccoed walls, tinted yellow and enclosed by gilt cornices, and on the *plafond* there was a ceiling-painting depicting the *Banquet of the Gods*,* a copy of the famous fresco at the Farnesina. Krach and Rutze were moving the glasses back and forth, as though clearing the decks for action; Drosselstein now turned, however, to the countess and, after paying the designer of the room and her good taste a few polite compliments, asked after Count Narbonne, the Emperor's first adjutant, who, so the newspaper reported, had on his return from Russia on Christmas Eve dined with the King.

'I heard of it,' the countess replied; 'General Desaix was also present. Count Narbonne, *oh je me le rappelle très-bien*.* He belonged to the old court, was a favourite of Marie Antoinette but skipped over very adroitly into the Empire. Do you know how he won over the Emperor's heart?'

Drosselstein replied in the negative.

'Through a piece of etiquette. That is to say, through a bagatelle, a nothingness, as people would say today. But in no domain are the *parvenus* so prepared to learn and reward as they are in this. I have the story from Count Haugwitz's* own mouth. It happened immediately after the Emperor's coronation; Narbonne, then a colonel, delivered a dispatch to the Emperor. He knelt down on one knee and presented the letter on his hat. "*Eh bien,*" the Emperor exclaimed, "*qu'est ce que cela veut dire?*" The colonel replied: "*Sire, c'est ainsi qu'on présentait les dépêches à Louis XVI.*" "*Ah, c'est très bien,*"* replied the Emperor, and Narbonne was installed as a favourite. The Desaix too, by the way, are of the *ancien régime*, old nobility from Auvergne.'

Rutze had pricked up his ears the moment he had heard the name of General Desaix mentioned. Now, when the countess repeated it, he leaned across towards her and remarked, in a voice firm and yet at the same time trembling with a suspicion he was about to commit a frightful gaffe, that so far as his knowledge went he believed that General Desaix had fallen in the war against Austria. He could recollect a piece of music, *The Battle of Marengo*, which in a parenthesis at the end had said: 'Desaix falls.'

A smile passed over even Krach's imperturbable countenance; Drosselstein was about to elucidate the matter but Bamme got in first and began with that mock solemnity of which he was a master: 'Yes, Rutze, it is a mad world indeed. Here you have a man falling *anno* 1800 at Marengo in the full heat of June, and on Christmas Eve 1812 he sits at table with His Majesty of Prussia. They are incredible fellows, these Frenchmen. Even their dead won't let you alone. They force themselves upon dinners; who knows what might not happen to us here today. Of course, it could have been an elder or a younger brother.'

The captain of Protzhagen flushed red and replied in annoyance that he thanked General von Bamme for having resolved the riddle but must permit himself to remark that such a task did not require the cunning of a hussar: openings-up of this sort still lay within the domain of the infantry.

Bamme laughed; he was satisfied with any kind of retort: he took offence at nothing, and was in the happy position of never having to load his pistols to assert a courage no one doubted.

The episode did not last long; the countess smoothed things down, assisted by an excellent Chablis that then made its appearance, while without needing to fear he would be fuelling the conflict anew von Medewitz again introduced the names Narbonne and Desaix into the debate. 'They are both men of family, it is true,' he began, 'but with what strange people His Majesty has been obliged to sit at table from the very first day of his reign! I myself met one of them in the White Room,* the Abbé Sieyès.* I was horrified when I heard his name. In 1793 he condemned a King of France to death, and in 1798 he sat opposite a King of Prussia as an ambassador. He wore a tricolour sash; of these colours I saw only the red, and whenever he said: "*Votre Majesté*" all I could hear was: "*La mort sans phrase*".'

'I have seen him too,' Krach said, tugging importantly at his neckerchief. 'Medewitz has no time for him, but he was at least an abbé. And it does mean something to condemn a King of France to death. But these marshals! Sons of coopers and innkeepers.'

'Perhaps,' Drosselstein interposed; 'but sons of coopers or not, they have been striking off so many hoops that the barrels have fallen to pieces over half of Europe. I do not like these marshals whose corporal's stripes are always showing through, but one thing must be allowed them: they are soldiers.'

'That they are!' exclaimed Bamme, attacking his *ragoût en coquille*; 'and whoever has ever led a platoon into the firing-line has a respect for them, rogues and cutpurses though they are.'

'Though they are,' repeated Medewitz, recalling the difficult days when he had been hard put to it to save his collection of boxes from Soult's* depredations.

'Only one of them fills me with rancour,' Bamme went on.

'Davoust?'* asked Lewin.

'No: His Neapolitan Majesty, King Murat.* He believes he

is something extremely distinguished, in great affairs and in small ones, including being a mighty cavalry general merely because he rode the Mameluke rabble into the sand.* But a *Zietenscher** once played a trick on him, and a disabled one at that. I mean the old steward, Kettlitz, at Charlottenburg.'

Everyone displayed curiosity and urged him to tell the story.

Such urging was hardly necessary. 'The story was in its own day known to only a few,' he began; 'I have it from Kettlitz himself. On 14 October we had the affair at Jena, and ten days later the French advanced guard was in Berlin; Murat himself, however, who was at that time still Duke of Berg, was in Charlottenburg. He had installed himself in the rooms on the side facing the park, the same that the Emperor Alexander had occupied a year earlier. Old Kettlitz was beside himself and worked out a plan. At five o'clock they had dinner in the great hall, and the portrait of King Friedrich Wilhelm I* gazed down with an earnest and morose expression on the newly baked duke, who ruled not only Berg but also the Old Prussian province of Cleves. There were not yet many French troops in the town. Then all of a sudden—the truffle pie had just been brought in—a fanfare started up, and twenty trumpets with drums beating with them played the Hohenfriedberger March. Was it coming from beneath the windows? Had Prussian squadrons ridden into the courtyard? Murat leaped up and made to save himself by flight. But no squadrons were there; finally the noise ceased and everything was cleared up. In the next room there stood a musical chest with a whole corps of trumpeters inside it and old Kettlitz had put his finger on its hidden spring. I would be delighted to see this monster music-clock pass to our von Medewitz of Alt-Medewitz for the completion of his collection, though to be sure under the one condition that he never releases the hidden spring in our presence. I like trumpets, but only in the open air.'

Unable to acquiesce in Bamme's teasing, Canon Medewitz accompanied it only with an embarrassed smile and then asked what had befallen the steward.

'Well, he was an old Zietenscher, and he lied himself out of it as well as he could. In any event he had had the pleasure of seeing the great cavalry leader, the destroyer of Mamelukes, take flight at the Hohenfriedberger March. This was in October 1806. In those days a marshal was still worth something: since then they have, I expect, become cheaper. But cheaper or not, the day my Quirlsdorfers bring in their first marshal, dead or alive, I shall add ten acres to the glebe land, though I cannot endure the reverend gentleman.'

'But Bamme, why are you always at odds with your clergymen?' asked Krach, who had been on good terms with his own parson ever since the latter had relinquished a strip of garden-land to him without recompense.

'I have not yet found him agreeable,' Bamme replied sharply. 'These parsons are malicious fellows, and the sharper they look the more malicious they are. Mine has a mania for allusions.'

'That sounds as though you are in the habit of going to church, Bamme,' the countess interposed. 'But I wager you haven't heard a sermon these ten years.'

'No, dear countess. But I have a *tendre* for funerals. Each has his own form of devotions and I have mine; and it annoys me to be disturbed in them by all kinds of stuff and nonsense. He starts with the young man of Nain, or with his celebrated female equivalent, * but before five minutes are up he has got to Babel, to Sodom or to some other such place of ill-renown, looks hard at me, has a quantity of brimstone fall from the sky, and then raises his voice and says: "Blessed are the pure in heart, for they shall see God." And all of it is intended for my address. That is how he was going on for five years. But last Easter I put a stop to it.'

'How?' asked the countess.

'We again had a funeral, a pretty young thing; so it was the turn of Jairus's little daughter. But her turn didn't last long; half-way through the *pastor loci* was again back with Lot and his daughters and looking at me as though I had been in the cave with them. I thought, it is time to remedy this. And so I invited him to the château, not for a disputation but simply to dinner. When we had got to the second bottle—he can certainly drink—I said: "And now, little parson, a heartfelt toast; let us raise our glasses: Long live Lot! A good fellow. Pity about his two daughters. And their mother hardly salted. *Apropos*, what was the elder daughter's son* called?" Imagine my triumph when he didn't know! Perhaps he was merely confused. I, however, gloating over his embarrassment, shouted into his ear: "Bamme." Since that day we have already had three corpses but he hasn't said a word.'

Lewin and Renate, who knew of Bamme's style of speaking more by hearsay than from their own experience, exchanged glances; but they were soon to learn that the high spirits of the old hussar did not shrink from even bolder flights.

The countess turned to the canon, who, hitherto drawn into the conversation very little, seemed to be prey to some slight ill-humour, and asked his advice on the subject of structural alterations, in the first instance to the Derfflinger banquet-hall in the opposite wing, which was near to collapse; then, however, she raised the general question 'fireplace or stove', which was decidedly among Medewitz's favourite themes. He had even written about it. Medewitz was in favour of fireplaces, though for the production of an improved draught of air he felt bound to urge the reintroduction of the portal-like folding-doors that had been unjustly banished from living-rooms. He then went on to a prolix explanation of how recent research had determined that all combustion depended upon a strong influx of air. Then he concluded with the following aphorism: 'The leaded window is the death of the open fire, the draughty old folding-door is its life.'

Bamme, who, as we know, also liked the sound of his own voice, and had a particular hatred of scientific explanations, thought the time had now come when he might properly draw the conversation back to himself. 'Dear countess,' he began, 'you seemed inclined to agree that such folding-portals ought to be installed. Permit me to sound a warning. I lay no weight on the fact that the large double-winged entry is really nothing other than the ancient barn-door transported from the farmyard into the salon, but what I do feel obliged to point to is the social, not to say moral dangers that are more or less inseparable from this form of door. To the highest degree solid in appearance, respectable, worthy and sedate, it leads to consequences that are precisely the opposite. Following

Medewitz's example, I would ask to be allowed a scientific explanation of this phenomenon.'

As no one objected, he continued: 'Every object has the roots of its existence in a particular something. In the case of the open fire, as we have just heard, it is the draught of air; in the case of the folding-door it is, in my opinion, the bolt. Now, you must accept my assurance that the bolt is a highly tricky customer, a thing that demands very special nursing and an unequalled loyalty and devotion. You could say that the folding-door stands or falls with the bolt.'

He paused, and Medewitz shook his head.

'What I say is so,' he expatiated further. 'You can close the doors, lock them, fix the latch, as much as you like; but no matter how safe you think you are, no matter how much you may feel "all secure", you will find this safety and security to be a mere delusion if their real guarantors, the great securing-bolts, have been ignored, if criminal thoughtlessness has neglected to throw out this lifesaving anchor in good time. And this neglect is the rule. In ninety-nine cases out of a hundred the servant, whose arms are not long enough, has given up shooting the top bolt, and in nineteen cases of out twenty has been too indolent to bend down to do the same to the bottom bolt. He has been content with the easier task, has confined himself to turning the key in the lock, and has thus created an appearance of security behind which there lurk all the forces of destruction. I myself have experienced an instance of this: may I tell you about it?'

Not without some hesitation the countess answered with a nod of agreement.

Bamme did not wait for this nod of agreement, however, but, growing livelier and livelier, continued: 'Well, the guards at Rathenow gave us a ball. The great hall at the inn took up half the floor, seven windows facing the street, but in the narrow side there were a pair of those barn-doors whose reintroduction Medewitz feels obliged to urge. A traveller, dead tired, drove up at the inn, and as all the regular rooms were occupied he was glad in the end to take one just next to the ballroom. The bed stood in front of the folding-doors. Sleep! he sighed again and again, and slim though his chances were of getting to sleep he resolved at any rate to try. Sometimes the god comes when you call him. Only not when the guards are holding a dance. The unhappy man finally shook off all his tiredness; dance music and the rustling of dresses disconcerted him; curiosity, the root of all evil, got the better of him, and, behold, he raised himself up so as to look through the never-failing chink in the door and silently witness the ball going on on the other side of it. Oh thoughtless, unsuspecting man! Given over to the most delicious reflection, he pressed his face and form harder against the door; he looked, he listened; the tricks and pranks of giggling couples had in him an unperceived eavesdropper; then, oh ill-fortune!—there suddenly came to pass that piece of knavery of which, of all the doors in the world, only the great folding-portal is capable, and, yielding slowly but with a solemnity that suggested the entry of a triumphant general, its two great wings opened to left and right, and the traveller lay in prostrate homage at our feet. Absolve me from going into detail. I shall hear the outcry that arose until my dying day. And those are the doors which, merely for the sake of improving the draught, our Medewitz wants to . . .'

He got no further. The countess, though herself not averse to accompanying the old general even on the most daring of his sorties, was on the other hand too well aware of her duties as a hostess, especially towards her niece, to hesitate any longer in inaugurating a retreat. She rose and, offering her arm to the count, begged her other guests, who had risen with her, to keep their seats and not to think of cutting short the treasured hour of dessert by so much as a minute. Renate followed with Krach. At the entrance to the salon the two ladies curtsied to their cavaliers, who, in obedience to the instructions thus indicated, returned to their companions at the table.

6

Nullum vinum nisi hungaricum*

IN the meantime, together with other dessert, bowls of fruit and Hungarian port and old Rhine wine had been brought

forth. Before Bamme there stood a long-necked bottle of
Ruster-Ausbruch: he filled a tapering wineglass half full, tested
the bouquet, slowly inbibed a draught and, having
encountered nothing but signs that the wine was genuine, set
the glass down before him again with an expression of satisfaction. Lewin, Rutze, Medewitz drew closer, all of them swear-
ing allegiance to the flag of Hungary. 'You have done right,'
said Bamme, and filled the glasses to the brim; 'a wine such as
this grows only in a land of the hussars.'

At the other end of the table sat Drosselstein and Krach; the
former was peeling a Gravenstein apple, the latter engaged
with a bottle of Liebfrauenmilch:* he was one of those who do
not get drunk but confine themselves to becoming first quarrelsome, then cynical and finally apathetic. 'Outrageous!' he
began. 'Why should these Hessians have such stuff to drink!'
He let the light play on the contents of his glass. 'The finest
wine for the foulest of fellows! Of all the bloodsuckers that
have come through Bingenwalde *anno* 1806 and now again this
year, none have such a bad name as they have. You can frighten
children to bed with it.'

'They were even madder than the Swedes,' Medewitz put in
from the other end of the table; 'they scorched my administrator over burning straw; they are worthless, but they are tough
and brave.'

'Brave, yes,' Rutze interposed as confirmation, 'as is everything that lives in the mountains. Even a mere ridge of hills
bestows character on those who live there.'

'Captain!' exclaimed Bamme, pushing away his dessert
plate, 'we are not yet deep enough in wine to suffer in silence
your delusion that Protzhagen is Switzerland. Is the parade-
ground at Potsdam a range of mountains?'

Rutze glared and seemed about to reply; but his wits left him
in the lurch, so that the gauntlet had to be picked up in another
quarter. 'Whether or not a Protzhagener has the right to feel he
is a Swiss', said Drosselstein, smiling across to the captain, who
was still struggling for words, 'must be a matter of dispute;
what seems to me indisputable, however, is that mountain
peoples are outstandingly brave. Only those who live hard by
the sea are their peers. And this is no more than natural.

Continual conflict with the elements engenders strength and courage, and out of strength and courage is born military efficiency. Do I need to supply examples? The Norsemen sailed all round Europe, founded states and conquered Byzantium, and when the cowhorns sounded down from the mountains of the ancient cantons into the valleys all Burgundy was filled with terror.* London trembled at the Highland clans. That is how it has always been, and that is how it is to the present day. When everyone lay meekly at the foot of the conqueror, it was down from the mountains that the first opposition came: Spain and Tyrol dared to resist him. The whole history of this century speaks for the mountains and the sea.'

'I am not sure', Lewin now put in, with a courteous gesture of his hand towards Drosselstein, 'whether I can agree with you, Count. Man is and remains a son of earth: and he thrives best where he has the most immediate and unalloyed contact with his mother earth, because here the conditions of his existence are fulfilled the most completely. And I therefore suspect that the apparent triumph of mountain and sea is due to exceptional cases or in part even to mere illusion. Mountains are natural fortresses, and all fortresses ask to be besieged. Whoever thinks he can precipitately storm them comes to grief, but he comes to grief against walls and moats rather than against the bravery of their defenders. Highlands represent the defensive, the element of conquest is at home on the plain. Our friend Seidentopf's Semnones, who subdued a world, where did they originate, where was their seat? *Here*, on either side of the Oder; perhaps in Guse, where we ourselves now sit.'

Bamme nodded; Lewin went on: 'No country is governed from the mountains. Rome, when it thought to become Rome, voluntarily descended from the hills to the banks of the Tiber. No capital lies in the highlands; the centres of government grew up out of the great regions of the flatlands, and in and with them the generals and the heroes, from Hannibal and Caesar to Gustavus Adolphus* and Friedrich.'

'Bravo!' cried Bamme. 'Considering what my *métier* is, I might even aspire to the proposition that world-history in the grand style, such as that represented by the progress of the Huns and Mongols, has never been made anywhere but from the saddle, that is to say, in plain terms by a kind of primeval hussar; but I renounce all vainglorious thoughts and would rather proclaim peace! Let us unfurl our Prussian banner: *Suum cuique*!* Viewed in the right light, what goes for individual men also goes for nations and races: they all have their uses. But each, of course, in his own place. That is the point. If you want to fight out the Battle of Trafalgar in the rigging of the Victory, with the sea raging and broadsides blazing away, you have to have swum in other waters than the Schwilow or the Schermützel; but conversely, if you want to go through the Russian square at Zorndorf as lightly and nimbly as a bareback-rider through a paper hoop, it won't be a bit of help to you even if you have slit open the bellies of all the sharks in the Indian Ocean. It is the same as in the old tale of the fox and the stork: one is suited to the plate, the other to the bottle. I myself am perhaps the only fox who is also suited to the bottle. Above all to such a bottle as this. Let us drink a toast. And let us do it in fair Latin: *Nullum vinum nisi hungaricum.*'

7

After Dinner

COFFEE was taken in the mirrored-room. When the men appeared there to chatter away the next half-hour again in the company of the ladies they found a scene different from the one they might have expected. Overcome by an indisposition, Renate had withdrawn; in her stead they were met by Berndt von Vitzewitz, who, just arrived from Berlin, had smilingly declined his sister's invitation to participate in the closing act of dinner: he was old enough to know from experience how disagreeable such belated entrances can be.

Lewin greeted his father, and the other guests too expressed their pleasure at seeing him. The one to do so most unin-hibitedly was Bamme: without a trace of pettiness in his nature, he did not allow his evaluation of others to depend on how high or low they rated *him*; the only thing he was vain of was what he called his 'social gifts', and these, though with qualifitions, Berndt von Vitzewitz granted he possessed.

The farther side of the mirrored-room was taken up by three right-angled low platforms set side by side which, amply decorated with flowers and pot-plants, formed a horseshoe-shaped enclave reflected in the standing-mirrors placed against the window piers opposite. Within this enclave the guests took their places around a long marble table that stood on four pillars and looked almost like an altar, and as the little cups were handed round were soon involved in a conversation that in point of liveliness seemed to seek to outdo the conversation at table that had only just ended. Berndt was speaking: he had excited the interest of the others by telling them he had been to see the minister.★

'Do we attack?' asked Bamme.

'*We*? Perhaps. If it were *my* decision: certainly! But the gentlemen in the government? No. Least of all the minister. His trade is diplomacy, not politics. Incapable of coming to firm decisions, he seeks salvation in compromises. He talks of "negotiations", a favourite word of his he still preserves from the old days. We have nothing to hope for from him. He will leave us in the lurch.'

'I thought I had understood you differently,' remarked the countess. 'I understood he had been largely in agreement with you.'

'Largely in agreement! Yes, with me personally, and so long as it was only a matter of words. Behind closed doors he will fight any battle. Our objectives are the same: the Emperor must be overthrown, Prussia re-established. But *how*? Here we come to the revelation. He wants to fight it out on paper, not with weapons in our hands; on a green table, not on a green heath. He has no conception of the fact that only a ruthless war can save us. Ruthless and reckless. The initiative can still be *ours*: but for how much longer! He fails to appreciate how vital these present days are. Every hour that passes in inactivity cries to Heaven and brands him a saboteur and traitor. Not out of malice, but out of weakness.'

'And did you describe to him the mood of the country?' Drosselstein asked.

'I did, and with an urgency that would have swept anyone else off his feet. But he! When I unfolded to him our idea of a popular uprising, when I entreated him to say the word, he was alarmed and tried to conceal his alarm behind a smile. "Let us arm!" I cried at him. This exclamation pleased him: I had myself uttered the word with which, with that adroitness in which he is a master, he hoped to assuage me. He came closer and with an air of mystery echoed what I had said: "Vitzewitz, we shall arm." But even this nothingness was still too much for him. "We shall arm," he went on, "though it is in the highest degree probable that we shall never *need* these arms; Napoleon is down, he will *have* to make peace, and we shall gain our objective without bloodshed. We are certain of England and Russia." I was benumbed. We parted on good terms, apparently even in agreement, though we were both aware of the chasm that had opened up between us. As I went down the stairs I said to myself: "*Still* uninstructed, then! *Still* out of touch with the times! *Still* ignorant of Napoleon!" '

Drosselstein, Bamme and Krach shared Berndt's displeasure and shook their heads; Medewitz, however, who liked to cloak his insignificance beneath a mantle of exaggerated loyalism, thought the moment had now come for him to assert his political orthodoxy.

'I cannot share your indignation, Vitzewitz,' he said. 'Your ardour is carrying you away. The couriers and dispatch-riders who arrive almost hourly from all the capitals of Europe—do we know what they bring? No. You see things, as we all do, from a position of partial knowledge: but the minister possesses that overview of the total situation which we lack. He is well informed, he has a network of agents encompassing Paris, the Emperor is shadowed night and day. If His Excellency says: "He is down, he will *have* to make peace", I see no reason to contradict him. He is the minister. He *must* know and, excuse me for saying so, Vitzewitz, he *does* know.'

Berndt laughed. 'Knowing is like seeing: we see what we desire to see, in that we are all alike, whether we are a minister or not. His Excellency desires peace, and so he invents for himself an Emperor who needs peace. His "network of agents" obliges him with appropriate reports: subordinates are not given to contradicting. A Napoleon who is down! Oh holy simplicity! He is more active than ever and as daring and defiant as ever. At the last reception he went up to the Austrian ambassador and remarked: "It was an error on my part to have let this Prussia go on existing"; and when the ambassador, no doubt confused by these words, stammered: "Sire, a throne . . ." he interrupted him with a "Bah!" and added arrogantly: "What is a throne? A wooden frame covered with velvet." '

Bamme smiled; the countess, however, said quietly: 'In that he is really quite right, *il faut en convenir.*★ We make too much of such external things and see grandeur and nobility where they do not exist. When you have knocked over as many thrones as he has, you can hardly think very highly of them; *cq se désapprend.*★ I do not like him, but in one thing he has my approval: *il affronte nos préjugés.*★ He goes through our prejudices as though they were spider's webs.'

'That he does,' Berndt responded, 'and it is not the worst side of him. But I am surprised, sister, to hear you express approval of it. For whom do we have to thank for this idol-worship in which we too are sunk, this daily sin against the first commandment: "Thou shalt have no other gods before me"? Whom other than your celebrated Frenchmen, and above all that pompous demi-god whose train you also bear: Louis Quatorze?'★

'*Ce n'est pas ça,*★ Berndt', said the countess, with an access of gaiety that reflected her pleasure in being in a position to correct a mistake. 'Quite the opposite. I hate those doctrines, *et ce Louis même, ce n'est pas mon idole.*★ *Sachez bien,* I love the French nation, but I do not love its *grand monarque*, because in his pomposity he belies his nation. For the true nature of the French is good humour, high spirits, lightheartedness. But this Louis is constantly haunted by something ponderously Habsburgian from his mother's side. All the Bourbons were. There was only *one* of them who had not a single drop of German blood in his veins, and he is my favourite.'

'*Le bon roi Henri,*★ Berndt supplied.

'Yes, *he*,' the countess continued, 'the most amiable and at the same time the most French of all the kings that ever were, a

Gallic fighting-cock, not a silly vain peacock, natural, gallant, free of all *grandezza* and swagger.'

'Freer, perhaps, than a king ought to be,' Berndt said laughingly. 'He was playing horses with the Dauphin when the Spanish ambassador arrived to see him; and when she was asked what impression the King had made upon her, Madame de Simier could only reply: "*J'ai vu le roi, mais je n'ai pas vu Sa Majesté.*" '*

'What you take for a rebuke, or at least *comme un demi-reproche*, was meant rather as praise. In any event, as equally praise and rebuke. And how could it have been otherwise? He was secure in his own self-confidence, and did not try to conceal his weaknesses because he was conscious of the excess of strength the gods had bestowed upon him in his cradle—a cradle which was, by the way, in fact the shell of a tortoise. He concealed nothing, and laughed at himself with the cheerful superiority of a *grand seigneur*. Every trait I know in him, even the smallest, I find enchanting. He had the habit of taking things wherever he went, and averred with the roguishness of a Gascon: "*Que s'il n'avait pas été roi, il eût été pendu.*" '*

This last assertion was taken up by Krach—who, like all mean and avaricious people, adhered to the most rigorous principles in questions of mine and thine—with as much indignation as deference to the narrator of the story permitted. He began with 'unkingly' and 'frivolous', and would have screwed himself up to an even higher pitch if Bamme had not interposed in a tone of irritation: 'He who gives on a grand scale may take on a small scale. But he has to *give* first of all: that is where the difficulty lies.'

Krach bit his lip; the countess, however, said to him with easy courtesy: 'You misunderstand me, Chairman; I am not defending my favourite when it comes to his morality. It is quite different things about him that enchant me. Listen what Tallemant des Réaux says of him in his memoirs. One of the courtiers, Count Beauffremont, knew that the fair Gabriele* had been unfaithful. He told the King, but the King refused to believe it: he loved her too much. Finally, the count offered to furnish proof, and conducted the King to Gabriele's bedroom: but at the moment when they were about to enter, *le roi Henri* turned back and said: "*Non, je ne veux pas entrer; cela la fâcherait trop.*" '*

Medewitz, who had himself suffered a comparable mortification, remarked that he could not understand the King; but the countess went on: 'In this anecdote you have the King *tout à fait*. He agreed with the epigram that François Ier cut into a window at Château Chenonceaux:

> *Souvent femme varie*
> *Et fol est qui s'y fie.**

'He reminds one of this earlier king in many ways, except that he excels him. Our sex, in its weaknesses and its advantages, has never been better understood or treated more gallantly, and the women of every land ought to erect statues to him. There would, of course, be no lack of those who would begrudge him this honour; one appeared, indeed, in his own France.'

'In his own France?' asked the count: he was very well read in French memoirs and seemed to be questioning the possibility.

'*C'est ça,*' the countess went on, 'and it was in the shape of his own grandson, the "*grand monarque*". When the town of Pau wanted to erect a statue to its beloved Henri, it petitioned the court for permission. Louis XIV didn't say yes and didn't say no: instead of an answer he sent a likeness of himself. But he had underestimated the ingenuity of the good citzens of Pau: they erected this memorial and gave it the inscription: "*Celui-ci est le petit-fils de notre bon Henri.*" '*

'And how did it end?' asked Rutze, who like a child made no distinction between an anecdote and a story and took more interest in the course of events itself than in the point for the sake of which it was narrated. The countess smiled.

'It is a story without an ending, my dear Rutze. It is hardly likely that the King even heard about this inscription, let alone read it. No one would have been so disagreeable as to have drawn it to his attention. And in any event it was just at this time that the excitements of the campaign on the Rhine were drawing the King's eyes in another direction. It was the harvest-time of his fame, including his military fame. And yet there was not the slightest trace of a general in him. *Le bon roi* Henri fought battles, *le grand roi* Louis had them fought for him: yet poets and painters have ransacked Olympus and the world of legendary heroes in search of figures with which to compare him.'

'I believe I heard', Berndt remarked, 'that he did not lack a certain military talent, such as those who live in high places so often acquire.'

'Count Tauentzien★ was of the opposite opinion. And I dare assume that his opinion accorded with the prince's judgement.'

'The judgement of the King would seem to me more competent.'

The countess, offended, fell silent; but after a brief interval she went on: 'You know, Berndt, that the King himself said: "*Le prince est le seul qui n'ait jamais fait de fautes.*"★ This seems to me to contain an admission that, in theory of warfare, in all that concerns knowledge and judgement, he was the superior.'

Berndt shrugged. 'He who can practise something must also command the theory of it. What is decisive are the flashes of genius.'

'But genius appears in manifold forms. The prince would not have been surprised at Hochkirch.'★

'And would not have won at Leuthen.★ You overrate the prince.'

'You underrate him.'

'No, sister, I merely assign to him the place that belongs to him: the second. There has at all times existed a desire, when it comes to questions of personalities, to correct world-history. But never yet, thank God, has anyone succeeded in doing it. In spite of all the supposed superior knowledge of the experts, all the subtleties of the scholars, the people stick to their great men.'

'But it should, *de temps à temps*,★ come to recognize better who its great men are.'

'It is precisely in this that it shows itself infallible, or at least our people do, whose slow and sober judgement is a sure protection against sudden surprises. For long it harbours doubts, and resists for even longer. But in the end it knows where its love and admiration belong. I was able to observe this more than once during the last years of the Great King, when duty or pleasure called me to Berlin.'

'I, for my part, have heard of voices raised in opposition, and have had notice of threatening speeches on the part of the "infallible people" which I would not venture to repeat here.'

'There will have been no lack of them, too. A just king, though he has earned the gratitude of thousands, will have hundreds to complain about him. But what he was to those thousands was apparent when, coming from the grand review, he paid his regular autumn visit to his sister, old Princess Amalie,* whom he often hadn't seen for the whole year.'

Rutze, recollecting such visits, nodded his head in agreement; Berndt however went on: 'I can see him before me as if it were today: he wore a three-cornered service-hat, his white general's plume was torn and dirty, his coat old and dusty, his waistcoat tobacco-stained, his black velvet breeches worn out and discoloured. Behind him there were generals and adjutants. Thus he rode on his white horse, Condé, through the Hallesche Tor, across the Rondell, and into the Wilhelmstrasse, which was packed full with people, all bareheaded, the profoundest silence everywhere. He was constantly nodding in greeting, from the gate to the Kochstrasse about two hundred times. Then he turned into the courtyard of the palace and was received by the old princess on the steps of the entrance. He greeted her, offered her his arm, and the great folding-doors closed again. It was all like an apparition. Only the crowd still stood there bareheaded, their eyes fixed on the door. And yet nothing had happened: no pomp, no salvoes of cannon, no drums and fifes; only a man of seventy-three, ill-dressed, covered with dust, returning from a hard day's work. But everyone knew that this day's work had not been neglected for a single day for forty-five years, and reverence, admiration, pride, trust stirred in the breast of everyone who beheld this man of toil and duty. *Chère Amélie*, that includes your prince at Rheinsberg too. Have you ever witnessed such scenes, or even so much as heard of them?'

The countess was about to reply when the huntsman entered and announced that the sleighs had driven up: thus the conversation was interrupted. All that remained was to issue an

invitation for New Year's Eve, by which time let us hope
Baron Pehlemann will have recovered from his attack and Dr
Faulstich eluded his Ziebinger enmeshment. A quarter of an
hour later the sleighs were flying along their various paths out
into the Oderbruch. Berndt accompanied Drosselstein to
Hohen-Ziesar for the purpose of taking care of a quantity of
official business. Lewin and Renate had the longest journey: all
the way to the other side of the Bruch. When they stopped
before the manor house at Hohen-Vietz, Jeetze reported with
an access of familiarity that the 'young people from Berlin' had
arrived an hour before but, tired by the journey, had already
retired.

'Until tomorrow, then!'—with these words brother and
sister parted.

8

*Chez Soi**

THE countess's bedroom lay above the salon, with which it
was connected by the spiral staircase: a quiet room, tall and
spacious, with windows facing north. In the ordinary way you
might have thought this an undesirable situation: here,
however, where the occupant had no wish to be awoken by the
sun before midday, what anywhere else would have been a
misjudgement appeared as an advantage. In the middle of the
room, touching the wall only at its head, stood the bed: a large
structure furnished with heavy curtains, apparently designed
for comfort and not like one of those coffin-like boxes that
make sleep seem a matter of secondary importance, or even a
punishment—a strange arrangement, since if a man is to be
sound and solid he must not only be properly awake but at the
right time also properly asleep.*

Still affected by the contention she had had with her brother,
and annoyed at having been deprived of what she did not doubt
would have been a victorious rejoinder to his last remarks, the
countess slowly ascended the spiral staircase; behind her came
her maid, a pretty, very youthful little thing, decidedly

Wendish in appearance and wearing an expression compounded of roguishness and cunning. This maid was Eve Kubalke, the youngest daughter of the old sexton at Hohen-Vietz and the sister of Maline Kubalke. Both girls occupied a similar privileged position: Eve was the favourite and confidante of Aunt Amelie, Maline of Renate.

For some time the countess remained silent; at length she appeared to have mastered her displeasure, sat herself before a mirror and began to prepare for bed. The little maid fastened an unwavering gaze upon her; at length the countess smiled and said: 'Well, Eve?'

'Your Ladyship is so quiet.'

'Yes. But now talk to me. Take the comb. What has been happening?'

'Oh, lots of things, your Ladyship. Fräulein Renate was so nice again. She told me about everything. I'm always glad when she has a headache and comes upstairs, because then I hear all about Hohen-Vietz and my sister Maline.'

'How is her young man? Wasn't it young Scharwenka?'

'Yes, but she has given him the push.'

'Given him the push? The wealthy innkeeper's son?'

'That was why. They are hard people, the Scharwenkas, hard and full of peasant pride. He held it against her that she was poor. But by then it was all over, because she didn't care much for him anyway. Now she wants to go and work in town.'

'Let us hope it is the right thing for her.'

'But does your Ladyship know that the parson at Hathnow has got married?'

'The Hathnow parson?'

'Yes, yesterday, on the second day of Christmas. It was said to be something quite unusual.'

'And whom did he marry, then?'

'A woman from Berlin. And how he came to do so is a whole story in itself.'

'Well then, let me hear it.'

'Last summer he went to Berlin to visit a friend, also a parson. I've forgotten his name but I shall think of it.'

'Don't worry.'

'Well, his friend lived in a big house, two storeys high. A storm came up and it rained bucketfuls. When it was over, and the rain was only falling lightly, the two friends leaned in the open window and looked out on to the street, which was under water so that the street-boards were floating about. But shall I go on?'

'Certainly.'

'Well, they were looking out on to the street and the street-boards, but also on to a large pair of rose-trees that had been moved to take advantage of the rain and were sticking out of the window right beneath them. The friends went on talking, and the Hathnow pastor was just going to go downstairs to see the landlord who lived below when an arm came out just above the rose-trees holding a little earthen flowerpot with two or three leaves growing in it so that the leaves could catch the rain. A couple of drops fell on to the leaves and also on to the arm; and then it vanished again. "It was like an apparition," the Hathnow parson is supposed to have said. The next day he proposed. She is the daughter of a tax-assessor.'

'I would not have believed it of the little man. He has always been so shy.'

'People don't really know what to make of it, either. Some think it was the tender care she showed for the three little leaves that did it, and he said to himself "She would make anyone happy"; but others think, begging your Ladyship's pardon, it was the arm that did it.'

'It will no doubt have been the arm,' said the countess with quiet conviction.

Eve, who was a little rogue, rejoined that 'he *was* a parson, after all', and then continued with her evening report: 'The mill at Manschnow has been broken into.'

'Old Kriele's mill?'

'Yes, your Ladyship. They took all his savings and the horse in the stables too. They must have known the place well, because the money was under the floor; but they took up the boards.'

'Is anyone under suspicion?'

'The thieves had old soldier's coats on, half torn so that you couldn't see exactly what they were. The Manschnowers believe they could have been plunderers, Frenchmen, who are never able to keep their hands off anything. They had blackened their faces.'

'Then they were not Frenchmen. If you blacken your face, it is because you are afraid of being recognized. And you said yourself they knew their way about in the mill.'

'But the soldier's coats.'

'That will be explained.'

With that their conversation was broken off: the countess's toilette was finished, her hair loosely pinned up, and she bade Eve goodnight. Before leaving the room, Eve went to a large standing-mirror and, as though letting down a window-blind, lowered a green silk curtain in front of it. She did the same every evening, and a word needs to be said about it. Like all ancient châteaux, Schloss Guse too had its resident ghost: in this case a 'Woman in Black'. By connoisseurs of the subject, these women in white or black are regarded as the most genuine ghosts of all, precisely because they lack what seems to the layman the main thing: a history. They possess nothing but their existence; they merely appear. As to *why* they appear there is either no information at all or the information is contradictory. So too it was at Guse. The tales told of her varied very widely; one thing was certain: that whenever the Woman in Black appeared death or misfortune followed. The countess, stout-hearted in other respects, lived in constant fear of this spectre; but what she feared even more was that she might one day possibly fall victim to a mere blunder, to the sight of her own reflection in a mirror. As she herself always wore black this apprehension was to some extent justified, and she took precautions accordingly. The installation of the aforementioned spiral staircase was among these precautions: she wanted to avoid passing through the mirrored-room late at night on her way from the salon to her bedroom. When she had attained the latter, the big standing-mirror naturally became an object of particular attention and apprehension, and Eve would hardly have been forgiven if she had even once neglected to lower the curtain in front of it.

Today it was still early, barely eleven o'clock, and the countess, who would in any case have preferred to turn night into day, felt no disposition to seek sleep prematurely. There were still letters to write.

She sat herself at a table inlaid with tortoiseshell and boule-work standing between the bed and the window, perused a brief letter that lay to her left hand, and then began to write:

Mon cher Faulstich.

*Tout va bien!** Demoiselle Alceste, as she informed me today in a misspelled letter (*le style c'est l'homme*),* has accepted. She will be in Guse on the 30th, *et comme j'espère** find Dr Faulstich already here. You must not let me down.

Many thanks for the suggestions you made. You appear to favour de la Harpe* but I cannot share your enthusiasm, either for the *Barmecides* or for the *Comte du Warwick*. The passages underlined in red (*Tome VII* returned herewith) I consider good.

Après quelque hésitation I have decided on Lemierre;* not *Barnevelt*, which caused such a stir and is more mature, but *Guillaume Tell*, *justement parce qu'il n'a pas cette maturité.** In compensation for this it has verve, fire, passion. Demoiselle Alceste has assented without any cajolement from me. I will not deny that considerations of effect also helped to determined my choice. Cléofé's expostulations to freedom are exactly what people want to hear nowadays, *et comme Intendant en Chef du Théâtre du château de Guse,* I am obliged to present new things with contemporary relevance and to accommodate myself to the taste of my public. *S'accommoder au goût de tout le monde, c'est la demande de notre temps.** Demoiselle Alceste will have to do her best, *et encore plus la surprise.** So it must be kept a secret, even from Drosselstein.

But one thing is still lacking, *cher Docteur, et c'est pour cela que je recours à bonté.** What is lacking is a prologue, an epilogue, a chorus, or something or other that points forwards or backwards or sidewards, for that is perhaps how one could define the chorus. You will be able to devise something. *J'en suis sûre.** Perhaps it could also do with a song. But it would have to be something easy, that Renate could sing at sight.

*N'oubliez pas que je vous attends le 30. Je suis avec une parfaite estime votre affectionnée**

A. P.

A second letter was addressed to Demoiselle Alceste: it contained only the countess's assurance of how pleased she felt they would very soon meet. Then she sealed both letters, extinguished the candles on the writing-desk, and retired to bed. Only the Italian lamp was still burning. She tied a saffron-coloured cloth around her brow, as she had done for many years, and attempted to read; but the book fell from her hand. The day's impressions passed before her; she heard Berndt's voice raised in vehement discourse, then it died down and the great portal-like folding-doors Bamme had described so impressively opened slowly and softly: but into the hall in which the guards were dancing there stepped none other than Mademoiselle Alceste, Lemierre's words on her lips and victory on her brow. Everyone applauded.

The dream spun on; the countess slept.

9

Unfaithful Darling

THE following morning saw the two brothers and sisters, Lewin and Renate and Tubal and Kathinka, assembled for breakfast. They greeted one another warmly and plied one another with questions about Christmas at the Ladalinski house and the previous day's reunion at Schloss Guse: then they got down to making arrangements for the day ahead. Kathinka and Renate wanted to call in at the parsonage, then collect Marie for an hour's chatter, while the young men agreed to pay a visit to the nearby little town of Kirch-Göritz. The suggestion they should do so came from Tubal, who had read in the Jena *Literaturzeitung* an article, *Versions and Perversions of Romanticism*, signed with his full name by Dr Faulstich, and had at once resolved to go and see the said doctor when he was next in Hohen-Vietz.

Only after all these things had been disposed of did the conversation, hitherto conducted in fits and starts, assume a calmer course; and the Hohen-Vietzers now urged Tubal to tell them about the Christmas session of Kastalia Jürgass had improvised, but especially about Hansen-Grell, its most recent acquisition. Kathinka too wanted to hear about him.

'I can do little to satisfy your curiosity,' Tubal began. 'Although I talked with Jürgass again on Christmas Day, I know hardly more than what I wrote to you in my long letter.

He is not handsome, has a bad complexion and is *gauche* and awkward. But this impression is dispelled when he speaks. His name might be considered a brief abstract of the story of his life, and elucidates much about him. His father, called simply Grell, born in Gantzer and originally a soldier, somehow landed up in Denmark. There he married the daughter of a well-to-do artisan. It was in Schleswig, and in that region everybody is called Hansen; and they also have a widespread custom of sending their children out into the world with a double-barrelled name constructed of the family name of the father and that of the mother. Thus originated the Hansen-Grells. After a few years the father, who had done some schoolmastering and had tried his hand at making church-clocks and playing the organ, felt a strong desire to return to his village in Brandenburg, and wrote a long letter to the lord of the manor at Gantzer describing how homesick he was. The reading of this letter touched a soft spot in old Jürgass, and a month later Grell and wife, together with a whole colony of Hansen-Grells, arrived in Gantzer.'

'And old Jürgass devised the means, of that I am certain,' Lewin interposed. 'It is a family as fine as any we have. They are related to the Zietens by marriage, and to the Rohrs; from the one they have the hand, from the other the heart.'

'It is as you say,' Tubal went on. 'A house, a job, a plot of land were found, and our Hansen-Grell went to the Havelberg school. But when he was half-grown his mother's blood and name sprang to life in him, and one day he appeared at his grandparents' house in Schleswig. He had walked the whole fifty miles on foot. It was a risky thing to do, but it turned out well for him, even in Gantzer, where old Jürgass explained to old Grell that every man who had ever come to anything had sooner or later committed a desertion. Even Crown Prince Friedrich.* In the meantime, our Hansen-Grell grew to manhood with his grandparents and departed for Copenhagen; it happened in the same year as the English bombarded the city.* He was able in various ways to show how he possessed courage and prudence in equal measure, and this led to his being engaged as a tutor in the house of one Count Moltke, where he spent several happy years. It was during this time that he pursued his Scandinavian studies. But when Schill, whose progress he had followed with a glowing feeling of patriotism, was surrounded by Danish troops and then hacked to pieces in the streets of Stralsund, the Grell in him came so emphatically to the fore that he gave up his post in Copenhagen—though without rupturing good relations with the Moltke household—and returned to Brandenburg.'

'I am surprised not to have heard of him before,' Lewin observed. 'Where has he been all the time since then? Our Jürgass doesn't normally hold out on us.'

'I would imagine he has been dividing his time between literary activities in Berlin and temporary jobs in the country. He has been in Gantzer only now and then. If I have heard correctly, he has been a preacher in Stechow. However, he will be able to fill in the gaps himself in the course of the coming week. And if not he, in any event Jürgass, who, though he appears to treat him sarcastically, in fact has a predilection for him that is almost respectful. He lauds above all his talent as a story-teller, when it involves the natural description of Scandinavia or the narration of personal experiences. This stood out even in "Hakon Borkenbart", which he read to us. I was intrigued to observe what close attention Bninski paid first to the poem, then to the poet, and perhaps even more to the man. But I wrote to you about that, I recall.'

'It seems to me, Tubal,' Kathinka here put in, 'that you attribute to the count feelings that are in fact your own. What *he* demands is beauty, form, *esprit*, all those things which this bird of the north, who I suspect is really a goose, appears not to have. It is southern plumage that appeals to Bninski: Prussian theology students and assistant schoolmasters, who are never more prosaic than when they grow poetic, not to say excited, are quite outside his range.'

'There you misunderstand the count,' Tubal retorted, and Lewin added, with a bow to his fair cousin: 'I too must contradict you, Kathinka; Bninski's inclinations are as you have described them, but at the same time he is also capable of being more serious-minded and has a glimmering of an understanding that it is in precisely the Hansen-Grells that we excel the Slavic society virtuosos, the practitioners of salon fripperies and everlasting love-intrigues. However, it is time now to break off. Kirch-Göritz is an hour away and the days are short. We shall take the guns, shall we? It may be a hare will cross our path.'

Tubal agreed. Saving their goodbyes for the moment of parting, the two friends left the room to prepare for their hunting and visiting expedition.

The young ladies also rose, and Renate began to crumble the remains of the bread to feed it to her doves, as she did every morning. Kathinka, in a close-fitting Polish skirt of dark green that revealed the beauty of her figure only now she was standing up, helped her to do so. Lewin's feelings towards her were only too comprehensible: a trace of coquettishness, combined with that sureness of movement such as is imparted by an awareness of superiority, made her dangerous to anyone, but doubly dangerous to anyone still young and inexperienced. She was taller than Renate by half a head; and her especial glory, an inheritance from her mother, was her chestnut-brown hair, which, in defiance of the current fashion, she usually wore loosely caught up in a gold net. Her complexion was as lovely as her hair, and her eyes were as lovely as either: though they were bright blue, they shone like fire.

'See,' said Renate, making for the window with a bowl full of crumbs, 'they are reporting already.' And a satin-grey dove had indeed landed on the snowy window-sill outside and was pecking at the window-pane. 'That is my favourite,' she added, and turned the lock so as to strew out the crumbs. Kathinka was behind her: the moment the window was open the dove fluttered in and settled, not on Renate's shoulder but on Kathinka's, and, cooing and daintily revolving, began to nestle its head against Kathinka's cheek.

'Unfaithful darling!' Renate exclaimed, and there was something resembling genuine ill-humour in her voice.

'Don't,' said Kathinka. 'It is the way of the world. Unfaithfulness everywhere: doves are no exception.'

At that moment the two friends reappeared to take their leave of the young ladies until they met again late in the afternoon. They were wearing hunting-jackets, fur hats and rubber boots, and their guns were slung over their shoulders. 'Are we taking a dog with us?' Tubal asked.

'No. Tiras is lame, and Hector scares everything off and ruins the shooting. The best creature there is, and the worst dog.' Thus they departed.

10

Kirch-Göritz

KIRCH-GÖRITZ lay on the other side of the Oder, south-east of Hohen-Vietz. There were two ways of getting there, and the friends decided to take one of them on the walk out and the other on the walk back. They passed first the village, then the woodland acre: when they came to Hoppenmarieken's house, which stood silent and shut up, they stopped and looked curiously in through the window; but they saw nothing. Then they took a footpath that ran along halfway up the rising ground beside the river. Now and then a magpie flew out, but nothing that would have rewarded a shot.

They spoke of Faulstich, and Tubal outlined the article in the Jena *Literaturzeitung*, which Lewin had not read. 'I am almost afraid', the latter said, 'that the author is not going to live up to the impression he has made on you through his work. He is a clever and interesting man, but in the last resort of a somewhat doubtful character.'

'All the better. As you may know, I am sufficiently like Aunt Amelie to prefer things with a "sting" to them partly on account of this sting. And Faulstich will prove no exception. The fact that he lives in Kirch-Göritz in itself makes him interesting—a man who ventures to treat of the sublimest questions! What wave of destiny cast him upon this shore?'

'We know little about him, and that little probably needs correcting. If I am not mistaken he is from the Altmark, from the region of Gardelegen, where his father was the parson: a man of rigidly orthodox beliefs, which the son resisted from the first. Nevertheless he did what his father wanted and went to Halle and studied theology. But he was distracted by his literary interests and did not really get on. Even then he had already become a kind of aesthetic epicure. He got to know Ludwig Tieck, who was several years younger, and played at being his patron and at the same time the supreme critical judge of his work; and it was this acquaintanceship, brief and superficial though it was, that finally led him, after all kinds of vicissitudes, to Kirch-Göritz.'

'Tell me about these vicissitudes.'

'Certainly, for they are characteristic of the man. It finally came to a complete breach between father and son, and the latter was already considering whether or not to join a company of travelling actors when, through connections he had established in Berlin, he found himself drawn into the Rietz–Lichtenau circle. As you will often have heard from your father, this circle was better than its reputation. Though she possessed many other things, Madame Rietz also possessed a sunny disposition, an incisive mind and a natural feeling for the arts. She was suited to her role. She and Faulstich had much in common, and he soon learned how to make himself indispensable. He arranged tableaux, invented *bon mots* for princely personages, supplied anecdotes and scandal, and composed the celebratory odes. All this naturally came to an end when the Lichtenau soap-bubble burst★ and, as he had four years previously in Halle, Faulstich once again found himself in the direst straits.'

'. . . from which Tieck, like the starry prince in the pantomime, rescued him.'

'That is correct. The sundered connection was again rejoined; Faulstich took the first step. Tieck, for his part, had just published *Puss in Boots* and was working on *Zerbino* and *Genoveva*,★ and it was easy for him to see how valuable Faulstich would be to him in the feuding that lay ahead. For he was no ordinary critic: full of imagination, he understood the intentions, and even the caprices, of the new school. So, half out of self-interest, half from goodnaturedness, Tieck recommended him to the Burgsdorffs at Ziebingen. The rest you will easily guess.'

'No, no, I can't: at least give me some indication.'

'Very well. Thus he went to Ziebingen, which further led to

his becoming acquainted with Count Drosselstein and soon afterwards to his removal to Hohen-Ziesar. I can still remember it. It fell to him to restore order to the library, which had become somewhat disorganized, and, so far as his pleasure-grounds left him time for it, the count lent him a hand. They discovered ancient prints richly endowed with illuminated initials, books of chivalry from the end of the fifteenth century, which, borne to Ziebingen in triumph, provided material he wanted for new romances and, even more, for critical researches. In about 1804 the post of second teacher fell vacant at Kirch-Göritz. Family influence did not find it too difficult to procure this post for Faulstich. Aunt Amelie, too, played her part. It is practically a sinecure, and the couple of lessons he *is* obliged to give occasionally fail to take place. The Kirch-Göritzers have to console themselves with the reflection that every hour lost by their town school is an hour gained by the Romantic school.'

'Do they find that easy to do?'

'I doubt it. You cannot gather grapes from the brambles of provincial councillors. Nor must it be supposed that Dr Faulstich makes it easy for them.'

'Is he arrogant?'

'On the contrary, he displays the courtesy that dwells in all those who defray their ethical costs out of the aesthetic fund. He is obliging, always joking, at the very least not a killjoy. He will listen to the most convoluted tale with every appearance of attention, and then reply to it with a courteous "It follows from what you say", under which cloak of politeness he proceeds either to reduce the chaos to clarity or establish precisely the opposite of what has been said. It is his prudence and his affable manner that sustain him, but he none the less gives offence through his mode of life.'

'So it was no mere accident he felt at home in the house of Madame Rietz?'

'I fear that is so. He lives with a childless widow, a woman of almost forty; you will see her. She dominates him, naturally, and the efforts he occasionally makes to put her in her place always miscarry.'

'But why doesn't he shake her off?'

'He lacks the resolution. His is a weak nature. And in this weakness of nature there is also something that gives more offence than anything else: his lack of convictions.'

'Are such shocking things to be discovered in a place like Kirch-Göritz?'

'They are, I would think, to be discovered in any place. And Faulstich doesn't bother to conceal what he is like: he openly admits to his sybaritism, to a voluptuous indolence at the furthest possible remove from a concern for duty and the categorical imperative. He recognizes only himself. Great deeds of any kind interest him only as material for poetry, preferably in poetic garb. A ballad about Arnold von Winkelried* can move him to tears, but it would seem to him a ludicrous inconvenience to participate in a bayonet-charge himself.'

'He shares that view with many other people: whether it constitutes a fault is a moot point.'

'Under certain circumstances I could agree with you. But if we are in general more eager to assert our principles than we are strict in putting them into practice, there are exceptional times when we are not entitled to put into practice things which seem to us valid in theory. I do not know for certain, but I am willing to wager any amount, that that which has moved the heart of every Prussian this Christmastide has been merely a nuisance to our Kirch-Göritz doctor, assuming, that is, that he has noticed it at all. My edition of Shakespeare against an Uhlenhorst tract that he hasn't read so much as a line of the 29th communiqué. An invitation to Guse or Ziebingen is more important to him that a conference of monarchs or a peace-treaty. He is at home nowhere but in his books; the people, the fatherland, morality, religion—he knows what they mean, yet they are only concepts to him, they do not affect him emotionally. If today he were called to be curator of the library in Paris, he would be ready tomorrow to glorify the Emperor. And the ordinary folk among whom he lives realize this. They are now planning to mobilize the people into local militias; sooner or later the Kirch-Göritzers too will have to march. But Dr Faulstich? He will watch them depart, laugh, and stay at home.'

While they were thus conversing the two friends had reached

the point at which the path running along the rising ground beside the river branched off to the left and began to rise steeply. They turned to the left with it and a few minutes later were standing at the top of the incline, the river at their feet and beyond it the flatlands of the Neumark. Everything was buried in snow, the features of the landscape invisible beneath the white level surface; even the course of the Oder itself would have been hard to make out if an avenue of fir-trees marking through the snow the highway from Frankfurt to Küstrin had not at the same time indicated where the river lay. Other avenues struck across this highway at right-angles, maintaining communication between the opposite banks of the river and leading eventually to the towns and villages scattered sparsely on either side of it.

The friends took pleasure in the picture before them, which, its monotony notwithstanding, was not without charm and a certain solemnity.

'Where does that church-tower belong to, with the big belfry windows and the gold cupola?' asked Tubal.

'To the village of Ötscher.'

'Ötscher! I have never heard the name before.'

'And yet it plays a part in our history. Two miles to the south of it lies Kunersdorf, where Kleist* fell and the King uttered the historic words which catch the mood of that moment better than anything else: "Is no accursed bullet going to strike me?" It was towards here, in the direction of Ötscher, that the army, melted down into individual companies, withdrew in those dreadful August days; pontoon-bridges were put together, and in sight of the spot where we are now standing the remnants crossed over the river. That place there to the right is Reitwein. An estate of the Finkensteins. That is where the King spent the night.'

'It is fortunate I have you as a guide: I would have denied that anything of historical importance had ever happened in this wilderness.'

'You would have been quite wrong. There are treasures here wherever you step. Over in Frankfurt there is War Councillor Wohlbrück, who has been collecting material for a history of the province of Lebus for years, and who was also in Hohen-

Vietz to search through the estate archives. I have heard him
say more than once: "We have no lack of events here, nor of
history, what we lack is a knowledge of how to appreciate
them.' You see that collection of houses covered in snow over
there behind the two sloping fields: that is our goal, Kirch-
Göritz *dans toute sa gloire*. At the present moment it looks about
as impressive as a beaver-colony, yet it was once the summer
residence of a bishop, in the fourteenth century possessed a
famous church of pilgrimage, and in the sixteenth century an
even more famous image of the Virgin. But let us now descend
from these heights; the hawk that soars there is outside our
domain. I will tell you about the nest that lies before us,
assuming you wish to hear any more. Your compatriots from
the Bug and the Vistula* play a role in the town's history, you
know.'

'That arouses my curiosity,' Tubal replied, 'though I fear I
am unlikely to hear anything flattering.'

'History seldom flatters,' Lewin went on as they moved off
again.

'Well, one time—I am starting *in medias res**—the Poles were
in this country, burning, plundering and murdering, and they
broke into a nunnery that stood somewhere here just next to
Kirch-Göritz. One of the nuns, hard pressed, sought to defend
herself against the ringleader and begged him to desist; by way
of thanks she would teach him a strengthening spell whose
efficacy he might immediately test on her herself. As she said
this she knelt down. The man was willing and desisted as the
nun repeated the words: "*In manus tuas, Domine, commendo
spiritum meum.*"* But imagine his horror when her head flew
off!'

There was silence for a time; then Tubal said: 'But you spoke
of other happenings; let us hope there is nothing Polish in
them.'

'There isn't. The rest may be considered an event local to the
Neumark; yet it is all the more depressing for that very reason.
The Kirch-Göritzers had a miracle-working image of the
Virgin, and it seemed destined to survive all the changes of the
times. The new teaching was already being preached from
every pulpit in the region roundabout, but the pilgrimages to

the Holy Virgin, whose miracles increased with every passing day now that she herself was oppressed, still went on. The fact incensed the margrave at Küstrin, a keen Protestant, and he ordered the provincial governor of Sternberg, Hans von Mink-witz, to put an end to the mischief. Minkwitz took ten or twelve armed citizens from the town of Drossen, which belonged within his jurisdiction, and marched with them towards Kirch-Göritz. He thought simply to remove the miracle-working image. But things worked out differently from the way he desired and intended. For in every village he had to pass through local peasants and other dishevelled rabble attached themselves to his procession, people who only a few weeks before had offered their prayers to the Virgin and laid their pennies at her feet: so that when Minkwitz's force broke into Kirch-Göritz it did so, not as an orderly squad, but as a wild, unruly horde. The image of the Blessed Virgin was thrown down and smashed to pieces; everything else—choir-stalls, carvings, memorial banners—was burned or ripped apart. Some of the gold-embroidered vestments, however, escaped this fate, and the rabble dressed themselves in these and went home to their villages in a dissolute masquerade. The whole story is a fearful example of how little faith there was in the so-called ages of faith, and how much brutality. That the latter wears the former as a dress is itself a proof of its strength.'

'I would like to disagree with you,' Tubal interposed.

'Do so, but not now. These here before us are the first houses of Kirch-Göritz; and we cannot enter the presence of Dr Faulstich arguing with one another.'

I I

Doctor Faulstich

KIRCH-GÖRITZ consisted of little more than a single street which halfway along broadened into a narrow irregular tri-angle containing two corner houses.

In one of these corner houses lived Dr Faulstich. It was a

two-storey house with a tall roof and belonged to Frau Griepe, the widow of a rope-maker, who had let the upper storey to the town's revenue officer and the front room of the ground floor to Dr Faulstich; a large room at the back, with facilities for cooking, she occupied herself. What space was left was taken up with a deep, vaulted gateway, inside which there stood rake-like trestles that came from the yard of the late rope-maker.

Tubal and Lewin stepped into this gateway and knocked on the lefthand door. A somewhat shrill but otherwise pleasant-sounding voice cried 'Come in', and the next moment our friends found themselves being welcomed by Dr Faulstich. His outward appearance accorded with the character-sketch Lewin had drawn of him: all that was at first sight prepossessing about him notwithstanding, there was much that was missing; and if the lightly curled hair, and even more the wide trousers with bold checks, gave him the momentary appearance of a man accustomed to maintaining himself in a style not much inferior to that of those around him, the shirt and neckerchief, and the coat-hook that stuck out above the coat-collar, proclaimed him a scholar of the traditional stamp who was *au fond* indifferent to cleanliness and indebted for the greater part of his semblance of elegance to Drosselstein's tailor.

He seemed to be genuinely glad to see the two young men and, brushing lightly aside the eulogies Tubal heaped on his critical labours, with a jocular 'You see, gentlemen, the seats of honour on the sofa are occupied,' he drew two rush-chairs to the table. Tubal and Lewin sat down, while the doctor, seized with the kind of restlessness that infects the conscientious host, hastened to the rear wall of the room, knocked on it three times with the knuckle of his index-finger, and listened attentively to hear if there was any answer. This answer seemed not to have been denied, for he now returned to his guests wearing a satisfied expression and with a trace of irony informed them that barely an hour previously he had received a letter 'from the private cabinet of her Ladyship your Countess Aunt'. Its contents: a New Year's Eve secret.

This secret would certainly have shared the fate of all such secrets—namely that of being immediately let out—had the conversation just under way not been interrupted by the appearance of the Widow Griepe.

She remained standing in the doorway and, regarding the doctor, who had suddenly become uneasy, with an extremely disrespectful expression that totally distorted a countenance on the whole still pretty, concentrated all she had to say into a half-questioning, half-threatening 'Well?'

'I would like to ask you to bring us some fruit, Frau Griepe; Hasenkopf and Reinette apples. Also some bread and butter.'

'Now?'

'If you please. The gentlemen have come from Hohen-Vietz.'

This semi-introduction did not fail to produce an effect, especially as Tubal, who lacked punctiliousness in such things, followed it with a slight bow in Frau Griepe's direction. She was pleased by such a show of respect, and even more by him from whom it proceeded. She examined Tubal with that glance of complicity in which, according to circumstances, her charm or offensiveness lay, and then disappeared again without having said Yes or No to Faulstich's request.

In the meantime, Lewin had been looking around the doctor's room, which, though spacious enough, still seemed cramped and uncomfortable. The accumulation of objects was partly responsible, but the greater part of the blame lay with the predominating disorder: exercise-books and printed volumes lay, together with whole confused heaps of literary pamphlets, around it; the worst turmoil, however, was that on the sofa—an article of furniture covered with an ugly, blue-and-yellow worsted material and designed also for sleeping—in regard to which Faulstich himself had remarked with all too great justification that 'the seats of honour are already occupied'. To mention only the corner immediately beside the doctor's workstool, there was a hastily disposed-of coffee-set standing there, with an elegantly bound book on top of the porcelain sugar-bowl, a teaspoon serving as a bookmark. A more gratifying impression was produced by the little portrait gallery drawn up in two rows above the back of the sofa. There were silhouettes, almanac and calendar pictures, plaster and wax medallions, which Lewin easily recognized as a Parnassus of our Romantic poets: the heads of the two Schlegels,★ and those of Tieck and Wackenroder,★ with their characteristic profiles, leaped out at him.

He had just begun discussing some of these pictures, and heard with interest how hard the doctor had found it to assemble the collection in anything like completeness, when a clattering outside the door announced the return of Frau Griepe. She entered, pushed aside a pile of pamphlets with a barely concealed contempt and set the requested refreshment on to the table in the space thus vacated, delivered in succession to the 'Well!' and 'Now?' of their first conversation an equally brief 'There!' and departed again with that overweening expression on her face which commonplace women never spare their victim whenever for this or that reason they have been obliged momentarily to exchange their role of despot for that of servant.

Faulstich drew a breath of relief, became more relaxed, and asked if he might be permitted to elevate the repast offered by Frau Griepe on to a higher level of things. 'I am not always so well assorted as I am today,' he said, and went to a wall-cupbard which, so far as Lewin could tell in a fleeting glance, was in a condition of chaos, and returned to the table with a whole armful of things. It was not hard to see that they were the remains of the Christmas fare at Ziebingen: they included spiced gingerbread, marzipan and a long-necked bottle of maraschino. Faulstich also fetched a couple of tapering glasses. The bottle of maraschino, however, had yet to be opened; he therefore took a little Karlsbad knife whose accessories included a tiny corkscrew and attempted to draw the cork. But what might have been expected to happen did happen: the corkscrew broke. What was to be done? He threw the little knife aside, reflected for a moment, and said, in a jesting tone that none the less rang somewhat hollow: 'I haven't the courage to put Frau Griepe's tenderheartedness to any further test; we must try elsewhere.' And with that he inserted two forks, and the cork came out.

He then sat down himself, filled the glasses, and proposed the health of the house of Hohen-Vietz. Lewin responded, but Tubal drank to 'the versions and perversions of the Romantic school'. Faulstich, who was not impervious to such tributes, smiled, as Tubal went on: 'I do not want to involve you in a conversation about things you have already disposed of, honoured Herr Doctor; *Roma locuta est*;* but there is one point you must forgive my curiosity for touching on: have you not overrated Novalis* at the expense of Tieck?'

'I hardly think so,' replied Faulstich, who was prudent enough to see in such questions a commendation of himself rather than a censure; 'I doubt whether it is possible to overrate him. The entire school is united in this view.'

'Even Tieck? Does he not regard such a promulgation as a dethronement?'

'Not at all, since the promulgation came from him himself. He is a good enough critic to recognize in Novalis the high point, the consummation of the school, and he is honest enough to admit as much, even at the risk of diminishing his own standing.'

'I am surprised, however, to find one who died so young esteemed so highly.'

'It requires a particular temperament, and hardly less an exhaustive familiarity with him, if you are to be able to follow this darling of the Romantic school, as I may call him. This applies equally to his prose and his verse. From the impression I have received of you, I would conclude that you are disposed by nature to enter the little Novalis community. And that is the main thing. Whether, on the other hand, you are as familiar with this poet as your nature disposes you to be seems to me, in the light of more than one experience, doubtful. I know how even his confessed followers sometimes shrink from him.'

'I have no reason', Tubal replied good-humouredly, 'not to admit to a superficiality which, here as elsewhere, is among my virtues. I know his novel* and two or three of his songs: the "Hymn of the Crusaders", the "Miner's Song" and similar things.'

'These are counted among his best things, but the best is not always the most personal. When I saw you coming up the street I was reading his *Hymns to the Night*.* In these hymns you have the real Novalis.'

So saying, the doctor took up the elegantly bound book, laid

aside the curious bookmark without any sign of embarrassment, and leafing through the pages said: 'I cannot resist the
temptation to acquaint you with something of what I have just
been reading.'

The two friends consented.

'We are generally regarded as fanatics,' Dr Faulstich went
on, 'and fanatics try to make converts. However, I shall impose
no excessive demand on your patience. Just a few lines: a
glorification of Greece.' Faulstich read the passage he had
referred to, and then, laying the book down again, said: 'Has
the world of Greece ever been described better, with more
profundity of insight? And yet this description is no more than
a transition to a description of the Christian world. Hear for
yourself. Every line moves me as if it were music.'

And he read on: ' "Amid the people, despised though it was
and grown obstinately alienated from the blessed innocence of
youth, there appeared the new world with a countenance never
seen before: in the poverty of a poetic hut the son of the First
Virgin and Mother. In solitude his heavenly heart unfolded to a
flower-cup of almighty love, and with deifying ardour the
blossoming child's prophetic eye beheld the days of the future,
untroubled by his days of earthly fate." '*

The doctor fell silent. The two friends had followed him
attentively. 'Strange,' Lewin said, 'but I almost feel that this
passage, heartfelt though it is, is inferior to the passage glorify-
ing Greece. Could the longing for beauty have been stronger in
him than the Christian legend together with his belief in it?'

Tubal shook his head. 'I had a similar feeling to you, but I do
not draw the same conclusion from it. Power of poetic expression is no measure of our convictions, or even of our inclinations. I love peace *de tout mon cœur*,* but I would find it much
easier to glorify war, and I could do so much better. What is
colourful always had the advantage, and even black is better
than white. Take even our most devout poets: where they
describe God or the Devil they all fall short.'

Dr Faulstich, who while Tubal was speaking had been
leafing on through the volume of Novalis as though looking
for a particular passage, nodded in agreement and then
observed to Lewin: 'That our poet was most intimately

attached to Christianity cannot be doubted for a moment; if such a doubt should arise, however, it would put an end to the position of supremacy he holds. For it is not the quality of his talent but the quality of his faith that raises him above his competitors. There is also such a thing as a Romanticism attaching to the classical world, but the actual root and cradle of all Romanticism is the Crib and the Cross. This is the note that, loudly or softly, is sounded in all that is best in what the school has created, and longing for the Cross is its criterion. In no one is this longing stronger than it is in Novalis: he was consumed by it. You have already mentioned the "Hymn of the Crusaders"; but lovelier and more profound than that are the stanzas with which he introduces his collection of *Sacred Songs*.* I shall read you only a few lines, since I am sure of the effect they will produce:

> 'When all become unfaithful
> I'll yet be true to thee,
> That gratitude extinguished
> Shall yet survive in me.
> For my sake didst thou perish,
> For me didst suffer sore,
> And thus with joy I give thee
> My heart for evermore.
>
> How oft I think, with weeping,
> That thou thy life didst give,
> Yet those for whom thou suffered'st
> Forget thee while they live.
> By love alone inspired,
> What marvels thou hast done,
> And now thou art departed,
> And no one thinks thereon.'*

The doctor, who had read with a voice growing more agitated with every line, laid down the book; then he went on: 'Not since Paul Gerhardt* wrote "O sacred head sore wounded" has anything like this been composed in the German language. And that it should have been written in this age of apostasy!'

Tubal was more agitated than Lewin: like all sensual natures he was greatly influenced by dreamy, euphonious sounds; so, while Lewin continued to discuss Novalis with the doctor, he went to the window and looked out. Girls and schoolboys in red headscarves and fur caps were coming up the street, chasing and throwing snowballs at one another, while hundreds of sparrows hopped about pecking at the ground, though none of them flew up. The breath of peace lay over it all; the reading of Novalis had aroused in Tubal a feeling of happiness whose roots were a quiet sense of longing, and at the sight of this scene he felt this feeling grow; he turned from the window and, walking back to the table, extended his hand to the doctor and said: 'How I envy you these days at Kirch-Göritz! Instead of the babble of mankind, depth and beauty, and in addition the leisure to enjoy them.'

Lewin stayed silent: he knew too much of the reality of things to be able to agree. The doctor, however, replied: 'You have only sipped from the cup; when one has to empty it, one tastes the dregs too. And this sediment rises higher and higher. Books are not life, and leisure and poetry, however many happy hours they may fashion, do not fashion happiness itself. Happiness is peace, and peace exists only where there is unison. But in this solitude of mine, whose appearance of peacefulness has ensnared you, all is opposition and contradiction. What seems to you freedom is dependence; wherever I look I see disharmony: sought yet only tolerated, a teacher at a ragged-school, and a champion of Romanticism, Frau Griepe and Novalis.'

He had leaped up and was pacing the room. 'Do not envy me,' he went on, 'and above all guard yourself against that lie of existence which cries to Heaven, dumbly or aloud, wherever the way we live stands in contradiction to what we believe. For our convictions, too, what are they but our beliefs! Truth is supreme, and the supreme truth is: "Blessed are the pure in heart." '

At that moment Frau Griepe, who had in the meantime smartened herself up, reappeared in the doorway, ostensibly to ask if she should now clear away, in reality out of curiosity and in order to show herself. The doctor's eyes blazed at her a glance of the most fervent animosity, but, at once sensible of the chains he wore, he straightway twisted his mouth into an amicable smile. 'Let us leave it, Frau Griepe, till later.' At that the lady again withdrew.

The friends had risen; it was already late in the afternoon and the time had come to depart. Tubal shook hands with the doctor. 'I have listened to all you have said; your words have affected me more than you can know.' The doctor smiled: 'Novalis is profound, but the word of the Gospel I have just repeated is more profound. Mother Nature has inscribed it on your heart, dear Lewin. And that is the guarantee of your happiness.'

'Let us not boast of it for fear of losing it.'

With that they separated. Frau Griepe stood at the house-door to seize another farewell greeting, and gazed after the two friends and laughed.

12

Help Me!

IT was striking four as Lewin and Tubal reached the end of the little town. A few minutes later they were standing beside the river, and Tubal, who was a few paces ahead, was already beginning to climb down the steep bank when Lewin called to him: 'Let's stay on this side; here we have the highway; let's not cross until we get between Neu-Manschnow and the duck-snare at the church at Hohen-Vietz.'

Tubal was agreeable. So they walked back a short distance until they were standing in the middle of a broad avenue of poplars which they had passed five minutes previously, and only then did they set off in the direction of the Rathstock ferry and beyond that to the outlying farm at Neu-Manschnow. This farm was their halfway mark. The road ascended a little; when they had reached its highest point they could see the church-tower at Hohen-Vietz standing against the glow of the evening like a silhouette on the ridge of hills on the far side of the river.

'It will be dark in fifteen minutes,' said Lewin, 'but we

cannot go wrong; now we have the road to follow, afterwards the tower.'

Tubal nodded in agreement; but it proved impossible to make him communicative. What Dr Faulstich had said about the 'contradictions of existence' was still ringing in his ears: it was only too applicable to his own way of life, and even more to that of his house and family, and his desire now was to make sure that his acquaintanceship with the doctor, only a few hours old, should continue; for, though he detested anything that smacked of preaching, he was always deeply affected by views and pronouncements clearly originating in rich experience and a lively sensibility.

The two friends walked on side by side in silence. It was evening by the time they reached the Rathstock ferry: a few stars were flickering dully, and towards the north a glow appeared in the sky.

'I believe the moon is rising,' said Lewin, and pointed to a bright spot on the horizon.

'So early?' asked Tubal indifferently, and felt absolved from passing any other remark by the appearance of a cart coming towards them on the road ahead, the iron chain of the horses' collars clattering against the shafts. Lewin recognized the team: it was the miller from Manschnow.

'Good evening, Kriele. Out on the road so late?'

'No choice, young sir. You know what's happened to me?'

'Yes, Kriele. But whatever possessed you to put your money under the floorboards?'

'What am I supposed to do with it, young sir? One place is as bad as another. I'm off to Frankfurt now. There's a hearing tomorrow.'

'Have they got the thieves already, then?'

'They've got Paschke and Pappritz, who're always up to something. But Justizrat Turgany had them tell me it isn't Pappritz. And with Paschke too it's touch and go.'

'Well, the magistrate knows what he's doing. Give him my regards.'

'That I will, young sir.'

And with that the horses moved off again; for a time the

miller's 'Hi! Hi!' and the clattering of the chain could still be heard. Then all was silent.

The encounter, trifling though it was, had at least loosened their tongues. Tubal asked questions, Lewin answered them, and before the Manschnow miller's family history had been fully narrated the friends had arrived opposite the church-tower at Hohen-Vietz. They turned left out of the avenue of poplars, followed the course of a narrow ditch that ran across the field, and were soon standing on a snow-covered declivity some twenty feet high from which there was no footpath or steps down to the river. It was too steep to walk down, and too high to jump, so they lay on their backs, pressed their shoulders firmly against the snow and, cradling their guns in their arms, slid to the bottom. Once there, however, they found them-selves faced by another, more serious obstacle: a number of fir-trees were visible in the middle of the river, indicating the course along it, but there was nothing to mark out where they might go safely across. Tubal strode forward, however, intending to march out regardless of danger, but Lewin prevented him.

'You don't know what you're doing. It's very tricky terrain. The villagers hack great holes in the ice all around here, so that the fish won't suffocate. These holes freeze over and the snow drifts across them.'

'We do have to get to the other side, all the same.'

'Certainly, but not here. We shall soon find a place to cross. About a quarter of a mile upstream the way branches off to Gorgast. That's a large village, and I'm sure the villagers must have made themselves a gravelled pathway.'

'Very well, you should know.' And with that the two friends walked on along the path at the edge of the river, which was often so narrow that their right shoulders brushed against the snow-covered incline beside them. It was a difficult march, especially where they had to clamber over great thickets of brambles. At length they came in sight of the spot where a kind of excavated path emerged from the right and continued on out across the ice.

'Our wanderings are coming to an end,' said Lewin, and indicated the little black pointed pine-trees that, as was soon apparent, marked out the path across. 'More adventure than I would have thought possible between Kirch-Göritz and Hohen-Vietz.'

'And we are not in harbour yet,' Tubal replied. 'A Russian campaign in miniature. Snow, snow. *Et voilà la Bérésine*.'

'But in this case we shall not have a bridge break under us,' Lewin said, and led the way along the path which in a few minutes brought the two friends safely to the other bank.

Here they first of all scaled the ridge of hills, from which they recognized on their left the church-tower at Hohen-Vietz; they now saw themselves compelled to retrace the quarter-mile stretch by which on the opposite side of the river they had overshot their goal. Their path led them first of all along the foot of the hill and then towards a thickly set plantation of young trees, from whose furthest corner it was at most a rifle-shot's distance to the village and scarcely half as far to the highway that led from Küstrin to Hohen-Vietz.

When they had reached this far corner the footpath ceased or became lost in the darkness. They were still hesitating whether to turn back and continue along the hillside path they had just abandoned (which would have led them to the Hohen-Vietz park) or to make across the snowy ploughed field and thus gain the highway, when they caught sight of several figures among the trees that lined this highway. Immediately afterwards they seemed to hear the sound of voices, and the next moment a violent quarrel appeared to be in progress. They could distinguish words of invective and abuse in the local dialect, and suddenly there came across the field to them the cry: 'He's choking me; help me, Lord!'

To obtain a better view of where he was, Lewin had jumped on to a large stone that lay here at corner of the wood as a landmark, but he would hardly have succeeded in doing so had not the moon at that same moment emerged from the clouds which had drifted across it an hour before. Now he could see everything clearly.

'That is Hoppenmarieken!' he exclaimed, at the same time leaping from the stone, tearing the gun from his shoulder and loosing off a shot to indicate that help was at hand. 'That will at least have scared them: forward, Tubal!' And with that the two friends set off across the field at a trot. Lewin stumbled but quickly recovered himself and at the next moment was again at Tubal's side.

When they were halfway to the road it became clear what was taking place: one of the vagabonds had been posted as a guard, while the other was wrestling with Hoppenmarieken and tearing and tugging at her neck.

'Hold on!' cried Lewin, who was now in the lead; but this admonition was no longer needed. The highway robber released her and, describing a wide arc, ran towards the same little wood from the opposite corner of which Tubal and Lewin had begun their run across the ploughed field. The other, who had been posted as a guard, vanished in the direction of the village.

By the time Lewin and then Tubal had reached the roadway Hoppenmarieken too had disappeared. But they soon found her again: she was lying between a heaped-up pile of stones and a group of poplars whose highest branches were full of crow's-nests. Her basket was still on her back, her stick in her hand.

'Is she dead?' asked Tubal.

Though he had not yet discovered whether she was or not, Lewin shook his head, bent down to her and drew her arms out of the linen bands by which the basket was carried; having thus freed her from it, and assured himself that she was only unconscious, he lifted her up from the ground and set her with her back against a tree.

'Give me some snow,' he called to Tubal, at the same time opening her tight bodice, whose top hook had in any case been wrenched off in the tugging and struggling. From the red and bloody state of her neck and throat he could now clearly see that the robber's exertions had all been directed towards tearing away the money-purse she always wore round her neck on a thin leather strap: the strap, however, had not broken, and the man had been unable to wrench it over her head.

At this moment Hoppenmarieken opened her eyes. The first thing she did was to feel for her purse; only then did she inspect the people tending her. A goodnatured smile—a thing normally foreign to her and one which, when it did occur, was enough to reconcile you to her ugliness—fluttered across her face as she recognized Lewin, the only human being to whom she was really attached. She stroked and patted him; but when she noticed how Tubal was continuing to rub her brow with snow, she grew impatient at this unwanted attention, pushed him away, and pointed with increasing vigour towards the basket standing beside her. Lewin grasped to some extent what this gesture meant, and began to rummage around in it: and when he straightway found near the top of it a bottle wrapped in sacking he thought he had grasped Hoppenmarieken's meaning completely. He bent over her and made as though to pour some of the brandy into the palm of his hand; but at that she lost patience even with him and, wrenching the bottle from his hand in annoyance, took a deep draught from it. At once all her vitality was restored to her; she thrust the cork back into the bottle and cried to Lewin: 'Now help me up, young sir.' Then she set her basket on the heap of stones, laid her crooked staff beside it, and inserted her short arms into the linen bands attached to the basket: she was now ready to march off again.

'Won't you come back with us?' Lewin asked. 'We can accompany you.'

She shook her head and strode away in the opposite direction, talking to herself incomprehensibly.

The friends gazed after her. From time to time she halted and gestured threateningly with her stick towards the wood into which one of the robbers had vanished.

13

In the Administrative Office

WHILE Tubal and Lewin were paying their visit to Kirch-Göritz, Berndt von Vitzewitz had returned to Hohen-Vietz. Fatiguing days lay behind him, and days full of disappointments. The minister had, as we have already heard, eluded with smooth words any binding commitment, and in other influential circles of the capital, in so far as he had had access to them, he had encountered the detested phrase: 'We must wait.' Nowhere had there been any understanding of the significance of the present moment: only in Guse had Captain von Rutze, whom he had succeeded in engaging in further conversation just before the party broke up, shown any sympathy for his conviction that caution must be abandoned and resolute measures taken. Drosselstein had vacillated; but on the journey to Hohen-Ziesar he had allowed himself to be swayed by Berndt's eloquence and had finally agreed, not only to a general arming of the people, but, if there should be no formal declaration of war, to the plan for unleashing a popular war on their own initiative.

On his arrival at Hohen-Vietz Berndt was pleasantly surprised to find a visitor present. He needed to be torn away from time to time from the plans and cogitations that ruled him with the force of an *ideé fixe*, and no one was better qualified to do that than Kathinka, who, while avoiding all talk of politics, was sufficiently inventive to conceal the deficiencies in the conversation which thus arose with happy inspirations or with piquant stories of life at court or in society. The appearance she presented contributed to her success. On this occasion too Berndt gave himself up to her chatter; in her description of a ball at His Excellency Baron Schuckmann's, where the Bavarian ambassador had said or done this or that, he momentarily forgot all his cares and plans; and he was drawn out of this cheerful distraction again only when the appearance of Tubal and Lewin, and their account of the adventure they had just had, propelled his thoughts back on to their customary track. He rang the bell.

'Jeetze,' he called to the servant as he came in, 'send Krist's Willem to the mayor. Or, better, go yourself. I have to speak with him. At half-past ten tomorrow morning.'

For Kathinka's sake, if for no other reason, he sought to restore the conversation to the level of small talk it had been on before this interlude, but, since Tubal and Lewin were likewise unable to strike the right note of cheerfulness, the attempt was unsuccessful.

That was in the evening.

On the following morning we discover Berndt in his Administrative Office on the first floor—a large corner room from which, since the side-door had been walled up, only a single exit led out on to the corridor. The spare rooms also lay along this same corridor.

The Administrative Office exhibited little that might have answered to the solemnity of its name. It was a study and work-room like any other, and Berndt liked to withdraw there especially in the summertime, when its two great windows were overgrown with trellis-vines: it was airy and shady at that time of year, and the birds twittered among the thick vine-leaves and gazed in through the windows into the spacious room beyond. For it had remained spacious, notwithstanding the accumulation of ancient lumber, of book-stands laden with books and documents, of iron-bound chests, and the presence of an old-fashioned tiled stove reaching almost to the ceiling. One of the chests stood to the right of the door and was fastened with a padlock, while along the ledges of the book-stands there was a chaotic array of Wendish funeral urns and Italian alabaster vases, two dragoon's helmets, and a red-clay portrait-bust of Friedrich the Great. A sense of order and beauty was clearly lacking: the things in the room just happened to be there, that was all.

A desk heaped high with papers and documents stood with its end touching the pier between the windows, and at this desk was sitting Berndt, a large sheet of cardboard in front of him which, with the aid of a ruler and drawing-pen, he was dividing into columns. He had just started to furnish the columns with headings when he heard out in the corridor the sound of someone carefully arranging his dress, immediately followed by that of a knock on the door, gentle enough to be polite but loud enough not to sound nervous.

'Come in!' It was he whom Berndt had expected.

'Good day, Kniehase. Punctual to the minute. We older ones have that in our blood; the young can no longer be persuaded to it. Take a seat, there, the chair by the stove, and then draw near.'

The mayor laid his hat and gloves on the big chest with the padlock and then did as he was bidden.

'I have summoned you, Kniehase,' Berndt resumed, 'because something has to happen. And you are the man I need. But I don't want to anticipate: first things first. You have heard of the assault which might have cost our old witch her life, or at least her money-bag.'

Kniehase nodded.

'A few hundred yards from the village, on the open road, practically in daylight. If it were an exceptional event it would be different—but it's the third case in a week. On Christmas Eve the smith at Golzow had his cow driven from its stall, on the day after Christmas the miller at Manschnow had his floorboards taken up, yesterday Hoppenmarieken was nearly strangled. What have we come to?'

'It's the hooligans from Quappendorf, your worship. Miekley was in Frankfurt on the third day of Christmas and he saw them bring in Paschke and Pappritz.'

'No, no, Kniehase. That is just the thing that gets me so annoyed, this foolish seizing of people without sense or reason. Always the same poor devils, and in five cases out of six they have to be let go again for lack of evidence. And that is what they call administering the law! It's pitiable. And it's all due to indolence: the justices won't think and the mayors won't act. Of the peasants I say nothing: they will never bring water until their own roof is burning. But all this has to change, and we must make a beginning. Our people of Hohen-Vietz are the best: no pack of colonists grown rich overnight. No offence, Kniehase, I know you're a Pfälzer yourself.'

Kniehase smiled. 'Your worship is quite right, the old Wendish stock is better: stubborn, but tough and reliable.'

'And shrewd as well, or they wouldn't have chosen a Pfälzer from Neu-Barnim as mayor of Hohen-Vietz. That is what I have always said. But now pay heed, Kniehase: what you call hooligans from Quappendorf are foreigners, Frenchmen.'

'No, no, your worship. I talked about it with Pastor Seiden-topf, and in his opinion the French are still up at the frontier, or even on the Vistula.'

'He is right. And yet I am right too. I am not referring to the much-shrunken "Grand Army", not to the divisions smoked out of Moscow which are now crawling across Russia like flies in November across a white wall, I am referring to the little scattered pockets of trash left behind here in fifty different places: a couple of thousand at Küstrin, five thousand at Stettin, but most of them stuck in their little nests in Poland. How far is it to the frontier?'

'Ten miles, as the crow flies.'

'There you have it, Kniehase. These pockets of trash, that could not possibly be accommodated in military strongholds, are now flooding over the country like water from a burst barrel. Neapolitans, Würzburgers, Naussauers, an army composed of them is bound to break up anyway. And once discipline is gone, it is only one step from a soldier's life to a bandit's. What is haunting these parts is deserters from Poland, and perhaps also marauders from the regiments of reinforcements that the Emperor is scraping together wherever he can in Germany as a kind of provisional payment on a bill still to be presented. And this rabble, from Poland or wherever else they come from, we must put an end to; at the very least they must not be allowed to overwhelm us. And then if the remnants of the Grand Army should arrive here, a hundred today, a thousand tomorrow, we shall have learned on the ones and tens how to deal with them. "He who keeps a penny shall one day have many" says the proverb. So let us get on! And the sooner the better.'

The mayor of Hohen-Vietz sat up straight and seemed about to reply, but the lord of the manor had not yet spoken his final word.

'What I mean, Kniehase, is this: we have to get ready; local militia, village by village.'

'And if the King then calls on us . . .'

'Then we shall be at hand,' Berndt completed the sentence, at the same time adding in more emphatic tones: 'And if he does *not* call on us, we are at hand *anyway*. And that is why I have summoned you, Kniehase.'

'It's not possible without the King.'

Old Vitzewitz smiled. 'It's possible. Times change. There are times for obedience and for watching and waiting, and there are other times when our first duty is to act. I love the King; he has been a kind lord to me and I have sworn an oath of allegiance to him, but I will not for the sake of an oath of allegiance be unfaithful to a natural allegiance. And that belongs to the soil on which I was born. The King exists for the sake of the nation. If he divorces himself from the nation, or allows himself to be divorced from it through weakness or bad advice, he absolves himself from *his* oath and releases me from mine. It is a vile thing to want the weal and woe of millions to depend on the whim, perhaps even on the madness, of a single individual; and it is blasphemy to invoke the name of the Almighty in aid of this puppet-show. We have seen over there what that leads to: to blood and the axe. Away with this heresy fostered by fawning court-clerics; it is a human institution and these come and go. But our love of our homeland, that will endure as long as the land itself.'

Kniehase shook his head. 'It's not possible without the King,' he repeated. 'Your worship was born here and knows the Bruch and its peasants. But, by your leave, I know the peasants better. The King is everything to them. The King built the dikes for them, the King erected the churches for them, the King dug the ditches for them. Their fathers and grandfathers told them so, and they tell themselves so, too. Whenever I am sitting over in Scharwenka's, with Kallies and Kümmeritz and the other farmers, every other word is "Old Fritz". He is their god and they speak of him as if he were still living. Only one thing is closer to the heart of the peasant: his hearth and home.'

'It's just for the sake of his hearth and home that he ought now to take up arms. It would not be the first time in this country. When the Swede was dwelling beyond the Elbe in the Altmark the peasants rose in revolt without much hesitation: and that is what they ought to do again.'

'I know about that,' Kniehase replied; 'they were farmers and peasants of Drömling. But they had banners, and on them was written:

'We are poor peasants who live on the land
And serve our Lord Elector with our heart and our hand.'

Old Vitzewitz, who was happy in his mayor and in the determination with which he knew how to espouse his cause, gave him his hand and said: 'Let *us* have such a banner too, Kniehase, and let us hold it high. But if the King forbids to us this banner, then we shall have to bear it without his permission, and not in his name but in the name of our *country*. And this legal title is not the worst we could have: for our country is our native earth, which made us what we are.'

Kniehase again shook his head. 'Our native earth cannot give us such a title, your worship.'

'It can, Kniehase,' Berndt responded, 'our native earth can do it, *must* do it, because it is our be-all and end-all. And, in an earthly sense, our finest possession. We are earth, and we shall return to earth, and this it is that makes our native earth so precious to us. We all sense this from the very first, but a clear understanding of it can come to us only through experience. I *have* experienced it. You were there, Kniehase, when we bore the coffin up the hill; you know whose I mean. It was winter-time and the snow was falling. But when the snow melted, and the first crocus appeared in March, then I went to the earth up there that lay over my happiness and kissed it with my lips, and kissed it again and again. And since that day I have known what is meant by a precious and beloved native earth.'

As he experienced this recollection, Berndt passed a hand across his forehead and over his eyes. Kniehase knew well enough why he did so, but his was a nature easily abashed by such an event and he banished the knowledge from his mind and sat staring silently ahead.

'That was in the spring of *anno* seven,' old Vitzewitz resumed after a brief interval, 'but I was to learn that lesson even better. I still did not fully understand what is meant by one's native earth. It was at this same time, you remember it, Kniehase, when they hauled the treasurer of Kyritz,* who was as innocent as you or I, before one of their cowardly and corrupt courts-martial and condemned and shot him. Shot, did I say? It was a butchery. The execution of the sentence was as wretched as the sentence itself. The courageous and unfortunate man lay on the ground and could not die. Then a Westphalian, more feeling than the rest, ran forward and shot him in the heart: "From love of you, innocent creature, I shall help you to die," he said.'

Kniehase nodded. He recalled the affair, which at the time had filled all who knew of it with horror.

'From that day on, Kniehase, I never ceased to hear those five shots, and it was as though I felt them enter my own heart. I no longer slept, but I knew what would restore to me my peace of mind and I finally set out for Priegnitz. When I arrived at the little town I inquired and was shown the way. It was before one of the gates, an avenue of poplars and an empty field beside it. Then I sent away the child who had accompanied me there, and when I was alone I threw myself down on to the hill and tore a handful of earth from it and held it up to Heaven. And my heart was full of hate and full of love. Then I learned a *second time* what is meant by native earth, the earth of our homeland. There must be blood on it. And all around here the earth has been fertilized with blood; at Kunersdorf there is a spot they call the "Scarlet Field". And is all this to be given up because a King hasn't the strength to defend himself against feeble advisers? No, Kniehase: *with* the King as long as we can, *without* him if that is what it comes to.'

Berndt fell silent. At that moment there was a knock on the door, and Jeetze entered with a letter: large paper with a large seal. Berndt recognized Turgany's hand. He quickly scanned its contents and then read aloud: 'I request you, most respected Sir and Friend, to have a search conducted in your district, perhaps also in the woodland acre. All the signs are that the crew we are looking for are hiding somewhere between Hohen-Vietz and Manschnow. Today we have a second hearing, the Manschnow miller has been summoned as a witness. But it will only confirm the findings of the first, and our two traditional scapegoats will, as usual, have to be released again. I may communicate with you further during the next few days. Your Turgany.'

Berndt laughed. 'You see, Kniehase, cost of transport and legal process once more gone to waste. But Turgany is on the wrong track. They aren't anywhere around here. Where they actually are will appear in due course. Who brought the letter, Jeetze?'

'Konrektor Othegraven.'

'Is he still here?'

'Yes, Fräulein Renate invited him in. They are in the living-room with the other young lady.'

'Ask the Herr Konrektor if he will come and see me.'

Jeetze departed and the mayor made to follow him.

'No, Kniehase, you stay here: Othegraven's happy arrival promises me timely aid, and I don't intend to forgo it.'

No sooner had he said these words than the schoolmaster appeared, and Berndt received him warmly. After a few brief words of greeting had been exchanged, the lord of the manor of Hohen-Vietz went on: 'I am not going to burden you with commissions to Turgany, my dear Othegraven; the post goes to Frankfurt tomorrow in any case. But I want to assure myself of something while my old friend Kniehase is here. He intends to leave me in the lurch, he believes that we in this monarchical land of Prussia will never do anything unless it is authorized from above. Seidentopf agrees with him. Do you?'

'No, and thrice no,' Othegraven replied, 'and I am only too glad at last to be able to bear witness to that fact for once before a heart that feels as I do, instead of to deaf ears only.'

Kniehase, who knew how strictly orthodox the schoolmaster was, pricked up his ears; Othegraven himself, however, went on: 'It is a monarchical land, this land of Prussia, and if God wills it shall stay monarchical. It was created by great princes, and if they enjoyed the loyalty of the people, they were loyal to the people in return. A people will always follow where following is needful; there has never been a lack of joyful obedience in our own people. But to seek to exalt blind obedience to the status of a people's highest virtue is execrable. For us the highest thing is freedom and love.'

Berndt had been striding up and down the room; now he stopped before Othegraven: 'I knew it. Thus we are at one and I may count on you. This moment, which will never recur, must not be let slip. If those in the highest places are so deluded as not to want to use the weapon we forge, very well, then we shall wield it ourselves.'

'Then we shall wield it ourselves,' Othegraven repeated. 'But the breach which we fear shall *not* come to pass. A new day is coming, a better day. Impotence will give way to resolution, and the surest way to help bring that about is to show resolution ourselves. They doubt our capacities, and even mistrust our intentions, I know that well enough: so let us show the King that we are for him even when we are at variance with him. Schill and his men acted against his will, after all, and yet they died with the cry "Long live the King" on their lips. There is a kind of loyalty which is not wholly itself until it learns how to disobey.'

Kniehase stared into space. He felt the ground he stood on had been undermined, but he was not yet vanquished.

'I swore an oath', he said, 'and I did so with the intention of keeping it, not so as to violate or quibble about it. Authority is from God, kings come out of the hand of God, the strong and the weak, the good and the bad, and I must take them as they come.'

'Kings come out of the hand of God,' Berndt exclaimed, 'but so does much else. And if these things come into conflict, the decisive thing must always be one's own heart, an honest opinion and—the courage to die for them.'

'It is so, Mayor Kniehase,' Othegraven said, taking over from Berndt, '*and making up one's own mind is harder than obeying*. Harder, and often more loyal as well. Your lord of the manor is right. Look about you: the nations as a whole have given up, almost everywhere it is single individuals alone who dare to do their duty. Hofer,★ too, was a man like you, Kniehase, true as gold: but when his Emperor made peace he said: "Franz'l★ was compelled to, I'm *not*; I shall keep this old land of Tyrol for him." And when he spoke and acted like that he broke his Emperor's peace and brought misfortune upon friend and foe. He paid for that with his life. But do you believe, Kniehase, that when the Emperor hears the name Hofer he thinks of disloyalty and broken oaths? No, his heart beats higher, and blesses the land and prince who know themselves served by a living love that pays more heed to itself than to proclamations and commands.'

Kniehase had now risen. He offered Berndt his hand: 'Your worship, I believe the Konrektor has put his finger on it. Making up your own mind is harder than obeying. I *have* made up my mind. We shall prepare ourselves and we shall go into action without asking for a Yes or a No. For asking creates difficulties. None of them must get across the Oder. And if things turn out differently, and if these foreigners are going to trample us under foot for ever, then may God give us the strength to die as Hofer and Schill and his men died.'

'I have *you* to thank for this, Othegraven,' said Berndt; 'I could not have convinced the mayor by myself. I hope we shall henceforth see one another more often. The plan has been talked over with Count Drosselstein. A network over the entire country. Beginning with Lebus: we are the vanguard. The great highways come together here between Frankfurt and Küstrin. I count the hours to the moment of decision.'

They stayed for a while longer; then Kniehase and the schoolmaster departed; they descended the stairs and crossed the hallway, and Hector, exhibiting signs of unusual pleasure as he recognized the mayor, accompanied them across the courtyard.

They made their way towards Scharwenka's inn, still engaged in lively conversation: but what they were discussing seemed to be something remote from war and local militias, and it was only after they had measured the front of the inn together at least a dozen times that they finally bade one another farewell.

As the schoolmaster's little sleigh was again jogging southward on the road to Frankfurt the mayor was seated with his wife engaged in deep discussion. They talked together for a long time, and, although Frau Kniehase solemnly promised to keep it confidential, before the day was out what they had talked about was all over Hohen-Vietz.

Only one person knew nothing of it: she who had been the subject of that discussion.

14

Something Happens

St Jonathan's Day, 29 December, had from of old been the day of processions in Hohen-Vietz: there were masquerades of all kinds, and from the beginning of the afternoon not only St Nicholas and the Christ-child, but Joseph and Mary and the Three Magi too, went from house to house. To this ancient stock of characters, however, new figures were added from time to time, and this year they were 'Summer' and 'Winter', the former wearing a hat of straw and bearing a rake and scythe, the latter wearing furs and clogs and bearing a flail. They conducted a colloquy:

> I am *winter*, cold and proud:
> I build bridges without using wood—

and boasted of their antithetical merits, until their drawn-out contention finally ended in reconciliation and the pronouncement of good wishes for whatever house they happened to be in.

On this occasion the schoolchildren added greatly to the fun by passing through the village as 'Snow White and the Seven Dwarfs'—Snow White with long blonde hair, the dwarfs with flaxen beards and brown hoods. When they at length arrived at the manor house they found the young people together with Aunt Schorlemmer assembled in the same great hall in which the Christmas celebrations had taken place; and after a short speech, in which Snow White asked permission for her attendants to propound their riddles, the dwarfs stepped forward and did so.

'What is it no one can say?'

That he is dead.

'Who can speak every language?'

The echo.

'Who is cleverer, the rich man or the poor man?'

The poor man: for he has need, and need is the mother of invention.

So went the questions, but the answers here provided were not forthcoming, and Maline Kubalke, who was with them in the hall, had to fetch several platefuls of apples and nuts to fill the dwarfs' little sacks.

So passed the afternoon. As darkness fell it grew still in Hohen-Vietz, because everyone, young and old, was getting ready for the dance and social evening to be held in Scharwenka's inn; and it was not until six o'clock, when a cracking of whips and jingling of bells heralded the arrival of the carriages and sleighs from the outlying farmsteads, some of which lay far off in the Bruch, that the silence in the village was again broken.

At the manor house, too, everyone, family and servants alike, was preparing to go out, and half an hour after the dance had started anyone regarding the long front of the Vitzewitz home from the village street would have seen lights at only two windows. These two windows stood beside the Administrative Office and drew attention to themselves, not merely through being the only ones illuminated, but more especially on account of the dark vine-branches which, extending out from the trellis, traced two or three fantastically shaped lines across the oblong of light. Behind these windows, at a sofatable covered with a piece of red baize, sat Renate and Kathinka, together with Marie, who had joined them fifteen minutes previously for an evening's gossip. It was a joy to all three, not excluding even Kathinka, to know themselves alone for once, and to enhance this pleasure they had removed themselves from the big reception-room on the ground floor to this much smaller one on the first.

Aunt Schorlemmer was absent. Contrary to her usual habits she had gone out and was sitting chatting at the parsonage; while old Vitzewitz, supported alternately by the mayor and by Lewin and Tubal, was holding forth at the inn. The farmers he was addressing showed themselves amenable to everything he said: it seemed to be the right kind of evening for striking the iron while it was hot.

The gossip our three young ladies were meanwhile engaged in was, as might be imagined, very different from the political talk at the inn: Renate was being especially lively, Marie, on the other hand, distinctly reserved—notwithstanding the warmth with which, on this as on previous occasions, Kathinka had approached her, she had a definite feeling that it would become her to assert as little as possible the sisterly intimate relationship she enjoyed with Renate, and to participate in the cousins' conversation only when occasion demanded and preferably only when directly asked to. Listening to this conversation was itself sufficient enjoyment for her, and her enjoyment increased by the minute when Kathinka—who, half sitting, half lying, was now resting her right foot on the sofa cushions—began to talk about social life in Berlin and, at length, of a grand *soirée* held by old Prince Ferdinand.

'Isn't he the father of Prince Louis, who fell at Saalfeld?' Renate asked. 'What wouldn't I give', she went on after her question had been answered in the affirmative, 'to attend such a *soirée*! Papa promised me we should do so this winter, but, times being what they are, it doesn't look as if we shall.'

'You are missing less than you think. They are composed of the same people as you can see anywhere: generals, counts, magistrates, just as though you were at Ziebingen or Guse. The dresses have somewhat longer trains, and there are a couple of hundred more candles burning: that is all.'

'But the prince will not have surrounded himself with Krachs and Bammes, will he?'

'Not exclusively: but he cannot avoid them altogether. He has no choice: birth and position are what count, not personalities. You regard the select company at Schloss Guse with so little respect because you know them; but you have only to satisfy your curiosity and vanity for a single winter and the charm of this society at court would vanish for ever.'

'I doubt that is so, though I believe you yourself cannot say otherwise. For you make demands that I know nothing of. I, for my part, would be content to be allowed just to take a glance into this world where everybody is somebody. Take the old prince himself: he is the brother of Friedrich the Great; that alone is enough to make him estimable in my eyes; I could not look at him without awe. He would perhaps ignore me, or direct at me words of absolutely no consequence, but for me it would not be a matter of no consequence to have seen or spoken to him.'

Kathinka smiled.

'You laugh at me,' Renate went on, 'but reflect that I live the life of a poor country girl, lonely and empty, and instead of a mother I have only our good Schorlemmer. Give me your hand, Marie; you are a great joy and comfort to me, but you are no substitute for a ball at court. What a glittering sight it must be! And then the King himself. Tell me a couple of names, Kathinka, so that I can try to picture it all.'

'Oh, there is old Count Reale, the chief lady-in-waiting's

husband, who paid a visit to Guse two years ago, and the court marshal, von Massow, of Steinhöfel, and Herr von Eckardt-stein of Prötzel, and Herr von Burgsdorff of Ziebingen, and Count Drosselstein of Hohen-Ziesar.'

'But I know all those already.'

'That is why I named them.'

'And foreign ambassadors!' said Renate, ignoring the brief pause that followed Kathinka's last remark. 'How I would like to see Count de St Marsan, and the minister, Hardenberg, whom Papa is always reproaching and finding fault with. I think he must be a very nice man. *Apropos*! Has your Count Bninski, excuse me for calling him that, also been presented at court?'

'No. He declined the honour.'

'Ah, now I know why court society finds so little favour with you. Lewin has described him to me, but I would like to hear how you see him.'

'Think of him as the opposite of the schoolmaster to whom I had the pleasure of being introduced this morning. I've forgot-ten his name.'

'Othegraven!'

'That's right, Othegraven. A fine name, originally aristocratic. But what a bourgeois decline, what a pedantic appearance! He holds himself straight, but it is the straightness of a ruler.'

'You have to judge him in the light of what he is.'

'In that case he must be adjudged perfect: for he is a perfect image of a schoolmaster.'

'I can see well enough how right Aunt Amelie was when she recently said of you: Kathinka is a Pole. Only we Germans—as Pastor Seidentopf had occasion to remind me only yesterday —know how to see through the outward forms. Don't you think so too?'

'No, little fool, I don't think so too: all that is German is self-flattery with vanities of that sort. However, I don't intend to go on about that, or about the calumnies that have for so long been heaped on the heads of us Poles. Only there are two things you will have to allow we possess: passion and imagination. And now admit, my treasure, that if there is anything in the world capable of seeing through outward forms it is *these* two things. The count is a handsome man, but I assure you he would be just the same to me even if he looked like this Othegraven's twin brother. For this perfect similarity would cease as soon as you looked beneath the surface, because beneath the surface he is completely different.'

'Different, yes. But better?'

'Different suffices. There are prosaic virtues and poetic virtues: let us not dispute their relative merits. All I want to convince you of is that it is not outward form and appearance—though I certainly do not underestimate them —that make me esteem the count.'

'So what is it, then?'

'For instance, his loyalty. For, incredible though it may sound, Poles too are capable of loyalty.'

'Indeed, though it is not the quality they are most noted for.'

'Then he who has it is the more adorned by it. And I would number Bninski among them. When, in the last encounter that decided the fate of Poland, Kosciuszko* lay unconscious from loss of blood at the edge of a grove of fir-trees that he had defended for three hours against superior forces, an ensign, still hardly more than a boy, stood beside him and defended him with his young life. He could have saved himself but scorned to do so. At last overcome, he asked only one thing: to be allowed to tend his general and share the same cell with him. This ensign was the count.'

Marie, who until that moment had not looked up from her needlework, gazed at Kathinka with her big eyes.

Returning her gaze in friendly fashion, Kathinka went on: 'That, Renate, was loyalty; not of the kind that you are fond of, which would like to make every secret kiss a binding chain for all eternity, but a kind of loyalty none the less, and not the worst kind. And as the ensign was then, so he is now. He fought in Spain. The Polish regiment of lancers he led—Tubal told me of it—captured a defile; I've forgotten its name; but they say it was an event unique in the history of warfare. The count was one of the few who survived that day. Sent back to Paris severely wounded, he received from the Emperor's hand the red sash of the Legion of Honour. And I may say it becomes him . . . No, Renate, you misjudge me, and yourself no less. We feel the same. We are enraptured by everything poetical, and stiffness and pedantry, even if they are called Othegraven, leave us cold. That isn't Polish, it is feminine. Ask Marie.'

'I shan't ask her,' laughed Renate, 'for you must know—'

'Then I shall answer without being asked,' Marie interrupted her unaffectedly. 'All the world esteems the schoolmaster, our parson loves him—'

'But *you*, could *you* love him?'

'No, never: not even if he had defended Kosciuszko or stormed a defile. He has courage, perhaps, but I cannot imagine him as a hero. I am sorry if I am doing him an injustice. If I am to love someone, he will have to engage my imagination: he, however, doesn't engage me in any way.'

'But you engage *him* all the more. Our old Seidentopf whispered to me yesterday: Othegraven has secrets.—But it is already striking nine, and in our chatter we are forgetting our supper.'

With that Renate rose and walked to a rococo chest of drawers, upon whose mother-of-pearl top Maline had before she left the house set a large tray of cold cuts of meat, with cutlery and plates to go with them.

The sofa and the chest of drawers stood against the same wall, and between them there was only the space formerly occupied by a door leading from this spare room to the Administrative Office: as it had been walled in only with half-bricks, the place where the door had stood formed a shallow niche that was clearly visible.

Kathinka removed the lamp and, without interrupting her flow of chatter, Renate was in the act of placing the tray, which after the custom of the time stood in a wooden holder, on to the table when she heard something clatter.

She looked at the other two girls. 'Did you hear nothing?'

'No.'

'I heard something clatter.'

'You must have knocked the tray against the plates.'

'No, it wasn't in here, it was next door.'

With that she placed her ear against the wall at the spot where the door had formerly been.

'All you're doing is frightening us,' said Kathinka: but before she had finished speaking all three clearly heard the sound of a window being opened in the neighbouring room, followed at once by that of someone leaping down and then of footsteps moving cautiously across the floor—though perhaps they were cautious only because it was dark. They seemed to hear two people in there: and there was no one else besides themselves in the whole house; there was no possibility of their being assisted, they were quite alone. Marie flew to the door and locked it; without being able to account to herself why, Kathinka lowered the lamp: only a faint glimmer of light was left in the room.

Renate again placed her ear against the wall. After a while she clearly heard a sharp, metallic sound such as is produced by striking flint against steel; she continued to listen, and by the time the sound finally ceased her imagination had been so greatly aroused she believed she could follow everything that was going on in the next room as though gifted with clair-voyance. She saw the spunk begin to glow, the sulphur-match to blaze, and the two house-breakers, after having searched around the desk, ignite the wax candle with which her father was accustomed to seal his letters. It was all fantasy; but when she turned her head for a moment she saw a real light, a bright beam falling from the neighbouring room on to the snow-roof of the ancient dwelling-house lying opposite and reflected from there back over the dark courtyard.

The girls said nothing: they had the vague idea that if they kept quiet it would lessen the danger they were in. They took one another by the hand and gazed out towards the driveway and, so far as they could, to the village street, for it was from there alone that help could come.

In the meantime there had been further signs of activity next door. It became apparent that the raiders had no fear of detection. As though deliberately disdaining caution, they threw a bunch of keys noisily on to the floor and set to work on the big chest standing beside the door in which money and documents were kept. They tried all the keys one by one, but the ancient padlock withstood all their efforts.

A curse was now heard: the first audible word. Then they

sprang up again—presumably they had hitherto been kneeling at the chest for greater comfort—and, if the noise they made told a true tale, began to rummage among the book-shelves standing against the dividing wall. They tore out whole rows of books, and, when they failed to find what they were looking for, swept the ledge clean with a single sweep of the arm, so that everything standing on it—Chinese vase, busts, dragoons' helmets—fell to the floor with a loud crash. Their rage seemed to grow with the unsuccess of their search, and they could now be heard shaking at the ancient door that led out into the corridor. Suppose it should give way!

The girls trembled like aspen leaves: but the heavy door-lock withstood the assault as the padlock had done before it.

The danger seemed to be past: there again came the sound of cautious steps, as though they were retreating in the dark back to the window, then all was still.

Renate breathed a sigh of relief and stepped across to the table to raise the lamp again; but she at once started back: she had clearly seen a head craning out from the side of the window and staring into the room.

Incapable of speech, and remaining upright only because she was holding on to the back of the sofa, she pointed to the window: a whole figure was now silhouetted in it, clinging to the vine-branch with its left hand while its glove-encased right hand smashed the window-pane and groped for the window-bolt so as to open the window from within.

All three girls screamed aloud and rushed away in different directions; Kathinka, all her normal resolution gone, clasped her hands together and tried to pray; Renate tugged at the bell-rope, even though she was well aware there was no one in the house to hear the bell; while Marie, seized by an extremity of fear, rushed into the danger and, not knowing what she did, raised her fist to strike at the man standing outside. But before the blow could land the laths of the trellis cracked and broke, and the dark figure plunged down on to the snow of the courtyard below.

None of the girls dared to go to the window and look out, but they could now clearly hear the sound of the downstairs bell which Renate was continuing to ring, and immediately afterwards the baying of a dog. Hector, it was plain, had preferred his warm rush-mat beside the hearth-wall to the pleasures of the dance at the inn and, although no one knew it, had been guarding the house. Now he was standing below in the hallway uncertain what the ringing meant, and his barking and whimpering seemed to be asking: what now? But he had not long to wait for an answer: opening the door, Renate called down the corridor in a loud voice: 'Hector!' and before the echo of the cry had died away she heard the faithful animal bounding up the stairs with mighty strides; a moment later his feet were resting on his young mistress's shoulders. All the fear she had felt now fell away; she seized the dog by the collar and, keeping hold on it for support, fled with him down the stairs and across the courtyard. Just as she was about to turn out of the driveway into the village street her father was suddenly standing before her.

'Thank God, Papa—burglars—come!'

A moment later Vitzewitz was in the first-floor room, where Kathinka threw herself weeping about his neck and Marie, her lips still trembling, covered his hands with kisses.

15

The Search

THE following morning saw the family and their guests assembled as usual in the corner room on the ground floor. Only Renate was missing: she had a fever, and a messenger was already on his way to fetch old Dr Leist from Lebus. Conversation naturally revolved around the events of the previous evening, and Kathinka, who was indulging herself in an exaggerated account of the anguish she had endured, sought to conceal a feeling of injured vanity she was unable to shake off behind a pretence of self-mockery; she thereby fell into a half-jocular tone which appeared, however, not to appeal to old Vitzewitz at all. He, for his part, shook his head and grew increasingly stern and serious.

From the details of the conversation it emerged that, so as

not to disturb the dance at the inn, Berndt had forbidden any raising of the alarm and even postponed inspection of the plundered room, and had contented himself with having the grounds and the park patrolled by a sentry-guard composed of Krist the coachman and Pachaly the nightwatchman. Jeetze, who had also volunteered, was, on account of his age and decrepitude and with the assurance that his willingness of spirit had been noted and recognized, sent off to bed.

It was striking nine as our friend Kniehase, who was expected, came across the courtyard from the direction of the driveway. Tubal and Lewin, who were standing at the window, saw and waved to him. Immediately afterwards, Jeetze announced: 'Herr Kniehase, the mayor.'

'Let him enter.'

Berndt went to meet him, gave him his hand, and pushed a chair to the table.

'Take a seat, Kniehase. What we have to say is brief and no secret. Stay, Kathinka! It has all happened quicker than I expected but, whether we are ready or not, we dare not delay. There is not a moment to be lost, we have to know whom we are dealing with. Our own villains would not have attacked Hoppenmarieken. I stick to the view they are foreigners: marauders from the frontier.'

Kniehase shook his head.

'Very well, I know you think otherwise. We shall see who is right, you or I. How many people can we count on? If we have ten or twelve, we shall move: today, at once.'

'We can make up ten, if your worship will include yourself and the young gentlemen here. I have sent the nightwatchman, Pachaly, out to the outlying farms, to Schwartz and Metzke, and to Dames as well; they are the youngest. But he cannot get back before midday: so we shall have to take those we can find here in the village.'

'And they are?'

'Not many.'

'Kümmritz?'

'He can't, he's got the colic again.'

'The miller, Miekley?'

'He refuses. He has heard something about rebelling and

waging war without the King that has disconcerted him: "All they that take the sword shall perish with the sword." We shall have to get at them through Uhlenhorst, he has the Old Lutherans in his pocket.'

'And Kallies?'

'He is willing, but I know Creampot, he is all nerves and cannot stand the sight of blood.'

'Well, Krull and Reetzke, then?'

'Yes, they'll come, and Dobbert and Roloff as well: that's four good men. And then the two Scharwenkas, the old one and the young one, and also Hanne Bogun, the Scharwenkas' young cow-herd.'

'The cow-herd?' questioned Lewin; 'but he has only one arm.'

'But eyes like a hawk, young sir, and these we shall need. And he can climb.'

'Very good, Kniehase, that makes us ten. It will have to do for a first search; and now, before the rest come, let us inspect the office, perhaps we shall find something that will give us a clue.'

They went up to the first floor; Kathinka, too, went with them, walking beside the mayor and chattering away to him how his foster-daughter had been the bravest of them and also the instigator of their rescue.

Thus, old Vitzewitz always a couple of paces to the fore, they arrived at the door of the office, which they now opened with a certain sense of foreboding that would in the next few moments prove only too justified. A scene of limitless devastation met their gaze: books and debris lay scattered together, the room was covered with spots of wax fallen from the candle, and the top of the big desk was scarred with a burn mark caused by the sulphur-match which the raiders had thrown heedlessly aside; a paring-chisel still lay beside the chest, and on the window-sill there lay a heavy, half-torn glove.

These objects, even when passed from hand to hand and examined, were not calculated to supply any definite evidence as to their owners, and so it was in a certain sense disappointed that they all returned to the ground floor, where they discovered the farmers now assembled, together with the young

Scharwenka and Hanne Bogun, the cow-herd. It was decided that the first thing to be done was to search the courtyard, or at least that part of it from where the break-in had taken place. There they found the ladder still standing which the burglars had dragged from the farmyard and used to gain entry: Lewin climbed up it and examined the exterior window-sill, while Tubal and the young Scharwenka inspected the snow on the ground beneath it; but even the numerous footprints which ran from the gables of the house across to the avenue leading to the park and then into the park itself proved valueless, since in the end they could not decide whether they were made by the burglars or by Krist and Pachaly.

'Very well,' said Berndt, 'let us give this up, and see whether we can find anything on the road to Gorgast and Manschnow.'

Jeetze fetched the guns, and the squad was about to march out into the village street when they heard a whistle from behind them and, turning, saw the Scharwenkas' cow-herd gesturing agitatedly at them with the empty sleeve of his jacket: he had stayed behind when they moved off, had shifted the ladder from the office window to the window of the neighbouring room, and had continued the search on his own account; and from the signs he was now making it was apparent that he had discovered something.

The men retraced their steps, and when they had drawn close to him Hanne Bogun held out towards them a brass button.

'Where was it lying?' old Vitzewitz asked in lively excitement.

Without replying the cow-herd ran up the ladder again and laid the button back on the spot from where he had taken it. It was the transom running close beneath the window, so there could be hardly any doubt that when the lower part of the trellis had given way the sharp edge of the higher laths had ripped off the button. It belonged to a French uniform: in the middle there stood an N, while the inside rim bore the inscription: *14e Rég. de ligne*.

Berndt was exultant: the find seemed to confirm his suspicions, and the farmers now assented to them. Only Kniehase continued to shake his head; but it did not come to any further argument, and after the button had been handed round they all set off again, the cow-herd bringing up the rear bearing two game-bags.

They first took to the highway in the direction of Küstrin. When they had arrived at the spot where two days previously Hoppenmarieken had been attacked and almost choked, they turned right and made for the grove of trees from which Tubal and Lewin had begun their chase across the snowy ploughed field: the peasants, however, knew their terrain better and employed a firm-trodden footpath which led to the middle of the wood.

Once there, they took counsel together as to whether the wood should be searched. The elder Scharwenka, who had slept in nothing but a feather-bed for twenty-five years, considered it impossible for anyone to spend the night outdoors in twelve degrees below freezing and hope to get some assistance from a blanket of snowflakes; Kniehase, however, was of a different opinion and, going by his campaigning experience, argued that there was nothing warmer than a hut of snow inlaid with straw. In the light of this testimony a search was decided on; but they reached the other side of the wood without having discovered anything whatever: no disturbance of the snow, no broken twigs, no signs of a fire.

They now had to resolve whether they wanted to confine themselves to the terrain between Gorgast, Manschnow and Rathstock lying on their own side of the river, or whether to cross over to the other bank as well and scour the whole stretch from the pulp-mills at Küstrin to the duck-snares and from the duck-snares to Kirch-Göritz. They decided on the latter course, so that their route would be essentially the same as that traversed by Tubal and Lewin when they paid their visit to Dr Faulstich. Having settled this point, they then agreed that the most suitable thing would be for them to divide their numbers into two squads, one to march off to the left, the other to the right, a procedure which—if nothing went amiss and if they wheeled about correctly at the predetermined spot—would lead to a midday rendezvous in the neighbourhood of the Neu-Manschnow farm. Kniehase led one of the squads, Berndt the other: the latter included, in addition to Tubal and Lewin, the younger Scharwenka and the cow-herd, Hanne Bogun.

Berndt's squad went to the right. To obtain a wide view of the ground they deserted the footpath that wound along the incline and ascended to the top. The weather was fine but not sunny, so that there was no glitter to disturb the view. Berndt and Tubal were fifty paces ahead and were soon sunk in a conversation that more than once distracted even the former's attention from what he was supposed to be observing. Tubal told of his childhood years, of his mother living in Paris, of Kathinka, and freely poured out his heart about the restless and contradictory life he had led from his youth onwards.

'I have no right to criticize the motives that may have moved my father to emigrate, but this step he took has certainly brought us no benefit. Our name is Polish, and so is our past, and so is most of our property, so far as we have managed to save it from confiscation. And now we are Prussians! Our father is one with a kind of fanaticism, Kathinka somewhat unwillingly, I willingly enough, but all of us out of considerations of interest rather than from love and a sense of affinity. And just as we do not really have a fatherland, so we do not really have a house, a family, either. And that is the worst thing about it. We lack a centre of gravity. Kathinka and I grew up but were not brought up: what education we enjoyed was an education for social life. And so our days are gay but not happy, we amuse ourselves, we have partial satisfactions but never complete ones, and certainly there is no peace in our hearts.'

Vitzewitz had not missed a word. Hitherto he had known the life of the Ladalinskis only in the broadest outline, and the respect the father enjoyed in individual princely circles, the means he possessed, which notwithstanding his removal were still ample, but above all the complete absence of narrow-minded exclusiveness which distinguished every member of the family equally, had always made an alliance with them seem to him something highly desirable. Now, though he listened to Tubal's confessions with the liveliest sympathy, for the first time there crept over him a doubt as to whether it would after all be advisable to link the destiny of his two children with that of this family.

Lewin and young Scharwenka were also engaged in lively conversation. They were of the same age and, yielding to the wishes of his old playfellow, Lewin was still addressing him with the familiar '*Du*' they had formerly employed. Hanne Bogun walked behind them whistling and entertaining himself with imitating bird-calls.

'How are things with Maline?' asked Lewin.

'In a bad way or all over with: she has given me the push.'

'I heard about it. But you are supposed to have offended her by reproaching her with being poor.'

'That comes from Fräulein Renate, who believes everything Maline tells her. But you see, young sir, that is the rottenest thing about her: she doesn't tell the truth and she spreads all kinds of stories about me. And I only put up with it because you can't know how it will end. And then since she may perhaps become my wife after all I don't want her to become the talk of the village first.'

'But you must have hurt her in some way, or said something to her that she could take amiss.'

'Yes, because she takes everything amiss. In the letter breaking it off she said we Scharwenkas were "full of peasant pride"; but, young sir, if we are full of peasant pride, then the Kubalkes are full of sexton's pride. Her father, old Kubalke, has the key to the church, and some Sundays, when the parson can't do it, he also reads the Gospel to us. And he can also make epitaphs and verses for weddings and christenings. All that makes them much better than peasants; that at least is what they believe, as firmly as if it too were as true as the Gospel. And that little Eve over in Guse, she is the worst, for the good countess spoils her more every day.'

'But Maline?'

'Maline, yes! She isn't as bad as that Eve, but she is just as vain and stuck up. And since St Martin's, when the old Justizrat was here and told her Maline was a Wendish word and meant raspberry, and that she wasn't merely called one, she *was* one, since that day there has been no getting on with her at all. And how did that happen? And how am I supposed to have offended her? She told me to fetch her her large check shawl, and when I had fetched it for her she wanted me to put it on her, so I told her: "You aren't a princess, Maline, you're a poor school-master's daughter." And now she tells stories about me and complains to people that I reproached her for being poor! And what happened really? I reproached her for being stuck up, that's what really happened. But twisting words and decking out lies to look like the truth, she knows how to do that all right. And if I weren't so fond of her—for the old Justizrat was quite right in what he said—it would have been all over between us long ago. And now it really is finished; but I can't help thinking it ought to start up again.'

Involved as they were in this and similar converse—which had occupied all the attention of the communicative innkeeper's son and most of Lewin's, who had confined himself mainly to asking questions—neither of the young men had noticed that the whistling behind them had stopped. When they chanced to turn round they saw that Hanne Bogun had halted some way back and, having dropped the game-bags from his shoulder, was in the act of climbing a pine-tree divided towards the top into two branches set wide apart. They had reached the highest point of the whole region, and it was quite clear that his intention was to obtain from here a view of the land roundabout; but all speculation as to what he did or did not intend was submerged in the spectacle of the climbing skill exhibited by the one-armed boy: grasping the slender trunk firmly with his stump, as though he felt the absence of his arm not at all, and employing the remnants of broken-off branches as though they were the steps of a ladder, he had reached the top even before the two youths had covered the distance back to the tree.

'What is it, Hanne?'

From the fork in which he was now standing he gestured with his hand, as though he wished not to be disturbed, and looked first up and down the river-bank, then also across the river to the Neumark. He appeared to discover nothing, however, and after once more surveying the entire circle he slid down again as easily as he had climbed up five minutes before.

As the two young men strode quickly on, he now kept level with them and to the brief questions Lewin from time to time directed at him he gave even briefer replies.

'Well, Hanne, what do you think, are we going to find them?'

The boy shook his head in a way that could have been interpreted as affirmation or denial.

'I don't understand how it is the Gorgasters and Manschnowers haven't spotted them: there's nowhere to hide, hardly a scrap of woodland; and there's all this snow about, too. I think they must have accomplices: otherwise we would be bound to have had some information about them by now.'

'One of them may well know all about it,' said the boy.

'Yes, but who is "one of them"?'

The boy smiled and, starting to whistle again, began imitating a bird-call: perhaps merely by chance, but perhaps intending to offer a clue.

'You give the impression of knowing something, Hanne. Whom are you thinking of?'

Hanne was silent.

'You won't lose by it. Will he, Scharwenka? We'll buy him a felt-cap, and hang a shining groschen from the tassel! Well, Hanne, who is "one of them"?'

Hanne walked placidly on, looking neither to left nor right, and said as though to himself: 'Hoppenmarieken.'

Lewin laughed. 'Naturally, Hoppenmarieken is bound to know everything. What her cards don't divulge to her, her birds do; and what her birds don't know, her magic mirror does. But the rogues who would have strangled her won't have divulged their hideout to her.'

But the boy did not allow himself to be disconcerted by this assertion, and only repeated in a categorical tone: 'She knows all about it.'

While they were talking they had reached the point at which, in accordance with the arrangement made back at the grove, they had to desert the footpath running along the height, descend the lefthand incline and cross over the river. Already they could see the tower at Kirch-Göritz glittering on the far side, but it was still a good two hundred yards away to the right, which made it clear to Lewin that the pine-tree-lined path at their feet was not the same path he and Tubal had passed along the day before yesterday, but a parallel path probably leading to the ferry at Rathstock.

Berndt and Tubal were already halfway across by the time

Lewin turned into the path over the ice. He had fallen silent but his mind was all the more occupied with Hoppenmarieken. What he had said against the idea that she was the raiders' accomplice now seemed to him untenable: that thieves should fall out among themselves was, after all, not unheard-of, and if a slight feeling that the thing was improbable remained it vanished before the certitude with which Hanne Bogun had pronounced his 'she knows all about it.' He was, Lewin told himself, probably only too justified: for who within the boundaries of Hohen-Vietz had a better opportunity of following Hoppenmarieken on her secret paths, or even of observing her activities on the highway, her encounters and whispered plottings, than Hanne Bogun had, who watched over the Scharwenkas' cattle all summer long and slept in a dried-out ditch or hidden among the tall corn.

Sunk in such reflections Lewin had reached the middle of the river; Berndt and Tubal had already attained the opposite side and were clambering up the steep bank. Young Scharwenka was walking to Lewin's left, both silent as before and paying no heed to Hanne, who had again fallen a couple of paces behind them.

But at that moment he came slithering forward over the ice and, having reached the side of the young Scharwenka, tugged at his coat; then, gesturing to the left with his empty sleeve, he said: 'Look there!'

The innkeeper's son halted, Lewin did likewise, and both stared out in the direction Hanne had indicated.

'I can see nothing,' Scharwenka exclaimed, and made to move off again.

But Hanne kept a tight hold of him and said: 'Wait a bit, straight ahead, among the poplars; now.'

He had seen aright: between two of the poplar-trees that seemed to be standing in the midst of the ice a thin whisp of smoke was curling up. Now it vanished: but the next moment it was back again.

'Now we have them! Where there is smoke there is fire. Forward!'

With that the two young men turned out of the path on to the wide highway that ran down the middle of the river and was made firm for sleighs and carriages; while Hanne was sent off to report on the situation to Berndt and Tubal and to invite them to turn back.

Lewin and young Scharwenka at first made their way slowly, with frequent pauses; but after they had observed Hanne overtake the others on the far bank and make his report to them they hurried on again quickly. Soon they discovered that what they had taken to be a neck of land jutting out into the river and occupied by two tall poplars was in fact one of those little reed-islands so often encountered in the Oder. The enclosing reeds, though here and there crushed down by the weight of the snow, were clearly visible; but they effectively concealed anything that might be lying behind them.

They now abandoned the broad highway as well, and through the snow lying heaped a foot high to the side of it groped their way towards the island. As they drew close they lost sight first of the curls of smoke, then of the two poplars, and a moment later they stood before the girdle of reeds itself. Lewin wanted to make his way through by force but was soon convinced that this was impossible. It was also superfluous, for Scharwenka had by then discovered a passage as broad as a man which someone had cut through the reeds with a sickle; he beckoned to Lewin, and the two then passed forward—it was not without difficulty, as the wind had blown countless stalks into the passageway, which had at many places become blocked with them. At last, however, they were through the girdle of reeds—which was some fifteen paces thick—and, employing the few that still remained in front of them as a kind of screen, from this secure position now looked out upon the interior of the island.

The scene that presented itself to them was a sufficiently startling one: they were gazing into what looked like a well-maintained farmyard. Everything exhibited a certain cleanliness and order: the snow had been swept away to either side; a cow tethered by the left foreleg to one of the poplars was nibbling at a bundle of hay fastened together with bands of straw; while close beside the other tree there stood a heavily loaded sleigh whose sail-canvas, tied round with cord, might be thought to conceal the proceeds of the latest raid.

This was the courtyard, and the sense of peace it exuded was exceeded only by that of the wooden shed that served as a dwelling-house. This shed, so amply clad in snow on both sides that it seemed almost to have been carved out of a snow-mountain, appeared to consist of three rooms of differing sizes. The two small rooms, which served as stable and kitchen, were open, while the third, larger room was closed up with two old planks and a brand-new door whose latch, hinge attachments and covering of red oil-paint placed its origin in Gorgast or Manschnow beyond doubt. Before the brick hearth, on which a frugal fire of twigs was burning, there stood a woman, still youthful, occupied with skimming and moving pots about, and now and then addressing a blond-headed child who was sitting on a corn-sack near the threshold. A stove-pipe extending a foot above the snow-roof served to carry away the smoke. In the open stable a horse stood and rattled its iron chain.

'That's Kriele the miller's bay,' said Scharwenka.

Having completed this reconnaissance, the two men retreated back to the outer edge of the reeds to keep a look-out for the arrival of their reinforcements. They had not long to wait. Berndt and Tubal, with the boy bringing up the rear, were already close at hand; and very soon all five were making their way along the narrow passage back to the place from where Lewin and Tubal had observed the island. A whispered council-of-war was held and they came to an agreement that Tubal and Hanne Bogun should rush upon the woman, while the two Vitzewitzes, backed by the innkeeper's son, should force their way into the room with the two planks and the red door. It seemed highly likely that, deprived of sleep through their nocturnal expedition, the villains were now reposing in this room; if this supposition proved erroneous, however, they would at least have the woman, with whose assistance it would surely not be difficult to capture these birds if they had flown.

'One, two, three!' they leaped across the farmyard and the next moment the woman screamed aloud, while Berndt and Scharwenka, followed by Lewin (who had had no difficulty in breaking down the door), pressed into the room, which was full of smoke and reeked of brandy. The daylight flooding in quickly revealed the state of things. To left and right against the walls there stood two fir bedsteads which, like the red-painted door outside, might once have seen better days; now they were loaded with straw paillasses on and under which two men, fully clad and wearing satiated rather than savage expressions, were lying fast asleep.

'Had enough sleep?' thundered Berndt, and jammed the butt of his gun against the chest of the man lying beside the right wall.

Still half asleep, the man thus addressed passed a hand across his brow, then stared up at Vitzewitz with an expression which fear and cunning twisted into a grimace; the latter, when he observed the excellent effect produced by the surprise attack, slung his gun quietly back over his shoulder and told the two villains: 'Get ready to move!'

In an instant they were on their feet; both were in their forties and of medium height. One was, after the custom of the country, dressed in a thick woollen labourer's jacket, the other in a French soldier's coat, and both were wearing wooden clogs out of which protruded long stalks of straw: there was neither time nor opportunity to improve on this garb. On a chest that served as a table there stood a low-smouldering lamp; beside it, two convex bottles of green glass, a shako and a felt cap: they put on the caps, slid the bottles, which may still have contained something, into their pockets, and then stationed themselves in a kind of military posture, as though to indicate they were ready to march off. Berndt gestured with his hand: 'Forward!'

Outside, the man clad in the soldier's coat made his way to the side of young Scharwenka and asked in a half-confidential tone: 'Where are we going?'

'To the gallows!' Scharwenka replied.

The rogue grinned: 'No, Scharwenka my lad, it isn't going to come to that.'

'You know me?'

'How should I not know you? Aren't I Muschwitz from Grossen-Klessin?'

'I see; and the other one?'

'Rosentreter from Podelzig.'

Scharwenka tossed his head, as though to say: 'He looks like it.' Then they crossed the yard to the narrow passage that led through the reeds.

Half an hour later the little column had reached the place of rendezvous, the outlying farm at Neu-Manschnow. The Knie-hase squad had had no occasion to stop and was there already. After everything had been told that needed to be told, Krull and Reetzke offered to assume responsibility for the transportation of the prisoners to Frankfurt: an escort of two was deemed sufficient, since Muschwitz and Rosentreter both seemed glad to be able to exchange their winter-hut for more restricted but more comfortable quarters. The woman, in regard to whom doubt reigned as to which of the two men she belonged to, followed dumbly, pulling behind her a little sleigh-box into which she had placed the child.

The Hohen-Vietz troop set off on their return journey at the same time as the prisoners were marched away. They travelled through Manschnow, where, passing the mill, they informed the old miller, Kriele, in what stable his bay was residing; at the mayor's office, however, they left instructions that the Manschnowers, to whose preserve the island belonged, were to conduct a thorough search and excavation of the shed there and to consign to Frankfurt any stolen goods they might discover.

16

Of Kaiarnak, the Greenlander

BY two o'clock our Hohen-Vietzers were back in their village, and half an hour later everyone even out as far as the last outlying farms knew that the villains had been found and were on their way to Frankfurt. At the inn, where several farmers, Kallies and Kümmeritz among them, were soon assembled, they recalled Muschwitz very well: he had always been a good-for-nothing idler, and they indulged in speculation as to how he could have acquired the French soldier's coat—speculation which started with murder and travelled, via petty larceny, to simple barter or purchase. This last was the most probable: in

Küstrin, where every day the ranks of the garrison—French but also Hessian and Westphalian troops—were thinned by typhus, there was ample opportunity for such 'backstairs trading'. Of Rosentreter no one knew anything. Praise for the young cow-herd was universal.

In the manor house, too, there was no end to the telling of what had happened. Kathinka and Aunt Schorlemmer wanted to know every last detail, and when there was nothing left to report in the living-room downstairs the relation was continued upstairs in Renate's sickroom. Lewin sat on her bed for an hour and brought it all vividly before her eyes in chronological order, from the searching of the grove to the surprise attack to the prisoners being marched away. Nothing was omitted: in recounting his conversation with young Scharwenka he was careful to emphasize that Maline had been in the wrong, he lauded Hanne Bogun's skilful circumspection, and concluded by describing the impression that had been made upon him by the woman they had also captured on the reed-island.

Thus mealtime drew round. Old Vitzewitz was in the best of moods, and however embarrassing it might have been for him that his hypothesis that the culprits were 'marauders' and 'deserters' had sustained a severe defeat, he prevailed upon himself (which was not usually the case) to make merry at his own expense and over his miscalculation. For he knew he would carry the day in the end: it was only a question of time.

As soon as the meal was over they were to drive across to Count Drosselstein at Hohen-Zeisar: Tubal and Kathinka likewise owed him a visit, and if they were to pay it at all they could not put it off, since on the following day they were due to set out from Schloss Guse on their return to Berlin. When they rose from the table Krist was already stationed before the steps with the ponies; and a few minutes later the carriage turned out of the driveway into the village street. In obedience to one of her passions, Kathinka had taken the reins and was driving. As they passed Miekley's mill they encountered Doctor Leist from Lebus, who was faithfully reporting to look after his patient: they exchanged only a brief greeting.

After exchanging a few words with Jeetze and being told of the great event of the day, old Doctor Leist, who for twenty years had known his way about the manor house of Hohen-Vietz as well as he did about his own, ascended the stairs and went in to Renate.

Only Maline was with her. The bedroom, now also a sickroom, lay on the side of the house opposite to the Administrative Office and was separated only by a wall from the oft-mentioned transverse building which had formerly served as a banqueting-hall, then as a chapel, and had long since exchanged its earlier vocations for the more modest one of fruit-store and lumber-room. At the end of the corridor there stood a narrow doorway which, with the aid of a tall-stepped stairway, led through to this ancient transverse building. Doctor Leist approached the invalid's bed, felt her pulse and then, unwrapping a bottle of medicine, said:

'I have brought something. Old Doctor Leist is like Santa Claus: he always brings something with him.'

'Only Santa Claus brings something sweet and Doctor Leist brings something bitter.'

'Not so, not so, little Renate. You ought to know old Leist better. He knows what is fitting, and knows too his German proverbs. Like will to like. And that means that bitter things are not for dear little girls.'

'Sour things, then?'

'Sour and sweet: a lemonade.'

'That's better. I am afraid of every spoonful of medicine: but a lemonade will be all right. And what about diet, doctor?'

'Not too strict. Let's say a biscuit and a little stewed fruit.'

'No fresh fruit as well?'

'In case of need, fresh as well. But with circumspection. Perhaps a ripe Gravensteiner or a Calville.'

'Thank you, thank you. They are just what I like. And can someone chat to me a little? Maline?'

'Fine, fine.'

'Or Aunt Schorlemmer?'

'Even better. I think she will have a calming rather than an irritant effect. And that is precisely what we need.'

With that Doctor Leist took his departure and promised to return the following day. He had hardly gone before Renate beckoned Maline to her.

'Now bring a footstool and sit beside me; here, close to the bed. We have the doctor's permission, after all. And now give me your hand. Ah, how nice and cool you are. If only I could have a peaceful night! But there are always pictures before my eyes.'

'That is the fever.'

'Yes, the fever. And it torments me that I keep seeing that poor woman and cannot shake off the sight.'

'What woman?'

'The one they tracked down today on the island. Lewin told me that not a single rough word, not even a complaint, passed her lips.'

'But, Fräulein, she's a thief. And no one knows whom she belongs to. Krist told me: "She has two men or none." And the one is as bad as the other.'

'I feel pity for her all the same; and she cannot be as bad as all that, because she didn't think first of herself but of her child, which she packed into a sleigh-box and took with her. And now I continually have before me an image of the long avenue of poplar-trees leading away to Frankfurt and going on and on and the lines of trees meeting far, far away at a point on the horizon. And the woman is walking between the trees pulling the sleigh-box with the child in it behind her, and when she at last reaches the point where the lines of trees seem to come together a new avenue opens out which is even longer and again ends at a point on the horizon. And all the time the woman gets weaker and wearier. The scene is an agony to me; I wish I could shake it off.'

'Krull and Reetzke are good men, though, and won't make her do more than she can.'

'They are peasants, and peasants are hard and unfeeling. I wish it were young Scharwenka who was taking them. He's not like the others; one can talk to him.'

'*Him*?' asked Maline.

'Yes, *him*. And you must not straightway colour up at the mere mention of his name. He has spoken with Lewin and complained of his troubles to him.'

'He complains about me to everyone.'

'That is what he says of you. And now listen to me, Maline,

and don't toss your head like that. We have always been good friends, so don't be obstinate and be willing to take advice.'

But before Renate could go on, Maline hid her head in her mistress's pillow and began to sob violently.

'Now you've even taken to crying! Well, have a cry, then: it is the first admission that you have been in the wrong, only the stubborn little thing won't yet confess it.'

'He reproached me with being poor.'

'No, he didn't. He reproached you with being proud. And he was right. And he is right, too, in everything he says about you Kubalke girls. You are everlastingly turning up your noses and giving yourselves airs, you and that little Eve over there, and the peasants don't find that pleasant. You would both like to go and live like city girls.'

Maline nodded.

'And what would the big city have to offer you? A little more finery and a couple more admirers. And what would that mean for you in the end? Genteel poverty as the wife of some garrison bugler or bank messenger. No, Maline, stay in Hohen-Vietz; you don't realize your good fortune; the Scharwenkas are the richest people in the village, and not the worst either. And he loves you and cannot get free of you, even though he may really want to. And you see, that is just the kind of love I myself have always wanted to have: that a man is so angry with you he would like to kill you and desires you so much he would like to kiss you to death.'

'How well you know how to describe it all, Fräulein. But *he* has to make the first move.'

'No, *you* must make the first move.'

Maline sighed. Then, however, she suddenly covered Renate's hand with kisses and, drawing a deep breath of relief, as though a great burden had been lifted from her, she said: 'How light my heart feels again now. Ah, Fräulein, Fräulein, he is the best man in the world. And it is also a good thing in him that he doesn't put up with everything. A man has to be a man, after all. And yet I can really twist him round my little finger.'

It struck seven, and Maline got up to give the invalid her medicine.

'Doctor Leist is right: it tastes like lemonade. And now go and get me a couple of Calvilles. Out of the old hall just below us over there. But take a candle with you and be careful on the stairs: the steps are terribly worn. And don't get tangled in the beanstraw.'

Maline gazed before her. Then, overcome with confusion, she said: 'I would rather get the apples from the dining-room, not from the old hall.'

'But why go so far. It's only on the other side of the wall: down a couple of steps and you're there. The Calvilles are by the left of the altar.'

'I can't go, Fräulein.'

'What is the matter with you?'

'I'm afraid.'

'What of?'

'He has started praying again.'

'Who?'

'*Old Matthias*.'

Renate shut her eyes for a moment, and then said with feigned composure: 'I have never encountered him. Do you believe in him?'

'I don't know. All I know is what Ruschen, the old garden-ing woman, has always told me: "If you say you don't believe in him, he appears to you." '

'And who has seen him?'

'Pachaly, the nightwatchman.'

'When?'

'Last night.'

'Tell me what you've heard.'

'I don't want to. It will only frighten you, Fräulein, and make you worse.'

'No, no, I want to know.'

'All right then. Well, Krist and Pachaly were keeping guard. Jeetze came too; I saw him when I came home at about ten o'clock, because I wasn't enjoying it at the inn and I didn't want to dance. But I am bound to say that *he* didn't dance either.'

Renate nodded, as Maline kissed her hand again and then went on:

'Jeetze had put Krist's grey cloak on and buckled an old sabre on top of it. It looked really comic. When the master saw him he got annoyed and said: "This isn't work for you, Jeetze. You're past it." And then he went up to Krist and Pachaly and ordered them to stay close to the house. "Krist, you take the park side, and Pachaly, you take the village side, and meet one another at the big middle-window of the old hall. And make sure you never get out of earshot of one another." I heard all this with my own ears, but the rest I had from Pachaly.'

'Well?'

'Well, they patrolled in this way for almost two hours. It was all quite quiet. They only heard music coming from the inn, where they didn't yet know what had happened. Krist, who was now starting to get cold, went over to the gate so as to fill and light his pipe and keep himself warm with it: and that was why for this one time they didn't meet one another at the big middle-window, and Pachaly had to walk past the old hall alone. When he got to the last window he saw a light; he went up closer and stood on tiptoe. Then he saw that the old picture was lit up and that there was someone kneeling at the altar and praying. He wanted to call out but couldn't. Then Krist came up and he beckoned to him. Krist also saw the light in the window, but as he was about to go and stand on the spot where Pachaly had stood the light suddenly went out and it was dark again. They only heard the sound of a footfall and a rustling in the straw that lay in front of the steps.'

Renate had raised herself higher in the bed. The wall against which she was lying was the wall on the other side of which, and only a short staircase below, there stood the altar. A deathly fear seized hold on her: she needed support and reassurance of a kind Maline could not provide; so she said: 'Go and get Aunt Schorlemmer, will you?'

Maline went: but as she was about to open the door Renate called after her: 'No, stay!' And then, ashamed of being so afraid, she added: 'No, go; I must keep control of myself.'

Minutes passed. Shadows flitted to and fro in the dimly lit room; her feverish eyes followed this shadow-dance and finally came to rest on the row of pictures hanging on the wall opposite. They were English colour-prints, and one of them depicted a Gothic doorway: a hanging-lamp was suspended in

it, and the view through it was of an altar; all was done in
excellent perspective and the altar was a mere dot. She could
not see it, she only knew it was there. And then the doorway
grew bigger before her eyes, and the altar grew bigger, and
someone was kneeling before the steps of the altar. Her heart
beat wildly, yet she could not tear her eyes from the picture.

Then she heard footsteps outside, and immediately afterwards Aunt Schorlemmer came in; she was still wearing her
overall, a sure sign she had been called from the hearth or the
kitchen. Maline, who may have had a bad conscience on
account of the effect her ghost-story had produced, had
remained behind.

'How good of you to come, dear Schorlemmer. I have had a
real longing to see you. You must stay and talk to me a little.
But first give me your hand; there—and now give me something to drink.'

'God, how feverishly you talk, child. You can't be left alone
for half an hour. But I had to get the hares ready. You can't rely
on Stine; she calls herself a cook, yet she hardly even knows
that a hare has seven skins. Now drink, my little Renate. I'm
going to put a spoonful of raspberry vinegar in it; it will
help to cool you down. Have you taken any of your medicine
yet?'

Renate emptied the glass Aunt Schorlemmer had handed
her, and then sank back on to her pillow. But the fear that had
dominated her had gone from her, and as though she suddenly
felt herself in the protection of benevolent spirits she said
quietly: 'Do you believe in ghosts?'

'I thought as much. That Maline hasn't been able to keep her
mouth shut again. She's already been babbling the whole day
long in the kitchen. And there one is as bad as the other. Only
Pachaly is a disappointment to me: I would have thought he
would have had more sense. For he is a follower of Uhlenhorst;
and one thing you can say for the Old Lutherans, they will have
nothing to do with such weakness and foolishness. They have
the faith, and that means they cannot have faith in
superstitions.'

'Dear Schorlemmer,' said Renate, 'you are so good, but you
have one little fault. Whatever doesn't suit you, doesn't exist;

and if it does exist in spite of that, you believe you can banish it from the world with a pious saying.'

'Yes, my little Renate, and I *can* do so, too. Much can be accomplished with a pious saying. And he who believes in God and Jesus Christ fears no ghosts.'

'You mustn't try to evade the question. I don't want to know who is afraid of ghosts and who isn't, I only want to know: are there such things as ghosts?'

'No.'

'And yet you live here with us, and, like so many old houses, we have had a domestic ghost for a hundred years. At least, that is what people say. Lewin is convinced they are right; you smile; very well, that may not mean very much. But Papa believes it too, and you know better than I how firm his faith is. It is not six weeks since we had the affair with Krist's Wilhelm. And now Pachaly! He's a sensible man, after all. I do not say Yes where you say No, but I would at any rate not like to discount the possibility.'

'I would, and do. Where it is not deliberate lies and deception it is a delusion. The dead are dead.'

'Let me tell you something. I once discovered a book in which I read that nothing perishes and that on a certain day *everything* will return, the great world and the small, man and beast, and also the so-called inanimate things. I would therefore meet not only you and Maline again, but also Hector and the English picture with the Gothic doorway and the altar that hangs over there on the wall. And this world, passed through a purifying fire, this transfigured reflection of everything that has ever existed, would be bliss and salvation. The book in which I discovered all this was a devout and pious book, and I have never read anything that made a deeper impression on me. And now I ask you: what is a ghost but an advance messenger from this world of glory?'

'It is as I say none the less: the dead are dead. And the world of glory to come will not be a world of this world. It awaits us, but not here, not in this life. There has been only one who reappeared among men, and it was on the road to Emmaus. But this one was Christ the Lord, the Son of Almighty God. Look, little Renate, there has to be a reason why ghosts appear only in certain places. There are ghosts in Hohen-Vietz, but not in Herrnhut. Nor where, at the North and South Pole, Herrnhut builds its huts and houses. Not *in* these huts and houses, at any rate. I discovered that for myself. In Greenland, all round about us, the Greenlanders, who have a hundred spooks to haunt them, kept on contentedly seeing their ghosts, but no one ever saw any in our mission house. A Herrnhuter and a spook cannot exist together. And the cause of that, my little Renate, is the pious sayings with which you think I imagine I am able to banish all evil from the world.'

'Don't be annoyed, dear Schorlemmer. And to show you aren't annoyed, tell me about the Greenlanders.* You have been at Hohen-Vietz six years now and I hardly know the name of the place where you lived and worked for so long and buried your nearest and dearest. Tell me about it, but don't tell me about the Greenland ghosts: I have had quite enough of our own one. Talk to me about something peaceful and cheerful, something with devout religion in it, that will raise my spirits and waft over me like a divine cooling wind. For coolness is what I long for. But first give me some of the medicine: it must be gone eight o'clock.'

Aunt Schorlemmer did as she was bid; then, looking about for Renate's knitting so as to have something to occupy her hands, she sat herself in the tall armchair and, when she had made herself comfortable, said: 'Well, what shall we begin with?'

'With the beginning, naturally; that is, with the land itself. I once saw a picture of it: cliffs and water and icebergs and snow; on the bank there lay a seal; nearby, on the other side of the spur of land, sat a white fox, while on the edge of the cliffs were squatting plump birds with short legs. I think they were called penguins.'

'It is not quite right but it will do, and I shall refrain from improving on it.'

'But do, do: I don't want merely to be entertained, I want to learn too.'

'Very well then. So imagine an endless stretch of coastline, many hundreds of miles long but only a few hundred feet wide. Before this stretch of coastline lies the sea dotted with a thousand little islands, and behind it lie the mountains, cleft by ravines, and out of these ravines the waters plunge down into the sea.'

'I would love to see it.'

'It was in one of these ravines that our colony lay. I say "lay", but it lies there still and shall, God willing, outlast many days yet. And this colony is called Neu-Herrnhut. In my time it had twenty houses.'

'That is very few.'

'Few and many. But you would be astonished if you could have seen them. When Lewin today described the wooden shed built in the snow on the reed-island, there suddenly stood before me the house I lived in for ten years with my dear late husband. It too was divided into three parts, stable and living-room and a kitchen between them. And what did we have to call ours? A bed and a chest, and above them a rail where our chattels hung from a couple of pegs. On the table there stood a lamp, and beside it lay God's Word. That was missing on the reed-island, to be sure, yet it was the best thing we had, our only comfort in danger and distress.'

'And were you then in danger?'

'Not from people, or only very seldom. For the Greenlanders are a gentle, quiet and well-behaved race and know how to contain their emotions.'

'I had thought they were dwarfish and superstitious and looked like Hoppenmarieken.'

'There you have again got it half right. But only half. For Hoppenmarieken is rude and the Greenlanders are polite. You hear no quarrelling or brawling; abuse and invective is, indeed, missing from their language. When they are offended they revenge themselves with jokes and mockery: the accuser challenges the accused to a kind of duel, and the one who has the most laughter on his side has won. They have the gift of fluent and elegant speech in general. They are sociable and hospitable, and at the time of the winter solstice there are dances and ball-games and singing with the accompaniment of a drum. They are well aware, too, of what good manners they have, and when they want to praise a stranger they say: "He is as well-behaved as we are."'

'This self-satisfaction of theirs must often have been a severe obstacle to you. For I recall that, when we were still going to him for religious instructions, Pastor Seidentopf told me and Marie: "A simple mind and a great mind are both equally open to the revelations of Christianity, but a vain mind obstinately resists them." '

'How very right he was: and the truth of what he said was brought home to us many a time in our colony. We made no progress: if today we thought we had gained an inch, tomorrow we lost it again to the angekoks.'

'To the angekoks?'

'Yes. The angekoks are sorcerers and soothsayers, mostly cunning deceivers, though there are some who are genuine, who have visions or at least claim to have them. They mediate between the people and the two great spirits: they are able to call on the good spirit and banish the evil spirit; the good spirit, by the way, is male, and the evil spirit female.'

'Indeed! That shows a lack of gallantry surprising in a people so polite they don't even have words of abuse or invective.'

'And yet, my little Renate, we have to put up with it with all the patience we can, for everywhere it is Eve who leads astray and gets mankind expelled from Paradise. But I was speaking of the angekoks. Their natural sharp-wittedness was useful to them in their resistance to us, and such mockery as our Lord and Saviour had to endure was also visited on us who in humility confessed him. But then God had mercy upon us in our distress, and the story of it is the story of Kaiarnak, which I will gladly tell you, if you still have the patience.'

'What is Kaiarnak?'

'A name. The name of a Greenlander from the south. For there are south Greenlanders and north Greenlanders: like all half-nomadic peoples they put up their tents in this or that part of the country and then after a certain length of time return again to their former dwelling-places. And so it was that a band of south Greenlanders on one of these hunting and wandering trips arrived in our colony to rest with us for a day or a week. There were a hundred or more of them. We made them welcome, and Matthäus Stach, who was at that time in charge of our colony, with Friedrich Böhnisch and my good

Schorlemmer as his assistants, asked them if they would like to take part in one of our meetings. That may strike you as strange: but the fact is that they like nothing more than to engage in a controversy and to think how fine they are when, with the aid of the sharp minds they possess, they come out on top. And so many of them came to the meeting. We had just taken our places, and Matthäus Stach read to them a chapter from the Gospel of St John which he had shortly before translated into Greenlandish. They listened attentively; most of them smiled; but a few showed an interest. To these our brother then turned and asked them if they believed in an immortal soul.'

'But you were going to tell me about Kaiarnak.'

'I am already telling you about him. Well, Matthäus Stach asked them if they believed in an immortal soul. They answered: Yes! And then he began to speak to them of the Fall of man and of his Redemption. I can still hear his voice, for he was a man of great gifts. Then the Lord opened up the heart of one among them, and though I have witnessed many conversions, and read of many others, none has ever moved me more profoundly. It was because it was all so plain and simple. No doubt seeing that his words were falling on fertile soil, Matthäus Stach spoke more and more affectingly, and after he had just described Christ's suffering on the Mount of Olives a Greenlander stepped up to the table and said in a loud and agitated voice in which the note of salvation already trembled: "How was that? I want to hear that again." These words penetrated us who heard them to the very marrow, and they have never been forgotten in Neu-Herrnhut. From that moment on, the blessing of God was upon all we did.'

'It could hardly be otherwise. Words such as those continue to echo: I can feel their effect even now.'

Aunt Schorlemmer kissed Renate on the brow and then went on: 'A week passed and the band of Greenlanders was still in our colony. But then they departed to pursue their hunting further north, and only Kaiarnak stayed behind; with him there stayed his two brothers-in-law, together with their wives and children, fourteen people in all. We approved their staying and held prayer-meetings with them. The children were given lessons: a very difficult thing, since the Greenlanders know nothing at all of what we call education. For they love their children as tenderly as monkeys and allow them to grow up without insisting on obedience or punishing disobedience. After six months had gone by, Matthäus Stach posed the question whether they had not by now been sufficiently prepared and ought to be baptized; but my good Schorlemmer, who had conducted the lessons, thought the time had not yet come and they should wait. And so it happened. It was not until the day after Easter that four members of this family, the first fruit of Greenland, were torn free from the power of darkness; Kaiarnak received the name Samuel, his wife was named Anna, his son Matthäus, his daughter Anna. There was great rejoicing in the colony over this event: but the rejoicing was not to last long. A month later there came the news that the elder of the brothers-in-law, who had left us for a time and joined up with a hunting party making for the north, had been treacherously and horribly murdered in revenge for having bewitched to death the son of a heathen Greenlander by means of Christian sayings and spells. At the same time it was added that the angekoks had entered into a great conspiracy to mete out the same fate to Kaiarnak's younger brother-in-law. At this news our little Greenland congregation, those who had been baptized as well as those still preparing for baptism, was seized with fear and trembling, and they resolved to return to the south, where they hoped to find greater safety among their own relatives. Alas, hard though we found it, we had to let them go, and I can still see Kaiarnak weeping bitterly and promising again and again that he would remain faithful and then tearing himself away; and the sleighs then gliding past us in a long line, making for Fiskenäs and Frederikshaab and the south.'

'And did he keep his word?'

'We had little hope that he would, for a new defection was abroad, and even those who stayed close to us again took to heeding the angekoks. We were very downcast; I too, who all this time had stood, so far as my poor powers permitted, loyally at the side of my good Schorlemmer. A year passed without bringing news of Kaiarnak, let alone Kaiarnak himself. Then, it was on St John's Day, we celebrated the wedding of Anna Stach and Friedrich Böhnisch, and as we were sitting at the wedding-breakfast and singing devotional songs—accompanied, you may be surprised to hear, by three violins and a flute—Kaiarnak entered the room and greeted us. Our joy was so great that the wedding feast turned as though of its own accord into a feast of reunion: for we had again our prodigal son, or at least one we had come to regard as such. And then Kaiarnak had to tell us everything, the great things and small that had happened to him, and how his own people had received him back. He concealed nothing from us: at first they had listened to him often and with visible enjoyment; but then they had grown bored with what he said, and he had withdrawn into silence and pursued his devotions alone. At last he had felt the strong desire to be with us, his brothers, again, and he had felt it more and more, until this longing denied him all repose and rest; and so here he was. My good Schorlemmer, who it was really who had brought him to salvation, wept for joy, and Friedrich Böhnisch said he would never forget that hour and that his wedding-day was now consecrated twice over.'

'Well might he say so. It was a wedding-day such as anyone would wish for! To me that reunion would have been a happy omen.'

'And that it was, too. The young couple prospered. So did Kaiarnak. But his days were numbered. I almost believe that, in his loyalty, he felt he could never do enough and that his zeal exceeded his strength, for he was not strong physically. He was taken ill with a violent pain in his side and lungs that quickly put an end to his life. He preserved a quiet demeanour even in the greatest agony, and when his people began to weep for him he said: "Be not troubled. You know that I was the first of you to be converted to the Son of God, and now it is his will that I shall be the first to come to him. If you are faithful to him we shall meet one another again and eternally rejoice at the mercy he has shown us." After that he fell asleep, while our prayers commended his departing soul to the Redeemer. His wife insisted that he be buried in a Christian manner, and not after the custom of the country. And so it was done. Not only the brothers and their relatives attended his funeral but the tradespeople of the colony did so too, and the ceremony consecrated our new cemetery. The Greenlanders marvelled at all they saw; but our brothers were much affected by this death. For they lost much through it: an awakened, gifted and blessed witness to the Gospel.

'And that is my story of Kaiarnak, the first we baptized.'

Renate seized her old friend's hand and said: 'Ah, how grateful I am, dear Schorlemmer. All fear has now fled, and it is as though I had never heard of spooks and ghosts. And now I want to sleep. But first repeat to me the rhyme of the fourteen angels. Let us repeat it together:

> 'Fourteen holy angels bright
> Stand about my bed at night.
> Two at my head,
> Two at my feet,
> Two upon my righthand side,
> Two upon my lefthand side,
> Two who cover me up tight,
> Two who see I sleep all night,
> Two to take me by the hand
> And lead me to the Heavenly Land.'

For a while they were silent. Then Renate said: 'And now go. I am protected. Only leave the side-door open, so Maline can hear me.'

'Goodnight, little Renate!'

'Goodnight, dear Schorlemmer!'

17

A Jackdaw's Nest

THE next day was New Year's Eve.

Hoppenmarieken rose very early: she wanted if possible to be back home by midday so as to get everything scrubbed and polished and to prepare for herself a punch with which to celebrate New Year's Eve. Today she was making the short trip, to Küstrin and back. It was only seven o'clock when she passed the manor house and waved across the courtyard to Jeetze, who was just opening the folding shutters of the big corner-window; the ingenuous way she waved made it clear that, since the arrests of the previous day would in all probability have severe repercussions on her herself, she did not yet know of them. She had not returned from a walk across the Bruch until after midnight; she had found no one awake, not even the inhabitants of the woodland acre, who normally liked to turn night into day; so that when she got up in the morning she was probably the only person in all Hohen-Vietz unaware of what had taken place.

It was two hours later before hosts and guests at the manor house assembled around the breakfast table. Even Berndt was no early riser when business did not oblige him to be, and the journey to Guse appointed for four in the afternoon could supply no reason for breaking a comfortable habit that had long since become a kind of household regulation. Having been detained by Renate, Aunt Schorlemmer appeared even later to satisfy their curiosity as to the condition of the invalid.

After she had, in addition to her own, communicated Dr Leist's reassuring words too, conversation turned to the previous evening's visit to Hohen-Ziesar, the events of which were relived in the to and fro of a chattering that grew increasingly animated. What emerged from it all was that Drosselstein had shown himself to be the most engaging of hosts, full of encouragement towards Berndt, full of attentiveness towards Kathinka. When the latter, who was visiting Hohen-Ziesar for the first time, had expressed her wonderment at the grandeur of the château and its environs, which was of a kind to be found nowhere else in the March, the count, disregarding the lateness of the hour, had seized the occasion to conduct her and his other guests through the long flight of rooms on the first floor—the ancestral hall, the armoury and the picture-gallery—with two servants bearing branched candlesticks preceding them. In this dismal half-light, all that you would in the daytime pass by with hardly a glance assumed a strange significance, and the knights with half-closed visors that lined the wall, the crossed lances, and the ancestral portraits themselves, which seemed to ask: 'Why do you disturb our peace?' did not fail to make a profound impression on Kathinka. A portrait of a young woman, described by the count as a likeness of Wangeline von Burgsdorff, a close relative of his house, remained fixed especially firmly in her memory.

Kathinka had asked about this picture—the product of a Netherlander of the school of Van Dyck whose uncanny bright blue eyes had invaded the dreams of many earlier visitors to Hohen-Ziesar—on the previous evening, but had received only a cursory answer; now she asked about it again, and Berndt, who was a real encyclopaedia of knowledge in regard to the history of every family and château in the entire region, was about to satisfy his fair interrogator's curiosity with a detailed account of 'Wangeline' (considered by many researchers into the history of the March to be the historically authenticated original of the 'Woman in White'), when a knock on the door put an end to a discourse but barely begun. An elderly man with thinning hair combed back off his forehead, whose Spanish cane and, even more, the long blue coat he wore with a coat-of-arms affixed to the chest, proclaimed him a beadle, came in, handed a letter to old Vitzewitz and then retreated again a few paces in the direction of the door. Everything about him bespoke the old soldier. Berndt broke open the missive and read:

Respected Sir and Friend!

I hasten to inform you of the outcome of a first examination I conducted yesterday afternoon of the gang of thieves apprehended and delivered up through your circumspection. From the two villains, with regard to whom Hohen-Clessin and Podelzig share the honour of being the birthplace, no amount of cross-questioning could extract anything; the woman, however, who has belonged with this pair only for a short time and who fell among the gang on the reed-island through the fault of others rather than her own, has made a comprehensive confession which embraces firstly the robberies perpetrated, mainly in the suburbs of Küstrin, but secondly the receivership of these stolen goods which subvented the undertaking. The person most heavily implicated is our lady-friend, Hoppenmarieken. I request you to be good enough to have her house searched, or to conduct such a search yourself, in connection wherewith I would, having regard to the peculiar cunning of the suspect, have you direct your attention to the walls and floorboards of the building. I would be obliged if the stolen goods, of whose discovery I have no doubt, were to be delivered here as soon as possible. As to whether it will be advisable or, given her mental condition, even permissible to bring the full weight of the law to bear on the accused, I await the favour of your opinion in due course.

Turgany.

Berndt laid down the letter, which he had read half-aloud, and turning to the beadle said: 'My dear Rysselmann, my compliments to his honour, and tell him I shall do as he asks.' Then he pulled the bell. 'Jeetze, provide some refreshment. It is a long way from Frankfurt, and our old friend here must be halfway between you and me. Am I right, Rysselman: sixty?' The old man nodded. 'And then dispatch Krist to Kniehase: he is to collect the nightwatchman and wait for me at the woodland acre.'

'Renate complains', old Vitzewitz continued when Jeetze and Rysselmann had left the room, 'that nothing ever happens in Hohen-Vietz! But say yourself, Kathinka, whether since you have been here we have not lived as though in the Land of Adventure. First a highway robbery in the public street, then a burglary in our own house, then a regular thief-hunt organized on proper tactical-strategical lines, and now a house-search in the domain of a dwarf—name me any peaceable place in the world where you could find more happening in the space of three days! I am curious, moreover, to see whether the island-woman's statements turn out to be true.'

'I have no doubt that they will,' said Lewin. 'From all that Hanne Bogun said yesterday, and even from all he did not say, I hardly expected anything other than what Turgany now writes. When do you intend to go up to the woodland acre?'

'Now, or at any rate soon. We have to get it done before noon.'

'May we come with you?'

'Certainly. The more eyes there are the better; considering the cunning of the old witch we are going to need them.'

So they broke up. Berndt took leave of Kathinka with a few words, and the latter for her part took herself upstairs to discuss with Renate the most singularly varied topics: Count Drossel-stein and old Rysselmann, Wangeline von Burgsdorff and Hoppenmarieken.

A quarter of an hour later Vitzewitz left, accompanied by Tubal and Lewin. They walked quickly. Before they had reached Miekley's yard they were overtaken by Kniehase and Pachaly, who were already on their way, and together they then turned and made for the woodland acre. Soon they were standing before Hoppenmarieken's house. They had already agreed to proceed in an orderly manner: that is to say, to begin with the kitchen area and conclude with the alcove, but in any event not to try to go through the house too quickly.

The door was only on the latch. They opened it, and then propped it open, so that the daylight now coming in would enable them to see into every last corner. Nothing could have been buried in the mud-floor, which was as hard as a rock, so there remained in the kitchen-hallway only the hearth and, opposite the hearth, the chimney through which the stove in the living-room was heated: but the proximity of the fire made this an unlikely hiding-place. The door-stop lying within the hallway, the strange situation of which might have aroused suspicion, likewise proved much too big and heavy; Lewin and Kniehase tried in vain to shift it.

There was thus nothing in the kitchen, so they went to the living-room. The great birds in the cages, already sitting on their front perches, gazed at the unfamiliar visitors. The latter then began to divide their tasks. Throwing back the red-and-white checkered coverlet, Pachaly felt about in the pillow and the paillasse on the bed, while Berndt knocked on all the walls and Tubal did the same to the tiles at the base of the stove. Again there was nothing. It was hardly worthwhile to look into the open plate-rack or the drawers of the cupboard or table. The floor was covered by a single board which ran from the window to the opposite wall: it had lately been scrubbed and there was nowhere any sign of its having been cut open or removed. The place of concealment, then, had to be the alcove.

The alcove was dark and hardly more than seven feet square: it was thus virtually impossible for five people to move and rummage about within it, so Berndt and Kniehase, who were in any case troubled by the stifling atmosphere of the over-heated room, withdrew to the door, where they were joined by Lewin a few minutes later, after he had tried in vain to strike up a friendship with a black bird with red spots on its breast.

Only Tubal and Pachaly were still in the alcove. They lit a candle and here too began knocking on the walls: on one side, where great bundles of herbs hung from four or five pegs, they experienced difficulty in doing this; they succeeded, however, though with no better result than in the hallway and living-room.

'We shall have to fetch the Scharwenkas' cow-herd,' said Tubal; 'he has the best eyesight.'

'No,' said Pachaly, 'the fame he has got and the fur cap he has been promised have already gone to his head. I know the boy. He cannot see better than others, he is only better informed: he's from the woodland acre himself and knows all the tricks and dodges of the people up here.'

'Maybe so. But where are we to look now? There are no hollows in the walls, the floorboards are nailed down, and in the whole of this alcove there is nothing but a red chest of drawers with the drawers empty. And there can't be anything hidden in the ceiling: Hoppenmarieken is a dwarf and her hands can hardly reach five feet.'

'Not in the ceiling, young sir, certainly: it has to be down here around the chest of drawers. Such creatures as Hoppen-marieken are vain, dress themselves up, and like to show everybody what they have. Why has she stuck the chest of drawers in this dark alcove, where no one can see it? That must mean something!'

'Let us take a look, then,' said Tubal, pushed the object of Pachaly's suspicions away to the right—where it knocked against a large bundle of ground-ivy, which fell from its peg with a loud rustling—and, moving close to the wall, stepped upon the wide middle floorboard whose left extremity had at just this spot been concealed by the chest of drawers standing over it. As he did so, the board, which at this point lacked any joist beneath it, sank several inches, its other end at the same time rising into the air in the manner of a see-saw.

'Just as I thought,' said Pachaly, and he sprang forward and removed the board. It came away easily, and what was revealed was sufficiently surprising. Along its entire length the soil beneath had been removed to form a shallow trench which deepened, at the end where the board had see-sawed up, into a cavity more than two feet deep; and these two sections had been so employed that the shallow trench appeared to be Hoppenmarieken's dry goods and hardware store, the cavity her grocery and provisions warehouse.

Pachaly then began to remove the objects they had discovered, and handed them to Tubal, who for want of a better place laid them on Hoppenmarieken's bed. From the trench came women's things: a piece of red flannel, the remains of a length of velveteen, coloured hat-ribbons and black silk kerchiefs such as are worn by the women of the Oderbruch. In the cavity they found bags containing sugar, coffee and rice, and in addition soap cut into bars and tallow-candles tied together by their wicks. From all this it was apparent that Hoppenmarieken's business had been conducted with the aid of this storehouse, and that goods she had supposedly been bringing back with her from Frankfurt or Küstrin she had as far as possible been in the habit of supplying from her own stock of stolen property. The board was now replaced and it fitted like the lid of a box; even the nails which would be found in a regular wooden floor were not missing: but before being inserted they had been cut short with pliers and had no other purpose than to display their heads.

The three pacing up and down outside had meanwhile ceased their promenade and come back in again. Berndt examined everything and then said: 'I know Hoppenmarieken: we shall achieve nothing with this. She will claim it is all her own property and it will be hard for us to prove otherwise. She is in cahoots with all kinds of devious tradespeople who would be ready at any moment to swear she acquired it legally. But I am sure it is stolen; all we lack is something personal to someone, something so obviously private property she will have no way of wriggling out of it. Let us search further: Muschwitz and Rosentreter, not to speak of our own villains up here in the woodland acre, will not have confined themselves to women's goods and bars of soap.'

Pachaly, who had continued assiduously with his investigations while Berndt had been speaking, now appeared at the little entrance to the alcove and beckoned to Lewin, who was standing closest to him. Lewin stepped into the alcove, and without more ado Pachaly went up to the thick wooden peg from which the bundle of ground-ivy had fallen, held the candle close to it, and said: 'Take a look, young sir; the peg is loose, the mud around it has been chipped away; something is stuck behind it.'

'That could be it!' Lewin exclaimed, and seized the peg and tugged at it: it came away without the slightest difficulty.

A deep hole, much deeper than that required by the relatively short wooden peg, was revealed in the wall. For that there had to be a reason: Lewin therefore searched around in the cavity and found a little packet not much bigger than half a hand: it was wrapped first in a piece of sugar-loaf paper, then, when that was removed, in a patch of coarse linen. When Lewin had taken off both wrappings, what lay before him resembled the contents of a jackdaw's nest: a little silver needle-case, a pocket-watch in a tortoiseshell case, a child's rattle, an amethyst brooch set with little topazes whose pin had been broken off, a signet-ring with an indecipherable name and a little golden oval frame which had probably once contained a miniature portrait. Though nothing in the find was of any great value, it was precisely what was needed to establish their case.

'Now we have her,' Berndt said quietly, wrapping up the objects again and putting them into his pocket.

The other pegs were also investigated but were set firmly in the wall: it could thus be assumed that nothing remained to be discovered, and it was decided to search no further. In the kitchen they found an old back-basket, and Pachaly was ordered to pack into it everything they had discovered and carry it to the manor house. He was reluctant to obey, for it seemed to him beneath his dignity to walk down the village street in broad daylight carrying a back-basket; but his position left him with no choice and, venting his annoyance in brief exclamations under his breath, he at length did as he had been bidden.

In the meantime Berndt and Kniehase, the two young men

immediately behind them, had reached the driveway of the manor house and were just about to turn into it from the village street when they saw Hoppenmarieken not a hundred yards distant coming along the highway from Küstrin: the tiny figure, the rapid walk and the animated gestures made it easy to recognize her.

'There she comes,' said Berndt, and, turning to Pachaly, who had already caught up with them, he added: 'Now be quick: arrange two or three chairs in front of my desk in the upstairs room and display what you've got with you.'

Hoppenmarieken waved while she was still some distance off. She appeared to be in a very good mood, and when she reached the group at the entrance to the manor house she handed Berndt a letter she had drawn out of her bodice as she came along.

'There's only this one,' she said, and added as though in explanation: 'The post from Berlin was late.'

She made to walk on and had already taken a few steps when Berndt called after her: 'Hoppenmarieken, I've got something for you. But it's up in my study. Come with me.'

Notwithstanding his effort to sound natural, there must have been something peculiar in his tone: in any event, the expression of complacency which the dwarf's countenance had hitherto worn faded from it as she followed the lord of the manor across the courtyard and up the stairs. Kniehase and the two young friends followed behind.

They had been obliged to restore the Administrative Office to some kind of order, and Pachaly, already there, had by now finished arranging his display. The ribbons and kerchiefs were not greatly in evidence: what caught the eye most of all was the length of red flannel lying smoothed and folded and the pyramids of bars of soap and bundles of candles.

'Well, Hoppenmarieken,' said Berndt, 'how does this length of red flannel appeal to you?'

'Lord, your worship, it appeals to me very well. It's of the English kind: seven groschen a yard.'

'Have you perhaps seen this length of flannel before?'

'I don't know.'

'Think.'

'I see so much, your worship, I may have seen it.'

'Where?'

'At the Jew Ephraim's.'

'Or at your own house!'

'My own house? Yes, by thunder, at my own house. Ha ha ha! Now I see. You've been there and discovered my little warehouse. Under the floorboards. Keeping it there makes things a bit difficult, but I wouldn't feel safe otherwise.'

'I can see that, Hoppenmarieken. You have to be careful, certainly. There are so many villains about nowadays . . .'

'Oh, there are!'

'Very good. But, you see, you are taking the bread from the mouths of our tradespeople. Do you have a licence to trade?'

'No, your worship, I don't.'

'Well then, if this goes on we shall have no alternative but to fine you.'

At these words, spoken as they were in a relaxed and cheerful tone, her former complacency returned: she suddenly had the feeling that all was going to turn out well, and in a voice that mingled simpering and pleading she said: 'Your worship surely won't do that.'

'Who knows, Hoppenmarieken? Take a look here, I've got another little present for you which you can perhaps explain!' And with that he drew out of his large jacket-pocket the packet he had put there after the house had been searched and placed it before her on the table.

She at once fell to her knees and cried: 'I don't know nothing about it!'

'But we know something about it.'

'I don't know nothing. They both came in to me . . .'

'Who?'

'Muschwitz and Rosentreter . . . and said I had to hide it. But I wouldn't and I started to scream, so Muschwitz took out his pocket-knife and said to me: "Woman, if you scream I'll cut your throat." So then I took it.'

'You are lying, Hoppenmarieken; you are a receiver, as you always have been. You gave them money; but not enough, I think, for they recently tried to take some more from you when they attacked you on the highway. They were sure you would not betray them. But they have betrayed *you*.'

'Yes, that they have. They think they're going to slip through the noose and put me in it instead. But I won't go along with it. I will swear an oath, a *true* oath. Call in Seidentopp; yes, let Seidentopp come . . . Oh, dear Lord God, what troubles we have! Oh God, oh God!' And as she thus exclaimed she crawled closer to Berndt and kissed the hem of his coat.

'Stand up!'

But the repulsive dwarf remained on her knees and went on: 'None of it is true. Oh, that Muschwitz, and the other one from Podelzig! They have both lied like the Devil. I will swear an oath, a *true* oath. Pachaly, fetch a Bible. And here is my hand; and I will swear an oath, *in* the church or outside of the church or wherever you like.'

'You shall not swear an oath, for your oaths are false. What shall we do with her, Kniehase?'

Convinced they had no other object but to make away with her, Hoppenmarieken cried out pitiably and wrung her stumpy little hands. At length she saw Lewin, who had remained standing at the door, and she made to crawl towards him, presumably to give a repetition of the scene she had just enacted before his father; but Pachaly held her back.

'Let it go, Papa,' Lewin now exclaimed. He spoke as though Hoppenmarieken, of whose complete imbecility he was firmly convinced, were not present. 'Just consider: she is mankind at its lowest level. Threaten her—it is the only thing she understands. She will obey the law only if she is afraid not to. And Turgany knows this as well as we do: he will make no great objection. But if he must do, then he will have to depict her as she is, and that is her best defence. Set her free, I beg you.'

'Do you hear what he says?' Berndt asked the dwarf, who while Lewin was speaking had finally risen to her feet. She blinked and replied: 'I heard it all; I know, I know. Yes, the young gentleman, he knows me and I know *him*. And I knew him when he was still tiny, *that* tiny. Yes, the young gentleman . . . !'

'He pleads on your behalf', Berndt went on, 'and wants me

to let you go. Why? Because you are Hoppenmarieken. But I know you better, and know that you fancy yourself exceedingly wise. You are cunning and worthless: that is the top and bottom of it. Take your basket; we shall shut our eyes to it this time. But be careful: if we catch you again it will be all up with you. And now go and behave better in this new year than you did in the old.'

She looked around for her stick and basket, both of which she had laid down beside the ironbound chest when she entered the room. When she was again ready to march off her glance glided over the goods spread out on the chairs: it was obvious she would have liked to lay claim to them as her own rightful property. Berndt saw what she was doing and felt that Lewin must after all be right about her.

'Go!' he repeated; 'all this stays here and will be delivered to Frankfurt. And perhaps you will be, too, even yet!'

She took this last remark for a joke, and grinned again.

A minute later she was crossing the courtyard; she saluted with her stick, and from the tempo of her gait you might have thought she was departing from the scene of some commonplace everyday contention, or indeed that nothing had happened at all.

18

Othegraven

FORTIFIED with a snack in Jeetze's little servant's hall, and nicely warmed up again, Rysselmann was just passing through the village of Podelzig on the highway to Frankfurt when he encountered a light calash-carriage upon whose leather driving-seat he recognized the schoolmaster Othegraven, the friend of his magistrate. Othegraven pulled up.

'Good day, Rysselmann, how are you? What in the world brings you to Podelzig?'

'I've just come from Hohen-Vietz. A duty trip: a letter from the Herr Justizrat to Herr von Vitezewitz. A fine man, and it's a fine village, too.'

'That's where I'm going,' said Othegraven. 'Will I find the mayor?'

'He's in the village, but I cannot be sure you will find him. For I heard his worship sent for him, because they wanted to search the house of the postwoman they call Hoppenmarieken. She is supposed to be a receiver of stolen goods.'

'Many thanks, Rysselmann. Give my regards to the magistrate. God be with you!'

With that the schoolmaster drove off again at a fast pace in the direction of Hohen-Vietz. What Rysselmann had told him was ill news to him, and if he had been one of those people influenced by signs and omens he would have felt obliged to turn back. But there was no trace of superstition in him: he regarded everything that happened as unchangeably determined. By confession, and even more by partisanship, he was a strict Lutheran; yet at the bottom of his heart there reposed—innate and thus inalienable—a goodly portion of Calvinistic belief in predestination.

From Podelzig he had only an hour more to travel. It was chiming noon as Othegraven halted before the parsonage. Seidentopf, whom he had not visited when he was in Hohen-Vietz two days previously, greeted him warmly on the threshold of his study, which with the winter sun shining in wore a particularly friendly appearance. Everything was altered, and the housekeeper whose presence had been so noticeable on the day after Christmas as she bustled about with her air-clearing perfume now demonstrated the most perfect composure as, in accordance with the custom of the house and without having to be requested to do so, she placed some lunch upon the table in front of Othegraven.

The two men had taken their seats on the little sofa close to the stove under the dust-covered bookshelf of the *bibliotheca theologica* and were gazing out at the snowy garden. An ash-tree stood before the window: a beautiful tree in summertime, it was now, with its branches hanging like tangled strips of hemp, a sorry sight. But neither man was in the mood to pay much attention to the scenery; and while the schoolmaster, whose purpose in being there was unfavourable to the possession of a good appetite, was sustaining himself more with a glass of wine than with his lunch, the parson told him of what had happened in Hohen-Vietz since the day before yesterday, of the break-in at the manor house and of the discovery of the gang of thieves on the reed-island.

'Adventures and military expeditions, as though the foe were already here,' he concluded.

Othegraven, whose mood at that moment was plainly the opposite of warlike, took little interest in the pastor's account of these things; it was aroused only when the subject changed and he began to talk of the events of the day after Christmas, of the merry party they had had that evening, of Pastor Zabel's embarrassment over the games of forfeits, and above all of Marie, of how charming she had been and how well she had spoken about his colleague of Werneuchen, even though on that subject he had been unable to agree with her.

'You could have said nothing', Othegraven interposed, 'that could have given me more pleasure. For you know, dear pastor, I have a great affection for this lovely child.'

Seidentopf was severely startled, the more so in that he held Othegraven in such high regard. Such a thing had never crossed his mind, and now he was presented with it he still regarded it as an impossibility. At length he pulled himself together and asked: 'Does Marie know of this?'

'No. I spoke with the mayor the day before yesterday. He replied that Marie was a town child and belonged in the town; when he thought of her at the side of a worthy man who loved her it did his heart good. And that she should be the wife of a scholar, perhaps soon the wife of a pastor, was exactly what he had always desired for her. The child was the apple of his eye, and he felt honoured by my proposal; but she herself would have to decide. I could not but agree with him; and now I am here to learn what her decision is.'

'I wish you luck, Othegraven. But, all things considered, is Marie right for you?'

Othegraven began to reply; but when it appeared from his first words that his answer was going to apply only to the 'dress of gauze with the little gold stars' and to everything connected with it, Seidentopf interrupted the schoolmaster and said quietly: 'That is not what I mean; what I mean is, have you considered whether two natures can get along together one of which is all fantasy and imagination and the other all strength of character?'

'I have considered it, but I confess I have done so more in hope than in doubt and apprehension. A wife with fantasy and imagination and a husband with strength of character—if I really do possess this distinguishing quality you have been good enough to confer on me—is precisely what seems to me an ideal. What else is marriage but a complementing and completion?'

'That is what it is in books and treatises, and I can think of cases, or rather I know cases, where it is so in fact. But when I consult the book of my experience it is on the whole quite the opposite. Marriage, or at least happiness in marriage, rests, not on complementing and completion, but on mutual understanding. Husband and wife have to possess, not opposite qualities, but different gradations of similar qualities, they must be related in temperament, they must share the same ideals. Above all, however, my dear Othegraven, we have not yet reached consideration of marriage: the immediate question is one of inclination of the heart, which is almost always towards a heart of the same kind; at least it is so with natures like Marie's.'

Othegraven smiled. 'In that case, my dear pastor, ought not the question you put to me to have been, not whether Marie was right for me, but whether I was right for Marie? As to the first point I am certain; and it is to acquire certainty as to the second as well that I am here. Please let me leave my carriage in your courtyard; I shall see you again in half an hour. You shall be the first to know whether or not the dice have fallen in my favour. An unchristian phrase, that; but I shall maintain it, for it exactly expresses how I feel at this moment, in spite of all conviction that what in the end decides our destiny is no dice-game. We ought, perhaps, to be less afraid than we usually are of contradictions of this kind, in which the heart of a believer too can become involved: we should then gain more for ourselves, and for others, than we lose. What is inflexible is dead.'

They parted, and Othegraven walked over to the mayor's house.

In the room to the left, where on the second day of Christmas Kniehase had read the chapter from the Book of Daniel, he discovered only the mayor's wife. She came to meet him with a warm greeting but also showing a certain embarrassment, and expressed her regret that her husband was absent on account of official duties with the nature of which she would not burden the young gentleman. Least of all today, for she knew why he had come. She would call Marie. Then she fetched him a chair and went upstairs to the gable-room, where the daughter was engaged in sewing and darning and all kinds of little needle-work tasks, so as not to carry anything untidy or unfinished over into the new year. Here, in the resolute manner of a woman who set little store on cautious preparation or sparing anyone sudden surprises, she said briefly and bluntly: 'Come Marie, Othegraven the schoolmaster is downstairs; he has asked your father for your hand. You can say Yes or No, either will be all right with us. We have no other desire than your happiness, and you must know what will make you happy.'

Marie was violently alarmed by these words, but composed herself and followed the mother down the stairs. Othegraven had not taken the chair that had been offered him; he was standing at the window pounding the knuckles of his left hand with the fingers of his right like a man full of inner turmoil.

'Here she is,' said Frau Kniehase, and returned to the door.

'Stay, mother,' Marie pleaded.

Frau Kniehase abandoned her intention of leaving and sat herself at the spinning-wheel. 'Marie, you know why I am here,' Othegraven began after a brief interval.

'Yes, mother has just told me.'

'Did it surprise you?'

'We have known one another only a short time.'

'If the heart is going to speak at all, it speaks quickly. It is now six months, Marie, since I first saw you; it was in the park, where the round bed is. I remember every little detail.'

Marie nodded, as a sign that the day had remained in her memory too.

'There were visitors,' Othegraven continued, 'Herr von

Massow from Steinhöfel, young Herr von Burgsdorff and Dr Faulstich from Kirch-Göritz; you were playing quoits, and I could already hear you laughing as I came with old Herr von Vitzewitz up the great avenue of elm-trees. Fräulein Renate was playing opposite you in a light-blue summer dress. When I joined in the game I was very unpractised, but whether I threw the quoits too far or not far enough you were always able to catch them. Your dexterity made up for my lack of it. I have forgotten none of this, and when I drove back to Frankfurt that evening I knew that I loved you.'

Marie was silent; the spinning-wheel hummed, and you could have heard a pin drop.

'Have you nothing to tell me, Marie?'

She now walked impetuously up to him, gave him her hand, and said in a tone of resolution in which there was only the lightest echo of her former fear: 'It cannot be. You yourself set this answer on my lips when you said the heart speaks quickly if it is going to speak at all.' Then she hid her face in her hands and exclaimed: 'Ah, am I ungrateful?'

'I have no claim to your gratitude, Marie.'

'And yet perhaps I am ungrateful, not towards you but towards my fate. I was not so young when I came to this house to have forgotten what I was before. And if I ever had forgotten, the cross standing above my father's grave up there would have reminded me every day. The way God has guided me lays on me a special duty of gratitude, and I do not know if I am fulfilling this duty if I now simply say: my heart does not speak. Perhaps it *ought* to speak; but it stays silent. And so things must remain as they are. Something divides us, a difference in our natures which I do not know how to name but which I know exists because I feel it.'

Marie fell silent.

'So at least I know the truth for a certainty,' Othegraven said then, 'and the saddest of all things, to hope where there is no hope, has been spared me. You have been frank and straight-forward: I thank you for that. I shows me how rightly my affection judged: rightly, but not fortunately. And it is without bitterness, Marie, that I leave you; for the heart will not let itself be compelled. And though I could wish that your heart had decided differently, I know that it has decided as it *had* to decide.'

He gave his hand first to Marie, then to the mother, and left the house in which a brief conversation had condemned him to a life of unhappiness.

An hour later he left again for Frankfurt.

'Dear friend,' the pastor's final words had been, 'I have now observed life for forty years, and I have seen again and again how men of your kind feel irresistibly drawn to natures like Marie's, without these natures ever being able to return the love they are offered. Strong character is drawn to fantasy and imagination, but fantasy and imagination are not drawn to strong character.'

Othegraven weighed Seidentopf's words in his mind and smiled sadly.

'It is so; the old man is right. And so I shall go through this life without love; for only that side of existence that I lack has any charm for me, that alone draws me to it. And so I know my fate. I shall endure it: not only because I must, but also because I *will*. Do what it is fitting you should do. But I had a fairer dream: even as late as today.'

As he was thus talking to himself the schoolmaster had arrived in Podelzig, and he now passed the spot where he had encountered the old beadle, Rysselmann. He recalled the elevated mood he had been in as he talked with him, and he repeated to himself: 'Yes, a fairer dream: even as late as *today*!'

19

New Year's Eve at Guse

THE letter Hoppenmarieken had handed to Berndt with the remark 'There's only this one' had been forgotten during the scene that immediately followed. Only as our little friend from the woodland acre, as merry and cheerful as if nothing had happened, had turned out of the courtyard into the village street did Berndt recall it: it came from Kirch-Göritz and bore the inscription 'To Fräulein Renate von Vitzewitz. Hohen-

Vietz, near Küstrin'. He gave the letter to Lewin, who retreated down the long corridor to hand it to Renate in person.

In the sickroom all was bright; the fever had gone, and Renate was merely weak. Kathinka was sitting beside her bed, while Maline was standing at the window peeling one of the Calvilles she had declined to fetch from the ghostly hall the previous evening.

'May I?' Lewin asked, and took a chair. 'I have not come with empty hands; here, a letter for you, Renate.'

'Oh, lovely! I wish letters came every day. Kathinka, take that to heart, and you too, Lewin. You pampered people have no idea what a letter means to us solitaries.'

While speaking these words she had broken the seal and now looked at the signature: 'Doctor Faulstich'. But who else could it have been—who in Kirch-Göritz apart from him could have had occasion to write to Fräulein von Vitzewitz? The letter was dated the 29th, and was thus a day late.

'Read it to us,' said Kathinka, 'unless you and the doctor have secrets together.'

'Who knows; but I will take a chance.' And she read:

My dear Fräulein!

A judgement from which there is no appeal has decreed that you are to participate in the performance to be given on New Year's Eve at Schloss Guse. More, you will be required to inaugurate the festivities and to recite the enclosed Prologue, which, the directorial tone of this latter so far notwithstanding, I recommend to your friendly consideration, and especially to the indulgence of the two members of Kastalia who yesterday gladdened me by their visit, with a poet's vanity and trepidation. Full of justified misgivings as to the efficiency of our Kirch-Göritz postal arrangements, I have hesitated whether or not to send this letter to you by express messenger; but twenty-four hours for a distance which even with the detour via Küstrin is no more than a mile and a half seems quite sufficient; and so I cherish the hope that these lines, together with the enclosure, will reach you in good time. *Que Dieu vous prenne, vous et ma lettre, dans sa garde!*★ With this wish, which in form and language is already almost more of an obeisance to Schloss Guse than to Hohen-Vietz, I remain your very devoted

Doctor Faulstich.

'How marvellous,' said Kathinka.

'I'll now read you the postscript,' Renate said, and read on:

The question of costume, my dear Fräulein, need not concern you, even though the personage into whose mouth I have placed my prologue-verses is no less a person than Melpomene* herself. However many difficulties the Nine Sisters may make, from Clio to Polyhymnia they are on one point complacent: that of dress. The cast of the drapery is all. But if we should need any advice I shall rely on Demoiselle Alceste, who with the assistance of Racine* and his school has for the past forty years dwelt in the house of Atreus and been constantly running up and down between Electra and Clytemnestra.

'Oh, what a shame!' exclaimed Maline from the window; like all spoiled servant-girls she liked nothing better than to involve herself in whatever conversation was going on.

'Yes, you are right,' said Renate, half in jest and half in sorrow, as she folded the letter again. 'For a moment everything lit up, but only to make me all the more aware of the darkness of my days at Hohen-Vietz. Forgive me, Kathinka, for being so ungrateful as to forget your visit and the many hours you have spent entertaining me with talk, but this trip to Guse and Demoiselle Alceste and my Prologue are beyond my wildest dreams. To be a muse, to be Melpomene: how grand that sounds! And to be dressed by a French actress with her own hands! I could live to be sixty and never receive so wonderful an invitation again.'

'But is it so very impossible?' asked Kathinka. 'You feel better, the fever has gone. Come, we'll put you in a fur coat and a foot-muff.'

Renate shook her head. 'I couldn't do that to old Leist. If I should die on him—he'd never forgive me as long as I lived. No, I shall stay here; and *you* must speak the role, Kathinka.'

'I?'

'Yes, you have no choice. As you know, except for you and me there are no young ladies at all in our aunt's salon, and if Demoiselle Alceste—I have just glanced at the verses—is not to appear as her own herald, announce herself and perhaps also extol and glorify herself, there is nothing for it but that you must speak the Prologue. Besides, you have the figure for Melpomene. But I almost think you don't want to do it.'

'Not at all: it's only that I don't trust my memory.'

'Oh! We shall find a way around that,' said Lewin. 'It is still two hours before we have to leave; but above all we have the journey itself; on the way I shall recite you the verses, several times, and by repeating them you will learn them. Fresh air makes memorizing easier, anyway.'

Kathinka was content, and so they separated, for the Ladalinskis needed the time they still had available to prepare for their departure rather than merely for a trip to Guse. If their aunt did not detain them, they intended to return that same night to Berlin.

At four o'clock the sleigh with the bays with the snow-blankets and the red plumes—the same that had drawn Lewin and Renate across to Guse on the third day of Christmas—halted before the entrance to the house and, after a warm farewell from Aunt Schorlemmer, and from Jeetze and Maline, who dried her eye with a corner of her apron and repeated 'how nice it has been' and 'such a nice young lady' again and again, the Ladalinskis finally made themselves comfortable on their cushioned bench and Lewin took his place in the driving-seat. Berndt von Vitzewitz, who still had to write to Turgany and submit a report on the results of the house-search, had promised to follow in fifteen minutes with the ponies.

'But I shall overtake you! What do you bet, Kathinka?'

'You'll lose.'

'No, I'll win.'

And thereupon the horses moved off and the lightweight sleigh flew away at a speed which, for the moment at least, would seem to have loaded the odds against Berndt.

As on the short journey to Hohen-Ziesar the previous evening, Kathinka had again taken the reins, the bells jingled and the red plumes nodded. Their route first took them five hundred yards between the poplars along the road to Küstrin before they turned off to the left into the broad snowy expanse of the Oderbruch. As they passed the spot where the attack had taken place, Tubal pointed across to the grove of trees and laughingly described to his sister the race he and Lewin had had across the field.

'And all that in the knightly service of Hoppenmarieken. Who was ever more faithful to his device: *Mon cœur aux dames!*'*

'But it needs lady dwarfs to spur you on to knightly deeds: otherwise you leave knightly deeds and knightly song to others, even if they be Doctor Faulstich. However, it is time for us to start reading, Lewin. All I know as yet is that the first stanza ends with a rhyme on Guse: Muse, Gus'. I believe the whole Melpomene idea owes its existence to the existence of this rhyme.'

With much laughter they now began to recite the verses, and whenever a new stanza had been conquered Lewin saluted with his whip and the crack, now and then awakening an echo, resounded across the broad expanse of snow. In this manner they had passed Golzow, and soon afterwards Langsow too, and the church-tower at Guse was already visible between the trees of the park, when the ponies, their black manes standing erect like combs with the fury of their gallop, suddenly appeared beside them and, raising himself in his calash-carriage, Vitzewitz called across to Kathinka: 'I've won!'

'No! No!' And with that there commenced a race in which the first thing to go overboard was the doctor's *ottava rime*, followed at once by all thought of Melpomene and the Pro-logue. To the bays, too, it was like an ambitious revival of the glories of former days; but the advantage they derived from their longer legs soon proved less decisive than the disadvantage of their longer years of service, which the youthfully gay snow-blankets had been able to disguise only for a few moments, and the calash thundered across the sphinx-bridge two horses' lengths ahead and was the first to come to a halt before the château. Berndt had already thrown back the splash-leather and alighted when the second sleigh drew up, and was ready to offer Kathinka his hand to assist her to the ground.

'Here is your reward for winning,' she said, giving the old man a hearty kiss; then, turning to Lewin, she added: '*Voilà notre ancien régime.*'

Whereupon they entered the heated entrance hall, where servants took from them their furs and cloaks.

Today it was the 'outer circle' that was assembled in the countess's blue salon: in addition to several immediate neighbours from Tempelberg, Quilitz and Friedland, it included the prefect and the new rector of Selow. They had already been together for half an hour, dividing their attention between their hostess and her favoured guest, Demoiselle Alceste.* As she had promised, the latter had arrived a day earlier, and she and the countess had chatted until after midnight about the days at Rheinsberg, about the Wreechs, the Knesebecks and the Tauentziens, but above all about the actors and actresses at the prince's court, the inspired Blainville and the beautiful Aurora Bursay. For more than twenty-one years there had always been some risk attached to their meeting, but this time both ladies were contented beyond their expectations —an outcome for which both might have ventured to claim the credit. But the greater part of it went, of course, to Demoiselle Alceste, who united in her person all the attractive qualities of her profession and her nation. Very large, very formidable and very asthmatic, of an almost copper-coloured complexion and clad in a black silk dress that looked as if it dated back to the Rheinsberg days, she could none the less make you overlook all this through the great goodness of heart betrayed by her expressive little black eyes and above all by her willingness to enter into the spirit of everything cheerful or playful and, if it was enunciated with *esprit*, anything ambiguous as well. What enhanced even more the attractiveness of her presence were the attacks of artist's dignity to which she was subject; attacks which, if they were not in themselves slightly comic, in any event gave rise to the liveliest hilarity when, as a reaction to them, she herself mocked them. Her mental alertness, together with her care for her figure, made her look younger than she was, so that, although she had performed Phaedra at the coronation of Louis XVI,* she could boast of having conquered first Drosselstein, then Bamme, in the space of less than half an hour.

Of these two conquests her whole nature inclined her to value the second more highly. She had encountered many Drosselsteins but hitherto no Bammes, and with the days of amorous adventures far behind her, she had long since grown accustomed to assessing the value of her conquests only according to the quantity of entertaining conversation they might guarantee her. In this she resembled the countess, but with the difference that the countess preferred in general the exceptional and singular, while if it was to please *her* a thing had to bear the stamp of cheerfulness and gaiety. In the light of this it was perhaps surprising that she had never been successful in comedy, but had enjoyed her true triumphs on the stage only in roles involving incest or conjugal murder.

Coffee was already being handed round when the party from Hohen-Vietz came in and approached Aunt Amelie. The latter greeted them warmly and rose from her seat on the sofa to introduce her favourite, Kathinka—who had hardly had time to tell her of Renate's indisposition and the momentary peril in which this had placed the role of Melpomene—to her French guest.

Demoiselle Alceste broke off her conversation with Bamme and went over to the two ladies.

'*Je suis charmée de vous voir,*' she began vivaciously, '*Madame la comtesse, votre chère tante, m'a beaucoup parlé de vous. Vous êtes polonaise. Ah, j'aime beaucoup les Polonais. Ils sont tout-à-fait les Français du Nord. Vous savez sans doute que le Prince Henri était sur le point d'accepter la couronne de Pologne.*'*

Kathinka had never heard of this, but thought it prudent to refrain from admitting the fact; whereupon Demoiselle Alceste continued with a conversation which, growing more and more political, included expressions of admiration for the prince and aversion to his royal brother such as even Aunt Amelie would hardly have dared to utter. The subject of the Polish crown offered the best opportunity for expatiating on this theme.

To the '*grand Frédéric*', she went on, placing a mocking emphasis on his name, the idea of having his brother beside him as the king of a great nation had been simply unendurable. There had of course, as always, been no lack of efforts to disguise the real motives with reasons of 'higher policy', but she knew better: envy alone had been decisive.

Kathinka, who knew nothing of the prince except that he was a misogynist, found in this pathological trait, which could hardly have recommended him to her, a momentary reason for feeling a sense of loyalty towards the Great King, so that at last she interrupted, smiling, with the words: '*Mais quelle bêtise; je suis polonaise de tout mon cœur et me voilà prête à travailler pour le roi de Prusse.'*

With that the political section of their conversation came to an end and they passed to the more peaceable theme of the theatrical performance they would shortly be giving. But even here complete unanimity proved unattainable: Kathinka repeatedly insisted that, as the Prologue-speaking Melpomene, she had a natural right to be initiated into Dr Faulstich's mysteries and those of his principal performer, Demoiselle Alceste, but she insisted in vain; the latter maintained that one of the greatest delights of theatrical life was to see the actors and actresses repeatedly surprising one another, and so pleasant a game ought not to be wantonly spoiled.

While this conversation was being conducted in the great window alcove with its view of the park and the setting sun—only a narrow band of evening twilight still lay along the sky—Tubal and Lewin had settled themselves beside their aunt to report to her the latest events at Hohen-Vietz. Their audience soon expanded. First Krach and Medewitz, then the prefect of Lebus and the rector of Seelow, finally Baron Pehlemann, who, disregarding the traces of gout that still lingered, had loyally put in an appearance: they all drew closer to hear of the break-in, of the discovery of the two vagabonds on the reed-island and of the search of Hoppenmarieken's house. No one followed the story more intently than did Aunt Amelie herself, who, in addition to a natural predilection for stories of break-ins, also derived a hearty satisfaction from seeing her brother's supposed French marauders transformed into Muschwitz and Rosentreter: Berndt's superiority of character had annoyed her too often for her not to have welcomed the trace of comicality which this transformation injected into his undertakings.

And yet, as his sister was silently triumphing over what she took to be his discomfiture, Berndt was again busy promoting these very undertakings. At almost the same moment as the introduction of Kathinka had interrupted the conversation between Demoiselle Alceste and Bamme, Berndt had succeeded in engaging the old general's attention and, taking him aside, had immediately begun to develop his ideas, previously no more than fleetingly sketched out to him, for an insurrection in the land between the Oder and the Elbe. The chief issue was still what it had always been: the arming of the populace *à tout prix*,★ that is to say *with* the King if possible, *without* him if necessary. It was in regard to this issue, however, that Berndt wondered whether he could expect the old general's support. For Bamme belonged to that military aristocracy raised under the rule of absolutism which would have done anything provided it was ordered by the cabinet and have been truly at home only under a king who governed by *lettre-de-cachet*.★ That was how Berndt knew the general. But there were two things he overlooked: first the general's strongly marked patriotism which, if offended, could at any moment intensify itself to the point which finds expression in the assertion, commonly made by our aristocracy, '*We* were here *before* the Hohenzollerns'; then his inclination for risk-taking and adventurousness in general, which was so great that any conspiracy whatever was attractive to him, so that he might well find an attempt to overthrow a ruler directed from *below* more enticing, because more uncommon, than an attempt to crush a revolt ordered from *above*. Without ideals or principles, his most pronounced characteristic was the need to gamble; he lived on excitements.

When he had outlined everything, Berndt added: 'There you have my plan, Bamme. Its loyalty can be called into question. We are true to our country and, as God is my witness, also to out King. But if we take up arms against his will we could be considered to have committed high treason. I am aware of this fact and I do not conceal it.'

During these last words Bamme had been smiling and twisting his white moustache: 'It is as you say, Vitzewitz. But what of it! We have to take our own life in our own hands: that is the custom in this country. I know exactly what they will do in the capital, or let us say rather what they will *have* to do; for I can see they have no choice. At first they will disown us, again and again, very earnestly and more and more menacingly. In the meantime, however, they will wait and follow what we are doing with great attentiveness and pious good wishes. If we succeed, they will accept what we have won, a country and a crown, without further ado, and reward us by—forgiving us; if we fail they will have us all put to the sword so as to save themselves. It could cost us our heads: but I, for my part, don't find that stake too high. I am your man, Vitzewitz.'

While in various parts of the salon conversation was thus in progress on so great a variety of topics—the Polish crown, Hoppenmarieken and a popular uprising between the Oder and the Elbe—the entire weight of the organization of the evening, together with the entire responsibility for its success or failure, rested upon the shoulders of Dr Faulstich. Reserving to herself only the supreme command, an ultimate Yes or No, the countess had, with a casual '*Vous ferez tout cela*',* devolved everything else upon the doctor from Kirch-Göritz. 'What will do for the count of Ziebingen', she had said, 'will do for the countess of Guse.' He had been obliged to obey and had, indeed, done so willingly, but he had also done so in fear. It was a fear that was only too justified. When he reviewed the situation he found the only person he could really trust was himself, and of himself he was not wholly certain. A hundred questions crowded in upon him. What kind of showing—to cite only one of the most pressing and vital questions—would be made by the flute-and-strings quintet which, combining the musical forces of Selow and Kirch-Göritz, had been entrusted to the direction of the youthful cantor of Guse, according to Aunt Amelie an unrecognized musical genius? Leaving true declamation aside, would Kathinka even prove capable of speaking the Prologue fluently and without making mistakes? Would Alceste not treat the whole performance condescendingly as a mere trifle? Could the servants, male and female, who had been entrusted with changing the scenery, holding certain properties in readiness, and with opening and closing the curtains, be relied on?—for the theatre at Guse had not yet acquired the curtain that rolls up and down like a window-blind, but still possessed the type that falls together from left and right. More than once the blood rose to the doctor's head and awoke in him the desire even at this eleventh hour to go to the countess and offer his resignation; but, seeing the impossibility of such a step, he had each time been fortified by the motto that in similar predicaments had so often before come to his assistance: 'Just get started.' He also derived unexpected succour when his need was greatest from the appearance of little Eve: she had hardly arrived to place herself at his disposal than a new spirit of co-operation entered into the servants, who had good reason not to want to incur the displeasure of the countess's declared favourite.

Thus nine o'clock arrived; Mademoiselle Alceste and Kathinka had been called from the salon an hour previously. Eve now went over to her mistress to whisper to her that all was ready. The countess rose at once, offered Drosselstein her arm, and walked through the dining-room to the theatre situated behind it: about half the space was occupied by a stage and half by an auditorium. The latter was lit only dimly, so that the figures on the stage would appear all the brighter. Some twenty seats were arranged in two rows, in front of them five high-backed chairs for the musicians, and in the centre, his eyes directed at the curtain and a manuscript-roll in his hand, there stood the conductor, the cantor of Guse, by name Herr Nippler. On the seats there lay theatre programmes, printed at the instance of Faulstich by the bookbinder and publisher of school-textbooks, P. Nottebohm of Kirch-Göritz, and after everyone had taken their places they were at once eagerly perused. The programme read:

Théâtre du Château de Guse.
Jeudi le 31 Décembre 1812.
La représentation commencera à 9 heures.

1. Ouverture exécutée sous la direction de M. Nippler, chantre de Guse, par 3 violons, 1 flûte et 1 basse.
2. Prologue. (Melpomène.)
3. Début de Mademoiselle *Alceste Bonnivant*.

Scènes diverses, prises de Guillaume Tell. Tragédie en cinq actes par Lemierre.

    a. Cléofé, épouse de Tell, s'adressant à son mari:
       Pourquoi donc affecter avec moi ce mystère,
       Et te cacher de moi comme d'une étrangère?
    b. Cléofé, s'adressant à la Garde de Gesler:
       Je veux voir mon époux, vous m'arrêtez en vain etc.
    c. Cléofé, s'adressant à Gesler:
       Quoi, Gesler! quand j'amène un fils en ta présence etc.
    d. Cléofé, s'adressant à Walther Fürst:

C'était-là le moment de soulever la Suisse. Tu l'as perdu!
4. Finale composé pour 2 violons et 1 flûte par M. Nippler.

Le Sous-Directeur Dr Faulstich.
Imprimé par P. Nottebohm,
relieur, libraire et éditeur à Kirch-Goeritz.*

The majority of those present had not read halfway through the programme before the signal was given by the bell. Nippler tapped on his desk with the roll of paper and the violins immediately set to work; then the flute came in, while from time to time the 'bass's fundamental force'* could be heard grumbling away. At length it came to an end, Nippler mopped his brow, and the curtain opened. Melpomene stood there.

An 'Ah!' went through the whole assemblage, so heartfelt that a more timorous nature than Kathinka's must have discovered the courage for speech.

Before she began, Rutze softly inquired of Baron Pehlemann, who was sitting next to him: 'What is she supposed to be?'

'Melpomene.'

'But here it says Prologue.'

'They are one and the same.'

'Ah, I understand,' Rutze whispered, though the expression on his face made it seem highly unlikely that this assurance was true.

Kathinka took a step forward. She wore a white robe which showed off Demoiselle Alceste's art of draping to perfection, and had propped against her left hip a long, green-bound notebook to whose covers there was stuck a copy of the stanzas she had to speak. In her right hand she held a stylus. Thus attired and accoutred she resembled Clio rather than Melpomene. Composedly, as though she had been born on the boards, her eyes directed alternately at the audience and at the notebook, she spoke:

> 'Ye know me! Once a favoured child of Hellas
> In exile now I stray from land to land,
> And weeds and moss and ivy twine together
> Where now the ruins of my temple stand;
> Ah, in my sadness oft the longing takes me

To end my wanderings on some homeland strand—
Brief *halts* alone are granted the transient Muse:
Her favourite one is *here*, here in Schloss Gus'.

And do you ask what happened to my sisters?
They hardly reckon on their daily bread:
Thalia plays in inns and public houses,
And poor Terpsichore with dancing's dead.
Thus unaccompanied through the world I wandered
Until my darling met me on the road:
Ye know her, and ye know she is the best
I have to offer to this feast: *Alceste.*'

Here she paused for a moment, unaffectedly turned the notebook over so that the back cover, to which the final stanza was attached, was now uppermost, and then went on:

'She has but one desire: to give you pleasure;
But whether she succeeds, 'tis yours to say.
And should her words sound strangely to your hearing
As strangers grant them hospitality.
As though 'twas *I* who speaks I pray receive her,
Ye noble guests assembled here today.
She is my emissary and she must prevail:
"I have no second if the first should fail".'*

The curtain fell. There was lively applause, the liveliest coming from Rutze, who repeatedly averred that he was now completely clear as to everything and was full of admiration for the way Faulstich had contrived it all. The only one to persevere in silence at this little triumph of Kathinka's was Lewin: the assurance with which she had recited verses she had previously barely glanced at, though it aroused his admiration, also filled him with a painful sense of foreboding. 'She can do anything she wants,' he said to himself; 'will she always want what she should?'

In the giftedness of her nature, and in the exuberance to which it gave rise, he saw something that would sooner or later drive them apart.

The interval was over, the violins softly intoned to indicate that the next number was on its way. All eyes turned to the programme: '*Scènes prises de Guillaume Tell. Scene One: Cléofé, épouse de Tell, s'adressant à son mari.*' At the same moment the curtain opened. A backdrop of lake and mountains had been pushed in front of the Greek temple, a cowhorn sounded and the jangle of cowbells was audible. The scene was thus very different, but what now appeared on it was more different still. In place of the youthful figure in white there stepped forward an old woman in black: Mademoiselle Alceste, who, treating the question of costume with extreme contempt, had retained her black silk frock (her one and only) and had been content to represent the spirit of Switzerland with a long shepherd's crook and a bunch of rhododendrons taken from the Guse green-houses and the style of grand tragedy with a skull-cap with a glittering brooch attached to it. The 'Ah!' of admiration with which Kathinka had been received was not accorded her, but to this she paid no heed: she knew from long experience that the decisive thing was not the entrance but the exit, and she was quite sure her exit would be effective.

Now she spoke, avoiding all false *échauffement*, first the words addressed to her husband exhorting him to tell her his secret: '*Pourquoi donc affecter avec moi ce mystère?*'; then in quick succession the brief sentences addressed to Gessler's servants and finally to Gessler himself. The excellence of her style was revealed in every word, and by the end of this third scene she could without vanity tell herself she 'had her public in her hand'.

But the fourth scene, '*Cléofé s'adressant à Walther Fürst*', was still to come. Aunt Amelie, who was intimately acquainted with the play, anticipated a supremely exciting effect from these iambics of wrath, and was just saying as much to Drosselstein when the director's bell behind the curtain announced that the piece was about to continue.

But who could describe the universal astonishment when, as the curtains now opened again, instead of Cléofé a similar yet essentially different character gazed down on them. Who was this novel figure? The question hovered only for an instant. The shepherd's crook, the bunch of rhododendrons, the skull-cap with the brooch were gone, and a short jacket with a green collar which covered at any rate the upper half of the silk frock permitted not the slightest doubt that the huntsman's figure standing defiantly on the rock was meant to be no less a person than William Tell himself. With the head of his crossbow he was pointing at the figure of Gessler, who had just been struck down: and in the *German* language, strangely but not distractingly accented, Alceste—who had agreed to this surprise, planned by Faulstich, very readily—spoke the closing words of the drama, which, now and then transcending the immediate Swiss context, could be interpreted as a universal hymn to the liberation of the peoples:

> 'The tyrant's dead! Come here, all ye oppressed,
> Behold his downfall: from his castle, see,
> That stands ablaze, how rise the flickering flames
> Like banners waving in the wind, that say:
> Gessler is dead and our dear land is free,
> Oppression now is dead, and tyranny!'

As she said these words Demoiselle Alceste descended the rocky steps and, advancing to the front of the stage, continued in elevated tones:

> 'And should the foe assemble for revenge,
> We can destroy him, we have strength enough:
> Let him but come, as soldiers he shall find
> Each one of us, behind our mountain wall.
> And should he press down to our deepest vale,
> Where every path to flight or rescue ends,
> Then down upon him stones and rocks shall fall,
> And, backing this confusion, *we*, with sword
> And spear and scythe, shall fall upon him then:
> "Despair, surrender, foe, all hope is lost!"
> So shall his pride and plumes defeated lie:
> For mightier than these is *liberty*!'★

A storm of applause broke forth that completely eclipsed Kathinka's triumphs, and the cry 'Demoiselle Alceste', beginning as a murmur, grew louder and louder. After a pause during which the applause rose to a crescendo Demoiselle Alceste appeared and bowed dignifiedly; and, since no one had thought to provide either garlands or bouquets, Aunt Amelie herself stepped forward and extended her hand up to her on the stage as a token of gratitude. Nippler then straightway struck up a brief finale he had composed himself, to the sound of which the guests rose and departed to take supper in the front-rooms.

Here in the front-rooms little tables had been laid and, as soon as those who had truly borne the burden of the day had also arrived, as they soon did, everyone took his place as choice or chance determined. Nippler too had been invited: Bamme, who had a preference for the singular and exceptional, paid him particular attention, assuring him again and again that the music had been 'something really remarkable. Especially the flute.'

The main table, on which six covers had been laid, stood in the mirrored-room: here sat the countess, with Mademoiselle Alceste and Kathinka beside her, and opposite them Drossel-stein, Berndt and Baron Pehlemann, who could make some small claim to a familiarity with French literature, having read the *Henriade* in translation and the *Charles Douze*★ actually in the original. As kindred of the house, Tubal and Lewin were doing the honours in the blue salon; several of the gentlemen had withdrawn to the billiard-room, among them Medewitz, whose falsetto was audible from time to time at the countess's table.

This was the same marble-topped table standing on four rounded legs at which coffee had been taken on the occasion of the Christmas dinner and which later, when the ancient con-tention '*Roi Frédéric* or *Prince Henri*' had again come up, had been the scene of a somewhat acrimonious debate between Vitzewitz and his sister the countess. And the table was not to be spared a dispute between brother and sister again today: but this dispute as yet stood far off; it came only at the conclu-sion of a long-drawn-out conversation whose subject-matter was at first limited to the 'perfect performance' given by Mademoiselle Alceste and only after every conceivable form of compliment had been exhausted came to include also the play itself. This transition was effected with much dexterity by the countess, and she knew well what she was doing. She was the only one present who had read the tragedy, and at the same time instructed herself on Lemierre's life from a biography which prefaced her copy of it, so that she saw herself in the pleasing position of being able to triumph over Drosselstein, her rival in matters of French literature, and at the same time shine brilliantly in all directions—and most of all before Demoiselle Alceste, who, as a true child of the theatre, contended herself with learning her roles and had felt not the slightest instigation to plunge into forewords and epilogues, let alone annotations or notes on literary history.

It was a pleasant picture the countess gradually unrolled before them as she described the life of Lemierre, and, because he was always moved by genuinely human traits in a person, even Berndt evidenced an unfeigned interest in it. In the manner of poets, Lemierre had always remained half a child. His unpretentious existence had been consecrated to only three things: poetry, self-denial and piety. He had already attained sixty before he acquired fame, but even when famous he was still poor. Performances of his plays brought him only small sums; when he received them he made his way to Villiers le Bel, where his nearly eighty-year-old mother lived. There he divided the money with her, talked to her of his hopes and plans, and then returned to the capital as he had come, by foot, to resume his work.

Like so many writers of tragedies he was of a cheerful disposition, and society was amused and enlivened by his jests, his anecdotes and his occasional verses. He was as generous as he was poor; himself without malice, he aroused no malice in others. A nervous affliction, which had seized him several months before his death, rendered him blind: he died in July 1793, in the midst of the days of the Terror, which he had lived to experience but was spared from seeing with his own eyes.

This, in summary, was the information the countess imparted piece by piece. She was very much enjoying the feeling of knowing more than anyone else and therefore received a somewhat unpleasant jolt when Drosselstein, repeating the name Lemierre several times as though recalling something half-forgotten, said with a faint hint of sarcasm: 'Yes, it can only have been Lemierre; your ladyship will surely remember the *bon mot* made on the occasion of the second performance of *Guillaume Tell*? I discovered it in the *Anecdotes dramatiques*.'

The expression on Aunt Amelie's face as this question was being asked left no doubt as to its answer, so that, to spare her the embarrassment of having to say 'No', Drosselstein went on without pausing: 'Although the piece had been enthusiastically received, even at the second performance the theatre was empty, and only a hundred or so Swiss were there for reasons of patriotism. One of the Frenchmen present noticed this strange composition of the audience and whispered to his neighbour: "It used to be: no cash, no Swiss; here it's a case of: no Swiss, no cash." '★

The countess was herself sufficiently fond of humour for this well-turned piece of wit to conquer her depression of spirits; and, soon lulling herself again with the euphonious sound of the titles of Lemierre's tragedies, with *Idomeneus* and *Artaxerxes*, she wound up her enthusiasm to the point of asserting that the superiority of the French mind was nowhere expressed more clearly than in the fact that even its productions of the second rank were superior to that which in German literature was regarded as being of the first.

Berndt, who may have suspected what the countess was aiming at, turned in her direction and asked quietly: 'Could you give examples?'

'Certainly; and I shall take that which lies nearest to hand, this same *Guillaume Tell* to which, with the aid of our honoured guest'—and here she indicated Mademoiselle Alceste—'we owe such a pleasurable hour. *Lemierre, n'est qu'un auteur de second rang.*★ But how much superior is his *Guillaume Tell* to the *Wilhelm Tell* of Herr Schiller,★ a play with more characters in it than the four Forest Cantons have inhabitants and with its continual changes of scene; someone sings a song and a lunar rainbow appears; all as though in an opera. Finally Gessler enters on a horse . . .'

'. . . And the prompter is in danger of being trampled to death, like Max Piccolomini.★ Isn't that so, sister?'

'I accept what you say and overlook the mockery in the way you say it, which is, I know, directed rather at me than at the poet. In any case, he is quite able to get along without my approval: the Duke of Weimar ennobled him.'*

'That he did. But have you, for your part, ever read Schiller's *Tell* with proper attentiveness?'

'I have at least tried to do so.'

'There you have the advantage of me in our little contention, since I, for my part, cannot boast of even having tried to read Lemierre's. One thing, however, is certain: he is come and gone. They may, for all I know, have given him a seat in the Academy, loaded him with garlands, erected a picture or a bust of him in some Hall of Honour, but what I said still stands: he is come and gone. He has left no vestige of himself behind.'

'And yet it is only an hour ago that we were tracing these vestiges, that you say do not exist, and were carried away by the beauty of his words.'

'His words, yes; but not by anything more. He may have touched the heart of his nation but he did not *move* it. For such words of consolation as are spoken in Schiller's *Tell*:

> When the oppressed on earth can find no justice,
> They reach for consolation up to Heaven
> And thence draw down their everlasting rights,

you will, I am sure, seek in vain in your Lemierre's. Otherwise I would know of them. For this "Herr Schiller", as you call him, is no cold, formalist poet, he is the poet of his *people*, and more than ever now, when this poor downtrodden people is wrestling for salvation. But forgive me, sister: you know nothing of people and fatherland, you are familiar only with society and the court, and your heart, if you look into it, is with the enemy.'

'Not with the enemy, but with that in which he has the advantage of us.'

'And in your eyes that is nothing more and nothing less than everything. I can see where he is superior to us, as you can, but the difference between you and me is that you will allow of no exception and fancy that his admitted general superiority is to be encountered in every single individual case. Remember, there are fruit-trees that bear little fruit: perhaps Germany is such a tree. And then, if there is to be any reprimanding at all, reprimand the tree but not the fruit. These are usually the finer the rarer they are: and a rare fruit of this kind is *our Tell*.'

While this contention was in progress a circle of listeners had grown rapidly around Vitzewitz from the salon and the billiard-room, and it was only now, as he fell silent, that the latter was sensible of what was painful in the situation: not for his sister, who was always challenging him to argument, but for Mademoiselle Alceste. He therefore rose and went up to her and, taking her hand and kissing it, said: '*Pardon*, Madame, if I should have offended you by anything I said. I know what we owe to a guest from a foreign land, but at the same time I also know what we owe to our own land. You are a Frenchwoman: I ask you what you would have felt if, anywhere in France, you had heard your Corneille* declared inferior to a second-rate poet of another country! I know I am not deceived in you, you would have spoken according to the dictates of your heart, not according to the demands of social convention. Madame, I count on your forgiveness.'

Mademoiselle Alceste rose with such an air of dignity you might have thought she was at least about to perform a scene from Corneille, and said: '*Monsieur le baron, vous avez raison, et je suis heureuse de faire la connaissance d'un vrai gentilhomme. J'aime beaucoup la France, mais j'aime plus les hommes de bon cœur partout où je les trouve.*' Then, bowing respectfully to the countess, she continued: '*Milles pardons, Madame la comtesse, mais, sans doute, vous vous rappelez la maxime favorite de notre cher prince: la vérité c'est la meilleure politique.*'*

The countess extended her hand to the ageing Frenchwoman and gave a forced smile. She avoided the eyes of her brother. She could forget scenes like this—but not straightway.

It was past eleven o'clock. Conversation, which had for too long been literary, now turned to discussion of the most ordinary things and revolved around the question when carriages or sleighs should be summoned, who should go and who should stay. Against Tubal and Kathinka's departure the countess imposed a decisive veto, to which brother and sister found no difficulty in acceding. They agreed to remain, together with Dr Faulstich and Mademoiselle Alceste. Immediately thereafter Kathinka left the room, ostensibly to give the keys of her case and *étui* to Eve, in reality to chatter with her. For Kathinka was a woman of the world in this too, that the tittle-tattle of her chambermaid meant a great deal to her and the probings of professors very little.

In the meantime the conversation continued, but exchanges became more and more cursory and even Bamme's sarcasms could no longer really bring it to life. At last the clock struck twelve: Berndt opened one of the casement windows to let the Old Year out and the New Year in, and exclaimed as the cold air steamed past him:

'Be welcome, New Year! Often have I seen you arrive, but never yet as I do now. I feel a sweet and painful shudder and I know not if it is hope or fear. We have no New Year wishes, we have but one wish: May we be free when you depart again!'

Their glasses rang together, Mademoiselle Alceste's making one with them. She divided her feelings of patriotism between the *ancien régime* and the republic; for the Emperor, who was to her a foreigner, a Corsican, she entertained an honest hatred: so there was nothing in her heart to begrudge the unhappy land in which she had spent so many happy years a return to liberty and autonomy.

The excitement engendered by this brief toast to the New Year was still in evidence when Kathinka came back into the room.

'We have been casting lead,' she said, laughing, and laid a piece of the metal before her aunt: an image of a wreath was clearly visible on it. 'Eve says it's a bridal garland.'

The lead was passed from hand to hand, and everyone agreed that Eve had seen correctly and very probably prophesied correctly too. The last person to take it was Lewin, who was in his superstitiousness struck by the fact that the garland was not completely closed.

Servants entered to announce that carriages and sleighs were waiting. Berndt took his leave first; then the remainder of the guests followed, mostly in groups of two or more. The prefect of Lebus left with Drosselstein; they were going the same way.

Only Lewin journeyed alone. There was still music coming from the first villages he passed through, and mingled with it he heard the sound of gunshots welcoming in the New Year.

Then all grew silent, and only the barking of a dog could be heard from time to time in the distance. Where the road was bad his sleigh threw the snow to left and right and piled it into heaps; Lewin, however, gave himself up to dreamy reflection on the events of the past day.

Kathinka was again sitting in the upholstered seat; 'it is time to think of studying our poem, Lewin,' and he inclined his head so that their cheeks touched and began to recite the verses to her. Then he saw her standing on the stage, calm, sure of her success, and he seemed to hear the melodious sound of her voice. 'How beautiful she is!' He was seized by a passionate desire to throw himself at her feet and with a thousand oaths and kisses confess to her his love—a love she had ridiculed because he had not had the courage to avow it. But he shook his head, for he felt convinced it would be in vain and that he would never possess her.

The stars began to sparkle more and more brightly; he looked up at the sky, and in his soul there suddenly resounded the words he had read on the tombstone at Bohlsdorf: 'And she can walk on stars.'

And with that all desire fell away from him. He still beheld Kathinka's image, but it was growing fainter and fainter, and a feeling of peace descended upon him as he flew alone across the broad white expanse of the Oderbruch.

BOOK THREE

★

ALT-BERLIN

I

At the Johanniter Palace*

BERNDT VON VITZEWITZ had arrived in Berlin soon after six in the morning and alighted at the King of Portugal, a hotel, much favoured in those days, which stood in the Burgstrasse just along from the Langenbrücke; and after giving a number of instructions to Krist—who then removed himself to the Green Tree,* where he and the equipage were traditionally accommodated—resolved to recover in two hours of morning sleep whatever he might have lost on the preceding night (which had, indeed, been very little, since he was one of those fortunate people who, when they feel tired, can fall asleep anywhere).

At nine o'clock—he had adhered strictly to the two hours he had allowed himself—he was sitting refreshed at breakfast. The mantelpiece-clock was ticking, the fire in the stove was crackling, the ice-ferns on the window were melting, and all breathed contentment; Berndt stepped to the window and gazed out across the river at the Gothic parapets of the castle gleaming in the bright morning sunlight: from this aspect the castle still retained its medieval appearance.

'That is not something that can vanish overnight,' he said to himself, and then, stepping back from the window-alcove, began with military rapidity to dress himself. For the majority of the visits he proposed to make today his Neumark dragoon's uniform would no doubt have been the most suitable, but he chose instead the red dress-coat of the Order of the Knights of the Electorate of Brandenburg, and he had just finished arraying himself in this when a servant entered and announced that Privy Councillor von Ladalinski awaited him before the hotel. Berndt seized his hat and gloves, turned the key in the lock, and a minute later was seated at the privy councillor's side: they had agreed by letter to undertake a number of New Year duty-calls together.

The privy councillor was in court dress. They greeted one

another warmly but forbore to enter into any real conversation, since the objective that lay immediately before them claimed all their attention. They spoke only the names of certain ministers and ambassadors with whom their cards were to be left; until finally the carriage rumbled on to the broad sloping approach to the palace of the Johanniter Order at the corner of the Wilhelmsplatz.

In this palace there dwelt the Grand Master of the order, old Prince Ferdinand: Privy Councillor von Ladalinski had for many years enjoyed with him a relationship that was almost that of a friend, while Berndt von Vitzewitz, who knew him only slightly, revered him simply on account of his being the brother of Friedrich the Great. In this Berndt was by no means alone: the eighty-two-year-old prince was at that time accorded a general honour and respect which he had previously been denied throughout a long and eventful life. He had witnessed the 'great times' and participated in their battles; that bestowed upon him in these days of humiliation a lustre and authority greater than he had formerly possessed, and many hopes and aspirations were centred upon him. The heroic death of his eldest son,* too, inevitably contributed to enhance his fame and the sense of gratitude many felt towards him: this eldest son was the much celebrated Prince Louis, who, foreseeing the catastrophe about to break in upon them, had on the day before the Battle of Jena fallen at Saalfeld.

The old prince was ready to receive the two gentlemen when they were announced to him, and he had them requested to be good enough to await him in his study. On entering it they divided up the roles they were to play in the ensuing conversation: Berndt would as far as possible do most of the talking, with the privy councillor only now and then seconding him.

The prince's study embraced the lefthand corner of the front of the building, and two of its windows looked out on to the Wilhelmsstrasse. It possessed a greater degree of ease and comfort than the rooms of princes usually do. Thick Turkish carpets, damask curtains only half-drawn and curtains hung before doors and windows lent it repose and intimacy—which, seeing it was not very big and had four windows and two doors, would seem a difficult achievement; and the light and warmth emitted by the fire in the fireplace enhanced the impression of cosy well-being. Low bookcases and *étagères* stood against the piers between the windows, leaving space for numerous busts and pictures, the finest of which was a land-scape with buildings representing Schloss Friedrichsfelde, the prince's summer residence. A life-size portrait of the prince himself, by Graff,★ hung over the fireplace; beside it a wide backless sofa extended as far as the nearest doorway, while in the right-angle formed by the sofa stood a round table decorated with an alabaster flower-vase.

Berndt, who had never been in the room before, had hardly finished inspecting its contents when the prince, throwing back the curtain that concealed the door leading to his bedroom, entered sooner than expected. Responding benignantly to the obeisance with which the two gentlemen received him, he gestured them to take a seat on the sofa, and himself took up a position with his back to the fire, his hands clasped behind him and plainly endeavouring to secure as much warmth as poss-ible: it was the only thing he did that betrayed his age, for in no other respect, either in his bearing or in his face, did he give the impression of a man of eighty-two. Berndt recognized at once what particularly characterized this face: it betrayed, so he thought, a strange combination of unpretentiousness and self-awareness. And so it did in fact: by nature insignificant, and aware of his insignificance his whole life long, especially when he compared himself with his brothers, he was none the less permeated with a sense of the exalted mission of his house, and this bestowed upon him a majesty which, when he knitted his brows in a frown (as he often liked to do), could rise to the likeness of a *Jupiter tonans.*★ A large Roman nose assisted him in the production of this effect. It could not escape those who observed him more closely, however, that his posture as the Thunderer was no more than an act, and that the pride and haughtiness he occasionally felt obliged to display was likewise an imposture, performed as a kind of family duty.

'You have come to offer me your good wishes for the New Year,' he began. 'I thank you for your thoughtfulness, and I do so all the more in that it is the customary lot of the aged to be forgotten. Though the events of our day are, to be sure, preventing that from happening to me.' He fell silent for a moment and then, concluding a train of thought whose earlier stages had remained unspoken, added with dignity: 'I wish I could be more to our country than a mere memory.'

'Your Royal Highness is an example to our country,' Ladalinski replied.

'I take leave to doubt it, my dear privy councillor. If I have ever been anything to my country it was as one who obeyed orders. Never, in war or in peace, did I in any way oppose the intentions of my brother, the King: I never even felt the desire to do so. But things are different now. Obedience has departed from the world and everyone is loud in his own opinion, even in the army. I put it to you, would the resignation of three hundred officers have been possible, or even thinkable, in the days of my exalted brother, as a public protest at the policies of their commander-in-chief? A spirit of insubordination haunts this people, and whatever I am to them I am certainly not an example.' Though he was sure the prince knew nothing of his plans, *could* know nothing of them, Vitzewitz none the less flushed at these observations, each one of which struck home.

'Your Royal Highness will forgive me,' he interposed, 'if I take a different view of the events of our day and seek their origin elsewhere. Even the Great King experienced opposition and had to tolerate it. If such opposition was rare, that was because prince and people knew themselves to be at one. And most at one when times were hardest. But today there is a rupture: that unanimity of heart is lacking without which the Great King himself could not have waged a war demanding greater sacrifice than any war hitherto; the measures our present government takes disregard the views of the people, and thus implant in them a spirit of disobedience. The people are in conflict with the government, not because they desire to be, but because they have to be.'

'I recognize that there exists a conflict of opinions: personally, however, I place myself on the side possessing the greater experience and the better judgement. And where this better judgement is to be sought and found cannot be in doubt: you must put your trust in the wisdom of my great-nephew, my gracious Lord and King.'

'We do put our trust in His Majesty . . .'

'But not in the count, his first minister.'★

'Your Royal Highness expresses it precisely.'

'Without, however, concurring with you: for, my dear Major von Vitzewitz, to draw this distinction between the King and his first servant is inadmissible and contrary to Prussian tradition. I have no love for Count von Hardenberg; he has abolished with a stroke of the pen★ the order at whose head I stood as Grand Master for fifty years, he has confiscated our property, he has taken from us our commanderies:★ but I have never offered opposition to these measures of his. I know only obedience. We live in a monarchy, and whatever happens, happens in accordance with the will of His Majesty.'

'Supposedly,' Berndt replied with a tinge of bitterness. 'The will of the King—who can now say what or where it is? Under the Great King, your Royal Highness's exalted brother, it was the duty of his ministers to carry out his will, now it is His Majesty's duty to sanction the suggestions, that is to say the will, of his ministers. What was once the concern of the King is now the concern of his advisers; the King still decides, but his decisions are no longer based on the facts of reality, for he does not know them; they are based on the picture of them provided for him. He sees friend and foe, the world, the state of things, his own people through the spectacles of his ministers. The will of the King, as it is made known to us in decrees and ordinances, has long since been a mere fiction.'

The prince betrayed no sign of displeasure. He paced once or twice across the carpet; then, resuming his place before the fire, he replied in a tone of winning familiarity: 'You misunderstand my great-nephew the King, as do many others. I cannot boast of being acquainted with the plans and intentions of His Majesty: it is not the custom of Kings of Prussia to ask advice of members of their family, old or young, or even to initiate them into the daily routine of state affairs; but I believe I can give you the firmest assurance that the personal rule you believe has gone to the grave is very much more alive than you suppose.'

'Your Royal Highness surprises me.'

'I do not doubt it; and it may be that in some particulars I am mistaken; but in one particular I am not mistaken, and this one is our chief concern. What should our attitude be towards our great ally, the Emperor? That is the question with which all our minds are at present engaged. You believe that our policy of delaying and deferring and gaining time with promises and assurances originates with the minister: I tell you that it originates with the King himself.'

'Because things are presented to him in such a way that he can come to no other decision.'

'No, because he sees a policy of procrastination as being the only policy to pursue. Time alone will resolve our confusion and perplexity. He is convinced that the state of things at present obtaining cannot endure, and more than once I have heard him say: "The Emperor is boundlessly ambitious, and he who cannot keep his ambitions within bounds will lose his balance and fall." He regards the Empire as no more than a soap-bubble.'

'But it is a soap-bubble of such solidity that thrones and states are shattered when they collide with it.'

'It is not my task to defend my great-nephew's pronounce-ment, even though it does accord with my own opinion. But he spoke too, I think, of a storm that is bound to expend its fury and abate. And you may take the word of an old man who has seen the changes time has wrought over almost three gener-ations: it *will* expend its fury, and abate.'

'To be sure, your Royal Highness, but not before it has struck down even the highest summits.'

'Or would have struck them down if they had not known how to protect themselves in such a way that the lightning-bolt passes them harmlessly by.'

'Through an alliance?' The prince nodded.

Berndt, however, went on: 'There may indeed have been a time for that, but that time is past. Each new day brings its own duties and its own demands. One day demands submission, the next an alliance, a third day demands rebellion. I would like to think, your Royal Highness, that the day of rebellion has dawned.'

'Rebellion? With what? We have no army.'

'But we have the people.'

'The King distrusts them.'

'He distrusts their strength?'

'Perhaps that too; but he distrusts most of all the new spirit now active in the heads of the mob.'

'It is in precisely this spirit that salvation lies, provided one knows how to employ it and, within the bounds of good sense, rely upon it.'

'I do not contradict you; but the King does not feel himself equal to this task, it is contrary to his nature. To him many heads mean many minds. Expect nothing from him in this direction.'

'I hope then that he may acquire the needful sense of confidence, and with it faith in a good and loyal people whose only desire is permission to die for their King.'

Again changing his position, the prince pushed an armchair towards the sofa and, lowering himself into it, took Berndt's hand and fastened upon him a firm and friendly gaze.

'I know the people; I have lived among them. In my old age, now that my feeling for so many things has been extinguished, it has also been ignited for other things, and so I can say, because I know, that our people are good people. I can see them as clearly as though I had them before my eyes. But the King is intimidated and overawed by them; he has been through many painful experiences, he has never known the greatness that distinguished the days of my own youth. I know him perfectly. He would rather make an alliance with his enemy, provided this enemy approaches him in the shape of a firm ruler or a properly regulated government, than with his own people, when this people is split and sundered into a hundred different factions and has deserted the path of obedience. For he places good order above everything. With a unified enemy he knows where he is, with a many-headed mob he never does. Today they are with him, tomorrow against him; and while the Napoleonic storm hovering over him may strike him down but may also spare him, he sees in the unfettered might of the people only an onrushing sea which, once the dams have gone down, will drown the whole social order indiscriminately in its flood. He values the social order more highly than the political. And in that he is right.'

There followed a brief period of silence; then the prince

stood up again, a sign that he wished to conclude the audience. He shook hands with both gentlemen and thanked the privy councillor for having accorded him the opportunity of becoming more closely acquainted with a man so truly devoted to the fatherland.

'It is very gratifying to encounter a man with firm and independent views; but do not make the responsible minister's job harder than it is. We shall maintain the alliance until it disintegrates of itself; and, if signs do not deceive, the time when it will do so is close at hand. The foundering demon will then drag down with him the chains that fettered us to him.'

'But only to leave us *still* in bondage, and perhaps so for ever. We shall have done nothing but exchange masters. For what determines our fate is our own action or inaction; and if we bear this burden so compliantly, others will come and lay a new burden upon us.'

'Let us hope otherwise.'

With that they parted. The two gentlemen bowed, the carriage drove off along the sloping approach, and the French double-guard posted before the palace saluted. 'How did you like my prince?' the privy councillor inquired.

'Very well; I fear he is right, and that the resistance I thought emanated from the minister in fact emanates from the King himself. But even that shall not make me waver. I have no fear of the people and it is with them that I shall go forward. It is folly to allow yourself to reckon on the mistakes or the forbearance of an opponent when you have in your hands the power to dictate the law to him. To sit idly by with your hands in your lap is not only to put your trust in God, it is just as often to tempt Him. *Aide-toi même et le ciel t'aidera.*'*

With that the carriage turned right into the Unter den Linden and halted before the Sun hotel, where they had agreed to have lunch.

2

On the Windmühlenberg*

In the 'Wiesecke Room on the Windmühlenberg', where only the previous evening the grand New Year's Eve ball had taken place, there were now assembled some hundred of the establishment's regular patrons, together with their wives and children. Everything had been restored to its usual place, and on the floor where not twenty-four hours before the dancing couples had whirled and turned there now stood (as though the ball never had taken place) the somewhat rickety green tables with the regulation four chairs stationed around them; and between the tables there pressed and crowded back and forth and in all directions the horde of vendors and hawkers who had for many years been indigenous to the place and, indeed, almost a constituent part of it: old women with cream buns and cinnamon pretzels, simple pedlars with trays strapped before them containing sulphur-matches, flints, glass-beads and other wares, and peg-legged newsvendors selling, in addition to the two Berlin newspapers, all kinds of pamphlets and broadsheets. Over the whole lay the sour odour of pale ale which, made more oppressive by the exhalations of the lamps and the clouds of tobacco-smoke, was freshened only now and then when a steaming glass of punch was carried through.

At one of these tables, standing halfway under the music-gallery, sat four citizens of Berlin, two of them engaged in passionate conversation, the other two equally passionate listeners. They were neighbours in the Prenzlauerstrasse: Rabe the chimney-sweep, Stappenbeck the brush-maker, Niedlich the lace-maker and Schnökel the provision-merchant; all four were forty years old or more, and Niedlich and Schnökel lived in the same house, their dwellings being separated only by the hallway.

Rabe was the most distinguished and respected member of the company: he possessed not only a fine bearing, a fresh complexion and white teeth—which chimney-sweeps usually have—but also a wonderfully striking head of an authoritativeness that would have done credit to a chief magistrate. He was well aware of this fact and behaved accordingly: he preferred to be addressed rather than to address others and, although he was descended of an old Berlin family, eschewed all vainglorious boasting. He was the Drosselstein of this circle, the aristocratic element—as, indeed, chimney-sweeps in general, a trade in which the business passes from father to son, do in fact constitute a kind of citizen-nobility.

If Rabe was the Drosselstein of the circle, Stappenbeck was its Bamme. Niedlich said of him, in reproach, that you could never for a moment doubt that he was a brush-maker: for his hair, his manner and his mode of speech were all of them bristly. He was a genuine Berliner, in fact. Less distinguished and respected than Rabe, he was vastly superior in wit and knowledge, and even in experience: he had travelled in pursuit of his business, which he attended to with zeal and circumspection, he had been in Poland and Russia, and since the beginning of the campaign against Moscow he had counted as an incontestable authority on all things Russian. Even Rabe, who was in any case too grand and noble to stoop to lengthy contention, submitted to his words of wisdom, though they were words of wisdom which, although originating in the firm ground of a genuine knowledge of the country, preferred to disport themselves in the fields of politics and military affairs.

His antithesis was the lace-maker, Niedlich, a pleasant-mannered little man whose loquacity was restrained only by his timidity. He wore a bright-green coat and, because he suffered from head-colic, a little cap of flowered velveteen with a tassel attached to it—'as a mark of his profession', Stappenbeck maintained. Accustomed through his trade to continually springing back and forth, he was unable to remain sitting still for longer than five minutes at a time, like a canary which cannot refrain from hopping up and down the ladder in its cage. On his lean cheeks there burned two sharply defined red blotches, as though he were consumptive or over-heated, though he was in fact neither the one nor the other.

Finally there was Schnökel: the bass of this little male-voice choir, in voice as in figure; a large, strong man with a short neck, apoplectic in appearance, and a thoroughly knowledge-able connoisseur of the light ales of Berlin and Cottbus.* In regard to this last, he was able to distinguish by tasting them not only the different brands, but also the day on which they were laid down; then he would drink, smoke and sit quietly. Only now and then, when repeated clattering of his beer-mug had failed to attract attention, would he call in his stentorian voice across the intervening tables for 'another light'.

Stappenbeck had the *Berlinische Zeitung* under his left elbow. It was the edition of 26 December, and he had just read from it to his three companions the chief passages of the 29th communiqué, which was reproduced in it. To refresh himself he reached with his right hand to the large box of snuff standing between them on the middle of the table; Rabe was smoking quietly, Schnökel emitting great clouds of tobacco-smoke, while Niedlich, an avowed non-smoker—who, to Stappenbeck's intense annoyance, had been noisily breaking a whole dozen sugar-biscuits, and consuming them, throughout the entire reading—gestured to one of the old women so that he might now turn his attention to the cream buns.

The description of the crossing of the Beresina with which the extracts from the communiqué printed in the paper concluded had, together with patriotic rejoicing, also awakened a feeling of sympathy for the human beings involved in it; this was especially so in the case of Rabe, and it was not without emotion that he murmured to himself: 'The judgement of God! What will become of him, Stappenbeck?' he added. 'Can he ever recover from this campaign in ice and snow?'

'As a carp recovers when the ice freezes to the bottom: he must suffocate. I tell you, Rabe, it is all up with him. Don't forget what he is facing: first the terrain, and then the snow, and then the people. I know the place. It's not like it is here. Suppose you want to go to Potsdam; well, first there's the Black Eagle, then Stimmings, then Kohlhasenbrück, and everywhere something hot to eat. But now take Russia. There you march straight ahead the whole day long, and when in the evening you meet someone and ask him: "How much further?" he answers: "Five miles." Only you can't ask, because you don't meet anyone.'

Rabe nodded. Although he recognized the element of exaggeration in what Stappenbeck had said, he realized just as clearly that it was no more than a jocular way of saying something that at bottom was meant seriously. Niedlich, however, said: 'You are only forgetting one thing, my dear Stappenbeck: they are already in Vilna, and from Vilna to the frontier is a mere ninety miles.'

'A mere ninety miles,' Stappenbeck repeated slowly, in a tone in which vexation and good humour counterbalanced one another. 'How far is it to Alt-Landsberg, do you suppose?'

'Three miles.'

'Very well, three miles. Now tell me, my old friend, whether you still remember the Maundy Thursday—it is now getting on for three years ago—when we made an excursion there together? You had a warm coat on, and thick boots; I won't mention the food we took with us. And now recall the state the lace-maker Niedlich was in when we arrived at the Blue Lion at Alt-Landsberg! There's no point in denying it, for I myself helped to take care of your blisters. And you talk about "a mere ninety miles".'

Schnökel laughed. 'Yes, ninety miles is a fair distance. But even so, Stappenbeck, it is very far from being all up with the Emperor. Why should it be all up with him, anyway? Hasn't he got out with his skin whole? And isn't he back again in Paris, nice and warm and with all the grub he wants? And as for his Frenchmen who didn't go out and freeze with him, I know them well enough: they'll soon produce a new army for him.'

'No, Schnökel, they won't,' Stappenbeck replied. He had now lit a pipe himself and had just extinguished the blazing spill against the edge of the table, so that it was now barely glowing. 'Blow on this spill as much as you like, it won't burst into flame again,' he went on. 'I don't believe the French will produce a new army for him, and if they do, who's going to command it? That's the difficulty. He's a devil of a fellow, but he can't do *everything* by himself.'

'But he doesn't need to: he has his generals,' Rabe said.

'That's just what he *doesn't* have. For the moment they are still stuck in Russia with frozen toes, and I tell you, Rabe, it would be a very odd thing if even one of them got back to Paris and told his Emperor: "Here I am." '

'Are we going to kill them all, then?' asked Niedlich, with an expression that mingled roguishness and horror.

'No, you aren't. Your clean lace-maker's hands ought not to get dirtied with the blood of French marshals. For all I care you can supply them with their tassels and epaulettes if they ever get back here. But, Niedlich, *if*. It is, as you say, a mere ninety miles from Vilna to Memel, but if I know the Russians they will make good use of this little stroll. And then, between Memel and our Prenzlauer Tor there's enough ground to bury a dozen marshals and everything that goes with them.'

'Who's going to do that?' Rabe asked in dignified disapproval. 'That's not the way we do things.'

'But it could become the way we do things,' Stappenbeck went on. 'Need teaches us to pray, but it teaches other things too, and there are other people in the world besides lace-makers. I tell you, Rabe, the people in Lithuania and Masuren* will make short work of them, and even if they don't, if no one lifts a finger, then God Almighty will do it for us. They will fall dead like flies. And the few who manage to crawl as far as here we shall have to accommodate somewhere ourselves.'

'But where, though?'

'In the new French colony, behind a wall in a ditch.'

'And if the Emperor should want them back again?'

'Then he can come and get them. But he won't, because by *that* time the Russians will be here.'

'Perhaps.'

'No, for sure. Don't take offence, Rabe, but I understand these things better. When someone has got into a rage he doesn't just stand still. It is the same everywhere. When my wife is having a go at me—and she does have a go at me sometimes—and I go into the next room because I've had enough of it, what does she do? She comes after me and carries on there. That's what's called human nature. And your Russian is human, too. Very definitely. I tell you, Rabe, the Russians are coming, and the Emperor is *not* going to come. Because the French have had enough of him; and you can take my word for it that not all that many of them have ever been with him. I said as much as long ago as *anno* six, when he came riding into here on his fiery mare, with his yellow face and his piercing eyes. "Children," I said, "he's only a tiny fellow; Old Fritz was small too, but not nearly as small as this." I am for tall men, like Saldern* was, or Möllendorf.'*

Stappenbeck appeared not to have finished, but before he could go on a cripple with the stumps of his feet bound in bandages, who had been gliding among the tables, held out towards him a pamphlet and said: 'This will interest you, Herr Stappenbeck: one groschen, but I am willing to take two.'

It was a single folded sheet, made of inferior paper: *New Songs, printed this year*, with two woodcuts, one of which depicted the three Graces within an oval garland of roses, and the other, on the back page, a little Cupid.

Stappenbeck paid the cripple the double price he had asked for and opened the sheet, in hope of discovering some anti-French rhyme such as were in those days circulated with the aid of broadsheets of this kind. He glanced over the titles: 'Ännchen von Tharau', 'Courage, my comrades, to horse, to horse', 'Herr Schmidt, Herr Schmidt', 'The Tegel Ghost'. He grew impatient and turned the sheet over: 'The Battle of Gross-Aspern', 'O Schill, thy sabre doth hurt';* could the cripple have meant these two? But they were already familiar to everyone. Wait a minute: *this* must be it; it bore no title, but the first two lines could be considered a substitute for one.

'Read it,' said Rabe, who could tell from Stappenbeck's face that he had finally found what he was looking for. And Stappenbeck read:

> 'Await,*
> Bonaparte, your fate:
> Just wait, Napoleon,
> We'll have you off your throne.
> It's the Russians who
> Have shown us what we have to do:
> Within the Kremlin wall
> Nothing to eat at all,
> And always at your backs
> Nothing but hunger and Cossacks.
> Yes, it's the Russians who
> Have shown us what we have to do.

The sun that shone
At Austerlitz* is gone,
All your former show
Lies buried in the snow.
Await,
Bonaparte, your fate:
Just wait, Napoleon,
We'll have you off your throne.'

The immediate consequence of this recitation was that the cripple was gestured to return: each of them now wanted to take the poem home with him to show his wife. There was no longer a trace of the feeling of sympathy that had attended the reading of the communiqué, and Schnökel especially was overcome by increasing delight as, his delivery interrupted by intermittent coughing, he repeated: 'Within the Kremlin wall nothing to eat at all.' Their reading and laughter had been noticed at the surrounding tables, and an elderly gentleman, who was greeted by Rabe as 'Herr Klemm' and by Stappenbeck with somewhat mocking emphasis as 'Herr Sergeant-Major Klemm', came over to join them, though to judge from his face he had been in no way prompted by a desire to participate in their merriment. The rank by which Stappenbeck had referred to him was explicable in part by the peculiarities presented by his appearance. He held himself as erect as a pillar, his scanty white hair was fastened together at the back with a large comb, and with his long blue coat and sulphur-yellow waistcoat he wore a pair of riding-boots polished to the knee like a mirror. His thin neck was encased in a stiff cravat.

'Won't you take a seat, Herr Klemm?' asked Rabe.

'Have you read this, Herr Sergeant-Major Klemm?' Stappenbeck added, handing to him the broadsheet, which he had in the meantime folded in such a way that the song referred to lay uppermost.

Klemm thanked him and read the poem, emitting little clouds of smoke from his Dutch pipe as he did so. His face remained expressionless, and when he had finished reading he laid the sheet on the table again and said: 'The police, who concern themselves with so many things that have nothing to do with them, close their eyes where they ought to keep them open. What will this lead to? To riot and rebellion. And what will be the outcome? Instead of being tied by the left hand we shall be tied by both hands, and by the feet as well.'

He struck the sheet lying before him with the knuckles of his right hand and went on: 'And are we not allies of the Emperor? Too late, unfortunately; if we had always been so we should be better off than we are. But this past mistake can be rectified, and precisely at the present time. If it is, good; if it *isn't*, if we again miss the opportunity, then we are lost. I am not speaking of loyalty, public policy doesn't need to be loyal; but it needs to be prudent, gentlemen, prudent.'

'What would now be prudent is clear,' said Stappenbeck. 'All he has now is ruins; the Russian will press after him, we shall press him from in front; thus we shall come together and have him in a fly-trap.'

'A fly-trap! You are making up the bill without the landlord, Herr Stappenbeck. The Russian will not press after him, take my word for it. But *if* he does, if he crosses the Niemen and then the Vistula, then you will have something of the kind, to be sure; only it won't be a fly-trap, it'll be a mousetrap. And who will be in it? The Russian.'

'Oho, that I'd like to see!' said Rabe.

'Herr Niedlich, would you please give me a piece of chalk.' Niedlich leaped up.

'No, many thanks, I find I have a piece in my pocket.'

With that the strategic sergeant-major pushed the glasses together into one corner and drew a line down the green table from top to bottom. 'Well, then,' he began, 'this thick line is the frontier, Russia to the right, Prussia and Poland to the left. Take note of that, gentlemen; Prussia *and* Poland. This blob here to the left is Berlin, and these two little wavy lines here between Berlin and the thick Russian frontier-line, these are the Oder and the Vistula. Now you must know that along the Oder and the Vistula, stationed in six fortresses large and small, there is a force of thirty thousand French, and an equal number are stationed down here in Poland in a so-called flanking-position, half of them already moving into action. Take note of this, I repeat, for it is this flanking-position that will prove decisive. At present the Russian is in pursuit; he is weak, for when one army freezes the other also freezes, and by the time he crosses the Vistula he is tottering. And now what happens? From the fortresses on the Oder he is met by a force of thirty thousand well-rested troops, from the flanking-position another thirty thousand, the one takes up a position in advance of him, the other cuts off his line of retreat. And bang! he's caught. That is what is called a mousetrap. I will even undertake to show you the place where the trap will be closed. This spot here. It is bound to be at Köslin, or perhaps Filehne. I will bet any amount that somewhere between Köslin and Filehne the Russian army will capitulate. Like Mack at Ulm.* Whoever doesn't capitulate is dead.'

'I don't believe a word of it,' said Stappenbeck, and with the sleeve of his greatcoat erased the entire mousetrap from the table.

'I cannot compel your belief,' said Klemm, with an expression of calm superiority. 'The science of warfare is a difficult thing: brush-makers—'

'And sergeant-majors—'

'Can't understand it,' Klemm concluded his sentence.

'Can't understand it,' Stappenbeck repeated.

Schnökel had followed this exchange with a heavily asthmatic laugh; Rabe, however, to whom anything that might lead to strife and contention was repugnant, rose from his seat and said: 'It is time for me to go, gentlemen. Anyone coming with me?' They all accepted this invitation, put the pamphlets they had bought into their pockets, and with a brief 'Good evening, Herr Klemm!' walked past the sergeant-major in the direction of the door. When they had almost reached it, a yellowish dog of medium size came running in pursuit of them and, because he thought he had been forgotten, shot with a speed born of anxiety between the legs of the diminutive Niedlich, who was able to retain his balance only with difficulty. It was Kratzer, Stappenbeck's Pomeranian: an ugly animal, as peevish and crossgrained as his master, he had occupied himself the whole time they had been in the Wiesecke Room with visiting all the tables where children were sitting and being fed with buns; now he leaped high in the air at Stappenbeck, barked and whimpered and, as soon as he was outside, began to race back and forth across the plateau of the Windmühlenberg, plainly exhilarated at again being able to give vent to his energy after the social constraint of the past few hours.

The four citizens kept to the wide footpath trodden in the thick snow by Wiesecke's numerous patrons from the door of the establishment to the Prenzlauer Tor. In spite of the cold, Rabe contrived to maintain his dignified bearing; the other three, however, who cared little for their outward appearance, had drawn their caps down over their eyes and wound their thick knitted scarves up around their ears. Schnökel, who found it too cold to talk when an east wind was blowing, lingered a little to the rear; Niedlich kept level with the other two, but only with effort by moving along at a trot.

At first conversation would not get going; finally, Rabe, whose thinking was peristent rather than rapid, began: 'You treated him too disrespectfully, I think, Stappenbeck. I've been reflecting. First he is an old man, second he is a soldier, and third he won the Battle of Torgau.'

'That he did,' Niedlich interjected: he had a strong inclination to agree with any firm assertion made by another, and especially when it was made by Rabe.

Stappenbeck halted and whistled for his dog. Kratzer came up with great bounds, barked a couple of times, and then raced ahead in wild zigzags across the snowy Windmühlenberg as fast as though the Devil were behind him. 'Look,' said Stappenbeck, 'that's how Klemm won the Battle of Torgau. He kept his head down and ran.'

'But he is supposed to have rallied the army when it was about to scatter,' Rabe put in. 'I can remember it all exactly. "What is your name?" the King asked him when he saw him bringing the grenadiers back into line. "Klemm, Your Majesty," said Klemm. "You have done well, my dear Klemm," said the King; "*I* shall not forget your actions this day." And then the King rode on. I have heard him recount the incident himself.'

'Who? The King?'

'No, Klemm.'

Stappenbeck laughed. 'Rabe, you have only one fault: you believe everything you hear. I know this fellow better. He is not one of the grenadiers who rallied the ranks at Torgau, but one of the grenadiers in the ranks that were rallied. And Old Fritz did it himself with his own walking-stick. "You rascals, do you want to live for ever, then?" Among those thus graciously addressed our Klemm has his honourable place.'

'You can't stand him, Stappenbeck, and once you've got your knife into someone—'

'I knife him, but I haven't knifed this Sergeant-Major Klemm nearly enough. He's an evil bastard through and through. A coward, a braggart and a tramp.'

'A tramp?' said Rabe.

'Yes, he is a tramp,' interposed Niedlich, who had been quick to see that the duel was again going to be decided in Stappenbeck's favour. 'He is a tramp. In the summer he stays put on one of the estates, with the Bredows or the Rohrs, they don't mind him being there. That is what you might call his feeding-time. And when they start the slaughtering about the beginning of December, along he comes wishing everyone a happy New Year, simply so as to remind them he exists. He also takes charity. And plenty of it! I myself have seen him polishing his ducats.'

'Come, come,' said Rabe, 'if he is a man in need of assistance—'

'He's a skinflint, and a blackguard as well,' interposed Stappenbeck, growing more and more excited, and pulled the thick scarf that was hindering him from speaking lower over his chin. 'I know what I'm talking about; he lives in my wife's brother's house; they know him; he's a time-server, an informer.'

'Come, come,' Rabe repeated.

'And if he isn't an informer—and I can't prove he is, though I am absolutely convinced of it—then he is certainly an ungrate-ful wretch. What Niedlich has said about how he continually spunged on the nobility of the Havel-land, and I know all of them on account of the brushes, that was in the past and was his good time. I mean the time when he was honest and honourable. I don't really begrudge a man getting his fill of bread and butter, and something to go with it as well. But since *anno* six our Klemm has been a stranger to the Havel-landers. Also to those where he used to have his sergeant-major's quarters. He has changed masters. Even a dog doesn't do that. Kratzer! See, here he comes. Lie down, Kratzer! He's a loyal animal. But this Klemm, no sooner had their Spoon Guards★ rabble come marching through the Hallesche Tor than he was in there sucking up to all and sundry, and making it clear he was available for anything. After that he polished *louis d'or* instead of ducats. He's a flatterer and go-between. And just as before Jena he devoured the French and their Emperor, so now he devours the Russians and draws on the table with chalk the "mousetrap" he intends to catch them in. But I rubbed out his mousetrap for him.'

At that moment there came across the air the sound of two French bugles, joined soon afterwards by the dull rolling of a drum, and Stappenbeck's torrent of speech, which seemed not yet to have come to an end, was interrupted. All four stopped and listened, for Schnökel too had in the meantime overtaken them. The last to come up was Kratzer: he laid his neck against his master's knee, sniffed about him, whimpered, and gave himself the appearance of also being immersed in profound reflection.

'They are blowing the retreat,' said Stappenbeck, in a tone intended to convey the twofold meaning of the phrase.

'May God grant it!' Rabe responded.

Then, as the sound of the bugles died away, the men resumed their homeward journey. Before them lay the city with its thousand lights; until at length, entering an excavated path that led from the plateau down to the gate, they saw the lights no more.

But the stars still stood above them in the winter sky and cast their glitter ahead into the New Year.

3

Privy Councillor von Ladalinski

THE house in which Privy Councillor von Ladalinski lived stood in the Königsstrasse, diagonally opposite the old Berlin law courts. It was one of those late Renaissance buildings constructed at the instance of King Friedrich I in the early years of the previous century whose outward appearance had suffered from much tasteless restoration but whose interior retained all its former elegance. This was so in the case of the courtyard and staircase, and especially so in that of the entire first floor, where the reception- and drawing-rooms lay. Here could still be seen those stucco ornamentations that lend so much life and charm to Schlüter's baroque buildings, while from above there still gazed down, even if considerably darkened, the great ceiling-paintings copied from Giulio Romano's* originals in the Corte Reale at Mantua with which the splendour-loving King had had the entire first floor decorated. To left and right of these drawing-rooms there stood two smaller rooms, each with only one window and large expanses of wall: because they were used more frequently they had suffered more from depredation, and of their once rich embellishments only the ceiling-paintings, among them a *Night and Morning* and a *Fall of Phaethon*, had been rescued.

One of these smaller rooms was the privy councillor's study; the wall facing the door was occupied by two tall bookcases containing enough files and documents to constitute an entire records-office; while between these bookcases and an empty stretch of wall there hung the portrait of a beautiful young woman whose likeness to Kathinka was unmistakable: it possessed the same chestnut-brown hair inclining to red, and above all the same expression of the eyes, so that the only respect in which they differed, that of the less clearly defined profile, seemed not to matter. A large desk extended half the length of the room, so situated that when the privy councillor looked up from it his eyes could not avoid alighting on this portrait. For the rest, the study had much about it that recalled a bachelor's quarters. Next to an old-fashioned stove decorated with pictures illustrating stories from the Bible there was visible a large, low basket filled with a red patchwork cloth which served as a lodging for an English greyhound, while several goldfish were swimming around merrily in a glass bowl standing in the window-alcove. The half-lowered blind rendered even dimmer the already very moderate amount of light falling into the room, and all was warmth and comfort.

The wall-clock was just striking ten as the privy councillor entered: a man in his sixties, tall and slim, with thick, short grey hair brushed well back. He was wearing a violet velvet dressing-gown, under which he had plainly already made an immaculate toilet. His bearing, above all his aquiline nose, lent him an air of uncommon distinction. The greyhound welcomed him respectfully though with signs of annoyance at having to fulfil this duty, nuzzled up to him briefly and then, the little bell around his neck tinkling as he moved, returned trembling to the warmth of his basket. The privy councillor, for his part, went over to the bowl and fed the fishes with a few breadcrumbs and insect's eggs; he occupied himself with this for several minutes and then took his seat at the desk, on which there lay spread out official letters and documents and several newspapers, French and English ones among them. It was his custom to dispose of all written work before he did anything else; today, however, he reached first for the newspapers, and took up the *Moniteur.**

Let us leave him to read undisturbed for fifteen minutes and, while he buries himself in receptions, ceremonials and addresses of loyalty, relate something of his life.

Alexander von Ladalinski was born, in the middle of the last century, at Château Bjalanovo, which stood at the centre of the domain of the same name. The nearest town of any size, though still several miles away, was Czestochova. Some of the estates belonging to the domain stretched out to the west and extended into the dukedom of Silesia, which had at that time just become Prussian.

Young Ladalinski received a painstaking education, which

he completed first in Paris, then in Vienna, and had at the age of twenty-three just assumed the management of his estates when developments in the affairs of the country drew him into the struggles and conflicts of politics. Though he had little taste for such conflicts, he none the less engaged in them conscientiously once he had committed himself. He sat in Parliament and was counted among the most prominent of the leaders of the anti-Russian party. Even then the attitude he adopted revealed on more than one occasion his inclination towards Prussia; and it was no doubt this inclination, together perhaps with the circumstance already noted that a part of his property was in the state of Prussia, that led him to attend the court at Berlin on the occasion of the accession of King Friedrich Wilhelm II.* He found there a flatteringly warm welcome, especially on the part of the King's minister, von Bischofswerder,* at whose house he was soon a daily visitor. It was here, too, that he came to know the youthful Comtesse Sidonie von Pudagla. What from the first moment enchanted him even more than her beauty was the cheerful exuberance of her disposition, the art she possessed, and which she practised with a graceful ruthlessness, of taking life and skimming the cream off it. A certain pedantry of temperament which characterized him, and of which he was, at least in his younger years, uncomfortably aware, induced him to admire this art and to see in it nothing but a virtue and advantage. Before he left Berlin they were betrothed, and during the following Christmas week they were married: the ceremony, in which the entire court of Prince Heinrich participated, was organized by the bride's brother and sister-in-law, Count and Countess Pudagla, at Rheinsberg.

If the wedding festivities had been glittering, the honeymoon journey was even more so. It was like the ceremonial reception of a princess. At every stopping-place there were new surprises, and they grew more dazzling the nearer the couple approached their goal. At last Bjalanovo lay before them, set high and clearly recognizable in the evening twilight; and as the foremost of the sleighs turned into the broad, leafless avenue four great fires were ignited on the four round towers of the château, which then, half dilapidated as it was, appeared in the light they cast like a castle in a fairy-tale.

Their entry into the courtyard of the château was attended by cheers of rejoicing from all its inhabitants.

In the pleasure he took in the successful accomplishment of this spectacle, which he himself had arranged, the husband failed to pay any very close attention to his young wife's reaction to it: for if he had done so he must have remarked her total lack of appreciation of what all these attentions were really worth; that they contained an expression of love either escaped her notice or failed to move her, and she felt no gratitude for them.

In this frame of mind she persisted. Her husband, who saw that she was cheerful, thought that she was happy; but she was so only on the surface, and, recognizing no other obligation than the enjoyment of pleasure and distraction, she found his attentions, which were indeed inclined to be excessive, only wearisome and tedious.

It was a year after their wedding that a son was born to them. He received the name Pertubal, a name belonging to the family from earliest times and worn with distinction at least once every century: a Pertubal von Ladalinski had participated in the campaign against Ivan the Terrible,* another Pertubal was at the Battle of Tannenberg,* a third fell before Vienna* with Sobieski. The name was supposed to be Syrian and to have been acquired during the Crusades: but, as ancient records show, all who bore it preferred to abbreviate it to 'Tubal'.

The birth of a son, though an event all the world thought an occasion for congratulation, was felt by his mother as being little more than an annoying inconvenience; and when, while still confined to bed, she was handed the infant, she declared she had always found little babies ugly and could make no exception in order to oblige her own. The child acquired a Polish nurse with a red headscarf and an even redder stomacher, and together they were banished to the floor above; no sooner had the mother been churched, however, than the extravagant social life that had been interrupted only a few weeks by the 'happy event' began anew.

Among those who frequented Château Bjalanovo was Count Miekusch, the owner of a neighbouring estate, small, elegant, with a long auburn moustache, a typical Polish

cavalryman. The similarity between his character and that of
the young wife gave rise from the very beginning to an
intimacy which, since it was pursued without any concealment, Ladalinski must have noticed but did not regard with
any suspicion. He was completely trusting; rumours communicated to him from time to time he dismissed as gossip and
maliciousness, and if the sky of his happiness was none the less
now and then troubled by a little cloud, his young wife's
bravado, which countered such impulses of jealousy with
cheerful mockery, knew how to restore his trust in her again.
He was happy at the birth of Kathinka, doubly happy when he
perceived that his joy was shared by his wife. And she did in
fact look upon her second child differently from the way in
which she had regarded Tubal; it was not banished upstairs but
was allowed to remain in her immediate vicinity; indeed, she
liked to approach its cradle and, without saying a word, enjoy
looking at the baby. Did she see herself in it?

This was in February 1792. An unclouded summer followed, but when autumn came it brought the collapse of a
happiness that had from the first been only an illusion. What
happened was what always happens in such cases: what is
forbidden, weary of submitting to any constraint at last finds
gratification in revealing itself to all the world.

The way it did so was typical of the young wife's character.
A fox-hunt was announced, to be held on the estate of Count
Miekusch, the wide, open terrain of which offered a splendid
venue for such an event. The ladies of the neighbouring estates
were also invited, and no one failed to attend: in addition to his
other social advantages, the count had the reputation of being
an excellent host. It was a wonderful September day, the sky
clear as a bell, here and there a little plantation of pine-trees, and
on the horizon the church-spire of the nearest village. The air
was still and gossamer lay on the grass. The fox was soon
unearthed, and the riders, men and women, hurtled over
meadows and stubble-fields in a brilliant procession, eager to
overtake one another. Only the young Frau von Ladalinski
held back, Count Miekusch at her side; both seemed content to
forgo the honours of the day. But soon the picture changed:
more and more couples began to drop out of the chase, and

before an hour was up the count and his companion were the only ones left still following it, or at any rate appearing to be doing so. Those who had fallen behind gazed after them and marvelled at the endurance of these two riders, whose forms grew ever smaller and more shadowy as they drew nearer to the village lying in the distant blue haze. Finally they vanished altogether, and as it was nearly noon it was decided to return to the count's château. An hour went by, then a second and third; evening arrived, and they were still waiting. At last the guests departed and rode back to their own estates: Ladalinski too did likewise. 'It's happened, then' he repeated to himself again and again. Only on the third day did a courier hand him a note fastened with a seal:

Do not expect me back; you will not see me again. It was a mistake that brought us together. Forget me. A kiss for the child.

Sidonie von P.

The letter fell from his hand. Every word was a humiliation, even her signature: Sidonie von P. She had readopted the name of her own family and erased the six years she had passed at his side as though they were an uncomfortable interlude. He was crushed, and yet he could not fulfil her abrupt demand to 'forget me': with a sense of the bitterest shame he had to admit to himself that, if she were to return, he would joyfully receive her back without a single word of reproach or demanding a single word of explanation. The hidden, enigmatic tug of nature was stronger in him than any conscious resentment.

He fell into a state of dejection, until he was wrenched out of it by the calamities befalling his country: those events were impending which would in the end strike Poland from the roster of nations. Russia was making its plans, and, like those of all patriots, all his efforts too were bent on their frustration. He attached himself to the party of Kosciuszko and drew up a liberal constitution that gained the applause of the leaders of the Whigs in the English Parliament; at last, when there was nothing left but force of arms, he joined the army. What he lacked in military experience he made up for in zeal and courage. There was no one Kosciuszko would have trusted more. At Szczekociny* he was among the last to hold out.

When, after the defeat at Maciejowice, the retreat to Praga★ began, he was entrusted with the command of the rearguard, which was composed of only four decimated battalions: with this force he covered the crossing of the Pilica for two hours, and while he was still battling the enemy on the far side he employed the time he had thus gained in laying bundles of tarred straw around the wooden pillars of the bridge and eventually setting fire to them; when he at last successfully led the remains of his battalions across the river the bridge was already engulfed in smoke and flames. The Russians pressed after him, and a small unit gained the opposite bank at the same time as he did, though they were immediately taken prisoner; but when the main part of the Russian force, marching in serried ranks, attempted to follow, the middle pillars of the bridge collapsed and everyone on it was plunged into the stream below. Suvorov★ himself halted a bare hundred paces from the scene of the disaster. It was the last major achievement on the field of battle: Praga fell three days later.

Ladalinski laid down his command: even if he did not join his brother-in-arms in pronouncing 'Finis Poloniae', he none the less felt the truth of the words. It was clear to him that the country was going to become Russian, perhaps with some semblance of an illusory independence, and he found the thought unendurable. Poland no longer existed; he therefore resolved to leave it. He went first to those of his estates that lay on the other side of the frontier in Silesia, and from here he offered to place himself in the service of the court of Prussia. In his reply to this offer, Bischofswerder expressed his joy at the courageous decision, and, subject to the King's approval, proposed he should take up a position in the Foreign Office. The King's approval followed a few days later. Great expanses of Polish territory were being incorporated into Prussia at precisely that time, and this fact alone encouraged the authorities not to reject such offers as Ladalinski had made.

He settled into his new way of life very quickly—that he was by nature more inclined to be Prussian than Polish assisted him in this, and, a foe to all capriciousness and disorder, he found the machinery of government in which he was now participating the incarnation of his ideal. What was pernicious in it he

failed to notice, or accounted it negligible by comparison with
the disadvantages of the opposite procedure which he had for
so many years witnessed. He soon became more Prussian than
the Prussians. The distinctions he was accorded, his ambas-
sadorial missions, first to Copenhagen, then to the English
court, on which Tubal, then still a child, accompanied him,
played their part in this evolution. Recalled from London after
the death of the King and the resignation of Bischofswerder, he
adopted the Protestant religion, in the justified belief that in
doing so he was confirming his new nationality: he chose the
Reformed Church★ because it was the church of the court—
scruples of conscience in such matters were foreign to the Age
of Enlightenment. The importance of the position he held was
not affected by the change of government, though the position
itself was: he left the Foreign Office and joined the Department
for the Crown Lands of the Directory of Finance, where his
considerable knowledge of farming and agriculture could be
put to excellent use. On assuming this position he had been
required to take up residence in the old palace in the Königs-
strasse: he had now been living there for fifteen years, and
Kathinka had grown up there.

Whether he was from time to time homesick for Bjalanovo,
and for the ancient château with its four brick towers where he
had spent the fairest and the most grievous hours of his life,
who can say? No word that might have suggested as much ever
passed his lips. He seemed happy in his adoptive fatherland,
and perhaps he was so in fact; and, firmly resolved never to
return to his former homeland, even if, as for a moment
seemed possible, it were to be given back its national
independence, he adhered to the princely courts, so that from
this firm centre he might enter on an ever more intimate
relationship with the country's nobility. His life became
devoted to the fulfilment of this design, in which he knew he
enjoyed the support of his sister-in-law, 'Aunt Amelie', more
exclusively than he would admit to himself, and thus nothing
gave him greater gratification than the presence of his children
in Hohen-Vietz. A double marriage with an ancient
Brandenburg family would seal and secure the step he had
taken, and he therefore felt no qualms over Kathinka's Polish

sympathies, which, whatever the grounds for them might be, were no secret to him.

In the meantime the privy councillor had finished reading; he pushed the papers aside and rang the bell. A servant entered with the chocolate, and before he had had time to leave the room the greyhound was already out of his basket, on this occasion with no sign of reluctance, and rubbing himself against his master. The privy councillor smiled and threw him the biscuits whose acquisition had been the real object of these loving attentions. Only then did he notice a letter that lay on the same tray and exhibited the characteristic hand of Aunt Amelie. He was a little surprised to see it: Tubal and Kathinka had arrived back from Schloss Guse only late the previous evening; he had not yet even had time to see them, and now here was a letter, which must therefore have accomplished the journey to Berlin more or less at the same time as they did. The privy councillor broke the seal and read:

Mon cher Ladalinski! Tubal and Kathinka left me only an hour ago, with them, to my regret, Demoiselle Alceste, whom you, my dear, will remember from the old Rheinsberg days. Now they are gone I feel, quite unusually for me, a sense of emptiness, and I can best fill it by talking about the children, whose presence has made these past days so pleasant for me. The more delight they gave me (*et en effet ils m'ont enchantée*),* the more I began to desire that *liaison double* we have discussed together so often. I have got altogether used to the idea of seeing Tubal ruling the roost at Guse, and the ancient seat of the Derfflingers, which in my hands is merely existing from day to day, raised again to its old splendour. The support he would need to accomplish this he would certainly receive from Hohen-Vietz. Beautiful women of various nationalities have always made their home there: my grandmother, *avec un teint de lys et de rose*,* was a Brahe, Berndt's wife a Dumoulin, and it would make me happy to see our dear boy extend this circle. *Vous savez tout cela depuis longtemps. Mais les choses ne se font pas d'après nos volontés.** I am sure about the young people of Hohen-Vietz but not about those of the house of Ladalinski. Kathinka accepts Lewin's attentions, but otherwise she only plays with him; Tubal has a feeling for Renate, *qui ne l'aurait pas*?* But this feeling amounts to no more than that sensation of pleasure that youth and beauty know how to inspire everywhere. Thus I foresee difficulties arising, it seems to me, from indifference in the case of Kathinka and superficiality of feeling in that of Tubal. *Et l'un est aussi mauvais que l'autre.** It is plain that Kathinka entertains a different inclination; the presence in your house of the count disrupts our plans, and yet it must be allowed to continue; the only proper course must be to keep a wary eye and to avoid anything that might stoke the fires. Your good sense, *mon cher beau-frère*,* will, I know, hit upon the right course. For my part, it seems to me that separations offer the best hope. Lewin must emerge from his narrow circle; above all, he must throw off the allures of literature. He takes these things more seriously than is consistent with the life of a nobleman, who may certainly take an interest in them but ought not to engage in them professionally. If our relations with France remain good, *comme je souhaite sincèrement*,* I would regard a year's stay in Paris as a very good thing for him. He would acquire the attributes of a man of the world which he at present lacks and on which alone Kathinka sets any store at all. *Et je suis du même avis.**

Je faisais mention de la France.* My brother would have me indicted for high treason if he knew I had spoken of a "continuation of good relations". And yet, though I certainly desire it in general, it is precisely his conduct that makes me desire it so emphatically. *Il organise tout le monde.** Up and down the entire Oderbruch he is taking steps to organize an arming of the people, an action for which he has a hundred names: local militia, national levy and 'call to arms'. In his enthusiasm he fails to see how this last designation, far from inspiring fear, can appear only tragi-comic.* He has won over Drosselstein; of Bamme I say nothing, for whenever anything happens in which folly contends with recklessness he has to be mixed up in it. *C'est son métier.** I have to laugh when I think of his Gross- and Klein-Quirlsdorfers as Brandenburg guerrillas. These little villages, where on average they cannot muster half-a-dozen fowling-pieces, want to set upon Marshal Ney,* *à Ney, le héros de la Moscva. Quant à moi*,* all this extravagant behaviour impresses me only as madness, and I hope that the wisdom of the Chancellor, whom I trust unconditionally, will save us from a policy that will destroy us and not even ensure to us the sympathy of other nations. *Car le ridicule ne trouve jamais de pitié.**

I am confident that quieter times and more stable conditions are coming; Russia is not an aggressive power; France will bury its plans for world conquest and allow an epoch of twenty years of unrest to be succeeded by an epoch of peace. *J'en suis convaincu.** Paris will again become what it always was and what it ought never to have ceased to be: *le centre de la civilisation européenne. Je le désire dans l'intérêt universel et dans le nôtre. Dieu veuille vous prendre dans sa sainte garde, mon cher Ladalinski. Tout à vous votre cousine Amélie P.**

The privy councillor laid down the letter: the political opinions it contained had made little impression on him, but the remarks concerning Kathinka and Bninski had impressed him very much. He read the passage through again: 'the presence in your house of the count disrupts our plans, and yet it must be allowed to continue; the only proper course must be to keep a wary eye and to avoid anything that might stoke the fires.' As he looked up his glance fell on the portrait hanging opposite him, and memories of all kinds, in which for the first time fears for the future were mingled, arose within him. He knew the history of so many families. 'Like an eternal . . .'* but before he could complete the thought the cry 'Good morning, Papa' rang through the room, and, turning in his chair, he beheld the smiling face of Kathinka peering from behind the door-curtain. In an instant she was at his side, and the gloomy notions that were troubling his soul were banished by her loving embraces.

4

At Frau Hulen's

ON the same evening there was a social gathering at Frau Hulen's. She could no longer delay it if she wanted to make an impression that accorded with her social station and open up her entire array of rooms, for Lewin had announced his return from Hohen-Vietz for the very next day. Immediately his letter had arrived, therefore, invitations had been sent out, with the assistance of a little crippled boy who washed the glasses in the beer-cellar next door and who, strangely in view of his physical disability, was employed as an errand-boy; and not one of them had been declined.

At seven o'clock lights were burning throughout the entire Hulen household, which, in addition to a small kitchen in a side-wing, consisted of two front-rooms and two dark alcoves. Half of them were rented to Lewin, who, given the friendly relations that reigned between him and his landlady, had not expressed the slightest objection to his part of the premises being taken over for the festivities in his absence.

And festive the rooms certainly were, quite apart from the lights and candles, which were blazing even out in the hallway. In both the rooms the stoves had been heated, and on the window-sills black and red fumigating-candles were smouldering, while all those mementoes and *objets d'art* to which Frau Hulen desired to draw her guests' particular attention were illumined individually, each in its own particular way. Taking pride of place among these objects were the cardboard structures produced by her dead husband, who, by profession a foreman at a small dye-works, had in his leisure hours been a practitioner of the plastic arts. The majority were of an architectural description. In addition to an open stage covered with figures representing the scene in the camp from *Die Räuber*,* he had bequeathed his widow a Doric temple and a model of Strasburg Cathedral, standing three and a half feet high and with rose-coloured paper stuck over all its windows and apertures, which with the aid of little oil-lamps was today glowing brightly to the very top of its spire. This cathedral, it may be remarked, stood on a tall-legged chest of drawers and usually obscured a little mirror situated behind it; not today, however, when, to obviate any suspicion that the room was not furnished in a manner entirely appropriate to Frau Hulen's social situation, the mirror had been raised a foot higher up the wall. Only the spire was still visible in the somewhat leaden glass.

And what of the appearance of Frau Hulen herself? In addition to the tall white cap, without which no one could remember ever having seen her, she wore a brown dress dyed by her late husband himself, with a black velvet band fitting close around her neck and embroidered with alternate blue and yellow stars.

'How will it go?' she asked herself and rehearsed again all the important points, trimmed the lamps in an attempt to overcome her anxiety, and smoothed the bedcover in Lewin's alcove, which today had to serve as a cloakroom. Then she looked again at Strasburg Cathedral and its illumination, and

felt like getting inside it. 'How will it go?' she asked herself
with a tightening of the heart, as she cast a glance in the mirror
and pulled at her neckband, which had slipped a little.

At that moment the bell rang. Frau Hulen hastened to open
the door and was somewhat put out to find it was only Frau
Zunz, a deaf old lady who lived on the same floor and who
owed her invitation to the present reunion solely to fear of her
tittle-tattle: for she had nothing in the world to do, and
whenever she saw anyone enter the house and heard him reach
the top of the stairs, she would station herself behind the
peephole of her double-door to discover who it could be and
what he was doing there.

'I seem to be the first, dear Hulen. Well, well, someone has to
be first.'

'Of course, dear Zunz, and you wouldn't want to keep your
closest neighbour waiting, I know. Won't you remove your
shawl?'

The old woman, who did not properly grasp what Frau
Hulen was saying but had gathered the gist of it from her
gestures, shook her head peevishly, drew her crêpe de Chine
shawl, a relic of better days, more tightly about her and, as
though secure in the feeling of fear she inspired, walked gravely
into the nearest room. It was Lewin's. Here she looked about
inquisitively, nodded once or twice as though to express her
surprise that the room was being used that evening even
though it was rented out, and then asked: 'The young gentleman is away, no doubt?'

'Indeed, dear Zunz, you know he is.'

'Yes, yes,' grumbled the old woman, and ran her index
finger over the little piano to see whether the dust was away
too. Then, coughing once or twice as though she found the
smoke from the fumigating-candles troublesome, she passed
into the 'best room' and sat down on the sofa.

This action, however, was completely contrary to the social
arrangements envisaged by Frau Hulen, so that, annoyed at the
old woman's presumption, she began to lose her fear of her.

'Here, please, dear Zunz,' she said, and pointed to a stiff-
backed grandfather-chair standing between the stove and an
étagère. 'And I'll fetch you the picture-book.'

The old woman murmured something that sounded almost like a protest and certainly resembled amazement, but she none the less did as she was told and sat in the chair Frau Hulen had indicated. The latter returned in a moment bearing in both hands a large and heavy book, upon whose title-page (the front cover had been torn off) it said in thick letters: *Songbirds of North Germany: ninety coloured copperplates.*

Frau Zunz opened the book, but she had not yet reached the third page when the bell rang again.

She who now appeared was Demoiselle Laacke, who taught music and singing and was the particular friend of Frau Hulen, who felt herself flattered by this acquaintanceship: an old maid of forty, tall, lean, with a long neck and thinning auburn hair. Her watery blue eyes, almost devoid of eyelashes, were quite devoid of independent movement: they always followed the movements of her head and thus smiled at the world horizontally, as though to say: 'I am Fräulein Laacke, the pure and irreproachable.' On the occasion of a charity concert she had once received an amethyst brooch from Queen Luise:* since that day she had worn it constantly. For the rest, the three Graces that had stood at her cradle and accompanied her through life were named Poverty, Humility and Pride. She bowed politely, if a little stiffly and condescendingly, to Frau Zunz, and then took her seat on the sofa as though it were a matter of course that she should do so.

Frau Hulen sat herself down beside the new arrival, patted her on the hand and said: 'How glad I am to see you, dear Laacke. You are always so good and make no distinctions.'

'Ah, dear Hulen, how can you even speak of it; that would be uncultivated. For are we not all human?'

Here a brief pause ensued, during which the piano-teacher allowed her shawl to slip from her narrow sloping shoulders. Then she asked: 'Whom else may we expect, then?'

Frau Hulen shifted uneasily, and replied with some embarrassment: 'The Ziebolds.'

'Oh, the Ziebolds! That will be nice. I recall he has a voice, tenor or baritone.'

'Yes, he has a voice,' Frau Hulen went on, 'and he is always amusing and polite, but still no one likes to sit next to him. And much less next to his wife. The reason is the pawnbroker's shop. You see, the old Ziebolds, who were the parents of these Ziebolds, they were very good people, in fact you could say, refined. They had the linen and hosiery shop at the corner of Jüden and Stralauer streets, and we used to live in the same building. That was the year previous, before Old Fritz died. And my old mother was took ill, and because she had to get her strength back and I couldn't do the cooking because I always had to be out on account of the fact I did sewing, oh yes, dear Laacke, I had my work cut out, I can tell you, well, the Ziebolds used to come and one day there was soup and the next day a roast or a chicken, never anything but wings or the breast, and on Sundays the old man, who was a skinflint really, though I can't say that of him, I'm sure, used to send half a bottle of wine. And that's how it went on until her death, I mean my mother's death.'

At this recollection the speaker passed the knuckle of her index finger across her right eye.

'That, however, was the *old* Ziebolds?' Mamsell Laacke observed, emphasizing the word as an indication that she had really been hoping to hear about the young Ziebolds. Frau Hulen understood what she meant and went on:

'Yes, that was the old Ziebolds, only they weren't all that old, they were only about their middle fifties, but even so they didn't last much longer and they died in the same winter as my mother had died. First her, on the third day of Christmas, or it may even have been the second, but he dragged on right up to March. As you know, dear Laacke: "March winds and March sun have made an end of many a one." He always had a weak chest.'

'And then no doubt the business went to the *young* Ziebolds?' asked Mamsell Laacke, exhibiting every sign of a lively interest in the fast accumulating death-toll.

'Yes, to the young Ziebolds,' Frau Hulen confirmed; 'that is to say to *him*, for at that time he still didn't have a wife. For he was a very handsome man, and because he could talk well and wore gold spectacles, they always said he looked like an attorney, and they used to call him "Herr Attorney Ziebold". He used to be flattered by that, and he was always going about with actors and their mamsells, and one day he found himself with one of them round his neck.'

'His present wife? Ah, I understand.'

'Yes, his wife. Well, then of course they thought that everything was coming up roses. But you can go to the well once too often, and before a year was out everything had to be sold up and they were broke, or so Frau Zunz told me, for in those days I still lived in the Rossstrasse.'

Frau Zunz, who had understood most of what had been said in spite of her deafness, nodded her head.

'But the young Ziebold wife,' Frau Hulen went on, 'she wasn't the sort of person to let anything get her down, and she soon knew what to do, and when I got married and moved back here to the Klosterstrasse they were already living in the Hohensteinweg and running the pawnbroker's shop. Well, you see, dear Laacke, the pawnbroker's shop, there was nothing wrong with that, and I said at the time to my late husband that I had known the old Ziebolds and they had been very good people. And so we got together again and used to visit one another. But that didn't last long, because we found out that the business with the pawnbroker's shop was no more than a sideline and that their real business was lending money at high interest, and that they were no better than usurers and that if you borrowed ten talers from them you had to pay twenty talers back. And that is why nobody wants to sit next to the Ziebolds.'

'Seat me next to Herr Ziebold, if you would,' said Mamsell Laacke, with the quiet composure of an abbess who knows herself safe behind the shield of her position and calling. 'And whom else do you expect?'

'Herr Sergeant-Major Klemm.'

'Ah, the stiff old gentleman with the top-boots who won the Battle of Torgau. He is always arguing and wears a yellow waistcoat.—And who else?'

'Herr Nuncio Schimmelpenning.'

'Schimmelpenning!' repeated Fräulein Laacke. 'The apparitor at the Court of Appeal, I remember now. He is supposed to be the son of old Judge Schimmelpenning, only he came by that status on the wrong side of the blanket. How did you come upon *him*, dear Hulen? A not very agreeable man, and so self-important.'

At that moment there was another pull on the bell, and, since Frau Hulen's social gatherings were no different from other social gatherings, the person who came in was the person they had just been talking about: Herr Nuncio Schimmelpenning. He was a well-preserved man in his fifties with pouting lips which he pressed together and then opened again with a little smacking sound, exposing as he did so a set of marvellous white teeth. The old judge had had a similar habit. For the rest, however, Fräulein Laacke had been quite accurate: in conceit and self-importance he was a match for any cockerel, and he gazed out at the world as though he were at the very least his own father or even the whole Court of Appeal itself. And, in truth, he probably believed he was.

Frau Hulen made the introductions; Schimmelpenning however, taking not the slightest notice of the obeisance of Mamsell Laacke, whom he appeared to find only in the way, made directly for the aged Frau Zunz, who had also been introduced to him by name, and said in a loud voice: 'Zunz, at Count Voss's, Wilhelmsstrasse? Recall you; knew your husband.'

'I too,' said the old lady, who from awe of the stately appearance presented by the nuncio had risen to her feet but, because he had spoken so loudly, had misunderstood everything he had said. Schimmelpenning, not knowing what to make of the old lady's 'I too', and, ever on the alert for signs of mockery, was at once inclined to assume that he was being ridiculed in some way; he pulled a sour face and seemed through his whole bearing in general to be trying to say: 'Strange company: how do I come to be in it?' Then he went across to the chest of drawers, drummed on the roof of Strasburg Cathedral and gazed into the mirror—and again he was surprised at how closely he resembled the old judge.

From the cloakroom—in which, if signs did not deceive, two couples who had arrived soon after one another were engaged in disposing of their outdoor garments—there now came the sound of loud and lively voices, of the kind people adopt when they are anxious to demonstrate either that they are utterly at ease or that they are utterly in the right, and immediately afterwards the first of these couples stepped into Frau Hulen's room. They were Herr Ziebold and his wife, he recognizable by his locks and his golden spectacles, she by her theatrical demeanour and silk dress, which was as close fitting as it was low cut.

Instead of greeting the arrivals, Schimmelpenning only depressed his chin gently against his chest, and his reserved demeanour, which extended even to clasping his hands behind his back, would have been even more strikingly impressive if the entrance of the second couple, which followed almost at once, had not drawn all attention away from him. They were Herr Grüneberg the mat-maker and his daughter: he was a lean, waxen-faced man who, because his trade was the weaving together of all kinds of strips of material to form floor-coverings of all kinds of sizes, was sometimes also called Herr Grüneberg the carpet-manufacturer. He himself cut an insig-nificant figure, and that in spite of an owlish physiognomy in which forehead, chin and nose formed a straight line with one another, while mouth and eyes lay far back and so to speak in shadow; the figure cut by his daughter, however, was by comparison all the more considerable: she was tall and formi-dable and completely unlike him in every way (she was, indeed, not his daughter at all but the child of his late wife by a former marriage). She was called Ulrike: verging on ugly, with large, empty, excessively protuberant eyes, she was none the less firmly convinced that she was beautiful and, by virtue of her beauty, destined for some higher place in the world than the one she occupied. Her association with Frau Hulen seemed to her something beneath her station, and even more beneath the station she thought her due; she fostered it, however, because she knew that a young gentleman of the nobility had lodgings with the old lady—a fact upon which her thoughts never ceased to dwell.

Herr Ziebold had seated himself on the sofa beside Mamsell Laacke; Ulrike approached the model stage and removed several figures—Karl Moor, Roller and the handsome Kosinski—from the boards; Frau Zunz was now silent and ignored. Schimmelpenning, leaning with his back against one of the windows, was gazing at the ceiling with a blank expression, and only Ziebold and Grüneberg were engaged in discussion, though their contribution to it was very unequal, a torrent of words issuing from Grüneberg, while Ziebold put in only a few terse and occasionally caustic observations. Frau Hulen became more and more agitated: she felt things were not going as they ought to be going and, repeatedly attempting to bring her guests together, said for the third or fourth time: 'But of course you have already met before.'

Those thus addressed, however, seemed very reluctant to acknowledge the fact. Most reluctant of all was Frau Ziebold: she toyed with the gold chain she was wearing (as to whose origin many dark rumours were in circulation) and cast at her husband admonitory glances not to go too far in intimacy with that stupid fellow Grüneberg. These glances excepted, her face wore no expression at all; but when she observed the air of self-importance worn by Ulrike she could not forbear to smile, for she knew the Grünebergs 'by way of business' and had rescued the daughter, who behind her father's back did exactly as she pleased, from more than one embarrassing situation.

The only guest still missing was Sergeant-Major Klemm; at length he too arrived, and Frau Hulen, who expected marvels from him, breathed a sigh of relief. He was in the same costume—top-boots and a high-buttoned yellow waist-coat—in which he presented himself everywhere, and after having, to Ulrike's annoyance, greeted Mamsell Laacke with a particular show of respect, proceeded to devote himself with especial attentiveness to the Ziebolds: either because, in his capacity as tale-bearer and go-between, he had all kinds of undisclosed connections with them, or simply because he wished to demonstrate his right to ignore people's chatter and allow his sun to shine upon the just and the unjust equally. Schimmelpenning, who had in the meantime changed his position and was leaning against an old-fashioned corner-cupboard, he passed by in silence; each measured the other with an expression of contempt.

'Now we are all here,' Frau Hulen then declared, 'and I am sure we are all going to have a very merry time. Aren't we, dear

Laacke? You will sing something for us afterwards, won't you? The "*Schweizerfamilie*" or "*Bei Männern, welche Liebe fühlen*".'*

'But dear Hulen.'

'Why not, dear Laacke. It's only a song, after all. And I'm sure Mamsell Ulrike would like to hear it, and so would we all. And you will accompany, Herr Ziebold, won't you? But now let us have something to eat. Please help me to bring in the table, dear Zunz.'

Our good Frau Hulen had spoken these last words very loudly; this fact notwithstanding, however, the old lady—who perhaps had really not heard, but perhaps too was annoyed at being called upon to render this service as though as a matter of course—replied: 'Oh, until ten, I think'; whereupon Mamsell Laacke, anxious to obviate any further discussion of the matter, rose with almost youthful celerity and helped to carry the dining-table in from the kitchen. Chairs were fetched, and in a moment everyone was seated: Klemm at the top of the table, Frau Hulen at the bottom, with Frau Zunz close beside her; then, opposite one another at the corners, came the pawn-brokers; beside Ziebold there sat, as she had stipulated, Mamsell Laacke.

All the food was already laid at the centre of the table: as the first course a large tureen of soup with seed-cakes, to its left a herring salad, to its right a jelly. Everything was heavily seasoned; on the cakes there lay a thick layer of powdered cinnamon, and little onions, alternating with pickled gherkins and morello cherries, were scattered over the salad. A typical Berlin repast, in fact.

'Please help yourselves; Mamsell Ulrike, would you be good enough to pass round the cakes? Lord, what pleasure it all gives me!'

'The pleasure is entirely ours,' replied Herr Ziebold, and polished first his spectacles, then, covertly, his fork, on a corner of the tablecloth.

So far as the conversation went, the only real question was whether Klemm or Schimmelpenning was doing the talking: Grüneberg was too artless to participate, and Ziebold, who in his younger days had been a genuine Berlin chatterbox, had by now abandoned this profession and contented himself with accompanying the conversation of others with a few commonplace interjections.

'Tell me, dear Hulen,' Schimmelpenning began, 'what is actually the name of the young man who lives with you?'

'Vitzewitz, Herr Nuncio.'

'Vitzewitz,' the latter repeated. 'A strange name.'

'We can't all be called Schimmelpenning,' said Klemm, and exchanged looks with his antagonist. 'Besides which, if I am informed correctly his name is *von* Vitzewitz.'

Schimmelpenning was sufficiently astute to sense the malice in this interruption but, ignoring it completely, turned again to Frau Hulen and went on: 'What actually does he study?'

'He studies . . . it is something foreign and Latin, and if he goes on with it for another couple of years he will get to the Court of Appeal.'

'Well now,' said Schimmelpenning, and sat up a little straighter.

"But he won't stay there; he's got something else in mind and reads all day long from comedies about a Moor who strangles his wife and an old king who goes mad because his children, daughters moreover, leave him in the lurch. I can always hear him, because he talks so loudly even Zunz could hear him through the wall, isn't that right, dear Zunz, and sometimes when I knock on his door and take him a letter or a fresh bottle of water I see he has been crying. Yes, you laugh, Herr Schimmelpenning, but he has a soft heart, and there's no harm in having a soft heart. I could tell you a lot about how good he is.'

'Well, do so, then,' exclaimed Ulrike, whereupon Frau Ziebold and her husband looked at one another knowingly.

'Very well, then,' said Frau Hulen, 'I will. Our beds, you see, stand wall to wall, and the wall is quite thin. And then I have my stomach-spasms and when I have them nothing is of any use, not the doctor or the chemist. And, that's right, it was about Martinmas, and perhaps it was partly my own fault because I had some of the roast goose, which is always poison to me, and then, lo and behold, I had them again. And I couldn't think of anything else to do, for the pains were getting worse all the time, so I knocked on the wall. Just softly at first;

and when I had knocked a second time he called out: "I'm coming, Frau Hulen, I'm coming." And while I was still wondering what the best thing to do would be he was already standing there, booted and spurred, and he said simply: "Stomach-spasms? That's what I thought. I know what to do, Frau Hulen." And not half a minute later I heard him in the kitchen, splintering up wood and raking around in the ashes and opening the drawers of my kitchen cupboard one after the other. And then I could tell what his idea was, and called from my bed: "Second compartment on the right!" "It's all right, Frau Hulen," he said, "I've found it," and it wasn't a long time at all before he was back again. And what had he made? A real cup of camomile tea, only a bit too strong and still too hot. But then he poured it out of the cup into the saucer, two or three times, until it was ready to drink. And then I drank it. And would you believe it, I was better straightaway. I won't say it was the camomile tea that went to my heart, it was the good deed, and the stomach-spasms were gone.'

'But dear Hulen!' exclaimed Fräulein Laacke, who had been gazing at her plate in embarrassment throughout this narration; she spoke slowly and accentuated every syllable. Frau Hulen, however, quite unabashed, replied with some acerbity: 'Dear Laacke, it is plain to see you have never had stomach-spasms.'

'Right enough,' Ziebold observed, taking the old lady's hand familiarly; 'I have made the acquaintanceship of that tormenter only once, but it was a sufficiently intimate acquaintanceship to teach me what it's really like. That was in *anno* six, on the day the Spoon Guards marched in. It was raining gently and was already cold. When exactly was it, Herr Sergeant-Major Klemm?'

'The end of October.'

'Quite right; I caught my death of cold and the pains I had were agony; but still, I wasn't sorry to have been there and seen the Spoon Guards march in.'

'Why ever were they called the Spoon Guards?' asked Ulrike.

'Because instead of a cockade they wore in their hats a tin spoon. The other ladies and gentlemen will all have seen it at the time, but if Mamsell Grüneberg would like to hear about it . . . '

'Please,' said Ulrike politely, and Ziebold, now beginning to free himself from his wife's control, which was becoming increasingly irksome to him, carried on without more ado: 'The Spoon Guards, as Herr Sergeant-Major Klemm will confirm, were given to all kinds of weird behaviour, and when they marched in anywhere they sent one of their number ahead of them, who walked twenty or thirty paces in front of the advancing column and announced with his strange manner-isms and deliberately tattered costume: here come the Spoon Guards! For they were proud of their name and their insignia.'

Ziebold, who as a skilled narrator knew the value of a pause, here asked for a glass of water, and only when Frau Hulen had met his request did he again resume his story.

'I can still see the first of them coming through the Hallesche Tor. He belonged to the evil Davoust Corps, and all that this corps meant was apparent in this one man marching ahead of the rest. He was tall and lean, with a pale face and pitch-black hair hanging down low over his forehead. His trousers, made of some kind of linen-stuff, were dirty and torn, and his feet were half bare and stuck into shoes that were really only soles tied together like sandals. A poodle which he led along on a string was walking beside him on two legs and snapping up the pieces of bread he was throwing to it. He was wearing a heavy cavalry sword instead of the usual infantry sabre, and from it there was hanging a goose; and in the little red hat he had put on at a crooked angle there was sticking the tin spoon, the field-badge of the whole gang.'

'Oh, how nice,' said Ulrike, for whose sake the story had been told. 'A tin spoon: that's too funny for words.'

Sergeant-Major Klemm, however, who neglected no opportunity of exhibiting his Francophilia, and who had not been quite won over by Ziebold's calculated appeal to his authoritative verdict, called across the table: 'The only com-ment I would wish to make on what Herr Ziebold has just said is that it was not exactly a "gang" which, under the command of Marshal Davoust, Duke of Auerstädt and afterwards His Highness the Prince of Eckmühl, marched through the Hallesche Tor. If it *was* a gang, however, then it was an altogether extraordinary one, for it came *recte* from Jena, where we failed to make a very good showing against this gang, to put it mildly.'

'No, we didn't make a very good showing,' responded Frau Hulen. 'But, no offence Herr Klemm, we ought not to speak of it, for it is an ill bird that fouls its own nest, and the misfortune of that time, or the disgrace of that time, I don't know which it is, must now be buried and forgotten. I admit that I thought too, at that time, that it was all up with us, because everybody said so and I am only a poor woman who cannot say No when the others say Yes. But I can assure you now, Herr Klemm, that it was only the next year, when I saw the two green coffins, that I knew we would rise again.'

'Two green coffins?' asked Ulrike, and attempted to laugh.

'Yes, the two green coffins the two old Sängebusches were buried in. Him and her. Haven't you heard of it, Ulrike? You must have been, pardon me for saying so, quite grown up by then.'

'No,' Ulrike assured her.

'Well,' Frau Hulen continued, 'them it was, the two old Sängebusches who lived just round the corner from here, nearly next door to the Waisenkirche. He was a registrar, but earlier he had been a soldier and had served under four kings, and when the Rheinsberg memorial* was finished and Prince Heinrich invited all the old soldiers he invited old Sängebusch as well, so that he should be there too. I have seen the letter myself, all written in German, except Henri was in French. Well, when he came to die, I mean old Sängebusch, they found a note which he had written, saying he wanted to be buried in a green coffin, just to show his faith and conviction that his dear fatherland Prussia would rise again . . . And then the wife, who was also old and ill, died as well, on the same day, and so it came about that *two* green coffins were ordered. But old Pastor Buntebart, when they were going to be buried, had a black pall put over them, because he was afraid there might be a scene or a demonstration, which he didn't want. But he didn't know the Berliners, though, because as the procession set off they pulled the pall away, so that the green coffins became visible again, and that is how they bore them, through a crowd of many thousands of people, and everyone removed their hats and wondered to themselves whether old Sängebusch would be proved right or not. And he *has* been proved right. Lehwess the baker, when I went this morning to buy breakfast, said to me: "Listen, Frau Hulen, Prussia is rising again." And old Lehwess the baker doesn't usually say things he doesn't know are true.'

Herr Ziebold nodded his head amiably to Frau Hulen; Sergeant-Major Klemm, however, inserted his left index-finger between his neck and his cravat and, moving it agitatedly to and fro, said half-impatiently, half-condescendingly: 'It is a moving story, Frau Hulen; but, with all due respect to old Sängebusch and his green coffin, he could have been wrong.'

'Who cannot be?' responded Schimmelpenning, who rarely neglected an opportunity of contradicting Klemm. 'Who cannot be? I say again; you, I, everyone. To err is human, but this Sängebusch did *not* err. Don't misunderstand me, I beg of you: green coffins have nothing to do with it; I am a Protestant and despise all superstition. These green coffins are childishness. But we are certain to rise again; and why? Because we possess a sense of justice. That is the point. *Justitia fundamentum imperii.*★ Show me anything in all history, ancient or modern, to compare with the mill at Sanssouci★ or the trial of Arnold the miller.★ The Court of Appeal, my friends. And even our enemies have admitted "there are still judges in Berlin."★ I want to say nothing against the French, but one thing I *must* say: they have no sense of justice. And where there is no sense of justice there is no moderation, and where there is no moderation there is no victory. Maybe there was a victory, but it will not endure, it will be transformed into defeat. The beginning of this defeat has arrived. The Russian is in pursuit, we shall appear in front, and we shall grind this French glory to pieces as though between two millstones.'

'You speak of millstones,' smiled Klemm; 'very well, I allow the millstones, but as for what will be ground to pieces between them, it will not be the French but the Russians.'

'Not at all, not at all,' exclaimed Ziebold and Grüneberg simultaneously, and then added: 'or at least show us *how*.'

This invitation Klemm had anticipated.

'It would be a good thing if we had a map,' he said; 'but a couple of lines will do as well. Frau Hulen, have you a sheet of paper?'

Frau Hulen hastened to supply the desired article, and then, with that self-assurance that only daily repetition can bestow, Klemm began to draw upon it the same lines he had drawn on the table with chalk on New Year's Eve.

Then he commenced: 'This thick line here, please observe, is the frontier, Russia to the right, Prussia and Poland to the left. Take note of that, ladies and gentlemen: also Poland. Here to the left is Berlin, and these two little wavy lines here between Berlin and the thick Russian frontier-line, these are the Oder and the Vistula. Now you must know that along the Oder and the Vistula, stationed in six fortresses large and small, there is a force of thirty thousand French, and an equal number are stationed down here in Poland in a so-called flanking-position, half of them already moving into action. Take note of this, I repeat, for it is this flanking-position that will prove decisive. At present the Russian is in pursuit; he is weak, for when one army freezes the other also freezes, and by the time he crosses the Vistula he is tottering. And now what happens? From the fortresses on the Oder he is met by a force of thirty thousand well-rested troops, while from the Polish flanking-position another thirty thousand come up, take up a position in front of him and cut off his line of retreat. And bang! he's caught. That is what is called a mousetrap. I will even undertake to show you the place where the trap will be closed. This spot here. It is bound to be at Köslin, or perhaps Filehne. I will bet any amount that somewhere between Köslin and Filehne the Russian army will capitulate. Like Mack at Ulm. Whoever doesn't capitulate is dead.'

Everyone was amazed; only Schimmelpenning, who was almost as much at home in the beer-houses of the city as his antagonist was, said, with cutting imperturbability: 'It is well known, Herr Klemm, that nowadays you repeat these sentences, literally word for word, every day, and you don't mind whether you draw the Vistula on paper with a pencil or with chalk on a table. Sooner or later it will get you into trouble; but that is your business. One thing, however, is my business, and that is to tell you that I find everything you do and say unpatriotic.'

'Do I need to learn patriotism from you?' roared Klemm, striking the table with the palm of his hand. 'Before your mother—my apologies, ladies—fitted you into your first pair of trousers, I was already at Torgau. I rallied the grenadiers . . .'

'I know of it,' Schimmelpenning interrupted, 'but it wasn't *you*, it was Major von Lestwitz.'*

'I don't know what Major von Lestwitz did,' cried Klemm, growing more and more excited, 'but I do know what *I* did.'

'And make sure no one forgets it,' Schimmelpenning continued to mock. 'It has never yet been noticed, Herr Klemm, that you ever failed to mention even one of your great deeds.'

At the word 'great' the nuncio made a long, malicious pause; Frau Hulen, however, who would have liked to have seen all contention banished from the world, turned to Herr Schimmelpenning and asked him in urgent tones if he would mind passing round the jelly that was still standing on the table untouched. Agitated though he was, he did not fail to hear or observe this request. As the new dish was passing Frau Zunz —who suffered from coughing fits from time to time and thus had to be careful with things that might irritate her throat—leaned towards Frau Hulen and asked softly: 'Much pepper?' whereupon the latter replied: 'No, dear Zunz, English spice.' The old lady appeared to understand this comforting declaration correctly, for she proceeded to help herself generously from the dish she was still holding in her hands. The threatening conflict, however, had been happily averted. Soon afterwards they rose from the table and departed in couples to Lewin's room, where punch and biscuits were handed round.

'And now, dear Laacke, sing something to us; but nothing sad, eh Ulrike, nothing sad?' Ulrike agreed, whereupon Mamsell Laacke observed that she did not wish to sing anything sad, but neither did she wish to sing anything cheerful. She disliked cheerful songs because they were shallow and trivial; the tender and sentimental was more to her taste, and you should sing only that which was in accord with your own nature. For 'in our voice there lies our heart'.

Lewin's sheets of music were now subjected to repeated inspection, until finally a couple of operatic arias were discovered in which Herr Ziebold's much lauded tenor could also participate. Mamsell Laacke handed him a volume with a sky-blue cover on whose title-page were the words: *Fanchon, das Leiermädchen, by Friedrich Heinrich Himmel. Piano arrangement, Act II*, with, beneath it, a picture of Fanchon in short sleeves and a headscarf and carrying in her hand a kind of mandoline.

Nothing could have been better, all things considered: a duet always had something of the charm of a dramatic scene. Fräulein Laacke caught the note and began, while Herr Ziebold placed his left hand on the back of the low-backed chair:

> 'Where the Alpine roses clamber,
> Bathed in a cheerful evening sun,
> Thus shall I have a picture painted,
> A picture of my childhood home.
>
> May no foolish whim constrain thee
> Such as base souls alone can feel:
> Do gifts dishonour when the giver
> Has given us his heart as well?'

After the tender and sentimental Fräulein Laacke had sung this last line three times with great warmth of feeling, the tenor of Herr Ziebold struck in, and both sang the concluding stanza:

> 'Love divides with hand impartial
> Whatever fortune may bestow:
> Giving, taking: love can never
> Tell the difference 'twixt the two.'*

Ziebold's strong point had from of old been the power of his tremulando, and today too he achieved such an effect with it that the tepid mood that had reigned hitherto was transformed and, momentarily at any rate, a feeling of general benevolence broke through. The evening was now definitely at its height: Frau Hulen felt this to be so and immediately suggested a peripatetic Polonaise, which everyone then performed, weaving through all the rooms and dextrously encircling the dining-table, which had been left standing where it was. Towards its

conclusion, however, Fräulein Laacke played too quickly and
deliberately omitted several bars: 'Have I been invited so as to
sit here and play on this jingle-box for the benefit of that frog-
eyed Mamsell Ulrike?'—this and similar questions arose in her
mind, and the final moments of the party were again
discordant.

Fifteen minutes later the couples departed in their various
directions down the Klosterstrasse; the Ziebolds had turned left
towards the Hohensteinweg.

'That was the last time,' said Frau Ziebold; 'you won't get
me there again. I have no wish to sit on the same sofa with
Mamsell Laacke. And that stupid thing, Ulrike! She looked at
me as though she had never seen me before; I even believe she
thought *I* ought to say hello to *her*. And how is it really? She
doesn't help us, we help her. The yellow Moorish dress and the
sugar-tongs have been with us now nearly ten weeks.' Here the
speaker paused for a moment to catch her breath, for the air was
keen and cold: then she went on: 'And then look at the men she
has there! I really don't know which is more unendurable, that
Klemm, who is always harping on the same thing, or that
Schimmelpenning, who gives himself such airs you would
think he invented the Court of Appeal.'

Ziebold laughed and said: 'You are forgetting Grüneberg;
didn't he sit next to you at table?'

'He did, certainly: but do you think he said a word to me?
And why not? Because he is an old fool and does nothing but
gape at that dear little daughter of his and wait for the prince
who is going to take her away in a golden coach. And then,
don't think I'm carping, Ziebold, Frau Hulen is a good
woman, but what cakes she serves up! Bits of roll, and the seeds
were hard enough to break your teeth.'

The Grünebergs had turned to the right. As they rounded the
corner into the Stralauerstrasse, Ulrike said: 'I really don't
know what Frau Hulen is thinking of. She doesn't behave like a
poor woman at all: three courses and then biscuits and punch. I
don't like it and I don't think it's right. And then she always
uses the two rooms, as though they both belonged to her!
When I let a room I've let it; young Herr von Vitzewitz, who

opened the door to me the last time I rang because Frau Hulen wasn't at home, would have been very surprised indeed to see that Mamsell Laacke tinkling about with her long bony fingers on his piano. And the singing! I'd rather listen to the street-singers. But it's always the same. A little blind-man's-buff or a couple of card-tricks are never enough for her . . . And the people! He, Ziebold, it's true enough, is a businesslike man, and you can see he doesn't let the grass grow under his feet. But that person, his wife! Always in silk and coral earrings—don't ask me who they really belong to. She must be forty if she's a day, but look at the dresses she wears! But one thing I know, I shan't be going there again. I have my reputation to think of.'

The others, too, were prey to similar thoughts. The only one who was contented with the evening was Frau Hulen herself.

5

Soirée and Ball

AT four o'clock on the following day—the sun had just set—the Hohen-Vietz ponies, who had hardly been out of their harness for the past week, halted before the house in the Klosterstrasse familiar to us from the commencement of our story. Lewin had taken the reins and waited patiently for the return of the coachman, who had dismounted to carry the old-fashioned portmanteau up into Frau Hulen's dwelling. The vehicle he sat in was not the former roofed sleigh with the leg-covers, which was suited only to a night journey, but the light, two-seater calash in which Berndt was accustomed to make his flying excursions. Our friend did not find his waiting tedious, for the whole sky to the north-west was still aglow, and the little, ivy-covered Klosterkirche that lay almost directly to his left stood like a shadowy silhouette against this evening glow and riveted his attention. Crows came flying in from all directions, landed on the row of gable-ends and, as was their custom, settled themselves down for the night. There was only a little life in the street; the lamps were lowered on their long chains, lit in a leisurely fashion, and then in a leisurely fashion creakingly hoisted again. At last Krist returned, and while he led the sleigh across to the Green Tree, Lewin opened the heavy housedoor, that closed itself again by means of a stone weight hanging behind it, and climbed up the stairs.

When he had reached the third and last flight he could already see the light of the lamp Frau Hulen had brought out into the passage: she had done so partly to demonstrate respect for her young Herr Lewin, partly so as to reveal the thick garland of ivy she had woven and fixed up over his door, to mark his arrival.

'Good evening, Frau Hulen.' With that he stepped first into the alcove, then out into his main room, which the old lady's love and care had also prepared in a similarly festive fashion. On the round table before the sofa there stood two little lamps, a coffee-set and a pound-cake, while a second garland, also of ivy but small and dainty and sewed together out of individual leaves, encircled the damask napkin.

'But all this is as though prepared for a bridegroom, Frau Hulen; where does all the ivy come from?'

'It's church ivy, young sir.'

'From across the road?'

'Yes, from the Klosterkirche; I picked it from where the sexton Susemihl's Johanna lies buried with her baby. All in one grave, mother and child. It's three years now. Can't you recall it, young sir?'

'No. What happened?'

'It was supposed to have been a marshal; but Herr Ziebold, the merchant, laughed at the idea; he said it was a marshal, certainly, but only a French billeting-marshal, what they call in our army a quartermaster. Well, dear God, I really don't know, I'm only an old woman, but what I do know is that, marshal or not, he will have been put to a lot of trouble, because she was a good girl, Johanna, and even old Frau Zunz, who knows something about everyone, could say nothing against her. And it was a good thing, too, that the child died. Some say, I know, that it wasn't dead, but I don't believe it and you shouldn't say what you can't prove. And now fall to, young sir, and pour out the coffee before it gets cold.'

'Yes, Frau Hulen, that is easier said than done. What are you thinking of? With this graveyard ivy . . . '

'Ah, young sir, I know you better than that. When the Tuesday gentlemen are here, the fat captain who is always so funny, and Herr von Jürgass and Herr Himmerlich, who has such a thin voice, and I listen from next door, I know that the louder they read and the more stirring it is, the more cups and glasses I have to bring in. And the one who makes most use of them is my young gentleman.'

'Well, Frau Hulen, if you have provided, I ought, as you say, to fall to,' and with that he poured the coffee and made himself comfortable, while the old lady, anxious to disturb him no longer, left the room.

Upon the table there also lay, arranged into a little fan, four or five letters that had arrived during his absence. One of them, from Jürgass, contained a brief inquiry as to when the next meeting of Kastalia was to take place; another, written only a few hours previously, was from Tubal. It was only a few lines. Lewin read:

4th January. We have been back since the day before yesterday. Papa, who had expected us to return from Guse sooner, has arranged a *soirée* for today (Monday). If you arrive in time do not leave us in the lurch. We have a superfluity of men but not of dancers. The mazurka, which was performed before the holiday at Wylich's and in which, as you will have heard, Kathinka celebrated one of her triumphs, is to be repeated. You were missing then, be present today. Your T.

Lewin laid down the letter; it had put him out of humour. During the journey he had been occupied in depicting this first evening to himself as a domestic idyll, everything light and bright, in which Frau Hulen's white cap, the white teapot and several sheets of white paper (each of which he hoped to cover with writing) had been the most attractive features; and now this dream had faded at the very moment he thought it had been realized. He had no desire to dance or to watch others dance, least of all Kathinka, whose mazurka partner, as he well remembered from his friends' enthusiastic descriptions, had been Count Bninski. And yet the invitation could not be declined. He still had two hours and, tired from the journey, he

employed his weariness to overcome his disgruntlement by
leaning back into the hard sofa cushion and going to sleep.

When he awoke the room was in darkness, the short-wicked
lamps burnt out. He disentangled himself from a blanket with
which Frau Hulen had covered him while he slept; but it cost
him an effort to orientate himself. Where was he? He groped
his way to the window and looked down on to the street. There
were the dimly burning street-lamps; across the way the
shadow with the two little towers, that must be the
Klosterkirche. Someone had told him some story about it? Ah
yes, Frau Hulen. And there was the garland; and Johanna
Susemihl and her baby; and now he was aware how stifling the
air in the room was, and that the narcotic odour of the ivy and
the fumes from the lamps had given him a dull headache. What
was he to do? He opened a wing of the window on one of
whose bolts he had been unconsciously leaning, and as the cold
night air came into the room he began to breathe more freely.
Then he knocked, and Frau Hulen entered.

'What's the time?'

'Eight o'clock.'

'Oh, then I've overslept. And this headache. A glass of
water, Frau Hulen, and some light. I must hurry.'

The old lady ran back and forth, the drawers of the chest of
drawers opened and closed, and an hour later Lewin was
mounting the wide stone staircase that led, past niches containing three or four periwigged electors, to the first floor of the
Ladalinski house. He threw off his cloak, listened as he
straightened his clothes in the cloakroom to the subdued sound
of the violins, and then stepped across the vestibule decorated
with orange-trees and through the open entrance which, situated between the two great reception-halls, constituted the
precise central point of the whole flight of rooms. Except in this
particular it was an entrance like many another, plain, with a
single tall window which also served as a door to the balcony,
and was distinguished only by the picture that adorned its
ceiling: Venus sinking unconscious into the arms of Zeus at the
destruction of Troy. It was the best of the old ceiling-paintings
and at the same time the best-preserved.

Little at home in the world of the pictorial arts, our friend

would at the best of times have exhibited but slight appreciation of the lineaments of this composition; today, when
headache, disgruntlement and the press of people congregated
at precisely this spot in any case hampered any searching
inspection of it, he exhibited virtually none at all. To the left lay
the ballroom. Lewin looked into it, and saw that twelve or
fourteen couples had taken the floor for an *anglaise*; Kathinka,
however, was missing. Where was she? At this question there
rushed in upon him ideas and images which yielded only
slowly and with reluctance to his efforts to banish them as
foolish. He then allowed his eyes to glide along the rows of
chairs against one side of the hall on which the older ladies had
taken their seats; but here too he looked in vain.

In the middle of this row sat the old Countess Reale, chief
lady-in-waiting to Princess Ferdinand, a lady of seventy or
over, with a nose both arched and pointed. Everything about
her was grey: her dress, her shawl, her high-piled hair; she
resembled a wicked cockatoo, and especially so now, as she
raised to her eyes a black lorgnette with two large crystal lenses
and regarded Lewin, whose hurried inspection she may have
noticed, with an amazed and almost vengeful stare. The latter
lowered his eyes and directed them in some confusion at the old
countess's neighbour. This was a Fräulein von Bischofswerder, daughter of the former minister and *dame d'atour* to the
Queen Mother.* She wore the little blonde hair that still
remained to her wound into two plaits, which had however
been deprived by the heat of the room of whatever elasticity
they possessed and now hung unbecomingly down to her
waist. Everything about her, indeed, was lengthy: her neck and
the Danish gloves which extended up to her elbows; and all his
ill-humour notwithstanding, Lewin could not repress a smile.
'Mamsell Laacke!' he said to himself.

At length he abandoned all further search and walked across
to the righthand room where refreshments were being handed
round and tightly knit groups were exchanging the news of the
day. They were mainly composed of the more elderly men:
adjutants and chamberlains of the various princely households,
which were at that time very numerous, ambassadors of the
smaller courts, notabilities from the Foreign Department and

departmental chiefs of the Finance Ministry and of the War and Crown Land Office. Several of them were particular friends of the house: the Intendant of Royal Castles and Gardens, Herr Valentin von Massow,* for instance, Palace Governor von Wartensleben, the General Director of Royal Entertainments, Baron von der Reck, and Councillor of State and Police President Le Coq. University professors, doctors, clerics and Berlin celebrities had also put in an appearance; in the first of the window-alcoves Court Chaplain Eylert and Councillor Sack of the High Consistorial Court were standing in animated conversation, while Professor Dr Mursinna, at that time the city's most celebrated surgeon, and Herr Fleck, the actor, were conducting an equally lively colloquy just beside the spot where Lewin was standing. He could understand every word, and clearly heard Dr Mursinna object to the way in which Herr Fleck had represented Richard III's limp: under different circumstances he would have had the liveliest interest in following the course of this conversation, but in his present state of agitation he felt only depressed at being unable to discover a more familiar face in this room either. Of the younger men there were none present whom he knew: Bninski, too, was absent, and on perceiving this Lewin again felt the blood rise to his head and was aware he had changed colour, though he at once also felt ashamed of the notions with which his jealousy was repeatedly persecuting him.

Finally he caught sight of a Baron Geertz, a Holsteiner and gentleman-in-waiting at the court of the Queen Mother, who, an intimate of Jürgass's and always in and out of the Ladalinski house, had in the course of the winter attended several meetings of Kastalia. Our friend approached him and asked after Jürgass and Tubal. 'I am just on my way to them,' the Baron said, and, making for a door at the opposite side of the room, drew back the door-curtain and gestured Lewin to enter, while he himself followed.

It was the privy councillor's study with which we are already familiar, though today it had undergone a complete transformation in order that it too should be utilized in the festivities. Where the greyhound and the goldfish had formerly had their favourite places there stood flower-tubs filled with the hydrangeas then coming into fashion, while a dark-red curtain with a black Grecian border had been extended in front of the bookcases, which had mocked every attempt to remove them. Only the picture of Frau von Ladalinski still remained as it was. The large desk had made way for a multi-coloured divan and a number of delicately gilded ebony chairs grouped around a table decorated with Chinese designs. Here Lewin's friends were sitting with an excessively large number of empty glasses of the most various shapes and shades before them; and upon his entry they greeted him with a cry of welcome as loud and joyous as social good manners could possibly have permitted. Hauptmann* Bummcke and Rittmeister von Jürgass, who had made themselves comfortable on the divan itself, received him into the space between them; Tubal sat opposite them on one of the ebony chairs; Baron Geertz and a Count Brühl joined them and closed the circle. Bummcke, who fifteen minutes previously, before the *anglaise* began, had waltzed with Kathinka and, to judge from the way he was ceaselessly fanning himself with his cambric handkerchief, had not yet recovered from the exertions involved, was speaking.

'I can't manage it any more, Tubal, yet dancing with your sister is like dancing with a fairy.'

'Wherever is she?' Count Brühl interposed. 'I've been looking for her for ten minutes, but I can't find her.'

'She is changing for the mazurka,' Tubal replied.

'And how she snubbed me,' Bummcke went on, gesturing to a servant who had just appeared in the doorway with a tray of sherry. 'I wanted to say something polite to her—delicious sherry, Baron Geertz, don't miss the opportunity—and so I said to her, my dear Fräulein, I said, whenever I hear your full name, Kathinka von Ladalinska, it always sounds to me like a military band, yes, upon my honour, it rings and sings like the bell-chimes of the Alt-Larish Regiment.'

'And what did she reply?' asked Jürgass, while Lewin and Tubal exchanged glances.

'Well, she replied abruptly: "There we are in agreement, then"; and when, sensing disaster, I asked in some confusion: "May I ask *how*, my dear Fräulein?" she said: "But, Hauptmann Bummcke, I am a little surprised to see your subtle ear attuned only to the musical significance of *other* people's names. Do I really have to name to you the instrument that lives, so to speak, on the first syllable of your name?" And as she said that she took me by the arm, and in the end I even felt grateful to her that I could conceal my embarrassment in the dance just beginning again.'

The whole company joined in the narrator's laughter; only Jürgass, carefully extracting a fragment of cork from his sherry-glass, refrained and adopted instead an artificially serious expression.

'You are beyond help, Bummcke. Why do you still go on dancing? He who places himself in danger is likely to perish. But I know you, you gentlemen of the infantry! All fat captains have the vanity to think they can prove they are really slim through going into a quick waltz, or, God help us, even become slim through doing so. No, Bummcke, you dance either too much or too little: too much for pleasure, too little for slimming. Dancing is for lieutenants. At thirty-nine one is a *déjeuners* man, a man for sitting at sessions, brief or lengthy, even if should be a session of Kastalia. *Apropos*, Lewin, when are we having the next one?'

'If we are to stick to Tuesday, tomorrow.'

'That's all right with me, and I will let Hansen-Grell and the others know. We can be sure of Himmerlich and Rabatzki; but what about you, Tubal? Our friend Bummcke, who I have reason to think is angry with me for indiscreetly revealing his age, I shall personally vouch for. No one must be absent: for, diligent as ever in providing the failing source and spring of Kastalia with renewed effervescence, I have once again attended to the supply of fresh forces. I say forces: note the plural. For I shall come along with two of them, two wounded comrades. More tomorrow, if I have the honour of introducing the two gentlemen to you. For today, this merely. They have been in their time poets, as for good or ill so many of our young lieutenants are nowadays, but the campaigns, the Spanish and the Russian—for the two gentlemen came indeed from north and south to meet together here, in our fair city of Berlin—yielded them nothing in the way of poetry. Smolensk and Borodino were unfavourable to lyricism. What they have brought with them is wounds and diaries. But even these must be welcome.'

'And are,' Lewin confirmed, and rose to return to the ballroom. This was the signal for all to do likewise; even Bummcke, disregardful of the admonition he had just received, pushed aside his only half empty glass and followed.

They could not have chosen a more propitious moment: the four mazurka couples—Bninski and Kathinka, and with them the Silesian Counts Matushka, Seherr-Thoss and Zierotin and their young and beautiful wives—had just stepped forward to dance, ladies and gentlemen both in a costume which, without being in a strict sense national, at least suggested the Polish element in their square-cut caps and short fur jackets. They were the same four couples Tubal had referred to in his note and who had already shone at the Wyliches' *soirée*. And then the dance began: it was just coming into fashion at social gatherings in our capital at that time, but whenever Poles or Silesians from beyond the Oder were present the others usually abandoned it to them, out of a well-founded fear of their superiority at it.

Everyone had pressed forward to view the graceful spectacle, so that it was difficult to gain a place near the door. Bummcke, whose *embonpoint* made the difficulty double, abandoned any attempt to assert himself against the gigantic Major von Haacke and the bloatedly consistorial figure of Chief Court Chaplain Sack, and returned to the sanctuary, where he was not a little surprised to find Jürgass and Baron Geertz already ensconced in the corners of the divan.

'*Tres faciunt collegium.** I record this day as the day of your conversion,' Jürgass received him. 'Better late than never. Next to dancing itself, watching dancing is the worst, even if only on account of the seductive power which notoriously lies in all *conspectus*.'*

A liveried servant, obviously clad in this attire only for the present occasion, passed through.

'Good God, Grützmacher, where did you come from? But it's a good thing you're here, anyway: a Cliquot, good soul.' Then, turning to Baron Geertz, who may have been surprised at this familiarity, he said: 'Our former regimental barber of the Goecking Hussars.'*

The servant returned and placed on the table a bottle with its cork drawn.

In the meantime Lewin had pushed his way forward to the front row of the spectators and had the same view of the ballroom as he had had half an hour previously. Of the four couples in graceful motion on the floor he was aware of only one; and, while he was ravished by the beauty of what he saw, at the same time there also crept over him that most painful of sensations, the sensation of being obliged to stand aside, of being overcome, not through the operation of chance or one's own caprice and humour, but because one's rival is actually the better man. And he felt that this was, indeed, the case: everything he saw indicated strength, grace, passion; of what account was his own mere good-heartedness beside these? A smile played about his lips, and he seemed to himself insipid, prosaic and boring. Catching sight of him, old Countess Reale again raised her lorgnette to her eyes and, after briefly inspecting him, lowered it again with an expression that seemed designed to set the seal on the verdict he had just passed upon himself. Fräulein von Bischofswerder's two plaits were hanging even lower and looking even more despondent. It all seemed to him a sign and an omen.

The dance was over, and everyone pressed into the ballroom to thank and congratulate the four charming ladies; Bummcke and Jürgass also showed themselves, and seemed by their sudden reappearance to be trying to conceal the fact that for the previous half-hour they had been absent.

Among the crowd was old Ladalinski himself; he was in the act of congratulating the lovely Countess Matushka, who, so far as figure and complexion were concerned, could have carried the day even against Kathinka, when one of the footmen approached him and whispered something into his ear.

The privy councillor continued with his conversation for a moment, then he bowed to the young countess and followed the servant. In the vestibule he discovered a messenger from the Foreign Department, who handed him a sealed letter. Undecided where he should go to discover its contents, the privy councillor stepped into the cloakroom and broke the letter open. It was very brief:

'*York has capitulated.** One of Macdonald's adjutants brought the news to the French ambassador. The Chancellor is on his way to the King.'

'Who gave you this letter?' Ladalinski asked.

The messenger repeated the name of a close friend of the Ladalinskis who was at the same time Hardenberg's right hand.

'Convey my thanks and respects to His Excellency.' With that the privy councillor put the letter into his pocket and rejoined his guests.

He had resolved to say nothing; but when he saw Kathinka and Bninski, and immediately afterwards Tubal too, engaged in eager conversation before the middle window of the hall, his resolve weakened and he went up to them.

'I have something to tell you, you too, Count; but not here.'

Without waiting for a reply he turned towards the nearest side-room, which, normally occupied by Kathinka, had today, like his own study, been commandeered as a reception-room. Several couples whose affairs of the heart were perhaps no older than the evening itself had sought refuge in the stillness of this boudoir, which was likewise illumined only dimly by a few lamps and a ruby-red hanging-lamp; now startled, they fled from their hiding-places—cheerfully or with a trace of ill-humour, according to temperament.

Kathinka indicated the chairs that had been vacated; but Ladalinski said: 'No, we mustn't sit down, we cannot desert our guests. What I have to say is brief: York has capitulated.'

'*Eh bien!*'* observed Kathinka, plainly disappointed that, after all the earnestness of his demeanour, her father had no more than *this* to tell them. She was altogether indifferent to politics: her only interest was in personalities and their private lives.

'Kathinka!' exclaimed the count, forgetting himself in the excitement of the moment; but he immediately corrected himself, and added with formality: 'My dear Fräulein!' His tone contained a mild reproach. Then, turning to the privy councillor—who had not failed to notice this change in mode of

address from familiar to formal—he said: 'Capitulation! That is
to say, he has gone over to the Russians.'

'I presume so.'

Bninski stamped his foot: 'And that is what they call loyalty
in this country!'

Now and then a head appeared in the door-curtain, only to
vanish again as quickly as it had come; the count, however,
oblivious in his excitement to both appearance and disappearance, continued in a voice filled with bitterness:

'Oh this everlasting song and dance about German loyalty!
Everyone learns it, everyone sings it, and they sing it until they
even come to believe it. The starlings in this country even have
to learn to whistle it. I am quite sure this General York despises
everything that doesn't wear a Prussian jacket, and what it all
comes to in the end is—capitulation!'

An awkward pause followed; none of them was able to find
the right words, and while in Ladalinski Polish blood and
Prussian doctrine contended with one another like fire and
water, Kathinka felt that through her thoughtless '*Eh bien*' she
had been half responsible for conjuring up this storm.

Tubal was the first to recover himself. 'I think, Count, you
are allowing your passion to get the better of your judgement.
You know how I stand; and my birth, moreover, guards me
from the suspicion of any narrow-minded Prussianism.'

The privy councillor was disconcerted by this scene; but
failing to notice this, or not wishing to do so, Tubal continued
quietly:

'Let us consider the case objectively. What has taken place is a
political act. Throughout history, changes of course, including
the most beneficial, have been inaugurated by faithlessness or
disloyalty. I will spare you, and myself, an enumeration of
them. There may have been exceptions, but if so there have not
been many, and perhaps even those have been the product of
clever concealment.'

Ladalinski breathed a sigh of relief as Tubal continued: 'He
who is set tasks that transcend the commonplace must not seek
to evade them, least of all make himself the slave of current
everyday notions of reputation and good name. He must not
turn faint-hearted and shrink from his responsibilities, which is

what all this scrupulosity over one's honour leads to. He has to account only to God and to himself. He must be able to sacrifice himself, *himself*, his life, his honour. If it is done in a true spirit, he will gain back twofold the honour he has staked. It is the eternal story of a conflict of duties. Loyalty in one direction can exclude loyalty in another. Where adherence to one can be purchased only at the expense of injuring the other, there will always remain a bitter aftertaste, to be sure; but he to whom this aftertaste tastes bitterest is precisely he who will have acted from the purest motives.'

'And it is General York you have in mind?' asked Bninski with a trace of sarcasm.

'It is precisely General York. In short, Count, you are at liberty to condemn him, but not to inculpate him. The true significance of what he has done will become apparent in due course; his honour, however, just as it does not require my protection, so it ought not to be subjected to doubt or assault.'

Bninski seemed about to reply, but the music had started up again and the by now half-open door-curtain revealed that the couples were uniting for a *contre*. Kathinka, who was engaged to dance with the young Count Brühl, suggested they end the conversation, which had in any case taken a different course from the one intended by the privy councillor and had lasted longer than he had expected it to. Much about it had been distressing to him; only Tubal's laudable attitude had enabled him to regain his composure.

Before the *contre* had ended the whole assembly knew of the great event. Its effect was very much slighter than might have been expected. The gentlemen averred that they 'were not surprised, it had always been inevitable'. Most of the ladies thought as did Kathinka, only they were sufficiently prudent to refrain from an indifferent '*Eh bien*'. But, slight though its effect may have been, it was sufficient to produce a certain air of preoccupation, and thus to disrupt the atmosphere of gaiety. It was only midnight when the first carriages drew up, and within half an hour the festive rooms were empty.

Bummcke, Jürgass, Lewin, who had been joined by Baron Geertz and Major von Haacke, who towered almost a head taller than all the rest, descended the steps of the house together. At the bottom Lewin went his separate way; the other four, however, were going in the same direction and walked off towards the Lange Brücke. Halfway across the bridge they stopped and looked up at the equestrian statue of the Great Elector,* the upper half of which was illuminated by the lights still burning in the Royal Stables and the old Post Office. Its magnificent head seemed to be wearing a smile.

'Look,' said Jürgass, 'he doesn't look as if he thinks we're done for.'

6

In the Lecture-Hall

LEWIN, having turned to the left, walked down the Königs-strasse and hurried towards his house by the quickest route. A gentle but icy cold wind was blowing from the Alexanderplatz and freezing his face; he pulled up the collar of his cloak and called a greeting to the watchman who for protection from the wind had stationed himself inside the gateway of the Town Hall.

'Cold wind, Ehrecke.'

'Yes, young sir. It's a Bernauer,* and that always cuts right through you.'

With that they wished one another goodnight, and Lewin could now hear only the creaking of the lamps suspended over the roadway as they rocked slowly in the wind on their chains. He passed Hohensteinweg, turned into the Klosterstrasse, and here, keeping to the righthand pavement, he observed as he walked along the familiar houses on the opposite side. The lights were on in Lehwess the baker's and the smell of newly baked bread emerged from the open window of the bakery in the basement and wafted right across the street to where he was walking. Close beside it, before the old 'warehouse' (the former Electoral Palace) that now served as a magazine, a French sentry, his rifle leaning against his sentry-box, was stamping with both feet in the snow and beating his arms across his chest in the fashion of a sailor trying to restore the use of his fingers. Then came the 'Graue Kloster',★ and then the Klosterkirche, its two spires wearing tall caps of snow; where the bricks of the church were crumbling most, the caps sat the most firmly.

As he came in sight of the church. Lewin suddenly felt a desire to pay a visit to the grave of Johanna Susemihl. He crossed the road and passed through a dilapidated arched gateway into the churchyard. Everything was thickly covered in snow: but he soon saw that a path had been trodden through it, skirting the graves or, where they were sunken, going over them, and leading around the church. He took this path until he came to the grave. Of the ivy that grew over it little could be seen beneath the white blanket that covered it; but ivy was also climbing up the wall beside it as far as just under the roof, and here there was only a fine scattering of snow on it. Against the same wall leant the wooden cross which, though it had been standing for barely three years, had already half fallen down, with its inscription—so far as he could see there was only a name, with no date or epitaph—gazing, in prayer or protestation, up at the heavens above. Lewin was deeply moved at the sight and unconsciously he clasped his hands; then he followed the narrow path through the snow further, until he arrived back at the place he had started from; and then he crossed over the roadway and walked to his house.

Frau Hulen was still up: she did not like to go to bed before she knew her young gentleman was safe indoors.

'Can you guess where I have just come from, Frau Hulen?'

'From the privy councillor, who has the pretty daughter.'

'I was there too. Beforehand. I mean just now.'

'I can't guess.'

'From Johanna Susemihl.'

'And at midnight!'

'That's the best time. You know, Frau Hulen, I feel sorry for Johanna. Who can be virtuous all the time?'

'Lord, Lord, young sir, what has got into you!'

Lewin did not reply; instead he stood whistling softly to himself. He seemed detached and hardly aware of the old lady's presence. At length he began again: 'I am not tired yet, Frau Hulen; that's because I had a sleep this afternoon. Would you fetch me the lamp with the green shade, the little one with the round base; I want to read a little.'

Frau Hulen did as she was asked, in addition recommended that he should lie still and count three times to a hundred, and then left him to himself.

He was indeed in a state of excitement that more than justified the excellent precept the old lady had given him. Visions and images rushed in upon him and succeeded one another with feverish speed; ever changing forms and figures pressed and whirled around him: Kathinka commenced a mazurka, but her partner was not Bninski but Bummcke; then he saw the count standing with Johanna Susemihl beside the church wall, and then General York came riding across a broad expanse of snow that grew narrower and narrower until it was the churchyard, where he waved an admonitory finger at the couple, who were trying to hide in the shadow of the wall. At last the figures faded; the fever fell from him and a condition of sweet languor supervened in which he even felt a faint flame of hope now and then flicker up. At the same time there arose in him the desire to give artistic expression to this mood of hope and sadness. He went over to the old-fashioned bureau, fetched the lamp from the table and set it on the sloping writing-leaf that creaked with every pressure placed upon it, took from one of the drawers a number of sheets of paper he always kept in readiness, and wrote:

> Be consoled: the hours hasten,
> And the woes that on thee weigh,
> Yes, the worst of them will vanish:
> There will dawn another day.
>
> In this world forever changing
> Griefs will come, of that be sure;
> Yes, but they in turn will vanish,
> Happiness come back once more.
>
> Wait in hope and count the hours,
> Not in vain they pass away;
> Changing is the lot of mortals:
> There will dawn another day.*

The weight that had lain on his heart had grown lighter with every line. He put the sheet with the other sheets of paper that lay on the bureau, laid himself down, and went to sleep.

It was already past eight o'clock when Frau Hulen—who knew precisely how Lewin divided up the week and, within the week, the day, and that Tuesday was 'lecture day'—having tried unsuccessfully to awaken him by rattling cups and opening the door of the alcove, finally let fall a metal shovel with a noise like the clashing of cymbals. This produced the desired effect: Lewin leaped up, groped about the night-table still half-asleep, and sounded his repeater-watch. A quarter past eight! He was horrified at the lateness of the hour, but resolved at once to make up for the time he had lost by hurrying more than usual, and twenty minutes later stood in his boots ready to march off.

The night's sleep had done him good, the turbid thoughts of the previous evening had departed, and it was only the sight of his own verses lying half-concealed on the ledge of the bureau that reminded him of the mood he had been in. But it was no more than a recollection: he did not experience it again. He hastily read over the lines he had written, and concluded half-aloud: 'There will dawn another day.' And as he read he felt as lively and invigorated as though this 'other day' had already broken. It was in high spirits that he made his way over the Lange Brücke, past the Stechbahn and the Schlossfreiheit, and on to the university, the former Prince Heinrich Palace.

He took this route only twice a week. With many semesters behind him—he had, indeed, finished his triennium the previous autumn—he found it sufficient to attend only those lectures that made a particular appeal to him or were lucky enough not to occur on days he wanted to keep free. He thus attended the lectures of Savigny, Thaer and Fichte,* all three of whom lectured on Tuesdays and Fridays, and did so one after the other in three successive hours. On other days he stayed at home and devoted himself to the study only of those subjects that appealed to him. He read a great deal, was wholly at one with the adherents of the Romantic school, followed with particular passion the feuds they engaged in and occasionally engaged in them himself. His favourite books, which never left his table, were Shakespeare and Percy's *Reliques*;* it was for the sake of these that he had learned English, which, though he understood it well, he was unable to speak. Now and then he attempted verse himself: Kastalia thought them successful, but he himself considered they showed no genuine poetic gift. In this, by the way, it must be said he went too far, and on at least one point, and that perhaps the decisive point, he was guilty of an excessive severity in his judgement of himself: for what he interpreted as a weakness was in fact his strength. He did not compose poems, they came to him, and he thus enjoyed the happiness and reward (the only reward the poet can be sure of receiving) of being able to throw off from his heart all that tormented it by setting it down.

The first lecture today was Savigny's. He spoke on 'Roman Law in the Middle Ages', and, to judge by the perfect composure with which he began and ended, had not yet heard of the great event of the day, knowledge of which had, indeed, become general only during the course of the morning. Nor was there any mention of the capitulation in Thaer's lecture, which followed, either because the professor was likewise still ignorant of it, or because he felt there was no way in which the subject of his lecture—'Crop Rotation and the Significance for Agriculture of the Cultivation of Potatoes'—could tactfully be connected with it.

From eleven to twelve Fichte lectured on 'The Concept of the Just War'. It was a *collegium publicum* for which, having regard both to the subject and the popularity of the lecturer, the largest of the lecture-halls had been selected from the first; none the less, all the seats had long since been taken by the time Lewin entered, and it was only with considerable effort that he succeeded in commandeering the end of the rearmost bench. Expectations were high, and they were not to be disappointed. The fifteen-minute interval normally allowed between lectures was not yet up when the little man with the sharp profile and the blue but penetrating eyes appeared at the lectern. He had had difficulty in fighting his way up to the platform. 'Gentlemen,' he began, after having, not without a smile of contentment, allowed his glance to glide over the full auditorium, 'gentlemen, we all have in our minds at this moment a piece of great news, and for me to pretend *not* to know it would appear an affectation or an act of cowardice, the one being as bad as the other. You will understand what I am referring to: General York has capitulated. The word usually has an ill sound, but there is nothing in it that can be called good or evil in itself; we know the general, and we therefore know in what spirit we have to interpret his action. I, for my part, am certain that, while it may seem to humiliate us, this is in fact the first step on the road which will lead us out of humiliation to renewal and revival. Your ears will be assailed with other expressions and other constructions. Cowardice, because it is ashamed of itself, seeks to conceal itself behind a false code of honour or dicta handed down from above; it takes refuge, indeed, behind the highest escutcheon of this country. But the nest of the eagle is not a crow's nest. It cannot be that the great deed should be the subject of timid disapprobation; and if it *is*, then let us be fortified in the belief: it is not, even if it is. Let us be full of hope that gives courage, and full of courage that gives hope. Above all, let us do what the brave general did, i.e. *let us come to a decision*.'

The auditorium replied to these words with enthusiasm; then everyone fell silent and there were no further demonstrations, not even when, at the stroke of twelve, the lecturer broke off and hurriedly left the platform. Many followed after him, however, as though to demonstrate their veneration, and pursued him down the long corridors until he left the building from its west wing.

Lewin had stayed behind in the auditorium to meet Jürgass, whose figure he had noticed during the lecture in one of the front rows. He discovered him in lively conversation with a young man who, from the description Tubal had given in his Christmas letter, could be none other than Hansen-Grell. And he indeed it was.

After Jürgass had introduced them—and had, as usual, given rein in doing so to his love of raillery—all three left the building, and then, passing through the trellised gate that stood between the stone sentry-boxes, turned right into the Unter den Linden.

Although the day was, if cold, a splendid one, there were few people about in the Linden, and only the hurrying to and fro of a large number of carriages signalled the agitation that must have been reigning in diplomatic circles.

At the corner of the Redern Palace, which had not yet been subjected to Schinkel's renovations,* our three friends encountered Major von Haacke, who had just left the Prince.

'Good day, Haacke. How are things going?'

'Not very well.'

'How so?'

'The King feels affronted; Natzmer has been sent to head-quarters this very day with orders that leave nothing to be desired in the way of trenchancy. Kleist* is taking over the command. The old man is going to be court-martialled; if he's lucky it could cost him his head.'

'This is all play-acting! It cannot be real. I know York: he's got guts, certainly, but he's also got brains. He has had secret instructions.'

'I don't believe so. This is not a time for secret instructions; they bind not only him who receives them but him who gives them too. And the worst is, they compromise a third party. The only sensible thing to do nowadays is to keep quiet, and the only secret instructions anyone receives are: Do what you think best and be prepared to take the consequences.'

With that they parted again, and our friends made their way along beside the Tiergarten to a place known as Mewe's Floral Garden. They sat themselves at a small table, embarrassed the waiter with several demands none of which could be satisfied, and finally contented themselves with ordering a coffee; in view of the fact that it was one o'clock, none of them could decide whether to count it as the last morning-coffee or the first coffee of the afternoon.

All this time Lewin had been occupied less with the capitulation than with the coming session of Kastalia. These reunions rotated among its members, and it was the ambition of each of them to make of *his* session the greatest possible literary event; today Kastalia was to assemble in Lewin's quarters, yet he had so far done nothing to ensure the success of the evening.

He complained jokingly of the fact to Jürgass, who, replying in the same tone, referred firstly to the two guests he had advertised would be attending—and whose names, it now emerged, were Herr von Hirschfeldt and Herr von Meerheimb —and then, since they would probably prove to be not quite enough, to Hansen-Grell, who always, he knew, had something fresh and tolerably readable in his pocket. '*Sans doute, aujourd'hui comme toujours.*'★

Hansen-Grell maintained the opposite, though he did so in a manner that made it permissible to doubt this assurance. Jürgass shook his head, and even Lewin resolved on a direct confrontation.

'Do you have anything?'

'No.'

'I know that,' Jürgass interposed. 'Seek and ye shall find.'

A brief pause ensued; then Hansen-Grell said finally, drawing a thick notebook from his pocket: 'Very well, I do have something. But it is not really finished, and never will be, either.'

'In that case', Lewin responded, 'it is as good as finished, or even better than finished. Besides, there exists a whole literature of fragments. The best any of us can manage is "fragments". Give it here.'

Without more ado Grell tore the page out of the notebook and gave it to Lewin, and while Jürgass laughed heartily at, as he put it, 'having once more caught out a poet up to his tricks', he read the lines over quickly and, nodding his head repeatedly, indicated his pleasure and approval.

In the meantime the coffee had arrived; they only sipped at it, and since the rhododendrons and magnolias set out in pots, with a few camellias appearing here and there as an extreme rarity, made little appeal either to Jürgass or to his two companions, they quickly departed and made their way back into the city. At the corner of the Leipzigerstrasse and the Friedrichsstrasse their paths diverged.

7

Kastalia

LEWIN went to lunch. In the part of the Taubenstrasse built up like a cul-de-sac from which, then as now, a narrow thoroughfare led to the Hausvogteiplatz, there was an old-fashioned wine-shop in whose smoke-stained guest-room Lewin was accustomed to take his simple midday meal. Today he had finished it more speedily than usual, and it was not yet four o'clock when he arrived back in his quarters. Two letters had been delivered in his absence, one from Dr Sassnitz expressing his great regret that he was going to be prevented from appearing at Kastalia, the other from Himmerlich containing, in addition, a lyrical contribution to the session: four very long stanzas under the collective title 'Sabbath'. Lewin smiled and, after having marked it with a figure I in red pencil, placed it in a card-folder lying ready prepared which served as the Kastalia file; he then inserted into it the verses he had received from Hansen-Grell and his own lines of the previous evening. These contributions, too, had first received their number pencilled in red.

With that the first preparations were completed, but they were certainly not the last. Very much still remained to be done, notwithstanding it has to be admitted that many individual questions had been happily regulated and as it were resolved in advance through wise legislation. The question of entertainment, for example: Paragraph Seven of the statutes, indited by Jürgass, read as follows: 'In the matter of entertainment Kastalia must show itself worthy of its name and origin. The basis of its hospitality is undeviatingly pure water and, what is closest to it, tea. A Rhine or Moselle may be offered only exceptionally. The great Society Cup is entrusted to the priestly hands of our fellow member Lewin von Vitzewitz, as the society's founder. *Substantia,*★ even in exceptional cases, not permissible.'

This was Paragraph Seven: but the foresight it embodied had

not sufficed to solve all of Lewin's difficulties, and especially not the always burning question of the seating arrangements, which arose partly from the comparative narrowness of his room, partly from the inadequate amount of furniture that Frau Hulen possessed. It was a delicate point which Lewin dared not venture to raise with the old lady. And so, today as before, he was put to the bother of repeated experimentation, until he had arranged his two round tables, not merely side by side, but in a diagonal line across the room, since if they had been set up in a position parallel to the wall it would have proved impossible to open and close the door and thus led to an obstruction of this vital, because sole, line of communication with Frau Hulen.

At length everything was done, lamp and candles were burning, and Lewin stood back and admired his work. On one of the tables there stood grandly the symbol of Kastalia, the large water-decanter, while in the middle of the other arose the pearl-embroidered tobacco-box whose chief embellishment (on the lid) was a representation of the death of Queen Dido. Between the sofa and the door, beside a spot on the wall which could be reached from at any rate most of the seats at the table, there stood, as was in those days customary, a pedestal-like pipe-table, with cherry-wood and other makes of pipe decorated with knots and tassels, while on a corner of the window-sill a number of bottles of Rhine-wine, together with the silver-plated Kastalia cup, awaited their moment.

Frau Hulen's Schwarzwald clock, whose ticking could be heard even in Lewin's room, had only just struck seven when the doorbell rang. It was Rabatzki and Himmerlich, who had encountered one another on the third flight of stairs and, the prevailing darkness notwithstanding, had recognized one another or greeted one another by chance. As though by an unspoken agreement they were always the first to arrive, however, and they employed the time before the appearance of the other members in the settlement of editorial questions: for Rabatzki published a small Sunday paper, and it may be said without exaggeration that the whole poetry-and-fiction section of each edition of that paper was fixed and determined during the minutes before the opening of the preceding session of Kastalia.

Today, however, it was not to be. Rabatzki had hardly found time to put a first question to his 'right hand', as he liked to call Himmerlich, before the appearance of the Rittmeister rendered all further discussion impossible. With Jürgass there also appeared the two guests he had advertised, von Hirschfeldt and von Meerheimb, the latter still wearing his arm in a sling. Lewin said how pleased he was to see them, and doubly so if, as Herr von Jürgass had intimated, they were prepared through communicating something from their diaries and memoranda to help to enliven the sometimes somewhat sluggish spring of Kastalia. The two gentlemen bowed, while Jürgass handed to Lewin two manuscripts of whose existence and content he had previously taken care to reassure himself.

Lewin hoped to find an opportunity, before the session began, of becoming acquainted with the new guests, who until that moment had been unknown to him; but he had hardly begun to bid them welcome before another ring at the door interrupted a conversation that had barely started. It was Tubal and Bninski who came in. Lewin expected to see a state of tension evolve at once between Hirschfeldt and the count, for though both had fought in Spain they had fought on opposite sides: but precisely the unexpected happened. Already prepared by Tubal, Bninski immediately approached Hirschfeldt with a courteous greeting in which there sounded a note of genuine cordiality rather than one of mere politeness; and if interruptions and interrogations of all kinds such as Jürgass especially liked to interpose prevented a connected conversation from developing, the count none the less managed to convey by the little attentions he paid him the particular partiality he felt for his antagonist.

Hauptmann Bummcke was the last. Jürgass could not let him get away with that with impunity and held the clock up to him.

'Military men, my dear Bummcke, do not recognize any academic fifteen-minute intervals. In consideration of your particular circumstances, it might be let pass in the summertime; but with twelve degrees of frost no *embonpoint* in the world can excuse an unpunctuality amounting to nearly twenty minutes.'

'Begin, begin,' cried several voices, among which those of Rabatzki and Himmerlich were clearly recognizable. While members and guests arranged themselves around the two tables as best they could, Lewin opened the proceedings by knocking with a sugar-hammer and then himself took his seat in an armchair which by means of a sofa-cushion had been transformed into a kind of presidential chair. He was far from being a master of oratory, but his office and situation left him with no choice.

'Gentlemen,' he began, 'I bid you welcome. Unfortunately we do not have a full complement. Our finest critical mind is missing: Doctor Sassnitz has apologized for his absence by letter. On the other hand, I am happy to draw your attention to a magnificent collection of texts, among them texts in print. At the head of these printed texts stand those publications originating with former members of Kastalia. They are *The Forefathers of Brandenburg*, an epic hymn by Friedrich Count Kalkreuth,★ and the *Dramatic Poems* of Friedrich Baron de la Motte Fouqué★ published only a few days ago by J. E. Hitzig here in Berlin, among which are to be found, together with Old Norse pieces, 'The Hallersee Family' and 'The Homecoming of the Great Elector', which were first read and received with so much acclamation in our circle last winter.'

Here Lewin paused as the books he had named were handed round. Then he went on: 'As new contributions for today's session five works have been submitted, of very varying compass: lyric or lyrical-epic poems, and diaries and reminiscences from Spain and Russia. It is a rule that we commence with lyrical pieces and then go on to whatever belongs to the domain of prose narration. I request Herr Himmerlich to be good enough to read to us his stanzas, which, if I have seen aright, are translated from the English. They bear the title: "The Sabbath".'★

With these words Lewin handed the sheet to Herr Himmerlich.

At the annunciation of the title Jürgass had rubbed his chin demonstratively with the palm of his left hand.

In a patently nervous condition and struggling to smooth out the much folded sheet of paper, Himmerlich began by repeating: 'The Sabbath. A poem by William Wilberforce.'

'Is this the same Wilberforce', asked Jürgass, 'who abolished the slave trade?'

'No, on the contrary.'

'What, has he introduced it again?'

'Not that either. The young poet with whom I would like to acquaint you today, and who bears so celebrated a name, is a factory worker. When I said "on the contrary", what I meant was that he himself still exists in a kind of slavery. I sense the illogicality of the phrase I used and I beg to apologize.'

'Very well, Himmerlich. No need to be so sensitive.'

'I am altogether a stranger to sensitivity, I assure you. But, now that I have the floor, I ask to be allowed to make some preliminary remarks. As you will all know, the English language is blessed with a very large number of short words, and, not always but often, it can say in a single syllable what we require three to say. It may also be remarked that the English have virtually no feminine rhymes at all.'

'How reprehensible!'

'From these linguistic differences there arise difficulties which, with your kind permission, I should like briefly to examine.'

'No, Himmerlich, saving the chairman's decision you do *not* have our kind permission. I have hitherto kept silent, in the knowledge that every hen cackles before it lays its egg. But this natural law, which must to a certain degree be indulged, stands, when it threatens to go too far, in contravention of the written law of Kastalia. Paragraph Nine of our statutes determines once and for all the question of preambles, and assigns to them their proper bounds. The words of the poet —"Beneficent is the fire's flame, so long as man its power can tame"*— applies also to the fire of oratory. I have the impression that the statutory bounds have already been overstepped, and I therefore ask our chairman to require that the speaker proceed to the poem itself.'

Lewin nodded in agreement and, colouring slightly, Himmerlich began in a vibrant voice:

''Tis morning, but yet the full and cloudless moon
Pours from her starry urn a chastened light:
'Tis but a little space beyond the noon—
The still delicious noon of Summer's night;
Forth from my home I take an early flight,
Down the lone vale pursue my devious way,
Bound o'er the meadows with a keen delight,
Brush from the forest leaves the dewy spray,
And scale the toilsome steep, to watch the kindling day.

The lark is up, disdainful of the earth,
Exulting in his airy realm on high;
His song, profuse in melody and mirth,
Makes vocal all the region of the sky;
The startled moor-cock, with a sudden cry,
Springs from beneath my feet; and as I pass,
The sheep regard me with an earnest eye,
Ceasing to nibble at the scanty grass,
And scour the barren waste in one tumultuous mass.'

At this point the recitation experienced an interruption
through the appearance of Frau Hulen with the tea-tray.
Always full of empathy with the vanities of poets, even if only
because he had gone through them himself, Lewin made
repeated gestures to the old lady to go back; but it was already
too late, and Himmerlich had to endure a martyrdom lasting
many minutes. He said a terse 'thank you' when the circulating
tray reached him, dispatched a look of tragic-comic hatred after
the old lady as she finally vanished again, and then continued in
an elevated voice:

'But lo! the stars are waning, and the dawn
Blushes and burns athwart the east;—behold!
The early sun, behind the upland lawn,
Looks o'er the summit with a front of gold;
Back from his beaming brow the mists are rolled,
And as he climbs the crystal tower of morn,
Rocks, woods, and glens their shadowy depths unfold.
The trembling dews grow brighter on the thorn,
And Nature smiles as fresh as if but newly born.

God of the boundless universe! I come
To hold communion with myself and Thee!
And though excess of beauty makes me dumb,
My thoughts are eloquent with all I see!
My foot is on the mountains,—I am free,
And buoyant as the winds that round me blow!
My dreams are sunny as yon pleasant lea,
And tranquil as the pool that sleeps below;
While, circling round my heart, a poet's raptures glow.'

Hardly had the last lines died away before the bookseller, Rabatzki, rose to his feet and said, in a tone in which self-importance was in continual struggle with modesty: 'Gentlemen! Without wishing in any way to anticipate your more competent verdict' ('Well said, Rabatzki!') 'I merely wish to be allowed to state, from the standpoint of one who is preponderantly a businessman, that I would account myself fortunate to be able to present these stanzas in the next number of my Sunday paper, and indeed quite exceptionally on its main page. I would ask Herr Himmerlich to authorize me to do so, and at the same time be good enough to furnish me with a note containing a few brief biographical details of the English poet, who seems to me altogether worthy of his famous namesake.'

These flattering words seemed to Himmerlich a favourable omen for his whole future, and something like a transfiguration passed across his face. He was not to enjoy his triumph for long, however. Jürgass knocked out the spill with which he had just ignited a fresh pipe, and said: 'With all respect to our friend Rabatzki's Sunday-paper enthusiasm, there is one thing I should like to know: is it a fragment?'

'No.'

'Then permit me to say that your Sabbath may have an ending but it has no conclusion.'

'That is a matter of opinion. I don't believe it was necessary to accompany my morning stroller back to his lunch table.'

'And I, for my part, would hardly think that your poem would have suffered from such a pleasantly idyllic addition. However, let us leave that aside. But the form, the form, Himmerlich! Tell us, what *are* these curious stanzas?'

'They are the so-called Spenserian stanzas.'

'Spenserian stanzas?' Jürgass went on. 'I find this name almost more curious than the verses themselves.'

'I assume, Herr von Jürgass,' Himmerlich replied, in a voice growing ever more excited, 'that you are familiar with the structure of the *ottava rima*, that fair eight-lined stanza in which Tasso and Ariosto* wrote their immortal works, the *Orlando Furioso* and the *Gerusalemme Liberata*.'

Jürgass, who was anything but at home in this domain, puffed more vigorously at his pipe and sought to conceal his growing sense of insecurity behind a brief 'And so?' enunciated in a superior manner.

'And so', said Himmerlich, seizing on this expression, 'the Spenserian stanza may be regarded as a first cousin of this stanza employed by Tasso and Ariosto. Its rhyme-scheme is different, to be sure, it has, not eight lines, but nine, and in this ninth line passes from the five-foot iambus to the Alexandrine . . . '

'But is none the less one and the same thing. I envy you this conclusion, Himmerlich.'

A heated debate seemed unavoidable; Lewin dextrously cut it short, however, by observing that to determine the precise degree of relationship between the Spenserian stanza and *ottava rima* was not a task for their circle. He would have to ask them to apply themselves to the poem itself, if indeed they did not prefer that, certain minor criticisms on the part of Herr von Jürgass notwithstanding, the encomium already expressed by their faithful fellow member, the bookseller Rabatzki, should simply be accepted as representing the verdict and vote of thanks of Kastalia itself.

This proposal was not merely agreed to, it was agreed to with a readiness the ironical flavour of which was very well perceived by the unhappy Himmerlich.

'We now turn to the second of the submitted contributions', Lewin went on. 'They are stanzas by our highly honoured guest, Herr Hansen-Grell; I hope—and I am sure every member of Kastalia will join me—that Herr Hansen-Grell will very shortly cease to be a guest and become a member of this circle. I now ask him to be good enough to read his poem.'

Hansell-Grell drew the lamp a little closer to him—for

tobacco-smoke was beginning to obscure the air—and then without more ado began in a quiet but very penetrating voice: '*Seydlitz*: born at Calcar★ on 3 February 1721.'

'Is that the title?' Jürgass interrupted.

'Yes,' was the terse reply.

'In that case, I am bound to say that I am even more surprised by it than I was by the construction and rhyme-scheme of Himmerlich's Spenserian stanza. "Born at Calcar on 3 February 1721" is the title of an obituary notice, not of a poem!'

'And above all', Hansen-Grell replied cheerfully, 'it is a title for which no one but Herr von Jürgass himself is to blame. Were it not for his aversion to anything resembling a *capitatio benevolentiae*★ the title of my poem would have been simply "General Seydlitz"; but, deprived of all possibility of bringing the indispensable "born at Calcar" to your kind attention, by the traditional means of a brief prologue, I had no other recourse but to include this biographical detail in the poem's actual title.'

'And thus we have had another prologue after all . . .'

'Because we ought not to have any.—But I have finished.' And Hansen-Grell read without further interruption:

'*General Seydlitz*

For reading and for sitting
He had no taste at all,
He much preferred the tending
Of horses in a stall;
Two shining spurs of silver
And a steel-blue blade he wore—
And he was born at Calcar,
And Calcar means a *spur*.

The windmill sails are humming,
A rider and horse come by,
They make full tilt for the windmill
And under the sails they fly.
Then, bending without stopping,
He reaches to the floor,
Plucks up of corn a bushel—
Hey, Calcar, that's a *spur*.

They're riding over the bridges,
The King exclaims: "Well now,
We've foes before and behind us,
Seydlitz, what would you do?"
Over the ledge he vaulted
Without the least demur,
The river surged like the ocean—
Yes, Calcar, that's a *spur*.

And other times and heroes;
How transient acclaim!
He, lying on his deathbed,
Says smiling: "What is fame?
The horn of a better horseman
Wherever I turn I hear,
But even *him* I challenge—
For Calcar means a *spur*." '

A burst of jubilation such as Kastalia had not heard for a long time erupted on every side and—as Hansen-Grell jocularly remarked to avoid further ovations—bore ample witness to the cavalier composition of the Tuesday society. The remark was quite justified: Bninski, Hirschfeldt and Meerheimb were cavaliers by profession, Tubal and Lewin were excellent horsemen. But the minority too were loud in their applause; Bummcke, if not a horseman, was at any rate a soldier, Rabatzki always applauded, and Himmerlich was relieved to be able to conceal his ill-humour behind enthusiastic, if brief and somewhat forced exclamations of delight—in addition to which they gave him the pleasant feeling he was a man capable of ungrudging magnanimity.

At length the uproar died down, and Tubal asked to be heard—a thing which, a private feud between Bummcke and Jürgass over the admissibility of the expression 'without the least demur' having broken out, he found somewhat difficult to achieve. Finally, however, he succeeded, and Tubal said: 'Perhaps I may be permitted to recall a dictum propounded in this place not long ago by Dr Sassnitz: "Our severity is our pride." You will feel that this dictum is the bridge across which I intend to proceed to an attack. The charm of the poem we have just heard resides exclusively in its tone and in the way it treats its subject; it is audaciously conceived and audaciously executed, but of this audacity it has palpably too much.'

'You cannot have too much audacity,' Jürgass interposed.

'You can,' Tubal retorted. 'Our honoured guest himself sensed the truth of this.'

Hansen-Grell nodded.

'Every work of art—this at least is my point of view in this matter—must be comprehensible in itself, without the need for historical or biographical notes. But I do not see that this poem fulfils this requirement. It is eminently an occasional poem and intended for a narrow, even the narrowest circle, like a toast at a wedding. It presupposes an acquaintanceship with half a dozen anecdotes about Seydlitz, and I believe it is hardly too much to say that it is capable of being understood only by a Prussian. Read the poem to an Englishman or a Frenchman, even in the finest translation, and he will be unable to find his way in it.'

Bninski shook his head.

'Our honoured guest, Count Bninski,' Tubal went on, 'appears not to agree with me. I am glad, for the poet's sake, to see a champion appear on his behalf from so unexpected a quarter. Perhaps the count would be kind enough to elaborate on his view in this matter.'

Lewin repeated the request.

'I need to say only a few words,' the count began, in good German though with a Polish accent. 'I know of General Seydlitz nothing except his name and his reputation, but I believe that I have completely understood Herr Hansen-Grell's poem. I learn from his stanzas that Seydlitz was born in Calcar, that he had no taste for learning but a great partiality for riding. Then there follow anecdotes whose meaning is quite clear and which at the same time glorify his horsemanship, until in the last stanza he succumbs to that better horseman to whom we must all sooner or later succumb. This small amount is enough, because it is a sufficiency. Here is the mystery of the thing. More years ago than I like to remember I used to be concerned with the folk-songs of my homeland and I collected many of them, and I noticed, in these and in those from elsewhere, that one of the marks and beauties of this species of poetry is the way in which it progresses by leaps and bounds. The imagination has only to receive the correct stimulus; if this is achieved, then it is not too much to assert: "The less said, the better." '

'I resign myself', Tubal replied, 'so as not to interrupt the progress of our meeting longer than would be desirable. If an unauthorized glance into our chairman's file has not deceived me, the next thing we can expect is some more stanzas of his own composition.'

'Our friend Ladalinski has once again demonstrated his sharp-sightedness. It was my intention today to present as the last of our lyrical pieces a piece of my own; but my contribution still needs revising and polishing, and I request permission to withdraw it.'

It was not without a feeling of embarrassment that Lewin spoke these words, for this departure from his original intention proceeded in truth from a cause very different from the one he had stated. He knew all too well to what faint-hearted mood the three little stanzas in question owed their existence; and however much this faint-heartedness may in the end have clad itself in the raiment of hope, he had come to think that Bninski would be bound to detect in the song the elegiac tone that was its keynote and then divine what had occasioned it. He found this thought extremely painful, and he thus moved his poem down to the back of the folder and, handing to Rittmeister von Hirschfeldt the prose manuscript now lying at the top, asked him to commence his reading.

The captain composed himself and, with that frankness of demeanour which constitutes both the charm and the prerogative of the soldier, began in a ringing voice and without any preamble:

'*Recollections of the War in Spain*
*The Engagement at Plaa**

'My elder brother, Eugen, after having fought first under Schill, then under the Duke of Brunswick, and having also participated in the embarkation for England,* had there engaged himself for service in Spain and in the summer of 1810 had arrived in Andalusia. When I heard of this I followed him and met him, just landed, in the great market place at Cadiz. Our joy at seeing one another again I shall pass over. He had on that same day been commissioned as major, and he found it easy to use his influence to obtain for me a post as a lieutenant.

'We disliked life in Cadiz, so that we were glad when orders came that we were to join the army detachment stationed in Catalonia which was daily engaged with the enemy. We departed thither, and after a highly uncomfortable sea voyage, during which we were made very well aware how different a Spanish man-o'-war is from an English one, we landed in the harbour at Tarragona. This was at the end of November, exactly two months after my arrival in Spain. Catalonia looked a lot better than Andalusia. We were attached to the Alcantara Regiment of Dragoons, my brother as lieutenant-colonel, I as first officer. The reception we received was comradely; all Prussian officers were regarded as being particularly reliable.

'In its time the Alcantara Dragoons had been a very much favoured and very splendid regiment; under the Old Regime they wore three-cornered hats with white lace, yellow long-coats with red linings and red collars, also green cuffs and blue knee-breeches. Every colour was represented. After the reconstruction the entire army had undergone since then, however, little was left of this magnificence and splendour, and the Alcantara Dragoons *we* discovered had to rest content with a low leather shako and a long blue coat with regimental number and brass buttons. They were armed with a very long sword with a narrow blade and a heavy iron basket-hilt, so that the weight lay in the hand, and in addition carbine and pistol.

'Our regiment belonged to the army of General O'Donnell, more particularly to the advance division of General Sarsfield. The latter, only twenty-six years old, a brilliant soldier, steely calm in battle, conceived an especial liking for my brother, in whom he at once recognized all those qualities by which he himself was distinguished. All the information we could have desired was made available to us. The division was numerically weak and comprised two infantry and four cavalry regiments, in all five thousand men at the most. They were the Almeria Infantry Regiment and the Baron Wimpfen Regiment of

Switzers, with the Alcantara and Numancia Dragoons, the Catalonia Cuirassiers and the Granada Hussars.

'In the very first days after our arrival an *avant-garde* of four hundred horse was formed and placed under my brother's command. Opposite us stood General Macdonald, who with a strong force held Barcelona, which lay to the north of us, and aspired through the performance of an outflanking manœuvre to seize Tortosa too, which lay to the south of us. If he should succeed, we would be shut in and would have to count ourselves lucky to be able to withdraw to Tarragona and there again take ship. Catalonia would then be lost. And that is what happened. But before it happened we had a series of bloody engagements.

'Of this series of engagements I shall describe only that at Plaa, because it proved to be a decisive engagement for me personally.

'It was on 7 January that we learned that it was all up with Tortosa. We were then ensconced, the entire Sarsfield Division, on the northern slopes of a high mountain range running parallel with the coast and some distance from it, and, while engaged in daily skirmishing with the advance guard of Macdonald's force, were occupying the road leading straight across the mountains from Lerida to Tarragona. As long as we continued to hold this road, together with the defile, the so-called Plaa Pass, the loss of Tortosa, though a serious matter, would at least pose no immediate threat to our own safety; possession of the pass secured to us our line of retreat to the sea. If we took into consideration the quantity of effort the enemy was making, which was on the whole not very great, there was no reason for us to change our position. Where we stood we appeared to be on the attack, whereas if we were to abandon our position on the northern slopes and cross to the other side of the mountains we should have displayed that state of apprehension and irresolution that is already halfway to a defeat.

'We had, however, underestimated the zeal of our antagonist, or at least that of General Suchet, who, operating in co-operation with Macdonald, exceeded him in energy. On 14 January we received reports that a strong enemy *avant-garde* was marching towards us from the coast, that is to say in our rear, with the unmistakable intention of closing the Plaa Pass. The village of Plaa lay hard against the foot of the mountains on the side opposite to us. On receiving these reports, General Sarsfield made up his mind at once: he strengthened our own *avant-garde*, which until then had consisted of only four hundred horses of the Alcantara and Granada Regiments, with two battalions of the Wimpfen Switzers, and ordered my brother to conduct a night march across the mountains and to occupy the village of Plaa before dawn. The detachment left at once; but a dreadful storm, with wind and rain, which made it impossible to traverse the narrow path across the mountains in any way but in single file, delayed our entry into Plaa until ten o'clock in the morning. We had arrived at the last possible moment: the French *avant-garde* division under General Eugenio (which meant that the commanders of the opposing forces bore the same name) were already attacking the village, and it was only with the utmost effort that my brother succeeded in holding it until noon.

'At this hour General Sarsfield appeared with the main force and restored the position, for our detachment was already in retreat. But we were still unable to gain ground, and when an hour later the enemy too received reinforcements of all kinds, he again went over to the attack, this time with a regiment of dragoons at a full strength. At that moment the only force available to oppose him was the cuirassiers sent forward to relieve our *avant-garde*, the Catalonia Cuirassiers under their commander, Don Pedro Gallon. Directly behind the cuirassiers we had the Alcantara Dragoons and the Granada Hussars. Our cuirassiers, who amounted to hardly two hundred horse, were too weak and began to waver; but when my brother saw what was happening he gave the signal to attack, and in line formation we fell upon the enemy dragoons on their left flank. They immediately gave way and involved in their flight a regiment of chasseurs stationed behind them. We pursued them for the distance of a mile and took many prisoners; General Eugenio, who had personally tried to halt the flight, was cut down and died the following day.

'It was a complete victory, and bought at not all that high a price; only *I* lost a great deal that day: like General Eugenio, against whom he had stood, my brother Eugen succumbed to his wounds. What there remains for me to say concerns only him and me.

'By five o'clock the engagement was over, and I led what was left of the Alcantara Regiment back to Plaa. On the whole I had got off lightly, except that a French dragoon whom I was trying to lay hold on in the *démêlé* had struck me in the face with the hilt of his sword, so that, black and swollen as I was, I presented a worse appearance than many who were severely wounded. It was thus that I came before my brother, of whose injuries I had already heard on the way back. I found him in one of the farmhouses at Plaa, with good people looking after him. When he saw me he insisted that I should be tended first, which I then was. When I went back to him I sat down and we began to talk. First we talked about the affair that now happily lay behind us. I had to tell him every little detail, and he followed my words with great attentiveness; my horse, for example, a fine black stallion, had had one of his ears cut off close to the head, a fact my brother greatly deplored. His attention, however, was especially attracted to a diary which happened to be in a portmanteau that had fallen to my lot during the division of booty. It had been kept, with the greatest scrupulousness, from the time the French first entered Catalonia until 14 January 1811, and contained descriptions, accompanied by little sketch-maps, of almost all the engagements in which we too had been involved. Eugen leafed through the book for half an hour and commended the impartiality with which events had been narrated. After all this, the last thing I thought of was that he might be in danger, and I had to agree with the doctor, who, in spite of the violent pains my brother complained of from time to time, spoke only of superficial wounds. They were sword-wounds in his left side. The only thing that seemed to me unusual was his gentleness; he was in a tender mood, spoke a great deal of our home and of our old father, and asked me to write to him, since for a few weeks he would be prevented from writing himself.

'Thus we spent the evening. Weary though I was, I intended to sit by him during the night, but things fell out otherwise.

Soon after midnight the alarm was sounded and I betook myself to my regiment, which was bivouaced before the village; as soon as I had arrived we received the order to reconnoitre a small town named Valls lying in the direction of the coast. I had left my wounded brother in good hands; I had begged of the Switzers a number of men to mount guard over him, and it chanced that the corporal who commanded this guard had been with him in the same company of the Duke of Brunswick's Regiment when my brother was still garrisoned in Halberstadt. Both were delighted to see one another again.

'Our ride to Valls passed without incident, but it cost a great deal of time and effort, and it was not until the afternoon of the following day that the troops who had carried out the reconnaissance returned to Plaa. Several officers I encountered told me Eugen had improved, and I did indeed find him more composed and without pain, though he was very weak. Nevertheless, he listened attentively as I told him of the little events of the day, and when, out of consideration for his condition, I fell silent, he demanded I go on. Suddenly, however, he interrupted me, and said: "Do you still remember the evening on the voyage from Cadiz to Tarragona when with our German companions we thought of our homeland, and someone asked the question: 'Which of us will see the homeland again?' I now know one who will never do so." I bent over him and begged him not to excite himself with such gloomy thoughts; but he paid no heed to me, but went on: "There is much still to happen today: I see a black future. If it comes to an engagement, look out for yourself. Our horses are tired enough to fall down. And don't forget, you don't always have to go charging in at the risk of your life. That is the way to sacrifice yourself needlessly." These were his last words. I had just lifted him up to give him a spoonful of medicine; as I was laying him back on his pillow it seemed to me he had grown very pale. I grasped his hand and it was cold; he pressed mine convulsively, gasped for air, and was dead.

'This was on the afternoon of the 16th. When he heard of my brother's demise, General Sarsfield sent me his condolences and added the observation that it would be a good idea to have the deceased removed as soon as possible up to the monastery church that lay above Plaa; every hour could bring a fresh engagement of whose outcome we could not be certain.

'I paid heed to these words. Out of some old boards—"four long planks and two short ones"—we constructed a coffin as quickly as we could and laid Eugen in it in his regimental uniform. Then some of my dragoons carried him up into the church and laid him near to the altar steps.

'Utterly exhausted by the exertions and excitements of the past few days, when night came I laid myself down on a pile of straw. I was quite dissolved in grief; visions of my childhood and early youth passed before me; now I was alone, utterly alone, and the brother I had loved so much was dead.

'I was about to fall asleep when I was awoken by an orderly officer. He had come from the general and had been sent to fetch a paper that Sarsfield had given to Eugen almost immediately before the beginning of the encounter at Plaa. It was a matter of importance and he must have it.

'I at once recalled the incident, I had seen my brother put the paper into his riding-cloak, and I therefore asked the officer to be good enough to accompany me up to the church, since my brother was still wearing the same coat he had worn before the start of the engagement. He refused, however, pleading he had other duties; and when I looked for him I found that my servant, Francesco, too had disappeared. So there was nothing for it but to go alone.

'I took a small lantern with only one window and walked up to the monastery building, which I saw was fairly extensive. One of the brothers opened the door to me, but was alarmed when I asked him to be good enough to open for me the church door too. "No one can get me in there at this time of night," he said. It was in vain that I tried to persuade him. "It is not safe," he persisted. Finally he agreed to give me the keys to the church, together with the instruction that, when I had turned it in the lock twice, I should push against the door as hard as I could, because it was warped and difficult to open.

'To reach the church you still had to pass through two long cloisters. Here a bitter infantry battle had taken place the day before (our troops being the Switzers) and traces of the battle were still to be seen everywhere: the bodies had been removed, to be sure, but the pools of blood remained; the statues, torn away from the walls, lay shattered on the floor; even the air was dank and smelt of putrefaction. Past these images of destruction I walked through to the church, inserted the key in the lock, and pushed hard against the door, which opened slowly with a groan. I removed my cloak, which could now only be a hindrance to me, took my sword in one hand and the lantern in the other, and made my way up the high-vaulted centre aisle. There reigned an uncanny silence, and I was startled by the echo of my own footsteps.

'Thus I reached the altar. There the coffin stood, provisionally covered only with a board. I lifted it, and my brother's glassy eyes stared up at me. As there was nowhere else to put it, I placed the lantern at his feet and began slowly to open his uniform button by button; it fitted firmly, almost tightly, across his chest. I did it with my face averted; but however much I might avoid looking at him, I had his deathly countenance before my eyes. At last I found the paper and put it into my pocket. Then came the hardest part: I had to refasten the buttons again, for I could not bring myself to leave him lying with his uniform undone as though he had been robbed. And when that too had been done I returned the way I had come.

'The following afternoon—the enemy had failed to attack—my brother was buried with full military honours by the Wimpfen Switzers in the same monastery church in Plaa before whose altar he had lain for the previous twenty-four hours. His sabre, gloves and spurs were hung above him, and it was only several months later that, on the order of General O'Donnell, who wanted to see the dead properly honoured, they were taken to the cathedral at Tarragona. They are to be found there still.'

When he had read thus far, the speaker rolled up the manuscript and laid it upon one of the window-sills; his listeners sat in silence gazing at the table. The first to rise was Bninski.

'I am also a guest in this circle, and I am almost afraid of encroaching on the preserves of those more fitted to speak if I now do so myself. But my position is an exceptional one, and that may serve to excuse me. Two years before you, Herr von

Hirschfeldt, I fought on the same fields as you did, if on the opposite side to you; I know the places you have referred to; recollections, hardly faded, reawoke within me as I listened. What does it matter who was friend, who foe! All were involved in the same peril. I ask to be allowed to call you a dear comrade of mine henceforth.'

While Bninski was speaking, Jürgass had uncorked the bottle of Rhine-wine standing close beside him, and with a celerity appropriate to the situation filled the great silver Kastalia cup to the brim. 'Gentlemen, one of those exceptional cases which Paragraph Seven of our statutes, in what I have no hesitation in calling its wisdom, foresees, is now upon us. And so I drink to the health of our honoured guest, Rittmeister von Hirschfeldt. Long life to him! Many honours have been heaped upon his head, as many honours as wounds; but one thing has until this day been denied him: he has not yet drunk from the silver cup of Kastalia. Now this hour too has struck. I drink to him, and let him drink with me in return.'

And, to the accompaniment of repeated cheers and toasts, the cup was passed from hand to hand.

After acts of homage such as these, Lewin's only remaining duty was to find a few concluding words. 'The advanced hour', he began, 'and even more the elevated state of mind in which it finds us, demand that we do now adjourn. I anticipate your agreement.' ('Agreed!') 'Our next meeting will, unless any objection is raised' ('No, no!') 'open with the diary of our honoured guest Herr von Meerheimb, which to our regret there has not been time for today, any lyrical pieces that may by then have been submitted being put back until afterwards. I declare the meeting closed.'

With that everyone departed, in larger or smaller groups. The majority kept to the left; only Jürgass, Bummcke and Hansen-Grell turned to the right at the corner of the Königs-strasse and made for the Alexanderplatz, where, in the depths of Mundt's wine-cellar, they concluded the evening in talk and critical chatter, naturally taking as their text the session of Kastalia just ended.

8

Light Cloud

THE following morning was clear and sunny, and the privy councillor's study too was lighter than it usually was on a winter's day. A ray of sunlight was falling on to the basket in the stove-corner, where the greyhound lay in a state intermediate between sleep and quivering. The pendulum clock struck ten and, with the punctuality that characterized him, the privy councillor entered the room and took his seat at the desk, upon which there again lay a number of newspapers and several letters addressed to him personally, weighed down by a paper-weight of black marble. Beside them lay an ivory paper-knife with a carved spiral handle.

It was a clear day, yet there was also a certain amount of 'light cloud', at least there was in the spirits of the privy councillor, who, reversing the customary order of things, had today deferred his morning visit to the goldfish and instead had taken up the newspapers straightaway. His eyes flew across the columns, but it was not difficult to see that he was not reading but only endeavouring to conceal from himself the disquietude that filled him.

'Good morning, Papa' came from behind him, as it did on an occasion described earlier, and before he had time to turn and reply to the greeting Kathinka was at his side. She too seemed disconcerted, and, looking him in the eyes with some intensity, said: 'You wanted to see me, Papa?'

'Yes, Kathinka. Please sit down.'

'Not until you cease to look so serious and solemn, as though some great historical event were about to take place.'

The privy councillor tapped on the table with the supple tip of his ivory knife, and then, shifting his chair round slightly, he turned to the window-alcove in which Kathinka had taken a seat with her back to the light: the semi-shadow in which she was as a consequence sitting was extremely becoming, and in the joyful pride he felt in his lovely daughter the father forgot for a few moments what was weighing on his heart. Kathinka herself was well aware of the impression she was producing. She was wearing her hair in a gold net, as she usually did in the morning, but the net had become half undone, so that some of her chestnut-brown locks had fallen out on to the collar of her wide, domino-patterned morning gown. Her feet, lightly crossed over one another, were clad in little morocco-leather shoes; and, quickly perceiving the advantage her father derived from his toying with the ivory knife, she took up the little trowel that lay beside the goldfish in order to toy with it in retaliation.

'I have asked you to come, Kathinka, to put a couple of questions to you, questions that have been troubling me for weeks. Aunt Amelie's letter again urged me to consider them and I would have spoken to you as soon as you returned if the distractions of the past few days had not prevented me.'

'How good our aunt is,' said Kathinka. 'She thinks of my happiness more than I do myself. I ought to be more grateful to her than I am.'

'I wish you could be. The desires she cherishes are also mine. And their fulfilment seemed to me so close. But you yourself have again called everything into question. I am distressed at it, I will confess. What terms are you on with Lewin?'

'Good.'

'That seems to be a complete answer but is in fact only half of one.'

'Very well, I shall candidly give you the whole answer. I like Lewin but I do not love him. He is all reverie and fantasy: he does more dreaming than anything else. You could regard this as a reason for my not loving him: but are reasons required in such a matter? Our aunt, who is so clever in other ways, or perhaps because she is so clever, completely forgets how small a role 'Why' plays in determining our inclinations. She wants me to be happy, but she wants it in *her* way, and what is to me an affair of the heart is to her only a family affair. I do not feel myself impelled, however, to become engaged, let alone married, as part of a game of domestic politics. Aunt Amelie acts as though Guse were Rheinsberg: well, their ways may mean a lot to her, but they mean very little to me. She treats everything as though what is involved is the union of two ruling houses; that may be very flattering, but Lewin is not a prince and I am no princess.'

'You are forgetting only one thing: Lewin loves you.'

Kathinka swung her left foot to and fro and tapped the trowel lightly against the rim of the bowl; the privy councillor continued, however:

'Lewin loves you, and it is not long ago that you returned his love, or seemed to do so. It is only during recent months that things have changed, and you now talk mockingly of the union of "two ruling houses". I have a great respect for the count, but I fear that the hour that brought him to our house was no happy one. Has the count proposed marriage to you?'

'No.'

'Do you believe he loves you?'

'Yes.'

'And you?'

It was lucky for Kathinka that the greyhound, which had deserted its basket very soon after she had entered and had posted itself beside her for the receipt of endearments and pieces of sugar, had in the meantime grown increasingly out of humour. Now, as the pieces of sugar had failed to materialize, it was pacing back and forth between her and the *étagère* containing the sugar-box and accompanying the conversation with a continual barking and tinkling of its bell. The privy councillor clearly experienced this as a nuisance, and Kathinka, who was keeping a close eye on his every gesture, seized the opportunity to create an interval. She rose from her seat, fetched the box and, biting and breaking one of the blocks of sugar into pieces, she threw the fragments to the greyhound, which was immediately pacified. Then she dipped a corner of her handkerchief into the bowl, wetted the ends of her fingers, and said: 'To answer your question, Papa, yes, I am very fond of the count.'

The privy councillor smiled. 'That will not be enough for the count, Kathinka. If you believe he loves you, you will have to ask yourself whether you are able to return his love.'

'I am able.'

'And will you?'

She was silent; the ticking of the pendulum-clock was clearly audible. At length the privy councillor said: 'You have told me enough, Kathinka, even by your silence. I perceive from it one thing on which I set great store: that, instead of simply following the dictates of your heart, you have also taken account of what it is I desire.'

Kathinka was about to reply but the privy councillor repeated: 'Of what it is I desire', and then continued: 'But this desire is inflexible and unalterable, and I cannot subordinate it to *your* desires. That is not possible. Listen to me. Your aunt desires a matrimonial match with Lewin; I desire it too; but I do not insist on it. All I insist on is that you do not marry Bninski. Such a marriage may not be, however sympathetic I may find the count personally. The Ladalinskis have left Poland and they cannot go back again. I have burned our bridges in that direction. There is no longer any point in wondering whether the course we took was the only right course: it is enough that we have taken it.'

'It was a joke, Papa,' Kathinka now said, 'when I spoke of a "prince and princess" and of a union between two ruling houses. It annoyed you, and I regret it. But was I not right, really? You say you find the count personally sympathetic; he is rich, respected, honourable, and our hearts and characters are attuned to one another. And yet all this means nothing because, forgive the expression, it doesn't fit in with your diplomacy. The kindest of fathers, always ready to grant me my slightest wish, denies me the greatest I have, because it upsets his political plans, because he is compromised by it.'

'I shall not dispute that word, provided it is understood as I understand it. Fear of being compromised is not always mean and petty, it can also be justified and a condition of one's existence. It is so for me. It is not a question of imagination or a quirk of fancy; all this touches upon my honour more than you think. Mistrust of me has never quite been silenced, not even after my transfer here. From the moment you return to Poland, with *my* concurrence and at the side of a man whose enmity towards Prussia is no secret, the suspicion will be nourished that, in the post I hold today, which gives me access to so many things, I have been only an eavesdropper. I repeat to you what you already know when I say that society has been reluctant to accord me the trust the court has vouchsafed me, and if I lose this trust, or even see it undermined, then the planks I cling to after the shipwreck of my life will vanish from beneath my hands. Whoever wants to can smile. I need the good will of the King, of the princes; if this good will were to be taken from me, I should be homeless a second time. And at that prospect my heart fails me. You may call that policy or you may call it fear of being compromised. Whatever it may be, it is a condition of my life, not a product of my vanity.'

Kathinka went up to her father, kissed him on the brow and put her arms around his shoulders. Then she said: 'Let me say again that no word has yet been spoken between the count and me. It is my belief he is deliberately avoiding a declaration, for—to repeat to you my complaint of him—he has, like you, the vice of being politic. For all I know, he has it in mind to rejoin the Emperor's Polish army. The present moment seems, indeed, to demand some such step. But whatever may happen, *one* thing I promise you: I shall not trouble you with desires or requests touching my own person. I shall stay silent, and nothing shall happen because of me that might endanger your position or expose your loyalty to this country to any fresh suspicions.'

It did not escape the privy councillor that, notwithstanding her apparent accommodation to his wishes, Kathinka's words had been chosen with particular caution; but he felt at the same time that to demand a less ambiguous form of agreement would lead nowhere: he therefore contented himself with the partial success he had achieved, and broke the conference off. 'I would like it', he concluded, 'if you would write a few words to your aunt. Do not disrupt her plans. For your own sake as well as hers. Times change, and we with them: but the most changeable of all things are the hearts of women. What today is nothing to you can tomorrow be something. There is no need for me to speak more plainly; for there are forms of expression that say only half what they mean—a language which, unless I am much deceived, you are very adept in yourself.'

'I shall write. And you may read what I have written, Papa.'

'I trust your word and your sagacity. And now make

yourself ready. I have ordered the carriage for twelve. Old Wylich is a fanatic for punctuality, especially when it comes to his matinées. We shall also be hearing a new composition of Zelter's;* Rungenhagen* is accompanying.'

With that they parted.

9

Renate to Lewin

A WEEK passed without anything worthy of report taking place in Lewin's or the Ladalinskis' circle of friends and acquaintances. And what applied to this circle also applied to the city as a whole. The excitement generated by the news of General York's capitulation had everywhere long since evaporated and given place to a vague but exhilarating feeling that a new era was about to begin. Very few had any idea of the mighty struggle that would still be needed before this new era could be inaugurated; the majority lived in the conviction that, as a result of the defeats already sustained by Napoleon, victory was going to fall to them as though of its own accord, and even the many repeated assurances that the King intended to maintain his alliance with France and to have General York, who had endangered this alliance, court-martialled, could make no difference to this sense of confidence. All such assurances were, indeed, regarded as no more than a game the authorities were being compelled to play and, quite in accord with the words Professor Fichte had urged his listeners to lay to their hearts, a mere mask which could at any moment be removed. The feeling of the people had, as is so often the case, hurried on far ahead of the decisions of their rulers: and this feeling persisted as the days passed by.

The stillness of the second week of January had not even been broken by a session of Kastalia. Jürgass, in whose quarters it was to have taken place, had in the early hours of the day for which it had been fixed taken the trouble to contact his friends and announce the postponement of the meeting, at the same time inviting them to accept an invitation to an 'extraordinary

meeting' on the following day. This meeting was to be confined to a narrower circle and would take the form of a lunch.

The following day had now arrived, but not the hour at
which they were to assemble. Lewin had made himself as
comfortable on his sofa as the construction of that article of
furniture permitted, and was leafing through Herder's *Völkerstimmen*,* a book he held in particular affection. It was a gift
from Kathinka, and even the fact that, possessing no appreciation of the naïve in poetry, she had handed it to him with a
trace of mockery in her voice, had deprived it of none of its
worth. He was just reading the passage:

> When a girl loves not one boy but two
> It seldom works out well,
> We two can tell
> What untrue love can do—

when Frau Hulen entered with a letter that had arrived by post.
The lines were in Renate's hand but they bore the postmark not
of Küstrin, but of Selow, from which Lewin concluded that it
must have been brought directly across the Bruch by express
messenger. He was struck by this circumstance, as, after he had
with a certain feeling of disquiet broken the seal, he was by the
length of the letter: for, of the two extreme parties to which all
letter-writing ladies belong, Renate usually counted as a member of the party of extreme brevity. What could this exceptional amplitude portend?

Lewin read:

Hohen-Vietz, Tuesday 12 January 1813.
Dear Lewin! Papa was going to write to you but has just been called
away; Count Drosselstein is here to settle some business affairs with
him. So the task of telling you of what has lately been happening
with us falls to me. We have been having a very difficult time. There
was a big fire last night;* the ancient hall-annexe has been burned
down.

You will want to know the details, so I shall give them to you.

It was hardly twelve o'clock when I was awoken by a noise. I sat up
and saw that the windows were glowing red, as though with the last
rays of the evening sun. I leaped out of bed and ran and looked out; the
courtyard was still empty, but flames were coming out of the middle

of the annexe and our old Pachaly was standing under the gateway with his back towards me and blowing into the village street on his cow-horn in tones that are still ringing in my ears.

I was overcome by an attack of fainting, and of the following minutes I know nothing. When I had again recovered myself I was sitting up in my bed, and Aunt Schorlemmer and Maline were beside me, both trembling with fear and excitement. They propped me up with more and more pillows, Maline had brought some smelling-salts, and Aunt Schorlemmer was praying over and over again: 'Lord God of Sabaoth, be with us in our hour of need!'

I do not know how it happened, but suddenly all fear fell from me, as though when my fainting-fit went away it took all my feeling of terror along with it. I said I wanted to get up, dressed quickly, and as there was nothing else to hand I put on the Polish cap Kathinka had left behind. Thus clad I went downstairs.

In the meantime the fire had progressed rapidly and there was still no means of putting it out. But hardly had I stepped into the courtyard than I heard a clattering from the direction of the village street, and the next moment our Hohen-Vietz fire-engine came in through the gate; Krist and young Scharwenka had harnessed themselves in the shafts, and Hanne Bogun, with the stump of his arm pressed against the water-cistern, was assisting them by pushing. They stationed them-selves close to the driveway but beyond it towards the farmyard; Papa had already posted men at the draw-well and at the little yard-pump, and soon buckets were being passed from hand to hand in a double row. All was life and activity, and before five minutes were up the first jet of water fell into the flames. Kniehase, the mayor, directed it all. Strange to say, in the midst of this terrible scene I felt my heart beating higher as though for joy. But what a sight it was too! I shall never forget those minutes: the night bright as day, every face illumined by the glare, shouts of command, and then sounding through it all at long, measured intervals the clanging of the bells from the tower. Despite his eighty years, old Kubalke had gone up there himself to cry 'Fire, fire!' to the whole Bruch. And it was not long before we heard the answering bells of the nearby villages.

'That's the Hohen-Ziesar bell,' said Jeetze, who stood beside me chattering with cold, and immediately afterwards the Manschnow bell too joined in. I recognized it myself by its deep note. Now the buckets were being moved quicker and quicker, because everyone knew that help must come from the neighbouring villages at any time. And come it did. Hohen-Ziesar was again the first; they came down past the woodland acre in a cart drawn by two of the count's horses, and we could already hear them as they turned the corner at Miekley's. They came in like a thunder-clap, were welcomed with loud cries of joy, and Kümmeritz, who had only just got over his gout, took command.

In the meantime half the village had assembled in the farmyard, though in such a way as not to interfere with the fire-engines. In the front row stood Seidentopf and Marie; he in his old black cloth cap with the jutting-out peak that made it look as though he was trying to protect himself from the blaze; she leaning on his arm and, like me, quite carried away by the exciting spectacle. I was again startled at her beauty. Her face was longer and narrower than usual, and under her red and black Scottish shawl, which she had thrown over her head like a hood, her great dark eyes themselves shone like fire.

The bucket-chains kept moving, the jet played on to the flames, but we were soon obliged to admit to ourselves that it was going to prove impossible to save the annexe, or even a part of it, and so Papa gave orders that the stream of water should now be directed only at the roof and gables of the house, so that the fire should at least be prevented from spreading. But even that seemed fated to fail; the vine-trellis was already alight in many places and, as the zinc at the top melted, the drainpipe leading down the side of the house came away from the guttering and fell into the courtyard.

At this moment Hoppenmarieken appeared in the gateway, came to a halt and gazed at the fire. She had not come from her house but was on her way towards it: who knows where she had been hiding up till then? When Hanne Bogun saw her, he waved the left sleeve of his jacket as though in triumph and exclaimed: 'Here is Hoppenmarieken', adding at once: 'Perhaps she can charm it away.' Papa well knew that the people, who know so much about her, also say of her that she is able to charm fire; but he was reluctant to turn for help to acts of sorcery he found repugnant or in which he did not believe at all. Seidentopf, who may well have seen the state of indecision he was in, went up to him and said: 'If God dwells in your heart, then all things stand at your service, good things and evil.' At that, Papa beckoned the old woman to him and said: 'Now show us what you can do, Marieken.'

This was all she had been waiting for. She marched between the two fire-engines rapidly up to the spot where the ancient annexe met our house at a right-angle and, after she had made two or three signs and uttered a couple of incomprehensible words, abruptly jammed her crooked stick into the corner. Then, marching straight back across the courtyard to the gateway, she said to the men with the fire-engines as she passed them: 'The Hohen-Ziesars can now go home again', and without looking behind her walked off down the village street in the direction of the woodland acre. Her great crooked stick, however, she had left at the scene of the conflagration.

The fire at once abated; the rafters and timbers fell in, but it was as though, having lost the strength to reach out for new nourishment, everything was consuming itself. At the same time the light breeze that had hitherto been blowing also abated, and it began to snow. It was an entrancing sight to see the snowflakes dancing in the dark-red glow of the blaze.

The engine from Hohen-Ziesar did in fact depart, and the courtyard was empty again; only Papa and old Kniehase still remained and made their arrangements for the night. I was among the first who went away, and, although my room gave directly on to the scene of the fire, I was so confident that all danger was over that I at once fell asleep. In my dreams what I had just experienced was mingled with that strange fire-apparition at the old palace in Stockholm which you told me and Marie about on Christmas Day as we sat around the fire and plundered the Christmas tree. In the dream I saw my windows glowing red; but when I rose to go and look at the light I was no longer alone; I became aware of a long line of people condemned to death being led with bared necks to an execution block. It was a terrifying picture, and wherever I looked everything was red. But at that moment Hoppenmarieken stepped through the door of the throne-room and everyone cried: 'Perhaps she can stop it.'

At that she raised her stick, and all the blood vanished; and the vision was swallowed up in darkness, and she with it.

This morning I went to breakfast early; Papa and Aunt Schorlemmer were already waiting for me. I had dreaded this encounter; the barn that burned down two years ago still stood a heap of ruins, and now a second disastrous fire which we could not possibly have the means to make good. But I discovered everyone to be in quite a different mood from the one I had dreaded. Papa was talkative and behaved with a gentleness that seemed indicative of hopefulness rather than despair. He took my hand, and when he saw that I was looking for words of comfort, he smiled and said:

> 'And one day the house will receive a princess,
> The bloodstain will fade in the heat of a fire—

'I am beginning to be reconciled to that ancient Hohen-Vietz folk-poem. The princess is still delaying her entrance, but the bloodstain has gone, faded in the heat of the fire. Yes, my dear Renate, we are encompassed by enigmas, and perhaps it is folly to want, in the twofold arrogance of our knowledge and our faith, to divest ourselves of all those things we call superstition but which are perhaps nothing of the kind. Wafted here from long ago, in superstition too there lie the seeds of revelation. "The bloodstain will fade in the heat of a fire": in the midst of all these trials it seems to me that other, better times are bound to come. For us, for everyone.' I was about to reply, but Jeetze came in and announced that Count Drosselstein had driven up.

Here you have the longest letter I ever wrote. Please give my regards to Kathinka, and to Frau Hulen as well.

Affectionately, your Renate von V.

Lewin laid down the letter. He had been moved by it, yet the feeling that had come to prevail in his father and sister attained the upper hand in him too: the feeling of joy that something uncanny had been removed from their lives.

He went quickly to his desk and wrote a brief provisional reply in which he gave expression to this feeling. He concluded with the words: 'The altar has gone, and if old Matthias wants to go on haunting he will have to look for another place to pray.' But when he read over what he had written he was seized with alarm. 'That sounds', he said to himself, 'as though I were inviting him to move across from the annexe into the house. That's the last thing I want. I've no wish to invite the stone guest to supper.' And he crossed the sentence out again with a thick line.

Then he hurriedly dressed, so that Jürgass, who was sensitive in this one particular, should not be kept waiting.

10

Luncheon with Jürgass

IT was not only His ancient Excellency Herr Wylich who was, as Privy Councillor Ladalinski had expressed it, a fanatic for punctuality: Jürgass was too. It was a fact the whole circle was aware of. And so it happened that at one minute to twelve all those who had been invited encountered one another in the hallway or on the stairs—including even Bummcke, who had not yet forgotten the jocularly clad but seriously intended reprimand he had received at the previous session of Kastalia.

Jürgass's quarters were in a voluted corner house on the Gendarmenmarkt and occupied half the *bel étage* giving on to the square. So far as their reception-rooms were concerned, they consisted of a narrow entrance-hall, a living- and drawing-room with three windows, and a dining-salon. The size of these quarters, and even more their appointments, might, in view of the fact that Jürgass was a Brandenburg officer of Hussars on half-pay whose father's estate could not have met the cost of even a third of these furnishings and decorations with the proceeds of three of its best harvests, have occasioned some surprise; but our cavalry captain was not only the son of his father but also the nephew of his aunt, an aged Fräulein von Zieten, who, as canoness of the convent at Heiligengrabe, had bequeathed to her favourite (our friend Jürgass) the whole of her not inconsiderable fortune. The actual words of the will and testament in which she did so read: 'In consideration of the fact that my nephew Dagobert von Jürgass, the only son of my beloved sister Adelgunde von Jürgass, born von Zieten, is, through his mother's blood, and also and in especial through the cultivation of his mind and body, a genuine Zieten, I bequeath to my said nephew, Rittmeister in the Göcking (formerly Zieten) Regiment of Hussars, in the supposition that, God willing, he will always maintain the character of the Zietens and never dishonour it, my entire monetary possessions, together with a picture of my brother, Lieutenant-General Hans Joachim von Zieten, and pray God to keep my dear nephew true to his Lutheran faith and loyal to his King.'

As chance would have it, this will and testament was indited by the old canoness, who departed this life the same winter, on that 14 October 1806 that was the day of the double Battle of Jena and Auerstädt, on which account Jürgass was accustomed to say whenever 14 October came round: 'A curious day, on which I never know whether to wear festive dress or mourning; Prussia fell but Dagobert von Jürgass rose.'

On the whole, however, his aunt had appraised him correctly: from his mother's side he had, together with an inclination occasionally to put on a glittering appearance, the Zieten talent for good housekeeping in his blood, so that, all the unfavourability of the times notwithstanding, he had during the six years since he had acquired it augmented his inheritance rather than diminished it.

He had fitted out the living-room already referred to in a particularly sumptuous fashion, as a consequence of which the attention of all those gentlemen who were today in these quarters for the first time was immediately directed to its walls and piers. Herr von Meerheimb at once discovered a miniature copy of a large Tintoretto* that was an ornament of the Dresden Gallery, while von Hirschfeldt rejoiced to encounter a long series of coloured prints whose originals he had seen in London on the occasion of an exhibition of the work of Joshua Reynolds.* The abundance of all these decorative objects, among which the presence of a number of sculptures was especially noteworthy, bestowed on the conversation conducted as the participants were walking back and forth something restless and detached that was unfavourable to the development of a cheerful and bantering tone; to Jürgass, however, though as a general rule he liked nothing better than to encourage cheerfulness and bantering, its absence on this occasion was not wholly displeasing, since it could not escape him that this erratic and disconnected quality in the conversation was entirely due to an admiration for his works of art or a curiosity in regard to other objects of interest on view, both of which he found flattering to his vanity.

Among these objects of interest pride of place went to the 'Great Boot',* which, six feet tall with a sole one and a half inches thick and a spur attached to it nine inches long, had in its time been a *cause célèbre* or at any rate the cause of one. The story of the boot was as follows.

At the end of the nineties Jürgass, at that time still a very young lieutenant with the Göcking Hussars, was strolling along the Friedrichsstrasse towards the Oranienburger Tor in the company of Wolf Quast of the Gensdarmes Regiment when, just before they reached the Weidendammer Brücke, they noticed a gigantic spur hanging in the window of an ironmongers standing opposite the Pépinière.* They stopped, laughed, discussed it, and resolved that the next one to be disciplined for an offence would have to purchase the spur. This next one was Jürgass. But the spur had hardly been bought when they struck up another agreement: 'The next one must have a boot made to fit it.' This time the next one was Quast, and scarcely more than a week had passed before the giant boot he had had made was borne with all imaginable formality, first into the barracks, then into Quast's quarters. All the younger officers of both regiments were present at the procession. There the colossus stood, and the giant spur was affixed to it. But the youthful high spirits now awakened were not yet satisfied and, in search of something still more exciting, they resolved to honour the Great Boot and its great spur with a festive party of a corresponding magnitude, at which the boot would naturally be used as a punch-bowl. No sooner said than done. The party went off to the complete satisfaction of all who attended it, but not at all to that of the Minister of War, who gave orders that this misconduct, as he regarded it, should cease, and the Great Boot be captured dead or alive.

The appropriate order had hardly been drawn up than all the young lieutenants declared they were unanimous in considering the rescue of the boot *coûte que coûte*★ to be a matter of honour; during the reorganization of barracks that took place soon afterwards, therefore, the boot was moved from one room to another, and finally transported in stages firstly to the Havel-land, then to the Ruppin★ and Priegnitz estates of the young gentlemen's respective fathers and uncles, who found themselves involved *nolens volens* in the game their sons and nephews were playing. By this route it finally arrived at Gantzer, where it remained forgotten for a full dozen years, until, on the occasion of a brief visit to his paternal house, Jürgass caught sight of the former *corpus delicti* and at once resolved to employ it as an original ornament for one of the rooms in the quarters he was at that time just in the act of furnishing. For the rest, he made no more and no less of the matter than the matter was worth, and whenever he told the story of the 'Great Boot' had on the one hand too much good judgement to treat an ensigns' escapade as though it were a deed of heroism, but was none the less still too dashing and unprejudiced to be ashamed of the high spirits of his younger days.

The servant entered, flinging open as he did so the folding

doors of the dining-salon and thus silently announcing that lunch was served; and Jürgass, advancing first, bade his guests follow him. Places had been laid at a round table. Hirschfeldt and Meerheimb seated themselves on either side of their host, Hansen-Grell sat opposite him; Tubal, Lewin and Bummcke, who alone of the membership of Kastalia had received invitations, inserted themselves to left and right.

Jürgass's luncheons were celebrated, not only on account of the selectness of the company that attended them, but also, and almost more, because of the little gifts and surprises with which he was accustomed to accompany them. And today too he had lived up to his reputation. Under Hirschfeldt's napkin there lay the 'Cathedral of Tarragona', a little picture cut out of a French travel-book, on the back of which were written the words: 'In grateful remembrance of 5 January 1813'; while, when he opened his, Hansen-Grell discovered a delicate silver spur attached to a card, with beneath it the inscription:

> Two shining spurs of silver
> And a steel-blue blade he wore—
> And he was born at Calcar,
> And Calcar means a *spur*.

Bummcke too had been taken care of, though the surprise prepared for him was more in the nature of a piece of raillery than a gift. It was a large paper-scroll lying beside his plate which, after removal of the length of red cord that held it rolled, revealed itself to be a much damaged copperplate print in crude mezzotinto. Below it read: 'Entry of Captain von Bummcke into Copenhagan'. And, unlikely though such an event might seem, the picture did in fact appear to represent something of the kind, if only because the street architecture of the Danish capital was faithfully reproduced and, to anyone who knew Copenhagen, the pointed tower of the Stock Exchange building constructed of three dragons-tails was clearly recognizable. Nevertheless, the actual subject of the picture, which portrayed an open carriage drawn by four horses and escorted by soldiers, was something very different, and depicted neither an *entrée joyeuse* on the part of Bummcke nor any entry of any sort, but the 'Transportation of Counts

Brandt and Struensee★ to their First Interrogation'. Bummcke, who had long known the picture from its display in an old antique-shop, quickly accommodated himself to the joke, or at least gave the appearance of having done so, which was certainly the best thing he could have done. For he had, it may here be inserted, a weakness for expatiating somewhat frequently on his 'travels in the north'—the only travels he had ever undertaken—and had as a consequence of this weakness, of which he was himself very well aware, not only fallen victim to Jürgass's raillery but made the discovery that keeping silent was the only way to avoid it or at least to cut it short.

The tray of port and sherry was being handed round as Bummcke, unrolling the picture again, began, with that calmness which a consciousness of being master of one's subject bestows: 'Poor Struensee! I have seen the spot, out before the Westerngade, where they chopped his head off. What was it? Envy, *rancune* and national prejudice. A judicial murder without equal. He was as innocent as the sun.'

'His intimacies seem, however, to be proved,' Jürgass observed weightily, his only object being to draw his infantry captain on to his beloved Danish territory.

'Intimacies!' the latter rejoined, unable to resist the bait even though he saw the hook. 'Intimacies! I assure you, Jürgass, it is all foolery and slander. During my stay in Copenhagen I had the opportunity of coming into contact with people who played a role, active or passive, in the drama. It was a game, with life and honour at stake, a bloodstained farce from start to finish. Canonization is out of fashion; if we had a remnant of it left, this Queen Caroline Mathilde would be declared a saint.'

'If it is not indiscreet to ask for names, where does your information come from?'

'From the Queen's personal physician,' said Bummcke.

'Well, he ought to know,' replied Jürgass cheerfully, 'but his authority does not suffice to silence the statements of those who have confessed themselves guilty. I appeal for the present to our friend Hansen-Grell. He must have heard something or other about the affair when employed by his count.'

'No,' Hansen-Grell replied. 'So far as I know, my count and his family had reason to keep silent about the case, and I have neglected to learn about it from books. I have in general to admit that, with the exception of individual, very remote centuries, I have not bestowed on the history of Denmark the attention it deserves.'

'And yet', Tubal observed politely, 'your Hakon Borkenbart ballad, with which you entertained us so greatly on Christmas Eve, gave us just the opposite impression.'

'Because you drew from my knowledge of the semi-legendary prehistory of the country all kinds of flattering conclusions as to my knowledge of Danish history as a whole. False conclusions, alas. It is more for the sake of poetry than for that of history that I have read Saxo Grammaticus and the ancient chroniclers; so much so that I have in the end neglected the modern Queen Caroline Mathilde for the sake of the ancient Queen Thyra Danebod.'

'Thyra Danebod,' exclaimed Jürgass in genuine delight. 'What a marvellous name! It gives you less of a tingle than Kathinka von Ladalinska: but nevertheless! What do you think, Bummcke?'

Bummcke, so unexpectedly reminded of the evening of the ball at the Ladalinskis, waved a finger in good-humoured warning; Hansen-Grell, however, went on: 'I entirely share the enthusiasm of our honoured host, and if I had to take an oath on it, I would have to confess that the real stimulus to my study of the history of ancient Denmark was the fascination exercised by this name and the many others like it. Sigurd Ring and King Helge, Ragnar Lodbrok and Harald Hyldetand entranced me by their mere sound, and whenever I hear them it is as though the mists dissolve and I behold a wonderful northern world, with bays surrounded by cliffs, the blue sea spread out before them and a hundred billowing white sails on the horizon.'

'It is the strangeness of the sound that captivates our ear,' remarked Hirschfeldt, who might have been remembering similarly attractive names from his time in Spain, and Lewin and Tubal agreed with him.

'Certainly', Hansen-Grell continued, 'this strangeness of sound plays its part. But, beyond that, it is ultimately something else that lends these ancient Danish names their peculiar fascination. For what speaks out of them is that gift, a gift related to the people's capacity for proverbial wisdom, for characterizing men, phenomena, whole epochs indeed, in a single epithet. The force of concision, much said in little, *there* we have the key to the mystery.'

Bummcke grew very excited—so excited, in fact, that, quite contrary to his usual practice, he waved the Château d'Yquem past him—and called across to Hansen-Grell as though to an old bosom friend: 'I know what you're getting at. Proverbial wisdom you said, quite right. It shows itself best in the case of the King Eriks, or at least the first six or seven of them: Erik Barn, Erik Ejegod, Erik Lam, Erik Plopenning, Erik Glipping. To each one I attach a picture, an idea of what he was like, especially the Plopenning and the Glipping. Glipping means "blink of the eyes" or the "winker". And, it's funny, but I really do see him before me, with his right eyelid blinking all the time.'

Jürgass threw himself back in his seat and said, through a fit of coughing that for sheer merriment refused to let up: 'That is the most capital piece of enthusiasm for foreign parts I have ever experienced in all my life. King Winker, I bid thee welcome.'

'If you knew more about him, Jürgass, you would treat this important figure with greater respect. He was a good king and was murdered at Viborg with fifty-six stab-wounds.'

'No more than he deserved. Why did he persist in winking? It is not yet the time for toasts, none the less I raise my glass. Long live Erik Glipping!'

'Long live Erik Glipping!' and their glasses rang together in honour of the old Danish king. Before the high spirits had completely died down, however, Hansen-Grell said: 'Excuse a schoolmaster's pedantry if he finds it impossible to abandon his theme: but I promise to be brief.'

'Brief or lengthy, Grell, you are always welcome to speak.'

'Good, I accept. Our honoured captain's predilection for King Glipping and, if I may so express myself, the plastic objectivity with which he brought the subject of his admiration before our eyes, opened to us at a stroke the golden gates of merriment; it is my task, however, to return us to seriousness once more. In our more recent history, in so far as it treats of emperors and kings, the *number* has come into fashion; the First, Second, Third, even the Fourteenth and Fifteenth; the number is in favour, and with it the most prosaic, unpoetical, characterless thing that exists. In contrast to this, the names of my old Scandinavian kings stand, with respect to their sound and content—I emphasize, with respect to their content too—in the realm of poetry, and that it is that makes me love them so much. More epigrammatic than an epigram, many of these names are at the same time like a poem, moving or impressive as the case may be. Judge for yourselves. I shall name only two: Olaf Hunger and Waldemar Atterdag! Is it possible to describe a person or an epoch more forcefully or sharply in one single word? It can never again be forgotten. Olaf was a good king, but the country wasted away through bad harvests and diseases, and neither his prayers nor his pronounced readiness to sacrifice himself for his people could serve to expunge the curse from the land, let alone turn it into a blessing. So it is that this king signifies in the pages of Danish history a time of evil, of want and death, and his ghostly image undeservedly carries the dreadful inscription: Olaf Hunger.'

'And treats *us* to a Lenten sermon over our lunch! Leave him be, Grell. What about the other one?'

'He stands as Olaf's antithesis.'

'Thank God for that!'

'He was handsome and victorious and loved women.'

'*A la bonne heure.*'*

'But more than that, he was also cheerful and benevolent. In the years of his youth he was carried away by his own passions and the counsel of others to hot-headed deeds; but when he became a man he regretted his youthful impetuosity, and he swore to himself he would never again do anything stern or harsh on the spur of the moment. When his court crowded around him and demanded of him a speedy verdict, sometimes even a sentence of death, he would gesture gently with head and hand and say merely: "Atterdag". That is to say: "Tomorrow". And an abundant cornucopia of blessings issued from this one word, and "Atterdag" has a fair sound in Denmark to this very day.'

'That is the man for me, Grell. Atterdag! And you are right, sound and content go together. I can see him before me as clearly as Bummcke saw Glipping. But my Atterdag doesn't blink. He has wonderful blue eyes, and endless wedding processions pass along behind him and the banner-bearers throw their sticks high into the sky. Pass round the pheasant again, Tubal, we owe that to Attertag, and even more to Olaf Hunger.'

Conversation then abandoned the kings of Denmark, and soon abandoned Scandinavia altogether, and only Bummcke made one more attempt, by now traditional with him, to leave Copenhagen for Aalborg, and thence, proceeding straight across Jutland, to take ship upon the great Limfjord. This was his favourite tour, and it was so because, eleven times out of twelve, he could count on being the only person in any given company to have made it and thus on having an uncontested right to hold the floor. Today, however, he found that he lacked that advantage; hardly had he begun to expatiate on the 'plaintive accent' of the landscape of North Jutland and the 'veil of melancholy' that hung over it than Grell was hard on his heels with contradictions, maintaining that *he* had never seen emerald-green water in the Limfjord or azure-blue sky over it, let alone a hundred thousand seagulls reposing on it like white water-lilies.

'There is nothing more common than that people should receive such opposite impressions,' von Meerheimb interposed, 'and it does not even require two people for contradictions of this sort to arise: we discover them in ourselves. What we call the mood of the landscape is as a rule our own mood. Joy and sorrow paint in different colours. When we were going along the Smolensk road and were getting near to the old Russian capital it seemed to us we were marching beneath a rainbow, and everywhere we looked the golden cupolas of Moscow rose up before us as though in a mirage. Our longing for them saw them long before they actually appeared in the mist of the horizon. That was around the middle of September. And four weeks later we were again going along the same road. The retreat had begun. It was not yet cold, and the October sun shone no less brightly than the September sun had done, yet all around us there lay desolation and solitude, and instead of babbling to us, as they had seemed to do before, the rivers seemed to creep along like the waters of the underworld. The country had not altered, but *we* had.'

Everyone agreed, even Jürgass, who made an exception only of the region between Neustadt and Gantzer, which, he assured them, invariably produced upon him the same impression. What that impression was he forbore to say, either out of prudence or because he did not wish to let pass the opportunity which now presented itself for ushering in a contribution to Kastalia that was still outstanding.

'Herr von Meerheimb', he began, tapping his glass with the back of his knife, 'has just led us across the fields of Mozhaisk, or lands lying close to it, not in a broad descriptive vein but discursively, if I may so express myself, in *aperçus* in landscape-painting, in antithetical mood-pictures. I recall to your minds that the lateness of the hour at the last session of Kastalia deprived us of an address which, if I am instructed correctly, also takes us to these same fields of Mozhaisk, though it there presents to us pictures very different from the cupolas of Moscow, real or imaginary. And so I permit myself to inquire of our honoured guest whether it would be agreeable to him to make up for what we missed at the session referred to and read to this smaller circle the segment of his diary intended for us.'

Von Meerheimb bowed, and said: 'I shall be glad to accede to your kind invitation, however much I may share the feeling of Herr von Hirschfeldt, who confessed it to me after the last session of Kastalia, that readings of this sort have something doubtful and disagreeable about them. This disagreeableness cannot be avoided by refraining from all mention of one's own heroic deeds—an expression I would ask should be taken as it is meant. For one still remains a part of the whole, and in extolling this one also, for good or ill, extols oneself as well. No account of great events at which one was present can avoid doing this, not even the most circumspect, and anyone who ventures upon such an account must throw himself upon the particular indulgence of his listeners. With *you* I am sure of receiving such indulgence. For the rest, I beg to state—despite the ban on prologues that obtains in this circle—that I have recorded only what I myself experienced, and thus make no claim to anything like a complete account of the event as a whole. Details lying outside my personal experience, as well as the names of people and places, I owe to communications from captured Russian officers with whom I afterwards lay in the hospital at Smolensk. And now I have concluded and beseech our honoured host at any moment he deems appropriate to command me.'

'Let us take coffee,' said Jürgass and, as they all rose from the table, offered Herr von Meerheimb his arm and preceded them into the living-room.

Here everything had been prepared and, although it was still early, the heavy window-curtains had been closed and the little crystal candlesticks affixed to the walls had been lit. In the polished English fireplace built into the large stove as the main ornament of the room there was a bright fire burning, and high-backed armchairs and upholstered seats stood on the free side of the sofa-table, which was covered by a Turkish cloth interwoven with gold thread. Coffee was served and, while host and guests took their places around the table, von Meerheimb drew a double-candlestick closer to him and read 'Borodino'.

II

Borodino*

. . . WE no longer believed the Russians were going to make a stand. They retreated along the great Smolensk road, avoiding any *rencontre* with our advance guard, and it seemed they were going to abandon Moscow without striking a blow. But it had been decided otherwise; there was a change of command on the Russian side, Kutuzov replaced Barclay de Tolly, and our entry into Moscow was preceded by an encounter of which, when night came, the Emperor himself said: 'Today I have fought the finest battle of my life, but also the most terrible.'

That was on 7 September at Borodino.

We had a foretaste of it as early as the 5th. When we made camp on the evening of that day we heard that a violent engagement had taken place at the front and that the Compans Division, to which the 61st Line Regiment belonged, had stormed a Russian entrenchment. The Emperor was supposed to have appeared immediately afterwards and, noticing the gaps in the said regiment, have asked anxiously: 'Where is the third battalion of the Sixty-First?', to which Compans was supposed to have replied: 'Sire, it is lying in those trenches.'

On the 6th we were certain the Russians were going to offer us a battle, and by early the following day they were drawn up before us a cannon-shot's distance away.

It was a clear day. The sun, which had just risen, hung like a red ball over a strip of woodland on the horizon and looked down on the bare plateau that, half unploughed land, half stubble-field, stretched out in front of us: it was of a considerable depth but only about half a mile wide. The height on which we had halted made it easier for me to survey the terrain, and I soon recognized that the plateau lying before us was by no means a smooth floor but was broken by many little hills and declivities. One of these declivities, to all appearances the bed of a dried-up river, was especially strongly marked and ran between our position and the enemy's like a moat, dividing the prospective battlefield in half. This dried-up river was called the Semenovska Valley. Whoever attacked would have to cross over this valley, and the nine-hour battle did in fact revolve around possession of it and of three positions lying partly on our side, partly on the other side of its rim. These three positions were the following: 1, the Bagration flèches; 2, the village of Semenovskoy; and 3, the great Rayevsky entrenchment. Positions two and three lay on the other side of the valley on the half of the battlefield occupied by the Russians, but position one, the Bagration flèches, were fortifications pushed forward like a bridgehead over to the rim on our side of the Semenovska Valley. The three positions together constituted the enemy's centre, upon which his right and left flanks depended. His right flank was at Borodino, his left at Utitsa. The enemy was ranged in long columns that seemed to go on for ever. We could see the flash of his bayonets on into the far distance, and in front of his positions, along the rim of the valley, the dark mouths of his guns.

So much for the enemy. But the bright morning light, combined with the heights in our possession, enabled us clearly to survey our own dispositions too. Immediately in front of us there stood in six massed divisions the army corps of Davoust and Ney, behind us Junot★ and the Guards, while we ourselves, ten thousand horsemen under King Murat, occupied, as regards both width and depth, the centre of the battle-array on our side of the field.

Napoleon's plan was first to take the flanking positions at Borodino and Utitsa, the former with the Viceroy's★ Italian Guards, the latter with the Poles under Poniatowski,★ and then, with these flanking forces wheeling in to assist him (for he never doubted they would advance rapidly), to break through the enemy's formidable centre. First the flèches, then Semenovskoy, then the Rayevsky entrenchment.

The first cannon-shot fell even before day had dawned, and the battle began at seven. The Viceroy took Borodino; but Poniatowski, encountering stronger resistance than he had anticipated, was unable to gain ground. Thus, and especially as the attack at Borodino also came to a halt, no assistance was available from the flanking forces, and the army corps of Davoust and Ney stationed at our feet were compelled to attempt to break through the enemy's centre by a frontal attack unsupported from either right or left. The Compans Division, the same that had been involved in the bitter engagement on the 5th, was again in the van. It threw itself upon the first object of attack, the Bagration flèches, took them, lost them and took them a second time, only to lose them a second time. The valiant Compans fell, Rapp and Davoust, more or less severely wounded, had to leave the battlefield, and more and more fresh divisions were brought forward to assure us of the possession of this advanced fortification. It was only after the fourth assault that the Russian grenadiers who had stood their ground and bled here under Prince Vorontsov★ abandoned any further attempt to regain the position and withdrew, as many of them as were left, back to the far side of the Semenovska Valley. Too enfeebled to form themselves into fresh units, they attached themselves to existing units they found there. They numbered only four hundred men, the remnant of six thousand. When he composed his report to the Emperor that evening, Prince Vorontsov concluded it with the words: 'My battalions of grenadiers no longer exist; but they did not vanish *from* the field of battle, they vanished *on* it.'

By eleven o'clock we had the flèches, and we now had to advance across ground in order to take first the village of Semenovskoy, which was already in flames in many places, then the great Rayevsky entrenchment situated to the left of it. But already our strength to do so was beginning to run out, at least at the front. Of the divisions of the Davoust Corps only the dregs remained, those of the Ney Corps were hardly any better, and only the Friant Division was still intact. It received the order to go forward and now assumed the van, while the divisions that had already been under fire opened out. The *bravoure* of the attack seemed for a moment to promise a grand success; but the moment the foremost battalions attained the far rim of the Semenovska Valley they were mown down in rows by concentrated fire coming from very close at hand; the battalions advancing behind them faltered, turned, and sought refuge in ravines and gullies on the near side of the gorge. The attempted assault had to be regarded as a disaster, and along our entire front, directly ahead of us as well as on both flank positions, there now remained no fresh infantry units of whom a renewal of the assault could have been demanded.

At this moment the order came to King Murat to make an attempt with his massed horsemen. Of these massed horsemen we too formed a part. On receipt of this order, Murat at once moved his four corps of cavalry to the front in echelon, first Grouchy, then Nansouty, then Montbrun, then Latour-Maubourg, and, holding the last-named corps provisionally in reserve, sent the other three one after the other against the positions at the enemy's centre. Grouchy led the way, Nansouty and Montbrun followed. The field thundered beneath the hoofs of more than six thousand horses; even the thunder of the guns was momentarily drowned out. But this tremendous cavalry assault succeeded no better than the repeated attacks of the infantry divisions had done: the foremost ranks fell on the nearside rim of the Semenovska Valley, and of the remainder the regiments in front involved those following behind in their headlong flight.

Another defeat; and a thousand riderless horses scattered away across the field. Grouchy, Nansouty, Montbrun had failed; only our 4th Cavalry Corps, Latour-Maubourg, was still standing untouched on our right flank, before it our division of cuirassiers under General de Lorges. We called him, jokingly but also in recognition of his cavalier virtues, our 'Sir de Lorges', and the moment was in fact not far off when the division that bore his proud name would rescue the 'glove out of the lion-pit'.* A cloud of dust appeared to our left, and King Murat himself, who had until then remained at the other flank, came galloping up in front of us. He was clad more splendidly and fantastically than ever, and perceiving that, notwithstanding the shot that had come over from time to time, we had maintained perfect order, he blew us a kiss as he rode past and saluted with the switch he carried instead of a sabre. At the same time he gave the order to attack, and we stormed across the field in two massed sections, one of them comprising the six-regiment strong Polish Uhlan Division under General Roznieski (we lost sight of them soon afterwards), the other, the only one I shall be speaking of, our De Lorges division of cuirassiers. But this section too became subdivided, and as the Polish Uhlan Division had just detached itself from our massed Latour-Maubourg Corps, so now, only a few minutes afterwards, the Von Lepel Westphalian Brigade detached itself from our De Lorge cuirassiers division. General von Lepel was considered the handsomest officer in the Westphalian army; he was the favourite of Friederike Katharine, the wife of King Jerome. We saw him riding in front of his brigade as a passing shot threw him from his horse. Mortally wounded, he uttered the name of his queen and died. His brigade then faltered and turned aside, and it was only later that it returned to participate in the engagement.

Thus we were now alone: the Saxon Thielmann Brigade, eight hundred horse of the Garde du Corps and the Von Zastrow Regiments. If we had in any case been positioned on the extreme right flank, our present situation demanded, as General von Thielmann* had realized from the way the engagement had gone so far, that we draw further and further to the right. What had every assault hitherto come to grief on? On the undiminished difficulty of crossing over the steep-sided Semenovska Valley in face of the row of enemy guns. Success therefore depended on the discovery of crossing-places on the river-bed where the slope was less steep and enemy fire less intense. Such places lay up-river in the direction of Utitsa, and, taking ourselves further and further out of the range of the cannon, at last, not a thousand paces beyond the above-named flank position, we came upon a gently sloping spot hardly touched by the Russian guns that seemed to make it possible for us to ride down comfortably into the Semenovska Valley. This was what we had been looking for. A minute later we were in the dry river-bed. Wheeling to the left, we again approached closer to the enemy's centre, and the closer we came the higher and steeper the banks of the river became: but this increasing height and steepness now afforded us protection, and the fire from the battery of a hundred Russian guns stationed around the village of Semenovskoy passed over our heads. We had almost reached the village without sustaining any losses worth mentioning; General Thielmann's skilled leadership had assured us of that. But now came the decisive moment, and the same steep slopes that had hitherto been our salvation were now a source of danger to us. And yet we had no alternative but to go up them. Our Garde du Corps Regiment led the way; 'Wheel to the right in squads, at the trot!' and the next moment we were trying to gain first the slope and then the height above it. A few turned a somersault and tumbled back to the river-bed; but the majority attained the crest, formed themselves into line and proceeded to the attack.

Only as we rode forward did we see where we were. Not three hundred paces in front of us the village of Semenovskoy was in flames; between us and the village, however, and then out beyond it, there stood as though on a chessboard six Russian squares: grenadier guard battalions, the famous Izmailov, Lithuania and Finland Regiments. We were right upon them as they started firing, but before a second salvo could follow the first the squares on the near side of the village had been ridden down, and the attack swept forward through the blazing Semenovskoy by its own impetus without any further command or bugle-call. Within the village many of our foremost riders fell into the underground cellars which had formerly served the demolished dwellings as store-rooms but were now filled with blazing rubble, but the squadrons following after them eluded these perilous places and all who were stationed beyond the village shared the fate of those who had been stationed before it. The Lithuania Regiment lost in ten minutes half its complement.

But the entire Thielmann Brigade was not employed in riding through the burning village; a small detachment of it, fewer than a hundred strong and made up of segments from both regiments, had, immediately after the foremost squares had been ridden down, ventured off to the right deeper into the Russian battle-line in order to counter an attack just being mounted by an enemy cavalry squadron. The move was successful; the enemy cuirassiers were put to flight, and in exploitation of this achievement, which might almost be called unexpected, we stormed on—I myself belonged to this detachment—through the massed columns of the battalions ranged behind and became fully aware of what we were doing only when we suddenly found ourselves in the rear of the entire Russian array.

From this position it would have been easier for us to ride on to Moscow than back into the Semenovska Valley. And yet we were obliged to attempt to regain this dividing line between friend and foe.

We therefore wheeled about. We all hung on the words of our leader, prepared to do whatever he said, but before we could turn huge swarms of Bashkirs and Kalmucks came at us out of coppices lying to left and right of us, troops of irregulars who, because they were not trusted at the front, had been assigned to these reserve positions. In an instant they were upon us with their pikes, and the defeat we had twice eluded in combat with the élite of the enemy's forces now awaited us at the hands of this rabble. Colonel von Leyser was struck from his horse, Major von Hoyer fell immediately afterwards, and before five minutes were up of our entire little troop only two were left: Brigade Adjutant von Minckwitz and I. We hacked our way through the ever-increasing horde and then raced back on our tired horses through the gaps in the ranks through which we had first come. What saved us was very probably the black cuirasses worn by the Von Zastrow Regiment, which led to our being mistaken for Russian cuirassiers as we passed along the long ranks of infantry. Our horses held out, miraculously enough, and within half an hour we had rejoined our comrades, as many of them as were still left. There was no time to tell them of our death-ride: for the Russians were even then in the act of preparing a large-scale assault with the aim of regaining the *position* of Semenovskoy (you could no longer speak of a *village* of that name), and everyone still on the far side of the valley had to return to the other side. That applied to us too.

By now it would have been midday or at most only a little after it. We could not conceal from ourselves that our exertions had been essentially as unavailing as the preceding cavalry attacks of Grouchy, Montbrun and Nansouty; we had scaled the hostile side of the Semenovska Valley, ridden down six battalions of guards, put Russian cavalry regiments to flight and seen the enemy's battle-array from the rear, but the end result of it all was that, though we might have moved forward a thousand paces, we were still standing on *this* side of the valley and were obliged to resume our task of driving the Russians from the *other* side all over again. That we should do so was never in doubt; not to do so would have amounted to losing the battle. The only question, therefore, was: *when?*

We waited expectantly for two hours; those at the top seemed to be vacillating; at last the order came to assemble together all forces available and to advance once more upon the whole front. Our Thielmann Brigade, reduced to half its strength, was to receive the lion's share of this operation: it received the order to storm the dreaded Rayevsky entrenchment, the firmest point in the enemy's central position. To storm an entrenchment with cavalry!

It was Ney himself who delivered this order. Instead of making any reply, General Thielmann merely pointed to the shattered brigade: four hundred horsemen on tired horses. But, in the fearful excitement of the moment, Ney drew his pistol from its holster and pointed it, as a sign he was ready to silence any attempt at opposition. Thielmann placed himself at the front, the trumpeters blew, and again we set off for the valley. This time we advanced half-left, since the Rayevsky entrenchment lay five hundred paces further downstream. What or whom we lost as we rode forward I no longer know, because everything that happened was compressed into a few minutes. I know only that our losses were considerable. Now we had arrived and the next moment we were down in the gorge; but it was no longer the empty river-bed in which three hours previously as we wheeled in from Utitsa we had found almost perfect cover from the enemy's cross-fire—fresh battalions drawn from the reserve were now firmly ensconced there and, taking up position in small tight groupings, they received us first with musket-fire, then, when we broke these groups up, with gun-butts and bayonets. But in vain; we went through or round them like a hurricane, for our task was not to exhaust ourselves down there in skirmishes but to take the towering Rayevsky entrenchment on the other side at the first assault. And now we had again ascended the steep bank of the river-bed and stood before the even steeper declivity of the entrenchment itself. Our foremost ranks involuntarily turned aside to the right and sought to gain the gorge of the entrenchment through a semicircular movement; but the body of our force following behind them stormed up the redoubt as though the declivity of the entrenchment were no more than a continuation of the slope of the river-bed we had just taken in our stride, and from there charged down into the middle of the entrenchment from above it. A man-to-man combat ensued; the gunners who reached for their sponges and rammers were hewn down; all who were left alive threw down their arms and surrendered. Only General Likhachev, who was here in command, asked for no quarter. An hour before he had left the entrenchment to report to General Kutuzov on the course of the engagement, which was then very favourable. 'Where does the entrenchment lie?' Kutuzov had asked, and Likhachev had raised his right hand to indicate the direction. A six-pound ball took his hand off; he raised his left, pointed directly south and said:

'Over there.' Then, only lightly bandaged, he had returned to his command. Now he lay among the dead.

The centre had been pierced, the Rayevsky entrenchment was in our hands. When the Morand Division came up to relieve us and General Thielmann gave the order for the brigade to muster, there was no longer a bugler left to sound the order. In the end a severely wounded cavalryman had himself lifted on to his horse and sounded the signal. Thus we returned to the other side of the valley.

It was only three o'clock, but the strength of both armies was as though burned out. On this day, we had lost a third of our numbers, the Russians a half of theirs. Kutuzov held a council of war and decided to retreat beyond Moscow. He knew such a decision would be regarded as discreditable, and said: '*Je payerai les pots cassés, mais je me sacrifie pour le bien de ma patrie.*'★

The following morning he began the retreat; Napoleon followed the next day. We did so too. We were only the ruins of what we had been; what we had been lay at Semenovskoy and in the Rayevsky entrenchment; but we had the right to inscribe on our standards the name: *Borodino!*

12

Through Two Gates

A HUNDRED questions followed this recital of 'Borodino', and while he was answering them von Meerheimb remained the centre of attention. He told of the march across the battlefield, still not cleared and presenting the most fearful scenes, of the entry into Moscow, of their hopes and disappointments, finally of the abandonment of the deserted capital, which had by then become a scene of conflagration. With the picture he sketched of this disaster—a week later he had been wounded —his account of the Russian campaign ended. A barely dissembled predilection for certain of the army commanders—Ney or Nansouty, or even more often Murat and the Viceroy—had been evident in the course of it; but the situation in Prussia, and especially in its capital, was at that time so peculiar that such a predilection could be expressed without the slightest fear of giving offence. No one knew where his political affiliations, and hardly where his heart should lie; for, while immediately before the outbreak of hostilities three hundred of our finest officers had entered the service of the Russians so as not to be obliged to fight for the 'hereditary enemy', an equal number or double the number of their brothers stood over against them in the auxiliary corps we had been obliged to furnish this same 'hereditary enemy'. We regarded ourselves essentially as spectators, clearly recognized the advantages that must accrue to us from a Russian victory, and therefore desired this victory, but we were very far from identifying ourselves with Kutuzov or Vorontsov to such an extent that a description of French superiority in war, a superiority in which, willingly or otherwise, we ourselves had played a salient role, could have been in any way wounding to us.

It was just striking six when von Meerheimb rose to leave: he was attending the opera—a performance of the *Vestale** was being given—and he did not wish to be late. As it emerged that he had made no arrangements with anyone else, it was decided to accompany him; only Hansen-Grell and Lewin declined and departed in different directions to their homes.

Lewin's mind was still full of von Meerheimb's address, which had made a great impression upon him, not so much as a description of a battle as for its skill in representation as such. He saw Semenovskoy in flames and how the horses, fleeting past the burning and smouldering houses, fell into the cellars treacherously covered with ashes and rubble; he saw the long Russian columns with Colonel von Leyser and his death-riders galloping between them as though running the gauntlet; and he saw, finally, a strip of meadow suddenly filling with riders in sheepskin, Bashkirs and Kalmucks, who then struck down their victims like a swarm of wasps. All this he saw before him, and mingled with it, like a tune he could not get out of his head, he heard the words uttered by old Compans: 'Sire, it is lying in those trenches.'

It was still ringing in his ears as he mounted the stairs to his quarters. Here he found everything light and bright. Frau Hulen must have precisely calculated the hour of his return or recognized his step in the hallway below: in any event, the little green study-lamp was already burning on his desk and seeming to invite him to come to it. And he did not keep it waiting long, but took his seat and glanced over the books, papers and letters which still lay just as he had left them that morning when he was preparing himself for Jürgass's luncheon. He read Renate's letter over again quickly without receiving any especially stronger impression from it; it was still as it had been; the outward loss was slight compared with the inner gain. On the other hand, he could not fail to recognize how worrying it must be to have a second fire take place within hardly more than a year, and to turn his thoughts if possible in a more pleasing direction he reached for the books lying to hand on the desk. On top there still lay the volume of Herder. As he opened it again his eyes fell on the song whose closing lines had affected him so much that morning and, superstitious as he was, he saw in this circumstance a sign of some foreboding. He closed disconsolately the book that refused him the pleasure he desired and, searching further, he at length discovered a paper-bound book on whose lemon-yellow cover there stood, beside the actual title: *Chants et chansons populaires*, the words, written in Aunt Amelie's characteristic hand: '*Dedié à son cher neveu L. v. V. par Amélie, comtesse de P.; Château de Guse, Noël 1812*'. Mistrustful of the literary taste of his aunt of Guse, Lewin had not yet been able to bring himself to look into the little book; now he took it up with a smile and leafed through the pages. One of the shorter sub-titles, which he translated to himself, perhaps not quite correctly, as 'Nursery Rhymes', fleetingly excited his curiosity, and he began to read:

> *Ma petite fillette, c'est demain sa fête.*
> *Je sais pour elle ce qui s'apprête:*
> *Le boulanger fait un gâteau,*
> *La couturière un petit manteau . . .*

'How delightful that is!' he said, 'and just what I was looking for. How much happier I feel now!' And he read to the end with increasing interest. The lines at once stuck in his memory; but that was not enough for him, he wanted them in his own language—whether or not thoughts of the next session of

Kastalia played any part in this desire may be left undecided. In any event, it was under the influence of a joyful mood that also speeded the translator's pen that, as though in haste, he wrote down the couplets of the charming little stanza. Only the '*petit manteau*' of the *couturière* presented him with any sort of difficulty.

The last line had hardly been put on paper before there was a knock and Frau Hulen entered. She was bringing tea.

'Sit down, Frau Hulen, I want to read you something.'

The old lady remained at the door and looked at her young gentleman in some embarrassment. Only then did the latter realize that, in the high spirits provoked by the sudden accession of good humour, he had made a boldly unconventional proposal, and it was his turn to be embarrassed. But, like so many before and after him, he consoled himself with the old story that even Molière had consulted the judgement of his housekeeper, and, as Frau Hulen set down the tea-tray, he was therefore able to say with comparative unaffectedness: 'Just listen; it isn't bad.

> 'On the nameday of my granddaughter
> Everyone has a present for her.
> The baker brings a loaf of bread,
> The tailor brings a cloak of red,
> The merchant sends for her delight
> A little doll's bed, so neat and white,
> And also sends a bandbox blue
> That opens when you want it to.
> And on it sheep and shepherd stand,
> A sheepdog, too, is near at hand,
> And in a tree a lark is trilling,
> Since dawn I've heard him gaily shrilling,
> He shrills and trills as best he may
> On my little dear's nameday.'

'Well, Frau Hulen,' Lewin said when he had finished reading, 'what do you think of it?'

The old lady pulled at the band of her cap, and said: 'Very nice.'

'That's not good enough.'

'Indeed, young sir, I really don't think it marvellous.'

'Why not?'

'It all goes so clip and clop, like a hornbook poem.'

'But that's exactly what it is; that's what it's supposed to be. You are a clever woman, Frau Hulen, that you are; and when I next write a hornbook poem you shall again be the first person who gets to hear it.'

The announcement of this coming mark of distinction seemed not to be rated at its full value by her to whom it was directed; Frau Hulen, while in the usual way she loved beyond all measure to stand and chatter, this time sought to secure her line of retreat, and only when she had the door-latch in her hand did she turn again and say: 'Ah, young Schnatermann was here to see you . . .'

'From Lichtenberg?'

'Yes, from Lichtenberg. He brought the compliments of his father, and said they were having a badger hunt in the Dalwitz Forest tomorrow. Other Berlin gentlemen are going too. And would the young gentleman also feel inclined? Eleven o'clock at the Lichtenberger Weg.'

Lewin nodded. 'That's just right; Thursday is a free day. Wake me early, Frau Hulen.'

And with that they bade one another goodnight.

Lewin was up early and, since it was only moderately cold and he was in any case inured to wind and weather, he required little to prepared himself for the excursion.

The way to the place of rendezvous was not very long, and from the Frankfurter Tor onwards followed the same avenue of poplars he had driven along countless times on his visits to Hohen-Vietz. He was familiar with every establishment as far as Lichtenberg and Friedrichsfelde, and whenever he passed the New World, a much frequented place of entertainment, he seldom neglected to take a glass of Bernau and conduct a long debate with the blue-aproned landlord, who invariably served his customers himself. Today, however, he thought it advisable to forgo any such debate, which was always easier to start than to finish, and he therefore walked past the establishment, before which a bread-cart harnessed to two enormous dogs was just being unloaded.

He had gone hardly a hundred yards further on when he saw coming towards him on the broad carriageway, which he was himself walking on for the sake of comfort, a disorderly troop of people, forty or fifty of them so far as he could make out from the distance they were at. It appeared that he, too, had been noticed, for, whether in response to a command or by individual initiative, the troop suddenly began to draw itself up in military fashion, whereupon Lewin, who did not know what to make of this phenomenon, stepped to the side of the road in order to let them pass. But he still had some while to wait, for the party now marching in his direction had slowed considerably from their former fast walking pace. At length those in the foremost ranks grew clearly recognizable. They were wearing grey cloaks, and shakoes, and at first sight could be mistaken for a troop of uniformed soldiers; but closer inspection revealed the full wretchedness of their condition. Their boots, in so far as they had any, had been cut open to ease the pain of their swollen feet, and when the wind blew their cloaks open it revealed tattered gaiters or none at all. They seemed in a desperate state. Their hands, some stiff with cold, others long since benumbed, were wrapped round with rags, and of their weapons they still possessed only their bayonets. They looked at Lewin as they passed and greeted him politely but with a certain bashfulness.

After this detachment of infantry there came cavalry, cuirassiers, ten or twelve men, the remnants of whole regiments. They were better clad, still had their white cloaks and some of them even their tall riding-boots, and as a sign that they had lost their horses through misfortune and not through some fault of their own they were carrying their saddles over their shoulders. A few still possessed their helmets with the long horse-tails, and this unintentionally provocative reminder of their days of glory bestowed upon them a somewhat gruesome appearance.

The rear of the column again comprised infantry, led by a corporal marching in an outfit which, though worn and tattered, was still complete. He was a tall, gaunt man with a black beard and deep-set eyes, and unmistakably a southern Frenchman. Lewin took his courage in his hands, went up to him and said: '*Vous venez . . .*', but his voice failed him and the corporal, laying a hand to his shako in salute, completed the sentence with: '*de la Russie.*'*

The next moment the column had passed by, a funeral procession bearing to the grave—itself. Lewin gazed after it for long minutes, and sensations such as his soul had never before known flooded through him.

'And these are the people we are supposed to waylay and set traps for and then strike dead from behind. No, Papa, that would be worse than to murder sleep, worse than the worst of all.'

He stood for a time absorbed in his thoughts, then he again moved on towards his rendezvous at the Lichtenberger Weg.

But soon he halted again, overcome by a profound feeling of pity for the unhappy men he had seen, and at the same time by an infinite longing to be of advice and assistance to them; and, abandoning without regret his rendezvous and Schnatermann, the Dalwitz Forest and the badger hunt, he resolved to return again to the city.

The advantage the little column had gained was not great, and he overhauled its rear section when they had reached only the exit of the Frankfurter Linden. Here he found many people crowding round the individual soldiers, but was relieved to see that they were mostly inspired by curiosity and sympathy: only a few expressions of hatred were to be heard, and derision and mockery were altogether silent. He therefore kept himself out of sight and followed the procession only at a distance as it made its way first across the Alexanderplatz into the Königs-strasse, then across the Schlossplatz into the Behrenstrasse. In the Behrenstrasse stood the office of the French commandant, into the courtyard of which, after they had knocked gently on the door, this advance guard of the retreat of the former 'Grande Armée' was admitted. The crowd outside, which soon grew bored, dispersed into the streets nearby.

Only Lewin remained. He had been pacing up and down in front of the house for perhaps a quarter of an hour when the big centre door was opened from within and five of the white-cloaked cuirassiers emerged again into the street. They were no longer carrying their saddles. With the keenness of sight necessity bestows they at once recognized Lewin, came up to him and, talking all at once, held out to him their billeting dockets, of whose content they could make neither head nor tail. Lewin read the forms: they were all made out in the name of a barracks-like house at the Rondell, as the present Belle-Alliance-Platz was then still called.

'*Suivez-moi*,' he said, and moved off to the right of the leading trooper. The others followed docilely without saying a word.

When they had almost reached the other side of the Wilhelmsplatz, and were on the corner where the statue of Winterfeldt stands, they heard the sound of warlike music which, if their ears did not deceive them, must have been coming from the Potsdamer Tor or the vicinity of it. Unable easily to resist such sounds, Lewin quickened his pace, then slackened it again when he perceived that his weary companions were finding it hard to keep up with him. He turned to the trooper walking closest to him and, as though to make good his mistake, pointed in the direction the music was coming from and said: '*Entendez-vous?*'

And a smile passed over the man's exhausted features as he answered: '*Ce sont des clairons français!*'*

In the meantime they had arrived at the corner of the Wilhelmsstrasse and the Leipzigerstrasse and saw extending back from the gate, for the line seemed endless, an entire French division marching in. The music had just ceased, presumably for the players to get their breath; but a vast press of people was crowding forward on the pavement to both sides of the advancing column, and had, indeed, to some extent hurried on ahead of it in order more quickly to reach the Lustgarten, where, as was well known, entry-processions and other military spectacles usually terminated. Lewin, together with his charges, had stepped under an archway and, from the loud cries coming from the crowd flooding past them, he had no difficulty in learning that what was proceeding up the Leipzigerstrasse with all military pomp and splendour was the Grenier Division newly arrived from Italy. He also heard that General Augereau,* the governor of Berlin, had ridden out as far as Schöneberg to meet the division and solemnly bring it in, so as to demonstrate to the Berliners, in a way that might give them seriously to think, that the Emperor could still draw on unexhausted resources and, in spite of Moscow, still possessed armies.

The exclamations of the crowd were a constant repetition of the same names and the same remarks; but now everyone fell silent, for the head of the procession, General Augereau himself, had arrived: a big, strong man, with an aquiline nose and a penetrating glance, wearing the uniform of a Marshal of France. When they caught sight of him, the horseless cuirassiers straightened themselves, and one of them who knew him from the Italian campaign whispered to the others: '*Voilà le duc de Castiglione!*'

A suite of orderly officers followed immediately behind him, and only when these too had passed was a clear view possible of the first ranks of the battalion marching in front. It was the Italian Young Guards. Ahead of them strode a drum-major, short and lean but with a red moustache that extended to his epaulets. Five paces behind him came a gigantic Moor, his head and neck towering above the regimental drum he wore, and beside him a fourteen-year-old bugler, a very pretty boy and, it was obvious, one much spoiled by the women, who was laughing and coquettishly displaying his white teeth. In his right hand he carried a little silver bugle, and as he marched along he glanced up at the windows to see whether he was being observed.

The band was still silent. But now, within thirty paces of the corner of the Wilhelmsstrasse, the drum-major raised his mace, threw it into the air and caught it again. At the same moment the Moor gave a beat of his drum and the little bugler at his side set the silver bugle to his lips and blared out a call. Then came a second drum-beat; the bugle fell silent, and the regimental band, forty or more strong, struck up. It passed by at the quick-march, followed by sappers and grenadiers, and down the long line of battalions words of command rang out incessantly.

When Lewin looked round for his companions they were standing with their backs turned. Of their former pride nothing remained but shame at the wretchedness of their condition. He had no desire to see what it was not right for him to see, and he thus directed his eyes back to the column, the last of whose battalions was now marching off. Only when this too had gone by did he lay a hand gently on the shoulder of the man nearest to him and say: '*Eh bien, hâtons-nous!*'*

Thus they walked down the Wilhelmsstrasse to the Rondell without another word being spoken.

When they separated there fifteen minutes afterwards the five white-cloaked cuirassiers drew themselves up as though in battle-array and placed a hand on the hilts of their swords in salute. In their eyes, however, there lay that which moves a noble heart the most: the gratitude of those in the depths of misfortune.

13

A *Billet* and a Letter

CONTRASTING scenes such as Lewin had observed on that morning when he had failed to attend Schnatermann's hunting party from now on became a daily event: through the northeast gates of the city there entered the misery of war, through the western gates its splendour. In the city's streets, however, both encountered one another and gazed at one another in amazement and almost with hostility. 'That is how we were' said the black looks of the former, but the levity and vanity of the latter extinguished the corresponding 'That is how we shall be.'

Among the Berliners, who rarely neglected the opportunity to witness either kind of procession entering, each drew his own conclusions from their very different aspects, and within the circle of our friends too, the house of Ladalinski included, there were widely varying views as to whether the returning veteran with his stained and dirty coat half-scorched from the bivouac fire or the giant, gold-braided and drum-beating Moor of the Grenier Corps represented the more accurate picture of Napoleon's Empire. Bninski, who conducted a lively correspondence with Poland and was well informed as to the disposition of the forces which, under the command of the

Viceroy, were even then concentrating themselves in the fortresses along the Vistula and in the regions of Warsaw and Posen, saw in the arrival of fresh divisions from the south, of whose existence he had hitherto had no suspicion, not only a defence against the immediate danger but, inasmuch as they seemed to demonstrate the inexhaustibility of the Emperor's resources, also grounds for the most sanguine expectations for the future; while, on the other hand, Jürgass, Hirschfeldt and von Meerheimb—especially the last, who had witnessed the total *déroute* with his own eyes—refused to believe that Napoleon's star would ever rise again.

'He may be able to conjure up new armies,' said Meerheimb, 'but not like those that lie buried between Smolensk and Moscow.'

Lewin, unpolitical as he was and by nature wholly subject to the impressions of the moment, had no firm convictions, but saw the Empire sink down and then raise itself up again entirely according to whether the scenes he chanced to witness were sad or cheerful.

A week had again passed without a meeting of Kastalia, the reason being its members' scrupulous insistence on meeting on a Tuesday. This last Tuesday, however, had taken about half the complement of Kastalia—Jürgass, Bummcke, Tubal, and with them Hirschfeldt and Meerheimb—to Potsdam, where on the following day the confirmation of the Crown Prince was to take place in the chapel, followed by a service in the Garrison Church. Tubal made the excursion in the company of his father, who had received a personal invitation to attend the ceremony. The privy councillor would have liked Kathinka too to be present, but to his visible annoyance his independent daughter had declined: she found nothing more wearisome than ceremonies, especially religious ones, and preferred to 'celebrate the solemn occasion' by calling on the beautiful Countess Matushka, which she did on the Wednesday evening, when those who had been invited to Potsdam were expected to return. For the Thursday there had been arranged at the beginning of the week a little reunion at the Ladalinskis to which Lewin had of course received and accepted an invitation: he was therefore not a little surprised to receive that morning a delicate little note folded into a triangle and sealed with blue lacquer which read as follows:

Dear Lewin!

I thought I might expect to see you yesterday or the day before, when Papa and Tubal were in Potsdam; but you are certainly not spoiling me with your attentions. Are you daydreaming? Don't be silly, Lewin. I am writing because I want to wish you good-morning, and also because I am not sure you still remember you agreed to come this evening. Poets are forgetful: you have long since forgotten the verses you wrote to me.

Kathinka v. L.

Lewin read the note two or three times, repeating the phrases: 'Are you daydreaming?' and 'Don't be silly, Lewin.' For a moment it was as though a tropical garden filled with intoxicating fragrance opened out before him, and Kathinka, emerging from behind the shrubbery where she had been hiding, ran towards him with arms outstretched and cried to him wantonly: 'What a bad seeker you are! Why couldn't you find me?' But then he read again: 'Poets are forgetful: you have long since forgotten the verses you wrote to me'; and he laughed bitterly.

'That is her real voice: full of mockery! What are verses to her? A favoured lover is not enough to make her happy, she needs one who is denied her favour too if she is to taste happiness to the full. That is why she makes sure I don't get away. That is the role she has assigned me! A foil to set off a more glittering stone.'

He was about to crumple the note but his hand refused to do so. A softer feeling overcame him and he touched with his lips the place which, for a few moments at least, had ignited new hope within him. Then he folded the sheet and put it into his pocket.

It was clear to him that if he passed the coming few hours at his desk they would be wasted hours; so he went out to seek distraction in the city. He found it sooner than he could have expected. At the corner by the Rathaus several hundred people were standing and studying a public notice printed in French and German on a large yellow placard. He stepped up to it and read it over the heads of those standing in front:

His Excellency the Herr Marshal, *Commandant en Chef* of the 11th Army Corps, has been informed that there have arrived in Berlin a large number of subaltern officers and officials of the *Grande Armée* who have abandoned their corps without authorization. His Excellency orders all such persons to leave the city, failing which all who have not satisfied this order are to be arrested by the Gendarmerie and their names notified to the Herr Minister of War. Hoteliers are directed not to supply accommodation to officers designated in this order and if apprehended doing so will be fined an amount to be determined. Signed: Augereau, duc de Castiglione.

Even more clearly than the 29th communiqué that had appeared at Christmas, this public notice contained an admission of the complete dissolution of the *Grande Armée*; discipline had gone, and with it the bond that held the army together. This was the impression received by everyone who read the proclamation and, since they were Berliners, there was no lack of pointed comment on it. 'Officials and subaltern officers! No mention of generals,' said one; 'and much less of marshals', added another. 'Of course not: dog doesn't eat dog.' So they talked back and forth, and more than once there could be heard the assertion that the hoteliers of Berlin were not agents of the French police.

Lewin soon disengaged himself from the crowd, and close to the Stechbahn encountered a couple of fellow-students who were easily persuaded to sacrifice a lecture hour and join him in a stroll to Charlottenburg. They were Marwitz* and Löschebrand, compatriots of Lewin's whom he had known since his schooldays at the Graue Kloster. They walked, via the Unter den Linden and the grand chaussée beyond it, to the Turkish Pavilion,* where, since twelve o'clock had meanwhile arrived, they ordered lunch.

In the lively conversation that attended their meeting, which veered from York and Augereau's placard to Spontini's *Vestale* to the confirmation of the Crown Prince, Lewin overcame the ill-humour the morning had brought with it, and was only fleetingly reminded of it when, in taking out his pocket-book, he let fall Kathinka's note, whose striking shape and colour ensured that his companions would notice it.

'I say, Vitzewitz,' exclaimed Löschebrand, 'a *billet-doux*!

There's no end to new revelations about him, eh, Marwitz?'
The latter agreed, and the next moment the incident was
forgotten.

It might have been four o'clock or just after when Lewin
again crossed the hallway of his house and felt his way up the
deeply worn steps of the stairway by the ancient banister-rail
long since rubbed smooth as a mirror.

Up in his room he discovered a letter in whose address he
could, in spite of the semi-darkness that already reigned, easily
recognize the hand of his father. The window was still glowing
in the red of evening twilight, and he went over to it and
read:

Hohen-Vietz, 20 January
Dear Lewin!
Renate has told you of the event that happened at Hohen-Vietz last
week, and from your reply by return I have been able to perceive that
you regard the misfortune, for such it is, with the same divided
feelings as we all do. The burned-out ruins of a barn in the farmyard
and now a wing of the manor house reduced to ashes certainly present
no pleasant spectacle, least of all a spectacle of good order; but is the age
in which we live an age of good order at all? And so the scenes of
conflagration are in keeping with everything else. No more of that.
There is more at stake than a couple of buildings.

Our organization is complete. I see Drosselstein, who is displaying
more zeal than, given his reserved nature, I could have expected,
almost every day; likewise Bamme, to whom I am beginning to
become reconciled. He is fire and flame, and his offensive cynicism, in
which even now he continues to indulge, is combined with a selflessness, indeed I must even say an occasional nobility of disposition, that
truly amazes me. Next to him, Othegraven is the most active. He has
great influence among the citizens and the pupils of the top two classes
hang on his every word. The pedantry which used to characterize him
he has either got rid of or, because it has its roots in a strong belief in
himself, it actually serves to enhance his effectiveness.

When I said our organization was complete, I was thinking only of
our own Barnim and Lebus; much is still lacking in other places,
especially in the villages *beyond* the Oder, which are so vital on account
of their situation. We on *this side* have created a brigade of local militia,
four battalions named after four of the towns of our two districts:
Bernau, Freienwalde, Müncheberg and Lebus. The *ordre de bataille* of
the last of these will interest you the most, so I give it here:

'*Lebus Battalion of Militia*

1. Hohen-Ziesar Company: Count Drosselstein.
2. Alt-Medewitz-Protzhagen Company: Captain von Rutze.
3. Hohen-Vietz Company: Major von Vitzewitz.
4. Neu-Lietzen–Dolgelin Company: (vacant).

The principle you will recognize in this—Bamme has assumed command of the brigade—we apply everywhere. There is still a shortage of officers, because here, too, we have a preponderance of those capable of sailing only when the wind blows from above. All this notwithstanding, however, everything must be ready for battle in ten or twelve days' time, even where they are now most in arrear.

This is in a certain sense too late, all the more so in that for what I had in mind at Christmas even *today* would already be too late. The whole body of French generals has—as Othegraven has written me from Frankfurt and Krach from a visit to Küstrin—succeeded in crossing the Oder. In sable cloaks and constantly supplied by our own eager lackeys with new relays of horses, they have followed after the Emperor, who set them the example. The harm our cause has suffered through this is incalculable; for the removal of the generals *in one way or another* (from this principle I shall not deviate) was more vital than the removal of the remnants of the army can ever be. Much has been let slip, irrecoverably lost. Our policy of wait-and-see is to blame for it.

But precisely this waiting-and-seeing, which has led us to let so many things slip, has also preserved us from many things, and if the good consequences were now finally to be weighed against the bad, it is possible or—I do not hesitate to make this concession—even very probable that the scales would tend to fall towards the good side. Three weeks ago I believed it would have to be done *without* the King, now I know—and I thank God for this transformation of affairs—that it will be done *with* him. We shall have a war after our old Prussian traditions. I would not be frightened of a people's war, for the country comes before the throne, but, as our Brandenburg proverb has it: better to be on the safe side.

Yes, Lewin, a transformation of affairs has occurred such as I had given up all hope of seeing, and the next few days will announce it to the world. It is quite possible that by the time you receive these lines the first of the steps in view will already have been taken.

And now listen. The court is to leave Potsdam and go to Breslau.* This step is more momentous than you can imagine. As to what has occasioned it there are only rumours. It is said that Napoleon intended to seize the King and have him abducted to a French fortress as a hostage for the peaceable behaviour of the people. I do not inquire how much truth or falsity there is in this rumour, it suffices that the King gave it credence. The departure will follow immediately after the confirmation of the Crown Prince, which takes place today. It will be carried out in five stages; the Garde Regiment will accompany or cover this removal. Breslau, Silesia are well chosen; the province is the only one with no French garrison, and Austria, which we count on, is not far off.

And now listen further!

The King is due to arrive in Breslau on the 26th: a week later he will call his people to arms. The draft of this proclamation has been in my hands; it speaks the language that now has to be spoken, and there is only one thing it lacks: the enemy is not named. But that, thanks be to God, is no longer necessary. York's capitulation, repudiated for appearance's sake but, as I now know definitely, in fact sanctioned in every respect, and the departure of the court, which will probably have taken place by tomorrow, so as to elude the whims and caprices of an incalculable ally: all this leaves it in no doubt *who* is meant.

Nor will this proclamation go unheard. I know our people. They are worthy to endure and they will fight for their continued endurance. That is all they can do. No one has more to give than himself. We have many faults, but many virtues too: it is not only our colours that know the antithesis of black and white. A feeling for our country as a whole has come alive in us since the days of the Great King, and if we see our country as a whole pass away we lose the desire to go on living as individuals. Think of the old major who bled to death in our church at Hohen-Vietz on the day after Kunersdorf. The stain his blood made speaks for him to this very moment. He thought Prussia's last hour had come: 'Children, I want to die,' he cried as they laid him down, and tore the bandage from his wound.

And there are many such men still dwelling among us!

For the rest, we are going to have a *proper* war, Lewin, and proper colours. Do you hear: proper royal Prussian colours. You should be pleased with me: for I have come over into your camp more than you have into mine. Write soon: better still, come! Everyone sends good wishes: Aunt Schorlemmer, Renate, Marie. Even Hector, who is gazing at me wide-eyed and plaintively whining, seems to want to be remembered to you.

As ever, your old Papa B. v. V.

14

The Inner Circle

THE invitation to the Ladalinskis had been for six o'clock: if he could avoid them the old privy councillor disliked social occasions that went on late into the night. Thus it was high time for Lewin to dress: and he did so, though not in the best frame of mind. Again and again he had been assailed by the question, which for many hours he had tried in vain to repress, of what Kathinka had really intended by her enigmatic second invitation, and again and again he had come to the conclusion: 'A coquettish game! She needs me; I am at the same time valuable and valueless to her; she holds me like a bird on a string and takes pleasure in not letting the string go.' This was the basic tenor of his thoughts, with the gentle voice of hope heard only now and then.

It was just chiming seven from the Marienturm, and immediately afterwards from the Nikolaiturm as well, as our friend entered the Ladalinski house.

The company was already assembled: it was occupying the little ladies' drawing-room familiar to us from that earlier evening of the ball at which the only two things of moment were the mazurka and the news of the capitulation; today, however, in place of the dim red hanging-lamp the room was lit by a large, bright astral-lamp, and it therefore presented a much more cheerful appearance.

Although she was engaged in an intimate whispered conversation with the fair Matushka when Lewin entered, Kathinka greeted him with unaffected affability, and as he took a chair and inserted himself into the semicircle formed by Tubal, Bninski, Jürgass and Ladalinski, she remarked that, although he was, as usual, an hour late, this was really nothing to wonder at in a poet, since unpunctuality was the sister of 'forgetfulness'. To this last word she imparted, not only a heavy emphasis, but also a tone of particular confidentiality, as though she wished through this one word to reiterate the entire contents of her note of that morning, which had concluded by gently reproaching him for his 'forgetfulnesses'. He, for his part, forbore to reply to her, either because he found this game annoying, or because at that same moment he felt pointedly directed upon him from the sofa the two big crystal lenses of her ladyship the wife of the Lord High Steward, who was today again sitting with Fräulein von Bischofswerder and was this time gazing at him with twofold malice because his unpunctual entry had interrupted a speech she had just commenced. Infused with the desire to be again reconciled with her, if that were in any way possible, he rose from the chair in which he had scarcely taken his seat and, in words somewhat jumbled and confused, attempted an apology; her ancient ladyship, however, closed her lorgnette with a clatter—an act that was unmistakably deliberate—and smiled haughtily, as though to say that silence and sufferance were very much to be preferred to any kind of response, and then, talking past Mademoiselle Bischofswerder in complete disregard of her, continued in a harsh and jarring tone with her interrupted communications. 'I tell you again, my dear Ladalinski, that His Majesty will leave Potsdam very early tomorrow morning. On the first night he will take up quarters in Beeskow, a little town that is better than its reputation; it has a castle that was formerly the residence of a bishop. The King will be accompanied by the Guards. Tippelskirch has taken over command in place of Kessel: Kessel is staying in Potsdam. His Majesty thinks to arrive in Breslau on the 26th.'

'I have just received identical news from my father in Hohen-Vietz,' observed Lewin, in his embarrassment again perpetrating a blunder, as a consequence of which he now had to submit—since looks alone seemed to be without effect—to a direct reprimand on the part of the old countess.

'Prussian chief ladies-in-waiting', she retorted tartly, 'are not accustomed to circulating news about His Majesty the King that requires confirmation. I am glad, however, to see your honoured father is so well informed. Please be good enough to remember me to him when you next have the opportunity. His mother-in-law, the wife of General von Dumoulin, was a friend of mine in our youth.'

Not knowing what to make of these words, in which for all their arrogance there did appear a trace of good-nature, Lewin considered it most advisable to ignore what was unpleasant in them and to content himself with a polite bow; the old countess then proceeded, with the air of one imparting matters of weight:

'Augereau has strict orders that, under certain clearly defined circumstances, and especially in the event of an uprising, he is to seize the person of the King, and His Majesty, who has known of these orders for more than three weeks, would have removed himself sooner from the danger threatening him if the desire had not prevailed to wait for the imminent confirmation of the Crown Prince, which, as we all know, finally took place yesterday. Moreover, His Royal Highness received—something that may have escaped you, my dear privy councillor, even though you were present at the solemnities—received from the hands of His Majesty, as a memento of this momentous day, a valuable ring.'

'Sans doute,' Bninski observed.

'Sans doute?' the old lady repeated, drawing out the words and inflecting them into a question: for the sarcastic tone of the remark the count had let fall had not escaped her. 'Why sans doute, Count Bninski?'

'Because a ring is a symbol of eternal and inviolable loyalty,' the latter responded, 'and in this country a solemn occasion, least of all an ecclesiastical one, is hardly to be thought of without one.'

The privy councillor shifted in his seat uncomfortably. He found it distressing in the highest degree to hear words uttered in his house, and before two ladies of the court moreover, whose ironical intention must, the earnestness with which they were delivered notwithstanding, be audible to everyone. He therefore looked across to the count in a visible effort to induce him to change, if not the subject, at any rate the tone in which he was discussing it. Bninski ignored these efforts, however, and continued in the same tone: 'It counts as one of the peculiarities of the German nation. Continual solemn oaths of duty, and a corresponding symbol to go with them, and I venture to say it would surprise me if the valuable ring His

Royal Highness received from the hands of the King his father was not accompanied by a direct demand for loyalty, either in the form of an engraved motto or in that of a saying from the Bible. "Be faithful unto death" perhaps, or something similar.'

The old countess pursed her lips. She was plainly uncertain as to how she ought to respond; quickly deciding for an attitude of conciliation, however, she said with forced good humour: 'I see you know about this ring, Count. If it is through inspiration I congratulate you and us. In any event, it bears inside it the inscription: "Revelation 2:10".* On this point you were quite right; but you were not right when you said that this confirmation ring was a custom of the court or of the country. On the contrary, it is the first instance of its kind.'

'Then it will become a custom. Good examples usually find a fruitful soil in the loyal hearts of the people.'

It is very probable that Bninski's continued caustic tone would in the end have transformed the countess's resolve to keep the peace into its opposite, for she was almost as impetuous as she was haughty, if Kathinka had not at that moment broken off the conversation she had hitherto continued to conduct with the fair Matushka and, bringing forward two low chairs for herself and her companion, introduced them into the semicircle between Lewin and Bninski.

'What blasphemies, Count!' Kathinka said, turning towards him. 'One would think, from the tone of your words, that you are inclined to believe that rings play no part at all in world-history. But in that you are wrong. Rings are found everywhere. Aren't they, Herr von Jürgass?'

'Sans doute,' said Jürgass, who felt free to repeat this phrase, that had come so close to precipitating a crisis, without fear of giving offence. 'I agree with Fräulein Kathinka: rings are found everywhere! Everything in life, legend, history revolves around them; my favourite has always been the ring of Polycrates,* for I prize people who are lucky. Now we even have a ballad on it. It was with the aid of a ring that the bishop married his church, the Doge the sea and Henry the Eighth, that gifted player who hazarded six-le-va,* his six wives. A retrospective exhibition of his six wedding-rings, by the way, would inspire in one strange reflections.'

'Oh, don't speak of that royal ogre, who appears to have forgotten that innocent women ought to be allowed to die a natural death.'

'But Anne Boleyn, my dear lady, was convicted.'

'Come now, Jürgass, surely you don't believe women have convictions? I could almost think you want to defend him: I had considered you more gallant than that. No, leave King Henry's six wedding-rings and tell me of better rings than those.'

'I can, then, tell you only of the three rings of the Puttkamers.'*

'You jest. From the Tudors to the Puttkamers! That is some distance. But I am sufficiently curious. What are the three rings of the Puttkamers? It had better be something amusing, though.'

'I don't know whether it is amusing or not. It begins with the fact that these three rings are actually only two. And these two are invisible.'

'Ah, that is a good beginning: something supernatural. But it is still early yet, we have plenty of time: so proceed.'

'Very well. So, then, there were three rings which the pixies or the "little people" or the dwellers underground made a present of to the Puttkamers many, many years ago when Pomerania had just been finished.'

'When was that?'

'Let us say a hundred years after Brandenburg was finished: this difference you must allow to my local patriotism. Well, the Puttkamers had their three rings which, so the pixies said, would, provided they kept them safe and treasured them, bring good fortune and blessings upon the house. And blessings did fall upon the house, especially in the form of children, until all of a sudden, no one knew how, one of the rings vanished and the blessings grew less.'

'Ah!' said Tubal.

'You say "Ah" and breathe a sigh,' Jürgass continued. 'But the Puttkamers had no wish to do without the blessings that had been falling on their house. And because they wanted to make sure of them, the wealthiest of the Puttkamers built a fine castle and in the tower, at the spot where the walls are thickest, he walled up the two remaining rings. And there they are to this day, and so long as they stay there secure they also secure the good fortune of the house.'

Fräulein von Bischofswerder, who had up till then been seated stiff and motionless in her place on the sofa, began nodding her head ever more vigorously in agreement as Jürgass spoke; now she interposed: 'We too had a similar ring, which, according to the legend, was supposed to ensure the good fortune of our house.'

'And *has* ensured it, surely,' the old countess put in. 'It was, I think, your honoured father's spirit-ring, that lulls the living to sleep and summons the dead.'

'To be sure,' replied Mademoiselle Bischofswerder, who felt her devotion to the old lady slipping away at this mockery, 'to be sure, Your Excellency. And among these dead there are to be found entire families who would have remained dead for ever except for my father's ring. Is gratitude not also a German virtue, Count Bninski?'

Somewhat startled to find his heresies supported in so unexpected a quarter, the latter bowed to Mademoiselle Bischofswerder, while the privy councillor, anguished by the idea that the peril only just surmounted was about to reappear in a new guise, turned to Lewin with the question: 'What was it you told me before Christmas, Lewin, about the Bredow's family ring? I can't recall it, and I would like to hear it again. Her Excellency Countess Reale will permit it, I know, and Kathinka, who pleads the cause of rings so eloquently, would surely be grateful to you for something that was an embellishment of her subject.'

'To be sure,' observed Kathinka, 'I should be grateful to see our silent friend taking part in our conversation at all, and doubly so if his contribution were a defence of the ring and its world-historic mission. For every cause requires its man, and I do not know what could go better together than a ring and cousin Lewin. Above all if it were a wedding-ring. There is a silent natural bond between the two, and a story could be written about it; indeed, I think I could write it myself, unpoetical though I am. I would interpret the wedding-ring as a little round king hollowed out in the middle who rules over all good people, all the honest and virtuous. And on the steps of his throne would stand his first minister, the most honest and virtuous of them all, and he would be called Lewin.'

Lewin changed colour, but, soon pulling himself together, replied quietly: 'After a character-assessment like that I shall be quite unable to refuse the invitation extended to me, all the less in that since the days of King Pharaoh it has been one of the privileges and duties of a custodian of virtue to interpret dreams and tell stories. And so, then, I shall begin:

'Well, there really was a family ring, broad and covered with all sorts of signs, and a young Frau von Bredow, whose lord and master, Josua von Bredow, was a captain of cavalry and high constable of Lehnin, wore it on the ring finger of her left hand. During the winter the young couple lived in the little garrison at Perleberg, but when May arrived they went off to Lehnin, as it was only proper they should, where, in the spacious abbot's house* that was the last remaining remnant of the days of the monks, they took up residence in what was at once their high-constabulary abode and a summer holiday resort. Then there followed many happy weeks, and they drove to Plessow, Göttin, Reckahne, to visit the various Rochows, and likewise to Gross-Kreuz, to visit old Herr von Arnstedt, but what they always liked best to do was to go walking beside the lovely lake at Lehnin, especially where the path ran between blackberry and hazel bushes out across the flower-covered meadow.'

'How pretty,' said Kathinka. 'I would like to have been with them.'

'And one evening', Lewin continued, 'they were taking their walk, and because the dog-roses were just coming into bloom the wife was seized with a desire to pick one. So as to reach it more easily she pushed aside one of the hazel bushes growing thickly around it, but at the moment when she was extending her left hand towards it the strongest of the hazel branches sprang back and took the ring from off her finger. She saw the golden arc it transcribed in the air, and then how it fell to the ground in the meadow close behind the hedge. A soft cry escaped her; then together they carefully parted the hedge, bent down and began to search. They were still searching when the crescent moon stood in the quiet evening sky; they were searching when morning came and when it was noon. But they searched in vain: the ring was gone. You wanted to be with them, Kathinka: perhaps, with your happy knack of succeeding, you might have found it.'

'No diversions,' Kathinka laughed. 'The story, the story.'

'And with the ring vanished the happiness of the young couple: not slowly and gradually, but all at once. "You should have been more careful," said the husband in a tone of reproach, and with these words the damage was done. Out of the first reproach grew the first quarrel, and within the space of a year everything designed to disturb the peace of a house entered into it: sickness and dissension, bad harvests and jealousy.'

'Jealousy too? Surely not. Don't wantonly deprive your hero of the sympathy of your audience.'

'I do so only so as to win it again. But only years later, I admit.'

'Then leave out the intervening years.'

'That's what I intend to do. The date of their silver wedding was at last approaching, and Josua von Bredow, who had long since left the army and withdrawn to the solitude of Lehnin, where he confined himself to carrying out his duties as high constable, thought to celebrate the day, notwithstanding the discord that continued as ever to reign in his house. They had, after all, been married twenty-five years! He was therefore seated with a large sheet of paper before him, and was in the act of writing down the names of those who were to be invited to the celebration, when Frau von Bredow, who in spite of her forty-five years was still a handsome and elegant woman, looked over his shoulder and demanded in the firmest tones that old Herr Arnstedt, who had acted unbecomingly at the last ball at Potsdam, should be crossed off.

'A scene seemed unavoidable: but all at once the housekeeper came into the room in great agitation and said: "Sir, here it is; old Holtzendorffen has just found it." And so saying, she placed before him a large early potato with, grown into its pointed end, the family ring. There it was, returned to them again. Mother Nature in her mercy had brought it forth, and

Josua von Bredow and his lady of the Ribbecks now knew that better days were ahead. He gave her a kiss and, without further ado, crossed old Herr Arnstedt out. And when, in the week that followed, they celebrated their silver wedding, they stood before the altar for a second time and the old parson at Lehnin, Pastor Krokisius, who at that time though was still in middle life, preached a beautiful sermon on the text: "All things work together for good to them that love God."* And when his sermon had at last come to an end—for Pastor Krokisius was incapable of brevity—he took the bride's hand and placed the ring on the same fourth finger from which the wicked hazel-branch had struck it and brought about a long interval of dissension and discontent. On the following day, however, they sent to Berlin for an engraver—for they refused to be separated from their treasure again—and had him engrave in the ring the date on which it was lost and the date on which it was found again, together with the fine biblical text upon which Pastor Krokisius had preached. And if they haven't died in the meantime they are still alive today.'*

During the course of this story the countess had sloughed off more and more of her haughty demeanour; and now, as though to seal their newly minted friendship, she tapped Lewin's hand gently with the point of her lorgnette.

Kathinka promised that, as soon as she became Queen, she would employ him in her court as interpreter of dreams and first story-teller, and only Mademoiselle Bischofswerder was unable to accommodate herself to the circumstance that this enchanting ring should have become involved with a potato: 'it is unpoetic', she said, with which observation Lewin unhesitatingly agreed, though he found it impossible to say why.

True to his natural inclinations, the old privy councillor lingered over unimportant details and wanted especially to know to which line of the Bredow family the ring had belonged. Then he came to speak of Lehnin, expatiated on the prophecy* whose first and last lines he knew by heart in the Latin original, and concluded by saying with a sigh that for a full seventeen years he had been denied an opportunity of visiting this ancient cultural centre, the burial-place of so many margraves and electors.

'But why not make an opportunity?' Tubal interposed; and before Ladalinski could reply Kathinka struck in, in a decisive tone: 'Let us make the excursion. Who shall be our courier? Tubal? No. Lewin? Absolutely not. You, Herr von Jürgass! If you are not a born courier I cannot tell a diplomat from a schoolmaster.'

'I would at once demonstrate my incapacity if I were to argue with you.'

'So you accept?'

'Yes.'

'And when?'

'Not before Tuesday. We have a change of horses at Potsdam; so there will be plenty of time if we start at midday. Rendezvous: Schöneberg, at the Black Eagle. Punctually at twelve. *Au revoir.*'

15

Lehnin

THE Tuesday agreed upon arrived. But it did not do so without something happening which always happens when such agreements are made: half the party had recalled they had a previous engagement. Not only the countess and the *dame d'atour* from the court of the Queen Mother, but the old privy councillor too, whose pedantic-romantic desire to recite the Latin lines of the Lehnin prophecy on the very spot they applied to had been the actual impulse for the excursion, had in the end been obliged to forgo it. But other participants had been drawn in to replace these self-excluded elements, and fresh snow fallen on the Monday night promised a swift and splendid journey: for it had also been agreed to make the excursion by sleigh. A light east wind was blowing, the sun was shining, and the sky stood as cloudless and blue as a bell.

It was just striking twelve from the Schöneberg Tower as four sleighs drew up before the Black Eagle, the rendezvous Jürgass had appointed. Their occupants were acquaintances from the Ladalinskis' ball: Count Matushka, Count Seherr-

Thoss and Count Zierotin, all three accompanied by their young wives. Only Bninski was missing: but Tubal had come along in his place and taken his seat beside Kathinka. A minute later a fifth sleigh appeared—somewhat bigger than the others and, like all hired sleighs, not very elegant—in which Lewin, von Hirschfeldt and Bummcke were sitting. Jürgass had preceded them to Potsdam three hours before to attend to the change of horses.

Salutations were hurried, for the brevity of the daylight demanded that no time be lost. Tubal took the lead, the three young couples followed, and the 'célibataire sleigh', as the ladies had good-humouredly christened the last arrival, brought up the rear. This good humour soon communicated itself to everyone; the horses threw the flying foam behind them, the bells jingled, and whenever they brushed against a low-hanging branch the snow flew into the air in a powdery spray or fell as glittering crystals down on to their muffs and bearskin blankets. And everywhere there was a continual lively chatter, even in the rearguard sleigh of the célibataires.

'I wonder where Bninski is,' said Lewin. 'He seemed very keen to come along.'

'So you haven't heard?' answered Bummcke. 'Jürgass asked him not to.'

'But how could he? I at least would not like to do such a thing.'

Bummcke laughed. 'You know Jürgass. I wager he found it easier than that tired crow just flying up in front of us does to flap its wings. He acts on the ancient principle: "Honesty is the best policy", and he told the count straight out that his presence would be an embarrassment. For I believe he has a surprise in store, something patriotically Prussian. You know how he loves that kind of thing. What Bninski replied to him I don't know, but this much is certain, it didn't affect the good terms they are on with one another. That doesn't surprise me, though. Jürgass is inoffensive and the count has a noble nature. You can forgive him even his prejudices. He hates us, but he hates us as a whole, not as individuals. Recall, Hirschfeldt, how well he took it when you read to us about Spain. There is nothing petty in him.'

Hirschfeldt nodded in agreement, and as, continuing with the conversation, they came also to recall the last evening at the Ladalinskis, the haughty countess, the stiff and ceremonious Mademoiselle Bischofswerder, and finally the feud the two were conducting between them, our friends found themselves gliding past the Steglitz Park, which the lighter and more elegantly constructed sleighs bearing the four mazurka-couples had already put behind them some time before. Lewin urged that they should catch up but the distance between them remained, and whenever the road came to a bend the rearward fifth sleigh beheld the flanking line of the four teams flying on ahead, the blue veils worn by the ladies and the white snow-covers blowing and billowing in the wind.

Past the outlying houses of Zehlendorf they flew, to the inn at Stimming on the Wannsee, where Lewin, pointing to the left, indicated the enclosed spot, recognizable only by its four poplars, where for the past year there had stood the grave of Heinrich von Kleist.* Hirschfeldt, who had at that time been in Spain, knew nothing of the lamentable event, and so it devolved upon his companions to tell him of the last vicissitudes, of the life and death of a comrade with whom, when both were residing in the same garrison, he had been at any rate superficially acquainted. From this account conversation soon passed over to a discussion of his work; and the character of Käthchen von Heilbronn, and the justification or otherwise of the dramatic employment of somnambulism, were not near to being thrashed out as their sleigh glided through the defile-like narrow passage constructed at Kohlhasenbrück through the close-encroaching fir-trees and from the other direction through the reed-bank along the Griebnitzsee. A minute later and the weavers' houses at Nowawes, covered in snow and little bigger than wintry grave-mounds, lay on either side, and then, slipping past the brewery and the castle colonnade, they entered the quiet little town of Potsdam—quieter than ever today, for, as the aged countess had foretold on the last evening at the Ladalinskis, the court and the guards had been gone for several days. Jürgass was standing at the Jägertor, ten yards further down was the relay-station, and, after all the ladies and gentlemen had greeted their courier and a couple of post-grooms had changed the horses and replaced the harnesses and the bells, they sped off without further delay faster and faster into the Havel-land: for they had to reach their destination before sunset.

It was now two o'clock. The domed roofs of the *communs*★ and the New Palace gleamed in the afternoon sun, the expanse of the Golmer fen stretching away behind them: the little village of Eiche and its church-tower seemed to sink down and disappear into it. Now these too lay behind them, and from the wilderness of ice and snow that the usually lake-like surface of the Havel★ had become there protruded only the mastheads of a score or so little boats overtaken by the frost and compelled to spend the winter frozen into the ice. Then came the town of Werder, discernible only by the column of smoke rising above its island brewery; and then, past low but precipitate hills on whose steep sides there was nothing to be seen but snow and fluttering crows, the sleighs raced on towards the villages beyond.

Conversation had ceased, or was confined to the occasional word; all their minds were filled with only one thought: to reach their destination. Jürgass moved up to the leading position, for they had just passed Gross-Kreuz and the road, now beginning to turn leftward into the great fir- and oak-tree forest at Lehnin, demanded both a sharp eye and an assured hand.

First came the fir-trees. Ah, how refreshing they found the stillness of the forest! The wind fell silent, and every word, though spoken in a whisper, resounded loudly in echoes all around. A warm scent of resin was in the air, enhancing their feeling of well-being. The tracks the wild boar had burrowed in the snow ran here and there across the path; the branches of the trees trembled as the redbreasted robins fluttered up from them, and from the depths of the forest came the sound of the woodpecker. Then they arrived at a large clearing on whose opposite side the leaf-bearing trees began, though at first intermingled still with firs. The sun was burning bright behind the trees and the brown leaves of the oaks glowed gold or copper-coloured according as the light fell upon them, while the black summits of the fir-trees stood like sharply etched shadows against the shimmering fire of the evening sky. They were all ravished by the beauty of the scene, and Lewin observed how one little hand after another emerged from the warmth of its muff to point to those places in the forest where light and shade were so bewitchingly mingled.

Bummcke recalled—from his time in Copenhagen, as goes without saying—a Claude Lorrain* that reproduced precisely these same evening colours, and he was about to embark on a discourse in aesthetics when the forest, which only a moment ago had seemed endless, suddenly opened out and a number of scattered buildings came clearly into view. And before our travellers had had time to realize where they were or give vent to their surprise, they had already come to a halt before the goal of their journey: the abbey church at Lehnin.

Whether it happened by chance, or whether Jürgass had announced in advance their time of arrival, no matter: without their having to wait or to knock, the little side-door close to the great Romanesque portal opened at once, and a meagre little man with long white hair came towards them; it was the sexton of Lehnin, an old man a mere two years younger than his colleague of Hohen-Vietz, Jeserich Kubalke. He greeted the ladies standing nearest to him by removing his cap, exchanged two or three words with Jürgass, and then, either because the latter had asked him to or because he himself desired to usher them in with the greatest possible solemnity, he opened the heavy, iron-bound middle door; and in this, despite the draught that was blowing through, he remained standing until the last of his visitors had entered.

The glow of evening still stood in the western windows and a red lustre that lent everything a blush of renewed life also fell on the bridal garlands hanging withered and with long faded ribbons on the church wall opposite. It was the best time they could have chosen: none the less anyone who observed them could not have failed to see that they were all disappointed, and especially so the ladies; for they had expected more.

'Where are the tombstones?' asked Countess Matushka, in the complacent tone affected by those who are in fact uninterested.

'Tombstones in the plural, dear Countess, I cannot provide,' answered Jürgass, who had detached himself, with the countess and Kathinka, from the remainder of the company and, because he had a thorough knowledge of the abbey, had undertaken to show the two young ladies around it on their own. 'Thanks to official and unofficial devastations, the Lehnin tombstones are limited to *one*. I shall at once do myself the honour of presenting you to it.' With that he mounted the steps to the upper choir gallery, where a monk carved in stone reposed on a tomb. Kathinka and Countess Matushka followed him.

'I had expected', said the countess, 'to see a soldier'; then, quickly improving on this remark, she added: 'I mean a warrior. You have no reason to laugh, Jürgass. It is to be assumed that the margraves were warriors, with shields and coats of mail and a crown. Or didn't they wear one? Again you are silent; that is not proper; a guide is supposed to talk all the time. Anyway, these margraves must have had something on their heads. They were Ascanians, if I have understood old Ladalinski correctly.'

'Yes, Ascanians or Anhaltians.'

'Not so. You are trying to confuse me. If they were Ascanians they cannot have been Anhaltians.★ The Old Dessauer who stands in the Lustgarten and whom the military march★ with the long trumpet solo is named after, *he* was an Anhaltian . . . But whatever is this?' The fair countess had stubbed the point of her toe against the stump of a tree which, itself as hard as stone, rose about a foot high out of the stone floor.

'This is the remains of the trunk of the oak-tree out of which, a certain number of centuries ago, I won't burden you with the exact date, the entire abbey of Lehnin grew. Under this tree, when it was still a tree and not a stump, Margrave Otto, the first of that name, had a dream which prophesied that danger lay for him in these forests. Margrave Otto was a son of Albrecht the Bear, of whom your ladyship will perhaps have heard.'

'Certainly, certainly; Heinrich the Lion,★ Albrecht the Bear.'

'Very good. Well, Margrave Otto had a bad, ominous dream, and when they came to hear of this dream his vassals, who were also Christian Ascanians, urged him to build a fortress as protection against the Wends.'

'Against the Wends? What are Wends?'

'Wends is the name of the heathen peoples who dwelt in these parts in those days.'

'I see. And what did the margrave then do?'

'He replied: "I shall establish a fortress against the Wends, but it will be a fortress from which our devilish foes", by which he meant the Wends, "shall be scared away, not by the noise of weapons, but by the sound of sacred songs." And so he built an abbey; and this abbey was called Lehnin.'

During this discussion they had been walking on further to the transept of the church, where pictures of every possible kind were hanging in worm-eaten, wooden frames so broken and battered that in many cases whole segments of them had fallen out. Kathinka, who had taken Countess Matushka's arm, came to a stop before the largest of these pictures and said to Lewin, who had meanwhile joined them from the other group: 'How ugly. It looks like a fairground picture.'

'It is indeed something of the sort. Even the division into segments has, as the ladies will notice, not been spared us. However, the artist has in this case contented himself with a mere division into two, a simple upper segment and a lower. The horrible confusion at the top is the murder of the first abbot of Lehnin,* who was slain by the Wends because they suspected him of an amorous adventure.'

'Without good reason, I assume,' said Kathinka.

'In my capacity as first ethical counsellor to King Ring it would ill become me to express any doubt as to that. I only wish the painter too had dealt with him more indulgently.'

'Perhaps the picture already belongs to the Protestant era.'

Lewin wanted to preserve the purified teaching from responsibility for this picture and was just commencing a discussion of it when Jürgass interrupted him and urged them to hasten, since, according to the programme he was determined to stick to, within the next ten minutes they would have to inspect not only the parts of the church that had fallen into ruin but also the remains of the cloisters and the buildings adjacent to them.

This loud admonition was heard not only by Lewin, and everyone hurried towards the exit in obedience to it. Only the Countesses Seherr-Thoss and Zierotin, who had been expending themselves in amusing suppositions before the picture of the murdered abbot, had remained behind and were now startled to find themselves alone among the bridal- and funeral-wreaths, which the draught from the open door was causing to rustle. The evening light in the windows had grown dimmer and dimmer; they looked around uneasily and sought for the exit, which, although they were standing quite close to it, they were unable to find. At length the sexton arrived and escorted them out of the church: they made no attempt to conceal from him how afraid they were, and nodded to him in a friendly fashion as he again turned the key in the lock.

The party found themselves once more united among the ruins outside—the later, Gothic half of the church had fallen in—but they did not remain among them for long. They confined themselves to peering into the staircase-tower that still remained standing and to pointing out to one another the rowan-bushes that seemed to be held in place against the sloping buttresses more by the snow than by the soil, and then they walked across a square courtyard which, enclosed by buildings recent and ancient and by heaps of cordwood and thick hedges, presented a scene in which magnificence and poverty were strangely mingled. Along the side of a stone wall with a kind of sunroof constructed over it there ran a bowling-alley, with the bowls lying as though fixed by concrete in the snow. Beansticks lay thrown together in confusion in a corner of this enclosure, while to the right of them, where the cordwood lay piled up, a pair of barberry bushes clung to a projecting pier of a building and seemed with their dark-red berries to mock at the neighbouring clumps of rowan, which were already turning yellow. All this was taken in only with a fleeting glance; and, tired of viewing but longing for a midday meal—to which all who knew Jürgass looked forward with perfect confidence—the couples now mounted several tall steps that rose beside the bowling enclosure and led to a long structure built partly of stone and partly of brick: the old refectory.

It was a high, half-ruined hall still covered by a protecting roof only at its lower end. Beneath this shelter a long table had been laid: at one end there blazed a huge open fire, while six monastic servitors clad in helmets and corselets stood along it three on either side, all bearing torches in their hands. The 'Ah!' that arose constituted the real triumph of the day for their courier.

They took their places. Lewin, who during the visit to the church had struck up a friendship with the fair Matushka more speedily than was his custom in such matters, was seated between her and Kathinka. Jürgass presided: with the flames of the fire flickering high at his back, he rose to address to them a few words of greeting.

'I bid you welcome, my friends, to these halls in which I myself am a guest. *How* I gained access to them is my secret. Whether it was Frater Hermannus* who, reciting his proph-ecies, conducted me in person around kitchen and cellar, or whether, from a time closer at hand, the family ring of my cousins, the Bredows, here worked its wonders, must be things hidden in the mists of obscurity. It suffices that we are here and that the table is laid. And now, attendant brothers, to your work!'

These last words were directed to four monks standing on either side of his chair who, in spite of a valiant endeavour to appear as Lehnin Cistercians, had been unable to prevent themselves from looking like fancy-dress capuchins. They were wearing brown cowls girded round with a length of cord, and while one of them began filling the tankards with Werder beer and a second to hand round the boar's head and then the haunch of venison, the two remaining strode slowly down the hall as far as the spot where the roof ceased and the last remnants of daylight fell on to the floor. Here there was a trapdoor, of ancient or more recent construction, through which one of the brothers now disappeared bearing a blazing wooden taper, while the other, who remained standing beside the opening, looked down from time to time inquisitively into the cellar below. Soon bottles—which, since they wore neither dust nor cobwebs, could not have been lying for very long —were handed up and taken into custody by the brother beside the trapdoor, who then, with a dexterity well worthy of the school of Jürgass, began to draw the corks and to pour the golden-shimmering Rhine-wine into the large drinking-glasses. His fellow monk (he of the burning taper) remained below in the cellar and was thought of no more.

In the meantime, conversation at the table had become lively; the ladies were in a frolicsome mood, but the most frolicsome of all was Lewin, who—not insensible of the fact that the fair countess seemed to have taken a fancy to him —derived most pleasure from knowing that he was finally playing before Kathinka a role other than that of the dreamer she mocked. The teasing she indulged in, which increasingly betrayed an element of jealousy or wounded vanity, served only to enhance his sense of well-being.

'Did you notice the White Lady,' he asked the countess, turning towards her, 'when we looked into the staircase-tower? I was horrified; she was a perfect picture of disappointed love.'

The countess laughed; Kathinka, however, talking past Lewin, said to her: 'Don't believe him, Wanda; he knows nothing of disappointed love. He is never to be trusted, the stories he tells least of all. What is lacking in them he invents.'

'All the better,' said Matushka. 'I don't care for true stories. True stories are always boring or ugly. Tell me about the White Lady, Herr von Vitzewitz. Use your discretion, of course, but make it something nice: a monk, love, desire.'

'Ah, dear Countess, there you have already told the story yourself. A monk, love, desire—that is all there is to it.'

'Oh, can't you add a little more?'

'I dare not, however much I might wish to oblige you: such stories are very sensitive, and take it ill if you try to touch them, let alone improve them. The White Lady goes up and down stairs looking for the monk she loves. But he hides from her. Then at sunset she steps out on to the balcony and, as though she has now seen him, stretches her arms out longingly towards him. But it is only an illusion. Then she goes and sits in the shadow of the wall and weeps.'

'That is nice,' said Matushka, and a trace of sorrow and understanding fluttered across her laughing countenance: for she was not as carefree as she seemed. Kathinka, however, tossed her head and said: 'I don't like to hear about disappointed love.'

'And yet the world is full of it,' Lewin replied.

'Perhaps that is why I don't like it. It is so commonplace, so deadly, always the same. I don't understand disappointed love.'

'The rich never understand that there are people who are poor.'

But Kathinka was not listening; instead, in her predilection for paradox not shrinking from even the most daring flights, she now indulged herself in a playful amplification of the sentiment she had just uttered:

'If love cannot be satisfied it ought not to exist at all. I do not recall having read in the Bible—I mean in the Old Testament, when human beings were more human—of any instance of disappointed love. David's love was satisfied, Solomon's was even more. If anything, perhaps it was satisfied *too* well. Disappointed love is a modern invention, like printing or the spinning-wheel. Yes, like the spinning-wheel, that hums and buzzes and goes on spinning its tear-stained thread for ever.'

The countess listened in astonishment; but, rather encouraged than abashed by this attention, Kathinka continued with increasing abandonment: 'And now we even have a "White Lady" in love with a monk. You don't fall in love with monks. Or if you do happen to do so—and it suddenly seems to me that from now on I intend to love only monks—then you must love him in such a fashion that no monastery in the world is able to hold or hide him. But *pardon*, Wanda! You are supposed to laugh: that's why I'm talking in this way. I shan't apologize to Lewin, because I can see that he believes everything I have just said.'

All this time it had been growing darker, and now the gable-topped wall on the side opposite the fire was illumined only by the grey of dusk, occasionally brightened by the flickering of the torches standing higher up the hall. In this uncertain light they could see, however, that outside it must have started to snow, for large flakes were visible falling one by one through the open roof. They all began to feel chilly, and the ladies tugged their fur coats higher up around their necks. This was the atmosphere Jürgass required; he now arose and prepared to append to the words of greeting he had spoken at the beginning of the meal the actual oration of the day.

'You have been pleased', he began, 'to be my guests in Lehnin, in that same Lehnin whose predictions, indited four hundred years ago by Frater Hermannus, the enemies of Prussia have so often and so triumphantly recalled, and especially now, in these days of humiliation in which spiteful ingenuity has thought to see that hour come foretold us in the prophecy: "And the last of his line shall have the sceptre struck from his hand." But these enemies of Prussia have not read to the end, and we who are of a different persuasion, we see in these days a different, fairer prophecy fulfilled, a prophecy which, after these words of grief, goes on to say: "And the March shall forget all its sorrows, and no stranger shall henceforth triumph over it." Yes, my friends, *this* is the hour that has come, and because it has come, here in this hall, which shall soon—this too is foretold to us—shine out upon the land in the splendour of a new golden roof—I cry: *Vivat Borussia*! But what was born of night, let it sink back into night. *Pereat Bonaparte*!'*

The *pereat*! died away without, for the moment at least, eliciting any response; for, as Jürgass was still enunciating these closing words, an obscure smoky light had become visible down the hall, rising out of the depths at just the spot where the trapdoor might be supposed to lie, and out of this smoky light there had appeared trembling and shaking first a hat of a very familiar shape, then a short French uniform jacket with limply hanging sleeves and an array of singularly fashioned fingers of which it was impossible to say whether they belonged to a human hand or were the truncated branches of roots. The apparition hovered for a moment, gazing down the hall headless and eyeless; then it sank again into the depths out of which it had arisen: and the trapdoor fell back with a crash that resounded round the hall.

Only then was the spell lifted; Counts Seherr-Thoss and Zierotin, who were seated nearest to Jürgass, re-echoed the *pereat*! and, swiftly recovering their mirth, all the other guests joined in. Only Hirschfeldt was silent; in the world outside he had in battle against the 'arch-enemy of mankind' acquired a respect for him that made it hard to take pleasure in such a scene as this, which recalled to him the braggart tone of the Gensdarmes Regiment.

Conversation continued a little while longer, and Kathinka proposed a brief and succinctly expressed toast to their courier; then the latter rose and, indicating the fire in the grate, which had almost expired, said: 'It is coming to an end, and with it our feast.'

This was the signal for the party to break up. The torch-bearers conducted them along the hall, and as they passed it they saw that, perhaps because the draught of air from above had driven the falling flakes harder against the wall, the trapdoor was buried more deeply in snow than was the rest of the open part of the hall. Jürgass, who was at the head of the procession, pointed to it and said: 'Buried in snow.' And with these words they reached the exit, descended the tall stone steps outside and took their places in the sleighs, which were already drawn up awaiting them.

Fifteen minutes later Lehnin and its church, the refectory and the 'apparition in the little hat' all lay behind them like a dream, and the chatter and laughter of the travellers echoed through the silent forest.

To re-enliven the conversation, it had been agreed that, at every change of horses, they themselves should change partners. Lewin made the journey as far as the first halt in the company of Jürgass, from whom he learned through what ancient connections at Lehnin he had been able to effect the theatricals at the luncheon party; at the exchange of places at Gross-Kreuz, however, Jürgass found himself by the side of Countess Matushka, while Kathinka requested Lewin for her partner.

'You seem to be afraid of me; but fear, my dear friend, is always folly. Since you neglected to choose me, I chose you. That is how it always is: the misfortune we think to flee runs after us.'

And before she had finished speaking the sleigh on whose

narrow back-seat Lewin had taken his place was flying along the avenue of oak-trees out of Gross-Kreuz; then it turned on to the narrow pathway beside the river that ran between the seemingly endless ice- and snow-covered expanses of the Havel-land and the precipitate banks of the Havel itself.

They had gone a considerable distance without attempting to converse or even exchanging a single word; at length Lewin, bending forward, said: 'Give me your hand, Kathinka.'

She did so, and he covered it with kisses. 'I cannot live without you,' he said into her ear. 'Have pity on me; tell me you love me. You write to me that I must not be silly and not daydream: ah, it is you, Kathinka, who must cure me of that.'

She did not reply. The only sound was the snorting of the horses and the jangling of the bells: but Lewin felt nothing but her breath and heard nothing but the hammering of his own heart.

'Do you still remember New Year's Eve, when we drove to Guse and memorized the verses? It was an enchanting journey and I was so happy.'

Kathinka nodded.

'But Tubal was with us then, and I said a hundred times in my heart: "Oh, how I wish we were alone!" And now we are alone, Kathinka . . . You said I was afraid. Yes, one is afraid in face of one's happiness.'

She withdrew her hand; but he felt she did not do so in displeasure and continued in a tone of increasing agitation: 'Yes, alone with you; in that lies all my happiness. Ah, if only this hour could expand and become my whole life, and I could ride on like this through the world with you, in wind and snow, and feel nothing but your hair blowing in my face.'

It seemed to him that his words had not gone unheeded, for her voice sounded different from her usual voice when she now said softly: 'Give me the reins, Lewin.'

'You have them, today and always.'

'But I need my arms freer if I am to take them; assist me.'

And he removed the silken cloak from her arms and shoulders and placed the reins in her hand.

As though they felt the grip on them tighten, the horses at once began to step out in a livelier fashion, and the cloak, caught in the wind they made, fluttered about Lewin's glowing face. In the pleasure evoked by the way they were flying along, Kathinka sank deeper into the seat and laid her shoulder gently on to his chest: an infinite desire filled his heart and burned and quivered in every drop of his blood. But the shy reserve that was his inborn inheritance again overcame him, and he tremblingly pressed on to her neck only a single kiss.

Thus they stayed for several minutes; then Kathinka said: 'The wind is too keen, Lewin; help me into my cloak again.' It almost sounded like mockery. He felt it to be so, but obeyed her.

Now they were both silent, and their sleigh flew over the Havel bridges. The stars stood icy clear in the winter sky, the fields of snow flashed and sparkled, and soon the domes of the *communs* and the broad bulk of the New Palace again rose to sight in the silvery grey twilight. Here stood the Jägertor, and there the relay of fresh horses was waiting. Lewin and Kathinka were the first arrivals; he assisted her from her seat and kissed her hand. She gave him a long but amicable look and, laying weight on each word, said merely: 'You are a child.'

It was not long before the other sleighs drew up; the horses were changed, and so were the places; Tubal again took the seat beside his sister.

And thus they raced off again in the direction of Berlin.

16

Kathinka

THE winter stars that had sparkled so brightly in the sky during the return ride from Lehnin had promised a clear day on the morrow, and that clear day had now arrived. Where the sun shone hotly down it melted the snow from the roofs, and when towards midday it had almost reached the highest point of its ascent it gazed hotly past the tower of the Nikolaikirche down into Kathinka's room. It was so blinding and oblique a ray of light that came in through the tall window that the green blind had had to be lowered halfway, yet even now every object was still brightly illumined, and it was this, together with the little flower-table set with fresh hyacinths, that enhanced the impression of comfort and cosiness the well-tended room at all times presented. Several things in it had been altered over the past two or three days. Before the sofa on which the aged countess had sat enthroned on the evening they had planned the excursion to Lehnin and, after at first waging war with almost every member of the company, had in the end concluded peace with them all, the little round table across which the clash of opinions had taken place was missing, and all that lay there was a large carpet, a masterpiece of Brussels weaving upon which Lady Venus flew through the air drawn by her doves. It was the same carpet whose vivid illustration had attended Lewin in his dreams on that Christmas journey to Hohen-Vietz where we first made his acquaintanceship: for the last visit he had paid that day had been to the house of the Ladalinskis.

That was now a month ago, however, and today it was Kathinka who sat on the sofa and gazed down at the carpet and its illustration. But, though she was looking at it, she did not see it: other pictures filled her mind, laughing and gaily coloured pictures, yet shrouded too in shadow. What was it that cast a shadow over them?

She seemed to be expecting someone—in any event she looked up from time to time and listened in the direction of the door. But all remained silent, and growing increasingly rest-less, she finally stood up and crossed over to the flower-table, then to the standing mirror to make some adjustment or other to her dress. She was wearing a morning outfit similar to the one she had worn during the conversation with her father on the day of her return from Guse: a dark white-bordered morning frock with a cape and large, pearshaped hooks fastened over mother-of-pearl buttons. No one would have noticed the slightest thing amiss with her appearance, only she herself seemed dissatisfied, continually rearranged her hair and fussed with the muslin scarf she was wearing lightly knotted about her throat. Then she went back to the sofa, threw herself into a corner and laid a foot on a low stool she had previously placed on the carpet. In the sofa-corner there lay a book: she opened it and attempted to read; but the effort was vain, she could not force herself to concentrate.

At this moment Count Bninski entered unannounced and she drew her foot down from the sofa-cushion without otherwise altering her position. It seemed as though they had already spoken together that morning; for now they uttered no word of greeting. He stepped up to her and kissed her hand.

'What do you have?' she asked, her calm restored.

'The decision.'

'Then tell me, tell me,' she went on, tapping the fingers of her left hand with her index finger. 'I know it all, and yet I still want to hear it from you. How did it go? I hope nothing was said or done to offend you.'

'No,' the count replied, seating himself on the stool and taking Kathinka's hand. 'He heard me out quietly. When I had finished, he laid aside the ivory knife which he had as usual been toying with and said, I think I remember his exact words: "You have not surprised me, Count; I have expected, I may say dreaded, this proposal. You will know without my assurance that this remark is not directed at you personally. To offer you the completest proof of the fact would be easy if in doing so I would not be obliged to touch on matters and impose conditions which would injure you in another respect and never secure your acquiescence." '

Kathinka smiled.

'The same old story,' she said.

'Yes,' Bninski went on, 'he will have it that he has broken with Poland, with our country, once and for all, and, to be brief, he concluded by saying that a union between us was impracticable and, he believed, impossible for two reasons: on account of the court and on account of the things he remembers. The latter I understand, the former not.'

'And yet both belong together,' Kathinka answered; 'we owe it to him to admit that. He needs the court. Because he burned his bridges and, for good or ill, transplanted himself and us from our own soil into a foreign soil, he cannot do without especially favourable conditions if he is to strike new roots in this foreign soil. And I don't need to tell you that, among these favourable conditions, the chief one is the sun-shine of the court.'

'Perhaps,' said Bninski, 'or, if you like, certainly. What I don't understand is why he should have chosen precisely *this* soil. And *that* he chose it now decides our fate. For what he seemed to suggest, that I too should conclude a peace with this country—never, never, Kathinka. Not even for your sake.'

He stood up and clasped his hands violently together. Then, as though trying to make clear to himself the cause of old Ladalinski's perversity, he continued in a kind of monologue: 'Whatever was it that drew him here? *Him*, of all people? It remains an enigma and a contradiction. For he possesses to superfluity that nobility of mind whose total absence in this country makes this country so repugnant to me. He is capable of great sacrifice and great resolution, and even the calamitous step that drove him into self-exile bears the stamp of an act of renunciation. And what is it that reigns here? Privilege, arrogance, and the swaggering braggart!'

'With you, too, it is the same old story,' said Kathinka.

But Bninski was not listening; without moving from where he stood he continued in growing agitation: 'He is a pedant. As such, of course, he is in the right place here. For all that flourishes here is rules and formalities, accounting and routine, and added to these that ugly poverty that is the mother, not of simplicity, but only of cunning and miserliness. Mean and stingy: that is the motto of this country. When I was a child I read in school at Cracow that Old Fritz's grenadiers wore waistcoats that weren't waistcoats at all but only triangles of cloth stitched directly on to the jackets of their uniforms. And whether that was true or not, I see this triangle of cloth here in all and everything. A system stitched together, cunning and deception, and with it all a deeply rooted idea that one is something very singular and special. And what is the purpose of it? It is all in aid of that belligerency and rapacity that always goes with poverty. They are never satisfied, this nation; without polish, without style, without anything beneficial or pleasing, they have only *one* desire: to grab more and more! And when they have finally grabbed too much they set aside what they don't need and woe to him who lays hands on it. A nation of pirates that operates on land! But always with a *Te deum* on its lips, always in the service of God or the faith or the most exalted ends. For in this country there has never been any shortage of banners and slogans.'

'I can no longer recognize you,' Kathinka interrupted. 'You start by being in the right and talk yourself into the wrong. You must yourself feel how much prejudice and bitterness are carrying you away into exaggeration.'

'No, I am not exaggerating. I am only reading the reverse side of the medal, because that is the side I *want* to read. Let someone else turn it over again and rejoice in the splendours that now become visible: that is quite all right with me. There may be something of greatness here, only I have nothing to gain from it, and neither has *he*,' and he pointed in the direction of the privy councillor's study on the other side of the house. 'Neither has *he*, I say, for he is a Pole from head to toe. He doesn't deceive me with his pretence of Prussian loyalism. Prussia! Why Prussia, which sold us for thirty pieces of silver? True, Prussia itself is now in fetters: but for how much longer? . . . Prussia! Prussia! Why not France? Why not Russia, radically rotten though it is? In the midst of its sins it at least has the courage to acknowledge them. But no, it had to be Prussia. And this Prussia, in which to satisfy a mere whim of fancy the Ladalinski line is to blossom anew and put down roots, must now step between you and me, and in an age in which, thank God, more princes are born on the battlefield than in princely beds, our happiness is to vanish like a feather in the wind in case a couple of contemptible little princelings should fail to smile. Shall it vanish, Kathinka? Are you resolved?'

She made no reply.

'Do we love one another?'

'You say we do.'

'Then I see only *one* course for us. And you will have the resolution to take it. I believe so, I hope so.'

Kathinka laid a hand to her brow; then, as though recalling something from the past, she said: 'I promised him not to do anything that could undermine his position or expose him to new suspicions of disloyalty to this country.'

'And this promise you shall keep. Flight will throw all the blame on *us*.'

'And yet I hesitate,' Kathinka went on. 'It is not that I am afraid of taking my share of this blame. You know how I am: if I feel any fear it is nothing to the thrill I get from the risk we are taking. No, it is not for my sake but for *yours* that I hesitate; for love of you. You ought not to put yourself in a false position. And that is what you will do. What bitter reproaches there will be . . . from Tubal . . . '

'. . . From Lewin . . .'

'Don't speak his name. I can't bear to hear it: for there is no one I have hurt more or to whom I owe more. And now I am going to hurt him more than ever! He loves me, and I have been fond of him since we were children. That is now over with. But you are wrong to think that bitter reproaches will ever fall from *his* lips. Not from him; but the others! Recall to mind when, at the ball, you heard of General York's capitulation, and think of the sarcastic "*Sans doute*" with which you spoiled the old countess's solemn story of the Crown Prince's confirmation ring. What was the meaning of all that? A profound contempt for what in this country calls itself "German loyalty". And now I ask you, are *we* being loyal, are *you*?'

'I am not being its opposite,' Bninski replied.

Kathinka shook her head.

The count, however, went on: 'And if it is as you think, Kathinka, then speak, let me see that it is so, and I shall not try to conceal what it is I am doing. I am no knight of La Mancha, set on expelling disloyalty from the world; I have no desire to abolish it, and least of all to foster the idea that I myself have outgrown it or am above it. Disloyalty! It was there at the beginning and will be there at the end: I am not afraid of the word and not even of the act. But the virtuous face it puts on in this country, *that* I hate. What I find repugnant is the lie. And I know one thing: it is *not* a lie when I call what is to happen neither breach of faith nor disloyalty but compulsion and cause and effect and self-defence. What has been taken from us we take back. Against the artificial rights of your father, which would sacrifice us to considerations that remain incomprehensible to me, we shall oppose our natural rights, the rights of our feelings.'

He stopped, and it was only to break the painful silence that followed that he added: 'Look to the future, Kathinka. There are better days ahead. They will be reconciled to it: the *fait accompli* is more persuasive than a thousand pleas and arguments.'

'You do not understand him,' she said: 'like all good and weak men, he is obstinate. I may call him that, for he has always been weak with regard to me ever since I was a child. He will not hate us, his love for me will still be what it was, but he will *not* be reconciled to what we have done and will *not* make his peace with us. I know what it is I am doing. When I leave we shall never see one another again!'

The count paced back and forth. When he again returned to the sofa she took his hand and, gazing up at him with an expression she had never worn before, said: 'And so be it, Jarosh! I feel that all is concluded, and not merely by us. We have inherited everything: first our blood and then our guilt. I have always been my mother's child: now I am her child entirely. Be good to me: for now I have no one but you.'

And she threw herself into his arms.

17

At Hansen-Grell's

Two days after this colloquy between Kathinka and Bninski, Lewin was sitting surrounded by letters that were awaiting a reply. Some, lines from Doctor Faulstich and Aunt Amelie among them, had already been lying beneath the paper-weight for so long that he could no longer delay responding to them and his failure to attend his three lectures—for Friday had again come round—could be regarded rather as a demand of duty than an instance of neglect. Frau Hulen, who passed through the room from time to time in her Old Berlin-style slippers stitched together from odds and ends of material, shook her head to see the letters lying spread out on the sofa-table accumulate every fifteen minutes, some of them not even finished but with only the first page written—for Lewin hated blotting with sand, a point on which he was, exceptionally, in accord with Kathinka.

'When you scatter sand on a love-letter', Kathinka was wont to say, 'you bury the love in it.'

He had been writing for two hours but had still not written the principal letter: the letter to Renate. He had saved it until last: a chatty discourse with his sister would make up for the toil and effort expended on the others. The letter to Faulstich had been a literary essay, that to Aunt Amelie had, as usual, been like dancing on eggs; but all these lay behind him and he could now relax and give free rein to his pen.

Dear Renate! [he wrote],
It is now the 29th, and it is not without shame that I read the date of your letter of the middle of the month. My hasty reply to it was no reply at all. Let me try to catch up on what I have neglected.

As you will have read in the newspapers, many important things have happened this week and last; what Papa wrote to me has in fact come about. The confirmation of the Crown Prince was followed by the King's departure for Breslau; the entire court accompanied him, even the Guards. Since then Potsdam has been as though dead, a fact we were able to confirm for ourselves on the occasion of an excursion we made to Lehnin. Perhaps I might tell you about this excursion, which took place last Tuesday. As you know—or possibly you don't—Lehnin is an ancient Cistercian abbey; most of the Ascanians were buried there, and some of the Hohenzollerns* too: Johann Cicero, if I am not mistaken, and Joachim Nestor. But these two were hardly in their tombs before the secularization came, and their great metal coffins were moved from the crypt to the crypt of Berlin Cathedral. There is also a Lehnin Prophecy, '*Vaticinium Lehninense*', in a hundred Latin verses, which foretell the destruction of the Hohenzollerns and the restoration of the Catholic faith in the March of Brandenburg; but it is all very obscure and imprecise, so that, as so often with such things, you can, if you want to, interpret it in precisely the opposite sense. Well, the previous week this Lehnin came up in conversation, and the privy councillor, who recited a couple of verses out of this prophecy, which he had got to know of years ago through our Director Bellermann,* suddenly betrayed a lively enthusiasm, quite unusual for him, for becoming acquainted with the abbey. All respect to the old gentleman, but I am bound to say I received the impression he had the idea of continuing his recitation at the place where it originated and of thus impressing us with a kind of medieval classicism. But his enthusiasm did not endure, and when the Tuesday came he was not among the participants. Jürgass had already been named as our courier. By Kathinka, naturally. In addition to her and the narrower Ladalinski circle, Counts Matushka, Seherr-Thoss and Zierotin with their young wives made up the party. We were treated to one surprise after another; Jürgass maintained his reputation as a master of ceremonies; Countess Matushka was enchanting, and I enjoyed the triumph of seeing Kathinka jealous. On the return journey we travelled some distance together. I addressed her very warmly, perhaps a little more than warmly, and she listened in a very amiable fashion. Bninski is soon to be leaving us; he is going to his estates, and from there to Warsaw to place himself at the disposal of the Viceroy, who is a friend of his. He does not get on well with Poniatowski. It would be stupid to say that I do not look forward to the day of his departure. Kathinka pays him a lot of attention, but it is not her way to concern herself with people once they are gone or to dwell on old memories: she lives for the hour, and the hour is, it seems, a favourable one for me. I have again come to believe in the possibility I may be fortunate and happy. She wrote to me recently: 'Stop daydreaming, Lewin.'

And now let me ask: How are things in Hohen-Vietz? What are our friends doing: Seidentopf, Aunt Schorlemmer, Marie? Just think, I dreamed of her last night, and what did I see her as? As a bride. She stood in a long, long veil before the altar but it was not at the church at Hohen-Vietz. Her dress was white and as light as her veil and strewn with little stars. She looked very lovely, and who do you think her bridegroom was? Drosselstein. Not our old Drosselstein but a younger version, tall and slim and clad in a uniform in which I have never seen our friend from Hohen-Ziesar. When I reflected on this dream this morning, I had to recall what you have so often said of Marie: that you wouldn't be surprised to see a golden coach drive up at Kniehase's and the little princess, her eyes full of tears but at the same time shining with joy, take her place beside her prince. In this you have read her nature aright. It was the right thing for her to have rejected Othegraven's proposal. I disapproved of it at the time; it seemed to me a piece of foolishness, if not something worse. But I did her an injustice. He is from the land of Münster and she is from Fairyland, and Westphalia is the last place on earth a fairy can come to terms with.

I wrote to Faulstich and Aunt Amelie this morning. I wasn't happy with either letter. I never know how to write to our countess aunt:

what I ought to do is collect anecdotes and *bon mots* in a box and whenever I owe her a letter simply empty out this box. But that is the kind of thing I am incapable of: I sometimes feel acutely my lack of adroitness, and do so all the more in that it is the trait in me Kathinka cannot forgive.

I shall be seeing her this evening, Tubal as well. Tubal is together a lot with Bninski, and with Captain von Hirschfeldt, an excellent officer who was in Spain (on the English side), a fact that doesn't prevent him from being on friendly terms with the count. The last time I saw Tubal—it was in Lehnin while we were visiting the church—he asked me: 'When we are going to Hohen-Vietz?' I leave it an open question whether he was thinking of enrolling in the Lebus militia or of his cousin Renate.

And now farewell. I look more cheerfully into the future than I have done for a long time. Everything promises well, great things and small: and the small things are the main things, for they concern us the most. Remember me to Papa and to our friends.

Your Lewin.

It was now one o'clock, and, since the walk he would be taking at midday would in any case take him past the main post office building, Lewin put himself to the trouble of personally handing in the five letters that were the result of his efforts of that morning. Next to the post office stood the Ladalinski house; he gazed up at it, but the blinds were down in all the rooms on the first floor, even the privy councillor's. He puzzled for a moment over what the cause of this could be, but forgot all about it again when, on the corner of the Stechbahn, he encountered Jürgass, with whom he proceeded to discuss the next meeting of Kastalia.

'Until Tuesday!' they said in parting, and, after he had taken a simple midday meal at his usual place in the Taubenstrasse, Lewin made for the Wallstrasse, whose lengthy course followed that of the former Berlin city wall. Thence he turned, not far from the Spittelmarkt, into the Kreuzgasse, a street consisting of old and stately houses somewhat come down in the world.

In one of these old and stately houses dwelt Hansen-Grell: his plainness and simplicity had drawn Lewin strongly to him from the first, as had the almost contradictory romantic traits that also characterized him; and, though an invitation to pay him a visit had never actually been proffered, when they had parted two days previously after a chance meeting and a long and very exhaustive conversation, Lewin had resolved to call on Grell at home even without one. He lived on a high ground-floor: eight or ten stone steps, well worn and enclosed by twisted iron railings, led up to it. On the door there stood, written in a thick pen on half a card, the name *Hansen-Grell*.

Lewin knocked.

'Come in!'

The door was divided into three panels and only the first opened, offering a gap just wide enough for a man to squeeze through sideways. Lewin traversed this defile and found himself in a large room some fourteen feet high in which at first glance he could make out only four bare yellow walls and a huge black Dutch-stile stove. As he entered four narrow strips of curtain began to sway sluggishly in the draught caused by the opening of the door. But this impression of bareness and desolation did not persist for very long, and the room's more cheerful features soon came into their own. Inside the stove the peat had burned down so far that the sight of the quivering blue flames served to reconcile you to this least pleasant of heating fuels, while from a folding table that stood beside it covered with books little curling clouds of vapour arose as if welcoming the arriving guest. Hansen-Grell was in the act of preparing his afternoon coffee.

'Just one moment,' he called and, setting the pot of boiling water, which he had only half emptied, back on to the glowing peat in the stove, he advanced towards Lewin and, after having removed at any rate the worst of the soot from his hand by rubbing it vigorously against the sleeve of his jacket, extended it do him.

'I am heartily glad to see you,' he said, 'especially at this hour, when the warmth of the stove and the steaming coffee are available to do the honours of the house. You will join me, I hope. As you can see, my domestic economy is somewhat restricted, but in the matter of cups I can compete with any gossiping housewife.'

Lewin made to reply, but Hansen-Grell went on: 'Oh, no, no, don't imagine you are depriving me: here is the coffee and there is the water. I could entertain the whole of Kastalia and not notice it. Do please take a seat while I look for my best Dresden china. You shall have the gilded cup with a cupid and a shepherdess who is laughing and weeping because she has been struck by his dart. Could you have imagined I had a passion for such trifles? It is an after-effect of my Copenhagen days. The old count was a passionate collector.'

While saying these words Hansen-Grell had betaken himself to a cupboard sunk into one of the thick walls of the room that Lewin had not previously noticed and begun searching not only for the promised Dresden cup but, in order to make a more respectable showing, also for a sugar-bowl which he clearly remembered having seen on one of the shelves. He himself always used sugar straight out of the paper bag it was bought in.

In the meantime, as his host, still somewhat embarrassed, continued to chatter on, Lewin had accepted his invitation and, brushing aside the curtains, had sat himself down in one of the deep window-bays. Here there stood two rush-chairs, on one of which a couple of books lay open, and while Hansen-Grell, whose conversation had by now deteriorated to hardly more than the utterance of exclamations of astonishment, carried on hunting for the still undiscovered sugar-bowl, Lewin took one of them up and looked into it. It was the poems of Hölderlin.* On one of the opened pages there stood four lines:

> In younger days I greeted with joy the dawn,
> I wept at evening; now, in my older years,
> My day begins in doubting, yet
> Holy and cheerful is to me its close.

Lewin was powerfully impressed by these lines, but he was not to be left to enjoy this impression for long: Hansen-Grell had now found everything he thought he needed and, after cautiously treading his path across the great distance separating the stove and the window, presented to his guest a cup of coffee filled to the brim.

The latter took, sipped and commended it, and then said: 'I am surprised to find you with Hölderlin. From the picture I had formed of you, I imagined you wedded for ever to "Lenore starting up at dawn".* I can allow you the "Wild Huntsman" or "Chevy Chase" at most, but Hölderlin? No.'

Hansen-Grell had seated himself on the other rush-chair and crossed his legs comfortably; now, clasping his hands over his knee, he said: 'There you touch on a sore point in my nature, a contradiction in it, if you like. Perhaps in many others as well. It is quite true that, so far as my sensibilities and, if I may speak of such insignificant things, my poems are concerned, I belong entirely to the new school; I hold, for good or ill, with the Romantics, and I shall never dream of anything but Nordic princesses and victorious dragon-slayers. And if the contrivances of Romanticism sometimes become too much for me, then, in compliance with the law of opposites, I am wont to throw myself passionately into things rococo, and am not afraid even of powdered wigs and hooped skirts. But never anything classical, either in form or content.'

Lewin smiled and indicated the book lying between them.

'I am coming to that,' Hansen-Grell continued; 'it is that which led me to speak just now of a contradiction. I shall never have a classical sensibility, never so much as try to construct a hexameter, let alone an Alcaic strophe, and yet whenever I come into contact with this classical world I fall beneath its spell, and for as long as this enchantment lasts look down on anything like a folk-song as though it were mere street-singing. All naïve poetry then seems to me like a pretty village girl at a court ball: she is still pretty, but the gaudiness and capriciousness of her finery make the charms she actually does possess seem inferior.'

'There I cannot agree with you,' Lewin replied. 'You yourself have supplied the phrase that seems to me the vital one: "for as long as the enchantment lasts". That is the point. "*Toujours perdrix*"* also applies in art, and all excess awakens the desire for its opposite.'

'Perhaps "*Toujours perdrix*" is the answer,' said Hansen-Grell, 'but my own experience none the less leads me to seek it elsewhere. Perhaps you have observed something similar. Our poetic productions—and this is the point I want to lay weight on—accord with our *nature* but not necessarily with our *taste*. The latter is able to rise above the former. If we want to bring them into harmony with one another; if our taste, which determines what we *read*, is also to determine what we *produce*; then nature, whose paths are different, leaves us in the lurch, and we come to grief. We have had our will, certainly, but what we have borne is dead.'

Lewin made to reply, but Hansen-Grell continued in an animated development of his idea: 'However, so far as our Swabian Hyperion★ is concerned,' and he tapped his finger on the book before him, 'the contradiction I confessed to at the beginning can perhaps be resolved in a much simpler way. All the classicism of his form notwithstanding Hölderlin is a Romantic through and through. May I read you my favourite poem of his?'

'Please do.'

It was already growing dark: but, since Hansen-Grell as good as knew the verses by heart, he needed very little light to read them by:

> 'One summer grant me, one, O ye Destinies,
> And then one autumn that my song may ripen
> And that my heart, replete with that sweet
> Music, more willingly may die then.
>
> Denied its right divine in life, the soul will
> Find no repose below in Orcus either;
> But if what's holy to me, what lies
> In my heart of hearts, the poem, stands
>
> Achieved, then welcome, silence of the shadows!
> I am content even if my lyre cannot
> Be with me on the journey; once I
> Lived like the gods, and more is not needed.'★

He laid down the book and continued without pausing: 'These are Alcaic strophes, classical in form and structure, and yet they have a Romantic sound in spite of Orcus and the shadow-world and gods of classicism.' Only now did he look up at Lewin.

The latter remained silent; but his silence said more than the wildest exclamations of enthusiasm could have done. At last he said, as though to himself: 'How lovely, and how he has caught the mood!'

'Yes, that's it,' Grell resumed. 'The mood has been *caught*; and that is the whole point, that is what is decisive. It is now fashionable to talk of moods and of getting into a mood. But to *get* into a mood does not amount to very much. Only he who knows how to arrest this mood he has got into—this enigmatic, indefinite thing that floats along and away like a cloud—and at the same time to preserve in it its magical twilight vacillation—only *he* can be called a master.'

Lewin nodded, but distractedly: he had plainly been only half listening, and instead of vouchsafing a reply he merely repeated the poem's closing words: 'once I lived like the gods, and more is not needed.'

Hansen-Grell had risen, and his homely face, with its short straw-coloured hair and red eyelids, was transfigured from within to genuine beauty. 'Whether for art or for love, whether for freedom or for fatherland, *once* to live as the gods and then—die. Die soon, before the mighty feeling fades from memory.'

They continued talking for a while, absorbed in this theme; then Lewin said: 'Let us go out, Grell, twilight still hangs in the evening sky and it is easier to talk outdoors.'

And with that they left the house and walked across the Opernplatz to the Lustgarten and the Schlossfreiheit.

Behind the Sophienkirche the crescent moon was just rising.

18

Gone!

AT six o'clock Lewin was again in his room; the conversation he had had with Hansen-Grell was still echoing in his soul. He had never before experienced so nearly unalloyed the fair power of the ideal. During his visit he had been compelled to think more than once of Faulstich: and yet, though there were similarities, what a difference there was too! In their involvement with the arts, and in the pleasure they took in them, they were alike; but while the one savoured beauty with a delicate palate, the other strove after it with all his soul. What enfeebled and enervated the one, steeled and strengthened the other: so that Grell was a model, while Faulstich was a warning.

The evening glow that usually hung over the roofs of the city at this hour was absent today, and total darkness already reigned in Lewin's room. He knocked at Frau Hulen's door but she was not at home; the lamp with the green shade was also missing and could not be found in the neighbouring room either.

'Where has the old lady got to?' said Lewin in momentary annoyance at the 'disorder' in the house; but he at once laughed to himself and added: 'Well, it's the first time in eighteen months.'

He felt his way to the kitchen, raked around in the ashes in the hearth until they began to glow, and lit the wax-taper he was carrying. And then, shielding it so that he would not have the bother of lighting it again, he returned to his room.

It was only now he saw that a letter was lying on the table; the address, to all appearances written very hurriedly, seemed to be in Tubal's hand. What struck him most about it was the uncommonly large seal with which it was fastened: its contents, plainly, were to be concealed from unauthorized curiosity; and if Frau Hulen had any little weakness it lay in this direction.

Recalling this fact, Lewin smiled as he broke open the seal and, unfolding the sheet, held it closer to the flame of the taper and read it. The smile faded from his face. There were only three lines:

Do not come this evening; Kathinka has gone. In a note we found on her desk she bade us all farewell. You can guess the rest.

Your Tubal.

The letter fell from his hand and he himself sank back on to the sofa. For a minute he lay as though stunned. Then he sat up and laid his head in his hands, then on the table and the back of the sofa: but none of these could cool the heat that pulsed through it, and he leaped up and ran to the window. The pale crescent moon, just emerging from the clouds, looked down on him; across the road a pair of crows fluttered up; from below came the creaking of the street-lamps. The coolness of the window-pane did him good, but the anguish he felt remained and seemed to be rising higher. He had to have air, so he took a felt cap from the peg and went out on to the landing; he had reached the first step of the stairway when, suddenly remembering what he had left behind, he turned and retraced his steps, seized the lines lying on the table and tore them to pieces, and extinguished the still-burning taper. Only then did he leave the house.

He turned into the Königsstrasse; but the weight of the buildings oppressed him as his room had done, and he felt he had to get out of the city. So he kept to the right and then, crossing the Alexanderplatz, made for the Frankfurter Tor.

It was the same path he had taken on the day the badger hunt was supposed to have taken place in the Dalwitz Forest. The New World inn had then been shrouded in morning stillness, but as he now approached it he saw that all its windows were illuminated; he heard the sound of clarinets, and youthful couples who had found it too hot inside were standing outside under the snowy lime-trees. What did they care that there was a wind blowing or that there was snow lying everywhere? The next dance would warm them up again.

Lewin had gone to one of the two posts which, with the aid of a crossbeam set on top of them, constituted the somewhat primitive entrance to the New World inn, and was leaning against it. The music within was growing more and more lively. He beat time to it with his right foot and found the dance delightful. 'How nice to be in there! He who wants to dance is easy to play to, says the proverb. Why doesn't it say: He who is played to, dances!'

At that moment an arm was placed around his waist from behind, and a young little thing who must have crept up beside the hedge without his noticing it said familiarly: 'Come on, they're already tuning up. There's a Scottish reel still to go, and then you can take me and Malchen home.'

It sounded more roguish than importunate, and Lewin therefore turned around and took her hand; at this, however, the girl, who may have mistaken him for someone else and only now had a sight of his troubled and wild-looking face, started back in alarm and ran off across the forecourt back into the inn. Once inside, she must have told of her encounter, for two or three heads immediately appeared at the window and looked out inquisitively at the stranger.

They did not remain there for long, though, for the Scottish reel soon began in earnest, and as he walked on Lewin tried to adapt its rhythm to the rhythm of his march. And for a while he succeeded; but the rhythm of the dance was more insistent than any other, and, lapsing again and again out of the constrained tempo, he marched on down the rectilinear avenue of poplars in a strange alternation of dancing and walking. He passed the spot where, on his way to Schnatermann's expedition, he had for the first time been brought up against the wretchedness and misery of the retreat; none the less he now no longer recalled that moving encounter but continued only to count the measures of the music, even though he had long since ceased to hear it.

'To dance along like that', he said, 'is really life. The point is to take nothing seriously. I have always missed the best things, and I did so again today. She was pretty and not at all prudish. "You can take me and Malchen home . . . Don't be silly, Lewin." No, no, she didn't say that; that was earlier.'

He fell silent for a while, letting his thoughts run quietly on. 'And what after all was the affair of Johanna Susemihl all about? And what does it matter whether old Madame Zunz begrudged her the child or not! Now they are dead and only the *maréchal de logis* is, so I think, still alive. He had braid upon his hat and a tassel too thereon.* And *foreign* braid; yes, that's what does it; the new, the foreign. It has to be something different. Curiosity as in the days of Mother Eve.'

He had now gone past Friedrichsfelde; only when he turned could he still see the lights of the village. Not a star in the sky; over the crescent moon the clouds raced thicker and thicker, faster and faster: but faster still was the passage of the images that raced over his soul.

'How surprised Frau Hulen will be! I can see her searching for me with her little lamp, as though I were a concealed lover. And that is what I really am, too; only too well concealed; I shall never be found. She will look as bewildered as she did that time I read her the French nursery rhyme. "Clip-clop", she said; that wasn't such a stupid remark. How did it go, now?

> 'On the nameday of my granddaughter
> Everyone has a present for her.
> The baker sends her sugar-bread,
> The tailor sends a cloak of red . . . *

'Yes, that's how it went. "*Le boulanger fait un gâteau, la couturière un p'tit manteau*: that appeared to be the easiest bit and turned out to be hardest. I can still recall it . . . But what strange things happen: a French nursery rhyme between Friedrichs-felde and Dalwitz. But why not? Even stranger things happen sometimes.'

He was now passing through the village whose name he had just uttered. The ancient elm-lined roadway lay in darkness, and the houses, most of which stood set wide apart, had their shutters closed; but light fell into the street through the heart-shaped ornamental openings cut into them.

'Burning hearts,' he said; 'tomorrow they'll be clapped back against the wall and as black as before. And four hours' burning is quite enough. Here lives the parson: he burns for six.'

A hundred paces beyond the parsonage the village came to an end, and Lewin stepped out into open country. He was cold. Was it the night air or was it fever? He turned up his coat-collar and pulled down the flaps of his cap: but the chill remained.

'Wherever am I going? I don't know. Shall I turn round and go back? No. I can't endure all those houses, I can't breathe among them, they kill me. So forward. I shall end up somewhere.'

He continued on the way he was going: a quarter of a mile, a half-mile. To the right, at a turn in the road, was the silhouette of a church-tower.

'I am tired and, I almost believe, hungry.'

He sat himself on a pile of stones heaped up at the side of the road and gazed at the withered leaves dancing towards him across the smooth-trodden snow: for the wind, which for hours past had been sending thick banks of clouds ahead of it, had now itself arrived and was scouring among the poplars. It was a south-west wind, moist and full of little raindrops, but some of these raindrops had frozen again and smote him in the face like needles. 'Warm wind,' said Lewin; 'how does it go? The warm wind came from the midday sea . . . that's how it starts, I think; but I've forgotten the rest. All I can still picture are the characters, the count and the customs officer and the honest man. Which of them might I be? The count? No. But the honest man; yes, that's who I am, that is my role.'*

He looked up and down the road, and then said: 'It resembles the avenue of poplars that runs through the Bruch, and the shadow down there could be the church at Guse . . . That was four weeks ago, but it seems like a year.' He plunged his face into his hands and dreamed, and in his dream he heard ever more clearly the sound of distant bells. He listened to them, full of an increasing feeling of desire and longing, and at last he seemed to feel the tears begin to flow and it was as though a weight was lifted from his heavy-laden heart.

But it was not to be: fate had decided otherwise. The ringing of bells that he thought he had heard only in a dream came closer in reality, and before he had had time to recover himself he saw a vehicle approaching between the poplars from the direction of Dalwitz. Strangely enough it was not a sleigh, as the jingling had led him to suppose, but a light open carriage whose two little horses had, whether for amusement or out of an exaggerated caution, had a bell-harness strapped to them. And now the carriage was level with him; the horses shied and turned off to the right. A young couple were seated in the front seat, he with his arms folded and wrapped in a cloak, she tall and slim in a tight-fitting coat and a cap trimmed with fur. He could not make out her face, but she was holding the reins and she started violently when she caught sight of the figure sitting at the wayside. Only when they had reached the nearest poplar-tree did she again turn her eyes back to her companion and, to all appearance, begin speaking to him in the liveliest fashion.

Lewin beheld all this and, unaware of what he was doing, leaped up and attempted to follow the fast vanishing vehicle. He wanted to shout and cry out, but no sound came. And thus he continued running until his last strength gave out and he sank down without a sound in the middle of the roadway.

An hour later a sleigh halted before the inn at Bohlsdorf; the tower clock was just striking. The driver, who had risen from the fodder-sack he had been sitting on to unharness the horses, counted the strokes and grumbled to himself in annoyance: 'Eleven already; I shan't get home 'fore midnight; but I couldn't just leave him lying there.' So saying, he went over to the hedge where a pair of feeding-troughs were standing covered in snow, while from the direction of the yard and garden the burning brushwood in the high-walled baking-oven sent a bright glow over the hedge into the street beyond. The man stared into the glow, enjoying the warm breath that came with it, then, tipping the snow from one of the feeding-troughs, he dragged it over to his team and opened the sack of fodder. Feeling, perhaps, that they had been waiting long enough, the horses thrust their heads into the empty trough and began rummaging about in it. He gave them a slap: 'Just a moment, there', and, having at last emptied out their fodder for them, he stamped off into the inn room, where the loaves of bread were lying on two great trestles ready to go into the oven.

'Evening, innkeeper.'

'Evening, Damerow. Still on the road so late?'

'Yes, more's the pity. This old slushy weather gets right into your bones.'

'That it does. What would you like, Kirsch or Kümmel?'

'Give me a Kirsch. But wait a bit. I've got someone on the sleigh. He was lying like he was dead up by the milestone. I nearly ran over him.'

'D'you know who he is?'

'No. He looks like he's from the town, like a Berliner. Someone come out with me.'

The innkeeper's wife, who was still drying up, took a little lantern from the trestle, lit a candle-end, clicked the lantern shut again, and followed the man out into the road. They went to the rear of the sleigh, which possessed only two basket-work sides and was open at the back, the man pushed aside a bundle of straw that may have been serving as a blanket, and the innkeeper's wife then shone her light into the interior of the sleigh. The lantern at once fell from her hand and she gave a scream. Then she ran back into the house, shook her husband, who had fallen asleep in the alcove, and cried: 'Get up, Drews. Come, be quick. I do believe he's dead.'

'Who, who?' asked the innkeeper, emerging from sleep.

But his wife was already back at the door. 'God, God, who do you think? . . . The young master of Hohen-Vietz.'

BOOK FOUR

★

IN HOHEN-VIETZ AGAIN

In Bohlsdorf

IT was three days later. The Bohlsdorf innkeeper's wife was sitting in the alcove behind the guest-room bent over her child. She was singing it to sleep: her voice was gentle, and even gentler was the motion of the cradle as she rocked it. But this degree of caution was not really necessary, for the sick man lying in bed in the room above the alcove was still sunk in a heavy sleep—it was now the third day he had been lying thus—and deaf to all that went on around him. They had not yet been able to get a doctor, but he had not gone without nursing, if mere attendance and observation such as two women had been undertaking without pause since the previous day could be called that.

Noon had gone by and it might have been two o'clock; the sun, already declining again, shone through the window of a little gable-room and, as though it emanated from him himself, the sick man was suffused with a friendly glow.

'His forehead is damp,' said Aunt Schorlemmer. 'Go and rest, Renate. Just for fifteen minutes.'

'I am not tired.'

'You must be. Go.'

And she went: but not to rest, but to write to Hohen-Vietz a letter she had promised.

The little room that had been given up to her as soon as she had arrived lay under the gables on the other side of the house and was still in that state of disorder always produced by the first moment of arrival. There had not yet been time to make it tidy. The open travelling-case stood on two chairs, while cloak and muffs and an array of shawls and scarves had been thrown on to one of the two beds.

Even now Renate appeared indifferent to this confusion: she left everything as it was, and only drew the table closer to the window to obtain more light. Then she pulled aside the red linen tablecloth—it bore as a design a white peacock with its tail spread—and took from her case a Karlsbad writing-case which, when it was opened, formed a sloping writing-desk. But the ink had dried solid, so solid that even the addition of a few drops of water had no effect on it; she therefore had to seek elsewhere: she took from her notebook a thin pencil which turned out, of course, to be broken, sharpened it as well as she could, and then, in characters whose illegibility was exceeded only by their faintness, wrote the following:

Bohlsdorf, 1 February.
Dear Marie!

We arrived here yesterday at four o'clock and found our invalid in a deep sleep from which he has not yet awoken. How deep this sleep is was demonstrated this morning. I knocked over a poker standing beside the stove and was full of alarm, for it made a great noise: but Lewin only opened his eyes and then at once shut them again. He seemed to have recognized me; I saw him smile, though to be sure it was only like a smile in a dream, for sleep immediately overcame him again. We are expecting Doctor Leist any minute, and I shall not send off these lines until we have heard what he has to say.

What has happened to him? I have been able to learn little more than we already knew. Or what you, too, already know. A driver found him lying unconscious in the road, loaded him on to his sleigh, and delivered him here in Bohlsdorf. The innkeeper and his wife took him in and have been looking after him. He is lying in one of the gable-rooms; Aunt Schorlemmer and I are occupying the other; we are separated only by the corridor.

As to why he left Berlin and came here through wind and storm I can only venture suppositions. And of these I have indeed very few. It must have been something sudden, for he was only lightly clad in jacket and cap even though the night was wet and cold. An hour before the driver found him, the Bohlsdorf administrator, who with his wife was on his way back from one of the neighbouring villages, had seen him sitting on the milestone on the chaussée. The young wife (very pretty) was with me this morning and told me of the encounter. She had been as startled to see him as if he had been an apparition. Then, she said, he had leaped up and followed their carriage along the road between the poplar-trees for some way. That, at least, is what she thought she saw; she cannot be certain. So all, you see, is dark and mysterious. The young wife, who was here about half an hour, bore a surprising resemblance to Kathinka, even in the way she dressed: she wore, to mention only one thing, a Polish white fur cap.

Alas, Marie, how changed everything is! I now long for the quiet days at Hohen-Vietz that I used so often to complain of. There is pressure from all sides, and I recognize that my heart is too weak and too small to give everything that is happening the attention it deserves. In peaceful times I should have been troubled by my aunt's sudden death, or at least been kept busy by it, but now there are whole hours when I do not give it so much as a thought. All that I think of is you, and I do that all the time.

I am still expecting today a couple of lines from Guse; Papa said he would write. I presume my aunt will be buried tomorrow; but I will certainly not be able to be there; I cannot leave here until we know Lewin is out of danger. And until old Dr Leist . . . But there is his voice on the stairs, loud and penetrating. Everyone in the house is talking in whispers, even the servants and farm-hands who come are enjoined to silence and meekly submit: only aged physicians are privileged to make a noise, and old Leist is no exception. I shall break off for the present and hear what he says.

Renate slid the letter under the writing-case and found the doctor already beside the bed in the room opposite. With his fur gloves hanging to left and right of the collar of his cloak by a thick cord, he presented a strange enough figure as, waving his free hand in greeting, he employed the other in feeling the patient's pulse. He seemed satisfied, passed a hand over forehead and temples, and then said: 'Let us leave him alone: he doesn't need us.' With that, the three left the patient to sleep on in peace and crossed over into the women's room, where the doctor now removed his cloak while Renate began to relate the circumstances under which Lewin had been found in terms similar to those she had used in her letter to Marie.

'Very good, very good,' interposed the doctor, who had clearly not been paying any very close attention; then, taking a seat in a rush-chair and complacently rubbing together his broad, brown-flecked hands, he went on in a tone of familiarity: 'And now, my little Renate, before we go on, I would like to ask for a coffee, that is to say, if you wouldn't mind, a coffee with cognac. I have sworn off coffee with milk: it is quite useless to an old physician with a practice in the country.'

Aunt Schorlemmer went away to procure what he had requested; as soon as she was gone, however, old Dr Leist, who like all physicians, even if they have not started as army surgeons, was greatly given to chattering and telling stories as an antidote to the everlasting monotony of case-histories and medical reports, repeated the words he had last spoken and then added by way of clarification: 'You see, my little Renate, the milky ones are useless. I mean as regards coffee. I have nothing against them otherwise. No, what I meant to say was this. You see, these French people are not usually my cup of tea, and all that business with the guillotine, what they called "La Terreur" or, as we say, the Terror, I can't forgive them that; but, honour where it's due, when they invented coffee with cognac they hit the nail on the head. There are some things they are superior to us in.'

Renate paced back and forth impatiently, but Dr Leist appeared not to notice and went on:

'And honestly to confess as much is nothing less than my bounden duty. For without this coffee with cognac I should no longer be alive and would not be sitting in this nice inn at Bohlsdorf. You have heard of *anno* 93, or *quatre-vingt-treize*, as the French say. They love anything that has a snap to it and sounds as though it meant something particular and special. Well, at that time, you see, we had the campaign in the Champagne and I was in it, with my grenadier company, the Alt-Larisch. Now that word, "Champagne", has a nice ring to it, and if you know no better it makes you think only of big-bellied bottles and corks popping out and hitting the ceiling. But, ye heavenly powers, we got to know the Champagne in a quite different way from that. It rained day and night, and we were all the time in tents in the open air on chalk and clay that didn't let the water through, and before a month was out half the Prussian army was no longer in tents but in hospital. And even though he was a doctor, old Leist would have been there too if he hadn't known how to look after himself. For he knew what the hospitals were like, and because he knew what they were like he preferred to creep off and drag himself as far as an isolated farmhouse in whose doorway he saw, if you will permit me, a fat old Frenchwoman. And she took pity on him and took him in. And, to cut a long tale short, she stowed me in a towering high bed, and when I then got into a shivering fit and my teeth, or as many of them as were left, started chattering with cold, she brought me a coffee with cognac, one cup, two cups, I don't know how many I drank. But what I do know is that by the third day I was on my feet again. And since then, whenever I am faced with a difficulty—and I consider a journey of seven miles in ten degrees of frost a difficulty—I drink a coffee with cognac: firstly out of gratitude, secondly as a precaution, and thirdly because I like it.'

At this moment Aunt Schorlemmer came back in, followed by the innkeeper's wife with the required cup of coffee. Beside the cup there stood a glass. The doctor ogled it, vacillated between decorum and desire, succumbed as usual to the latter, and emptied the glass in a single gulp. The process of blending with the coffee was not undertaken.

Renate's impatience with the old man had by now subsided and, bestowing a smile upon him and laying a hand on his arm, she said: 'But now, dear Dr Leist, how is our invalid really? Is he in any real danger?'

'Danger, danger,' the doctor replied in a tone of playful reproach; 'I shouldn't have sat here talking about *anno* 93 if there'd been any danger! No, no, my little Renate, if old Leist has something unpleasant to say it robs him of his taste for anything else, even a coffee with cognac. How is he? He is very well. His sleep will restore him to health. No danger at all. Over-excitation of the nerves. That's all.'

Renate was silent: she desired to explore no further, for she was beginning to have a suspicion she already knew the whole story. Aunt Schorlemmer, however, who was ignorant of recent events, asked half in annoyance: 'Nervous over-excitation? What is that supposed to be? And what caused it?'

'Ah, my dear little aunt,' Leist replied, 'that is more than a poor doctor can know. He is happy if he can as much as recognize what it is he has before him. As to what caused it, he cannot have anything to do with that. Only the invalid himself knows the answer to that question. And our Lewin must surely know it and will one day satisfy the curiosity of all of us, for it is a truly curious story, I'll be bound.'

And at that the old man smirked to himself as slyly as though he had already read the entire love-tale from start to finish.

'But now, instructions!' said Renate. 'What have we to do?'

'We have to wait. That is the best thing to do in all circumstances. Time, time. Time brings about all things. To the sick it brings health. Therefore let us wait.'

'But for how much longer?'

'Yes, that is another question. But let us consider. Today is the third day. The fifth will be the day, I think, the day after tomorrow. The day after tomorrow he will have slept his fill and will want something, perhaps some fried bacon or an onion. Whatever it is he must have it, for what is then speaking is the voice of nature, and we are obliged to pay heed to it.'

'Ah, how glad I am that I can conclude my letter with such good news!' said Renate. 'I was just writing to Marie Kniehase when you arrived. You know, doctor, you could dictate me the last lines.'

'That I will do,' said Dr Leist, 'and I will also be your postman, for I am travelling through Hohen-Vietz. Have you everything you need?'

'Everything.'

'Let us write, then: " . . . Dr Leist is now here and assures us there is no danger. In two days our invalid will be out of bed and in four as good as recovered. I am writing all this at the old doctor's dictation, and he himself will take this letter with him. Full stop, dash. Your Renate".'

Renate sprang up and, handing the letter to the doctor, said gaily: 'So, now we have it in black and white, and all you have to do now is write "Certified" and your name. But not in the usual doctor's scribble but clearly so that everyone can read it.'

The old man did as he was bid. Then he rose, and while Renate helped him into his heavy and many-collared cloak he concluded his visit with the words: 'And now one more thing, ladies. I must ask the healthy not to neglect themselves in their care for the sick. Otherwise you will merely exchange roles with one another. Therefore, no follies like all-night vigils or other superfluities. Little aunt, I shall make you responsible. And I shall look in again the day after tomorrow. And now, God be with you.'

They accompanied him down the stairs to the carriage standing under the awning. Soon the horses moved off and

Renate and Aunt Schorlemmer waved after the departing doctor. A real burden of care had been lifted from them; he had spoken so confidently. Towards evening a sick-nurse came to relieve them beside the patient's bed and, after two sleepless nights, they went across to their room for a peaceful one.

Renate was tired, but Aunt Schorlemmer was, as ever, wide-awake and active. She sat herself beside Renate and seemed inclined to go on talking for fifteen minutes.

'I wonder what things are like in Guse,' said Renate. 'Alas, dear Schorlemmer, I am afraid I shall dream of my aunt.'

'You won't do so.'

'And I wonder how she died,' Renate went on. 'I cannot believe she died a Christian death. I see her lying in her coffin, pale, with her black widow's-cap and the peak pulled down lower over her face than usual. And this picture fills me with fear. It may not be right, but I can tell you, dear Schorlemmer, that I am glad I am here in Bohlsdorf rather than in Guse. Is that wrong?'

Aunt Schorlemmer stroked her hand and said: 'If it is wrong, my little Renate, it is only a little wrong. I really don't know whether it is our Christian duty to gaze upon the faces of the dead. And she had something uncanny about her. Those who disdain Jesus have nothing of his halo of grace about them.'

'I wonder, too, what will become of Guse. It was a freehold and, being saleable, it does not revert to the Pudaglas.'

'I know of one heir to it.'

'Who?'

'Renate von Vitzewitz. But you would then have another name.'

'Away with you! How you do talk! A poor girl like me and that beautiful estate.'

'Indeed, little Renate, people aren't always what they seem, and while you believe I am thinking only about Greenland and New Herrnhut, I am thinking about quite other things. I too have my little passions and like to marry people off, and when I take a look into the future I see nothing but . . . '

'Well?'

'Nothing but bridal processions, big and small ones: you,

Marie, Maline. I have even taken care of Eve, even though she is a haughty little thing and really doesn't deserve it.'

'And Kathinka?'

'No, not Kathinka. She does everything for herself and has no need of my assistance.'

'Ah, how I envy you that you can think such nice thoughts. I see no bridal processions. And now, when I am trying to imagine one, I see it all in black.'

'That is because your thoughts are in Guse.'

'You are right, I think: at least, I hope so. Ah, how nice it is that you are with me. It reminds me of that evening, the one before New Year's Eve, when you talked away my fear of ghosts. You told the story of Kaiarnak, the first to be baptized; you see I have remembered the name. But now I would like to go to sleep. Say me one of your songs, a nice one, not one of the sugary ones about little lambs and little angels. I can't stand those.'

'Very well, then let us take one that is really firm and solid,' said Aunt Schorlemmer:

> 'Look down from Thy throne,
> Father, Spirit, Son.'*

Renate nodded in assent, and the old lady continued, her voice growing softer and softer, as far as the third stanza:

> 'Let my pain and smart
> Purify my heart;
> Let my will recline
> Peacefully in Thine;
> Everything I own
> Belongs to Thee alone.'

She went on no further. Renate had clasped her hands together, smiled and gone to sleep.

2

An Encounter

NEXT morning the sun was shining brightly on the roofs of Bohlsdorf. Renate had been paying a return visit to the administrator's wife and was on her way back to the inn when she saw that a splendid carriage had drawn up outside it. The gentleman to whom it belonged was pacing up and down the middle of the village street: a tall figure in a fur coat and fur boots, he was glancing from time to time up at the church-tower, whose grotesquely shaped cap of snow seemed to be engaging his attention. As she drew nearer, Renate recognized the old privy councillor.

'Uncle Ladalinski!' she exclaimed, and hurried towards him.

The privy councillor was visibly disconcerted, and a brief silence followed their first words of greeting, until Renate broke it by asking: 'Are you on your way to Guse?'

'Yes, dear Renate, for your aunt's funeral. But what brings *you* to this village? I expected to see you in Guse, you and Lewin and your father.'

'You will meet only Papa in Guse; Lewin is here.'

'Lewin is here?'

'Yes. He is ill, unconscious; this is now the fourth day. The people here sent a messenger to us. It was the same morning as we had news of our aunt's death. Papa went to Guse, I came here. Aunt Schorlemmer came with me, and we found Lewin as we expected to find him after all the messenger had told us. He was lying in a deep sleep. It is all a mystery, and we can only try and guess what could have made him leave Berlin in the middle of the night and come here. A driver found him lying as if dead beside the milestone on the highway.'

The privy councillor stood for a while in silence; then he took Renate by the arm and said: 'Then you know nothing? Alas, child, what days we have lived through! Kathinka has gone, and we shall never see her again.'

So *that* was it. Everything was now clear to Renate, though she may have shown less surprise at the privy councillor's words than he may possibly have anticipated.

'Can I see Lewin?' he asked.

'Yes; he is lying upstairs.'

They ascended the narrow stairway and found Aunt Schorlemmer beside the patient's bed. She made to leave the room but the privy councillor begged her to stay. Lewin's expression as he slept was of one in full enjoyment of sleep, and the privy councillor was much affected by the sight: he himself had not enjoyed a refreshing sleep for many days. He took the patient's hand and said: '*He* will recover'; and the painful tones in which he spoke these words seemed also to say: '*I* shall not.'

In this mood they again left the inn and returned to the village street, where in the meantime young and old had clustered round the chaise, from which the greyhound was gazing peevishly as though he were in a box in the theatre.

'I would like to say a few more words to you,' said the privy councillor, indicating with a slight motion of his head the crowd of villagers, who were now beginning to show more curious interest in the couple emerging from the inn than in the waiting carriage.

'Let us go into the church,' Renate replied, 'the door is open.'

He was content to do so. They climbed over the half-derelict stone wall and, passing beside a couple of graves, approached the same side-door through which Lewin had entered on Christmas Eve.

Inside the church all was deserted; only the numbers of the hymns sung the previous Sunday still stood on the blackboard. A bright shaft of light fell from a side-window on to the altar-piece: a Crucifixion. Mary and John were absent, and only a Magdalene knelt and embraced the cross. It was an ugly picture from the middle of the previous century, and the Magdalene was the ugliest part of it: she wore a tall auburn wig with large pearls embedded in it, and her expression was sensual and coarse. The privy councillor found it unpleasing; he turned and sought a place in the church where he would be spared the sight of it. He found such a place to one side of the altar, where, pushed into a corner, there stood four ancient choir-stalls which, to judge from their carvings, came from the Catholic era and had found accommodation here when the church had at some time or other been renovated. Ladalinski pointed to them, and they went and sat in the two foremost stalls.

Both of them were afraid to mention Kathinka, and conversation thus came to a halt before it had really begun. At last Renate collected herself and said: 'I am sorry Tubal isn't here. He was our aunt's favourite, and now he will be missing at her graveside.'

'And yet it was a justified feeling that held him back,' the privy councillor replied.

Renate looked at him questioningly.

'A justified feeling,' Ladalinski repeated after a pause, 'the feeling that he shared in the guilt. Alas, my dear Renate, the guilt we take upon ourselves we do not bear alone. Others are compelled to bear it as well. And that is what Tubal feels. He did not want to see anyone, not Lewin and not you.'

'And yet he should have prevailed upon himself,' said Renate. 'And that he did *not* do so is not to his credit, or at least not wholly. He listened to his own finer feelings but forgot that we too possess them. He should not have done so: he should have realized we would not have at all agreed that he had a share in the guilt, and that if he had said he had we would not have listened.'

She fell silent for a moment; then, as though with a view to changing the subject of the conversation, she asked: 'Do you know how our aunt died?'

'No, I have heard nothing. All I know is what I learned from a brief notification from your father. I was greatly shocked, for she was very close to me, and I had to comfort myself by thinking of what she was spared by this sudden and unexpected death. For she did not like to see her plans thwarted. So *thoroughly* thwarted!' He fell silent, then after a while added: 'And her plans, Renate, were what I too desired. All that remains of them I place in your hands.'

Renate gazed silently ahead and blushed. Then, however, she said quickly and in a tone that was almost cheerful: 'Uncle Ladalinski, let me be frank. I know I may. You are knocking on the wrong door, and you are aware you are; what you would like to place in my hands already resides with another.'

'No, Renate, it resides with you. One heart constrains another, and I know . . .'

She shook her head, and was about to reply when they heard a scratching on the door, and the next moment the greyhound came running up the centre aisle, stationed himself before the privy councillor with much barking and jangling of his bell, and then ran back to the side entrance continually looking round to see if his master was following.

'Coachman and servant are growing impatient,' said the old privy councillor; 'we must break off.'

With that the two left the church and walked back across the churchyard to the carriage, into which the greyhound was just being lifted. The privy councillor took his place beside it and, stroking it with one hand, extended the other to Renate in farewell.

'Thank you for our conversation; remember it well, I beg of you.'

With that they parted. Renate stepped beneath the awning of the inn and gazed after the carriage. Her thoughts were with Tubal, and she tried to picture him to herself—but she saw only the features of Kathinka.

'Are they so like one another?' she asked herself, and went back up the stairs.

An hour later the innkeeper's wife brought food, laid the tablecloth and apologized again and again for being so late, only 'the little ruffian' had refused to go to sleep. She did not know whom he had it from, certainly not from his father, for *he* did too much sleeping. Her speech as she chattered on was that of a higher class, though she spoke with fair fluency, and only now and then, when she grew more excited, did she let fall an occasional word in dialect.

Aunt Schorlemmer and Renate had taken their places and drawn a third chair to the table.

'You must stay,' said Renate, 'and see how much we like it. For you run a good kitchen, I already discovered that yesterday. Your little boy is asleep, and so you have time to sit and talk to us. We have been here nearly two days and have not yet even learned your name.'

'I am called Kemnitz . . . that is my husband's name.'

This she said in a tone of voice intended to indicate that her own maiden name was a little more genteel. Renate grasped this and therefore continued: 'You must be from the town? From Alt-Landsberg or Müncheberg?'

'No, not so; I come from here. My father had the school, and after I was confirmed by Pastor Lämmerhirt I went and worked in the office. Because we were three girls, you see, and I am the middle one; Christiane had married the miller at Marzahn, and Mariechen, who is our youngest, is still at home, because our mother is still living.'

'And then did you stay at the office?' Renate asked.

'Yes, until eighteen months ago. It was fine there. The young wife was the only child and we were always together, and so I knew everything that was going on. The present administrator was a friend of the mother and had married his way in; at first he was only a manager. And you could see that that was how it was; outside he was the big man, but indoors he was as quiet as a mouse; the mother ruled the roost, and the daughter was learning how to better every day.'

'And *your* husband, dear Frau Kemnitz, he was at the office too, I suppose?'

'Yes, he was the steward. He was already in his seventh year and was always looking at me in such a way I couldn't help laughing. And at first I didn't want to, but then Pastor Lämmerhirt told me not to "throw away my happiness", and so I accepted him and I haven't regretted it, because he is good to me, and now with the boy, you wouldn't believe how much he loves that child. There are other things, though, that you have to overlook.'

'That is what a good wife always has to do,' said Aunt Schorlemmer, smiling and raising an admonitory finger. 'A good wife has to keep her eyes open, but she also has to know how to shut them, all according. She must see all, but she must not *want* to see all.'

The innkeeper's wife, to whom, in the fashion of all village people, reference to 'seeing' and 'not seeing' suggested only love affairs, misunderstood Aunt Schorlemmer's words, which were intended in a very different sense, and answered with a smile: 'Oh, there's nothing of that sort.'

'Well, what is it then?' Renate asked inquisitively.

'What is it, miss? I am almost ashamed to speak of it. He is always sleeping, and that ought not to be. In the evening, when the guest-room is empty, I read to him an epistle from the hymn-book, that's how I was brought up, that is what my late father did, and that is what they did at the office. And at the office if someone didn't want to listen, they didn't. But my Kemnitz goes to sleep. For a while I got him to read instead, but that too was no good. He was still sleepy all the time.'

'But there's nothing very bad in that, my dear Frau Kemnitz,' said Renate.

'Oh, surely, miss,' the innkeeper's wife replied. 'And if he only slept when he was asleep; but he sleeps when he's awake, too. And that's the worst of all. He forgets everything, he doesn't keep his wits about him. At the last bird-shoot, for instance, we had the house full, all the rooms, and I have to be everywhere, upstairs and downstairs, in the kitchen and in the cellar, and we gave away half a cask of gin. Yes, gave it away, because my Kemnitz forgot to chalk it up, and when he tried to do it afterwards from memory, because he was afraid of what I would say, he got it all wrong and we should have had a fight on our hands if I hadn't arrived just as the row was starting up. So then I wiped my sleeve over the whole bill and said: "It's all free", and gave everyone an extra glassful and pretended to be all very jolly and happy about it. But in the night I wept my bitter tears.'

The innkeeper's wife had so agitated herself by this recital that even in recollection the tears again sprang to her eyes; but she felt at the same time that the best solace lay in speaking further, and she therefore went on: 'If only things were like they were the summer before last. But now of course we have the Red Jug, not a hundred steps from the village towards Tassdorf. He started building at Easter, by Whitsun the roof was on, and he moved in on Midsummer Day. He's called Bindemeier and he's a wheelwright who went out of business; a bad man who spends all he makes and is always changing wives. He's now got his third one; but the children are from the first, Line too, who's getting married tomorrow.'

'Married, who's she marrying then?' asked Renate.

'The son of a farmer at Dahlwitz. At first it wasn't going to happen. The old man didn't want it, he's a skinflint and has that peasant pride. But then Line went over to Dahlwitz and got the old man so bewitched he now swears that if the boy doesn't take her he'll marry her himself, for he is a widower.'

'Is she as pretty as all that, then?'

'No, she isn't pretty at all; but she has such a way with her. And where does she get it from? From her father. And that is the whole point. For you see, Miss, he's only got a retail licence, he isn't a real innkeeper, even though he does have the Red Jug; but I admit this much, he knows how to keep an inn. And my Kemnitz doesn't know how to. He forgets to chalk up the bill and the other one chalks it up double. But none of them who go to the Red Jug notice it, because he knows how to keep everyone happy and always has a tale to tell.'

'And would you like to change, then?' Renate asked, 'and have a husband like the man at the Red Jug?'

'Oh, good heavens, no,' exclaimed the innkeeper's wife in alarm, 'I'd never have another moment's peace.'

'There, you see, you have had to admit that you are happy. You have peace of mind, which is the best thing there is. Let your husband sleep if he wants to; he is a good husband, and that is what matters. If he sleeps a lot, then you must stay awake a lot: that will balance things out. Nothing is ever perfect, and everyone feels the shoe pinch somewhere: one it pinches here, another there.'

The innkeeper's wife sighed. 'That's what Pastor Lämmerhirt told me too,' and, so saying, she rose and collected the plates together. Then, returning to the place from where she had started, she added: 'But it isn't a good thing to have a sleepy husband, that I do know.'

And with that she left the room.

'Do you know whom she reminded me of?' asked Renate.

'Certainly; of Maline.'

'Except that young Scharwenka isn't sleepy. Perhaps he isn't sleepy enough.'

'There the shoe pinches in a different place,' Aunt Schorlemmer concluded.

Renate nodded and, tired by the exertions of the day, threw

herself on to her bed to sleep for an hour. Aunt Schorlemmer covered her with a cloak and went across to the other room. Here she sat at the head of Lewin's bed and began to work at a piece of knitting she had borrowed from the innkeeper's wife, for she could not bear her hands to be idle.

As the sun was going down, Renate and Aunt Schorlemmer left the inn to go for a walk, an exercise to which the air and the light outside strongly invited them. They went down the avenue of poplars leading towards Tassdorf, past the Red Jug where everything had already been prepared for the wedding. Neither spoke; at length Aunt Schorlemmer said, as though she knew Renate's thoughts were set on the same course as hers: 'And now taken off like this, unprepared, without communion, and in her hands nothing but a book in French. That is not the way to be received into Heaven.'

They had come to a stop and were watching the moon rise, pale and silvery, over a dark strip of woodland.

'Over there lies Guse,' Renate said.

Aunt Schorlemmer confirmed it.

'They are burying her now, I think. I seem to hear the singing.'

'May God have mercy on her soul!'

And they both clasped their hands together and went back to the village.

3

'That is the Voice of Nature'

THE innkeeper's wife and an old woman from the village had taken it in turns to watch beside Lewin throughout the night; now it was nine in the morning and Renate and Aunt Schorlemmer were again sitting by his bed. He was sleeping more restlessly than he had the previous day and now and then a few disconnected and barely comprehensible words emerged from his lips. Bright morning light filled the room and the ice was melting from the window-panes: the sound of it was the only sound audible except for the twittering of a canary and the clicking of Aunt Schorlemmer's needles. Thus there passed half an hour, during which the women sat gazing silently before them or down at the patient. Now the sunlight fell upon his face, and Renate whispered: 'Look, he is dreaming. And it looks like a pleasant dream.' And before Aunt Schorlemmer could reply there came the sound of bells ringing outside, and Lewin awoke. His first glance fell upon his sister: he recognized her and said: 'Renate.'

Renate had leaped up, and now she took him in her arms and cried again and again: 'My dear, dear Lewin.' Aunt Schorlemmer continued to knit, but her lips were trembling. When Lewin noticed her presence he nodded to her and gave her his hand.

It was clear that he was still very weak. They placed a pillow behind his back, so that he could sit rather than lie, and he now cast his eyes about the room.

'Where am I?' he asked.

They told him the name of the village. He shook his head, then seemed to reflect a little and asked: 'Where is Papa?'

'In Guse.'

'In Guse? Why in Guse?'

Renate and Aunt Schorlemmer looked at one another, and did not know what to reply. Renate, however, soon collected herself and said quietly: 'Aunt Amelie is dead.'

'I see . . . how old was she?'

The question remained unanswered, for he began again to lose consciousness and a moment later he was once more lying in a deep sleep. And yet he had been restored to life, he had spoken, and the two women extended their hands to one another in a gesture of joyful gratitude.

Another half-hour had gone by when the innkeeper's wife entered in visible agitation. 'The procession is coming,' she cried, for the first time forgetting to lower her voice. 'The organ is already playing. And the young people from the office are there too. That's bad enough. Only the old lady has stayed away, she's on our side. God, God, I'm all of a tremble.'

'But why don't you go and get ready?' said Aunt Schorlemmer, drawing the innkeeper's wife goodnaturedly towards the door. 'There is still time for you to join the procession, or at least arrive with it at the church.'

'But I can't,' the latter wailed. 'We count as enemies, and people would point the finger at us and say we were trying to blight their happiness. No, that won't do.'

'I would like to see the bride, none the less,' said Renate.

'Ah yes, miss, that's just why I have come. She isn't pretty but, as I told you, she has something about her. And then afterwards you can tell me what she looked like. God, I really don't know why I should care. Yes, miss, you must see the bride and so must dear Aunt Schorlemmer, if I may presume to call you that. Four eyes can see more than two. Oh, here they come now; that's the band playing, and I daren't even go to the window. And even if I did dare, the procession isn't going past here anyway. And why not? Because they think we'd put stones in the road to trip them up.'

Renate looked at Aunt Schorlemmer to see if she agreed it would be all right. 'You go along, child,' said the latter, 'and I shall come with you. It can never be wrong to be in church. You take a look at the bride; I know what it is I have to do.'

The innkeeper's wife was highly delighted, ran back and forth and expressed her gratitude to both the ladies. Then she fetched two thick copies of Porst's hymn-book* bound in velvet and secured with metal clasps, and promised again and again that she would remain with the invalid. 'I have things to do here,' she concluded, 'and that will make the time pass and I shall be best contented. He shan't be disturbed, not even by a fly.' Renate and Aunt Schorlemmer then put their cloaks about them, took one further look at Lewin, who was sleeping on peacefully, and left the room; the innkeeper's wife sat herself at the foot of the bed.

They could not so much as have crossed over the street before the bells began ringing a third time. Finally, however, it grew still again. 'Now they are singing,' the wife said to herself. 'Lord, Lord, I would so much have liked to see her; he is supposed to have given her a silver chain with a clasp and slide. He can afford to, she's got the old man in her pocket. A brazen little thing, with red hair and freckles as well. But I'll say nothing against her, for she's standing at the altar even now.

And perhaps she's not so bad after all. God, give her your blessing, and us too, because there's no relying on Kemnitz and I can't do everything all by myself.'

As she was still engaged in this pious prayer, Lewin, who a moment before had seemed to be sleeping peacefully, suddenly opened his eyes and fastened a friendly gaze upon her. The last hour's sleep had quite visibly strengthened him. 'Where is Renate?' he asked, 'I mean the young lady.'

'At church, young sir. And so is dear Aunt Schorlemmer as well. I am to blame, really, because I sent them off; that is to say, I asked them to go. We have a wedding today, you see: Line, the girl at the Red Jug. She has carried off a farmer's son, one of them at Dahlwitz. Well, I don't begrudge it her.'

Thus she chattered on.

In the meantime Lewin had sat up and appeared to be listening: but it must have been apparent to a closer observer that he was paying more attention to the twittering of the canary than to what the innkeeper's wife was saying. At length he turned towards her and said: 'I am hungry.'

'Yes, I know,' replied Frau Kemnitz, and having elicited with a couple of questions exactly what it was the patient required, she ran out to the kitchen. Here the fire was, as usual, burning in the grate; but everything else she had to prepare herself, since the servants were over in the church. She took a stew-pan down from the chimney-box, then a mortar, and, making much more noise than was really necessary, began pounding and clattering. She seemed to derive great pleasure from the noise she was making. When she saw through the kitchen door, however, that Kemnitz was lounging sleepily beside one of the windows and gazing out into the village street when there was nothing to be seen there, she went up to him, shook him violently, thrust the mortar into his hand and said in a tone of annoyance: 'Do a bit of work.'

'What is it, Lene?'

'Don't ask silly questions: just stir this pot.' And with that she was already back in the kitchen: during the intervals in his labours Kemnitz allowed himself he could hear her busy at the kitchen cupboard.

They continued thus occupied for some time, until the sound

of the organ starting up again indicated that the ceremony in the church opposite was at an end. The doors were opened and, with the band at its head, the wedding procession re-emerged and proceeded again down the street. Among the last to leave the church were Renate and Aunt Schorlemmer, who had found a good seat next to the organ-loft. They were discussing Pastor Lämmerhirt's address; Aunt Schorlemmer found little in it she could commend, Renate was less censorious. As they reached the inn, Dr Leist too came driving up.

He had encountered the procession and was in the best of moods. 'It is a good omen!' he cried to the two ladies, and they entered the inn together. The first thing they encountered was the innkeeper's wife in person: she was coming down the stairs carrying a tray on which there lay a plate and a spoon.

'How is he?' asked Renate.

'Well, miss.'

'Is he awake?'

'Yes.'

'Tell us, then, dear lady,' said Dr Leist. 'What has been happening?'

'Well, the ladies had not long been gone, and the preacher could hardly have yet started, when he opened his eyes. I mean the young gentleman.'

'And what did he say?'

'He asked after the young lady, and when I had told him everything, and about Line and her wedding, he looked at me wide-eyed and said: "I am hungry." And then I at once thought of all Dr Leist had said to us and asked him straight out what he would like and told him ten things or so he could have. But he didn't like any of them and shook his head again and again and started to get cross. But at last he said: "I've got it." And what was it? Would you imagine, miss, it was soup. And beer-soup, moreover. And so then I asked him straight out: "How would you like it, young sir, with Kümmel or with ginger?" And then he laughed quietly to himself and said: "With ginger".'

'With ginger,' repeated Dr Leist. 'He is getting better, you see. It was not a matter of indifference to him what he had. No, with ginger. Yes, ladies, that is the voice of nature. I congratulate you and us all, and now let us see the patient.'

They then mounted the stairs again and found Lewin sitting upright in bed. He recognized the doctor; but when he made to lift his left hand to offer it to him it sank back feebly on to the bed.

'How are you, Lewin?'

'Well, I think.'

'Well, I think! That is not good enough. How was the soup?'

'Very nice.'

'That's better. No headache?'

'No.'

The doctor now himself took up Lewin's hand and felt his pulse; by the time he had finished the patient had again fallen into an exhausted sleep. 'Let us not disturb him.'

Thus they left the room, and resumed their conversation only when they were out on the stairway. 'Everything is going along as it should. The crisis is past; all the signs of recovery are there. No fever; only he is feeble, very feeble. But every hour's sleep he gets advances him a week. Tomorrow he will want to get up, and the day after tomorrow he can travel.'

'And we?'

'We shall depart tomorrow and arrange quarters for him,' the doctor replied.

'And send Krist for him with the covered sleigh.'

'Just so. I was about to suggest it. And with a decent straw bolster in it, for he will probably still need something to lean on.'

They had now reached the lower landing and were standing before the guest-room, where the doctor was to be given another warmed beer. But he declined it, 'for I have to go on to Reitwein'. And when the innkeeper's wife ignored this refusal and continued to urge the beer on him he finally cut short all further discussion with the two words 'maternity case'. That sufficed. Aunt Schorlemmer was even more embarrassed than Renate.

The doctor's carriage was already drawn up under the awning, and he was in the act of climbing aboard when he stopped and removed his foot from the footboard. 'Old Leist is growing old indeed,' he said; 'I almost forgot the main thing.' And with that he began to rummage around in the depths of his cloak pocket. At length he found a thick, red-leather notebook that also served as a surgical case, and took a letter from it: 'To Renate von Vitzewitz'.

Only then did he enter the carriage. 'Goodbye until we meet in Hohen-Vietz.' Renate and Aunt Schorlemmer returned his valediction.

The letter turned out to be from Marie.

4

Recovery

EVERYTHING came to pass as Dr Leist had said it would. On the following morning Lewin desired to get up and, in spite of all the weakness he still felt, was sufficiently strong to leave his room and say farewell to Renate and Aunt Schorlemmer under the awning before the inn. It was the innkeeper's own team they were using, and Kemnitz himself was to drive. He was acting in a livelier fashion than was his custom, and when Renate drew attention to it and whispered a well-meant commendation of this celerity into his wife's ear, the latter responded, not without a certain pride: 'Oh, he's capable of it. When the mood takes him, that is.' The ladies then took their places; Kemnitz hooked on the leather cover and then himself clambered over the wheel on to the backless driver's seat. One more handclasp, and the carriage disappeared around the other side of the church.

Lewin returned to his room. He had exerted himself more than he should have done, and now he threw himself still dressed on to his bed: he did not expect to sleep, but he needed to rest. Visions of all kinds passed before his eyes, fantastic and ever changing but each formed out of the lineaments of its predecessor. He saw Frau Hulen's dark kitchen and the little wax-taper which he had had so much trouble igniting in the ashes in the hearth; then the taper turned into a candle, and the candle turned into twelve candles, and the twelve candles were burning on either side of a coffin, and in the coffin lay Aunt Amelie, her widow's-cap pulled down low over her forehead.

And beside the coffin there stood little cypress-trees, and they grew taller and taller until they were as tall as poplars, and now it was an avenue of poplars, and along the avenue there came racing a carriage, and he ran after the carriage and wanted to cry out but his voice failed him.

These visions came and went and came again without seriously disturbing him. A weight lay upon him, leaden but painless, and under the influence of an almost pleasant stupefaction what was closest at hand fled into the distance and reality became a dream. They were things of the imagnation merely; and of the emotions he might have felt he felt only one: a longing for Hohen-Vietz.

And now another day and another night had passed; bright morning light shone through the windows and it was about ten o'clock. Krist, who had arrived soon after midnight with the covered sleigh and an entire winter outfit of fur coats, scarves and fur boots, was already busy in the stables fastening the harness and the bells to the two bays, and the innkeeper's wife was standing in the stable doorway chattering about the affairs of Bohlsdorf but also in the hope of receiving news of the affairs of Hohen-Vietz in exchange.

While this colloquy was going on, Lewin was sitting in his room dressed ready for the journey. He had already taken a morning stroll, though only as far as the church across the street, where he had once again read the epitaph engraved on the tomb that he had long since known by heart. He had been back half an hour and was now holding in his hand a folded sheet of paper whose contents seemed to be engaging his attention. It was the letter from Marie Kniehase: he had obtained it the previous day from Renate at the moment of her departure. 'I will just glance through it again,' he said, leaned over towards the window and read it half-aloud:

Dear Renate!
I received your letter yesterday evening, when Doctor Leist came by. There was no time to talk with him; because of the late hour he wanted to go straight on. I read it and in the joy I felt I ran to the parson; he was hardly less overjoyed than I was. And yet it is really something sad. You write: 'Why did he leave Berlin?' and then add: 'I can only venture suppositions, and of these I have indeed very few.' Ah, my dear

Renate, I know why, and in dreams and waking I have seen this hour coming.

Here everything is quiet, many of the farmers and their wives have gone across for your aunt's funeral. For in her own way she was much beloved, and everyone spoke of her. Seidentopf too has been gone this past hour: he wants to go to Guse first, then to Küstrin and Hohen-Ziesar, and we don't expect him back before the end of the week. What a strange collection of mourners there will be around Aunt Amelie's coffin! Bamme, Rutze, Doctor Faulstich. And just imagine, Jeetze is in mourning too. It was funny and yet moving when I saw him today: he had got out a pair of black gaiters—'they're from the late countess,' he said—and a crape armband.

My thoughts are with you continually; they wander from one gable-room to the other, and it seems to me that I already know the village. It is the one Lewin told us about on the first day of Christmas, and I can still see it all before me: the Christmas tree with the pretty, young innkeeper's wife and the little blond-headed boy, and then the dark church with the stepladder at the altar and the little lantern; before the altar the gravestone lying with the lovely inscription which I must have repeated to myself a hundred times since then. When I do so I always feel as though I had grown wings and could fly.

Here Lewin paused a moment and repeated to himself the words: as though I had grown wings and could fly. 'How well she puts it,' he added. Then he took the letter up again and read on to the end.

God grant that old Dr Leist's prophecies will be fulfilled; he has promised to take these lines back with him, and I am sending them to Lebus by Hoppenmarieken. She is waiting outside and banging her stick on the paving-tiles, a sure sign she is getting impatient. I am much too much afraid of her to dare let her grow into a worse temper: and therefore farewell, my only beloved Renate, my happiness, my pride and my assurance. Remember me to Aunt Schorlemmer; and when Lewin opens his eyes, let your thoughts dwell on me too. Then I shall feel it in my heart.

Your Marie.

When he had read to the end, Lewin rose and went over to the canary's cage to give the little bird a piece of sugar by way of thanks for the entertainment his friendly twittering had provided during the long hours of the previous day.

He was in the act of reseating himself when Krist entered to announce that all was in readiness and the sleigh awaiting him; at the same time he loaded himself with the winter outfit that lay untouched on the bed and stamped off again down the stairs. Lewin followed him: but when he reached the door he stopped again and looked back into the room. He felt very little emotion, for the after-effects of his illness still had him in their grip: but, this apathy notwithstanding, he was clearly aware of what the days he had spent here signified to him, and that his former life was sinking behind him and a new life beginning.

The innkeeper's wife was waiting below. Kemnitz had not yet returned, but she had her pride and joy, her little blond-headed boy, on her arm, and she could not have presented herself to say farewell more becomingly. Of this fact she was well aware, and was full of loud and coquettish laughter until, when Lewin extended his hand to her and said how grateful he was for all the care she had shown him, she broke into convulsive sobbing: for although, at the office and in confirmation lessons with Pastor Lämmerhirt, she had acquired more education than was usually the case, she was still sufficiently a child of nature to be capable of releasing a stream of tears whenever the occasion seemed to require it. Lewin was familiar with this natural capacity from his experience of it among the peasant women at Hohen-Vietz, and he now made no more of it than he knew it was worth, but confined himself to patting the head of the child, who was busy groping for him with its hand; then he mounted up behind the horses on to the sleigh. 'Off we go, Krist,' he said, and settled himself comfortably against the tightly packed straw-sack that served as a back-rest; whereupon the horses moved off at a canter, circled the church, and drove past the nearest farmsteads out into the sunlit landscape beyond.

It was a wonderful day, brisk yet not cold; on the horizon there lay dark streaks of fir-tree forest, with the spires of the various villages and hamlets of the region rising between them. They passed through some of them, and Krist, who had many acquaintances hereabouts, exchanged a word or two, or brought them to a halt to rekindle his pipe. Lewin, for his part, breathed in the wonderful air and felt more and more recovered with every breath he took; his nervous system came to life again and the weight that had been pressing upon him faded and disappeared. The visions that passed before his eyes grew ever more cheerful, he thought of Seidentopf, and it seemed to him he was travelling towards the land of peace.

Thus the hours passed; the bells on the horses jingled as they galloped on, and already the sun was beginning to decline towards the horizon.

It was gone four o'clock when they halted before the inn at Dolgelin. Immediately opposite stood the parsonage. Lewin alighted to take a snack at the inn; Krist, however, after he had thrown a woollen blanket across the back of one of the bays and an old army cloak over the other, crossed the road to the opposite side of the village, where Pastor Zabel's sleigh had just come to a halt close beside the fence.

'Evening, Karges,' said Krist. 'Where've you been?'

'To Gus'.'

'What for? She's under the ground now, you know. Since the day 'fore yesterday.'

'I know. But the schoolchildren are still having their day. Lots to eat and drink: roasted venison, pork. And each one then gets a bun to take home.'

'Ah yes, the schoolchildren. But what did the parson have to do there?'

'What did he have to do there? I don't know. He always has to be there is all I know.'

At this moment Lewin again stepped out of the inn into the street; when he saw him, Krist hurriedly broke off the conversation and returned to the horses. Here he removed the old cavalry cloak from the back of one of the bays and held it spread open before Lewin as a sign that before he again entered the sleigh he would have to put it on. Lewin, however, declined.

'Put it away, Krist,' he said; 'it isn't cold.'

'It is so, young sir. The sun is right down. And I am to look after you, both of 'em told me, first one then t'other. And this isn't being any help.'

'Just put it by. I shall tell them I didn't want it.'

'No, young sir, that won't make any difference. With our young miss we might get away with it, but old Schorlemmer would never let me hear the last of it.'

'All right, give it here then,' said Lewin, and wrapped the cloak around him.

He was soon glad he had offered no further obstinate resistance to Krist's urgings: the air grew colder minute by minute and the warmth provided by the heavy cloak did him good. The stars came out; a sensation of sweet inexpressible sorrow overcame him and a stream of tears broke from his eyes, not more copious than those shed by the good Frau Kemnitz a few hours previously but much, much hotter. Yes, these tears were to him a promise of happiness and recovery. He thought of Marie and of how alike they were in the way they felt. 'I feel as though I had grown wings and could fly', he repeated from her letter and gazed up at the stars sparkling ever more brightly above.

Thus they journeyed on. The bays, who had covered twelve miles since the previous evening, gradually slowed to a walk, and it was only when they had passed Manschnow and had begun to scent their stable that they again broke into a trot. Seven o'clock was sounding from the church-tower at Hohen-Vietz when they came in sight of the outer extremity of the park, and before the last stroke had died away the sleigh came to a stop before the entrance to the manor house. The first thing Lewin saw was the annexe now lying in ruins, and the shock of beholding the scene of the conflagration was all the greater because the news of the fire had affected him but slightly. And the impression he received was enhanced by the fact that in the manor house itself all was darkness and silence.

There was no one to be seen. Krist cracked his whip and the bays shook their bells impatiently. At length a light became visible, and Jeetze's lean form appeared behind the glass door. He tilted the lamp a little to the side to secure the flame against the draught blowing through, then he came out to assist his young master to alight.

'Good evening, Jeetze. Everyone gone out?'

'Yes, young sir. We didn't expect you so early.'

'And where is Papa?'

'Still in Guse.'

'And Renate?'

'At Miekley the miller's. Uhlenhorst is there, and the

Lutherans are meeting there again. And those from over the way are there too: the administrator from Zehden and the old head forester of Lietze-Göricke. Our young lady didn't want to go along at first, but Aunt Schorlemmer wouldn't let her alone.'

'I see,' said Lewin in mild annoyance.

'Shall I go and fetch them?'

'No, don't bother. I'm tired.'

With that they moved from the hallway, where this exchange had taken place, to the rear hall of the house. There Hector was already awaiting his young master; but, as though he knew he had been ill, he refrained from all violent demonstrations of affection and, quietly wagging his tail, he confined himself to repeatedly licking Lewin's hand as they mounted the stairs together.

In Lewin's room everything had been made ready for him. The eiderdown had been folded back and the quilt lay folded on the chair beside the bed; on the table beside the sofa stood lilies of the valley, the only ones the greenhouse, neglected since the death of Frau von Vitzewitz, had produced: what made them precious, however, was that they were Lewin's favourite flowers. He breathed in their odour and said in a voice tremulous with emotion: 'Renate!' The happy feeling that he had returned to the security and loving care of his home settled upon his much tried heart.

An hour later Jeetze again opened the door softly. The lamp was still burning, and the old servant took it from the table to extinguish it. Hector, who was lying on his deerskin rug, blinked with one of his eyes but did not move.

And the next moment everything was still again.

5

Last Wishes

THE following evening saw our friends again gathered around the fireside at Hohen-Vietz. They presented much the same picture as on the first day of Christmas, except that the

Christmas tree was missing and, even more, the cheerfulness that on the former occasion had attended the game with the golden nuts. Aunt Schorlemmer was again knitting at her shawl, Renate, a strip of crape before her, was sewing a mourning-band, and Lewin—still suffering the after-effects of his illness, or at any rate those of the exertions of the previous day—was gazing languidly into space and toying with a fir-cone he had taken from a wood-box standing beside him. Only Marie was making an effort to stimulate conversation, but her remarks failed to elicit anything but the briefest responses.

The little clock on the mantelpiece struck eight. At the same moment Jeetze announced the parson, who entered immediately afterwards. They all exhibited great pleasure at his arrival, and in Renate's case it took the form of gentle teasing: it was not good for the shepherd to desert his sheep, she said; four hours were already too much, but he had been away four days! In his absence the wolf had broken in: Uhlenhorst in person.

'I know,' said Seidentopf. 'And who deliberately courted danger? Who went to see him again?'

'We did, of course. But this time we got away unharmed. And not we alone: the Zehden administrator too turned from him when he continually kept repeating: "All they that take the sword shall perish with the sword."* He has had this saying on his lips ever since Christmas and by now everyone has had enough of it. He always forgets he is talking to old soldiers. He is a Lauenburger, or from Eutin, and whenever I hear him speaking like this I come to think every different province must have its own different brand of Christianity. But that is going to lead to a quarrel: I can see Aunt Schorlemmer is already getting annoyed. So then, no more of that. And now, do come and sit down, dear pastor, here is your chair, between me and Marie. And now talk to us.'

'What about?'

'About all and everything, but first of all about Guse, for we know as good as nothing. Papa has been back here only once, and we were still in Bohlsdorf at the time. So it will all be new to us. Was it very solemn? Was the coffin open or closed? I should have been frightened to death standing for hours beside an open coffin. Who gave the address? Who was there?'

'Everyone, her entire circle of friends: Bamme, Drosselstein, Krach, the captain from Protzhagen in his old Pirch Regiment uniform—no one was absent. Faulstich was there too, with a kind of cantata which, if Nippler has finished composing it by then, is to be sung in the church at Guse the Sunday after next or the one after that. Our doctor of Kirch-Göritz had had the text printed in advance and gave each of us a copy.'

'A cantata,' said Aunt Schorlemmer. 'And by Faulstich! That is bound to be some awful pagan racket from beginning to end. Nothing about death and the grave, and even less about resurrection: only the underworld and shades and the names of a dozen Greek gods!'

'Not at all, dear Schorlemmer,' replied Seidentopf. 'You do him an injustice. What he has written is not Christian, but neither is it offensive. He has too much tact for that. But I have brought it with me, and our ladies can be the judge.' With that he drew a black-bordered sheet from his inner pocket and gave it to Lewin, who unfolded it apathetically and, after reflecting briefly and without having so much as glanced at its contents, handed it on.

'You read it, Renate.' And Renate read:

> *'At the Grave*
> *of Countess Amelie von Pudagla,*
> *born von Vitzewitz*
> Thou of the noble mind
> And noble brow,
> Thou hast departed:
> Where art thou now?
>
> Where? Let the questioners
> Not trouble thee:
> Thou hast attained the goal,
> Where'er that be.
>
> The best of life's favours
> Thou hast won thee;
> Now *peace* is thy portion:
> Light lie the earth on thee.'

There followed a short silence. Then Aunt Schorlemmer said: 'It is not offensive because it isn't scoffing. But, dearest pastor, it is offensive enough to a Christian heart. He asks: "Where art thou?" and doesn't know the answer. I know it, I thank God.'

Seidentopf, who as one of the world's universal defenders was always eager to put in a good word for everybody, was on this occasion too about to intercede on Faulstich's behalf; but Renate, who in the meantime perceived that the back of the sheet containing the cantata, which was as brief as it was lacking in faith, was also scribbled over with pencilled lines, did not permit this clerical response to take place but, running her finger over the lines, remarked: 'I wager, dear pastor, that we already have your critical commentary, here on the back of the sheet. Am I right?'

'No, dear Renate,' replied Seidentopf. 'I am quite uncritical, as Turgany assures me. In some spheres perhaps less so than he assumes, but certainly I am quite uncritical in the sphere of the cantata. I should be embarrassed if I had to state what a cantata *is*.'

'Well, if they are not a commentary, what *are* these lines?'

'The last wishes of your aunt of Guse. Not her actual testament—such a thing has never come to light—but a kind of funeral programme. It was discovered among other papers on her writing-desk, and with your Papa's permission, and naturally omitting certain French interpolations, I made for myself a hurried copy of it.'

'Oh, this we must hear,' Renate exclaimed gaily. 'But it is very tiny and impossible to make out. You yourself will have to come to our aid.'

'Gladly,' replied Seidentopf, 'and all the more so in that the provisions of this programme were carried out precisely. These last wishes are, indeed, the best description I can give you of the funeral itself.

'Well, then, do read it,' Renate begged.

Lewin and Marie agreed with the request, and only Aunt Schorlemmer objected: 'Oh, the things we are now going to have to listen to all over again!'

Then Seidentopf took back the paper and began without further preliminaries or delay:

'*Stipulations to be Observed on the Occasion of my Demise.*

'I fear death. But this fear does not prevent me from looking it in the face. It cannot be evaded. And therefore I, Amelie von Pudagla, born von Vitzewitz, stipulate as follows:

'*Firstly*. I wish to be laid in a coffin of cedar-wood clad in my widow's dress and then placed on a bier in the great hall on the spot where the satyr stands. The satyr must be content to be accommodated elsewhere for as long as this lasts.'

'On the spot where the satyr stands,' repeated Aunt Schorlemmer, and clicked her needles violently.

Seidentopf continued:

'*Secondly*. I wish to be buried at sunset on the fourth day: not in the church, however, nor in the Derfflinger vault attached to it, but in the château park at Guse, in the little cedar grove they call New Lebanon.

'*Thirdly*. On the way from the château to the park Nippler shall lead all the village children in singing the hymn: "*Was Gott tut, das ist wohlgetan*". I expressly forbid the singing of "*O Haupt voll Blut und Wunden*".'

Everyone appeared surprised by this stipulation and they looked at one another, though they said nothing. Only Aunt Schorlemmer spoke up: 'My God, what has the lovely hymn done to offend her! I should get no peace in the grave if I had written down such a thing in my last will. Renate, child, make sure *I* have that hymn sung. I mean when I come to be buried.'

'I shall do so, dear Schorlemmer. But let us hear on.'

'*Fourthly*. At the graveside the pastor shall give a short address in which he shall not commend me on account of what I was or did on earth, but shall say merely that throughout my life I detested all underhandedness, obscurity and dissimulation. He shall say this, not in commendation of me, but because it is the truth.

'*Fifthly*. A granite stone shall be placed upon my grave and in due course a metal tablet inlaid in it bearing the following epitaph:

> *L'éloge ou le blâme ne touchent plus celui*
> *Qui repose dans l'éternité.*
> *L'espérance embellit ma vie et m'accompagne en mourant.**

'*Sixthly*. Faulstich, to whom I bequest my miniature with

the ruby frame, shall write a cantata, and Nippler (who shall receive a *douceur* of ten ducats) shall set it to music. It may be sung either at the graveside or in the church at Guse, as may be thought fit, on the third Sunday after my funeral.

'*Seventhly*. On the third day after my interment, and then annually on the anniversary of my death, the schoolchildren are to be given a party and new clothes purchased for twelve of the poor of the village.

'*Eighthly*. I entrust the carrying out of these stipulations to my brother, Berndt von Vitzewitz, formerly major with the von Knobelsdorff Dragoon Regiment, lord of the manor of Hohen-Vietz.'

When he had finished reading Seidentopf folded the paper again and Aunt Schorlemmer murmured, without looking up from her work: 'Even Faulstich doesn't get forgotten.'

Lewin smiled. He had been growing perceptibly more cheerful paragraph by paragraph, and now he said quietly: 'You have always had your little conflict with our aunt. That was all very well so long as she was alive; now she is dead, though, I think we must all make our peace with her.'

Aunt Schorlemmer shook her head.

'You shake your head,' Lewin went on, 'but that doesn't make me change my mind. For all those things in her to which we took exception she now has to answer in another place; she now knows more than we do, and in all those things that lie beyond this life she is out of the reach of our judgement. Our opinion of her must now confine itself to what she was and signified to us on *this* side of the grave. And that was something of consequence. Her weakness lay in her faith, to be sure, but her strength lay in her courage. "I do not haggle," she used to say. And all we have just heard demonstrates to us that to the end she refused to compromise and knew how to remain loyal to her unbelief.'

Lewin's pale countenance had acquired colour as he spoke. As he now fell silent, Seidentopf declared he was in full agreement: a courageous confession of unbelief such as they had witnessed, all perseverance even in the face of death, met with his applause; he much preferred it to that Christianity out of fear shown by, for example, Baron Pehlemann, who reached eagerly for the Bible whenever he had an attack of gout and shut it again as soon as the attack was over.

No one was surprised to encounter such expressions from the mouth of Seidentopf. Even Aunt Schorlemmer was not surprised: but if she was not surprised she was even less in agreement with such sentiments.

'Perseverance!' she repeated vehemently. 'If only it were! But it was not perseverance, dear pastor, and least of all perseverance unto death. I knew Aunt Amelie and I saw into her heart. She found that an annoyance. A courageous confession of unbelief, indeed! Oh, how you misunderstand her! She wrote all that, not out of courage, but in the vanity of her heart, and she enjoyed the idea of the astonishment it would arouse when it was one day read after her death. By Bamme, by Krach, perhaps also by the tall captain. But death was not yet present: if it had been, if she had seen it face to face, she would *not* have written these words, of that I am certain. She possessed courage, but it was merely the courage to live, not the courage to die.'

The conversation was interrupted by the entry of Jeetze, who appeared bearing a tray on which there stood a pile of little painted plates and an old-fashioned silver fruit-basket. As no one seemed willing to give up his place at the fire, the tray was placed on a little round table inlaid with Tula work and this table was moved into the semicircle. Marie, who had her hands free, played hostess and peeled the fruit.

As the plate passed from hand to hand conversation gradually resumed; but, since everyone knew that agreement on the subject they had previously been discussing was scarcely possible, it turned to other topics.

Naturally Seidentopf continued to hold the floor: for, quite apart from his stay with Count Drosselstein, he had gone straight from the funeral at Guse to Küstrin, where he had spent a whole day during the course of which he had seen much and heard even more. He excited particular interest by what he had to say concerning the daily increasing desertions; though the fact that these desertions were taking place ought, he added, not to occasion surprise, since half the garrison from Westphalia was under the command of General von Füllgraf, an old warrior who, as every citizen well knew, was himself unable to resolve the conflict between his German heart and his French oath. His own soldiers knew it too, and were thus decamping in whole squads. Others, who were for the moment staying put, had nailed a poem to his door, which read:

> Art thou *Füll*graf? Say not so,
> Leave the legions of the foe,
> At our head as *Voll*graf go!*

To avoid the suspicion that he himself was in sympathy with this discontent, the old general had notified his superior, General Fournier, of the posting of this poem and had instituted an inquiry: but the inquiry had revealed nothing and the desertions had only increased. The latest squad to depart was said to have comprised seventeen men and to have made off in the direction of Kirch-Göritz. That was now three days ago. The warning-gun could have been fired on the 'Hohe Kavalier',* but to what purpose? The citizens of Küstrin would have laughed, and so would the French. For the latter no longer heard anything but tales of an 'arming of the people', and they were naturally intelligent enough to see that the very peasants at present engaged in preparing a rebellion were not likely at the same time to want to play the policeman and seize and hand over deserters.

At this point Lewin interrupted the pastor to ask how the organization of the local militia was proceeding, and learned, with many details, what progress the arming of the people had made during the course of the previous three weeks. At first Hohen-Vietz had been in the van, but Berndt's absence for almost a full week had slowed things down a little and now Drosselstein was ahead and Rutze was in advance even of him. He had learned these facts from Bamme himself during a walk through the park at Guse on the day of the funeral. It had been a very pleasant walk in general, for the old man was easy to talk to: that he could not be persuaded to enter the church at Gross-Quirlsdorf, or only exceptionally, was a matter for the pastor of Gross-Quirlsdorf. The latter had succeeded in preaching him out of it with his stereotyped Christianity: and stereotyped Christianity was no better than Pehlemann's Christianity out of fear. Be that as it might, however, they had had a lively conversation and had walked up the avenue of elm-trees and back through the line of bird-snares, and had finished back again at the little swan-house: here Bamme had looked up at the corner window for a time and had finally said quietly:

'She was a remarkable woman, you know, Seidentopf. She always knew best, even about Rutze. A hundred times I swore to her that Rutze's entire brains could be got into a hazel-nut, but she would never agree and repeated again and again: "Dear Bamme, it is character that is decisive." And she was right. Yesterday I was with him at Protzhagen. *A la bonne heure*. What he has assembled and trained up there is nothing less than our finest company. A triumph of discipline. Fellows to chase the Devil out of Hell!'

This quotation from Bamme was as far as Seidentopf got, for at that moment it struck nine, which was the time he usually liked to return home; and on this occasion there was the additional incentive that he did not like the look of Lewin. He therefore departed, in the company of Marie, who was going home in the same direction.

When they had passed through the courtyard, and had also put the low-built lodge in which Krist and the gardener lived behind them, Seidentopf said: 'What did you think of Lewin? I didn't like the look of him. He hardly spoke three times. And how tired and peaky he looked.'

'He didn't say much,' replied Marie. 'But we mustn't be surprised at that. It was too much for him today. And the journey yesterday. And after all he has gone through in body and soul.'

'You know what it was, then?'

Marie nodded. 'It was what I supposed. Kathinka has gone. But why am I telling you: you will have heard about it at Guse!'

'Yes, Vitzewitz took me aside and told me; but even if he hadn't told me, I should have read it in Ladalinski's face. He gave the impression of being a broken man.'

'She was his darling, the darling of everyone. And I almost believe I envy her.'

'Do not envy her, Marie,' said Seidentopf, giving her his

hand. 'You have chosen the better part: humility and peace of mind. Happiness lies in these alone. And now, goodnight.'

And with that they parted, and the pastor entered his house and went straight to his study. Here all was dark, but the shutters had not yet been closed and the snow and the stars outside provided him with just the amount of light he liked. He sat himself upon the little leather sofa and gazed out into the wintry garden.

'Things are going to turn out as they ought to,' he said. 'I am sure of it. And now more than ever. Kathinka gone. That is more than I could possibly have hoped for. She was the great incalculable in my calculation.'

He was about to continue in these reflections, but the housekeeper with the big cap came noisily in, placed the little study-lamp beside Beckmann's *History of the Electorate of Brandenburg*, and closed the shutters.

6

A Deserter

AT the same time as Seidentopf and the ladies were talking together at the manor house, the farmers of Hohen-Vietz were talking together at the village inn. They were the old friends we encountered there on Christmas Day: Kümmritz and 'Creampot' and Krull and Reetzke; but Miekley too, who on that previous occasion had interrupted the discourse on Crucible Schultze and the Schwedter Margraves by his late appearance, today was already occupying his place at the table. Old Scharwenka was, as usual, going up and down and playing host, while Kniehase the village mayor was sitting towards the window, where the Küstrin *Anzeiger* and the two Berlin papers lay.

It happened that farmer Reetzke, who normally kept Krull company in staying silent, was today holding forth: for on the previous day he had been in Küstrin, where he had had to deliver a load of Oderbruch hay to the fortress. What he had to report covered two days more than Pastor Seidentopf's account.

'So they are taking in supplies,' said Creampot. 'Tell us, Reetzke, what supplies have they got?'

'They vary,' replied the latter. 'All the warehouses are full, but they are short of animals for slaughter. The creatures can no longer endure it with them and are running away. A hundred and seventy of them the night before last, all from Tamsel and Quartschen.'

'A hundred and seventy?' asked Kümmritz.

'Yes, Kümmritz, as I say. The day before yesterday they herded the Tamsel cattle together and the day before that the cattle from Quartschen, and they were all standing on the "Gorin", not a thousand steps from the town, roped together in pairs. They had built a corral as well, and they had a sentry at the entrance. But after one o'clock the moon went down, and in the morning when the relief guard came they saw that all the cattle had gone.'

'How did that happen?'

'There was a gap in the corral, and the cattle had made use of it. At first the French thought the peasants had driven them off in secret, but there were no footprints in the snow, only hoofprints, and these went half the way to Tamsel. The French didn't dare go further than that, for the Russians are already close to it; yesterday they captured a patrol near Blumberg.'

'Our cattle,' said Kümmritz, 'they still have their proper instincts and so they run away from the French, but the Westphalians stay and so does old Füllgraf. And if only they *were* Westphalians! But they're from the Altmark, from the Salzwedel region and Stendal. I've talked with a couple of them myself. Why don't they run away? Why don't they desert?'

'They do desert,' said Reetzke. 'Fourteen last week, seventeen this. But they got one of them back, a very young fellow; they were bringing him in when I was standing at the big warehouse with my load of hay.'

'Who brought him in?' asked Scharwenka, sitting down at the table. 'Would our Neumark people over there capture a deserter?'

'No,' Reetzke replied, 'the French brought him in; they had

taken him prisoner in the Krampe. Yesterday morning. Haven't you heard about it?'

'No, we've heard nothing. Tell us about it, Reetzke,' several cried together, and Kniehase too laid down his paper.

'Well,' said Reetzke, 'there was a surprise attack and the French had to take to their heels. They lost four dead.'

'And in the Krampe?' asked Kniehase, who had been growing more and more attentive. 'And was it the Russians who did it?'

'No. The Kirch-Göritzers. Pfeiffer the glover, who is lame in the left foot and who is supposed to have done in one of their generals on Drewitz Heath in *anno* six—but they couldn't prove it against him—he was the leader. He is always spoiling for a fight and is a good shot and has been top marksman three times already.'

'The Kirch-Göritzers!' Kümmritz interrupted. 'Who would have thought it! But now forget about the glover and his left foot and tell us what you know. Don't let us have to drag it out of you in bits.'

'Well then, the seventeen men went to Kirch-Göritz and arrived at the rifle-house, and there was Pfeiffer, who never has anything to do, and he immediately stuck himself into his rifleman's uniform with its row of medals, and welcomed them and lauded them, for he can talk something remarkable. And when they had told him where they had deserted from and that every morning twenty men had to go to the Krampe to cut the brushwood for the fascines, Pfeiffer said: "Children, what an opportunity! I was with Schill's brigade and I understand these things. Tomorrow morning, then. Who's coming with me?" All the seventeen Westphalians volunteered, as they had to if they didn't want to appear complete cowardly rats, and of the Kirch-Göritz riflemen eleven more also stepped forward. And Pfeiffer was number twenty-nine, which was what he looked like.'

The farmers laughed, for they all knew him.

'So then the next day came, that was yesterday morning, and they crept out close up to the Oder, first past the duck-snare and then past the pulp-mills. And so they arrived at the spot where the French came to cut the brushwood, and the brushwood stood so high and so thick they couldn't see one another. But at one place there was a path and they forced their way through one behind the other, and then they came out running and shouting, and Pfeiffer let off an old pistol, and the eleven Göritz riflemen fired a salvo into the crowd of soldiers, so that four fell straightaway and the others ran off to the fortress. Now the Westphalians gave chase; but it was slippery with ice, and the one in the front, who was hard on the heels of two of the soldiers running away, slipped over and fell in such a way that he couldn't get up at once. Then the two he was chasing turned round to him and seized him and dragged him off with them. This was the young fellow I saw them bringing in about ten o'clock. So then I said to myself, for I had got curious about it: "Reetzke," I said, "don't go back via Manschnow, go back via Kirch-Göritz." And so I came back via Kirch-Göritz. But, heavens above, when I got there they were all acting like they were possessed, and Pfeiffer had driven them completely crazy with punch and speeches. And he now regards himself as Schill and Blücher* combined.'

'That sounds like him,' said Kümmritz, 'a bigmouth who always knows in advance just where to chance something and where not to. Shame the young man has to foot the bill. But that's how it always is: this lame Pfeiffer gets the glory and the poor Westphalian will get his brains blown out.'

They continued talking back and forth, and Creampot was expatiating on how the deserter might just possibly have been rescued at the moment he slipped over when young Scharwenka came in: he too had been delivering hay and straw to Küstrin, and was still wearing his tall boots, greatcoat and fur cap; he greeted each of them but was plainly in a state of great excitement.

'Sit down, Wenzlaff,' said his father. 'What is it? You don't look like very good news.'

Young Scharwenka wiped a hand across his forehead, and then said: 'They have shot him; I wasn't thirty feet away; they wanted everyone to see it.'

'The deserter?' they all asked.

'So you already know?'

'No. All we know is that yesterday they brought in a

deserter. Reetzke has just told us about it. But now tell us, what happened?'

Young Scharwenka inserted himself between Krull and Reetzke, and then said: 'I was going to make the delivery but I couldn't get a receipt, because the old general, Füllgraf, was not yet about, and when I asked at the warehouse how long he was going to be the inspector said he could be as late as four o'clock or even later. And the castle clock was then only just striking twelve. So I had to think what to do, and so I said to Mathis: "Well, Mathis, there's nothing to be done, we may as well take it easy. Let's go and see Kerkow. We have to go past his place anyway." Because I also had to go on to Menken. And then I went over the bridge. And I hadn't been chatting with old Kerkow at his gate for ten minutes, with the hens pecking about around us, when we heard the sound of drumming, God, such drumming as I never heard in all my life.'

'That's because you've never been with the army, Wenzlaff,' said Kümmritz. 'But I know it. A drum roll and then silence and then another drum roll. It is always a bad sign.'

Young Scharwenka nodded and went on: 'And then it wasn't long before they were coming up the street. First of all five drummers and the same number of fife-players; but the fife-players weren't playing. And then came the young fellow. God, how he looked. Not afraid and not sad—I was moved, I can tell you—and when he saw me standing there and saw too, I expect, the pity for him in my eyes, he took off his cap and saluted me.'

The farmers all drew closer; you could have heard a pin drop in the room.

'And then came old Füllgraf, with a couple of adjutants beside him, and then behind them the whole battalion, the same battalion as the young Westphalian had deserted from. But now it was thinned out, not four hundred men. Then old Kerkow said: "Come, young Scharwenka, let's go and see it." And I went with him.'

'And yet it is written: "Thy heart shall not be full of curiosity and thou shalt not stand with the gapers," ' said Miekley.

'Oh, come on, Miekley,' Kümmritz interposed. 'Come on, a thing like that has to be seen; it impresses itself on you. And if you aren't careful you also start hating the enemy. And there's nothing wrong with that either.'

'And so they went on,' young Scharwenka continued, 'drums rolling all the time, as far as the last houses, and at Günzel the clothmaker's they turned left into the open field, there where the rope-yard is. "Halt!" old Füllgraf commanded, and then they formed a square, only the fourth side was open and that was where the grave was. I stood with Kerkow among the poplars, and we saw the sand that had just been dug up lying on the snow. And I felt my heart quake, because five men and a sergeant had now stepped forward out of the square, and they blindfolded his eyes with his own handkerchief. An old blue handkerchief with white spots. And then he was supposed to kneel down. But all of a sudden he tore the handkerchief off again and went up to the general, who was not ten paces away from him, and said something I couldn't hear. But I saw old Füllgraf nod his head and pass his hand over his brow. And then it was as though the young fellow felt all relieved, and he stood up dead straight and gazed up at the sky for a good minute. And then he was ready, and with his left hand, in which he was still holding the handkerchief, he struck his breast and cried: "Here, comrades, here is where the Prussian heart sits. Fire!" And the salvo rang out and the next moment it was all over. Then old Füllgraf rode up and said to the firing-squad: "Give me the handkerchief." But the dead man was holding it so tight they had trouble getting it away from him. Then they broke up the square again and marched away in sections past where we were standing. Now the fife-players were also playing, and I could tell it was supposed to be something cheerful, only I didn't feel very cheerful as I followed on behind them. It was only one o'clock, and it wasn't until six that I got my receipt. What a five hours *that* was!'

And so saying, he placed the receipt, signed by General Füllgraf, on the table. Each of the farmers took up the paper and looked at the signature. Then Creampot said: 'And why did it have to be his own battalion! They have enough Frenchmen. But that is the kind of dodge the French are always up to: always something peculiar, with cruelty in it.'

'Do be quiet, Creampot,' Kümmritz said in annoyance.

'Everyone hasn't fallen into the milkchurn. You don't understand these things. Peculiar! What nonsense. A deserter gets
shot, it's the same everywhere. We caught one at Pirmasens:*
he was a good-looking boy, too, but that didn't help him. War
is war.'

Miekley made to second Creampot, but Kümmritz, who
had worked himself into a state of agitation, refused to let
him speak. 'I don't want to listen, Miekley,' he said. 'You've
got yourself stuffed full of tracts, and that is the worst thing
of all. Uhlenhorst wants to abolish war, but it is war that
will abolish Uhlenhorst. For once war comes here he will be
talking to empty benches. And that can happen any day.
We're having a war, I tell you, and we can talk about it
afterwards. The old Gross-Quirlsdorfer is up to something,
and I know him, he's a hard man to dissuade and Uhlenhorst
certainly can't do it. Local militia or not, he'll read you the
articles of war and whoever doesn't stand by the flag gets
hauled before a court-martial. And you know what that
means.'

Creampot and Miekley shook their heads.

'You can shake your heads; you'll find out it's no joke; things
are going to happen, and here we are going to get it the worst.
That I know from the old prophecy. Do you know what it
says? Fiery horsemen will be seen in the sky, and men will
become as rare as the storks were *anno* 57 when the great storm
struck them and you could see only one every five miles. And
as at that time God did strike down his divine bird, so now he
will strike down men. But there will be a peace concluded at
Chorinchen.'

'Yes,' said Krull, 'I read that too last Sunday in the Küstrin
Anzeiger; it was on the back page, where they have the news in
brief and the riddles.'

'And today they are carrying a reply,' said Kniehase, and
stepped over from the window to the middle table. 'Would you
like to hear it?'

'Yes,' they all cried.

'Very well: *Reply to the Prophet of Gloom in Number Five of the
Anzeiger.'*

'And what does he write?'

'In 1812 much snow will fall and there will be a great fire in Moscow.'

'He makes it easy for himself,' muttered old Scharwenka, 'he prophesies the past.'

'In 1813, however,' Kniehase read on, 'there will dawn an age the like of which has never been seen before on earth. In this age, old people will not be quarrelsome and young girls will not be inquisitive. Doctors will no longer tell tales and judges will sleep only at night. And wine will be made only in the autumn. The rich will be benevolent and the beggars industrious. And everyone will love everyone else of the same class.'

The farmers laughed, and Kümmritz said: '*Another* prophet. One who makes lamentations and another who makes jokes. But which is the true one?'

'The one who is serious,' said Miekley.

'No, Miekley,' replied Kniehase, 'the one who is cheerful. The world is not going to perish, and nor are we.'

All united in agreeing that Kniehase was right, otherwise life would not be worth living.

A couple of the farmers copied out the 'new prophecy' for their wives and daughters; Creampot, however, took young Scharwenka aside and had him repeat the story of the deserter: for, of all the members of that circle, he was the one with the weakest nerves and consequently took most pleasure in the thrills of romance.

And then they went their separate ways.

7

Frau Hulen Writes

THE following morning, brother and sister were sitting alone at breakfast: Berndt had still not returned and Aunt Schorlemmer was busy in the house. Lewin was visibly better but was little inclined for talk, so that Renate was glad to see Hoppenmarieken appear beneath the entrance and by the usual waving of her stick indicate that she had letters for them. A moment later she came into the room accompanied by Aunt Schorlemmer and laid letters and newspapers on the table. 'One of 'em is from Faulstich,' she said, which fact, since she was unable to read, she must have acquired from the seal or some other external mark. And she was right. Faulstich had sent them the oft-mentioned cantata and, since he could now no longer direct such things to Guse, had also taken the opportunity to enclose an ironically pompous communiqué celebrating the victory of the Kirch-Göritzers under Pfeiffer the glover. Interspersed in the said communiqué were a number of stanzas under the title 'The Battle on the Krampe'; they included the following:

> And when they'd got their courage up
> With *eau-de-vie* a'plenty
> They charged their way through the undergrowth,
> All of the nine-and-twenty.

> And Göritz and its griffin bird
> Came raging from the cover,
> Then King became the Thane of Fife,
> Valiant Pfeiffer, our glover.

Hoppenmarieken had listened as these rhymes were read and had done so with hands folded, as though they were verses from a hymn-book. At the end, however, when she heard the name Pfeiffer, she realized what they were about and said: 'Oh yes, that Pfeiffer, that little hobble-leg. He's always been up to some mischief; now I expect they'll do for 'im.'

And with that she reached for her basket and stamped off out of the room again.

Lewin had been little pleased by the letter and he now pushed it away. 'Altogether Faulstich; always an eye for the ludicrous and nothing further. Complete lack of engagement. In the end I am more on the side of Pfeiffer the glover. But let's see what's in the other letter.'

This other letter was a little square with a faith-hope-and-charity seal on the back and furnished on the front with a lengthy address running straight on and not exactly distinguished by the correctness of its orthography. 'To His Excellency Herr Lewin von Vitzewitz, at present in Hohen-

Vietz near Küstrin; postpaid.' Lewin was sure he had seen the handwriting often before, but could not say where. Full of curiosity he broke the seal and looked at the signature. 'It is from dear old Frau Hulen!'

'Oh, read it,' said Renate, and Aunt Schorlemmer added: 'This will please us better.'

'Perhaps,' Lewin said; but his voice betrayed that he shared the same belief. And so he read:

Your dear Lordship!
These are truly hard times we are having, as Fräulein Renate wrote to me from Bohlsdorf so that I would know where you were. And that was a truly good deed by the dear Fräulein.

Yes, hard times they are, and I would much rather not talk about it. But yet I must tell you as an old woman, she was not for you. I saw it at once; she was as slim as a wasp, it is true, but *they* sting too, and then you have to lay earth on it to get rid of the pain. And if the heart is involved then it is truly bad. Yes, dear young sir, so it was with you too, so that earth was to be laid on you. But our dear Lord God did not wish it and found another way, without death and dying, and has preserved you for a true happiness.

Lewin had read thus far when his eyes began to dazzle and he let fall the hand in which he held the letter.

Renate took it to read it in his stead; she repeated softly: 'Preserved you for a true happiness', then she went on:

That I know for sure. That I could see on the first day, when you rented the rooms from me and said straightaway: 'That is not enough, Frau Hulen', and added to it out of your own free will. Ah, he who has such a care for poor people, for him our dear Lord God also has a care and does not let him perish, and you have no doubt discovered yourself what we were singing again last Sunday:

> Oft hast Thou refreshed me,
> And fed with bread of Heaven,
> With consolation blessed me—*

Yes, dear young sir, these are true words of comfort, written and intended for poor people. And in the end we are all poor, even if we are rich. You already know why.

And all this is what I wanted to write to you, dear Herr Lewin, as I may I hope call you as an old woman. And when you are again on your feet you will no doubt want to live at old Frau Hulen's again. The dear young lady thought so too. You won't find other such lodgings, for everything is suited. The Green Tree and the musical clock and the Klosterkirche. But I will say no more about that, because it looks so Catholic.

Please give my regards to the dear young lady, who is so good and remembered an old woman, as which I am your most gracious servant and remain

Wilhelmine Hulen, born Petermann.

Lewin made to retrieve the letter, but Renate said: 'No, not yet. There's a long postscript to come.' And she read on:

I must also inform you, young sir, that Herr Rittmeister von Jürgass has gone. He was here and asked after you. And the comical young captain as well. They are both going to Breslau, where everyone is going now. For old Lehwess was right after all, and Prussia is going to rise again. And tomorrow it will be in the gazette. But people just can't wait and there is a hurrying and scurrying as though war was already upon us. And whoever is too old or too weak gives what he has, or he collects. The Potsdam cadets have collected forty talers.

Renate laughed; for this first postscript, scribbled close to the edge of the sheet, was followed by a second:

Just imagine, young sir, the lame cellar-boy from next door also wants to go. He says the King can make use of anyone. And the day before yesterday I went to see the *Fire of Moscow*★ in the Bölkschen Saal. God, what a blaze! I thought we should all go up with it.

Your Ditto.

Aunt Schorlemmer had listened to the chatter of this letter with a kind of reverence. 'That is a good woman,' she now said, and then added: 'Let's send her a present!—Shouldn't we, Renate?' And with that she departed, so as to leave brother and sister alone.

She had been correct in thinking they wished to be left alone; Renate especially wished it, and after a short while she reached for her brother's hand and asked softly: 'May I speak with you, Lewin?' The latter nodded.

'Frau Hulen is right,' Renate began. 'In the simplicity of her heart she divined the truth. And now listen to me. You have been here two days, and we cannot go on wandering about together anxiously avoiding all mention of what is weighing on our hearts. It surprises you I should say "our". But so it is, for I am as weighed down as you are.'

She fell silent and was about to go on to speak of Kathinka but was unable to utter the name, and so she continued: 'I loved her so very much, more than a sister. She had that air of nobility that is so attractive, and she bewitched me, me and you and everyone. I cannot help thinking of the morning you went to Kirch-Göritz, you and Tubal, and the doves came to the window and I had hardly opened it before they were fluttering lovingly around her. I was annoyed at it at the time, but I was wrong. Everything fluttered around her. Even the doves. And Marie, too, was quite absorbed in her and consumed with admiration; consumed, yes, for her heart was bleeding.'

Lewin, who had listened to every word, smiled and said: 'We like to hear praise of what we have lost. Strangely enough, by enhancing our sense of loss it consoles us. But you may also reproach her, Renate, if you wish, without being afraid of hurting me. For my heart is now free: it was not by any act of mine, I hardly even desired it, but as I drove here through the bright winter day I felt that an old life was falling from me and a new life beginning. There is still a little acheing echo of it in me, but I have none the less recovered.'

'Alas, if only I could speak as you do,' said Renate. 'Your days of sorrow lie behind you, mine are still to come. And even if I am spared them, it will always be a hard destiny that preserves me from a yet harder one. I know that is how things will be; I have a presentiment of it in my heart.'

Lewin made to reply, but Renate continued in growing excitement: 'Theirs is a dark house, and what they themselves do not possess they cannot give to others: light and happiness. It has always been their fate to inspire love but not trust. Trust, "the mother of all love and its child". I read that once, and was deeply moved by it. But since then I have learned differently. There is also a love without trust, and my love is such a love; you know whom it is for, and I cannot tear it from my heart. And that is why I shall *not* be happy.'

'Yes, Renate, you will be. Happier than I.'

She shook her head.

'Tubal . . .'

' . . . is his sister's brother,' Renate interrupted in painful agitation, 'is *Kathinka's* brother.'

8

Headquarters: Hohen-Vietz

THEIR conversation was interrupted by the sound of a carriage drawing up, and Renate, who had a clear view of the window, cried: 'It's Papa!' And he it was: he was already in the outer room when brother and sister reached it, and he embraced them warmly; Renate he kissed on the forehead, Lewin he took by both hands and drew to the window.

'Let me take a look,' he said, and inspected him closely from head to foot. 'Well, you seem all right to me; it was your first affliction, and that hurts the worst, but it also heals the quickest. When we are young our sorrows are brief. In time you will come to know the reverse side of that. And now not a word more about it. Let us sit down.'

Jeetze had come in to lay the table a second time, and Aunt Schorlemmer appeared to participate in the joy of reunion: for, however calmly her Herrnhuter's heart might beat, she forgot all about keeping calm whenever, after days or weeks of separation, she heard the voice of Berndt von Vitzewitz again resounding through the house. Hector, too, had put in an appearance, and so they were all together.

'How eagerly we have been awaiting you, Papa!' said Renate. 'Not out of love, for of that you do not love to hear, but out of curiosity. We know nothing or as good as nothing. Tell us! How did she die?'

'Has Seidentopf not spoken of it, then?'

'Yes and no. He spoke of her funeral but not of her death. I cannot get over the idea that it was a shock that killed her.'

'And so it was. Death must have come upon her suddenly. When I saw her she was still in the position in which Eve had found her that same morning: she was sitting in the flowered armchair at the foot of her bed, her eyes, which were still open, fixed on the standing-mirror. The book she had been reading, a volume of Diderot,* had fallen from her hands and was lying beside the chair.'

'And how was she dressed?'

'In black. The previous evening she had sent Eve away; she wanted to prepare for bed by herself. That was at eleven: and that was about the time it must have happened, or not long afterwards.'

'And . . .' Renate faltered.

'I know what you are going to ask,' Berndt continued. 'When I entered the bedroom, the mirror was draped in its green curtain. But Eve flushed red when I asked about it, and contradicted herself again and again. I was not inclined to press her further, the poor little thing, especially as I am certain that the previous evening she had forgotten about it.'

'He who nurtures a ghost is destroyed by it,' said Aunt Schorlemmer.

'We ought not to nurture it, but if it is there . . .'

'We should ignore it. Then it will go away. It cannot endure neglect, for it is vain, like all the creatures of Hell.'

Berndt smiled, gave Aunt Schorlemmer his hand and said: 'Our old contention! Perhaps we should again declare a peace. But now to other things. What I still have to tell you, children, is much more cheerful. We are rich! And when *you* look in a mirror, Renate, you will see the face of an heiress.'

'I knew it,' Aunt Schorlemmer cried in triumph. 'I prophesied it that evening in Bohlsdorf when Dr Leist paid his first visit.'

Renate flushed, for she remembered many other things Aunt Schorlemmer had said on that occasion. Berndt, however, ignored the interruption, and continued: 'No will and testament has been found. There can be no question of the Pudaglas having a legal claim to Guse. It is freehold. Thus it falls to me as the most immediate heir. I have discussed the matter fully with Ladalinski, whom I asked provisionally to represent the interest of the Pudaglas; he knows in what sense I would be more than happy to meet the wishes or claims of this house, which is so closely related to him, and above all his own wishes. I am speaking of your aunt's long-matured designs. You know what they were. From the moment you have made your choice, my dear Renate, Guse belongs to you: I am merely usufructuary and administrator. On the other hand, these words are intended to commit you to nothing: you may choose as you wish.'

Renate and Lewin were silent, and even Aunt Schorlemmer failed to find an aphorism adequate to express all that was going on within her. Berndt seemed to be content with this silence, and while, as was his habit, he fed Hector with the bread and meat that had been intended for him himself, he went on: 'And so, then, we have become wealthy, wealthy in these poorest of days. And as surely as God knows I have never thirsted after earthly possessions, just as surely do I now rejoice in possessing these. I feel I can breathe more easily: for, to tell you the truth, the hardship and distress of these times has weighed heavily upon me, more heavily than I would want to admit to you. The barn burned down . . .'

'. . . shall now be rebuilt, Papa.'

'And the annexe . . .'

'. . . shall not be,' Renate laughed. 'As the heiress, I shall deny the necessary means. No, there we shall make a clean sweep and bring the garden right up to the house, just as it is over in Hohen-Ziesar, and the count himself must help us. It is his passion, after all. I am for mignonettes and stocks, but only as a border-frame; the middle of the bed must be occupied by mallows. Cinnamon-coloured ones and those that look like satin, they're the ones I like the most. And we'll have the two Derfflinger cannons brought over from Guse, but we'll leave the satyr where it is, and on the driveway we'll put a sundial, or better still a big black glass ball, so that the village street will be reflected in it, and Hoppenmarieken when she goes past.'

'That's the ticket, Renate! You are quickly getting used to the better times ahead, I see. Only you mustn't want to rob your own château, as I for the present regard Guse, for the benefit of old Hohen-Vietz, even to the extent of a pair of Derfflinger cannon. And anyway, who knows how much is still left? The French are around there at the moment and taking away with them whatever they fancy. Unless we keep a pretty close watch on them, that is. Come, Lewin, we must have a talk about that.'

Berndt rose, Lewin followed him. They went into the single-windowed room in which, at the commencement of our story, father and son had had their first conversation about a popular uprising and the final removal of foreign domination. Nothing had changed since then: the sofa and the picture were still in place, and the map of Russia with its variously coloured pins was still affixed to the window-shutter; all as they had been on Christmas Day.

Berndt took his seat, placed his foot, as he usually did, on the footstool standing before his desk, and said: 'Sit down, Lewin. Before we speak of other things, one more word about you. I didn't want to go on about it in front of the women. We mustn't let them hear too much about such matters: if they do they straightway start giving themselves airs. For they all want to rule, and they are delighted to know they possess so much power over us. In this they are all the same as one another and in an everlasting silent conspiracy against us.'

Lewin stared ahead; Berndt took his hand and went on:

'It is easy to speak of afflictions we ourselves no longer suffer or perhaps never have suffered. Yes, that is so, indeed: what you are suffering, Lewin, has been spared me. But I have been afflicted in other ways! I know what suffering is; and I know, too, that to live means learning how to overcome. Supple and flexible natures, such as yours, have the easiest time of it in these struggles: and so I knew that, in this struggle, you would overcome. What is still to be done time will accomplish, and our time more speedily than any other: for everything urges us to action, and activity is as surely the best course as brooding is the worst. These coming days will make you free.'

'I am free, Papa. I was discussing it with Renate as you drove up. It all lies behind me. What is still to be done concerns only my physical condition. I have been very ill and I am still suffering from the after-effects: but that is all. And now, what about Guse? You wanted to speak of it.'

'Yes. Very well, now listen. Yesterday afternoon—I had just got back from the church, where Nippler had been playing me the music he had composed for the cantata—and the village was full of the rumour: the French are coming. And it was true. Fifteen minutes later a hundred men marched in and halted in front of the château. They belonged to various regiments of the

Oudinot Corps and they were carrying a military chest with them. When I went up to them I was greeted by their leader, a swarthy Italian who called himself the Conte di Rombello. His rank was that of captain. In an effort to intimidate me, he spoke of the "rest of the corps" which would be arriving the next day, and demanded quarters for his men. I was at once willing to comply (for I could have desired nothing better) and invited him into the château, where I told him he could have any of the rooms he wished. He chose the mirrored-room; a somewhat peculiar taste, but that is his affair. He is handsome, so he will wish to see himself. The military chest stands in the hall, which for the protection of the cash it contains has for the moment been transformed into a kind of guard-house. Thirty men lie in the neighbouring rooms, another thirty are accommodated in the old Derfflinger barracks, the remainder with the peasants.'

'And now, what is your plan?'

'The troop intends to move on tomorrow morning. So whatever is to happen has to happen quickly. Bamme knows of it; but I have been content simply to report the matter. We shall act with what we have here to hand. If we include the men from Manschnow and Gorgast as well, we have a force of a hundred. That will be enough, for they are as exhausted as flies and their morale has long since sunk to nothing. Add to that the factors of night and surprise. It cannot go wrong. Those billeted separately with the peasants will be glad to escape with their lives: so it is only a matter of the château. There is a double guard at the front, on the sphinx-bridge, but we shall let it alone. Instead we shall cross over the moat, at the spot where the swan-house stands, and come up in the rear. Kniehase will have to lead this operation. I for my part shall take the "*conte*" prisoner, and you and Wenzlaff shall be with me. If we do it efficiently it need not cost us a single man. The military chest will remain ours; for the time being, that is. On the day the King declares himself we shall take it to Berlin: there they will be able to make use of it, for money is always the scarcest thing in the land of Prussia.'

'And the prisoners?'

'Not a hair of their heads shall be touched. I have cooled down somewhat. Recall what I wrote to you: "Let us have a proper war." And so let us hand the prisoners over to the Russians. Of course, I do not say they will be particularly comfortable with them. And now let us go and see Kniehase and talk over the details with him. We must be ready to march by nine and in Guse by midnight.'

With that they seized their hats and sticks and made off across the yard in the direction of the village street.

An hour later Berndt and Lewin returned from the mayor's house, where they had again discussed the '*coup*' with Kniehase and agreed on all the steps needed for its accomplishment. They discovered Jeetze in a state of great agitation, on beholding which Berndt inquired: 'I haven't seen you running for ages, Jeetze, what has happened?'

'The general is here.'

'Bamme?'

'Yes, General von Bamme. Your worship hadn't been gone fifteen minutes when he came along on his little Shetland pony. Your worship will know it, the cream-coloured one with the black mane. Krist and I have put it with the other ponies.'

'The Shetland pony. But where is the general?'

'Upstairs. I had to put the heat on, because it was cold and clammy. He is sitting in the office and has kept his grey cloak and his fur hat on.'

Father and son now ascended the stairs and discovered the general just as Jeetze had described him. Before him on the desk standing more or less in the middle of the room there lay a large-scale survey map of Barnim and Lebus held down with an inkwell and a pair of scissors; the little man was bowed over it attempting to orientate himself on it—an attempt not exactly facilitated by the thick cloud of tobacco smoke which shrouded him.

'Good day, General.'

'Good day, Vitzewitz. As you see, I have established myself here without announcement or inquiry. Not my usual practice. But you must take into account that I am now a general and place the action to my credit. My native Gross-Quirlsdorf lies too much out of the way, and in plain terms I am thinking of making Hohen-Vietz my headquarters. Initially I was uncertain whether I ought not to prefer our aristocratic Hohen-Ziesar, but Hohen-Vietz is better. The highway runs along here, and whoever wants to head west from Küstrin has to pass your windows.'

'I am delighted, General, that your choice fell thus and not otherwise.'

'And to confess the truth,' Bamme went on, 'it is not only on account of its situation that I have established my quarters here and not in Hohen-Ziesar: it is also on account of you, Vitzewitz. You are, after all, the soul of the affair, it is you who planned everything, it is your *métier* and you know the locality. And that is the chief thing. Look, here I am poring over this map and playing my own quartermaster-general. But to what end! In the past half-hour I have been back and forth between Küstrin and Berlin thirty times and haven't been able to discover even three real wolf-pits.'

'Wolf-pits?' asked Berndt, and gazed at the old man in wonderment, while Lewin drew a chair up to the other side of the table, so as to be able to view the map at any rate from above.

'Yes, wolf-pits, or fox-traps, whichever you like. And now listen to what I say. On *one* point we are all united: that something has to happen. And also on the fact that it is high time for it to happen. The marshals and corps commanders have left, all the big names, but of the little ones there are still hundreds stuck between the Vistula and the Oder, and these we must have. Therefore we must catch them on the roads, become brigands, knights of the highway. One mustn't be afraid of words, *we* least of all: something of our ancestors' blood and *métier* must still reside in us. Whether we shall be thanked for what we intend to do, that, to be sure, is the question. I almost doubt it. You know my view of the matter. Self-help has always been "*suspect*" in this country, as your sister the countess would have said. They do not like us up there. And they are quite right not to do so, those gentlemen from Nuremberg: for you can see where it begins but not where it will end.'

Bamme, who whenever the question of 'the Hohenzollerns versus Quitzow and Company'* came up was always drawn into labyrinthine excursions, had today too lost the thread of his discourse, and Vitzewitz was obliged to bring him back to it with the still unelucidated question: 'What do you mean, wolf-pits?'

Bamme laughed, relit the little meerschaum that had gone out while he was speaking, and said: 'Wolf-pits, Vitzewitz? But we have already said what they are: brigands' hideouts, general-traps. They don't need always to be generals. We will take company commanders as well. Or anything else that falls into them. We mustn't be particular. Well, that's it. But would you believe, Vitzewitz, that in these ten miles I haven't been able to conjure out even three such general-traps! On my honour, not one. And why not? Because I am a Havel-lander and, to my disgrace be it said, I haven't been able to find my way about in Barnim and Lebus for all the seventeen years I have been here. Rathenow, Havelberg, there I'm at home, there I know every highway and byway. But what do I know here? Hohen-Vietz and Hohen-Ziesar.'

'And Guse.'

'Yes, Guse. That would have been the kind of trap I am talking about. But they've left.'

'Who? What?' cried Berndt.

'All of them! The hundred men, the *conte* and the military chest. And the last is the worst. Two hours ago I passed the whole troop not three hundred steps from the village, their cash-box in the middle of the column. Clever fellows. They must have got wind of something. And that *conte* is a delightful chap; and how he gabbles and chatters! I wish I could have introduced him to Aunt Amelie: no offence, Vitzewitz.' Berndt stamped his foot—not on account of Aunt Amelie but on account of his frustrated *coup*.

'It's as though it is doomed never to be,' he cried. 'Repeated failure, repeated postponement. Admit it, Bamme: the moment we are about to creep up on the deer there's a noise and he goes running off.'

'Let him, Vitzewitz; every day's a new day. You lose with one card and win with the next. In any case, I bet six bottles of Château d'Yquem to a Château Krach that for all his lovely eyes the *conte* won't get three miles. The general-traps aren't ready yet, I know, but sometimes they make themselves. And as for the money, I console myself with the thought that when an army corps is depleted so is its military chest. And this poor Oudinot has certainly had to pay a very heavy bill. So let's forget it.'

'We shall have to,' said Berndt. 'Go, Lewin, and tell Kniehase to leave the men where they are, above all those in Manschnow and Gorgast. We don't want to upset them by marching them about unnecessarily, or they'll be missing when we need them.'

And when this point had been settled, and the Guse disaster already half forgotten in the compounding of new undertakings, Jeetze entered to announce that dinner was served.

9

An Aide-de-Camp

THE hall had been decked in Bamme's honour. A large open fire was blazing, snowflakes were falling outside, and the ancient Vitzewitzes gazed down from their frames in amazement at the hoarsed-voiced little man who was again and again called 'Herr General'. In their days generals had looked somewhat different from this. But perhaps their amazement was directed at the opulent decoration of the table rather than at anything else: for today not only were the heavy, four-branched silver candlesticks blazing, but between them there also arose a disproportionately large rococo centre-piece depicting the Danube and all its tributaries and with the Empress Maria Theresia sitting enthroned on the top. The old bewigged Vitzewitzes had not beheld the object for a good thirty years, and even our Berndt had for a moment been as though struck speechless at the sight of it as he had entered the room. On encountering his look of surprise, however, Renate had pointed to herself and then whispered roguishly to her father: 'It is I, Papa, as the heiress of Guse!'

Then they had taken their places: Bamme between Berndt and Renate, Lewin and Aunt Schorlemmer opposite them.

There was also an empty chair, for Seidentopf, who had also been invited, had had to decline only a few minutes before: for the old cottager Maltusch had been lying dying since the previous night and had asked to be given holy communion. The imparting of this information had at once inspired Bamme to mutter certain tasteless remarks concerning last suppers and missed dinners: but his bad conscience in doing so had constrained him to murmur them so indistinctly that even Aunt Schorlemmer, who never allowed such things to pass unreprimanded, had been unable to call him to account.

The old cottager Maltusch, who was not much younger than our friend Jeserich Kubalke, lived three-quarters of an hour from the village, hard by the Hohen-Ziesar frontier and in fact on a tongue of land actually extending into Drosselstein's domain: and this circumstance soon led, after several minutes' scouting and skirmishing in the Maltusch–Seidentopf–Kubalke region, to a foray into that of the count, and thence to an investment of the count himself. All were united in his praise; Renate spoke with especial warmth, and even Aunt Schorlemmer commended his Christian-mindedness, 'of which he himself was not aware'.

'If the circle in which he moves had been different,' she said, 'and if he had lived in an age of revival instead of an age of apostasy, he would have become a man like *our* count.'

'Let us thank God', Bamme retorted, 'that he has stayed as nature and circumstances made him. I have nothing against the Lusatian count whom you, honoured lady, like to designate "*your* count"; but I am horrified at the idea of our Drosselstein—all honour to him, but he is not even now the most individual of men—as Zinzendorf the Second. It does everyone good to stand on his own two feet, whatever these two feet may be like. We have ours, Zinzendorf had his. When I say "ours" I have, I know, to apologize, since I realize it is not in precisely this direction that I have a right to any vanity. However, it remains true that "the saddest cases are the duplicates". What did Prince Heinrich come to grief on? The countess over the way is dead, so we may venture upon an answer to this question without risking forfeiture of her friendship. He came to grief simply on the fact that in the end he was nothing more than "almost his brother". In this respect I must commend old Ferdinand, whom you, Vitzewitz, recently visited in his Johanniter Palace. He never was anything, God knows, but at least he was himself. No, dear lady, let us leave our count of Hohen-Ziesar as he is. That will be the best thing, for him and for us. After all, he has only one failing!'

'And what would that be?' asked Berndt.

'He can't lay off the Pregelwater:* which is to say, he is too firmly fixed in his East Prussian prejudices. Pay heed to him when he talks about politics, especially in these times of ours when, he is unshakeably convinced, the people at the top are again busy making world-history and diligently intent upon creating a balance between freedom and order. I know him. East Prussia is the home of manliness and Königsberg is the home of wisdom. That stands immovable, that is Clause One. Everything that exists in the other provinces is measured against this standard. We Brandenburgers only just pass muster. We will do, though merely as raw material. We can be trained for service, for use in the army and the administration, but in ourselves we are nothing and are of no importance. We are unfree, tools, court slaves, mere bodyguards of the Hohenzollerns.'

Berndt smiled.

'Yes, General,' he said, drumming lightly on the tablecloth, 'but, taking everything into account, *is* that not what we are?'

'No, Vitzewitz, no. Naturally, there are exceptions: a few or, for aught I know, a lot. But what makes me annoyed is that in the midst of the Pehlemanns, the Medewitzes and Rutzes, who possess nothing but musical clocks, gout and stupidity, in the midst of these the Vitzewitzes and Bammes get forgotten. Court nobility! Bah! The hunting Junker von Otterstädt,* who wrote "Jochimken, Jochimken, watch yourself" on his gracious lord's chamber door, was also at court. Bodyguards! Nonsense! What we are is Frondeurs, all or at any rate the best of us, and our great passion would thus be setting-up and pulling-down, at least that is what mine is. When were the Bammes ever at court? Never. And the Vitzewitzes haven't often been. We didn't care what they did *anno* 95, and we don't care now. As long as it works they stick together. *Manus* *manum lavat.* When I feel happy I always speak Latin. Legitimacy, loyalty! Bah! It is all bargaining and pact-making and mutual advantage.'

'And *oaths*,' said Aunt Schorlemmer.

Bamme shrugged his shoulders.

'My good woman,' he continued condescendingly (for he knew Aunt Schorlemmer could not endure him), 'if oaths were what counted the Zinzendorfs would rule the world. I doubt that we would be the gainers by it. Imagine a world-history consisting of nothing but virtue. For my part at least I would rather not read it. Oaths are like laws: they exist only to be broken. Political oaths do, at least: I naturally exclude the oaths of love.'

And he turned as he spoke to Renate, who was sitting beside him, and kissed her hand.

'I realize you are joking,' Renate said.

'Ah, my dearest young lady,' continued Bamme, who was in his own fashion a devoted admirer of Renate's, 'I am not joking, I am only falling into my old error of failing to take proper account of whose ears it is I am speaking into. All that was material for the countess aunt, not for the lovely niece. At this moment I was in Guse, not in Hohen-Vietz. *Pardon!*'

As he was saying these final words the sound of bells had grown increasingly audible from the direction of the village street, and immediately afterwards a sleigh came to a halt before the steps of the house.

'That ought to be Drosselstein,' said Bamme, half-raising himself from his seat to obtain a clearer view of the forecourt. But it was not Drosselstein: to his astonishment, an astonishment shared equally by Lewin, there entered Hirschfeldt, Grell and Tubal; and as they disengaged themselves from their cloaks and scarves, this last introduced his two companions and apologized for their all appearing thus unannounced.

Berndt welcomed the unexpected arrivals with the liveliest expressions of pleasure—a pleasure which, as may easily be supposed, was shared by Bamme, who never ceased to delight in and to demand 'new blood'; there remained none the less a residue of embarrassment which Lewin and Renate, and to an even greater extent Tubal, sought to conceal behind a conversational chatter at once agitated and disjointed. Even Aunt Schorlemmer, indeed, failed to maintain her customary composure.

In the meanwhile chairs had been brought in, and since, in addition to Seidentopf's vacant place, the top and bottom of the table had also been left unoccupied when it had first been laid, no serious disturbance of the seating arrangements was occasioned. There was talk of quickly repeating some of the courses, but all the newcomers declined in the firmest manner and declared, not only that they had taken very substantial sustenance during their journey, but that to all appearance they had chosen for their arrival in Hohen-Vietz the most propitious possible moment, that of the dessert. This view of the matter was emphatically seconded by Bamme, who was engaged in cementing fragments of black bread and biscuit together with a piece of fresh butter, and who went on to assert that epicures of every age, from Lucullus to Friedrich the Great, had always regarded the actual dinner as no more than the pedestal for supporting the three great dessert-divinities Bacchus, Momus and Pomona.*

Thus the old general fantasized on, and the happy mood he was in began to infect the others, so that the constricted, disjointed chatter of the first minutes gradually gave way to less constrained conversation. In the end everyone was involved, especially Tubal, from whose communications there emerged, among other things, the actual goal of their journey. They were, he averred, on their way to Breslau, where they proposed to follow the example of Jürgass and Bummcke and join the volunteer army in process of being constructed there. The call to arms of which everyone was talking had not yet been uttered, it was true, but no one doubted that it would come ('Any hour', Berndt interposed), and a letter from Jürgass that had arrived yesterday already provided a picture of the new awakening. Among other things, a Silesian local militia was in course of creation: all men between eighteen and sixty who were not already bearing arms were to be conscripted into it. The purpose of this militia was to attack the enemy where he appeared in small detachments, to capture generals (Bamme smote the table with the flat of his hand) and to make short work of *fourrageurs* and *maraudeurs*. Scharnhorst was in command; Blücher was co-operating. But the weightiest consideration was that the King himself, who had hitherto been sceptical of the possibility of a vigorous patriotic revival, was now full of confidence. And in this new faith he would continue to be strengthened, for the new spirit was the same everywhere. Donations were streaming in from all sides: money, arms, equipment; everyone was giving whatever he had, and he who had nothing was giving himself. All this was taken from Jürgass's letter. He for his part, however, believed he could add that in the new few days nine thousand volunteers would be leaving Berlin for Breslau.

This information, which was received with jubilation, put to flight the last vestiges of embarrassment, if any indeed remained, and did so especially in the case of Berndt, who had from the first refused to take what had happened in the Ladalinski household too tragically. For what in the end did it amount to? It was the old privy councillor's obstinacy rather than his honour that had suffered a defeat. Bninski was a count and rich, and Lewin—was young. The Hungarian wine, of which not only Bamme but the whole table was beginning increasingly to partake, was in like measure raising everyone's spirits, and Berndt, full of designs which the continued presence of his guests could only expedite, at length directed at Tubal the question: 'How long are you here for?'

'Until tomorrow.'

That, to be sure, was not the answer he had wished to hear.

'You must stay', he cried, 'and join with us. Our Guse *coup* was a washout; that *conte* of theirs was cleverer than I took him for, and got his head out of the noose in time. But something's got to happen in the next few days, even if we have to storm the Bastion Brandenburg or the "Hohe Kavalier" itself. Bamme and I were the first to act in these parts and were already drilling before those on the other side of the Oder had moved a muscle, and now they have a nice little war going while we are still sitting like old women at evensong.'

A withering glance from Aunt Schorlemmer struck him, and Berndt, indulgent to the point of weakness to the rigorous principles of the old Herrnhuter, at once corrected himself and, repeating his final sentence in a different form, said: 'While we are still sitting quietly with our hands in our laps. But that has to change. Everywhere they are ahead of us: in Soldin, in Driesen, in Landsberg. And as if that were not enough, not an hour away from here the Kïrch-Göritzers have their battle in the underbrush, and before we know it Faulstich will be getting the *Pour le mérite*. Are we here to strike sail before Pfeiffer the glovemaker? We who were the first to crow, the first and the loudest. Shall we let it be said of us that we have been merely play-acting and idling our time away with exercises and drum-beating? No, I hate nothing more than this playing at soldiers. And why? Because I used to be a soldier and take the thing seriously. A citizen, a peasant, is not bound to take up arms, but if he *does* take them up he must use them, or he is a fool or a braggart.'

'There is something about this Hungarian,' said Bamme with a grin, and twisted his moustache. 'For example, it enables us to change roles. You, Vitzewitz, have been talking like Bamme, so I shall have to talk like Vitzewitz. That is to say, quietly and thoughtfully. No, friends, you are going too far, above all too far in your own condemnation. It takes two to make a quarrel, says the proverb. And the same goes for a war. First we must have an enemy.'

'Not so,' Berndt interrupted. 'Let's not hide behind *this* objection. The enemy is everywhere. All we need to do is to want to encounter him. "Seek, and ye shall find." One proverb is worth another, and mine even comes from the Bible. Troops of men such as that hundred at Guse are now on every street. We simply have to declare them prisoner, more is not needed. It is the kind of expedition (you were there, Tubal) which we mounted against Muschwitz and Rosentreter, my "French *maraudeurs*" of that time. There is no question of danger: for the sake of our reputation, indeed, one could wish there were more. But the page can turn, new regiments of the Viceroy's will soon become mixed in with the old, and there can be no doubt about it, you are going to stay, you and your friends!'

Tubal exchanged assenting glances with Hirschfeldt.

'So we'll stay!' they both cried and, turning to Berndt, Hirschfeldt added: 'The proclamation has not yet been made, and the formation of the volunteer corps has hardly yet begun: so we are not neglecting very much. In any event, Hohen-Vietz is on the way to Silesia: we can be in Breslau in three days, four at the latest. I, for my part, place myself at your service, and our friend Grell, eager for war though he is, will not consider a conversation about Hölderlin, such as he will have the best opportunity for here, in any way a waste of time. I ask the Herr General to be good enough to command me.'

'Done, Hirschfeldt', said Bamme. 'That I call a capture! You are more welcome to me than you can know. It is no small thing for an old Zietener who can do no more than keep his eyes open and stay on a horse to have an aide-de-camp with him who knows all about maps and lists and paperwork. For nothing gets done in the world nowadays without quill-driving playing some part in it. Therefore, to good comradeship!'

And their glasses rang together.

Fifteen minutes later they all rose from the table, and while the remainder of the company retired to the corner room the two ladies ascended to the upper floor to take care of the placing of their guests. They agreed to accommodate the Hölderlin enthusiast Grell with Lewin; Tubal and Hirschfeldt would be in the neighbouring room. All this was quickly accomplished and only Bamme's accommodation presented difficulties. 'Where shall we put him?' asked Aunt Schorlemmer. 'I don't want him in our corridor. He is objectionable and a horror.'

'I am afraid of him too,' Renate responded. 'That is to say, a little.'

'It is a good thing you are afraid. I am also, if aversion is fear. He can't come up here, ten steps from your room and mine. Perhaps he will ring, or certainly he *will* ring, and Maline will have to fetch him a glass of water.'

'Well?'

'Well?' Aunt Schorlemmer repeated. 'What questions you ask, Renate! I have brought you up too innocent. A man like Bamme never drinks water and always rings and counts on getting this or that when he does so.'

'But, dear Schorlemmer . . .'

'I have lived with the angekoks,' Aunt Schorlemmer went on, 'and the Greenlanders, who are also small, just as small as this Bamme, they too were all full of the lusts of the flesh. My dear Renate, one shouldn't talk of the Devil, certainly; but it is just as certain one shouldn't lock the stable door after the horse has bolted. And Maline is just a child, yes that she is in spite of all her worldly wisdom. For what worldly wisdom does for her is undone by vanity. And the vain are always his easiest victims. You know whom I mean. I feel as though we had the Evil One in the house.'

'It is not as bad as you are making out,' said Renate. 'He does not have a good reputation. But people exaggerate and, when all's said and done, he is an old man; he must be seventy or more. I recall Aunt Amelie saying of him: "If we do not flee from sin, in the end sin will flee from us." She said it in French, but you do not like to hear that language.'

Thus the two ladies talked together in the upstairs corridor, and while they were talking the object of their moral fears and anxieties was not only bathing in a sea of contentment himself, but was also succeeding in communicating his sense of well-being to all around him. He was being affable and racy, as he usually was, he was genuinely delighted that Hirschfeldt had agreed to stay, and he was forbearing to play the self-important general. For he knew he could let himself go without forfeiting anything essential in his authority: and if he did forfeit it he knew very well how to get it back again whenever he wished to. With Hansen-Grell, who was introduced to him under his somewhat outlandish-sounding double-barrelled name, he was at first unable to get along—it was due partly to the name itself, partly to its owner's peculiarly protuberant eyes—but he soon rectified this and while they were playing at tarot (which our Gantzer cantor's son had learned to perfection as a card-partner at Count Molke's house) repeatedly promised him the living at Gross Quirlsdorf, 'once I have succeeded in irritating the present incumbent to death or had him kicked upstairs to Berlin.' For that was where he belonged and that was where he was going. An identity of interests must unite patron and pastor if they were to get along together, and the finest cement had always been, and remained, tarot, or, if not tarot, card-playing of some sort.

The evening passed quickly. Shortly after nine o'clock the game was broken off and everyone retired, the younger men to the guest-rooms upstairs, the general to his room on the ground floor, which the entire female personnel of the house had been strictly forbidden to enter no matter how furious the ringing.

Half an hour later all was still; in only one of the rooms on the upper corridor was a light still burning, and Renate and Marie chatted about the events of the day: about Bamme and Aunt Schorlemmer's ridiculous fears, about Grell and his impressive ugliness, about Hirschfeldt and his scarred countenance.

'Scars make a man handsome,' Marie averred.

And then conversation glided over to Tubal, whose name had, very significantly, hitherto remained unspoken.

'Tell me,' said Marie, 'how was he?'

'He was embarrassed and avoided my eye: at the same time he talked a lot, about one thing after the other, but I could see that he was only trying to help himself and us to get through what was painful in this meeting—a piece of delicacy that touched me. But that is what the Ladalinskis are like. They are all possessed of that nobility which prefers to accuse itself rather than others. And, to say the least, it is as though they shared the responsibility for what happened. That is why Tubal was not with us in Guse. The old privy councillor admitted it to me when we met in Bohlsdorf.'

Marie shook her head.

'I see it differently,' she said. 'What you call delicacy is really their conscience, and the guilt they gently admit to is not imaginary. They are all alike and know nothing except the present moment. He loves you and yet he is not certain of his love. Full of mistrust of himself, he is shy and timid when he meets you. Perhaps he will openly confess all this to you, so as to gain, at least in his own eyes, the feeling he has some strength of character and something like a justification for the way he is acting.'

'You were always at loggerheads with one another,' said

Renate. 'If I didn't know better, I could believe you were in love with him.'

And with that the two friends parted, and Maline came to accompany Marie back home.

These final words had been spoken with a laugh, but when she was again alone Renate ceased laughing. Were these not the same apprehensions she had herself honestly expressed to Lewin only that morning, in the hope they would be contradicted? And now she heard nothing but confirmation of all that oppressed her heart with misgivings. Was Marie right? Worse, had *she herself* been right?

She would no doubt have gone on brooding and questioning in this way if Aunt Schorlemmer had not come in. She had come to say goodnight to her darling. 'The heiress is here,' she concluded, 'soon there is bound to be a wedding.'

'Alas, dear Schorlemmer,' Renate replied, 'there is one thing about you Herrnhuters: you may be pious, but you are no prophets.'

'You cannot say that, Renate. When we have the true faith we also see truly.'

'You see truly what ought to be, but not always what will be. Reality does not always keep faith with you.'

Aunt Schorlemmer smiled to herself good-humouredly.

'Those are tenets from Lewin's new catechism,' she said. 'But no more of that, my little Renate; for today be content to go to sleep. That is what you ought to do, and I prophesy you will.'

10

At the Wermelin

LEWIN and Grell were the first up, but decided to wait for the others to appear. They were not long in arriving, and soon everyone was assembled in the hall, where on account of the number of guests breakfast too was to be taken. Only the ladies were still missing: Renate had excused herself, at least for the present, while Aunt Schorlemmer, full of instinctive aversion to the old general, had simply stayed away, consoling herself with the thought that no one, with the possible exception of Berndt, would notice her absence. And he would understand the reason for it. Jeetze trotted busily back and forth, accompanying each new *double entendre* from Bamme with a soft jovial tittering and confessing quietly to himself that when he had put on the black gaiters the previous week he had not believed he would again see such merry days at Hohen-Vietz.

'Has Hoppenmarieken been yet?' asked Berndt.

Jeetze said she had not, and the old general, who, although behind his back he was constantly being likened to her had never heard of the dwarf, asked inquisitively: 'Hoppenmarieken? Who is that?'

'Let her tell you herself,' replied Berndt. 'I can see her coming across the yard now.'

And so she was: before any further questions could be asked—for Grell and Hirschfeldt had also displayed an interest —the object of this universal curiosity appeared in the glass door and was not a little astonished to encounter a cheerful company of the living in a place where hitherto only the dead Vitzewitzes had addressed her from the walls.

'Here, General, is Hoppenmarieken,' said Berndt.

And Lewin added: 'My lady-friend, are you not, Marieken?'

'Ho ho!' laughed Hoppenmarieken, set down her basket and began to rummage about in it, although everything she needed in fact lay on top.

'Letters?' Berndt asked.

'No, your worship, only the *Berliner*,' and she handed Berndt the newspaper.

'Ah, the "Proclamation"!'*

'Yes, that it'll be. The post said so too. And one of the people in Küstrin told me: "Now the balloon's going up, Hoppenmarieken . . . " Well, that's all right with me. The French have had it now, that's plain; they're all clearing out, and the old general . . . '

'Füllgraf?'

'No, the other one, the top one.'

'Ah, General Fournier. Well, what of him?'

'Yesterday he was down with Margrave Hans. He himself and five or six of his generals and officers. All down in the crypt.'

'Where they were looking for the twenty-four bushels of ducats the Margrave is supposed to have taken with him into his grave?'

Hoppenmarieken nodded.

'And who told you of it?'

'Old Mewes the baker.'

'And what else?'

'Not much, and at first I didn't understand him. But then Mewes burst out laughing, and said: "You're not that stupid, Hoppenmarieken. And now pay attention. The Russian is here, together with his Cossacks, and they have got their big popguns at Quartschen and Tamsel. And the French know that and they're clearing off, and they're taking with them whatever they can get. And that is why yesterday they were down with Margrave Hans in his crypt. But they didn't find anything." '

'I can well believe it,' said Bamme, and added, turning to Vitzewitz: 'Margrave Hans was a Hohenzollern, and they have their heads screwed on: they don't bury a penny, let alone twenty-four bushels of ducats; the Hohenzollerns want to collect interest. I could have told the Küstrin general that. But even if I had he would never have believed me.'

Hoppenmarieken, who had understood not a word of all this, none the less laughed at it, nodded her head familiarly to the old general, and then, saluting with her stick and mumbling her usual incomprehensible gibberish, she left the hall.

'A splendid specimen,' said Bamme. 'If I were a prince and ran a court, I would have her trained in hocus-pocus, in potions and fortune-telling.'

'Then you would be wasting your money and effort,' Berndt replied, 'for she knows it all already.'

'All the better; but now, the "Proclamation". Let us hear it, Vitzewitz.' And the latter began to read.

The first ten lines held everyone's attention; thereafter, however, attention slackened: which was hardly surprising, since the phrases they were hearing became increasingly lukewarm and gave rise in the end to a feeling of thorough disappointment. This feeling was so strong that the appearance of Kniehase, who entered before Berndt had finished reading, was scarcely felt as an interruption.

'Take a seat, Kniehase,' said Berndt. 'What have you got for us?'

'Good news, your worship: we have him.'

'Whom, the Viceroy?'

'No, not as high as that, but we have the Italian count. I have just seen the manager from Trebnitz: all hundred of them are prisoner in his church. They have taken the count to Selow, because he got a blow on the head.'

'Tell us about it.'

'Well, then: it must have been yesterday about midday, as they were going through Alt-Rosenthal. Just beyond it there begins the Trebnitz Heath, on the right tall trees, but to the left a nursery, and they didn't much like the look of it, or so the Trebnitz man thought. But even so they had to go through it, because they wanted to get to Jahnsfelde before it got dark. And so they marched off, keeping close together with the military chest safe in the middle, until they reached the little lake which lies inside the nursery and is really no more than a pond and which the Rosenthalers and Trebnitzers call the "Wermelin". And there they copped it, because that was where they were hidden and they all leaped out shouting "Hurrah", which the French who heard it at Moscow can't bear to hear again. So they threw down their weapons and surrendered.'

'All of them?'

'All except the count. He snatched up one of the guns and shot one of them out of the saddle. But Tettenborn* came at him from the side and gave him a blow on the head, so that he collapsed to the ground.'

'Tettenborn?' everyone asked.

'Yes, Colonel Tettenborn, with twenty Cossacks. He had crossed the Oder the same morning at Zellin. He is now in Selow: he took the count there, and also gave him back his sword, because he had shown himself a brave officer and a man of honour.'

Bamme was the first to collect himself. Like Berndt and all the others, at the commencement of the story he had believed he was about to hear of a Barnim–Lebus feat of arms, and at the mention of the name Tettenborn he had been for a moment seriously put out to see all the fancied glory of the local militia amount to nothing more than another tale of the Cossacks. But the old general was not the man to give way to any kind of vexation for more than two minutes: he possessed, on the contrary, a decided talent for at once seeing the good side of even the most vexatious matter.

'Taking everything into account, Vitzewitz, we have three reasons for congratulating ourselves: firstly I have turned out to be right (which in my eyes is always a major consideration), secondly we have the *conte* and his hundred men, and thirdly we have the Cossacks, or at any rate their vanguard, on *this* side of the Oder. Not an altogether pleasing prospect, you may think: but the way things are, we have no alternative but to sail with any wind that offers, even with that empty-headed windbag Tettenborn. So no despondency, Vitzewitz. Something will be left over for us, even if it is only the Viceroy, after whose health you so solicitously inquired of Mayor Kniehase.'

This sufficed to restore Berndt to his good humour, and it was agreed they should depart for Hohen-Ziesar, which, although he had been acquainted with Drosselstein for many years, Bamme had never visited. Vitzewitz decided that their arrival ought not to be unannounced and retired to his study to write the necessary note.

The others also rose from the table: Grell and Hirschfeldt to inspect the village and the church under Lewin's direction, the old general to pay a visit to Seidentopf. 'I must take another look at his potsherds,' he said, 'and perhaps his coins as well. Trajan, Hadrian, Antoninus Pius. I can never get any further. Strange that I should always get stuck at *him*.'

Only Tubal elected to stay indoors: he went across to the corner room, where he might reasonably hope to encounter the ladies—or at any rate his cousin. He had not deceived himself: Renate was sitting close to the window engaged in bead-embroidery and counting the stitches on a pattern lying before her.

'Am I disturbing you?'

'No, but I thought the men had gone off to the village and the church. Or do you, like the general, have an aversion to churches?'

'I preferred to remain behind. May I take a seat, Renate?'

She nodded in assent.

'Our hours here are numbered,' he went on. 'Hirschfeldt is growing impatient, he is itching to get away, and what I have to say to you can brook no delay.'

Renate recalled the conversation she had had with the older Ladalinski in the church at Bohlsdorf. She was anxious to avoid any declarations or avowals, at that present moment at least; and so, to ward off questions she feared to hear, she herself assumed the role of questioner.

'Have you received letters?' she asked. 'I mean letters from Kathinka.'

'Not letters, only hasty lines. I received them the day before yesterday, the day before our departure.'

'And where were they from?'

'From Myslowitz, a small town on the frontier. The count's estates are near there.'

'May I know what she writes?'

'I have no secrets, Renate. And if I had any, it would make me happy to be able to share them with you.'

'I never thirst after secrets, but I long to hear from Kathinka. Please, read what she says.'

And Tubal read:

> Myslowitz, 4 February
>
> My dear Tubal!
>
> Tomorrow we are going, via Miechowitz and Nowa-Gora, to Bninski's home. A Catholic priest will accompany us. I am thinking (Bninski wishes it) of returning to our old faith. There is nothing in me that could prevent me from doing so: all in all, I prefer Rome to Wittenberg. Write to me soon. I am eager to know what you are doing, what *everyone* is doing. I think of Papa every hour, and now I often think of our mother, too. You will understand. Bninski wants to go to Paris; he is as I thought he would be, and I am happy, *completely* happy. But no, I cannot say that. Is it *our* fate, or is it the fate of all mankind?
>
> Your Kathinka.

There followed a silence.

Then Renate said: 'And these are the lines you are to take with you. It is fine to have loving words for one's companions, but not words like these. There is such sorrow in them.'

'Ah, Renate, if only I had more comforting words to take with me. Say them. You know what it is I so much want to hear.'

She did not reply.

Tubal however went on: 'I know why you do not reply. There is something in the human heart we lack: that is the fatality of our house. It fell upon my father and consumed his life, and now it is falling upon me. It is as though we had trifled away something. For a moment it seemed all that might be going to change: now *this* has come upon us. And things are again as they were. Everything testifies against us, and the "Yes" I long to hear refuses to pass your lips.'

This, then, was the 'self-confession' Marie had prophesied only the previous evening, and Renate now recalled with pain the gently mocking tone in which she had done so. But it lasted only a moment, then it was overcome, and all that had ever moved her soul in Tubal's favour was there again, redoubled by the profound feeling of sympathy his words had evoked, and with that cheerful openness that constituted the magical charm of her nature she said: 'Hear me, Tubal, I will keep nothing from you. Lewin and I, we have often spoken of it together, we did so as recently as yesterday. Your fate is not the worst. One thing has been denied you, another thing has been granted you. And this other thing . . . '

She fell silent.

He however seized her hand and, covering it with kisses, exclaimed: 'Oh this little hand of yours, if only I could hold it all my life long, always, always.'

'I shall give it to no other. But desire no more of this present hour, and most of all do not bind yourself. *I*, I it is who am bound.'

'Oh say you love me, Renate. Say it, so much depends on this word.'

'No, not now. These are not the times for bonds and betrothals. But other times will come. And if you have then tried your own heart and taught mine to trust, then, yes then!'

11

Hohen-Ziesar

THE excursion to Drosselstein was fixed for two o'clock. Berndt and Bamme had agreed that, for their part, they would make the journey on horseback: the general would be on his Shetland pony. They were joined by Tubal, who after the conversation of that morning had been overcome by a reluctance to travel at the side of Renate which he himself could not account for. He seemed unsure what tone he ought to assume with her. Or was it something else?

The riders had the start of them: none the less, they could hardly have passed the stone at Miekley's mill before the sleigh that was to transport brother and sister, together with Grell and Hirschfeldt, to Hohen-Ziesar drew up at the door. Jeetze stood ready with cushions and coverlets, Lewin took the reins, and a moment later the bays pulled away and trotted up the silent village street.

The jingling of the bells mingled with the cheerful chatter of our travellers, with Lewin riding in front and Grell's continual assurances that he was perfectly comfortable on his rear seat, which was in fact merely a wooden plank, being refuted by his equally continual sliding back and forth. The most talkative of the companions was Renate. She felt happier than she had for a long time. The conversation that had left Tubal perplexed had been for her an unexpectedly potent source of comfort. What she had told the old privy councillor in the church at Bohlsdorf —'You are knocking on the wrong door'—had at that time, as at all times, been a true expression of her feelings. For as long as she had loved Tubal she had also been attended by the doubt whether he returned her love, and this doubt, a greater torment than anything else she felt, had now been taken from her. He loved her. What, compared with that, was the question whether his love would endure and remain faithful? What, compared with that, was the question 'Shall I be happy or unhappy?' which belonged only to the future? Now she *was* happy, and a trace of apprehension that still remained in her served only to enhance the sense of exultation she felt at that moment. It was as though she were walking through a forest the gloomy depths of which resounded dread and mysterious; but what was close at hand was brightness and sunshine and the jubilation of birds. Lewin, who had spoken of brighter days, and Aunt Schorlemmer, who had spoken of weddings, had both been right. Marie was a black pessimist, and she herself was one as well. But that now lay behind her: she *had* been one.

This happy mood was also reflected in the unrestrained conversation that soon began to revolve around the count.

'Is he related to the East Prussian Drosselsteins?' asked Hirschfeldt.

'Certainly; he belongs to them', Renate replied, 'and it is a fortunate chance that we have him in our province. He inherited Hohen-Ziesar during the first years of his marriage, and moved into it so as to live near the court. It was out of consideration for his young wife.'

'So he is married, then?' Hirschfeldt asked further.

'He was. The countess died; first consumption, then a haemorrhage that killed her. She was very beautiful, a Countess Lieven. When she died the count hid himself from the world; he was only in Dresden now and then, and it was said he would go over to Catholicism.'

'The rest of the Drosselsteins are accounted among the firmest of Protestants.'

'So no doubt is the count. But there are situations—at least so said our aunt, to whom I ascribe responsibility for it—in which Protestantism fails us and Catholicism offers the heart a softer bed.'

'And the count was in such a situation?'

'So they averred. Let Lewin tell you about it: it is a romantic tale, and romantic tales are his hobby-horse. All in all, however, I believe what people say. You will see the countess's portrait and you may then judge for yourself. It hangs in the drawing-room: a pale blue robe trimmed with white roses. Only one of them, close above the girdle, is not white but dark red. And yet the portrait was painted two years before her death.'

'Strange,' said Grell, who in the meantime had contrived to adjust himself in his seat.

'Yes, that it is. But it is less startling in Hohen-Ziesar than it would be elsewhere. The château is rich in things strange and singular, among them objects excavated at Herculanum and Pompeii: pins and brooches and, just imagine, a pair of nail-scissors. The count spent a long time there and brought all these things back with him.'

'I shall be glad to inspect them all,' Grell responded, 'but I would give preference above all to the prophetic red rose.'

'And you would be right to do so,' replied Renate. 'And you are also right to remind me of the theme I have let go of. The Pompeiian scissors severed my thread. But what was I going to talk about? Ah yes, about the strange pictures at Hohen-Ziesar. Of these too there is an abundance. For instance, there is a portrait of the "Woman in White".'

'The Woman in White!' exclaimed Grell and Hirschfeldt *a tempo* and as spiritedly as though the lady had at that moment just appeared to them. Then Hirschfeldt added: 'But since when have ghosts had their portraits painted?'

'No,' laughed Renate. 'You mustn't expect anything *quite* as singular as that. It is the portrait of a beautiful lady of the court from the last years of the Great Elector: Wangeline von Burgsdorff. She died young and in death is obliged to expiate her guilt by going around as the "Woman in White". Naturally it was a question of love.'

Hirschfeldt smiled. Grell, however, who was disposed to take everything somewhat pedantically, reiterated the name 'Wangeline von Burgsdorff' and then added:

'I thought it was a Countess von Orlamünde, who lived at Plassenburg and, if I am not mistaken, also at the château of Bayreuth. I can still remember how, as a child, it would give me the shudders to read of the "four eyes" that "stood between them" and had to be done away with. I only half understood it, but for that reason it excited my imagination all the more. And now I hear a different name: Wangeline von Burgsdorff.'

'You must not put me to an examination,' Renate replied. 'If you want to know more, the head of Kastalia will have to help you. What is the truth of it, Lewin?'

Instead of imparting the desired information, however, Lewin only transferred the reins to his left hand and pointed with his right to the château which had at that moment just appeared in sight behind the trees of the park. 'The count himself may be able to tell us,' he said.

A few minutes later the sleigh halted on the ramp before the garden, where Drosselstein was already awaiting his young friend and offered his hand to assist her to alight. Together they passed through the folding doors into the drawing-room, Hirschfeldt and Grell following behind.

The drawing-room was a large, square hall extending almost the entire depth of the house: behind it there ran only a narrow corridor. This corridor looked out on the inner courtyard, as the drawing-room did on the park and garden. It was apparent at first glance from the contents of this hall that the owner of Hohen-Ziesar must be wealthy and much travelled and possessed of good taste in the plastic arts. On one of the walls there hung a large tableau, half-architectural, half-landscape, representing the Drosselsteins' old East Prussian château. Opposite this tableau hung the portrait of the young departed countess. Grell sought the red rose, and found it: he had imagined that the rose would be redder and the countess herself more beautiful, and therefore sustained two disappointments, the second of which, however, was probably only a consequence of the first. Orange-tree tubs and flower-tables stood in all the window-alcoves, while black marble console-tables ran along the other three sides of the room with Roman emperors, their names inscribed in red, standing upon them. Bamme, who had already been there for fifteen minutes, had read two or three of them—Geta, Caracalla, Alexander Severus—and had then withdrawn from the row of tables murmuring to himself: 'Not too much all at once': a somewhat obscure remark which probably referred to the related numismatic studies he had undertaken that morning with Seidentopf.

Conversation had scarcely got beyond the opening round of superficialities when Drosselstein offered Renate his arm to conduct her in to dinner. A double door-curtain drawn back indicated the way to the neighbouring dining-room. Here the window-curtains were already closed, but two elegant octagonal candelabra gave sufficient light to illuminate every corner of the room: antique mosaics, representations of fish, flesh and fowl, were embedded in the stucco walls, while an imitation (a strikingly good one in view of the condition our art was in at that time) of Giulio Romano's fresco at the Palazzo del Té at Mantua, the *Wedding of Psyche*, had been placed on the ceiling. Of all these things Bamme saw nothing, but they had an appreciative audience in Grell, whose natural artistic sense had been greatly developed at the Moltke Palais.

Renate occupied the place between Drosselstein and Bamme. The latter had, perhaps from his youth onwards but in any event since the days of his attendance at Guse, agreed with the proposition that the best way of vaulting over the mere tedious preliminaries of a conversation lay through subjecting someone to a dose of mockery, and today he threw himself with impetuosity upon Seidentopf, whom he had doomed to be a sacrifice to that evening's entertainment when, a few hours previously at the Hohen-Vietz parsonage, Seidentopf had brought out Odin's chariot. On this occasion, however, success eluded him, and it did so because, to all appearance, he had again committed a misjudgement, or, to quote his own words, 'again mistaken the company' he was in. For Drosselstein was too elevated to laugh very much at anything, Lewin and Renate had already heard Turgany expatiating and expanding on the selfsame theme and doing so much better, and Berndt—who, like all more serious-minded natures, was customarily a very gratifying audience for the dispenser of jokes and merriment —was at that time far too deeply immersed in his plans and projects to be capable of deriving amusement from Bamme's excursions on the six suppositious birds of Odin. On the contrary, he took advantage of a fleeting pause to inform Drosselstein, with an abrupt '*ad vocem*★ Seidentopf', that, in his capacity as patron of the living, he had directed that the 'Proclamation' was to be read from the pulpit on the following Sunday.

And now, in place of 'Odin's chariot' the theme of the 'Proclamation' trundled quietly round the table for fifteen minutes, until Drosselstein produced the more or less provocative remark that what he found lacking in the Proclamation was anything *East Prussian*. He realized that by saying such a thing he must incur the reproach of being to a certain extent partisan; but the spirit characteristic of it differed in each different province, and he did not believe he would offend them if he said that the disposition of the Brandenburg nobility was too greatly influenced by personal considerations. It was something they in his own province were aware of being free of. '*Your* pride', he concluded, lightly inclining towards Vitzewitz and Bamme, 'is loyalty, discretion, reserve; *our* pride is freedom. In the hands of Dohna or Schön or Auerswald* this Proclamation would have assumed a different form. Its virtue is circumspection, it bears the stamp of the court; what it lacks is the language of straightforward manliness.'

Bamme was minded to offer a sharp retort, but restrained himself in the interest of preserving equanimity and said merely: 'It is strange, but these days the further north-east we look the more heavily are we indebted. We owe much to the East Prussians, but it seems we ought to be even more obliged to the Cossacks. Since yesterday we have had them on this side of the Oder. Have you yet heard of the skirmish between Alt-Rosenthal and Trebnitz? A hundred taken prisoner. It will create a stir.'

The count had not been in possession of that news. He now consented to hear it, followed Bamme's somewhat highly coloured description of the affair with evident interest, and was only surprised to find the account concluded with an abrupt invitation to him to 'participate in further such joint operations' —not, however, with Tettenborn, but with Chernichev* in person.

'You must come to headquarters, Drosselstein,' Bamme said with resolution, 'and you must do so tomorrow. Our condition at the top is better at this moment than it will be in a week's time. Now I have an aide-de-camp, but for how long can I be sure of him? Any minute he can get up and go. So speed is needed. We must undertake a *coup* of a larger sort, and I have laid my plans accordingly. But we need the help of the Russians. And you know Chernichev and everyone around him from your Petersburg days.'

Although he must have heard of the rumours that had once

circulated, Bamme spoke of these 'Petersburg days' as though of something the count would recall with a feeling of pleasure, and would have gone even more deeply into this somewhat ticklish terrain if Drosselstein had not brought him to a halt by abruptly accepting the mission and, to secure himself further, directed at Renate the question: 'Where shall we take coffee?'

'In the gallery, naturally.'

'I fear it will be too cold there.'

'No matter. The gentlemen must learn how to inure themselves to cold, and I shall put on my cloak and muffs.'

Drosselstein was content, whispered a few words to a servant standing behind his chair, and then steered the conversation in the direction of Faulstich and Nippler, whose work on their joint cantata might be regarded as neutral ground for any further converse. After Nippler's claim to the title of an 'unrecognized genius' had been explored, and affirmed and denied by an equal number of votes, Bamme took the opportunity to express the hope that the admirable brevity of the text would not in the event be called into question by the music.

This pointed remark presented an excellent way of concluding. Drosselstein rose and, after skilfully detaining his guests in the drawing-room for a few minutes, he invited them, as Fräulein Renate had commanded, to take their coffee in the gallery.

12

The Woman in White

THIS 'gallery', which lay on the north side of the château, ran through the entire left wing. It consisted of three halls, the first of which contained the family portraits, some of them embellished with great historical detail. Here too the curtains were closed, an open fire was blazing, and the coffee-table was laid in the middle of the hall. But what arrested the gaze of the guests as they entered was two silver vessels standing on either side of the fireplace on two tall tripods: out of the vessels there ascended in gently trembling columns two pale blue spirit-flames. The count had had them installed so as to heat the chilly room more quickly, but perhaps even more for the sake of their picturesquely fantastic effect. This effect was a success: the count was showered with congratulations.

They took their places in a wide semicircle, and, as coffee was being handed round, Renate, who was now seated between Grell and Hirschfeldt, pointed to a full-length portrait hanging immediately in front of her to which the two blue flames seemed to lend a spectral life.

'That is she.'

Grell pushed back his chair to obtain a better view, and then said: 'A beautiful head, but uncanny.'

'I presume', Hirschfeldt added, 'that it was from the uncanny expression of these eyes that the legend itself arose; they challenge one to think they were not destined to be closed in death, like ordinary eyes. They have something about them that makes it seem they must stay open and see for ever.'

'Such pictures are to be found in every older gallery,' said Berndt. 'Strangely enough, they are always of women, and of young and beautiful women at that.'

'A very instructive hint,' remarked Bamme, 'which will, however, like so many others go unheeded. In any event, I would be grateful to hear some time what it is all about. Those of us who had the good fortune to travel here in the company of Fräulein Renate seem now to have entered into a secret league. I presume, if I may presume to do so, that it is Wangeline von Burgsdorff.'

Drosselstein nodded.

'Thought so,' Bamme went on. 'Faulstich told me about it ages ago, but he didn't get beyond vague generalities. I should like to know more. Do you hear how the blinds outside are flapping against the window-panes? A wind must have got up. This is the right atmosphere for ghost-stories. Since we cannot have midnight we shall have to make do with six o'clock. So, to our subject: Wangeline. She must have been a great-aunt of yours, Drosselstein. What is it she did?'

'Her story is brief,' said Drosselstein. 'Wangeline von Burgsdorff was a maid of honour in the service of a ruthless and ambitious mistress who was married to a prince whose heir was the son of a former marriage: she had prepared for this son the familiar "poisoned orange", having first had him consigned to a sickbed. Overcome with a sudden remorse, she entreated her maid to hasten back to the invalid's room and save his life, if it still could be saved. And the lightly clad figure of Wangeline flew off along the corridors, until, suddenly encountering a young knight to whom she was passionately attached, she allowed herself to be detained by him for a few moments. A few moments only, but long enough to cause the death of the prince. She came too late, and what she failed to say in life she was cursed with having to say in death. Thus now she walks and utters her warning.'

In spite of the lacunae and obscurities that attended it, or perhaps indeed because of them, this brief account did not fail to make an impression on the majority of those present. Only Bamme shook his head with historical-critical reservation and, setting down his cup, said: '*Pardon*, Drosselstein, if I contradict you. At least I do not do so without sound reason. I have, you see, a couple of hobbies; in earlier years it was young women, now it is those in white, and I have read everything ever written about women in white, from Peter Goldschmidt's *Höllischer Morpheus*★ to Rentsch's *Brandenburgischer Zederhain.*★ And it is clear, it is the Orlamünde woman. I cannot suppress the suspicion that your relations the von Burgsdorffs have created a new woman in white for themselves simply out of resentment at the fact that one of them—no less a one, indeed, than your celebrated Konrad von Burgsdorff, sometime favourite of the Great Elector—was thrown down the stairs of the Berliner Schloss by the *real* woman in white, I mean my Orlamünde woman. Our Brandenburg families (who are, of course, all vengeful and malicious on account of their lack of straight-forward manliness) forget such things as good as never, and so the Burgsdorffs have tried to revenge themselves by setting up a pretender as a retort and rival to the old-established ghost.'

Drosselstein pursed his lips and said, in a more offended tone than was usual with him: '*Eh bien*, General, if you have read the *Höllischer Morpheus*, which I do not for a moment doubt, then I shall refrain from contradicting you.'

Bamme could hear very well the irritation in the count's

voice, but, choosing to ignore it, bowed in the count's direction and carried on in the same tone as he had previously employed: 'It is as I say: the putting forward of a pretender out of family resentment. None the less, Drosselstein, if I can do anything for your Wangeline, you may rely on me to do it. In the first place, I am in general all for overthrowings and dethronements, which are the only thing that makes world-history readable to me, and in the second place, and chiefly, I have to admit to you that for her part too my old lady friend Orlamünde carried things too far. She deserves a dethronement. And why? Because she oversteps the law. And that will bring down any dynasty, even in the realm of the shades.'

Renate laughed and then said: 'But, General, now you are badly contradicting yourself. First you proclaim your love of overthrowings and dethronements, that is to say of rebellion against the law, and in the same breath you regard it as a serious fault in your poor Lady Orlamünde that in the "realm of the shades" she fails to observe the law. How can you extricate yourself from that?'

'A tricky situation,' Bamme replied. 'I admit it, dear lady. But I shall at least attempt to overcome the dilemma. This past winter, you see, I witnessed a performance of an English tragedy, *King Richard the Third*. A very interesting character: brave, ruthless and, and this is the chief thing, diabolically cheerful. Well, I can certainly say I enjoyed myself watching him make away with his brothers and the other lords and finally gaining the crown; but I cannot assert I was in the least surprised to see the awkward situation his half-dozen delightful murders had got him into by the end of the play. In other words, I like to read of overthrowings and dethronements and I intend to continue to do so, but on the other hand I find it only right and proper—and an enhancement of my pleasure moreover—that in the end the overthrower and dethroner should himself be overthrown in his turn. Illegitimate acts are interesting and from a certain point of view even pleasant and desirable, but in the end they cannot be other than they are, namely things for which sooner or later their perpetrator has to pay. Men or ghosts, it makes no difference.'

'And what then are the "illegitimate acts" or improprieties

perpetrated by your poor Lady Orlamünde, in whose over-throw you yourself wish to assist?'

'There are two, dear lady. Firstly, she does not stay in the house, she is a travelling ghost, a quite inadmissible species. She haunts all about and frequents all the Hohenzollern châteaux, old and new: Plassenburg, Bayreuth, Berlin. This may seem a mere bagatelle, but is in fact a cardinal sin. There are itinerant preachers but no itinerant ghosts. That is counter to convention.'

'It may be counter to convention,' Renate replied, 'but it is nice and I prefer it for just the reason I prefer dogs to cats. I rate loyalty to the master higher than I do loyalty to the residence.'

'A subtle distinction,' said Bamme, 'and one for which I cannot at the moment think of any reply.'

'Good; but you spoke of two. What have you to say further? What was your second indictment against the Woman in White?'

'Something as to which I fear I may count even less on your being in accord with me, for it is a question of dress.'

'But fit to be recited?'

'Oh, totally: Seidentopf would be able to preach a sermon on it.'

'Well, then.'

'Well, then. The same steadfastness I demand of my ghosts in questions of location I also demand in questions of toilet. But what is in fact exhibited? The same libertinage. For three hundred years we have had a simple "Woman in White", clad like a nun with veil and scapulary. That was quite in order. But now hear what happened. One day, without any motive, she decides to ennoble herself and begins wearing a ruff. That was bad enough; *mais enfin,* still *une dame blanche.*★ Then suddenly the unthinkable occurs, and as though she wanted to mock at both herself and us, she appears *tout-à-fait*★ in black attire, with an astrakhan muff and ditto fur trimmings. And so we now have a "Woman in White in Black". That is the stage things have reached for the present, in Bayreuth at any rate. What stage they are at in Berlin will be known only when she next appears.'

'And how do you interpret all this: is it a real spectre or deceit and deception?'

'Conjurers and tellers of ghost-stories, dearest lady, are allowed to get away without any explanation. But I shall give one none the less. Leaving aside moonlight and the fluttering handkerchief, you may be certain that in three cases out of four it is a peevish steward, and in the fourth a pretty maid of honour, a youthful little thing . . . '

At this moment Justizrat Turgany was announced.

'Very welcome!' said Drosselstein, and Turgany entered.

13

The Frankfurt Project

'WHAT is your view regarding the Woman in White?' Renate cried to the magistrate as he came in. 'Favourable,' Turgany replied, in no way disconcerted by the question. 'Favourable, my fair young friend. I take a favourable view of all women.'

'Even of those in white?'

'Even of those in white,' Turgany repeated. 'But I take a quite exceptionally favourable view of the Lady of Bayreuth, who again got herself so much talked about last summer. In the newspapers I mean, naturally. I regard her as the country's most patriotic woman since she twice haunted the great Emperor out of her château. "*Ce maudit château*"* was how His Highness himself described it. But let us defer that. I would first of all like to be acquainted with the two gentlemen *ad latus** Fräulein Renate.'

Drosselstein introduced Grell and Hirschfeldt, who were astonished to discover from the brief, fragmentary conversation which followed that the magistrate was initiated into all the secrets of the latest session of Kastalia. When they gave vent to this astonishment, Turgany said: 'You forget, gentlemen, that a jurist's duty is to have eyes and ears everywhere, especially in times like these. I have just surprised you by expatiating on Calcar and the Seydlitz spurs, but what would you say if I went on to speak of the historically better attested spurs that General O'Donnell caused to be hung in the cathedral at Tarragona?'

Similar allusions followed, and everyone was intrigued as to how Turgany knew all this, until the enigma was resolved by the revelation that Himmerlich, a younger fellow-student of Othegraven's, was a regular correspondent of his and never failed to report to him on the literary events of the week; through Othegraven the information then reached Turgany.

The latter had taken a seat, and as he sipped at his coffee, and continued to scatter the *aperçus* in which he excelled, Drosselstein said: 'And now, Turgany, to what do we owe the pleasure of seeing you here? I am a man of sufficient experience to be able to recognize something businesslike in your expression. And I find your fiery sparkle suspicious, too: I fear a cold douche will follow. What is it? Something legal?'

'Not at all,' Turgany replied. 'Something more elevated. Political and military.'

'That's interesting,' said Drosselstein, and Berndt and Bamme pricked up their ears, though at first they did not believe Turgany was being really serious.

The magistrate, however, repeated: 'Political and military. Let me proceed straight *in medias res*. Is it all right to do so? We are quite by ourselves?'

Drosselstein nodded.

'Well, then,' Turgany began, 'what I have to tell you is in brief this: for three days now we have had in our city the French general, Girard, of the Viceroy's army, and with him two enfeebled regiments, not two thousand men.'

'Military chest?' Bamme inquired.

'No, but fifty cannon, bronze eight- and twelve-pounders. And that is not to be despised: the time is fast approaching when we shall be able to use them, and use them in the right direction, that is to say pointing westwards. There is nothing about it in the "Proclamation", but you have to read between the lines.'

Berndt and Bamme exchanged understanding glances; Turgany continued:

'Two thousand men, then, and fifty cannon. The question is whether the means exist to venture a surprise attack on these enemy forces. The citizens of Frankfurt, or at least a large part of them, can be relied on for certain. And it is in the name of these citizens that I am here. Othegraven, who is at their head, is resolved to capture General Girard with twelve men, old soldiers, who have volunteered for the task. And the general's staff and adjutants as well. So far as the garrison goes, it is stationed in the Dammvorstadt, on the other side of the Oder. So everything depends on severing the connection between the city and this suburb. The ice is already beginning to break up at both ends of the bridge: the bridge itself will be sacrificed if circumstances demand it. Here you have what we for our part are able to offer.' The magistrate fell silent for a moment; then he went on: 'Let me add a few words. So far as *I* am aware, the forces of your local militia will presumably be sufficient to carry out this undertaking, but they will *certainly* be sufficient if the Russians, who are only three miles from Frankfurt, agree to participate as well. This participation would have to be limited merely to a feigned attack on the Dammvorstadt, and would have as its objective merely to prevent the two thousand troops stationed there from attempting to cross the river over to this side. I was assigned to bring all this to the notice of our closest neighbour, Count Drosselstein; a fortunate chance, however, has ordained that I have been able to supply the Herr General himself' (and here Turgany bowed towards Bamme) 'with a picture of the situation.'

Everyone had grown very serious, and neither the clattering window-blinds nor the ghost of Wangeline herself could now be blamed for the chill which suddenly settled over the company: its cause was, rather, an awareness that all at once they were confronted by the need for a decision; everyone was seized with alarm, and even in Berndt and Bamme the sense of a heavy and perilous responsibility struggled with the joy they felt that the hour had come at last. After a while Bamme said:

'Hirschfeldt, you have seen more war than I have, what shall we reply?'

Hirschfeldt lightly shrugged his shoulders and accompanied the gesture with a motion of the head which could have meant either assent or refusal. At this the old general recovered his good humour and said: 'That is just where I am: halfway between Yes and No. Your war-making in Spain was, so far as I know (which is unhappily little enough), a long series of covert approaches and attacks. I wager you have dozens of such engagements behind you. So you must know something about them. What do you think of an assault on an enemy town? For that, with apologies to you, magistrate, is how we must for the present regard your loyal Frankfurt, since it is occupied by the enemy.'

'What I have to say', Hirschfeldt responded, 'is in brief this. Assuming the Russians agree to participate, everything depends on the condition of this enemy garrison: if the troops are in good shape, things will go badly, if they are in bad shape, things will go well.'

'Then things will go well,' Vitzewitz interjected. 'And at all costs we must not let these dogs get loose again, even if we risk them biting and scratching us. But they will not. These regiments are wreckage, like the hundred men we had in Guse. A Hurrah! and they throw down their arms. So forward with good courage. Or shall we rate ourselves lower than the twenty Cossacks and their Tettenborn! For myself, I accede to the project and reply with an unconditional: Yes.'

Everyone was in agreement; even Renate was for a moment gripped by the warlike spirit of her house. 'Yes, yes' resounded from all sides. At length the excitement subsided and, after Drosselstein had repeated his promise and fixed his visit to Russian headquarters for the following afternoon, Berndt and Bamme declared themselves prepared to undertake a reconnoitring tour of Frankfurt immediately after the count's return. On the occasion of this tour all further arrangements required for a speedy co-ordinated operation—in which, however, Turgany declared he would not *personally* take part—would be finalized with Othegraven.

They were now no longer in the mood for facetious conversation, and so the party broke up at a relatively early hour. First the sleigh was driven up; ten minutes afterwards the riders too mounted their saddles. The warm thawing wind that had been blowing during the afternoon had let up, and a sharp air was coming in from the east; the sky was growing clear and the stars were emerging ever more brightly.

Bamme rode between Berndt and Tubal. They were going at a walking pace, and it cost the Shetland pony an effort to stay *en ligne* with the other riders. Each was sunk in his own thoughts; at length Bamme said: 'Who is this Othegraven?'

'A schoolmaster,' Berndt replied. 'A little stiff and pedantic, but energetic and courageous by nature. And if he did *not* possess courage he would obtain it from his enthusiasm. A man of honour.'

'Strange,' said Bamme. 'Schoolmasters were different in my day. We used to hang paper pigtails on them or write things on their backs, and I cannot remember any of them being called a man of honour.'

He fell silent, but seemed to have been reflecting further when after a while he continued: 'Your sister, the countess, loved to talk of such things, and when she did so it always made her look annoyed, because she didn't really know whether she ought to laugh or cry. "That is the wind that blows from the west." It was French, that was the good thing about it, but the rise of the bourgeois she found vexing. For my part, I have nothing against the bourgeois. So far as I'm concerned it's the human being that counts, and if this general and universal *homo*—of whom as a good Latinist I am entitled to speak—has really grown a head taller since they made the poor king a head shorter, then it does not seem to me to have been purchased at too high a price. *Le jeu vaut la chandelle.** This too a reminiscence from Guse. Ah, Vitzewitz, the stupidest thing about us is our prejudices. How did you like Drosselstein today, harping on his East Prussian string again?'

'And at quite the wrong time, too,' laughed Berndt. 'I happened by chance to learn who it was indited that Proclamation. State Councillor Hippel.* East Prussian *pur sang.** But I wanted to spare Drosselstein the embarrassment. It is in our weaknesses that we are most sensitive, you, I, everyone. Let us be glad we have him: he is the *sanspareil* of our circle and a nobleman from head to foot. Most of them are only called so: he has the advantage of *being* one.'

Bamme agreed; and with that they broke off their conversation and put their horses into a trot.

.   .   .

When they reached Hohen-Vietz they were all in need of rest and withdrew to their rooms. Hirschfeldt and Tubal were occupying the same room; they talked on together for a short while, then Hirschfeldt fell silent, and slept. Only Tubal was still awake.

Thoughts of all kinds that he was unable to control revolved in his head.

'Am I betrothed?' he asked himself when he had at last extinguished the light. 'I believe so . . . In that case I ought to be happy! And am I? Oh I am, certainly, I *am* happy . . . But not happy enough; for if I were I would be full of joy and see and hear nothing but *her*. Do I see her? Strange, but I cannot picture her clearly. I can hardly picture her at all. . . . And yet I love her. "Who doesn't love her!" our aunt said . . . Ah, happiness, happiness. Am I happy? And I need to ask . . . ingrate that I am!'

Thus his thoughts ran on. The images that moved before his mind grew more and more shadowy, until he too fell asleep.

14

Locked In

THE next day, a Saturday, was a day of preparation. Bamme sat over maps and plans, while Berndt was out from early morning visiting and briefing their more distant units. He returned from this excursion just after three o'clock; and when, a few minutes later, he entered the general's ground-floor room, he found the latter deep in conversation with Drossel-stein, who was reporting on the result of his mission to Russian headquarters. Chernichev had not only received him with exquisite politeness, but had also informed him that proposals of the kind he was bringing, in other words acts of co-operation on the part of the local population, were precisely what he had been counting on: only this would bring the successes they were looking for in the limited war that lay before them in the coming weeks. An attack on Frankfurt would, if it were undertaken by all parties at the proper time, present fewer difficulties than might seem to be the case at first glance. The French soldiers were demoralized, but the emplacement of so formidable a quantity of artillery demanded, however, that their attempt on the town must unquestionably be made quickly. He therefore proposed Monday night; for his part, he would move up to the region of Kunersdorf during the course of the preceding day, and would do so with two thousand élite troops. His zeal for the operation could be relied on: he would be present in person and personally direct the attack.

Thus Drosselstein's report, which Berndt and Bamme had followed with increasing interest: both believed they could see in the happy outcome of this mission a pledge of further success, and fixed their projected 'reconnoitring of Frankfurt' firmly for the following morning. At the same time they thanked the count for the diplomatic tact with which he had conducted negotiations, and asked him if he would not stay at least until dinner-time; Drosselstein declined, however, on the pretext of business, and, after having again begged them 'not to let anything go wrong on Monday night, even if only for the sake of retaining the good will of Chernichev', asked to be kept in mind when it came to the carrying out of the undertaking.

Towards evening Seidentopf arrived, and Jeetze anticipated that the card-table would be demanded: but the game of tarot did not take place—a sign that his duties as commanding general were beginning to weigh heavily upon Bamme. He himself joked about it and sought through self-mockery alternating with high spirits to render the burden a little lighter; but he did not succeed very far, and only when Berndt began to talk of the sanctity of the Sabbath and, addressing himself to Seidentopf, repeatedly to express his regret that on account of the reconnoitring trip to Frankfurt he would be obliged to miss church, the pastor's sermon and the reading of the Proclamation, was his old spirit of contradiction aroused, and then he interposed a sharp and dry '*I*, for my part, will not be missing much' in the highest register of the voice. Shortly afterwards they all retired, having agreed to meet at the breakfast table the next morning half an hour earlier than usual.

And now this next morning had arrived, and the bells of

Hohen-Vietz church-tower rang out through the winter-clear air. In the manor house all was hustle and bustle; while some were getting ready to go to church, others were preparing to depart for Frankfurt. It was already ten minutes to ten; Krist drove up (again the ponies) and first Berndt and Bamme, then Hirschfeldt and Grell mounted the open carriage. Only Lewin and Tubal stayed behind: perhaps because there was not really room for all of them in the vehicle, but perhaps too so as not to allow the family choir-stall to remain unoccupied on so important a day as this. And now the church-bells began to ring for a third time, and as they bade farewell to the departing carriage and its passengers waved back in reply, Lewin and Tubal offered their arms to the ladies, who were standing ready to leave, and they all walked along the deserted paths of the park, then through the avenue of lime-trees, and up to the church. The little side-door was shut, so that today they had to use the main entrance and enter the church through the tower where the bier and the broken Turkish bell stood. The church was full, since everyone had heard that something concerning war and peace was to be said from the pulpit that day: only the major's seat close by the altar was, as always, empty.

Renate and Aunt Schorlemmer went up to the centre aisle, Lewin and Tubal following them. When they had reached halfway they turned right into a traverse aisle that led first to a narrow little flight of steps and, ascending these, to the family choir-stall. Here they took their places in the ancient, high-backed leather seats and joined in the hymn the congregation were singing. Lewin sat furthest back, Tubal directly behind Renate and Aunt Schorlemmer, so that between them he had a clear view of the great monument and a couple of the foremost rows of pews. In the second pew from the front the village mayor, Kniehase, was sitting with his wife and daughter; Marie had made a slight gesture of greeting to Renate, but thereafter had had her gaze fixed firmly on her hymn-book.

It was a lovely day; everything seemed to shine, and this impression was even enhanced when the luminous figure of our Seidentopf appeared in the pulpit. The singing ceased, and only the sound of the organ continued softly on as, following the example of their minister, the congregation bowed their heads in silent prayer. Then, however, a movement of lively anticipation passed through the church, all heads were raised and, sweeping back his long white hair with his right hand, Seidentopf began: 'My very dear people!* The day we have longed for has come. Weeks and months ago, when God gave us his sign on the battlefields of Russia, when brave and noble commanders, not fearing the appearance of disloyalty, dared to act in the true spirit of our King and his intentions and to take the first decisive step towards throwing off a yoke that had grown unendurable to us, even then we knew that this longed-for day would come. But it had not yet come. Now it has dawned. Our transition from servitude to freedom is now under way. The King has spoken, the word we have been waiting for so impatiently has been uttered. Each of you knows this already, but from this place let it once more be proclaimed.'

And then our friend unfolded the sheet containing the Proclamation and read in a loud and penetrating voice. The warmth of his delivery lent life and meaning to even the simplest phrases, and an effect was perceptible such as no one had experienced when reading the document at home alone: what moved the assembly most visibly were those words which spoke of love of fatherland and of that loyalty to the King which always proved itself most vigorously in times of peril.

And then Seidentopf went on: 'Thus, my friends, has the King spoken. Spoken as never before, because never before could he have been so greatly conscious of the sublimest and most elevating feeling a King can have, the feeling of being in pure and perfect accord with the desire of his people. It is a holy war that is beginning, a war full of hope *of inner liberation*; and so I shall take for my text the words of the prophet Jeremiah, from the eighteenth chapter: "At what instant I shall speak concerning a nation, and concerning a kingdom, to pluck up, and to pull down, and to destroy it; if that nation, against whom I have pronounced, turn from their evil, I will repent of the evil that I thought to do unto them." Yes, my friends, God has been against us too, that he was minded to pluck us up, and to pull us down, and to destroy us, on account of our sin and guilt: for our guilt was great.'

And then, gazing into the past, he began to paint for his congregation a picture of our guilt. Under the rule of a great king we had quickly climbed to the pinnacle of renown, a renown that had made us haughty, reckless and complacent. Dishonest gains had enlarged our domains to the point at which a half of our land consisted of people of other nations, so that we had hardly known any longer whether we were Germans or not. And while other nations had fought for great and vital issues, we had stood aside in selfish self-righteousness and had lived in the belief that we would grow mightier and more awe-inspiring through mere inactivity. And thus at the heels of the policy of defiant arrogance that had characterized the youth of our nation there had followed a policy of pusil-lanimous cowardice, and with the passing away of our renown our honour too had at last faded more and more to a mere phantom. A deluge of vanity and prodigality had undone the laborious achievements of better years, until at length the storm from without had broken over us and, to employ the words of the prophet, the Lord had 'spoken concerning us' as to a nation he intended to pluck up, to pull down, and to destroy. A crushing defeat in war that was still in the memory of all of us had finally hurled us down from our heights into the abyss.

Here Seidentopf paused. Then, bending forward in the pulpit, he continued in a more urgent voice: 'I said a crushing defeat in war. But worse than this war was the peace that followed. I am not speaking of the outward distress it brought with it, I am speaking of the dismal habit it created of *tolerating things unworthy and shameful*. It was a habit that struck so deep that in the hearts of many (not in yours, my friends) all desire for and hope of a better and worthier state of things was extinguished. With many, the only thought they had was how they could most comfortably accommodate themselves to the foreign yoke. Others, however, who still refused to abandon hope of a better time to come, with what were they contented, in what did they seek deliverance? In *lies* and *deception*. They became hypocrites in all they did, and when danger threatened the most they exhibited friendship, and begged for friendship in return, in just those quarters where their real feelings must be loathing and contempt. They had attained that state of shamelessness which forgets or disregards every nobler *goal* of life for the sake of merely living. That was our condition, my beloved, and we ourselves had become, in the words of the Scriptures, "like the heathen in the wilderness". Those were the days of our captivity which lie behind us; but, thanks be to the Lord, a *new* day has dawned.'

And then he began to unfold to his congregation what this 'new day' signified and demanded: a return to truth, a return to the courage that truth bestows. He elaborated on this theme, and hailed 'the valour of the people' proclaimed in the call to arms he had read that day as an endowment, a warrant of better times. In contrast to those decades when the soldier had in his presumption regarded courage as something exclusively his, courage had now become the duty of every individual man and woman. And *they* too would have to give practical expression to this courage, they could be called upon at any hour, and if this hour came they must show themselves worthy of it.

The congregation had followed his words with rapt attention. Even Lewin had on this occasion found no time look out for the robin redbreast; only Tubal had allowed his attention to be distracted, and it was soon alternating mechanically between the great tomb-monument and the silver altar-crucifix, attended by a string of curious questions. How much did the monument cost? What made the brass candlesticks gleam so brightly? Which of the Vitzewitzes had presented the crucifix? And then other questions followed, only in the end to give way to a repetition of the first. Why was all this happening? Were Seidentopf's words not sufficiently serious? Yes, they were: but on its unceasing progress between the monument and the crucifix his glance had alighted upon Marie. *That* was why. Her mouth quivered from time to time, and her big dark eyes seemed to be closed, so deep they lay in the shadow of her eyelashes. He regarded her pale, fine-drawn profile, until in the end he did *only* that, he was oblivious to all else save the reproachful voice that spoke within him as he gazed.

·   ·   ·

In the meantime the sermon had ended, only the prayer remained to be spoken, and everyone looked up at the pulpit expectantly. Marie did so too: although she must have felt she was being gazed at from the choir-stall she possessed the self-control to ignore the fact, or, more probably, really to ward off any impression it might have made on her, for she was pure of heart and a stranger to all dissimulation.

Seidentopf was now praying: 'Most merciful God. Thou hast done unto us a great thing in calling upon us to fight for a free and worthy existence. Be with us. Victory comes from Thee, and it is with trust and confidence that we pray to Thee for a blessing on our actions. Protect the King, lend strength and wisdom to our commanders, courage to those who bear arms, but to *all*, to us too, lend faithful endurance. And however the fortunes of war may change, give us as its final blessing *one* thing, give us *peace* and *freedom*.'

Then the organ again struck in, the last verse of the hymn was sung, and the people of Hohen-Vietz slowly rose and left the church. Marie remained behind to speak with Renate and Aunt Schorlemmer; then they walked together down the centre aisle, Tubal and Lewin following.

When they had all reached the archway in the wall that led out to the tower, Marie remarked that she must have left her hymn-book behind on her seat. She made to retrace her steps, but Tubal would not hear of it and himself went back up the aisle to fetch the book. Marie gazed after him and waited, while the others passed through the outer door and out of the church.

The book was not there. After having looked for it first on the seat and then on the floor, Tubal finally stood up again and made with his arms a gesture supposed to indicate that his efforts had been in vain.

Marie called to him: 'I shall have to come and look myself', and went likewise back up the centre aisle. But at this moment Tubal espied the book lying on a narrow shelf beneath the slanting desk of the pew; he seized it triumphantly and held it out to her. Thanking him, she took it from his hand, then turned and hurried again towards the exit; but before she had reached it she heard the sound of its being locked from without.

Coming down from his organ-loft, old Kubalke had failed to notice there was someone still in the church.

Marie gave a gasp, then quickly pulling herself together said: 'We are locked in, quick, go and hammer on the door.'

Tubal too was taken aback, but in a way different from his companion. He felt as though an electric shock had passed through him.

'Why do that, Marie?' he said. 'The old man wouldn't hear us. We are prisoners, it seems.'

'Yes, but prisoners in a *church*. And in any case the windows are not very high up . . . and Renate will notice we are missing.'

'She will, certainly: but let us hope she doesn't do so too quickly.'

Marie heard how his voice was trembling.

'Very well,' she said, 'we are prisoners, then. Let us make the best of it and employ the time. It is always worthwhile to learn, and I wager you do not yet know our church. No one knows it; everyone believes he has done enough when he has admired the great Dutch monument and laboriously deciphered the name of old Matthias von Vitzewitz or even that of his virtuous Veronika von Beerfelde. That then counts as knowing the church at Hohen-Vietz. But we have many other things here as well.'

She said all this in a tone that was almost cheerful and quite obviously in an endeavour to conceal her embarrassment; and when, instead of replying Tubal only gazed more and more inquiringly into her eyes, she added even more hastily: 'I must show you them all. Thus we shall not be wasting these minutes here. I won't tell you about the broken font that people say is a thousand years old, or not at first, because I know you will not believe it; but you must see the image of the Blessed Virgin here to the right. You see, Maria has let her Christ-child fall out of her hands.'

'Perhaps because she wanted to have them free again.'

'Oh no, no, that is godless mockery. And I can already see you are as little interested in it as in the thousand-year-old font. But here, this is something that will interest us both,' and she indicated an old, upright tombstone cemented into the wall close beside the image of the Virgin.

B.S.—27

Tubal stepped up to it and read: 'Katharina von Gollmitz.'

'Yes, that was her name.'

'Let us ignore the name,' said Tubal. 'What is it to us? What are the dead to us?'

'No, no, you must hear about her. She was a friend of a *former Fräulein von Vitzewitz*, I have forgotten her first name, but let us assume she was called Renate.'

'Not Renate.'

'Yes, let us assume she was called Renate. And her friend, this very Katharina von Gollmitz whose tombstone you see here before us, she died here and was buried here. But the dead Fräulein von Gollmitz had a longing for her homeland and wanted to leave here and escape from the grave that was in a land not her own.'

'I don't believe it.'

'Oh, you have to believe it, for it is true and every child here knows it. And whenever Fräulein von Vitzewitz walked over this tombstone, that then was still lying with the other tombstones in the middle aisle, she heard her friend calling: "Renate, open up!" '

Tubal smiled.

'And that is what *we* shall now call, isn't it?'

'Not I.'

'Oh yes, yes, you must call too, for so the tombstone exhorts us. And whatever tombstones exhort us to do, even though they are dumb, that we must do.'

'Yes, only not today, not at this moment. We are *alive*, Marie.'

'But for how long?' Marie replied.

Tubal was taken aback. There was something in her words that had hit home in him. But he thrust the impression aside again and said merely: 'Let us leave the tombstones.'

And with that they stepped back into the centre aisle.

When they had nearly reached the foremost pews Tubal broke the long silence that had supervened and said in a gentler voice: 'We shall be good friends, shan't we, Marie? Fate has brought us here together. Is it not as though we ought to belong to one another?'

'No, not we . . . But listen, I hear voices.'

'Whose?'

'I don't know.'

'Not *our* voices, Marie, not *yours*, not *mine*?'

'No, no, Renate's.'

She spoke the name with emphasis, and he knew well why she did so. But, by now beside himself, he seized her hand and said with rapidly increasing vehemence: 'Renate and again and again Renate. Why, what will it achieve? I beg you, not this name now; I don't want to hear it. It wants to set itself between us, but it shall not. No, no, Marie!' And he threw himself to his knees and clasped his arms about her, burying his glowing face in her dress. For a moment she felt she ought to call for help or in the pounding fear of her heart grasp at the altar-cloth, but suddenly inspired by a different idea she tore fully open the half-door that led to the major's seat and pointed to the bloodstain that filled all who knew of it with horror.

In vain.

'Even if life and death stood between us', he cried, 'I will not let you go, Marie . . . I will . . .'

Then there really was a noise outside, a key turned in the lock, and immediately afterwards old Jeserich Kubalke appeared and came up slowly towards them between the choir-stalls.

'My apologies, young sir, but at eighty-one your eyesight's no longer up to much and so I went and locked you in like prisoners. And two very pretty prisoners, that I must say. Yes, yes, Marie.'

Under the effect of this greeting both had regained their composure, and they proceeded to tell the old man how they had employed the time of their captivity and how they had been reading the great tombstones, including that of Fräulein Gollmitz.

'That of Fräulein Gollmitz too. I know it, she was the lady who didn't want to stay here. Yes, that is worth reading. But the young people don't do it, or if they do it doesn't make them think. Yes, the tombstones . . .'

Chattering thus, they were back again at the exit of the church.

'Father Kubalke,' said Marie, 'we go in the same direction.'

Tubal stepped up to her and offered her his hand as though as a sign there ought to be peace between them. 'It was a dream, Marie. Isn't that so?'

She shook her head.

Then she took the old man's arm—he had hardly heard these last words and paid no heed to them—and descended with him one of the narrow paths that led from the hill down to the middle of the village.

15

The Reconnoitring Tour

AT just this time the ponies were trotting on their way via Hohen-Ziesar to Frankfurt.

Hohen-Ziesar lay a considerable distance away from the direct route; but Berndt had not hesitated to make the half-hour detour, so as to do what he had neglected to do the previous day and invite Drosselstein to participate in their Frankfurt reconnoitring tour. It was, as it turned out, a pointless journey, for they discovered that the count had already left Hohen-Ziesar in the early hours, very probably to pay a second visit to Russian headquarters on the far side of the Oder. Certainty on the matter was not to be had; all that was certain was that he was not there, and this fact was accepted by both Berndt and Bamme with considerable equanimity, since *au fond du cœur* both had little desire to listen to observations made merely from a 'higher point of view' concerning matters of which they themselves possessed a superior understanding.

And so, with their compliments to the count, they continued into the clear winter landscape. The ponies seemed to want to compensate for the delay, and it was only when they arrived back on the great highway just before Podelzig that they relaxed their pace. In the village itself our friends learned that the vanguard echelons of the battalion ordered there the previous day had arrived barely half an hour before, and immediately afterwards they beheld various groups of local militiamen surrounded by villagers old and young and asking and answering questions of all kinds. For a moment Berndt considered whether he should dismount and speak with the people; he decided against, however, so as not to lose any more of the few daylight hours remaining.

The next village was Clessin. Here too there was apparent excitement and unrest—the Proclamation had just been read—and only in Cliestow, which they reached just as the chimes were ringing midday, did they find everything quiet: here the sparrows were sitting on the roadway in their hundreds, irresolute whether or not to take flight, and nothing but the sunlit smoke that rose straight and clear from the chimneys indicated the presence of life.

And then Cliestow too lay behind them. The way began to ascend a gentle incline, and an enticing view arose further and further before them. Numerous farmsteads were scattered across the broad plateau that extended far to their right, while away to their left the deep-lying Oder valley wound its way through the fields. In this valley, no more than another half-hour distant from our travellers, there now arose the goal of their journey, the city itself, clearly recognizable by the copper-covered coping of the Oberkirch and the many little golden spheres ranged around its green pointed roof like the buds of buttercups.

'I count seven churches,' said Bamme, who out of a kind of obstinacy had never been to Frankfurt before. 'It seems a big city, bigger than I thought.'

'The actual nucleus is small,' Berndt replied. 'But the suburbs extend far out. See the Dammvorstadt over there, almost a town in itself. And beyond it Kunersdorf of bloody memory. Here on our side of the river we are more peaceable. The long line of houses down there is the suburb of Lebus; but I will not bother you with such details before I have to. From the Spitzkrug we shall have a much clearer view and be able to look down the Sottmeiers' chimneys.'

'The Sottmeiers?' asked Bamme.

'Yes, here we may still call them that.'

'What does it mean?'

'It belongs to the teasings and feudings that go on everywhere between the "Old Town" and the "New Town".

Whether it is appropriate is a matter of indifference, so long as it irritates and makes for bad blood. Which it does. A hundred years ago an old woman, not much better than a witch, set fire to the whole suburb down there. She was called Widow Sottmeier and she was burned at the stake with six or seven of her confederates. Fire for fire: that was still the way of things in those days. Since then all the inhabitants have been named after the ill-famed old woman and are called "Sottmeiers". A strange logic: first injured, then insulted. But logical or not, the Old Town likes it, so it stays as it was of old.'

Thus conversing they had arrived at a whitewashed inn with a tall thatched roof which, situated at the head of three streets which came together at this place, bore the name of the 'Spitzkrug'. This was the look-out point Vitzewitz had referred to. They halted; a triangular garden constructed across the three streets lay in front of the inn, and here our friends posted themselves and, looking over the top of a hedge, gazed down at the picture that lay like a relief-map below them. Surveying the scene, Bamme realized at once that this was a site they must hold on to at all cost.

'Here we shall post our *soutiens*,'* he said. 'The Spitzkrug here shall mark our line of retreat. The three roads will give us a choice and confuse the enemy.'

'Why a retreat?'

Bamme laughed. 'A secured retreat is half the victory. If you intend to go forwards, you have to start with the thought that you might possibly have to go backwards. If I know I can get out again, I will attack Beelzebub himself in his innermost sanctuary. Ask Hirschfeldt, he understands war.'

As he had been speaking these words, Bamme had taken out his notebook and he now began to sketch the various streets. When he had finished, and had asked after the name of a little suburban church lying at their feet, he said to Vitzewitz: 'And this hillface here jutting out towards the town?'

'That is Gallows Hill.'

'I see. And the road running over towards it?'

'Execution Street. Presumably because it led from the town out to the place of execution. The remains of the three hanging-posts can still be seen among the cherry-trees.'

'Let's forget the hanging-posts, Vitzewitz,' said Bamme. 'I am in favour of a secured line of retreat, but if it can be managed I'd like it somewhere else. First the Sottmeiers and now Gallows Hill and Execution Street: they all go together, I'm sure, but I frankly admit I would prefer a little less consistency and a little more cheerfulness. *Nomen et omen*. I am superstitious about such things and like to avoid them. Let us go: I have orientated myself.'

They mounted again and rode downhill into the suburb, firstly past the little church of St George, then past the hospital of the same name. A single, long street. Proceeding thus, they arrived after ten minutes at the Brückendamm, where, in those days at least, the Old or Inner Town began, and which led over a wide though dried-up moat to the old Lebuser Tor. Immediately before this gate the Brückendamm broadened into a little angular square in one corner of which there stood a couple of two-wheeled though strongly constructed carts. Beside them lay a number of iron cannon-barrels, all rusty and a couple of them broken, as though they had been dragged from the Battle of Kunersdorf and left there. Bamme took note of everything. Then they rode through the vaulted gate—it dated from the time when the city was fortified—and past the guard that was posted behind it. The sentry stationed with the cannon was marching up and down, and as they passed by him he gazed at them with friendly curiosity and greeted them with a wave of his hand.

'It is lucky for him', said Bamme, 'that he will be relieved tomorrow evening and not standing sentry here. A handsome boy with such a friendly wave. I should feel sorry for him.'

A hundred paces beyond the guard at the gate a narrow street branched off to the left. It led along as far as the river, but before it reached the river it widened out into a church-square on which there arose, grey and towerless, the oldest church in the city. As soon as you had gone past this church you noticed at once how the square again narrowed down and became a street once more; but there were only two or three houses on either side, and then you were at the quay. In one of these houses dwelt Turgany. Berndt had taken the reins and now drove up to it. It was a large ancient corner-house with a balcony jutting out before it and a splendid view of the square and the ramparts: a perfect observation post. After he had given instructions that Krist should unharness the ponies and return to the Spitzkrug, or at any rate to an ancient inn lying that side of it at the end of the Lebus suburb, Berndt ascended with Bamme the broad flight of stone steps, with Grell and Hirschfeldt following.

The magistrate welcomed them warmly and introduced Othegraven, who had been awaiting the arrival of their guests from Hohen-Vietz even more impatiently than had Turgany. A table was laid close beside the window; they all took their places at it, and politely agreed when their host expressed his regret at the absence of Drosselstein. As was his custom, Grell at once began to inspect the room, which dated from the time when the Renaissance had been striving for mastery over the Gothic. The balcony was still Gothic, while the large expanses of wall, and especially the stucco ornamentation, indicated that the Renaissance was already asserting itself: as did the stove, whose green-glazed tiles bore a representation of the story of Tobias.

'A delicate Rauenthaler', said Bamme, 'will in due course procure for me the address of the action. Hopefully it is not a secret. But now to business, gentlemen. *Carpe diem.** Do not be surprised, Vitzewitz, to find me once again on the paths of classicity. Commerce with one's fellows educates one, and one owes something to the company one keeps. But now, your plan, Othegraven.'

Othegraven bowed somewhat stiffly, and then said: 'After our friend Turgany has had the honour of placing before you our plan of attack, what I have to say will essentially consist only of informing you of the locality and the arrangements with respect to timing; always assuming that you, for your part, Herr General, have no alterations or new suggestions to propose. If that is the case'—Bamme nodded—'I shall be recapitulating what you already know rather than adding anything new.'

'All the better. Many strands only become confusing. Well then, let us repeat our exercise.'

'Very good, Herr General, in that case may I ask you to be so good as to step over to this balcony window. The other gentlemen too. We shall then have our field of action before us, and what little remains to be said can be demonstrated as though on a map spread open.'

Everyone had risen and gone across to the balcony. Othegraven pointed to the left. 'Observe the third house in the square, Herr General, if you would be so good; the large one just past the church.'

'I see it; the one with the pruned lime-tree and the sentry-box in front of it. It looks like a hotel.'

'Quite so. In this hotel there reside General Girard and his staff. Plus three or four orderlies. The moment the first shot is fired we storm out of the church. It is not twenty paces away. Before the general has even woken up he is our prisoner. His staff and orderlies with him.'

'And then?'

'Five minutes later we must also have in our hands the men of the garrison who are billeted here in the Old Town in ordinary houses, either singly or in twos or threes. We know which houses these are and will have surrounded them beforehand. I hope to be able to guarantee the prompt execution of these actions and to report to you immediately upon your arrival here that they have been carried out. That is the *first* act.'

'And then?' Bamme repeated.

'And then,' the schoolmaster replied a little sharply, 'and then the second begins, *your* act, Herr General. For our citizens are ready to place themselves under your command in all respects from the moment of your arrival. Your reputation for resolution precedes you, and resolution is everything.'

Bamme bowed. He was not insensible to such expressions of admiration, least of all when they came from social circles in which he had the feeling he needed for one reason or another to rehabilitate himself. For he was very well aware what he lacked.

Othegraven continued: 'The issue in question in this second act is whether *we,* that is to say your local militia and our citizenry operating together, are in a position to resist the two thousand *voltigeurs* and grenadiers who, with the heads of their regiments and battalions, are lying across the river in the Dammvorstadt and who will undoubtedly be making every effort to force a crossing over to the Old Town from the moment the battle begins. Such a crossing must not be made easy for them. We shall sacrifice the bridge, and clearing the ice from the river is in hand. Our Kietzer fishermen have worked marvellously; they haven't been to bed for days; His Majesty the King shall hear of it. None the less, without wishing to pre-empt any better judgement of the situation, it seems to me that the outcome of the undertaking is dependent on the interven-tion or non-intervention of the Russians. If they keep their word, by the day after tomorrow we shall have taken prisoner a French brigade, captured fifty cannon, and, above all, given a sign, an example, to the whole province. If, on the other hand, the Russians leave us in the lurch, we cannot in the long run hold out against two thousand men. For they are well-rested troops, reserves who were not sent to Russia. I repeat my regret that the count is not with us, but console myself with the thought that he is absent only because he is paying a second visit to Chernichev's headquarters to reassure himself of Rus-sian participation.'

'Very good, Othegraven,' said Bamme. 'That is what I call a born quartermaster-general of the school of Prince Eugen★ or at least of Montecuculi.★ Don't you agree, Hirschfeldt? And all presented short and sharp. So: plan accepted. Only one small matter remains: to carry it out. But, Chernichev or not, it *has* to succeed; at least we must no longer allow ourselves to think otherwise. We have said A and now have to say B. All war is a game of dice. And we are throwing the dice in a good cause. *Alea jacta est.*★ Now I am speaking Latin again, so I must have recovered my good humour.'

They had by now returned to the table and resumed their places. But none was in the mood to continue eating, and Turgany thus read their feelings aright when he said: 'Let us now adjourn, my worthy friends. My programme is: first, inspection of the quay on this side of the Oder, then across the bridge, the Dammvorstadt, the Duke Leopold Memorial and the French artillery park. This done, I regard those tasks we can carry out on foot as completed, and offer the use of my carriage for anything further. It will be awaiting us at the artillery park or close beside it. Then back across the bridge, the Kleist

Memorial and return to my house or to the Lebus suburb, whither, if I am correctly informed, you have sent your own carriage.'

And with that they all left to commence reconnoitring.

From Turgany's house it was hardly a hundred paces to the river. The quay, bordered by groups of poplars set far apart from one another, lay in Sunday stillness. Little Oder craft, and bigger keeled ships belonging to Stettin but overtaken here by the arrival of winter, stood frozen into the ice. The bridge spanned the river to their right: twenty or more piles among which our friends observed the large icebreaker installed to protect the bridge. No work was being done; the bells of the Oberkirche were ringing, and women in their Sunday best hurried singly past them on their way to evensong.

Bamme surveyed the quay and the groups of poplars up as far as the buttress of the bridge, then said to Berndt: '*Voilà*, Vitzewitz, our *champ de bataille*, presumably.' Berndt nodded in agreement: he was in an excellent, almost a cheerful mood, and far less excited than Bamme, for he regarded the project they were bound upon not as an adventure but as a duty and a task to be performed.

Thus they arrived at the bridge and crossed over to the Dammvorstadt. Here the world seemed to consist entirely of Frenchmen; some were sitting balanced on the window-ledges as though it were a hot day in June, while others were playing leap-frog or standing in the doorways chatting with the girls and children. This was especially the scene before the Golden Lion, a large hotel close by the bridge which had been transformed into a barracks. Our friends turned at the corner of this hotel and made for the great memorial to Duke Leopold★ that had already been clearly visible to them as they left Turgany's house and walked towards the river: it stood directly on the opposite side, with only the broad stream separating them.

Now they stood before the memorial: on both sides of it, among the planks and cordwood of a wood-yard established there, forty bronze cannon had been assembled. The sight they presented excited very varying thoughts in the minds of the beholders: Othegraven gazed disconcertedly at the boards and planks and wondered how they were to be got rid of, while

Berndt and Bamme noted with satisfaction that there were no ammunition-caissons to be seen, which meant they would at least have no artillery to contend with.

In the meantime Grell had turned his attention to the memorial itself. Three female figures bore a star-wreathed urn; in the base upon which the whole thing stood, however, were inscribed the words: 'Philanthropy, Constancy, Modesty— three Heavenly Sisters—bear thy funeral urn, departed Leopold, and with the Goddess of the City whose citizens thou hastend'st to rescue, and with the God of the Oder beneath whose waves thou perish'st, they lament that Earth has lost her Jewel.'

Bamme had likewise come over to the memorial and now, indicating the urn, said: 'Funeral urn. I should say! It looks more like a giant punch-bowl, don't you think? And that, surely, is what it's supposed to be. I wager the sculptor—all honour to his memory—was a knave and in his own way wrote history. You know the story, Vitzewitz?'

'I know it,' the latter replied. 'But it has been refuted.'

'Pity,' Bamme continued. 'The best bits of world-history always get retracted or refuted. Pitt died of a bottle of Burgundy; but that wasn't grand enough for a hero of oratory, so we are now told he died of the Battle of Trafalgar. If I had the pedantry of Rutze I would think there was some confusion here with Nelson. But that is how it stands in all the history books. *Apropos* Rutze. His company is brilliant, perhaps the finest. No offence to you, Vitzewitz.'

While these words were being exchanged a sentry had approached Grell, who was assiduously engaged in sketching, with a '*Pas permis, monsieur*', but had refrained from voicing any further objection when our Hölderlin-enthusiast had shown him his comically inept portrayals of the three divinities and had thus incited the risibility of the little South Frenchman.

Turgany's vehicle now came clattering towards them from the direction of the bridge. They boarded it, made themselves as comfortable as they could, and completed their programme —even pausing at the Ewald von Kleist Memorial for a few minutes—in the order they had previously determined upon. Thereafter they separated and the visitors went off in search of

Krist and the ponies in the Lebus suburb. The last arrangement they made was that the brigade of local militia should arrive at the Spitzkrug not later than one o'clock on Tuesday morning. A trusted confidant of Othegraven's would be awaiting them there.

The little church of St George was just striking five as our friends arrived at the end of the Lebus suburb and before an ancient inn that stood there recognized the Hohen-Vietz calash-carriage. But the ponies had not yet been tethered.

Almost a half of the establishment was taken up by an uncommonly large gateway which ran down the whole depth of the house. It was already growing dark, and this arched entrance would very probably have been nothing but a large black hole if a stable-lantern had not been swinging in the higher reaches of the arch. With the aid of this it was possible to discern three steps which led to the left out of the gateway into a guest-room that to all appearance occupied all the rest of the building. Everything else lay in another building set diagonally to it. At the front of the inn, however, there appeared to be a second gateway, likewise furnished with a lantern: but when you looked more closely, you saw that this doorway was not a doorway at all but a large chapel-embrasure with a painted crucifix suspended within its depths. Beside this crucifix there were two whitewashed saints whose arms, extended in petition, bore a good half-dozen withered wreaths. Vitzewitz had gone into the courtyard to look for Krist and the ponies; accompanied by Grell and Hirschfeld, Bamme was patrolling up and down outside: anxious to learn more of the two 'gateways' he was looking about him and at length espied a man who, crouching on one of the low window-ledges, sat like a shadow in the feebly illuminated opening.

'Hi, Sottmeier!'

The man stood up and walked towards Bamme. It now became apparent that he was porter, cellarman and waiter all in one. He wore a green baize apron. One of his eyes, which appeared much larger than the other, was blemished by a white blotch, and this white blotch constantly bored into whomever he happened to be talking to. His hair was stiff and black: in all an ugly and uncanny figure.

'Hello, friend,' said Bamme, who had lost the desire to repeat the word 'Sottmeier', 'hello, friend, what is the name of your inn?'

'The Last Farthing.'*

'That is good. I like it. You can tell how the place comes by it. And here next to it, the gateway with the crucifix and the two nuns, what is *that* called?'

'The Last Farthing also.'

'Thunder, that I don't like; this continual "last farthing", as though there was nothing else in the world. It smells like a Miserere. Grell, where will it all end? We started out with Gallows Hill and now we're finishing with the Last Farthing. And the Last Farthing twice, no, that's too much.'

Grell laughed. 'We must take the most favourable view of it we can, Herr General. It is actually a piece of refinement, these two "Last Farthings" as close beside one another as Heaven and Hell. Yet it has always been thus. One gives all he has to the church, the other to the beer-house. It all belongs to the Catholic ages, but I don't believe things have got very much better since then.'

'Nor do I,' said Bamme, and thereupon strode to the three steps that led from the gateway up to the guest-room. Grell and Hirschfeldt followed. A moment later Berndt too entered: after protracted stumbling around in the unlighted stable he had discovered Krist fast asleep on a box of fodder and with some effort induced him to go and harness his ponies.

In the guest-room several Sottmeiers were sitting playing cards. Bamme was not in the mood for social pleasantries, and he therefore sought out a second room lying behind the first in which he discovered a large billiard-table, its cloth half torn but with the rents crudely sewn together again with a darning-needle. Over the table hung a smouldering lamp. 'It looks as though it's been taken from those nuns outside, don't you think?' he said to Grell, then, turning to the waiter, added: 'Another light.'

The waiter brought two and, since there was no table in the room, made to place one of them on the cue-stand and the other on the table of a child's high-chair standing beside the stove. Bamme, however, commanded: 'Not there: here, to left and right of the Karoline!'* and had the lamps put down in the middle of the billiard-table.

When this had been done and the man in the green baize apron had disappeared, the general said: 'I bet he hasn't shut the door; we'd better bolt it; best be on the safe side. Anyone who knows men mistrusts them. This place smells like a low den in any case, and where it smells like a low den it also smells like treachery.'

Grell bolted the door and then again placed himself beside Bamme, who continued with increasingly comical solemnity:

'Before we board our carriage, gentlemen, I shall inscribe our dispositions for tomorrow on this table. A piece of chalk, Hirschfeldt. All great battles have been won with three lines. And these three lines I have *in petto* for tomorrow too.'

Hirschfeldt had in the meantime rummaged through the ancient cue-stand and found a piece of chalk. He gave it to Bamme, who at once drew a circle on the billiard-table and then divided this circle into left and right halves with a thick wavy line.

'Here to the right,' he began, 'the Dammvorstadt, is a matter for Chernichev; may the Devil take him if he leaves us in the lurch. What *we* have to do lies here to the left, *here* at the three gates.'

And now he began to indicate each of the three gates with a short double line drawn obliquely through the periphery of the circle.

Then he continued with mounting fervour: 'At one o'clock we shall halt at the Spitzkrug and then march off down three roads towards the three gates. That is the prelude. And now for the play itself. We *take* the three gates, whether by stealth or by force makes no matter, and then press on to the church square in three columns. Here we have our three strategic lines. The church square is the rendezvous. There matters will be decided, one way or the other. Let us hope for everything and fear nothing. And there's an end of it. Password: "Zieten". And may the old Father of Hussars show us his favour.'

A smile passed across every face when they heard the old

'Father of Hussars' thus appealed to as though he were God and his saints. But Bamme noticed nothing: he only opened the window, took a handful of snow and with it expunged his three-line plan of attack.

The ponies were now waiting outside. Krist cracked his whip, and the black-haired waiter, who had in the meanwhile fastened his baize apron up into a triangle, pressed forward to assist Bamme in boarding the carriage.

'Do you have any French here?' Bamme asked.

'Not many.'

'Nice people, are they?'

'Oh yes, more or less. If you like them, that is. No worse than our own.'

While this conversation was taking place everyone had settled himself and the carriage moved slowly up the hill in the direction of the Spitzkrug.

'He has a hang-dog look, that fellow,' said Bamme. 'A forgotten remnant of the Sottmeier family; some Wend or other who can see before and behind at the same time. A squint-eyed rascal *comme il faut*. The Devil take him. I bet he eavesdropped at the door.'

'Not at all,' said Vitzewitz, and laughed. 'He is from Dolgelin. His father is the blacksmith. A spark flew into his eye.'

And with that they entered the Bruch at a fast trot and made for Hohen-Vietz, which they reached at the hour they intended.

16

Who Will be Struck Down?

At eight o'clock—Berndt and his guests had not yet returned—Renate, Tubal and Lewin were sitting in the corner room which we know so well. Seidentopf had agreed to come but had failed to do so; Lewin seemed ill at ease; Tubal, more disconcerted even than on the day he had arrived, was avoiding any encounter with Renate's eyes. So it was that every effort on the part of this last to encourage the straggling conversation to a somewhat livelier pace came to nought, and whenever a carriage drove by each of them sighed with relief, in the hope it might be the Hohen-Vietz ponies.

'Where can they be?' Renate now said. 'I haven't been able to shake off a feeling of dread the whole day long; I had it already in church, and then when I noticed you were shut in, you and Marie. I told Aunt Schorlemmer of it too. Do you know, Tubal, if I had been in Marie's place I should have been frightened. Midday has its ghost just as well as midnight.'

Tubal, who felt every word strike home, bent down and threw a couple of fir-cones on to the fire, and said with some embarrassment: 'We found the time passed quickly. We read the tombstones.'

'The tombstones,' Renate repeated. 'I wouldn't have had the courage to do that. But Marie, I believe, would be able to sit herself in the major's seat and ignore the fear she felt, provided she had to. For at bottom she has the same dread as I have, only she has more of the strength to subdue her fears.'

The pendulum-clock now struck eight and Renate grew more and more apprehensive. 'Do you think it possible', she said anxiously, rising and walking over to the window, 'that the French can have learned of our intentions? Our militia has been out in all the streets for three days now, and there are always mercenary creatures ready to play the spy for pay or other rewards.'

'Certainly there are,' said Lewin. 'But these spies cannot betray more than they themselves know. And what they know the French also know: simply that a storm is gathering against them. Not merely here, but everywhere.'

'And now this letter from Drosselstein,' Renate, who had been only half listening, went on. 'I do not believe there is much good news in it. I feel as though I had read every line of it. Refusals, doubts, something or other . . .'

At that moment the carriage awaited with so much suspense drove across the pavement of the courtyard and halted. 'Here they are!' everyone cried, and before Renate had had time to fetch the astral-lamp from the back of the room and set it before the sofa our travellers from Frankfurt had already entered.

Aunt Schorlemmer and Jeetze followed. A torrent of questions. Supper was refused, tea would suffice, and because they were all more or less frozen it was agreed to shun the sofa-table and to take their places around the fire. The report on the day's proceedings was to have been rendered in chronological order, but they did not get very far with it because, as soon as the diversion to Hohen-Ziesar was mentioned, Lewin and Renate at once recalled Drosselstein's letter, which had been forgotten in the joy of reunion.

Berndt broke open the letter and read:

Only a few words, my dear Vitzewitz. I have just returned from beyond the Oder and discover that you have been here with the general and two other gentlemen to take me off to Frankfurt. As you will certainly have supposed, I have been to see Chernichev a second time. I encountered him already on the march. He is advancing today to within two miles of Frankfurt. His intentions are unchanged. He informed me as we parted that he had reported to his immediate superior, the corps commander Prince Wittgenstein, and he anticipated receiving approval of the steps he had taken, or was still to take, by midday tomorrow at the latest. *Tout à vous*.

Drosselstein.

Each of them felt the ambiguity of this pledge of Chernichev's, which could also mean he was going to draw back if he had to, but no one gave utterance to this feeling, and least of all Bamme, who, to put an end to the disconsolate mood now prevailing, began an oration in which, among other possible and impossible subjects, he spoke of Othegraven and the Sottmeiers, of the two Last Farthings, the heavenly and the hellish, and even of the two nuns 'with the everlasting smouldering lamp'. In conclusion he averred that their undertaking was a well-planned one, above all clear in its design; three lines converging on a point guaranteed success. The Russians were good fellows and reliable allies (here he cast a glance at Vitzewitz, to see whether the latter would regard this remark as serious or ironical). Yes, they were good fellows, *had* to be, and all would go well. If all did *not* go well, however, then the world, including all notions of divine justice (about which he in any case had his doubts) wasn't worth a charge of powder.

All stood in silent perplexity, and Aunt Schorlemmer whispered to Renate: 'What is all that supposed to mean?' Bamme himself, however, began spooning Basle cherry-brandy into the teacup he had long since emptied and in his annoyance with Chernichev—whom he thought it prudent not to allude to in person—now began to empty the vials of his wrath over the '*Tout à vous* Drosselstein', who, he asserted, could have spared himself two things at least: firstly his renewed visit to Russian headquarters and secondly this letter. But he belonged wholly to that species of noble gentleman who, because they had nothing better to do, continually oscillated back and forth between polite visits and polite letters. And that was what they called good breeding and diplomacy.

After playing this trump—for he believed in making a 'good exit'—he suddenly stood up, bade them all goodnight, and departed to his room. Berndt followed his example and soon the others did too; and before ten o'clock had arrived all was dark and silent in the house.

Only in the rooms at the back of the upper floor were there lights still burning. Here the younger guests had made themselves comfortable and were enjoying the pleasure of talking over the events of the day just ended. The day about to begin was also in their thoughts.

Tubal and Hirschfeldt were, as already narrated, sharing a room. It lay on the staircase side of the floor opposite that middle chamber in which the three young ladies had been so paralysed with fright on the 'night of the break-in'. The little adventure and its epilogue with Hoppenmarieken had, in fact, been the subject of discussion a few days previously; today they returned to it again, and Tubal said suddenly: 'And now, Hirschfeldt, a change of subject which, since we have been speaking of Hoppenmarieken, is really no change of subject: what do you think of Bamme? You have been with him the whole day today. What about an hour ago, around the fire: did you mark him? He expended himself on Drosselstein and clearly felt quite entitled to do so. And what does it all amount to? Diogenes in his barrel getting annoyed with Alexander.

Partly cynicism, partly mere mischievousness. Prussianism is all very well: but this bandy-legged Prussianism of the Brandenburg March that most likes to disguise itself as a Hussar and wants to play at being Zieten all the time though it has nothing in common with him except his ugliness: that I hate. Yes, ugliness. Look at this man, who may count as typical of this region, and then tell me whether, if you leave Kirghizs and Kalmucks out of account, there is in God's wide world anything to resemble this "type Bamme"?'

'Perhaps not,' Hirschfeldt replied. 'But I am unable to become indignant at it. However much may be objected to in it, the "type Bamme" is at least honest. And the more hypocrisy that exists in this country, and perhaps in view of its origins and history *has* to exist, the more pleasure I take in individual figures who, if you will permit me the expression, endeavour to extirpate the national guilt *en gros* through honesty *en détail*. Whether they do so consciously or unconsciously makes no difference.'

Tubal sat up in his bed and regarded the speaker with amazement. It was as though he had been listening to Bninski. Hirschfeldt, however, trimming the candlewick with his fingers continued in the same tone of equanimity: 'You are surprised to hear me talk like that, Ladalinski. Me, an Old Prussian. But the explanation is simple. I was abroad a long time, and abroad is where you learn. Each of us who comes back home is astonished by nothing so much as by the naïve belief he encounters everywhere that all is for the best in the land of Prussia. In large things and in small, in the totality and in the individual. For the best, I say, and above all also the most honourable and honest. And yet it is precisely in this direction that we are at our weakest. What politics we have played over the past twenty years! Lies and deception, and they were bound to be our undoing. For he who shifts and vacillates, whether a state or a private person, he who is inconstant and unreliable, who breaks promises, in a word he who does not keep faith, is destined for death. And now goodnight. Let us extinguish the light and sleep. We shall not have so comfortable a bed tomorrow.'

He extinguished the light and saw events old and new pass

before his eyes. But one thing he did not see: how his final words had struck his room-mate in the heart.

In the room next door Lewin and Grell were chattering.

'This time tomorrow we shall be on the march,' said Lewin. 'Do you feel happy about it?'

'No,' Grell replied. 'I have never been under fire, and I am therefore now in fear, perhaps in fear of showing fear. And it is a strange thing about presentiments.'

'Do you believe in them?'

'Yes,' Grell said. 'Not everyone has them; but we have it from our mother. In Schleswig it is common.'

There followed a short pause. Then Lewin said: 'I don't want to press you, Grell, concerning things about which you would perhaps prefer to keep silent. But there is one thing I would like to say: I have the impression you are taking what we propose to do a little more seriously than it ought to be taken. It is a *coup* that will either succeed or fail: that's all. If we surprise the enemy he will give himself up; if we do not surprise him, or if the Russians leave us in the lurch, we shall withdraw: but in the one case as in the other, we shall hardly sustain any casualties worth speaking of. The enemy is at present intimidated, and, even if he does succeed in beating off our attack, will be obliged to confine himself to purely defensive measures.'

Grell smiled. 'Perhaps you are right, Vitzewitz. I hope so, at any rate. But you know what spring storms are like: a flash of lightning out of a clear sky and then it's all over. *One* bolt only, but each time it claims its victim. And who can say *who* will be claimed or *who* will be struck down?'

Both fell silent, sunk in serious thought. Then, endeavouring to turn the conversation in a different direction, Lewin said: 'Did you visit Kleist's memorial? It looks somewhat antiquated with its butterfly and its inscription in three languages, yet it has always made a profound impression on me.'

'Yes,' Grell affirmed. 'But the impression I received earlier from the Duke Leopold Memorial was profounder.'

'And why so?'

'Because it preaches even more clearly and decisively my favourite proposition that we receive what is truly our life only through our death. Already here on earth. Who would still have heard of the poor duke if he had simply lived out his life to its last hour. But he cut short the progress of his days and sacrificed himself; and now, because he knew how to die, he lives on.'

'It is our deeds, not our death, that secure us a fairer life.'

'But it is doubly secured us by a deed that is done in death.'

17

The Muster

AND now came the day on which all was to be decided.

The old general had been out of bed at the crack of dawn, had rung for Jeetze and had had Hirschfeldt summoned; the latter had appeared at once and half an hour later had ridden off to deliver the *ordre du jour* to all the battalions within a radius of half-a-mile. This *ordre du jour* stipulated that this or that battalion was to report just outside Hohen-Vietz at precisely twelve o'clock for the purpose of the muster to be held there, immediately afterwards take up alarm-quarters in the village, and at nine o'clock in the evening be ready to march off against Frankfurt.

Bamme had been occupied in composing these *ordres* during the sleepless hours of the previous night. Only now, when Hirschfeldt was on his way, did the old man grow more composed; now there was no turning back, or, to employ his own words, 'the playbills have been printed and the play must, for good or ill, go on.'

He had recovered his composure, but that did not mean he was feeling comfortably at ease. For, great though his self-confidence was, it was matched, even under ordinary circumstances, by his self-knowledge. And today it certainly was. He felt he was not really equal to the task that had fallen to him; and he admitted to himself frankly that the talents he possessed were not really the right ones and that zeal and good will were not adequate substitutes for those he did *not* possess.

The site chosen for the muster was a large unploughed field lying between the coppice and the highway close beside the tilled land our friends had chased across to rescue Hoppenmarieken on their way home from Kirch-Göritz on the third or fourth day of Christmas. But it was a long time until twelve o'clock and they all sought ways of shortening it. Tubal and Lewin drove across to Reitwein to see a grave-monument that was to be erected there; Vitzewitz made certain preparations 'which I would have had to make anyway', and Grell went to the parsonage; so it in fact seemed as though the full burden of waiting and counting the hours was to fall exclusively upon Bamme. But Kniehase came to his rescue by informing him that the neighbouring estates had furnished a number of horses for inspection and selection by the 'Herr General and his adjutant': they were, he said, standing at the fire station, between the inn and his own residence.

Among these horses there was a sorrel mare contributed by Drosselstein, a beautiful animal as red almost as fire, which seemed to Bamme extraordinarily fine. But he hesitated whether or not to select it.

'I like the sorrel mare,' he said, 'but I have my doubts too. Really I think I could get by with my little yellow pony, which you know of course; we are the same sort of size and we go together. What do you think, Kniehase, shall I take the Shetlander or shall I take the sorrel mare?'

'With your permission, Herr General,' said Kniehase, 'if the Herr General asks me, the little Shetlander won't do. A general has to sit high up, higher than anyone else; you have to be able to see him, like the colours. *This* here is the general's horse!' and he gave the sorrel mare a blow on the crupper.

'Good, Kniehase, you are a knowledgeable man. Very well, I'll take the sorrel. And firmly saddled and the stirrups high up, so that they don't jangle. And now one other thing, Kniehase: do I have to talk to these people, do I have to make them a speech?'

'Yes, Herr General, certainly you have to. It's always done. And give it to them strong, they like that and the old ones then say: "*He* knows what's what." And if they think you know what's what they obey you, and they follow you, even if they break their necks in doing so. That's what our people are like, I know them, a good example is everything, a good example and plenty of courage.'

Bamme nodded.

'And Herr General,' Kniehase went on, 'there's one thing more I wanted to ask with your permission: would the Herr General not like to put on a uniform? A uniform always makes an impression.'

'No, Kniehase. There are uniforms and uniforms. An old Hussar's jacket is in place only among its fellows; then everyone makes allowances for it. But by itself it's dangerous and finds itself being called names. Cloak and fur hat must suffice, and my savage whip here'—and he flourished about in the air a thick whalebone which served him as a cane or a switch according to need.

While they were talking the sorrel mare had been led aside, and with it a grey steed they had selected as a reserve horse for Hirschfeldt. Thus several minutes passed; then Bamme, who had been pacing up and down with the village mayor, said: 'What's the time, Kniehase?'

'Half-past eleven.'

'Then we still have half an hour; how shall I pass such a long time?'

'The Herr Pastor is at his window. Would the Herr General not like to pay him a visit?'

'No, Kniehase, not Seidentopf, thank you. I saw his funeral-pots only yesterday. But the air is very damp and over there I perceive the inn; who is it runs it?'

'The Scharwenkas.'

'Ah yes, the Scharwenkas, colonists from Bohemia.'

'Yes, Herr General; but the place is packed, on account of the muster, farmers and farm-hands both. Would the Herr General care to accompany me to my own home?'

'Certainly, Kniehase, very willingly. I have heard all sorts of things about you at the Vitzewitzes'. You are supposed to have a lovely daughter, a real paragon.'

'Foster-daughter, Herr General.'

'That's all one to me. The old Herrnhuter hen over there, who is so scared of me she mumbles charms whenever she sees me, told us yesterday about your little daughter, and made your place seem a cross between a poultry-yard and a swannery. I don't pay much attention to the chatter of old women, but I am inquisitive to get to know this miracle, this little swan.'

They had by then reached the residence of the mayor and they now entered the room to the left of the doorway, where Marie, who had been observing the presentation and selection of the horses with great interest, was sitting at the window. She stood up as they came in and made to depart; but the old general, surveying her with astute and cunning eyes, said: 'Do stay, please; I shall do nothing to offend you.'

And Marie stayed. Bamme took a seat and, addressing the mayor, said: 'Inform the captain, Kniehase, if you please, that he is to await me outside the village on the highway. I intend to ride out from here; and have another blanket put over the mare out there; she comes from Drosselstein, so I imagine she has been spoiled. In the meantime, your daughter shall tell me all about herself. Things which you, of course, will already know.'

Kniehase left the room.

Marie was aware of the general's reputation, yet she found she was more composed than she had been the previous day in the church. She soon realized he meant no harm by her and that what his words conveyed was interest in her, and even respect.

'I am an old man,' he began, 'and like to chatter. What I like best, however, is people who are different from other people. And when I meet them I am as inquisitive as a nightingale. So you must permit me a few questions. You are, it seems, not a child of Hohen-Vietz, not a native of the Bruch?'

'No, I am from Saxony,' Marie replied.

'Ah, from Saxony,' Bamme continued. 'I as good as guessed it; the old rhyme* does have some point to it. And you lost your parents early?'

'Yes. I hardly knew my mother. Then I travelled around with my father; but he was often unwell.'

'You travelled around with him: what may I take that to mean?'

'We travelled around and gave performances: dancing and

recitations and magic. First in small towns, then in villages; and it was here he died. His grave is up in the churchyard, and old Jeserich Kubalke, our sexton and the father of the pretty Maline, wrote an epitaph for him.'

'And what happened *then*?'

'I wept: not for my own sake, for I was not aware I was now in need and distress, but because I had loved him so much. Even now I am attached to him, and dream of him. You are looking at me, Herr General, in such a friendly way, such as I would not have believed you could look at anybody: and that gives me the courage to talk of my father. Ah, those people who are scorned and despised are, if they are good people, the best people of all. I learned when I was very young how little appearance means; and how what is in our hearts can appear only to God, who sees all and knows all!'

She had said all this in a voice of deep emotion; now she fell silent and observed how the old general's mouth trembled; then the latter repeated his question: 'And what happened *then*?'

'What happened then was what you see: the Kniehases took me in. It was before Christmas, and he persuaded his wife, and I became their little darling. I was well off, too well off; but the late lady of the manor came along and *she* saw what was happening, and when she realized I was growing up wild and having my own way too much she saw to it I was put on the right path. Or if it was not the right path, it was the path she thought was right. She took me into the manor house and there we were brought up together, Renate and I, I mean the young lady of the house and I. We were of the same age and inseparable.'

'And inseparable from Lewin too?' asked Bamme, who had again been tickled by the desire to tease.

'Yes, from Lewin too, until he went up to the city. But we have remained good friends.'

'And will continue so, no doubt?'

'I hope so.'

At this point in the conversation Kniehase entered to report that the time had come: three of the battalions had arrived at the rendezvous beside the coppice and the fourth would be there immediately. This was welcome news. The old general took his leave, draped himself in his hussar's cloak outside in the hallway, and as he tugged with an uncertain hand at the fastening of the collar he swore repeatedly that he would take six foster-daughters into his home if only one of them turned out like this little fairy. For a fairy she was, even though real fairies were supposed to have blue eyes. And with that he hoisted himself into the saddle, drew himself erect, and, turning to Marie, who was standing at the window, blew her a kiss: a gesture that seemed, however, more friendly than foppish. And thereupon he rode off: a singular figure, the little man on the tall, fiery red steed, in cloak and fur hat and with his stirrups strapped high.

For the rest, everything was as the mayor had said, and as Bamme now approached the open field appointed for the muster he saw that three of the battalions were already drawn up in regular formation. They were standing in a horseshoe, or in a square with its foremost side open. The moment he arrived, Drosselstein and Vitzewitz reported that the Lebus battalion too was marching on the village. Hirschfeldt confirmed this report, and the little man grew bigger up on his tall steed when he found himself thus saluted, the central and pivotal figure to whom all made report.

These reports had hardly been concluded when there came from the direction of the village the sound of a beating drum and they saw a long column making its way between the poplars towards them. It was the men from Lebus. They were marching at intervals of a hundred and fifty paces. And now the foremost had come clearly into view: the Lietzen–Dolgelin Company. An elderly man bearing a standard whose staff was stuck into a broad girdle was striding vigorously at their head, even though one of his legs was a little shorter than the other.

'Who is the old fellow?' Bamme asked Vitzewitz, who had halted beside him.

'Revenue officer Mollhausen of Lietzen. Already in service back in the time of Margrave Karl. Shot through the hip at Kunersdorf.'

'I see. And the standard he is carrying? Red and white. I've never seen it before in all my life.'

'That is the commandery standard with the eight-pronged Johanniter cross. Lietzen was an estate of the order.'

As they were thus talking 'Lietzen–Dolgelin' had reached the field and now wheeled to the right to attach itself to one of the flanks of the open square. As it did so, the company next in line came into view. It was the company from Hohen-Ziesar. It had a bigger military-band than the others: two drums and two fifes; and the entire forward section was composed of men on horseback: managers and administrators from the various farms and estates possessed by the count. The latter, when he saw his own people arriving, placed himself at their head and led them, their swords lowered in salute, past the old general.

Now the Hohen-Vietz Company drew nigh. Of all the companies it enjoyed the most respect, and was treated by the others as if it were an ancient noble family. This was because it was the company with a background of history. The Lietzner commandery standard with the eight-pronged cross carried very little weight, for the material it was made of was new, barely thirty years old; the Hohen-Vietz Company, however, still had the victorious ecclesiastical banner from the days of the Hussites and, above all, the great Swedish Drum known to every child in the villages of the Bruch and which now beat out its march with a hollow and monotonous sound. It was the blacksmith who bore it, on a broad leather strap set with seashells that was almost as wide as the leather girdle that sustained the bells of a sleigh-horse. The drumhead was blue, and the curly-haired Moorish head painted in a yellow shield on this drumhead had been identified by Seidentopf as that of Queen Christina.

And then the Protzhagen Company arrived, Captain von Rutze at its right flank and, instead of a drummer, a horn-player going before it. The latter, a fat, short-necked man and the Protzhagen cow-herd by profession, seemed lost in the coils of a huge horn which was supposed to be the same as that in which Junker Hans von Rutze had broken his neck a hundred and fifty years previously. It emitted only two notes, a deep one and a high one: the deep one was appointed to sound the signal for attack, the high one that of retreat. The company itself, however, which was, as before, the finest in the battalion, was in all its elements armed with pikes, in memory of the historical fact that Eusebius von Rutze had broken through the Turkish centre with a company of pikemen at the great Battle of Budapest;* as a consequence of which his great-grandson, our captain, in spite of individual objections had insisted on pikes, and Bamme—himself an advocate of naked steel and of fighting hand to hand—had been glad to let him have his way. It was with a smirk of pleasure that he now regarded Rutze as the latter, his six-foot-long spontoon grasped in both hands, filed gravely past him, and then, turning to Berndt, said: '*Voilà*, the entry of the Protzhagen highlanders. Look, Vitzewitz, at the monster in the brass boa constrictor. The horn of Uri* to the life.'

And with that the Rutze Company too wheeled to the right and joined the square.

This wheeling, like that of the other companies, would have closed up the open square if it had been performed *en ligne*; but since they all marched in behind one another in pairs, one pair going to the lefthand flank of the horseshoe and the next to the righthand flank, a wide gap was left between them, through which first Bamme, then all the other battalion commanders with him on the highway, entered into the square.

To distinguish themselves from the Lebus Battalion, the Barnim Battalion had brought with them a large number of small company colours, pieces of red baize on to which the 'Prussian cuckoo', as the men of the militia expressed it, had been sewn. These colours were now lowered, while all the drums, large and small, broke into a roll. The old general saluted, rode along to the front ranks, and then took his place in the middle of the square surrounded by his suite and several of the Barnim standard-bearers. The moment when he would have to address the troops had now arrived.

Bamme felt no trepidation, and he knew how to speak like one to whom it is a matter of indifference whether his words are well received or not.

'Men!' he began, 'in Frankfurt there are fifty cannon and a mere two thousand French. A couple of hundred more or fewer makes no matter. We want to take them in a surprise attack: are you willing?'

'Yes, Herr General!'

'Good, I expected nothing less of you. For what was it Old Fritz said? "Whenever I want to see soldiers," he said, "I go and see the Itzenplitz Regiment." And another time he said: "Whenever I want to see soldiers, I go and see the Margrave Karl Regiment." Yes, men, that is what Old Fritz said. Have you grasped what I mean?'

'Yes, Herr General.'

'The Itzenplitz Regiment and the Margrave Karl Regiment: where were they at home?'

'Here, Herr General.'

'Correct, here in Barnim and Lebus. Well, men, shall we be worse than our fathers were? When Old Fritz sees us, shall we blush for shame?'

'No, no!'

'It will not cost very much: the citizens are helping us, and so are the Russians. But "when you chop wood the splinters are bound to fly". A couple of us will have to foot the bill. Are you willing?'

'Yes!'

'I knew it. But now, look to your courage. Anyone who plays the scoundrel gets his brains blown out. I like a joke, but when there's serious work to be done you won't catch me joking. And now, forward! Battle cry: "Zieten!" and password: "Hohen-Vietz!" They'll never get their tongues round that. . . . And do you know who's going to get them, them and their Emperor?'

'Yes, we are.'

'No, the "cuckoo" is going to get them,' and he pointed to the little company colours the Barnim standard-bearers beside him were holding.

The latter then resumed waving their pieces of red baize, all the drums and fifes struck up, and Bamme had the satisfaction of seeing his last stroke of oratory accompanied by cries of Hurrah! that seemed as if they would never end.

When the uproar had to some extent died down, he rode out of the square waving his hand and returned to the highway. The battalions quickly broke up into sections and followed him into the village with drums beating.

And the 'horn of Uri', too, could be heard sounding amid the drumming, now with its deep note, now with its high one.

18

The Decampment

THE afternoon hours passed more quickly than they had anticipated; all the commanders were invited to dine, and conversation with them abbreviated time. Even Bamme survived these dreaded hours in good humour once he perceived that, the strained situation notwithstanding, his tales and anecdotes did not lack an attentive and appreciative public.

Long before nine o'clock the battalions began to assemble and were now standing scattered up and down the village: the vanguard in front of Miekley's mill, the two Barnim battalions in the street where it widened out between the inn and the mayor's residence, the Lebus battalion in front of the manor house. It was fairly dark, but the light that fell from the houses to left and right clearly illumined the pikes and rifles collected into pyramids in the street. The militiamen were standing before the houses conversing with the girls and women of the village, for everyone able to bear arms was now out and in battle order.

Bamme stationed himself at Miekley's mill beside a kind of bivouac fire that had been lit at this point in the middle of the roadway. With his fur hat pulled down deep over his eyes and his hussar's sabre buckled over his grey cloak, he presented, as he sat in the light of the fire high up on his tall, red sorrel mare, an even more grotesque sight than he had when he had ridden forth to the muster. Hirschfeldt was stationed beside him.

And now it struck nine, and before the final stroke had died away there came the command: 'Fall in!' All who heard it knew who spoke it: only one person possessed that shrill, penetrating voice. The militiamen of the battalion standing nearest obeyed at once and with the precision of old soldiers, while Hirschfeldt galloped up the village street to transmit the order to the other battalions. Then Bamme rotated his mare, took up a position between two wooden posts that formed the entrance to the mill-yard, and uttered the command: 'Battalion, forward march!' The drums began to beat, and to cries of Hurrah! the force moved off in quick-march past the old general, who, when a fresh battalion arrived, raised his fur hat in greeting to at any rate the foremost units. The last to file past was the Lebus Battalion, which constituted the rearguard: the Swedish Drum banged loudly, and the Protzhagen cow-herd with Junker Hans's horn blew along with it unceasingly. It sounded like a fire-alarm.

Vitzewitz and Drosselstein attached themselves to the procession, and only when the last man of their rearguard battalion had gone by did Bamme too abandon his position between the two posts and follow at the tail of the column.

Half an hour later all was again silent in the village street, and only the lights in the houses continued to burn far into the night: for there was not one whose occupants would not have been following the campaign in fear and hope, with anxiety and with their prayers.

So it was too at the parsonage. Hither Renate and Aunt Schorlemmer had come in search of advice and solace. At least, Renate had: Aunt Schorlemmer already possessed what she needed, and preferred to take refuge in the iron certitudes of her hymns and proverbs, which she regarded, not entirely without reason, as more efficacious than anything Seidentopf could offer her.

They had not been there long when Marie too entered. They greeted one another warmly, but conversation refused to flow and, after exchanging a few indifferent words, they all lapsed into silence. During the course of the day they had been repeatedly assured that in all probability the undertaking would be an easy one, that the French were demoralized and that any real resistance on their part, let alone an obstinate defence of their position, was hardly to be expected; nevertheless, Hirschfeldt's serious demeanour, and even more the unease that showed itself unmistakably through Bamme's pose of serenity, had spoken more convincingly than all these optimistic assurances. The danger could be denied, but it was there none the less. So it was that, as they sat, the thoughts that ran through their minds were gloomy, and especially so in the case of Marie. She feared nothing on Lewin's account, for it seemed to her that some guardian angel was bound to protect him; but when she thought of Tubal she shuddered. Was she affectionately inclined towards him, in spite of herself? No. But deeply embedded in her nature there was a belief in a balance and compensation, the sacred mystery of guilt and atonement was inscribed in her heart, and her busy imagination painted for her dark and dismal pictures whose settings might change but whose essential content remained the same.

Many minutes passed in this way; the silence grew painful, the more painful in that the sanguine Seidentopf, who was by nature always more inclined to hope than to fear, also participated in it.

At length Renate said: 'Which way will they go? I forgot to ask Papa. Along beside the river is shorter, but the high route is more comfortable and not so sad and desolate.'

'In so far as I understood Bamme', Seidentopf replied, 'they intend to divide up the column at Reitwein, or at Podelzig at the latest, and advance along *both* routes, the Barnim battalions below along the Oder, ours and the Münchebergers' over the plateau. Then they will meet together again at the Spitzkrug. Hirschfeldt suggested the square at the little St George's church, but Bamme insisted on the Spitzkrug.'

'That I can well believe,' said Aunt Schorlemmer. 'He always prefers the inn to the church. And that is what makes me so afraid and so depresses my hopes.'

Renate took her old friend's hand and said: 'I cannot see why. You know nothing about him, after all, except what people say.'

'And that is quite good enough for me. What people say is always true, even though the world is full of lies. But lies run themselves to death, and what is then left is truth. Have you ever heard anyone speak ill of the count from over there? No; and why not? Because he has a pure heart. He has not had an awakening and lacks the light of faith, that is all. But what this horrid Bamme lacks is nothing more nor less than everything, and what he has in its place is smoke and vapour. And he is always smoking, too, with a nasty little pipe, and ash and matches and tinder lie all over his room. He has burned holes in the floorboards, and everywhere it looks as though I won't say who had been staying with us for a week. What good can come of this? Oh no, Renate, what we need is the help of God. He has to send his angels to fight at our side; but they cannot fight at *this* man's side, for the pure cannot consort with the impure.'

'Dear Schorlemmer,' said Marie, 'surely you are doing him an injustice: he is not so black as he is painted; he has that in common with the person you compare him with. He came to our house this morning and sat with me and talked to me, it must have been for half an hour. I wasn't afraid for a moment, or at any rate a good deal less afraid than I am of many others who don't have Bamme's reputation. He was very polite and very interested, and I must say he said nothing in any way offensive. Perhaps he was different in earlier years. He is clever and he knows what people are like, and I believe he is well aware what he ought to say and what he ought not to.'

'Marie is right,' said Seidentopf. 'And he has in addition a great virtue: he does not play the hypocrite, he does not make himself out to be better than he is. On the contrary, he imputes to himself all kinds of follies and eccentricities, for the human heart is wonderful in its vanities. Most people seek their advantage in a pretence of virtue, he takes pleasure in a pretence of sinning. I don't want to exaggerate, but when I sum up his failings I would say merely that he is vain and flirtatious and lacking in firm principles.'

'Lacking in firm principles!' Aunt Schorlemmer exploded. 'That is putting it mildly, I must say. Principles? He hasn't any principles whatever, and that is the worst thing about him. For he who has no principles is like a beast of prey or a cat. And how do cats behave? One minute they are lying purring and warming themselves beside the stove, and the next they are at the throat of the baby in the cradle. "She thought it was a mouse", say those people who find an excuse for everything. But I have no time for such excuses. She may have thought it was a mouse, but the little innocent is still dead.'

Renate and Marie exchanged glances, but Aunt Schorlemmer, who, good woman though she was, in her zeal often forgot all charity, carried on with increasing vehemence: 'And it is with this man they are attacking the walls of a fortified city, as though he were a man of God and one chosen of God. But if he bids the fat man from Protzhagen with the ancient Rutze-horn round his neck to blow a call he will do so in vain, for the ancient Rutze-horn is no trumpet, and Bamme is, God knows, no Joshua. For Joshua possessed the Law God gave to Moses, and he swerved neither to left nor to right. And so it remained in Israel, and when bad times came, because they had mingled with the heathen and served the gods of the heathen, then God raised up a man of God among them, who then smote the Moabites and the Amalekites and many others besides. And why did he smite them? Because his chosen one served the true God and overthrew the temples of Baal. But this Bamme who is now going forth to smite our enemies is himself a child of the heathen who would build temples and altars to Baal every day if he could. And what is his Baal? Gaming and drinking and the lusts of the flesh. And so I say he will not return like Gideon . . .'

'But perhaps like Jephtha,' said Renate, laughing, 'and if he comes home victorious I shall go out to meet him with drums and cymbals.'

Presented with this picture, Seidentopf and Marie forgot, for a moment at any rate, the earnestness of their situation; Renate herself, however, took the old lady's hand and added sooth-ingly: 'Don't look so cross, dear Schorlemmer; it isn't right to speak like that. Here we are together at a heavy hour, and our nearest and dearest have gone forth to give the country the signal of rebellion. And what do you do? You paint for us gloomy pictures, as though everything must miscarry on account of this *one* man. That isn't right, and it isn't like you. For the sake of one good man God shows much mercy, so you used to teach me, but he does not condemn hundreds of innocents to perdition on account of one sinner. Am I not right, dear pastor?'

'Yes, and yes again,' said Seidentopf, 'and there is no point in making us anxious and depressed at a time when we should be bearing up. My old friend has been carried away by her zeal. We all have some subject on which when we think we are being fairest, we are in fact being completely unfair. And in my friend's case it is called Bamme. Let us leave contention and dejection, and let us read something of the omnipotence and the mercy of God.'

Marie had risen, and now fetched from the *camera theologica* the great Augsburg Bible with the iron clasps and opened them. Old Pastor Seidentopf then read from the Ninetieth Psalm: 'Lord, thou hast been our dwelling-place in all generations. Before the mountains were brought forth, or ever thou hadst formed the earth and the world, even from everlasting to everlasting, thou art God.'

Thereupon Aunt Schorlemmer and Renate rose and returned to the manor house. With them went Marie, for they wanted to be together that night.

19

The Attack*

WHILE Seidentopf and the three women were thus conversing in the parsonage, the companies of militia were moving towards Frankfurt. The few stars in the sky had vanished almost as soon as they had appeared, and only the snow that lay on the ground gave just enough light for them not to lose their way. The dark columns marched on in silence, and anyone standing a hundred feet away would have been aware of nothing but a long line of shadows, with here and there a spark or two from the militiamen's pipes. The crows gazed after the procession, surprised but without moving, and only a couple of them flew up, screeching, to report its coming to others further along the road. The clouds settled lower and lower as the march went forward, and even though a cold wind was sweeping across their path to everyone the air seemed sultry.

Thus they came to Reitwein, where there were still lights in all the houses. Many of the villagers, again mostly women, had come out on to the roadway to greet their relatives in the column, while others remained standing in the doorways and waved at them with white cloths and handkerchiefs, a sight that produced an uncanny impression in the darkness that prevailed all around.

Beyond the village the road divided. When the head of the column had reached the fork, the Barnim battalions wheeled to the left down into the low-lying country, just as Seidentopf had predicted they would, while the other half of the procession continued to march on along the plateau. This second half included, in addition to the commander-in-chief and his adjutant, our Lebus Battalion.

At its head, fifty paces ahead of the foremost units, rode Drosselstein and Vitzewitz. They knew the highways and byways of the region and at Bamme's express desire had taken over the leadership during the march. Neither was inclined for talk; finally, however, when the last houses of Reitwein already lay a rifle-shot's distance behind them, Drosselstein began: 'It's a piece of luck we have Hirschfeldt at the general's side. He has a clear head and is familiar with war.'

'Yes,' Vitzewitz affirmed. 'And all the more in that the old man lacks confidence in himself. When we offered him the command, and having regard to all the circumstances *had* to offer it to him, for good or ill, he was sufficiently vain to accept it; but now he is insecure, because he doesn't feel up to his task. He would dearly like to admit as much, and it is greatly to his credit that he has refrained from doing so and has constrained himself to silence, at least before the men. He is not given to calm reflection and is rash and foolhardy when it comes to his own person. Responsibility weighs upon him. However, these present hours are the worst. Once he is in action he will be himself again.'

'And this action, how do you think it will turn out?' asked the count.

'I hope it will turn out well; unless, that is . . .'

Drosselstein looked at him inquiringly.

'Unless, that is,' Vitzewitz repeated, 'the Russians leave us in the lurch.'

'I do not merely have Chernichev's assurance, I received it, as you know, for a *second* time yesterday. He is not a man given to petty prevarications.'

'Perhaps not,' Vitzewitz replied. 'But I know the Russians,

they are capricious and inclined to be passive. And with that they have their bland social forms and politenesses that only make things worse. They promise everything and know in advance they are not going to keep their promise, or at least they don't feel conscience-bound to do so. There are two things they lack: a sense of honour and a sense of sympathy. And Chernichev is like the others. It is possible that he will come, but on the other hand it is not *im*possible that he will *not* come. And that is why I feel the trepidation I do.'

Drosselstein tried to argue against him, but his words clearly betrayed that in his heart he shared Berndt's apprehensions.

All was still silent in the column following behind them. The mayor, Kniehase, was leading the first section, Lewin the second, Tubal the third. Between the second and third sections marched Hanne Bogun. Mistrustful of his tall sorrel mare, Bamme had insisted on a reserve horse, and the Scharwenkas' boy had been chosen to lead the Shetland pony along. In the whole column he was the only person who felt completely contented: vain and, since the day the 'search' had taken place, plagued by an ever-increasing self-conceit, he was now thirsting to distinguish himself again, and he did not for a moment doubt that an opportunity for doing so would present itself. Even his mode of dress indicated as much: he wore, as usual, a baize jacket and linen trousers, but over the jacket he had buckled a broad leather belt in which he had made a slit and into the slit inserted a long knife with a groove down the middle. As a whole, the boy presented a picture of an impudent ne'er-do-well.

Oppressed by the silence, Tubal went forward a few paces and asked him: 'Hanne, what is the next village called?'

'Podelzig.'

'Half a mile, isn't it?'

'Yes; but that's as measured by the fox.'

'How so?'

'He always adds his tail.'

'And Podelzig is halfway to Frankfurt?'

Hanne Bogun nodded.

'Listen, Hanne,' Tubal went on, 'how was it that time, wasn't one of those men in the reeds from Podelzig?'

'Yes, Rosentreter.'

'Right, Muschwitz and Rosentreter. Now I remember. Muschwitz, that was the one with the French uniform and the shako. Do you recall? What has happened to him, and the others?'

'They're still inside.'

'And the good-looking woman with the child in the sleigh-box?'

'Inside too.'

'Poor woman.'—Hanne grinned.

'It's not as bad as all that, young sir. Rysselmann keeps the stove on, and it's pretty cold up there in the reeds. In the winter they all like to be inside; but when the spring comes, it's different then, then they all want to get out again.'

Tubal went on to ask about the Spitzkrug and how far it lay outside the city, but Hanne Bogun was unable to enlighten him: he had never been beyond Podelzig.

Bamme and Hirschfeldt were riding at the tail of the column.

'Well, Hirschfeldt, how are you?'

'Fine, Herr General.'

'I am glad to hear it. To tell the truth, I myself am not very happy; I am not at all at ease, everything seems to me too tall, especially my mare. And a surprise attack like this is a peculiar thing; a horse neighs, a dog barks, and all is lost. Do you gamble, Hirschfeldt?'

'I have gambled.'

'In that case you will know that one day you know for certain that the seven of clubs is going to win and the next day you don't.'

'And today is such a day?'

'Deuce take me, yes. Look at the crows sitting up there: they don't even move. They know we're too frightened to touch them. Clever birds. I just rode down the column: God, how they all skulk along, so dark and silent, as though this ditch were the river in the underworld. What's its name?'

'The Styx.'

'Right, the Styx. A downright funeral procession. And I wager the men feel the same way. They would all rather be at home.'

Hirschfeldt smiled.

'It is always thus, General. The finest troops pull a long face before the action begins. And it's night, too, remember. Night is no man's friend, says the proverb, and the soldier, too, is a man. But these are good people. The company of pikes under the lean old gentleman . . .'

'Rutze.'

' . . . This company of pikes might be considered a model, and the Hohen-Vietz Company is its equal. Look at a man like that Kniehase, with a heart like a child and arms like an athlete. I took a close look at each of them at the muster today. All in all, I think things will go well, always assuming . . .'

'Always assuming what?'

'Always assuming the Russians do not leave us in the lurch.'

Bamme nodded in agreement, and then said: 'I don't trust that Tettenborn. He's a trickster. He wants to get himself into the papers. Berlin, Berlin. What's going on here is too small for him, it doesn't attract enough attention.'

It was clear that Bamme was confusing the earnest and almost solemn Chernichev with the somewhat giddy-headed Tettenborn, who for a full three days had been roving about in Hohen-Barnim between Küstrin and Berlin. Hirschfeldt made respectfully to correct him on this point, but the general carried on without pausing: 'You wouldn't believe, Hirschfeldt, what I haven't seen shipwrecked on such vanities! And what is even worse than these vanities are rivalries, twofold and threefold worse when they can cloak themselves in a political or patriotic mantle. And these Russians are among the worst! I wager each one of them would like to see us take a beating. What they want is to make the world believe, and perhaps to make themselves believe too, that nothing can go right without the Cossacks, and that where their assistance is lacking defeat is certain. They are enjoying themselves in their role of liberator, and all the more in that it is such a novel one.'

Talking thus with one another the column marched on, and

through the darkness of the night all that could be heard was the sound of the militiamen's heavy tread on the hard frozen snow, and from time to time the clatter of their pikes and rifles as they moved them from one shoulder to the other. At ten o'clock they passed through Podelzig, at eleven the sheep-fold at Lebus. From here they still had an hour and a half to go; the long shadowy procession began to move more and more slowly, until they heard midnight chime from the tower of the Oberkirche; a minute or two later they all came to a halt at the Spitzkrug. The two Barnim battalions were already there and standing on either side of the road. A brief rest was essential; Bamme had the rifles stacked together, and the militiamen then sat themselves down on fences and roadside stones and extracted from their handkerchiefs whatever victuals the women and children they had encountered on the way had given them. Not a word was spoken; each of them reflected in silence that this might be his last meal.

While this encampment was in progress, Bamme had gone into the Spitzkrug, where, in the large but low-ceilinged and frugally lighted guest-room, he found already waiting the expected emissary of the citizens of Frankfurt. From his report it emerged that every house on the Nikolaikirchplatz was occupied by the citizen militia, while in the ancient church itself there had been installed a select body of men with whom Othegraven intended to seize General Girard. Bamme was delighted to hear all this; a second communication, however, to the effect that a French sentry was standing down at the entrance to the suburb not a hundred paces from the Last Farthing, was less delightful and calculated only to cause embarrassing difficulties. What were they to do? How were they to get past this sentry?

The landlord of the Spitzkrug volunteered to go and have another look. Bamme agreed that he should, and in the meantime had the brigade reassemble. He himself was stationed on the right flank, at the head of the Lebus Battalion. Before long the landlord returned, and confirmed that a French soldier was on sentry duty in front of the St George hospital.

'Damn it!' said Bamme. 'This fellow is in my way. We must steal up on him and knock him down. Volunteers forward!'

But no one moved. Only Hanne Bogun stepped forth from the ranks, went up to the general and looked him in the face with a resolute, if also impudent and offensive expression. He had moved the knife, which had hitherto been hanging at his side, more to the front of his leather belt, and was holding it gripped in his single hand.

Bamme smote the boy on the shoulder and said: 'It's not a job for you, Hanne'; whereupon Hanne stepped back grinning and took again the bridle of the Shetland pony that he had for a moment surrendered to someone else.

A painful pause followed.

At length the voice of Kniehase was heard from the right flank: 'If it *has* to be done, Herr General . . . '

And there was something in the tone and expression of these words that could not fail to tell. They told on Bamme, certainly, and advancing his mare to the shoulder of the athletic old man, he said: 'No, Kniehase, let's forget it. It does *not* have to be done.' And with that a weight fell from everyone's heart. A proposal made earlier was again taken up, and it was decided to avoid the lengthy suburb altogether, to push on by a route running close beside it that lay in the shelter of the so-called 'Donischberg', a ridge covered with brushwood and undergrowth, and to gain the Old Town by this means. Only here, at the gate itself, would they then, *coûte que coûte*, commence the battle.

And now, leaving one of the battalions at the Spitzkrug to ensure their line of retreat, the others received their orders to advance. The two Barnim battalions set off along the plateau with the object of gaining the more southerly gates, while the Lebus Battalion moved down the hill on the aforementioned road beside the ridge. Just before the Last Farthing it turned off to the right and, marching at first in loose order and keeping always within the twists and turns of the Donischberg, made for the esplanade that separated the ring of suburbs from the Old Town.

The Hohen-Vietz Company marched at the front. When they had reached the square beside the moat and, with the celerity of old soldiers, formed themselves into ranks again, Vitzewitz placed himself at the head of his troops, drew his sword and rode at the gallop for the Dammbrücke which led over the moat to the old Lebus Gate. The gate was shut, and through the grating at the top there came several shots. Kümmritz, who had been accounted a 'target' as long ago as 'ninety-four, was grazed by a bullet, and immediately afterwards by a second one, though it failed to affect his composure or that of those standing near him; but the son of the old farmer Püschal collapsed with a bullet through the chest, and Vitzewitz, recoiling, murmured to himself: 'The first fatality.'

Everyone faltered, terrified and irresolute. The advance came to a halt.

At this moment Bamme came racing up the long column, reached the head of it and, pointing with his switch to the two-wheeled cart standing in the embrasure of the gate of which he had taken good note the previous day, cried to Kniehase: 'Four men forward! I know our city gates, they're as worm-eaten as the bungs of beer-barrels! Come on! And away with the rubbish!'

And with a crash the gate came down, and with a loud Hurray! the foremost ranks broke into Alt-Frankfurt. The enemy fled into the guard-room; only the sentry before the cannon, a *voltigeur* with a pointed beard, remained where he was, and Vitzewitz was in the act of raising his arm to cut him down in requital of the dead man who lay outside the gate when, as smoothly as an eel, Hanne Bogun shot past him and stabbed the *voltigeur* in the side.

'*Petit crevé*!'* the man exclaimed, and sank to the ground mortally wounded.

The remainder of the battalion followed after them, and when everyone had reassembled on the embankment of the moat, with some already standing beneath the tall arch of the bridge, Bamme gave the order that the Hohen-Vietz Company under the command of Kniehase should remain at the gate as a reserve unit, but that Vitzewitz himself (whose advice he did not wish to lose) should accompany him on their further advance into the town. Likewise Hanne Bogun with the Shetland pony.

Hardly had these commands been given when the long

column again began to move forward: the Hohen-Ziesar Company in the van, then Lietzen–Dolgelin, then Rutze with his pikemen. After the last man had gone by, Bamme pulled round his sorrel mare, dug his spurs into her, and placed himself *en ligne* with Drosselstein, who had in the meantime reached the tangle of streets that marked the inner city.

'Left wheel!' The company commanders repeated the order and, without any congestion or confusion, all three companies filed smoothly into the empty church square—the square on one corner of which Turgany's house stood. On the side at which they had entered all was still shrouded in semi-obscurity; but when our militiamen, having advanced on either side of the church, had reached the far end of the square, they were presented with a wholly different picture. In front of the hotel with its pruned lime-trees there stood a crowd of civil militia, lights were burning on every floor and, before Bamme had had time to survey the scene and decide what had happened, Othegraven reported that General Girard and his staff had been taken prisoner; on their word of honour that they would not try to escape, they had been allowed to remain in their rooms. The house and its prisoners were being guarded by only a small detachment under Major Rudelius.

Bamme nodded, commended the way the citizens had acted, and then led his companies into the wide but short street that, as has already been observed, emerged out of the church square at the quay, and from every throat there came a cry of astonishment. On the far side of the river the wood-yard was in flames and to their right the bridge was burning. The fire on the other side was rising high and bright into the night sky, but over the bridge, whose damp timbers were smouldering rather than blazing, there lay thick clouds of smoke and vapour, out of which only now and then a dark glow flickered up.

The old general uttered the command: 'Halt!' and ordered his right flank, Drosselstein's company, to take up position immediately in front of the entrance to the bridge. Here he also stationed himself: but when he perceived that from this position his view of the scene was somewhat obscured he rode out on to the bridge itself and positioned himself close to the fire, which also afforded him a concealment of a sort. And now there extended before him the long lines of friend and foe.

To the left stood his *own side*: a picture to rejoice the heart of an old soldier. First the mounted units from Hohen-Ziesar, then the commandery standard of Lietzen–Dolgelin (an eight-pointed cross on a red field), then Rutze with his pike dipped to the ground, and behind him the brightly decorated green and gold-bordered uniforms of the Frankfurt citizens' militia—all clearly visible in the vivid light of the blazing wood-yard. In front of the long array, at either flank, stood the seconds-in-command, Drosselstein and Vitzewitz.

And with equal clarity he could see on the other side of the river the enemy. The *voltigeurs* stood along the bank in squads of ten and twenty, plainly without leadership. But this was not to be long in coming: officers on horseback chased up and down the quay, from the tangle of streets of the Dammvorstadt there came the noise of drums and bugles, and before ten minutes were up companies of grenadiers in compact formation, clearly recognizable from their tall bearskin caps, appeared and took up position between the bridge and the blazing wood-yard, while the *voltigeurs* gradually made their way down the sloping river-bank and sought to find a pathway across the ice. They advanced with great dexterity, closing ranks and opening them as they received the signal to do so, and came to a stop only when, midway across the river, they perceived the wide channel which the fishermen of Kietz had hacked in the ice. It was too wide even to consider leaping over it; they were thus obliged to go back, either to fetch for themselves boards and planks, or so as to proceed further downstream, where they had presumably stopped removing the ice, and there seek to effect a crossing.

Bamme rejoiced to see this retreating movement. But, whatever it might signify for them in the short term, it would be without any significance at all if the assistance on which they counted failed to materialize. Had the Russians broken into the Dammvorstadt? Had the Barnim battalions taken possession of the other two city gates? Bamme listened sharp-eared to left and right, but he heard no sound that might have answered these questions in the affirmative. The certainty grew within him that, if Chernichev failed to appear, he was bound to be defeated in this unequal contest.

The picture that was meanwhile unrolling before him could serve only to confirm this gloomy expectation. Hardly had the *voltigeurs* who had pressed forward as far as the channel regained the river-bank than, with the celerity characteristic of the French soldier, they set about assessing their situation and exploring ways of remedying it. Without waiting for any word of command they began putting into effect whatever measures the moment demanded: and while some were endeavouring to push down the slope and on to the ice a number of flat-bottomed boats lying along the bank, others had taken possession of the boathooks stacked behind the quay in the direction of the coppice and run with them to the blazing wood-yard, where they hacked their way into the storehouse where the boards and planks were stocked in an attempt to tear it down. The attempt succeeded. Many of the boards were only beginning to catch fire and, dragging them rapidly through the snow until the flames were extinguished, they then drew them over the ice until they were again midway across the river, where at the same moment a couple of flat-bottomed boats that had just arrived were quickly and adroitly lowered into the channel. In less than fifteen minutes the pontoon-bridge was ready; and the vanguard then advanced across it, while ever larger squads of *voltigeurs*, and finally the grenadier companies too, set out from the far bank. *En avant!* And as they came there sounded from the quay and upon the ice itself the blare of the bugles.

On the near side of the river, the French, deprived of all positional advantage, had now to show whether or not they were the stronger. Their first assault against the Frankfurters miscarried; but, not in the slightest degree disconcerted by this second setback, the French columns simply moved off further to the left, where several wood- and peat-barges lying side by side offered them excellent cover—all the more excellent in that the hulls of the boats were exactly the height of a man, so that the attackers were almost invulnerable.

Across these ships' hulls there now ensued a contest whose final outcome was the less in doubt in that the pikeman positioned there had not only to endure the battle without cover but, worse than this, to receive the enemy's fire without being able to return it. The courage of Rutze's men was here put to a stern test. At length they began to waver, and since Vitzewitz hesitated to turn for help to Drosselstein's men stationed beside him, who, with the battle continually spreading out along the bank, could at any moment themselves come under attack, he resolved on his own responsibility to ride back to the gate and fetch his own Hohen-Vietzers stationed there and doing nothing.

From his position on the bridge Bamme, too, had observed Rutze's pikemen moving back, and racing up to them in a towering rage he shouted at them while still some distance away: 'Halt! Attention! Level arms, at the right!' And behold, they did actually obey, couched their pikes, and advanced again halfway to the river-bank. But enemy fire bursting at them at that moment from left and right made them not merely waver a second time but move back even further, so that Bamme perceived at once that it would be impossible to maintain Rutze's company *en ligne* with the other companies. None the less he pulled his horse around, with the aim of making at least an attempt to drive back the retreating men from behind: and in doing so he encountered, seeking cover with more anxiety than anyone, the Protzhagen horn-player.

'Blow, in the Devil's name, horn of Uri, blow!' he cried, and raised his switch to the confused horn-player. Obedient to the power of a word of command, the latter without knowing what he was doing righted his ancient Rutze-horn and began to blow: but instead of blowing the attack, in the bewilderment of his fear he blew the retreat. At this moment (a piece of good fortune for the Protzhageners) Bamme's red sorrel mare was struck by a bullet, so that she collapsed to the ground, taking her rider with her. But with remarkable rapidity the old man was again on his feet, mounted his Shetland pony, which Hanne Bogun had been holding in readiness, and a moment later was again seated firmly in the saddle.

'Ah!' he exclaimed, making himself comfortable; and, freed from all the constraint which the 'general's horse' had from the start imposed upon him, he was again himself. He pushed his switch beneath the saddle and drew the hussar's sabre which in '*anno* 95' he had sworn he would never draw again.

He was again himself, but there had been no other improvement in the situation. Extending their line further and further to the right, the *voltigeurs* had effected a crossing downstream at places where the ice was still in place, and were now preparing to storm out of every side-road and take our entire position from sides and rear. And, worst of all, those few French quartered in private houses who had hitherto stayed hidden and quiet had now regained their courage and were firing from the windows of their billets. It was Drosselstein's men who were especially hard pressed by this fusillade, and when immediately afterwards—'*pour combler le malheur*',★ as the count muttered to himself—the detachment of grenadiers standing over at the Golden Lion also fired a volley through the smoke and vapour of the burning bridge, the entire line began to waver.

The position was, in truth, hopeless; but hope once more flickered up when, at precisely this most threatening moment, the firm tread of the Hohen-Vietzers was audible as they came marching from the church square.

'Hurrah, children!' cried Bamme, 'that's the Swedish Drum', and to the loud rejoicing of the pikemen, who had been momentarily brought to a halt, our friends now marched forward into the foremost rank.

Berndt at once recognized, from his view from the saddle, that a cunningly constructed noose was at that moment beginning to be drawn around the hitherto victorious Frankfurt civil militia, and crying in the highest agitation to his three foremost sections: 'Forward! . . . No firing, bayonets!' he spurred his horse into the midst of the throng without waiting to see whether or not he would be followed, and made for the spot where he had perceived the schoolmaster defending himself to left and right like a madman with an old cavalry sabre. But before he could have reached him he would certainly have been struck from his horse and become a victim of his own courage and readiness to assist if his Hohen-Vietzers had not impetuously followed close behind him—so close, indeed, that in the midst of all the excitement and turmoil he believed himself able to recognize each one of them individually. He could see that Kniehase's forehead was bleeding, and he saw Grell, who in the confusion had lost his hat, hewn down by a French officer. But then everything grew dim before his eyes, he heard the sound of firing and of curses in French and German, and as a minute afterwards he emerged from the throng of combatants he had no choice but to recognize that all their efforts had achieved nothing and that their attempt to rescue Othegraven had failed. Who, apart from Grell, had fallen or been taken prisoner could not for the present be determined for certain. Lewin was not to be seen; but he might be among those scattered or forced to the ground who were reappearing in ones and twos at every moment.

After all this their only concern could be to get out of the trap Frankfurt had become as quickly as possible and with the fewest possible losses. Bamme gave orders, first to break off the engagement, then to retreat. The pikemen moved across the square, which was now dark and empty, followed by Hohen-Ziesar and then by Lietzen–Dolgelin. The Hohen-Vietzers, who still had the most cohesion, covered the retreat. It was in an orderly fashion until the head of the column reached the old Lebus Gate. Received with musket-fire from the French guard detachment, who had again collected themselves, the foremost units here began to waver, and were soon in a state of confusion which at once communicated itself down the entire procession and which grew worse rather than better during the march through the suburb. The long street lay in darkness; here a cart, there an upturned fishing-boat obstructed their path; and many of the wearier militiamen slid over or fell into the troughs and gaps of which there was no lack in the roadway.

'Light!' shouted Bamme. 'Damned Sottmeiers, they set fire to houses and want to save candles. Light, I say, or your roofs will blaze.'

And as he shouted he beat on the house-doors and window-shutters with his switch, which he had now taken up again. This proved of some assistance: several lights appeared, and they were able at least to see where they were. Thus they went on in a wavering line through the seemingly endless suburb, past the St George hospital, until at last they halted at the Last

Farthing. The companies were numbered off: Lewin was still missing.

The battalion left behind at the Spitzkrug had already descended to the foot of the hill on its own initiative. It was one piece of comfort, but the only one.

The little lamp was still burning behind the grating of the niche, and the two 'nuns' were still offering their faded wreaths to the Crucified.

Bamme gazed into the niche for a time, then he said to Hirschfeldt, who was standing beside him: 'Here, Hirschfeldt, our place is here, at the Last Farthing. Here it was planned, and here it is ending. I had a presentiment of it. The last farthing. We've paid ours!'

20

The Morning After

THE retreat went on through the night, and then into the gradual dawning of the next day, with the column becoming more and more depleted as the march continued. The Barnim battalions had detached themselves as they had left the Spitzkrug, the Hohen-Ziesar and Lietzen–Dolgelin companies had done so at Reitwein, and only those that remained, among them Rutze's pikemen, marched back to Hohen-Vietz.

They were approaching Miekley's mill as it struck seven. A heavy, yellow-grey fog was settling, and only those at the very front were able to recognize the mill-yard. Everywhere a painful silence reigned: the dense air muffled all sound, and it was as though they were creeping secretly along. Bamme sensed this and desired to put an end to it. 'Forward, Hirsch-feldt,' he cried, 'forward with the whole military music! Let's not march in silence, as though we had come from the penitent's chair. Let us demonstrate our good conscience, or at least pretend to.' And through the fog there came the rumbling of the Hohen-Vietz drum, with an occasional note or two from the Rutze-horn: it was a hollow and dismal sound, and it penetrated to the very marrow all who heard it. At last they halted. 'Order arms!' They had reached the spot between the inn and the residence of the mayor; there were lights in the houses, but no one was to be seen in the street. Berndt and Bamme had another brief deliberation regarding the accommodation of the pikemen; then the drum gave the signal and everyone repaired to his quarters. Within five minutes the only people left were our friends, standing silent and undecided what to do. None felt any desire to cross the threshold of the manor house again, for each knew that bearers of ill tidings always arrive too soon. At length Berndt indicated the mayor's house and said: 'I want to have another word with Kniehase. Will you tell my daughter I have returned, General? Or you, Tubal.'

Bamme took Hirschfeldt's arm, and Tubal followed: and thus they walked up the village street to the manor house. Jeetze was standing at the glass door, and the look of surprise on his face seemed to ask where the master and the son of the house were. 'Still in the village,' said Bamme, and then added half under his breath: 'Come, Hirschfeldt, I don't like family scenes. Least of all scenes like this.' And with that he went off to the corridor that led to his room. Only Tubal remained behind. What was he to do? Ought he to go in to Renate? He could not; so he threw himself into the old armchair by the fire, in which Jeetze had spent the night.

Berndt had not gone to the mayor's house; he had only wanted to be alone, and he followed the others along the street a short distance behind them. His heart was beating and, as though he were bearing too heavy a burden, he walked slowly and falteringly past the parsonage and then past farmer Püschel's large house and farmyard. In that house too, there was mourning: an only son fallen.

The next farm was that of Kallies. Between the two ran a privet-hedge, and several of the dry branches brushed against his face as he went by. He stopped and stood listening and sunk in thought; and then he thrust his hands into the branches and grasped them, for he felt he was about to fall down.

'All a failure,' he said. 'And I am to blame for it. A failure, total and complete. Shall I see it as a sign? Yes. But a sign that we must stake what we love most for the sake of a higher good.

Nothing else. This is no smooth and easy world. Everything has its price and we must be happy to pay it when it is demanded in the right cause.'

Thus he exhorted himself. But in the midst of this exhortation, through which he thought to strengthen and sustain himself, he was seized by a new and deeper anguish, and beating his forehead he now cried: 'Berndt, do not deceive yourself, do not lie to yourself! What was it? Was it fatherland and holy vengeance, or was it vanity and ambition? Did the decision lie in *your* hands? Or did you want fame? Did you want to be the first? Answer, I want to know; I want to know the truth.'

For a while he was silent; then he let go the branch with which he had been supporting himself, and said: 'I do not know. Bah, it will have been as it always has been and always will be: some of it good, some of it bad. Poor human nature, how petty it is! And I thought myself better and greater. Yes, to fancy oneself better than others, there's the cause of it; pride goes before a fall. And what a fall it has turned out to be! But I am punished, and this hour is my reward.'

Thus he had reached the courtyard of his house. In the hall he discovered Tubal, who, exhausted by his exertions, had fallen asleep in Jeetze's armchair. Beside him lay Hector. When the latter caught sight of his master he leaped up and pressed himself against him, though he gave no other sign of joy. Berndt stroked the sagacious animal, cast a glance of silent envy at the slumbering Tubal, and then went to the door leading to the corner room. He placed a hand on the latch and then hesitated. But it was unavoidable. Only the two girls were there. Renate flew towards him. 'My dear, dear Papa!' she cried and threw her arms about his neck. Then she let him go and, as though she were his conscience, asked him: 'Where is Lewin?'

Vitzewitz struggled for words. Finally, in a tone in which there spoke all the misery of his heart, he said: 'I don't know.'

'Taken prisoner, dead?'

'No, not dead, not yet.'

Renate was seized with fear and trembling, but at the same moment she saw Marie totter and fall to the floor as though lifeless. The sight seemed to communicate a faintness to

Berndt, who, almost overwhelmed by all that had rushed in upon him, seemed ready to collapse himself; at length he tore himself out of his bewilderment and pulled the bell. Jeetze came, followed at once by Aunt Schorlemmer; there was running about and confusion; he himself, however, was busy restoring Marie. When he had succeeded in doing so, he saw she was bleeding from a wound to her forehead close beside the left temple: she had fallen against the protruding foot of the fireplace. At last recovered from her fit of fainting, she asked to be taken home to the mayor's house, a service Maline at once agreed to perform, though she did so less out of sympathy for Marie than from her own curiosity: down in the village she might hope to hear more of what had happened than she would here in the manor house, where nobody was saying anything; even Bamme, though his room was no longer out of bounds, seemed unlikely to offer much in the way of information.

When Berndt and Renate were alone, Berndt asked: 'What was the matter with Marie? I had thought she was made of sterner stuff.'

Renate was silent.

'He is your brother,' Berndt went on. 'And yet *you* bore up.'

There followed a pause during which Renate lowered her eyes. At last she replied: 'She loves him.'

After all he had just witnessed, Vitzewitz appeared to have anticipated such an answer, for he replied quietly: 'And he—does he know?'

'No.'

'Are you certain of it?'

'Yes, quite certain. She has never betrayed it, neither by word nor action. And if she had, Lewin would not have noticed: he was blinded by his love for Kathinka.'

Berndt paced up and down the room, a prey to the most contradictory emotions. At one moment his mouth was twisted in scorn that the child of the 'mighty man' should find her way into the ancient house of Vitzewitz; then all such feelings vanished, and the distress that lay nearest to him, the distress he felt at the fate of his only son, obliterated all else. 'How can I rescue him?' And it was as though he swore to himself a solemn vow: 'God, I lay at Thy feet all my pride;

humble me, I shall submit in silence; anything, anything; only do not let me lose my son.'

As Berndt had been pacing up and down, Renate had been following him with her eyes. She knew exactly what was passing in his soul, and now she said: 'Please, Papa, tell me everything. What has happened to him? Do not keep anything from me!'

He took her hand. 'I have kept nothing from you, child. All is darkness and uncertainty. I know no more than you. But one thing I know only too well: we must be prepared for the worst, for the very worst, even if at this moment God's sunlight does still shine upon him. Taken with a weapon in his hand! They will bring him before a military court, and . . . '

'How did it happen?' Renate interrupted. 'Speak, I want you to tell me about him, I want something to sustain me, even if it is nothing but the vain consolation of knowing he did his duty or demonstrated his courage.'

'That consolation I can offer you. There was hand-to-hand fighting; Othegraven had been encircled and we wanted to free him. We plunged into the midst of them. When we emerged again, Lewin was missing. At first we weren't worried, for many who had been missing had gradually found their way back to us; but Lewin failed to reappear. He has been taken, there can be no doubt about it.'

'And what do we do?'

'The only thing left for us to do: pray that God will show mercy. May angels protect him! We can do nothing more.' And with that he left the room and went across to his office.

Here it was cold and inhospitable. Jeetze had forgotten the heating; and there was dust on the chairs and table. But Berndt either failed to notice or was indifferent to it, while, in the conflict of feeling which usually fills our soul at such moments, he directed his attention to other things towards which he was, if anything, even more indifferent. He noticed that the keys were hanging in the wrong order on the key-board and began carefully to arrange them correctly. Then he walked over to the window and stared for several minutes at the plans and maps of Russia still affixed to the wide folding-shutters. 'Minsk, Smolensk, Bialystok.' And he paced up and down repeating the names again and again. At last he halted before the picture that hung over his desk and his eyes filled with tears. 'Beloved,' he murmured to himself, 'how I thank God that, in his merciful providence, he spared you *this* hour. Oh, would I were where you are. Peace dwells only with the dead.'

He lowered himself on to the sofa, and began to feel a chill. There lay his cloak, which Jeetze, instead of hanging it up, had merely thrown over the back of the sofa. That was lucky. He pulled it over him and wrapped himself in it. 'Minsk, Smolensk . . .' And then consciousness faded and he slept.

He slept long and deeply. It was gone midday when a knock on the door awoke him. It was the third time Jeetze had knocked. 'Come in!' Jeetze reported that Rysselmann had come to the house.

'Bring him in. At once.'

Rysselmann entered, as stiff and straight as ever, his hair combed back, his cane under his arm and his badge of office fastened to his long, blue high-collared coat. He remained standing in the doorway and gave a military salute; Jeetze stood beside him, reluctant to leave the room. 'Stay,' said Berndt, who well understood why the old man was hesitating, 'you too can learn how things are. You too love him . . . Ah, who does not?' And he furtively clasped his hand over his eyes. Only then did he step over to the old beadle and say: 'Well, Rysselmann, what brings you?'

'A letter from the Herr Magistrate.'

'Does it contain good news?'

The old man stayed silent: he could not say Yes, and No stuck in his throat.

Berndt weighed the letter in his hand: he dreaded to open it, for then all would be known. He examined the old man, and at length decided that, all in all, he did not look like the bearer of a death-notice. 'I shall read this letter—but alone. . . . One more thing, though, Rysselmann: do you know . . . ?'

'Yes, your honour, one thing I do know.'

'And that is?'

'The young gentleman is alive.'

The letter fell from the hand of old Vitzewitz and his lips

trembled. He could not bring himself to speak. When he had mastered himself again he went up to Jeetze, laid a hand on the old servant's shoulder and, shaking him in joyful agitation, said: 'Did you hear, my old friend? He is alive! And now take care of Rysselmann. He has brought us something good, give him something good in return. Good, did I say? No, give him the best. Here, you have the key; the lefthand side, where the Spanish is. Fetch him a bottle, my good old Jeetze. And you can drink some too. Did you hear? He is *alive!*'

Jeetze kissed his master's hand and fussed back and forth; then he left, with Rysselmann following him. As soon as he was alone, Berndt opened the letter and read it through quickly. It was as the old beadle had said. He himself then left the office, and made his way to join the women in the corner room. He found only Renate, who hastened towards him, fear and inquiry in her face. 'There is still hope, child. And now call Aunt Schorlemmer.' Only when she had arrived did they seat themselves at the round table, and Berndt read:

Honoured Sir and Friend!
It is my sad duty to notify you that, following the engagement, two prisoners have fallen into the hands of the enemy: your son and the schoolmaster Othegraven. During the course of the morning your son will be taken under escort to Küstrin. Herr Othegraven was shot at dawn at the tanning-yard. After these brief preliminaries, it only remains to me to report to you on the death of this brave man. I had been asleep hardly an hour when I was awakened by a French orderly, who had come to notify me that one of the prisoners, the schoolmaster Othegraven, wished to speak with me. I dressed hurriedly, and the young soldier led me across to the old Nikolaikirche, at each of whose doorways the French had posted a double guard. Inside I saw the dead lying on a heap of straw: the first I recognized was Kandidat Grell.

In the vestry I encountered Othegraven. He was sitting in an old high-backed choir-stall, and the door was open, so that he had a clear view of the pulpit. He pointed to it and said: 'Look, Turgany, there is where I preached for the first time. My text was: Blessed are the peacemakers. And now, this is the end. The court has pronounced, and within an hour it will be all over with me.' I took his hand and, since there could be no question of his being either rescued or reprieved, I asked him if he had any last wish and whether he found it hard to face death. He said he did not, and added that he had once read that life was like a banquet. Everyone wanted to see it to the end; but anyone called away in the middle of it soon felt afterwards that he had not missed very much. And that, he said, was true. He, for his part, only wished that the drum-beating and the blindfolding were over; and he also distrusted the markmanship of the French. 'They do everything untidily, and their shooting of Hofer was a complete botch.' He continued to reflect on this thought for a time, and then, before I had put any further question to him, he said: 'I have no one; my little collection goes to Seidentopf, everything else to the hospital attached to this church. And now let us say farewell, Turgany. Give my best wishes to this valiant town, that I have so come to love, and tell anyone who is interested that I died in faith in Jesus Christ, but also in the firm belief that I have given my life in a good cause. I have preached: Blessed are the peacemakers; but we are also commanded to fight in our own defence and for our own way of life.'

And after that we parted. For ever.

An hour later I was summoned to General Girard. A true Frenchman, humane and noble-minded. 'I could do nothing to prevent it,' he said as I entered. 'An uprising at our backs, and directed by him; he had to die. The laws of war, and concern for our security, demand it. I do not ask after his fellow culprits; your people are now in revolt against us, and we shall have to see how we come through.' And thereupon he dismissed me, visibly moved, having added that the '*directeur adjoint*', as he called him, had died, '*comme un vieux soldat*'.

We buried him close by the church, where a part of the old churchyard still remains surrounded by railings. Beside him we buried Hansen-Grell.

I close with the heartfelt wish that your son's removal to Küstrin may be a first step towards his reprieve, or perhaps even his release.

Turgany.

Their first feeling as Berndt laid down the letter was one of profound thankfulness.

Renate embraced and kissed her father, and Aunt Schorlemmer, who never cried and was very proud of the fact, wept tears on to her folded shrivelled hands. She had no words to express what she felt, and even her proverbs failed her.

Lewin still lived, and so there was still hope. But their joy was very much tempered by the fact that, though previously they had all been appalled to think they might already have lost him, they were now prey to the fear they might still lose him at any moment.

Thus half an hour passed; Renate had departed for the mayor's to look after Marie, Aunt Schorlemmer had departed to look after the housework: for, whatever may happen, the home fires are still burning, reminding us of the rights and claims of everyday life. For his part, Berndt had remained alone; his mind was again absorbed in designs and plans. As the striking-clock was just striking two, Jeetze appeared and announced that lunch was ready.

As was usually the case since they had had visitors in the house, the table was laid in the hall. Bamme went up to Vitzewitz to congratulate him on the 'good news'; but his congratulations sounded chilly: it was plain for all to hear that Bamme had doubts, not of the accuracy of the intelligence, but of what it really amounted to. They sat down; Berndt asked after Marie, after Kniehase, after Rysselmann; but soon he brought to an end a meal at which, all efforts notwithstanding, little had been said. Everything seemed to him merely negligence and loss of time so long as they had not at any rate discussed a plan of action. He retired again to his work-room, and fifteen minutes later he had the other gentlemen requested to be good enough to join him there.

The little room had in the meantime grown more cheerful: a fire was burning, and the old cloak that had been lying on the sofa was now hanging from a peg. The general and Hirschfeldt appeared first, followed by Tubal. To find places for all three would not have been easy, given the narrowness of the room, if Bamme, who was fond of warmth, had not moved himself close to the stove. Here he sat smoking with his feet tucked under him, resembling an idol rather than a man.

Jeetze came and handed round coffee, for which they were all thirsting to a greater or less degree. And indeed the cups had hardly been drained when an improvement in everyone's mood became perceptible. Was the situation really as hopeless as all that? No. Berndt declared that, in his view, their chief hope lay in the fear felt by the French, in their presumable reluctance to make an example of anyone a second time. 'Girard or Fournier,' he concluded, 'it makes no difference; they know their days here are numbered, and they'll take care not to bend the bow any further than it is bent already.'

Bamme would hear nothing of this; Hirschfeldt, though he did not directly contradict the idea, thought their only real salvation lay in proceeding on their own account. As long as the neck was in the noose, he repeated, they could never be sure what would happen: a chance event, a whim, and the noose could tighten. 'If we can rely on Turgany's letter—and I believe we can—the gentlemen at Küstrin will not meet until before noon tomorrow or tomorrow afternoon. Even if the dice fall against us, which unfortunately they doubtless will, we shall still have nothing to fear until first thing the day after tomorrow. Executions are early morning affairs: that is an ancient custom. So whatever *we* are to do has to be done tonight or tomorrow night. Tonight? Assuming we shall need the assistance of our people, tonight will be impossible: even the best of them will not have recovered yet from such a blow as we received. Therefore tomorrow: tomorrow night.'

Berndt and Bamme were in agreement, and they agreed, too, that in carrying out the enterprise they would rely on cunning. In this, Hoppenmarieken was to assist. Hoppenmarieken, as Berndt very well knew, lived on the best possible terms with the garrison at Küstrin; there was none of them to whom she had not at some time been of service in the matter of purchases or procurement. Westphalians and French were equally attached to her; the latter, indeed, were greatly taken with her and, on account of her comically grotesque appearance, or perhaps also because they regarded her as feeble-minded, allowed her to come and go everywhere. That Hoppenmarieken herself, vain as she was, and liking adventure, would raise objections to assuming the role assigned her, of that there was not the remotest possibility; though the question did remain whether she was, with equal certainty, entirely to be trusted. This question was for the moment shelved, and Berndt sent to the woodland acre to have her fetched. But she had not yet returned from her customary excursions, and it was therefore decided to postpone the conference with her until the next morning. Bamme desired to be present at it.

They then separated and returned to their rooms. What still had to be done were things that could be discharged by

Kniehase better than by anyone else; he then arrived at the manor house, did everything that needed doing, and by the time it was growing dark was back at his house.

As soon as he was home again he went to Marie, with whom, paying little heed to his own wound, he had spent the greater part of the day.

He again sat himself beside her bed, and attended to her and asked her how she was; but she, as she listened to him and to his loving concern for her, was again assailed by the silent reproach that, through all the preceding hours, she had thought only of Lewin and not even once of him—of him who now spoke to her so lovingly and who from the first day on had shown her nothing but the tenderest consideration. She denounced her own selfishness and shed bitter tears. But he would not listen to her, and only repeated again and again: 'Don't child; you're young, that's all.' And then she quietened down and let him go on talking. Oh, how high did her heart beat when she heard of Turgany's letter: Othegraven was dead, but Lewin was *alive*. And that was all that mattered! The same selfishness which she had only a moment before denounced in herself was back again: and she hardly knew it.

Her brow had grown cooler; the loss of blood from her injury was accounted a good sign and her condition gave no cause for concern. She smiled to herself when Bamme and Rutze and their demeanour during the street-battle were referred to. It was only towards evening that a fever set in and she then began talking quietly to herself: 'If only Othegraven were here . . . he would help . . . to please me.' And then she said old Füllgraf's name and then that of the old steward at Küstrin, who was a cousin of the Kümmritzes and whom now in her imaginings she implored to hide the 'young gentleman' in his castle, 'in the middle of the great hall where no one will look for him'.

Thus the hours passed and the images circled around in her mind: but an hour after midnight the fever abated and she fell asleep.

21

'That We Must'

IT was not yet seven the following morning when Hoppen-marieken, clad in her usual fashion, came up the village street. When she reached the manor house she turned into the courtyard and surveyed the long dark row of windows. Only in the two corner-windows on the first floor did she see a light. 'He's already up,' she said and strode forward to the house.

She had observed correctly. Berndt had already been up for an hour and was sitting in his office. With him was Bamme, who, after having first tried once more to accommodate himself next to the greatly overheated, indeed almost glowing stove, had finally been obliged to beat a retreat to the window. Looking out of it, he now saw Hoppenmarieken coming across the courtyard. He was clad in a costume which, hardly less striking than that of the old witch of the woodland acre, had reduced even Berndt to momentary astonishment: a tight-fitting black velveteen dressing-gown, a red woollen shawl and yellow felt-slippers. In addition, he was smoking his morning pipe.

And now there was a knock.

'Come in!'

The old woman came in, but, leaning with her basket in the doorway, maintained a respectful distance from 'his worship', though she did so more out of habit than out of awe, since she was well aware that they needed her help.

'Good-day, your worship,' she said in her deep rough voice, and, when Berndt had responded, nodded with the same familiarity in the direction of the window corner. 'Good-day, General.'

'Do you know me, then?' Bamme asked, contentedly emit-ting a couple of clouds of smoke from his meerschaum.

'Aye, how should I not know our little general? I was down there at the muster and saw it all: Rutze and his pikers, and the fat Protzhagener with his fire-horn. God, what a sight! And then Drosselstein's red sorrel mare with the long legs. No, General, that didn't suit you at all.'

'You are right, Hoppenmarieken. I can see you have a good eye, and next time I shall consult you.'

She laughed.

'You do that, little general. The foolish, as I always say, are always the cleverest.'

Berndt saw that he would have to discontinue this conversation: familiarities of this kind were the last thing he needed. 'Set down your basket, Marieken, and come over to this table. Over here, so I can see you better.'

For a moment she lost her confident bearing, muttered to herself incomprehensibly, and then did as she had been bidden.

'You know, Hoppenmarieken—'

'I know.'

'And you know, too, that they are wasting no time. The schoolmaster has been shot at the tanning-yard, where the tall poplar-tree stands. It is a miracle they have still spared Lewin. But for how long? They have taken him to Küstrin, and we must get him free.'

'That we must, that we must.'

'And you are to help.'

'That I will.'

'Good, then take this ball of string and get it to him in secret. He is being held in the Brandenburg Bastion; Mencke wrote and told me last night. Don't rush it, take your time, even if it gets as late as midday. But be crafty, as crafty as you can be when you want to, and don't forget it's a matter of life and death.'

'I know, I know.'

Vitzewitz was silent for a while, during which time Hoppenmarieken stowed the ball away in her basket; then he continued: 'And now come back here and pay attention to what I have to say to you.'

Hoppenmarieken obeyed.

'Here, where you are standing now, Lewin pleaded for you, and because he pleaded for you, and only because he did, I let you go. Otherwise you would now be feasting on bread and water: and you wouldn't fancy that, for you like your food.'

'Aye, that I do.'

'Be silent. Listen to me. I am warning you: watch your step. I have shown you a great deal of patience and forbearance, and I have shut my eyes to your activities more often than I should have, but if you play a double game this time, may God help you. I shall trample on you, dwarf, and throttle you with my own hands.'

He had uttered this threat with the most heartfelt sincerity, but its effect on Hoppenmarieken was very slight. She merely shook her head, and without feeling in the least intimidated only continued to repeat: 'A fine gentleman, the young gentleman!' and as she spoke saluted with her stick as a sign that she could be relied upon. And this was, indeed, a better sign, and signified more, than if she had gestured emphatically with her finger. Then she again reached for her basket, rejected the advice proffered her to 'concentrate where possible on the Westphalians' with the rejoinder: 'Nay, I shall go for the little Frenchman: they're easy to get round', and a moment later left the room.

Only when she was between the two posts in the drive did she again turn with military precision and wave in the direction of the corner-window. She was quite sure the old general was gazing after her. The latter gave vent to a laugh and, transferring his little meerschaum to his left hand, he blew her a kiss with the fingers of his right.

'I still says she's a fine specimen, Vitzewitz,' he said. 'I wish I had such a thing at Gross-Quirlsdorf.'

Berndt did not reply; he rested his head on his hand. After a time he said:

'Bamme, you know human nature. Wasn't it risky to stake everything on *that* card? Can we trust her?'

'Unconditionally.'

'And why? Because her old witch's heart is set on Lewin?'

'Perhaps for that reason, too. The heart must have something, and the less it has, the firmer it clings to what it does have. It will die for it. Whether it is good or evil makes no difference.'

Berndt nodded.

'But', Bamme went on, 'that is not why I trust her. I trust her because she's shrewd. Do you know what she is thinking at the present moment?'

'Well?'

'The French will not stay in Lebus for ever, but the Vitzewitzes will be here for a long time to come.'

'And?'

'And you make alliances only with powers that are going to last. Even if your name's Hoppenmarieken.'

22

In the Weisskopf

At the same time as the letter informing them that Lewin had been taken prisoner was on its way from Frankfurt to Hohen-Vietz, Lewin himself was on his way from Frankfurt to Küstrin. They were separated only by the width of the river, and if old Rysselmann had kept a sharper look-out he must have recognized the French escort-squad as it moved along the road across on the Neumark bank. They were *voltigeurs*, selected men, placed under the command of an old sergeant who had already served in Spain. And there had been good grounds for taking such precautions, for, even though the Russians had the previous day shown how lacking they were in good will, or had at any rate failed to keep their word, they were none the less still in the neighbourhood, were swarming all over the Neumark, and seemed to be making a special point of waylaying small contingents of the enemy: that operation exacted few sacrifices and got itself talked about. The members of the escort were well aware of the existence of this state of affairs and thus neglected nothing in the way of care and attention for their prisoner: if the worst came to the worst and they themselves were taken prisoner—as they had every reason to fear they might be—their own captive might be inspired to intercede on their behalf.

But their fears were not realized: the Cossacks, for whom Lewin too had from time to time been keeping a look-out, never crossed their path, and, after passing the outlying houses of Kirch-Göritz at midday and shortly afterwards the pulp-mills, they arrived before the fortress on the stroke of two and delivered up their prisoner in the ancient castle-yard at Küstrin. General Fournier d'Albe asked a few questions which, their coldness notwithstanding, betrayed some interest in the captive, surveyed the slim figure before him, and then ordered that he be lodged in the 'Weisskopf'.

Lewin's heart sank when he heard that name.

The 'Weisskopf' was a round tower in the Brandenburg Bastion: more correctly, only the base of a round tower standing the height of a man which, so legend said, had been built two or three days before the execution of Katte* as the scaffold on which it was carried out. Several local historians, our Seidentopf among them, had, to be sure, demonstrated the baselessness of this tale; but, baseless or not, the associations the place had acquired on account of it were calculated to give a very gloomy turn to the thoughts of anyone standing before a court-martial.

To this 'Weisskopf' Lewin was now led away. A lance-corporal and two men marched him off, and our prisoner was already dreading the idea of being compelled to spend the rest of the day, and perhaps the night too, in a cellar-like confinement, when on approaching nearer he perceived that on top of the tower-base there had been erected quite an attractive wooden tower-house, to which a wooden ladder with eight or ten half-broken rungs led up from the ground.

Before this ladder the squad now halted. The key to the little iron-bound door was missing and the steward was summoned from the castle; he opened the door and admitted the prisoner. As long as the lance-corporal was there the old man was gruff and monosyllabic; but Lewin, though he lacked much knowledge of human nature, could easily see that this monosyllabic gruffness was only assumed, and he promised himself a greater communicativeness from the old man when they were alone. For the present the latter again locked the door, shot a superfluous bolt, and followed after the guard-squad as it moved away.

And now our prisoner was alone in his tower room.

But was it a room? Frau Hulen's attic accommodation had

not exactly spoiled him, yet that had been palatial compared with this first-floor room at the 'Weisskopf'. It was five paces across, and when he stood upright his hat touched the ceiling. 'It's like being buried alive!' he said, and went over to the window: at least he could have some fresh air. The righthand shutter, which he opened first, was hanging only by its upper hinge, so that the gale which blew through made him immediately shut it again; the lefthand shutter, however, was in better shape, and he fastened it open and gazed out at the river and the land around it, which lay there before him, a picture of winter beauty. All that he saw in this picture he knew, it was all so familiar to him. There, away to the left, the wide flat expanse with the willow-trees lining the bank, that was the Krampe, where the Kirch-Göritzers had had their battle; and beyond it, recognizable from the river gravel, the defile he and Tubal had passed along in the semi-darkness on their way back from Dr Faulstich. And there, away to the right, he could see the Bruch! There, extending into the distance, lay the farms of Gorgast and Neu-Manschnow, linked one with another only by the paths of poplar-trees; and now and then he imagined he could see Hohen-Vietz church-tower, with the cross upon it glittering in the afternoon sun. For a long time he stood immersed in the picture; then he closed the window again and turned and measured the tiny space he occupied.

Five paces. And measured the other way even less, for in this direction there stood a bedstead. Across it lay four or five boards, and at its foot was a sloping rush-chair, much dented and with the rushes hanging loose underneath it. That was all; only a couple of hearts had been scratched on the wall, with four or five names beneath them. French names. Therefore recent, not old, not dating from the days of Katte: and Lewin was so greatly in need of solace he took comfort even from this trifling circumstance.

It might have been an hour later that he heard the sound of footsteps outside, and the old steward reappeared: in the interim he had learned the name of his prisoner and had now come to see whether there was anything the 'Junker' wanted. The general, so he averred, permitted anything, and what he did not permit two fellow-countrymen could surely arrange between themselves. 'Don't you think so, little Junker? And then, little Junker, the dinner isn't eaten as hot as it's cooked. And the final consolation is always: a man can only die *once*.'

'Yes,' said Lewin, 'but when?'

'Oh, not for a long time. Your sands haven't yet run out, little Junker. The sermon's only just begun in your case. And it never finishes till all the sand's come through.'

Lewin thanked the old man for his words of encouragement and asked him for some supper, whatever there might be, though he would prefer a soup. But not before seven o'clock. If the old man had a book, he might let him have it; he wanted to seat himself by the window so long as there was daylight, and while away the time with reading.

The steward promised to perform everything, and it was not long—the little clock on the castle tower was just striking four—before there came from outside the sound of voices and a clattering as of wooden clogs could be heard on the ladder. Immediately afterwards the little door opened again, and there appeared in it the back of a broad-shouldered and, to all appearance, gigantic chasseur à pied* who, bent over double, was exerting himself to pull a wide tied-up bundle through the narrow opening. An old woman with a copper-coloured face remained standing on the steps outside, pushing at the bundle. At last it came through and the chasseur turned and greeted the prisoner with a half-mocking, half-goodnatured: ' *Bon jour, camarade*,' adding in the same tone: '*Voici votre équipage!*'

Lewin responded to this greeting and surveyed the chasseur, who was now standing upright before him and in his whole dress and bearing presented a perfect model of southern French nonchalance. His collar stood open, while his feet were encased in large wooden clogs stuffed with straw; plainly a good-natured, swaggering Gascon who, to escape from duties elsewhere, was serving in the castle as a warder.

'*Madame de Cognac*,' he said, turning now to the old woman, who was still standing on the stepladder, '*s'il vous plaît!* Come in, *Madame*, and unlace it.' Lewin smiled. '*Oui, monsieur*; unlace it; *c'est tout-à-fait allemand*. Oh, I have learned German good. *Moi. N'est-ce pas, Madame?*'

The latter nodded.

'*Vous voyez, Monsieur, notre marquise de Chaudeau a consenti.*'

While this conversation had been going on the bundle was in fact being undone, and the chasseur and his companion were now occupied in preparing a bed for the prisoner. Soon it was ready: a straw mattress, a stuffed bolster, and a discoloured cloak with an otterskin collar which, since he had been unable to discover any more bedding or blankets in the entire castle, the old steward had furnished from his own wardrobe. The large bundle had also contained three books, which, with affectedly reverential bows and '*Avec les compliments de monsieur le Châtelain*', the chasseur now handed over to Lewin. '*Et à sept heures le souper.*' Then the clogs clattered down the steps outside, and the broken gibberish with the old woman continued until it was lost in the wind that blew across Bastion Brandenburg.

Lewin pulled the chair to the window and examined the books the steward had sent him. Two of them, bound in black and with lemon-yellow edges, were, as might have been expected, a Bible and a hymn-book. But the third! It was no more than a pamphlet, two pasteboard covers with marbled paper rounded at the corners. On the title-page he read: *Report by Major von Schack on the Decapitation of Lieutenant von Katte, 6 November 1730*. That was a bad choice for the old man to have made: an icy cold shudder went through our prisoner, and he laid the Bible on top of the pamphlet so as not to see it.

Long, long hours.

He paced up and down and counted. 'A thousand paces.' At last it struck seven. The thought of seeing the Gascon come in again was not a pleasant one; but it was not he but the old steward himself who appeared, bringing with him the supper: a soup made of crusts of bread and rose-hips.

'Here you are, little Junker, here's something warm. The bread was baked by the French, but the rose-hips are from Margrave Hans's kitchen-garden, and my Lene, who is my youngest, picked them herself. It has been a real year for rose-hips. A real year for the French, too, of course; only they got the bristles.' And the old man set before Lewin the pot of soup and a stable-lantern in which a stump of candle was smouldering, and, already halfway through the door again, turned and

said: 'And now God be with you, little Junker. What will be
will be. And blow out the candle as soon as you've finished, for
there's no lights allowed. Otherwise I shall catch it. Do you
hear: lights out straightaway.'

Lewin was hungry, and the spicy odour enticed him to eat.
Yet he could not do so. The bitter taste in his mouth came, not
from the tin spoon he had been given, but from the fear of
death. He laid down his napkin, extinguished the candle, and
threw himself on to the bed. His watch was pressing into him
as he lay, so he took it out and placed it on the rush-chair
beside him. Only then did he wrap himself in the cloak, pull its
collar up under his chin, and look up from his pillow at the stars
that glittered down to him through the panes of the little
window. 'And she can walk on stars' resounded in his soul,
growing ever softer, ever more distant, and listening he fell
asleep.

He slept deeply and for many hours; the overworked body
asserted its rights. But towards morning he began to dream.
He saw a sleigh-ride and heard the jingle of the bells, and when
the sleighs came to halt it was before an old doorway with a
Roman arch, through which the couples clad in winter cloaks
and muffs entered a high-vaulted nave. Withered wreaths with
long ribbons hung from the pillars and moved in the wind
blowing through the nave, and they all walked between these
pillars (the fair Matushka was among them), down towards the
altar. And when they came close to the altar the organ began to
play. But at that moment the picture changed, and the grey
stone pillars became whitewashed wooden posts with green
garlands wound around them. And the women, too, were no
longer the same, they were other women, clad for summer
with flowers in their hair, and they were all following a couple
going on ahead of them whom he could not recognize because
he was walking behind them, and it was only when he had
reached the altar (there was a tombstone before it) that he saw
that it was he himself who was to be married in this place. But
he did not know to whom, for the bride was hidden in layer
upon layer of white veil, and on the white veil there glittered
golden stars.

The organ now fell silent, and when the minister demanded

the 'Yes', the bride threw back her veil, and instead of the 'Yes' that was on his lips he said: 'Marie.'

He had spoken the word aloud and started up, as though he wanted to hold fast to a vanishing apparition. Where was he? He saw the starry sky and felt the collar of the cloak grown damp and cold from his own breath. And gradually the whole terrible reality came back to him, and he listened to hear whether there were not sounds outside which meant that the guard was already coming for him. For he knew that it was in the grey of morning that such scenes were enacted.

But what time was it? He reached for his watch and made it repeat. Five. That was too early; it could not happen before six. So he still had an hour of life, but by the same token he still had an hour of death, and he wished the minutes away that he might have certainty: however dreadful it might be, it could not be so dreadful as the torment he was in now. He leaped up, opened the window and greedily sucked in the night air; but it was in vain; he saw it all, everything that would happen to him, and he called on God, no longer for his life, for that was done with, but for strength in his last hour: 'Not to depart this life without dignity: that is all I ask!' And then he again looked across to Hohen-Vietz, to the little piece of earth dear to him before all else, and he gestured with his hand. 'Farewell, all you I love.'

At that moment a ray of light flashed up in the eastern sky and vanished again: it was the first forerunner the day sends forth long before he himself rises up in his golden chariot. 'Could this be a sign to me?'

And he became more composed.

Six o'clock. No sound of guards could be heard from without, and the conviction grew firm in him that he would have at least this day to live. And a day was a long time: what might this one day not bring? And he repeated to himself the stanza that had once before sustained him in a mood of deepest dejection:

> 'Wait in hope and count the hours,
> Not in vain they pass away;
> Changing is the lot of mortals:
> There will dawn another day.'

Yes, yes, wait in hope. Another day, a whole day! And it lay now before him like life itself, and he looked ahead into it as though it contained a whole world of possibilities.

The first possibility to be realized, however, was only the reappearance of the chasseur, the unsoldierliness of whose attire was now enhanced by a basket with a lid suspended from his left arm. '*Bon jour, monsieur de Vietzewitz. Pardon, si ce n'est pas tout-à-fait correct. Mais votre nom, c'est un nom difficile.*'

Lewin agreed it was.

'*Voici votre café. Un bon café, sans doute. Cela veut dire: de la chicorée! Mais qu'importe! C'est un café allemand.*'

With these and other words—for he was certainly a chatterer—the chasseur opened the basket and placed the brown Bunzlau pot on to the window-sill, with a piece of black bread and a couple of freshly baked rolls beside it. Then instead of the basket he hung on his arm the large lantern that was still there from the previous night, and retired with a half-mocking: '*Votre serviteur.*'

Lewin was glad to be alone again, moved the chair to the window and consumed his breakfast. It was tolerably palatable, and when he had finished he leaned back and, relaxed and newly invigorated, looked out at the glowing orb of the sun just gilding the Göritz church-spire lying there below him.

'Now let me read.' And with that he took up the Bible and opened it:

'The Book of Daniel!' A smile flickered across his face, and he said to himself: 'No, not Daniel. Everyone in my situation imagines himself in the lion's den.' And he leafed further on until he reached the Book of the Maccabees, then back again until he reached the Book of Judges. 'Yes, this is a nice book: lively and spirited; this will cheer me up!'

And he began to read.

But his reading had not got very far when he heard the sound of feet stamping and a coughing and clearing of the throat, and, getting up, recognized Hoppenmarieken coming along close beside the edge of Bastion Brandenburg. She was no more than twelve paces away from him. Now she looked up, raised her stick in her left hand and at the same moment threw into his window a ball of string she had hurriedly brought forth out of her neckcloth. As the ball fell at his feet a couple of splinters of glass fell with it, and before he had had time to recover from his surprise the old woman had gone on again. He gazed after her and saw that she had now commenced a conversation with a sentry standing further down, a conversation conducted of course in sign-language. She offered him something from her bottle, and when others from nearby sentry-boxes also came to join them antics and shrill laughter ensued, until she finally saluted with her stick and made her way round the castle hill and back to the town.

Only now did Lewin take up the ball of string. It was not very big, but it was heavy and must consequently contain something. The next thing he did was to break a chip of wood from one of the boards lying on the bedstead, and he then began carefully to wind on to it the line of hempen string—it was as thin as a needle but very strong—with the clear objective of being able easily to hide both coils, the old and the new, if he was surprised. Soon he was finished, and was holding in his hands a flat stone encased in a threadwork net, to the firmly stitched knot of which one end of the hempen string was firmly tied. In the same knot, however, he found a rolled strip of paper; when he unrolled it, he read:

At the stroke of twelve (the guard is not relieved until one) throw this ball over the bastion; hold tight to the string and make sure it runs out. When it goes taut, pull up the rope. Then let yourself down. If the worst comes to the worst, jump! Below thick snow—and we too.

Lewin concealed the note: he could not bring himself to destroy it, for he felt he was going to read it again and again. Then he sank to his knees where he stood and thanked God for saving his life: for he no longer doubted he would be saved, and he was firmly resolved that, if all else failed, he would risk a leap from the bastion. If the leap misfired, he would at least die in the hands of his own people, and the walk to the scaffold, the rolling of drums and the blindfold would be spared him. It was this paraphernalia he dreaded the most. 'Death can be endured, but execution is unendurable.' He found the very word repulsive, and at the mere sound of it all that was coarse and ugly arose before him as though in a procession of grotesque pictures from a fairground.

And this repulsiveness he had now, whatever might befall, eluded. When the initial rejoicing in his heart had subsided, however, he soon came to feel that he had only exchanged one tyrant for another, and that subjection to the hour of his rescue was almost as excruciating as subjection to the hour of his death. He traversed the narrow room again and again, opened and closed the window, and read over the note, whose contents he had long since known by heart, for the tenth and then for the hundredth time. The chasseur brought the midday meal, but he asked him to take it away again; he longed only for clear air and coolness, and, noticing that long icicles were hanging from the roof almost down to his window, he broke two or three off and refreshed himself with their coldness. Then he read the note again, tested the ball of string, and calculated the height of the bastion. And his conclusion was always that it amounted to nothing, not nearly as bad as a leap from a second floor. And ten feet of snow below! It couldn't fail; and, carried away by these notions, he almost forgot that the leap was supposed to serve only as a last resort.

And now midday had gone by, and finally the afternoon too. The sun declined, evening twilight faded, and the day passed away. Only six hours left, soon only five. He counted the minutes.

At seven the old steward came. 'Little Junker, they are now round the table; the old general is there too, a "*bon garçon*", as that sluggard they have assigned to me as a warder says.'

'A court-martial, then?'

'Yes, little Junker. I had to heat the great hall. That is the one with the balcony, where Margrave Hans hangs over the fireplace, life-size with yellow leather boots and spurs as long as my hand. He'll be amazed at the sight.'

'I believe it.'

'And if the young gentleman wishes to write a last letter or a message to his father . . . '

'Is that how it is, steward?'

'I do not say that is how it is; but that is how it could be. A court-martial is a court-martial, and the outcome every time hangs by a thread. Ah, little Junker, it is always best to be ready for anything.'

'That it is,' said Lewin mechanically, while his soul, into which fear had flooded back, grasped at life with redoubled force. But the old man noticed nothing; he took up the covered basket which the chasseur had left behind, proffered a 'Good-night', and left his prisoner alone.

'So they are now sitting up there,' Lewin said, 'and Mar-grave Hans can gaze down as much as he likes, he won't save me from their death-sentence. I feel as though they were pronouncing it at this moment. And it is like a stab in the heart. But I want to live; God, have mercy upon me and protect me with thy grace. Though they condemn me to death, let them do so in vain.' And he again clasped his hands together and pressed his heated forehead against the window-pane.

The stars came out, and he tried to assemble the constellations so far as he knew them: but they again vanished behind the clouds. 'The hour runs even through the longest day.' And now at last it struck eleven.

'One hour more,' he murmured to himself, 'and this torment will end! One way or another.'

23

The Rescue

AT the same time as Lewin was speaking these words two sleighs were drawing up before the manor house at Hohen-Vietz. The foremost was no more than a sledge and resembled the covered sleigh in which Lewin had made the journey from Berlin to Hohen-Vietz on Christmas Eve, except that the basketwork sides were lower and the tall arched awning was completely lacking. In place of this arched awning a piece of black oilcloth had been laid over the carriage and its edges, which hung down low over both sides, fastened to the four spokes by means of holes cut into it. A little, shaggy farm-horse stood between the shafts, and Pachaly, the reins in his hand, was seated on the driving-seat. The second vehicle was an ordinary but very large travelling-sleigh which had been borrowed from Mayor Kniehase on account of its size. In this sleigh there sat six people: Berndt and Hirschfeldt in the back, facing them in the rear seat Tubal and Kniehase, at the front Krist and young Scharwenka. Krist was driving. The ponies were harnessed up, but without their bells.

What might have been found most surprising was that Bamme was missing, and yet that he should have been missing was, to anyone who knew him more intimately, wholly in accord with his character. The Frankfurt affair had rendered him neither inwardly discouraged nor outwardly despondent; but, dominated as he was through and through by ideas and conceptions deriving from gambling, he had since then been addicted to assuring everyone that he had 'not been dealt a lucky hand'. It would 'all go better without me', he had asserted again and again, and he had been shaken in this conviction only momentarily when the sleigh with the black oilcloth hanging from it had driven up. The following dialogue had then taken place between him and his aide-de-camp, who had been standing beside him.

'Whatever is that black box, Hirschfeldt? Black and sloping and a cover draped over it. A perfect picture of a coffin. Makes me wonder who they're going to put in it.'

'Me, perhaps.'

'No, not you, Hirschfeldt. You'll always escape with a ricochet or a bullet somewhere safe . . . But whatever is that, now, that that blockhead of a Pachaly is dragging up and stuffing into the sleigh? Take a look: "six long planks and two short ones". And now two grave-boards and a rope. I know what *that's* for, at any rate, but all the other things! Grave-boards and planks, and six of them, what's more. It savours of a funeral.'

Cool-headed though he was, Hirschfeldt in the end found these reflections made him feel distinctly uncomfortable, and merely so as to say something he remarked: 'You are superstitious, General.'

'Yes, that I am, Hirschfeldt, and I take delight in it. Rob me of the little bit of superstition I have and I have nothing at all and I collapse. But most people are like this, and those who aren't, the worse for them. Look at the woman Schorlemmer. She has no superstition. But what does that produce? A nutshell of wisdom and a bushel of boredom. With a nightcap on it.'

Bamme twirled his moustache and had the feeling he had said something exceptionally fine: but his whole *oratio pro domo*★ had fallen on deaf ears, for Hirschfeldt's mind had still been exclusively preoccupied with coffins and funerals; at length he said: 'So do you believe, General, that we shall return from Küstrin in not much better shape than we did from Frankfurt?'

'Not at all, Hirschfeldt. I am not with you, that is one thing; and the other is that they are not on the alert. I mean the French. So you will get him free; but it'll cost you something, a leg or a couple of ribs. You won't get it cheaper; but perhaps, too, it'll be more expensive. That's why I don't like that black box.'

Thus had run the conversation between Bamme and Hirschfeldt; immediately afterwards all those who were participating in the expedition had taken their seats and departed at an easy trot along the highway to Küstrin. When they had arrived at the spot where the 'muster' had taken place only two days previously they turned right, passed the coppice of fir-trees on its northern edge and then continued in a straight course for the river. Here the ways were narrow, and mostly snowed up, so that they had to go at walking pace. And yet they were counting the minutes. Berndt and Hirschfelt grew impatient. At last they had the river before them, recognized in spite of the darkness the carriageway marked out along the ice, and drove cautiously down the incline and then, with a gradual wheel to the left, into the low-lying path of river gravel. Now they could again advance at a trot—and it was high time they did so.

As yet no one had spoken. Berndt, oppressed by the silence, turned to Kniehase, who was sitting opposite him with his head still bandaged, and said:

'Everything in order, Kniehase?'

'Yes, your worship.'

'Rope, boards, planks?'

'It's all here. I handed them to Pachaly myself. And the little ladder, too, and two bundles of straw.'

'And Kümmritz?'

'He was sent off to the Manschnow mill at nine o'clock.'

'And Krull and Reetzke?'

'They're stationed over there between the duck-snares and the pulp-mills.'

'Good. And now, let come what may.'

For a moment he was silent, only his lips moved noiselessly. Then, putting all unease and anxiety behind him, he said: 'And now let's get a move on, Krist, or we shall be late. Look, Tubal, all dark and grey: the heavens are with us, they conceal our coming.'

As they spoke they had come to within five hundred paces of the fortress, and in the prevailing darkness there rose up a shadow even darker: Bastion Brandenburg. That their approach had been noticed by one or other of the sentries was hardly likely, for they were driving not only in the shelter of a wall of snow shovelled up on both sides of the path to the height of a man, but also in the shadow of the pyramids of gravel erected along it every ten paces. It was in the shadow of one such pyramid that the sleighs now came to a halt.

The little clock on the tower of the castle church struck the half-hour. That was as they had calculated: all was well so far. Berndt was the first out of the sleigh; then, ahead of the others, he crept across the ice up to the walls of the fortress directly below the 'Weisskopf'. When he reached them he saw that at the foot of the bastion everything was buried deep in snow; the west wind had driven up whole hills of snow at this point. But, deep though it was, the snow was still not deep enough and was lying too loose: it was thus in need of prodding. This was what they had brought the planks along for: with their aid they intended to push one of the mounds of snow—one that was ten paces wide and firmer than the others—hard against the bastion wall. Thus they went across to the smaller of the sleighs that Bamme had bluntly, and perhaps from some presentiment, designated a 'coffin-sleigh', and were about to pull out the planks destined for this task when the straw packed in on top of them began to move and vibrate. And behold, a moment afterwards Hector—well aware of the hazardous nature of his deed—was standing wagging his tail in an embarrassed fashion at the side of his master: embarrassed, but also expressing pride and joy, and his shrewd eyes seemed to be saying: 'Here I am; I, Hector, friend of my friend Lewin. I know this is a serious matter for him, and because I know I want to be there too.'

The first to collect himself was Berndt; he bent down to the culprit but did no more than shake his finger at him. When he stood upright again the dog, too, stood upright and laid his forepaws on his master's shoulders: and thus they stood and looked at one another.

'Hush, Hector,' Berndt whispered, and stroked and patted the faithful animal. The latter, however, when he saw himself thus taken into favour, passionately attacked his master's hair and beard, and nodded his head and wagged his tail again and again to demonstrate that he had understood everything very well. Then, at long last, he relinquished his hold and returned to the ground.

The planks had in the meantime been brought out and were now set upright on their sides. But the snow refused to shift: the slush that had seeped through during the day had frozen together with the ice on the river, so that they had to fetch spades to separate them again. Finally they succeeded: the mass of frozen snow began to move, at first slowly, then quicker and quicker, until, having pushed the soft snow aside, it at last stood firmly at the foot of the bastion. The snow that the west wind had blown higher up on the sloping wall now fell below to form a soft pillow on top of the wall of frozen snow. Then young Scharwenka, who was the nimblest and most agile of them, climbed on to it and quickly drew the rope after him, while the four others crouched down beside it. Krist held Hector by his collar; Pachaly had remained with the sleighs.

They all looked expectantly at the clock. Five minutes to go. At any moment they would hear it begin striking up at the castle.

And then it did strike. Lewin thrust open the window, counted to twelve, and on the stroke of twelve threw the ball of string, the loose end wound around his left hand, over the edge of the bastion. He heard it thud; then it began to unwind. After a short time he saw the thin hempen cord start to grow taut: which must mean his friends below had knotted the rope to it.

And now he began to pull with all his might. But the moment he did so a French sentry came into view tracing his prescribed course from one corner to the other. He was already near; if he kept close to the window his bayonet would pass under the rope, but if he moved further out to the right towards the edge of the bastion it would strike against it. Lewin had begun to think he would have to let it go, and then all that would be left was the leap: but, humming a tune, the guard walked past hard by the foundations of the Weisskopf.

The corner at which he would wheel and turn lay a hundred and fifty paces away. Lewin computed that he had two minutes. So he must be quick. He now pulled even faster and more vigorously than before, and soon he had the rope in his hands. But where was he to fasten it? The centre-frame of the window was far too decayed; so, as there was nothing better available, he wound it round the foot of the bedstead, and pushed the bedstead against the window-pier to prevent it from slipping. And then he climbed out. Once outside, he threw himself down, crawled to the edge of the bastion and grasped the rope: then he breathed a fervent prayer and launched himself forwards and down! When he was just over halfway the foot of the bedstead to which the rope was fastened either broke in two or came away from the bed; but there was hardly twenty feet left to go, and he glided harmlessly down the snow-covered slope of the wall: the only result was that his descent was accelerated by a few seconds.

He was saved, and he was permeated by a blissful feeling of being restored to life as he burrowed his way out of the loose heap of snow. Whatever dangers lay ahead were no longer real dangers: for a shot fired into the night could hardly be considered dangerous.

And then the first shot did in fact resound. It was answered with a Hurrah! from below; everyone waved his hat in the air, and Hector, now permitted to move, leaped upon his young master and covered his face and hands with joyful and affectionate licking. 'Stop it, stop it!' But before he could obey a whole salvo cracked out from above into the darkness, and the dog, who through his love and loyalty had covered his master, collapsed to the ground. Lewin stood motionless, not knowing what to do; Berndt and Hirschfeldt dragged him off with them, and they all made a rush for the sleighs: only Hector, abandoned, lay whimpering at the foot of the bastion.

'No,' cried Tubal, 'we can't do this!' And, turning back, he bent down to the faithful animal, who was vainly attempting to drag itself away, and took it up in his two arms. But long before he had reached the nearest of the sleighs the first salvo was followed by a second, and, struck beneath the shoulder-blade, Tubal stumbled and fell.

'Let's go, let's go!' and ten hands seized hold of him and dragged and carried him over the snow to Pachaly's sleigh, and laid him, grievously wounded, on top of the straw, with Hector at his feet. Then they drove away between the black heaps of gravel into the night. It was impossible for the enemy to follow them; but if he had done so, they would, with the aid of the units posted along their route, have had the strength to meet him.

When they drew level with Gorgast they wheeled to the right and drove slowly up the sloping river-bank. Tubal had a burning thirst and they gave him snow; thus they continued as far as the Manschnow mills. Here the road grew more and more uneven, and on Tubal's account Pachaly had to drive at walking pace. The other sleigh went on ahead faster.

Berndt had taken the reins. When he tried to pass between the posts at the head of the drive the ponies shied up, and he then saw that Hoppenmarieken was sitting on the lefthand kerbstone. She was, as usual, leaning on her basket and holding her crooked stick in her hand. But she did not salute them—she did not move at all.

24

Salve Caput

IT was twelve hours later; a bright noonday sun stood over Hohen-Vietz, and it was thawing from every roof. Even the ice that hung from the wheels of Miekley's mill, and had grown dull there through the winter, was again glittering crystalline and transparent, and the doves were perched on the long ridge of Kniehase's barn. All was bright and cheerful, and nature felt the first breath of spring.

And the manor house too lay bathed in sunshine. But anyone who, standing in the driveway, cast a glance at the entrance hall or up to the long row of windows must have perceived that it was a house of sorrow, or, worse than that, one that threatened to become so at any moment. A thick layer of straw had been spread over the carriage-way, and through the windows or the glass doors of the hallway there was no one to be seen. All seemed dead. Only the sparrows, sitting in multitudes among the straw and pecking up the loose grains, were in good heart; their twittering was the only noise to be heard in the profound silence.

Twelve hours had passed, and they had brought with them only one minute of perfect joy and happiness: that minute in which, after he had greeted his sister, Lewin had encountered Marie and the tears of rejoicing that had broken forth at their reunion had signified that henceforth they were betrothed. And it was a betrothal as fair as any human eyes had seen. For what had come to pass was simply that which ought to have come to pass: the demand of nature, that which had been determined from the very beginning, had been accomplished; and Berndt himself, his heart profoundly moved, had rejoiced in the happiness of the happy couple.

But how different were the minutes that had followed when, a short time later, the second sleigh had drawn up and Krist and Pachaly had slowly and gently carried Tubal up the stairs laid out on planks and pillows. Hector, too, had tried to go up, but his strength had failed on the first step and he had crawled away along the narrow kitchen corridor to his rush-mat. There he now lay and edged himself towards the warm place beside the wall behind the oven; for he was very cold.

At eleven o'clock Dr Leist had come from Lebus. He climbed —as soundlessly as his habitual manner and his snowboots permitted—up to the upper floor and entered the sickroom; its curtains were closed tight to shut out the morning sun, which was standing directly outside the windows. 'We need some light,' he said, and drew one of the curtains aside.

Only now did he see Tubal. The latter was in great pain, but he endured without flinching the probing of his wound, even though a 'light touch' was not precisely what Dr Leist was noted for.

'Well done, young sir, that is what I call bearing up bravely.'

'How is it?' asked Tubal.

'An ugly case: perforation of the spleen. But what is the spleen? The most superfluous thing possessed by man. There are people who have it cut out. And youth can overcome anything. In a month we shall be sitting here at the window, counting the jackdaws on the church roof and smoking a pipe of tobacco. You do smoke, I suppose, young sir?'

Tubal said he did not.

'Well then, we'll play *patience* or *mariage*.'*

'*Patience.*'

Dr Leist stroked Tubal's hand.

'That's the ticket: keep your chin up and stay in good spirits. Staying in good spirits is the best medicine there is.'

Whereupon he descended the stairs again to report to Berndt in his work-room on the results of his examination.

'Well, doctor?' Vitzewitz asked.

Dr Leist shrugged his shoulders. 'He is going to die.'

'Can nothing be done?'

'No; it was an oblique entry, and that is always the worst. Pierced everything: lungs, liver. And the spleen, too, into the bargain.'

'And how long does he have?'

'Until tonight, if he hangs on. Today is his last day, and tomorrow it will all be over with. If you want to inform his father, the privy councillor, it is high time to do so. To be sure . . . but it's too late. The news wouldn't reach him, even if it took the wings of the morning. And they are the quickest, if I remember my psalms.'

'Then let us wait. Better he should hear the whole story than half of it.'

Leist nodded.

'Alas, doctor,' Berndt went on, 'what a day this is! To rescue

Lewin at *this* price. How shall I be able to face his father! His only son, no, more . . . his only child!'

Berndt buried his head in his hands; after a time he said: 'What have you prescribed?'

'Nothing.'

'And what shall we give him if he wants something?'

'Anything.'

'I understand. And when will you return? In the afternoon or the evening?'

'I am staying,' said the old man; and then, since there was nothing further to be said, he went across to Bamme, whom he knew from Guse. And that turned out well for both of them. Soon they were sitting together by the stove, and they smoked their way through the next two hours, indefatigable in a discourse that began with Tubal and ended with Hoppenmarieken. The latter had that morning been found dead on the kerbstone where Berndt had seen her sitting. When they asked Pachaly, who also did doctoring, whether she had frozen or if it was a stroke, he had been unable to say; and Leist, too, evinced no desire to pursue any scientific inquiry into the cause of her demise. She was dead, and that sufficed. From time to time, whenever his patient complained of pain, he went upstairs to dispense his '*crocata*', the superiority of which to the '*simplex*'★ he seized the occasion again enthusiastically to extol; until—having finally succeeded in producing a condition of painlessness through the application of this opiate—he deemed the time had come for a little relaxation on his own part and prescribed for himself a *café au cognac*. Jeetze filled the order, Bamme had one as well, and, growing less and less straight-faced as time wore on, they both in the end joined in affirming that, all things considered, it had been a long time since they had chattered away so agreeable an afternoon.

And now it was evening. Everyone was assembled in the corner room; only Renate had retired to her own room. They were chattering idly when Jeetze, who was sharing with Lewin and Aunt Schorlemmer the tending of the invalid, came in and reported that young Herr Tubal wished to see the Herr Rittmeister.

Hirschfeldt went up. A lamp with a little green shade was burning, throwing a meagre light.

'I have asked for you, Hirschfeldt', said Tubal. 'It is so dark, but I expect you will be able to find a chair. Please come over here.'

Hirschfeldt did as he was bid, and sat himself beside the bed.

'I am dying, my friend. *Cita mors ruit.*'★

Hirschfeldt made to reply.

'No, do not assure me otherwise . . . I feel it is so, and if I didn't feel it I would be able to hear it in every word old Leist lets fall. He is an ill hand at dissembling, and his voice has a cheerful, goodnatured tone that carries with it the sound of funeral-bells. And after all, what does it matter? We must all die sooner or later!'

'You are rallying, Tubal,' said the captain. 'I believe the old man has told you the truth. You and us.'

Tubal shook his head.

But Hirschfeldt went on: 'You will live, and you *want* to live, Tubal. No one is glad to depart from this world. The weary alone excepted.'

'I am weary. But let's not talk of that. I have only a few hours left. Please let me have something to drink. Wine; over there. Leist has allowed it, he has allowed me to have anything.'

Hirschfeldt gave it to him.

'And now listen to me. I have two wishes. See to it that I am taken up to the church as soon as possible. I want to lie there before the altar.'

He clearly found speaking painful: but when he had drunk and set the glass down again he went on in a more tranquil tone: 'That is one thing. And now the other. I want to be buried here. But not in the crypt; there I would perhaps grow restless, like Fräulein von Gollmitz, who wanted to get out again. No: firmly in the earth.'

He was silent for a time, then he added with a painful smile: 'You are looking at me, Hirschfeldt, as though I were speaking in a fever. No, I am not feverish. But that about Fräulein Gollmitz, you must have someone tell you that story, Renate or Marie. Yes, Marie, it was she who told it to me. Not in the crypt, then. And now send me the doctor, I need assistance again. The pains are coming back, and his opium is the best thing for that.'

Hirschfeldt departed to send up Dr Leist. The latter prescribed for the invalid a further dose of his '*crocata*', talked about '*anno 92*' and the cannonade at Valmy in considerable detail, and concluded, not merely with the assurance that he would be as right as rain again in six weeks at the utmost, but also by recommending in the most serious fashion that, when he came to make the journey to Breslau, as he shortly would, he should consider spending the night at Sagan rather than at Sorau. He did this so well and convincingly that Tubal was momentarily deceived as to his real condition.

But not for long: for the end was in fact approaching fast, more quickly indeed than the old doctor had expected. At eight o'clock Seidentopf arrived, and Aunt Schorlemmer went up to ask the invalid whether he would not perhaps like to talk to the 'old friend of the house'—she did not want to say 'the priest'.

Tubal smiled, and said he would not: he felt a need for consolation, certainly, and a longing for elevation; but he also sensed that Seidentopf could not give him what he longed for.

Half an hour later he began to have hallucinations: he spoke of the Virgin Mary who had dropped the infant Jesus; then he asked them to stop the drumming and trumpeting; and finally he sat up and said: 'No, no, we can't do this; Hector, that faithful animal.'

But suddenly it was as though his mind had grown clear again; he asked for a drink, and immediately afterwards he asked Aunt Schorlemmer to call Renate to him.

'And the doctor?'

'No, not him. Every word he says is a lie, and his medicine also lies. I want no more of either of them. Send for Renate.' And Renate was sent for, and came.

When she was there it was plain to see that he wanted to be alone with her, and Aunt Schorlemmer left the room.

'Sit beside me, Renate,' he said. 'I want to say farewell to you.'

She broke into convulsive weeping, threw herself to her knees and hid her head in the pillows.

'No, no; don't make it so hard for me. Ah, you don't know

how hard. And you shan't know, either. Never, I hope never . . . Ah, Renate, parting is bitterer than I thought, and there is one thing alone that consoles me: nothing has ever gone right with me, and I would not have made you happy.'

She made to reply but he prevented her. 'Do not speak,' he went on, 'do not deny it. I know better. For what is it that makes us and others happy? Being loyal and being firm and constant, being constant in the things that are good. And we have always been inconstant and disloyal, all of us, all of us. My father was so. He gave up his country, his faith, his friends. And for what? For the sake of an idle fancy. And nothing good has come of it for any of us.'

'Do not accuse yourself, my love. Ah, Tubal, what are you dying for now? For love and loyalty. Yes, yes. First towards Lewin, and then, when he was rescued, you felt sorry for the poor creature lying deserted and whimpering in pain and misery, and now you are dying because you took pity on the faithful dog.'

'Yes, I felt for it, I took pity on it. That I have always had, pity and mercy. And perhaps, too, mercy now awaits me because I had mercy. I have need of it; everyone has need of it. In our last hours it is good for us to have some anchorage like this . . . I recall a long hymn I had to learn in the religious lessons with the old church councillor; I had no taste for it, but there was one stanza I did like; that one was beautiful.'

'Which? Say it, or would you like me to say it?'

'It was something about death and dying and about Christ being with us in the hour of departure.'

Renate had taken his hand, and now, without further questioning, she spoke in a soft but firm voice as though to herself:

'When I must be departing
Depart not then from me,
If death must be my portion
Do *Thou* my comfort be;
When fear and dread of dying
Shall come and seize on me,
Release me from my anguish
Through Thine own agony.'*

Tubal had raised himself in his bed.

'Yes, that's it.'

He seemed to want to say more, but he sank, growing ever more feeble, back on to the pillows and, in the manner of the dying, began to pluck agitatedly at the bedclothes; as he did so, it was as though he were searching for something in his memory.

At last he had it, and continued in disconnected phrases: 'It was earlier, much earlier, and we were still in the old church, and the chaplain recited a Latin hymn to me. And when Easter came I had to repeat it in front of my father and my mother and Count Miekusch. And my mother laughed because she didn't understand the Latin. But my father grew serious, and Count Miekusch did too.'

He was silent for a time, and Renate looked at him in alarm.

'That was twenty years ago,' he went on, 'or even more, and I had forgotten it. But now I have it again:

> *Salve caput cruentatum*
> *Totum spinis coronatum*
> *Conquassatum, vulneratum*
> *Facie sputis illita . . .* '*

With each new line he had raised himself higher and higher, and he was staring at the wall at the foot of the bed as though he saw something there. And a smile, in which pain and redemption struggled with one another, now transfigured his face.

'Kathinka was right . . . but now it is too late . . . *Salve caput cruentatum . . .* ' They were his last words.

He sank back on to the pillows and his eyes closed for ever.

25

Just as at Plaa

IN the same hour a mounted courier was dispatched to Berlin to deliver to the father in a few lines from Berndt the news of the death of his son. There had been no delay: none the less the old privy councillor could not be expected to arrive before the following evening.

In the morning the occupants of the house forgathered as usual in the corner room; only Renate was missing, and Hirschfeldt now took the opportunity to bring to Berndt's notice all that Tubal had expressed to him as his 'last will'. Berndt agreed to speeding the body to the church as soon as possible; but as for the funeral, that would have to wait on Ladalinski's decision. Thereupon they separated. Hirschfeldt and Bamme rode across to Drosselstein for an hour, and Lewin went to the parsonage to unburden himself of all his joy and sorrow: for he knew that there he might pour out all he felt, because there he would meet with understanding, and, more than that, he would find a quiet mind able to impart the peace it itself possessed. And his heart longed to be at peace.

At two in the afternoon a large rack-wagon approached the village: it was one of those seen swaying through the open barn-doors at harvest-time laden high with produce and a 'tree' set on top of them—a so-called 'Oostwagen'. It had come from Küstrin, and any Hohen-Vietzer who happened to encounter it would have known that the team belonged to Kniehase and the driver was one of Kniehase's men. The latter was seated on a board that jutted out somewhat from the wagon, with both feet resting on the shafts. Close behind him on the same board there stood two coffins, one black with white attachments, the other yellow and with ugly blue decorations. The yellow one was much the smaller. The driver was leaning against the black one and smoking.

'Gee up!' he cried and gave the horses a blow. When they had arrived in the driveway, Krist and Pachaly, who were already waiting, came forward to unload the foremost coffin. Kniehase's man assisted them.

'What time are they bringing him up?' he asked as he watched Krist take hold of the upper handle of the coffin.

'Today, straightaway.'

'And in front the altar?'

'Yes, so they say.'

'And why in front the altar? That's not how we do things.'

'I don't know. He's a Pole, and that may well be how they do things.'

This seemed to set the mind of Kniehase's man at rest, and he continued along the village street with the yellow coffin. He passed the mayor's house, and when he arrived at Miekley's mill he turned into the woodland acre and finally came to a stop before Hoppenmarieken's house. The old women standing there received the ugly yellow coffin.

'Look,' said one of them, 'yellow and blue. Just right for Hoppenmarieken.'

'And as tiny as a child's coffin.'

'Well, she wasn't no bigger than a child.'

'No, but the Devil is sometimes small, too. And what if she did do all that receivering? She'll be taken up there too, and buried with all the rest. Old Seidentopf was in favour of it.'

'Yes, he was. He thinks there's nothing he can't do.'

And with that the conversation concluded.

In the manor house, meanwhile, much activity had been taking place, though it all took place as though on tiptoe, and no one spoke a word. By four o'clock Tubal's body lay in its coffin, and an hour later six bearers bore it along the upper corridor and slowly down the stairs. When they had just descended the last step, and made to advance across the back hallway where the servants of the household were standing, they found themselves brought to a stop, for Hector lay in the middle of their path. He had dragged himself to this spot from his rush-mat, and was now trying to stand up. But it was in vain; he only lay and whimpered, and Berndt, who had hitherto succeeded in restraining his tears, now wept copiously. Thus they passed through the house and the courtyard, and at length turned into the oft-mentioned hillside path that led up to the church. As they drew near, the horizon began to glow with the reflection of the sun that had just set behind it. The old sexton, Kubalke, unlocked the door, and a little while afterwards Tubal was lying before the altar.

It was precisely nine o'clock when a chaise halted in front of the manor house; as the straw was still lying on the driveway no one noticed its arrival, least of all Jeetze, who was in any case hard of hearing. At length light appeared in the windows, and immediately afterwards Lewin appeared and came to the coach-door to assist Ladalinski (for he it was) to alight. The privy councillor's outward appearance seemed little altered; his bearing was stiff and erect, his clothing and hair were tidy and in order. He asked after Renate, who was not present, and then followed Berndt into the corner room, where a tall fire was burning in the grate and the tea-table was prepared in the Russian manner, as their guest liked it. Bamme and Hirschfeldt made to withdraw, but were invited to stay; Aunt Schorlemmer likewise. They all took their places, tea was served, and they spoke about the journey. It had not been possible to leave Berlin before midday: arrangements of all kinds had continually deferred the moment of departure.

They chattered on in this way for several minutes without any allusion to the event that had brought the privy councillor there. He asked for a second glass of tea, and it was only when he had emptied this too and, as he did so, expressed the wish to continue his journey as soon as possible, that Berndt said: 'Have I understood correctly? Continue your journey?'

The privy councillor nodded.

'So you will not be returning to Berlin?'

'No. I intend to remove the body of my son to Bjalanovo straight from here. All the Ladalinskis lie there. Life makes its demands of us, but so does death. It behoves me to act as my son would have wished: and he, as I am well aware, was drawn back to the homeland.'

Hirschfeldt made to report the manner of Tubal's death; but Berndt, who knew how obstinate Ladalinski was, and was aware from much previous experience that, although unpleasant communications might well disturb his guest's equanimity, they would in no way influence his resolve, forestalled the captain and hastened to express his agreement without further ado. Hirschfeldt divined his intention, and it was therefore settled that Ladalinski would continue his journey at nine the following morning, and that a sleigh, preferably a light, one-horse, covered sleigh, would be furnished for the transportation of the deceased. These arrangements were agreed upon swiftly, and only then did the privy councillor, rising from his seat, say: 'I would like to see my son.'

'He lies up in the church,' Berndt replied. 'Before the altar. It was his last wish.'

'Then I will go up there. But alone, Vitzewitz. I ask only that I may be accompanied by your sexton. He is an old sexton, I hope.'

They were able to meet this request, and conversation, which would otherwise have come to a standstill, now turned to a detailed consideration of the circumstance that in the entire Oderbruch there was no other village in which people lived to so advanced an age as they did in Hohen-Vietz. More and more examples were adduced: first the aged Wendelin Pyterke, and then Seidentopf's predecessor, who had celebrated his diamond wedding and three days later baptized a little great-great-grandson. On account of his feebleness, to be sure, he had had to conduct the baptism sitting down. Conversation was still dwelling on this predecessor of Seidentopf's and his great-great-grandson—whose existence was, by the way, disputed by Aunt Schorlemmer in a fashion that suggested it would have involved some impropriety—when Jeetze announced that old Kubalke had arrived and was waiting outside.

They all went out to meet him. He was standing in the hall and holding in one hand the keys to the church and a large lantern. With the other he raised his cap and greeted them.

'It's rather late, Papa,' Ladalinski addressed Kubalke. 'More bedtime than time for church. But you know—'

And with that they walked from the house together and out along the shrub-lined pathways of the park. Lewin and Hirschfeldt had followed them as far as the courtyard gates. 'Just as at Plaa,' said Lewin, adding after a brief pause: 'But for him it is worse.'

Hirschfeldt nodded in silence, and they returned together to the corner room.

Meantime, the two old men were walking up the hill, Kubalke two or three paces ahead so as better to light their way, for there were only a few stars in the sky and here and there roots had grown out over the pathway. When they were halfway up he stopped until the privy councillor had caught up with him, and said: 'Take care, your honour, there is slippery ice here.' Then, lapsing into dialect—a thing he often did from age and carelessness, notwithstanding he was a school-master—he concluded: 'Them young varmints have made a slide here. And more than one. They don't think as how many other people come up here too. And that includes *me*.'

'We'll walk closer together,' said Ladalinski, who found the way the old man spoke pleasant to his ear.

'Yes, yes,' the latter replied; then, resuming conventional speech just as unconsciously as he had lapsed from it, he went on: 'When I was what your honour is now, the mid-sixties or thereabouts, my Maline wasn't yet ten months old, and little Eve, who your worship also knows—up in Guse, but now I have her back with me again, for she is our little pet—yes, little Eve wasn't even yet born.'

'Then you must be over eighty, Papa.'

'Eighty-three. Next thirteenth August, that is.'

'. . . And must have married late in life.'

'Yes, your honour, that I did. My second wife, that is to say. When I went wooing the first time it was three years before we had the Russians here, and I had just come to the village . . . But here we are.'

And, so saying, he mounted the stone steps of the deeply notched entrance-way and unlocked the great church-door, which swung back inwards. They passed through the tower between the stumps of wood and the old Catholic altar-dolls that lay swept up together in a corner, and then walked up the broad middle aisle past the pews towards the altar and the pulpit.

When they had reached the front row of the pews the privy councillor made to enter the seat to his right and sit down for a moment: for he needed to collect himself. But old Kubalke drew him hastily back and said: 'Not there, your honour: that is the major's chair.'

The privy councillor looked at him in surprise.

'Not there, your honour,' the old man repeated, 'not there. It was in *anno* 59, and I can see it as if it was today. They brought him in from Kunersdorf, grenadiers of the Itzenplitz Regiment, and here they laid him down, here on his bench. But he had had enough of life. "Children, I *want* to die," he said, and tore off his bandages. And there he bled to death. It was the twelfth of August, the day before my birthday.'

As he had been speaking these words, Kubalke had drawn the privy councillor over to the other side of the aisle. The foremost row of stalls on this side was locked, but in front of them there ran a narrow bench on which the children sat while waiting to be confirmed. On this bench the two old men now sat themselves; and now they had the bier just in front of them, not three paces away.

When they had rested for a time Ladalinski said: 'Now I think we should remove the lid.'

'Not yet, your honour. You must at least be able to see the young gentleman your son. And it is still so dark. A fine young gentleman. Only last Sunday I shut him in here with Marie Kniehase; for I can see hardly anything any more. And when I came back fifteen minutes later he was standing there with his cheeks all flushed. Just there by the major's seat. But Marie was flushed even more. I will just go and light the candles, your honour.'

With that he went up to the altar, took the wax tapers from the great brass candlestick and ignited them. At first it seemed they would go out again, but at length they blazed up and, now removing the pall from the bier and laying it upon the altar steps, the old man said quietly: 'Now, if you please, your honour.'

Ladalinski had risen, and he now came and stood at one of the ends of the coffin.

'Am I standing at the head or the foot?' he asked.

'At the head.'

'But I prefer to stand at the foot.'

Thereupon they changed places, and then lifted the lid, the old privy councillor's eyes closing convulsively.

And only then did he look upon his son, long and unblinking, and to his own surprise he found that his heart was beating more and more calmly. What did it amount to, after all? He was dead. And in the depths of his soul he felt that there was nothing dreadful about it: no, no, it was freedom and redemption. Life appeared to him so poor, death so rich, and he was dominated by one feeling alone: 'Alas, if only I were lying there in his place.'

He prayed for him, and for himself; then, while everything undulated dreamlike around him, he stood for a further minute and then said: 'Now, Papa, let us close it again.'

He was ready to do so, and they also laid the pall back over the coffin: a faded piece of woollen cloth that only just reached the supports of the bier. And behold, that ancient Catholic sentiment, that had stirred first in Kathinka and then at last in Tubal too, now likewise came to life again in the heart of Ladalinski, and, indicating the coffin and its pitiful covering, he said:

'It looks so bare. What if I were to take the crucifix and place it upon the coffin. Or do you think it would give offence?'

'Not at all, your honour. That is the right thing to do with a crucifix. That's what it's here for, for the dead; it's they who need it.'

And so they took the crucifix from the altar, placed it on the coffin-lid, and sat themselves down again; Kubalke, however, continued in a confiding tone: 'It's not seven years ago that I last took that crucifix down from the altar. For we had the Spoon Guards here then, and the marauders; and you couldn't trust the rest of them, either, all that much, when it came to something silver. And so I said to my wife: "Wife, where shall we hide it?" And she said: "Hide it in the bedclothes"; but I didn't want to do that, so I hid it in my pillow and laid down and tried to go to sleep on it. But that wasn't right, either, and I got no rest, and it was as though I was lying on the wounds of my Saviour and hurting him. So I got up and took it out again and hung it on the wall. "Mother," I said, "there is no need for us to hide it. Even if the French trash do break into our church, they *won't* break into the house of a poor sexton. They won't think of looking for anything there. And if they do come, He will know how to look after Himself. For one thing we have learned around here is, He doesn't let Himself be mocked—no, and not pictures of Him, either." '

The privy councillor's heart had been moved as he had

listened: how much good it did him to hear this simple speech and this childlike faith. He took his companion's hand and said: 'Now let us go back.'

And they rose together; the sexton extinguished the candles, and they walked back to the door again between the pews. As they were passing through the tower it struck ten. The sound of the bell beating close above them refreshed old Ladalinski's heart, and thus they emerged again into the open air.

It had grown even darker, the last stars were gone, and Kubalke again went in front until, halfway down, they again came upon the spot where the slides had been made.

'Take care, your honour, here's the slippery ice,' Kubalke said as he had on their ascent, and seemed also to be about to speak again of the 'young varmints': but Ladalinski forestalled him and, resuming their interrupted conversation, said: 'You have been married twice, Papa? Is that not what you said?'

'Yes, your honour.'

'And did you also have children by your first wife?'

'A daughter.'

'And is she living still?'

'No, your honour. Long since dead: dead and rotted. It was what you might call a legacy from her mother.'

The old privy councillor looked at him inquiringly.

'Yes, her mother. She was a pretty handsome creature and all the menfolk ran after her. Well, there was a candidate in divinity come here, and one Sunday, when Pastor Ledderhose, who lived to be a hundred, had sprained his foot, our Herr Kandidat went into the pulpit and preached, and Wendelin Pyterke, who was our mayor in those days, said to me: "Listen, Kubalke, he knows a thing or two." And he did know a thing or two, I don't mind telling you. Come the evening they were both gone. Off to Pomerania, to Kammin or Kolberg. And there he became an inspector in a salt-works, but it didn't last long and they both came to a bad end.'

'And her daughter?'

'She stayed with me till she was seventeen; then she flew off as well, and it all turned out just the same. As you make your bed you must lie in it. But it's all buried and forgotten now.'

By then they had arrived at the rear of the manor house, and old Kubalke unlatched the yard-door. In the dimly lit rear hallway they encountered Jeetze.

'Goodnight, Papa!' said Ladalinski. 'You've lived to see a lot.'

'Yes, your honour. But all things get buried and forgotten in the end.'

26

Two Funerals

LADALINSKI had wanted to resume his journey to Bjalanovo at nine in the morning, and when this hour came he had said his farewells to the occupants of the house and was now ascending the wintry avenue of walnut-trees to fetch the coffin standing before the altar. Only Berndt and Lewin were with him. Beside them rocked a chaise-carriage decked with plumes, while they were preceded at ten or twenty paces by a covered sleigh drawn by a single horse: it was the sleigh that had participated in the journey to Bastion Brandenburg and upon which Bamme had bestowed the name 'coffin-sleigh'. Pachaly was again seated behind the shafts, just as he had been three days previously, and the only difference was that now, hung in an old sword-hilt fixed to the high horse-collar, a single sleighbell swung to and fro.

Now they were at the top; the covered sleigh drove directly up to the steps of the entrance-way, while the chaise-carriage halted at a little distance. The church stood open; Pachaly went in with them, and a moment later Ladalinski's servant also appeared. Thus they walked up the centre aisle to the altar; Berndt recognized the crucifix and realized who had moved it. They then stationed themselves on either side of the coffin without a word being spoken; at length the privy councillor said: 'Now carry him out', and took up the crucifix to return it to the altar. Vitzewitz prevented him, however, and said: 'No, Ladalinski, not so; that is now *yours*; my grandfather presented it to this church, and I shall present a new one. Take it, I beg of you. Willingly or not, you have given me your son, and all I can give you in return is this cross. Alas, I have borne it, too.'

Ladalinski's lips trembled; he could not speak, or he wanted not to. Then, however, in glad agitation he tore a strip from the pall, placed it around the middle of the coffin as though it were a sash, and inserted the crucifix, which had been standing unsupported, into the black bow of the sash. Then he stepped aside, and Pachaly and the servant took hold of the supports and carried the coffin and its tenant out of the church.

Fifteen minutes later the sleigh, having moved slowly along the top of the hill, turned off to the left and, when it had successfully negotiated the downward path, drove away between the willows in the direction of Frankfurt. The chaise followed after it, and as its covered cushioned seat rocked back and forth on the uneven roadway memories awoke in the heart of old Ladalinski, and he thought of that other journey to Bjalanovo he had taken long, long ago on roads snowed up just like this. And yet, how different that journey had been! It was a honeymoon trip, and the loveliest of women—just become his—was snuggling against him, laughing with high spirits; the snow was flying, the horses were galloping, and every new stopping-place brought more flowers and new tokens of admiration. He had been as inventive as love itself. And now he saw before him nothing but the sleigh, brushed now and then by the willows and slowly making for a tomb that was no longer his and at whose door he would have to beg hospitality for his dead son. That was more than he could bear. The little sleighbell rang out, gentle but sharp in the cold air; and gently but sharply fell his tears.

At the same hour as the old privy councillor, accompanied by Berndt and Lewin, had ascended to the church, Bamme too had donned his hussar's jacket and departed from the manor house, but had gone off in almost exactly the opposite direction. He had the intention of attending the funeral of Hoppenmarieken, which was due to take place in the course of the morning and which he hoped would afford him an opportunity of taking another look at this object of his particular interest.

When he drew near to the hedge that enclosed the little house he saw that vagabonds of all kinds, among them the old women who the previous day had assisted Kniehase's man with the coffin, had formed a line on either side of the pathway. Bamme waved a greeting, and it was not without satisfaction that he heard someone hiss behind him: 'That's him; doesn't he look dolled up.' Then he went into the house, whose door was standing open. There was a strong draught blowing, but in spite of this draught the house was warm, for the stove was steaming and in the hearth in the hallway there were huge logs burning with, strangely enough, several cooking-pots placed upon them. This had been the doing of the residents of the woodland acre, who intended to make a day of it at Hoppen-marieken's expense. She had left no heirs, and Kniehase had closed his eyes to it.

Bamme had promised himself this would be an experience, but he found even more than he had expected. The open coffin had been placed on two chairs in the manner of a travelling-trunk, and on the edge of the coffin was sitting a black bird, similar to a raven only much smaller. When the bird became aware it had a visitor, it hopped across to the opposite edge of the coffin and thence to the coffin-lid, which with its black and blue ornamentations lay on two other chairs. This change of places produced the distinct impression of having been per-formed out of respect for Bamme; the latter decided, in any event, to assume that this was the intention and, approaching the bird, commended it. 'You're a fine fellow, you have good breeding.' Thereupon, however, he recalled the actual purpose of his visit, pushed aside the table with the hymn-book and cards in it which was standing against the wall, and, after some experimentation, found himself a spot from where he could comfortably and in an adequate light observe the body of the dead woman. It was lying in state, and nothing pertaining to Hoppenmarieken had been overlooked. Her white hair was tied up under her black headscarf, the corners of the scarf were standing erect, and half the soles of her two thick waterproof boots were protruding above the coffin. In her right hand she held her hooked stick; but because it was too long it had been broken in half, and the lower half now lay beside her. Her facial expression had changed little: its cunning had been eradicated by death, but its stubbornness remained. Bamme was delighted; he turned the hooked stick a little to one side and then said to himself: 'A dwarf bishop'—a remark upon which, for lack of an audience to applaud him, he applauded himself. Then he looked into the alcove, in which the great bundles of ground-ivy were swaying back and forth in the draught, and here too he found everything '*superbe*'.

When he returned to the main room, the black bird had flown back to the edge of the coffin, and, inquisitive as to what it might be about, Bamme approached it and saw that it was literally being fed by the dead body; for the women of the neighbourhood had lain rowan-berries and grains of wheat in the open palm of Hoppenmarieken's left hand: a poetic touch, woodland acre style.

Bamme nodded in appreciation and made to return to his observation post; but it was soon borne in upon him that the scene was losing its charm.

The curiosity of Hoppenmarieken's birds gazing down on him and his red hussar's jacket through the bars of their cages could perhaps have been endured, but the gaping of the old women and children standing outside began to grow uncomfortable and annoying: so annoying, indeed, that in the end he was glad when they told him the bearers were about to appear. This they did shortly afterwards, closed the coffin and set off for the churchyard. One of the bearers was Hanne Bogun, who had hold of the lefthand front support, while beside him to his right there walked a lame good-for-nothing the lower part of whose legs formed an isosceles triangle. 'That's nice,' said Bamme, happy to have seen legs more grotesque than his own, and attached himself as first mourner, while the entire woodland acre followed *in corpore*.* Everyone was very cheerful, the children threw snowballs at one another, and Kniehase's doves fluttered above the procession as though they were burying Snow White or some princess in a fairy-tale.

Thus they came to the churchyard gate. Grown tired, the bearers here changed places, and only Hanne Bogun, because he had only his right arm, stayed on the lefthand side of the coffin. Then the procession moved off again between the graves, and came to a halt at the other end of the churchyard. Here, close by the stone wall at a spot overgrown in the summertime with thistles and yarrow and a favourite grazing-place for goats, a grave had been dug. Beside it stood Seidentopf and Kniehase, and opposite them Berndt and Lewin, who, when they had noticed the procession approaching, had remained on the hill after Ladalinski's departure. Except for a couple of small farmers and cottagers, the people of the village were represented only by Miekley, who, though he disapproved of this 'Christian burial' as much as everyone else did, had two reasons for determining not to show it: firstly, if 'something happened'—and he had little doubt something would happen—he did not want to miss it; and, secondly and chiefly, so that he could afterwards entertain Uhlenhorst, who had announced he would be lunching and dining at the mill, with a new piece of 'Seidentopfery'.

The bearers had set down their burden; now they lowered the coffin, and, while all the children of the woodland acre crowded round the grave inquisitively, Seidentopf said in a clear voice: 'Let us commend her soul to God. She did not lead a Christian life; but her last day, I may hope, compensated for much. There was nobody she loved, excepting one, and this one, who now stands with us at her grave, she rescued or assisted in his rescue. Her cunning, otherwise a source of evil, was here a source of good. And if this good should not weigh sufficient, then God's mercy will step in and in compassion make up what is lacking. Let us pray for her.' And so saying, he removed his biretta and said the Lord's Prayer, while two women of the woodland acre standing a little distance off giggled with one another.

'God, our old Seidentopp; I don't know, he prays for everybody. He wants everybody saved.'

'Yes. But his praying won't save Hoppenmarieken.'

Two hours later Uhlenhorst and Miekley were sitting at table; Creampot Kallies had also been invited. The third bottle of Graves had already been brought up from the cellar, for they all insisted on a 'nice glass of wine', and Uhlenhorst was growing more cheerful minute by minute. And this was comprehensible: for today the wealthy saw-miller was sawing to pieces, not merely treetrunks, but Seidentopf as well. When at length he had reported on Bamme's visit to Hoppenmarieken's dwelling, Uhlenhorst bent forward a little and said weightily: 'Nothing more natural, they are brother and sister.'

Accustomed though he was to oracular pronouncements from the mouth of his mentor, Miekley was none the less a little taken aback; Uhlenhorst himself, however, continued in the same tone: 'I do not mean in a worldly sense. But they both have the same father and were both born in the same place. As to what place that was, I am sure I don't need to tell you.'

Creampot had pricked up his ears (this was something for the inn), and before five minutes had passed both were convinced their mentor had once again seen to the heart of things and hit the nail on the head. 'I may be wrong,' said Uhlenhorst, slipping into a tone of humility, 'but I doubt it.'

And with that the colloquy concluded.

At the beginning of the afternoon the calash drove in front of the manor house; the ponies were harnessed; Bamme wanted to go back to his estate again to see to his affairs. 'It is on account of the pastor, Vitzewitz,' had been his final words when Berndt had invited him to stay a few days more. 'I have to keep him in the fear of the Lord, or he will get above himself and go into the pulpit and start telling my Gross-Quirlsdorfers that Hoppenmarieken killed herself because she was in love with me. All *sub rosa*,* naturally. With the aid of passages from the Bible. You can find anything you want in the Old Testament if you look hard enough.' And thereupon the old general had seized the reins and driven out of the courtyard like the Devil's chase, first past the open field, then past the fir-tree coppice, and then off in the direction of Küstrin.

That had been at three o'clock. Even before darkness fell Creampot Kallies made his appearance at the inn, where at first he had to make do with Scharwenka the innkeeper, for none of the other farmers was yet there.

'So now the general's gone too,' Creampot said, looking as portentous as though he were about to repeat the tale of

'Crucible Schulze' and the Margrave of Schwedt. 'I saw him this afternoon riding to Frankfurt on the fire-red sorrel mare. He rode via the woodland acre. It was on the stroke of four.'

'That can't be so, Creampot,' Scharwenka retorted.

'And why not?'

'First because the sorrel mare is dead; I saw her fall myself, not ten steps from the poplar-tree where they afterwards shot the schoolmaster, and then second because this afternoon I saw him (I mean the general) drive past me in our old man's calash-carriage. On the stroke of four. The ponies were in the shafts, and the Shetlander was being led.'

Kallies shook his head. 'You don't understand me, Scharwenka. That's just what I mean. Off to Küstrin in the calash and off to Frankfurt on the sorrel mare. You saw her fall. Good. But dead or not makes no difference. Such things do happen. Because you have to know what he's really like. Uhlenhorst . . .'

At this point he was interrupted by the entry of a number of other farmers, among them Kniehase, of whom Kallies was somewhat in dread—especially when he proposed donning Uhlenhorst's feathers and putting all kinds of mischievous conventiclist visions into circulation.

27

'And One Day the House will Receive a Princess'

A WEEK had passed. The straw lying before the house had been removed but everyone was walking softly, as though there were still someone there who must not be disturbed. Renate had not left the upper floor since that evening on which we saw her last, and it was on her account that the sounds in the house were subdued. Berndt was much occupied with work; on the specific instructions of Aunt Schorlemmer two or three windows were kept open on the ground floor to let out the 'odour of Bamme', and instead of Hoppenmarieken—who, it was said in the village, had three nights together been seen sitting on her own grave—Krist and Hanne Bogun appeared alternately to place letters and newspapers on the table. It was a time truly appropriate to Jeetze, all grey and still and with black gaiters; old Jeetze himself, however, who now had hardly any duties, would sit for half an hour at a time beside the rush-mat and chat to Hector.

Thus the days passed. Marie often came in the morning and went up to Renate to read to her or to talk. Tubal, however, she never mentioned. Afterwards she betook herself down to Lewin in the corner room; he was already waiting there for her, and they would then sit by the fire or in the deep window-bay and recall quiet days of the past; what they most loved to dwell on were the days of the Christmas just gone, and especially that lovely evening when he had thrown the golden nuts over the tall Christmas tree standing between them and she had caught them. Of their happiness they spoke no word, for they feared it might fly away if they alluded to it. Only once did they do so, as though by chance, and that was on the day the pastor of Bohlsdorf in the course of a tour of duty called on his colleague at Hohen-Vietz and at the same time paid a visit to the mayor. When Marie told him of it, Lewin said: 'Ah, Marie, you do not know how much I owe to that old village of Bohlsdorf and its church. Above all, *you*. It was there I began to recover even before I knew I was ill. How blind I was, and how egotistical! But now I have learned to see and I have you, you, my happiness and my princess with the golden stars.'

Immediately after he had spoken Berndt entered the room and, perceiving Marie was blushing, kissed her smilingly and with fatherly tenderness on the forehead. She cast her eyes down and trembled with emotion, for she well knew what this moment meant to her. Then she took leave of them, so as to leave father and son alone.

When she had gone Berndt said: 'I rejoice in your happiness, Lewin, even though I do not yet know what I shall say to all the Vitzewitzes hanging out there in the hall when sooner or later I appear among them. But I shall also have many other things to answer to them for. Disobedience and rebellion are not in the catechism of our house, either, and I think the one will be taken with the other and the less absorbed into the greater. And now no more of that. If the stars decree otherwise—which God forbid—then their agent will no doubt be a French bullet: but if we have you back, we shall also have a wedding. And I know one thing: it may spoil our pedigree but it won't spoil our profile; not our profile nor our character. And these are the two best things the nobility has.'

And again the days went by, and Renate, who in her lonely hours had recovered if not cheerfulness at any rate clarity of mind, was once more part of her family circle. The following day Lewin and Hirschfeldt were to depart for Breslau; they were preparing for their journey, and were engaged in packing their portmanteaux when through the corner window they suddenly perceived between the posts on the drive a rider entering the courtyard on a Shetland pony. Bamme, of course. Everyone ran to the window, and even Aunt Schorlemmer for a moment forgot her aversion in the welcome prospect of renewed contention. Most delighted of them all was Berndt, who had long since ceased to worry about the old general's whims and vanities.

'Well, Bamme,' he began, when the latter had seated himself and quickly polished off a tray of cordials one after the other, 'in what state did you find Gross-Quirlsdorf? The village, the parsonage, the church?'

'In an excellent state, Vitzewitz, better than expected. He had made his peace with me, I was told. There was church the very next day; so, inquisitive as I am, I wanted to find out whether or not there was any truth in it, and I didn't even wait for the third bell. I paid for that, to be sure, for the organ-playing seemed as if it would never end and a couple of times I thought they were going to sing through the whole hymn-book. But finally he appeared, and what would you believe he preached on? He preached on Saul and David. And repeated over and over: "Saul hath slain his thousands, but David hath slain his ten thousands." Well, Vitzewitz, we know better than anyone to what extent we are still in debt to our reputation for these ten thousands; but, *enfin*, who could this everlasting little David possibly be? At first I resisted the idea, finally I acquiesced in it. And so now you know, ladies, and most especially you too know, my dear Schorlemmer, who it really is who is sojourning under your roof. A fresh proof of the old saying: Everything happens to him who lives long enough.'

They continued chatting, and before midday had come —dinner was not until four o'clock—Bamme put forward the suggestion they should ride over to Drosselstein to 'try the heart and reins of East Prussia once again'.

Berndt was agreeable, and after a few minutes the horses were led out.

When they had gone by Miekley's mill, Berndt said: 'I forgot to tell you, Bamme, we have a betrothed couple in the house.'

'I say! Schorlemmer?'

'No.'

'I thought she would have been praying after Seidentopf. Good bait catches fine fish. Widowers and urn-collectors are as easy to snare as quails. And Seidentopf ought to present no problem at all. Just look at his display cabinet: everything his late departed wife left him all collected and preserved. To make a cult of it in that way is always risky.'

Berndt laughed.

'You're letting your ideas run away with you, Bamme, as usual. But the facts are stubborn. The case is otherwise. *Not* Seidentopf.'

'Well, who then?'

'Lewin.'

'My congratulations! But that is only one, half a couple. Who else?'

'Lewin and Marie Kniehase. The mayor Kniehase's foster-daughter.'

Bamme pulled the Shetland pony around so that he was standing at a right-angle to Vitzewitz and looked at him with his little eyes with every sign of genuine astonishment.

'You are surprised?' Berndt said.

'Yes.'

'And you disapprove?'

'No, Vitzewitz. *Au contraire*. Except for the 29th communiqué and the great robbery at Krach's, I have heard of nothing for the past ten years that could have given me so much pleasure. She is the most enchanting creature, and, like all who themselves have little to offer, my demands in this direction are high. So once again: *gratulor*! By thunder, Vitzewitz, that will produce a breed!'

Berndt made to reply, but, confronted thus unexpectedly with one of his favourite topics, the old general was little inclined to relinquish speech so soon.

'New blood,' he continued, 'new blood, Vitzewitz, that is the main thing. I did not acquire my views on this yesterday, and you know them. I abhor the whole principle of keep-it-in-the-family, and most of all when it comes to marriage and propagation. Your sister, the countess, thought likewise, and I have more than once heard her advocate rules of conduct that impressed even me. All honour to her memory! She was a *superbe* woman. Yes, Vitzewitz, we must get rid of the old humdrum routine. Away with it. How has it been till now? A Zieten marries a Bamme, a Bamme marries a Zieten. And what did it produce in the end? *This*!'—and he struck with his switch the legs of his high boots. 'Yes, *this*, and I am not so stupid, Vitzewitz, as to regard myself as a model specimen of mankind.'

Berndt remained silent, for he wanted to hear more, and Bamme was not long in obliging.

'We are by ourselves, Vitzewitz,' he went on, 'and may safely say what we think. Sometimes it seems to me as though we were brought up in a madhouse. There's nothing special about our kind. One thing at least we believed we had a monopoly of: courage; and now here comes along this white-faced Grell and dies like a hero with a sabre in his hand. I say nothing of the schoolmaster: such a death could put an old soldier to shame. And where does all this come from? From over yonder, borne on the west wind. I can make nothing of these windbags of Frenchmen, but in all the rubbish they talk there is none the less a pinch of wisdom. Nothing much is going to come of their Fraternity, nor of their Liberty: but there is something to be said for what they have put between them. For what, after all, does it mean but: a man is a man. It is all right for me to talk like this, Vitzewitz, for with me the Bammes will die out, an event which will not cause the veil of the Temple to be rent in twain, and I don't even have a namesake whose class-consciousness I could offend or affect in his pocket. For, between ourselves, here we begin to take offence only when we begin to be affected in our pocket.'

By now they had arrived at the wall surrounding the park, and a minute later they halted before Drosselstein's garden-room.

While this conversation was being conducted on the road to Hohen-Ziesar, Renate and Marie, who had withdrawn to the rear of the room and had sat themselves on the sofa with the large flower pattern, were also chatting with one another. Lewin had joined them but was visibly preoccupied and had been sitting between them for several minutes without taking Marie's hand or even casting a glance at her.

Marie herself, wholly unaffected and undemanding as she was by nature, seemed not to notice; but Renate said: 'You *are* a strange couple: you're paying no attention at all to one another.'

'Don't give up all hope of us,' laughed Marie, and Lewin added: 'We have been like brother and sister for too long. But all will soon be well. What do you think, Marie?'

And the blush that suffused her face exempted her from any other answer.

After this—it was again a Saturday—Lewin and Hirschfeldt went to the parsonage to take their leave of Seidentopf. They found him poring over Beckmann, and not only was the cabinet-door of his *arcus triumphalis* standing wide open, but the middle shelf, on which the three chief items of his collection and, since the day after Christmas, Odin's chariot too, had their place, had been pulled out. Anyone who knew how Seidentopf divided up his week would not have been surprised by this spectacle: for he was one of those wise preachers who prepared their sermon on Friday so as to be able to employ the intervening day for the refreshment of the soul. And what could be better suited to this end than the *ultima ratio Semnonum*! To disturb this process of refreshment would thus in the usual way be regarded as inadmissible; but today, for Lewin and Hirschfeldt to come and bid him farewell could hardly be called a disturbance. They intended, they said in the course of the ensuing conversation, to depart for Frankfurt at nine in the morning, so as to meet some friends from Berlin there at midday. All this was said as though by the way, but Seidentopf understood very well that the communication of these exact times was supposed to excuse their non-appearance at church. It vexed him a little, for, like all pastors, he was sensitive on this subject; but, quickly recovering himself, he expressed his good wishes for Lewin in the warmest possible fashion. Then he turned to the captain and spoke of the 'days behind us we have lived through together'.

'They were stormy days,' he concluded.

'And yet they were days *before the storm*!' Hirschfeldt replied.

And now it was nine in the morning. Hector had dragged himself laboriously to the sandstone steps, and for the last time in this book the ponies were led out. Their bells rang out brightly, and on Krist's ancient hat with the ancient cockade there fluttered today a long green ribbon. His wife had wanted it to be a red one, but he had insisted on green.

And now nothing more of farewells.

Past the woodland acre flew the sleigh in which Lewin and Hirschfeldt were sitting, past Hoppenmarieken's little house, and as immediately afterwards they again descended the hill and drove off in the direction of the river a sound like a dull roll of thunder suddenly welled up and died away into the far distance.

'The ice is cracking,' said Hirschfeldt. 'It is a good sign for us to set off by.'

And at the same moment the bells of Hohen-Vietz began ringing, and the two friends involuntarily turned and looked back.

'What does the sound of those bells mean to us?' asked Lewin.

'A world of things: war and peace, and now also a wedding; a wedding, the happiest of weddings, and I, I am among the guests.'

'You speak, Hirschfeldt, as though you knew,' Lewin rejoined, his heart beating.

'Yes, Vitzewitz, I do know: I see into the future.'

In the afternoon of that same Sunday the ladies were sitting in the corner room in which we have so often encountered them. Their tears had dried, Aunt Schorlemmer had surmounted the agitations of farewell with the aid of a powerful maxim, and only to Marie's long eyelashes there still clung a number of watery drops.

Renate kissed her, and said: 'Stop now, Marie, for you must know there are three things I believe in.'

'All sensible people do,' said Aunt Schorlemmer. 'All Christians, that is to say.'

'And what I believe in', Renate went on, 'is, firstly in the Hundred Year Almanac, secondly in conjuring fire, and thirdly in old sayings and folk-rhymes. And do you know the one I believe in most!'

'Well?'

'*And one day the house will receive a princess.*'

Marie smiled.

Aunt Schorlemmer, however, said: 'What foolishness! I will tell you a better saying.'

'Which is?'

'To them that love God all things work together for good.'

28

From Renate's Diary

BETROTHAL or wedding brings a story to an end. But a diary that lies in the manor house at Hohen-Vietz to the present day and is preserved there as a treasured legacy vouchsafes us a glance into what came afterwards. The pages are in Renate's hand, and it is from them that I borrow the following.

Lewin is back. I have waited only for this day to do what I have long wanted to do and begin writing a diary. The sabre-cut over his forehead suits him well; the tendency to softness he formerly had has now gone; Marie finds this too. How happy she was! And yet as calm as she was happy. And that was what I was most glad about. For I hate noise more than anything; and noisy feelings most of all! It was odd that, an hour before Lewin's arrival, we were unpacking the tombstone intended for Grell. A little marble tablet. It was not without emotion that we read the name and date and the lines from Hölderlin. Jeetze wanted to hide it, but Maline said: 'No, no, it means good luck', which naturally made my dear Schorlemmer explode in fire and wrath at the ineradicability of Wendish superstition. (Lewin is to take over Guse; they are to live there as newlyweds. It will be the best thing.)

The wedding was yesterday. In *Bohlsdorf*. Lewin had insisted; he wanted to be married where the course of his life had been decided. So we drove there in three carriages. With us were Drosselstein and Hirschfeldt (who has lost an arm, unhappily the right one). Bamme was mysterious and declared he had 'for the moment buried my wedding present'. But the day of its resurrection would come. Schorlemmer indignant at this expression, the rest of us intrigued. Seidentopf gave the address; he never spoke better; it is true what they say, it is the heart that makes the orator. He took his text from the Bible, but what he really spoke on was the line 'And she can walk on stars'. After the ceremony we had a snack at the administrator's office. The young wife even prettier than before; again reminded of Kathinka. Journey back in an open carriage. Delightful. The gossamer was flying and settled in Marie's green garland. It was like a second bridal veil. Bamme, who knew only the popular name for these gossamer threads, got excited over the 'ungallantry of this year's September', but calmed down again when I told him they were also called 'Maria's twine'. For the rest, Lämmerhirt and Seidentopf have drunk *Brüderschaft* and want to correspond. Lämmerhirt also collects death's heads and is Germanic. Thus an ally against Turgany.

Today we laid our dear Seidentopf to rest. Lewin and Marie came over from Guse with their three eldest children. They brought with them big wreaths of elder, which is blooming so beautifully in Guse this year. Pastor Zabel from Dolgelin spoke the funeral sermon; well-meant and commonplace. Papa won't admit this was so; but then he always adds something of himself. Turgany was present too; very moved. He accompanied me when we went back, and said in the way he has: Now I can undisputedly declare this region Wendish; but I would prefer not to do so.

Letter from Kathinka (from Paris). Interested, but very superior. She now thinks us very small fry. Only two things engage her now: Poland and 'the Church'.

Yesterday we were over in Guse, Papa, Schorlemmer and I. When we were at dinner the president of the court at Selow was announced; he had brought over in person a document deposited with the court there. Address: 'To Frau *Marie von Vitzewitz*. To be handed to the addressee after my demise. *Bamme*, Major-General.' We opened it and read. He had bequeathed all his wealth to Marie, and done so in very Bamme-like expressions. At the end it said: 'I learned when I was very young how little appearance means.' Marie recalled having said to him something similar. We all congratulated her; only Aunt Schorlemmer advocated sending it back, there was 'no good in it'. Marie, however, said she was 'not devout enough for *that*', at which we all laughed very much; in the end Aunt Schorlemmer did too.

And now I am alone, *quite* alone, and tomorrow Lewin, who has now left Guse, will move into this ancient Hohen-Vietz, into the house so dear to me and to him, in which may he be as happy as he was before. And he will be, for he is bringing his good angel with him. My dear Marie. She has passed the sternest test, and happiness has left her as she was: humble, true and simple. And so I could stay and go on living with and among them, but I don't want to be the Aunt Schorlemmer of their house. Besides, I don't know any hymns or proverbs. So I shall go to Kloster Lindow,* our ancient foundation for single ladies. That is where I belong. For I desire a life of contemplation and quiet works of charity. And there is but one thing I long for even more. There is a world of glory: my heart tells me so, and I am drawn up towards it.

Here the diary ends.

On a narrow neck of land between two lakes in the March there stands the aristocratic foundation of Lindow. It consists of old convent buildings: a church, a refectory, all in ruins; and surrounding the ruins a quiet park that serves as a burial-place, or a burial-place that has already become a park again. There are flower-beds, tombstones, elder-bushes, and children from the town playing among the tombstones.

And I stood on one of these tombstones and gazed into the setting sun that gilded the convent and the still surface of the lake just in front of me. How beautiful! It was a glimpse of a world of peace and light.

Only as I left did I read the name inscribed in the stone:
Renate von Vitzewitz.

NOTES

In the verification of facts and dates in the following notes I have been especially helped by Gordon A. Craig's *The Politics of the Prussian Army*, E. J. Feuchtwanger's *Prussia*, Peter Gerrit Thielen's *Karl August von Hardenberg*, Herbert and Elizabeth Frenzel's *Daten deutscher Dichtung* and Charlotte Jolles's *Theodor Fontane*; but my greatest indebtedness is to the detailed annotations furnished by Walter Keitel and Helmuth Nürnberger for the edition of *Vor dem Sturm* included in the Hanser Verlag's collected edition of Fontane (second edition, 1971): without these before me my task would have been a lot more difficult and protracted than it was.

BOOK ONE

3 *parish church:* built between 1695 and 1714; its musical clock played 'Üb' immer Treu' und Redlichkeit', a popular song to the tune of Papageno's aria 'Ein Mädchen oder Weibchen' from Mozart's *The Magic Flute*, on the hour and half-hour.

4 *Hohen-Vietz:* fictitious; in its layout—a village situated on either side of a single long street—it is at once a typical and an idealized *Strassendorf* of central and eastern Brandenburg.

   Waldteufels: homemade musical instruments, probably producing a sound like a comb-and-paper.

   Lewin von Vitzewitz: the name is invented, though the name Zitzewitz existed in Brandenburg. The description of him as 'the hero [*Held*] of our story' is inconsistent with Fontane's description of the novel as a '*Vielheitsroman*'; but it may be that the expression is intended ironically.

7 *the days of the first colonization:* the twelfth century.

   She now beholds the light . . .: the original of these verses is inscribed on a tomb in the Nikolaikirche in Berlin.

10 *The Pomeranians:* Pomerania lies to the north and east of Brandenburg; in the fifteenth and sixteenth centuries the provinces were in continual conflict.

   the Hussites: the followers of the religious reformer John Hus (*c.*1370–1415); after their founder's execution they took up arms and inaugurated what are known as the Hussite Wars, during the course of which, especially in 1431 and 1432, they 'ravaged' Brandenburg.

Lebus and Barnim: towns in Brandenburg and the counties named after them; the county of Lebus lies immediately to the west of the Oder; Barnim, Upper and Lower, lies to the west of Lebus and separates it from Berlin. Hohen-Vietz is supposed to lie in the county of Lebus.

Greek fire: a mixture of nitre, sulphur and naphtha employed to ignite enemy fortifications.

11   *Thirty Years War*: from 1618 to 1648.

Frankfurt: Frankfurt-on-Oder. Except for the suburb known as the Dammvorstadt (now incorporated into Poland under the name Slubice), which is to the east of the Oder, the town lies on the west bank of the river, fifty miles east-south-east of Berlin. During the period of *Before the Storm* its population numbered probably about 40,000 and it was under French military occupation.

12   *Nördlingen*: the Battle of Nördlingen took place on 5–6 September 1634; a victory of the Imperial Army over the Swedes.

14   *Münster and Osnabrügge*: The Peace of Westphalia, which ended the Thirty Years War, was signed at Münster and Osnabrügge (modern Osnabrück) on 24 October 1648; it accorded equality of rights to both Catholic and Protestant persuasions.

our most gracious Herr Elector: Friedrich Wilhelm (1620–88), known as the Great Elector; the 'Brandenburg army' to which Matthias refers was the nucleus of the future Prussian Army.

the Burgsdorffs: Konrad von Burgsdorff and his wife; von Burgsdorff was chancellor to the still youthful Elector.

post mortem Schwarzenbergii: after the death of Schwarzenberg; Adam Count von Schwarzenberg was the principal adviser to the Brandenburg Electors until his death in 1641.

Interim bene vale: In the meantime, farewell.

Schloss Eger: in north-east Hungary, also the scene of the assassination of Wallenstein in 1634.

15   *Peterwardein*: fortress in Hungary in possession of the Turks.

21   *'Now thank we all our God'*: the hymn 'Nun danket alle Gott' by Martin Rinckart; for the lines sung a little later I have used the familiar English version of Catherine Winkworth.

23   *Suhl*: in Thuringia, noted for its arms manufacture.

23 *Berndt von Vitzewitz*: modelled, with considerable modification, on Friedrich August Ludwig von der Marwitz (1777–1837). A general in the Prussian Army and lord of the manor of Friedersdorf in the Oderbruch, Marwitz, though a minor figure on the stage of history, is of some interest in his own right. He was the conservative Junker *par excellence*, implacably hostile to the ideas of the French Revolution and to the innovations of the Reform Era (as the years 1807 to 1813 are called in Prussian history); forced into a posture of permanent opposition to the liberalizing constituted authority, he developed certain radically un-Prussian traits, of which the most important for the present novel was a disposition to believe that political action on one's own initiative, without the sanction of King and government and if necessary in defiance of them, was not under all circumstances impermissible. This was a new phenomenon in someone as relatively highly placed as von der Marwitz, and to combat it the King and his chief minister, von Hardenberg, had him briefly imprisoned (an act which, like some of Marwitz's own acts, was itself unconstitutional). Seemingly as a result of this imprisonment, Marwitz became more radical and to some extent more irresponsible in his antagonism to the state; and during the period covered by *Before the Storm* he was advocating a popular uprising against the French which, though it did indeed come, would possibly have led to a bloodbath if it had come in the form demanded by Marwitz. Reconciliation with Hardenberg came after Prussia had repudiated its alliance with and declared war on France. The details of Marwitz's career correspond only slightly to those of Berndt's, but the connection between the two is none the less quite clear; certain specific correspondences will be indicated in the notes. Fontane published a laudatory essay on Marwitz in 1861, and the relation between Marwitz as he was, Fontane's attitude towards him, and the character of Berndt has been one of the main topics of discussion in critical assessments of *Before the Storm*.

thirteen: this is the age at which Marwitz says his military career began.

Zorndorf: Battle of Zorndorf, 25 August 1758; victory of Friedrich the Great over the Russians.

Pour le mérite: the premier Prussian award for bravery.

25 *'Here lies my happiness'*: these words were inscribed by Marwitz on his wife's grave at Schloss Friedersdorf.

29 *the Emperor's allies*: under the treaty of March 1812, according to which Prussia agreed to furnish 20,000 troops for Napoleon's projected invasion of Russia.

30 *our Queen*: Queen Luise, the wife of Friedrich Wilhelm III; the encounter took place on 6 July 1807 at Tilsit: the Prussians believed, wrongly, that Napoleon might moderate his demands if met by the Queen rather than the King.

32 *Castle Soltwedel*: the seat of Albrecht the Bear from 1134, when it was already ancient.

   The palace of Sanssouci: pleasure palace constructed at Potsdam for Friedrich the Great between 1745 and 1747.

33 *Malplaquet*: the Battle of Malplaquet, 11 September 1709, during the War of the Spanish Succession.

   Mollwitz: the Battle of Mollwitz, 10 April 1741, the first engagement of the War of the Austrian Succession: the famous occasion on which Friedrich the Great, advised the battle was lost, fled the field and narrowly escaped capture, while in his absence the Prussian infantry reversed the situation and won the battle for him.

35 *since the reformed doctrine had come to the land*: conversion to Luther's reformed doctrine was general in Brandenburg from about the middle of the sixteenth century.

36 *Lutheran or Calvinist*: the Calvinist doctrine penetrated the March during the first decades of the seventeenth century (the then Elector declared himself Calvinist in 1613), but never replaced the Lutheran as the preponderant confession.

   orthodox conventiclists: a 'conventicle' was a private domestic gathering for the purpose of religious instruction and devotion.

37 *Judas Maccabaeus*: the central figure of the Jewish rising against the Selucidae tyranny (170–160 BC); the words quoted, from the First Book of the Maccabees, are Judas's last words before his death on the battlefield.

39 *Zinzendorf*: Nikolaus Ludwig Count von Zinzendorf (1700–60), the founder of the Herrnhuter sect and a prolific hymn-writer. (See next note.)

40 *a Herrnhuter*: Herrnhut was the name of Zinzendorf's estate in Oberlausitz after which he named the sect he founded there in 1722; a Herrnhuter was a member of this sect. Not strictly an original creation but the German branch of the Moravian Brotherhood, the Herrnhut Community combined simplicity of

belief with missionary zeal and, sometimes to an extreme degree, with the 'Protestant' prejudice that discomfort and austerity are good in themselves. Aunt Schorlemmer is modelled on Fontane's wife's foster-mother, who was a Herrnhuter. There was in fact a Herrnhut mission in Greenland, and I take Fontane's sending Aunt Schorlemmer to precisely this outpost to be a piece of affectionate mockery of the prejudice above-mentioned.

41 *Bohemian Brethren*: forerunners of the Moravians and thus also of the Herrnhuter (all being ultimately heirs of the Hussites); compelled to leave Bohemia in 1620.

sal sedativum: sedative; *sal volatile*: stimulant.

42 *the third commandment*: 'Remember the Sabbath day, to keep it holy' (Exodus 20:8); the German Bible, however, uses the word 'Feiertag', and not specifically 'Sabbath', which makes it possible for Lewin to regard work done on Christmas Day as a breach of this commandment, even though Christmas Day 1812 fell on a Friday.

the eleventh and twelfth: of December 1812.

43 *Rostopchin*: Feodor Vasilievich Rostopchin (1763–1826), Russian general, governor of Moscow, made the decision to burn the city down and is said to have started the conflagration himself by setting light to his own residence.

the crossing of the Beresina: incident in the retreat from Moscow, 26–28 November 1812.

44 *Charles XI*: King of Sweden 1660–97.

46 *Gustav IV*: King of Sweden 1792–1809; he was removed from the throne by a palace revolution.

'While God protects me . . . ': from the hymn 'Jesu meine Freude' by Johann Frank.

48 *Archduke Karl*: commander-in-chief of the Austrian Army 1806–9.

the campaign of '92: Revolutionary France declared war on Austria and Prussia in April 1792; Austrian and Prussian forces penetrated Champagne but after their defeat at Valmy were compelled to withdraw.

50 *the Rhine campaign*: the war with France between the end of the 'campaign of '92' and the Peace of Basel of 5 April 1795, which temporarily ended Prussian participation in the anti-French coalition.

the Weissenburg lines: a pattern of defensive trenches laid in 1706 near Weissenburg in Alsace; the scene of much fighting during the Rhine campaign in 1793.

Kaiserslautern: a town in the Rhineland-Palatinate; there were two engagements there in 1794.

51 *Schwedter Margrave*: Schwedt is on the Oder, near Frankfurt; the Margraves, the heirs of the third son of the Elector Friedrich Wilhelm, died out in 1788.

52 *Kandidat Uhlenhorst*: 'Kandidat' here means a student of divinity reading for holy orders.

55 *Hoppenmarieken*: modelled on Anna Dorothea Hoppe, the daughter of a cottager in Letschin.

56 *Küstrin*: a town on the Oder, eighteen miles north-north-east of Frankfurt (destroyed in 1945 and deserted by what was left of its German population, now rebuilt as the Polish town of Kostrzyn). During the period of *Before the Storm* it was occupied by the French, who maintained a garrison there.

58 *Czernebog temples*: dedicated to the 'Black God', the chief of the underworld gods of the Wends.

61 *After having thus . . . syllabus of pleasure*: alludes to a couplet in Goethe's *Faust* I: Mephistopheles to Faust: 'Mit welcher Freude, welchem Nutzen/Wirst du den Cursum durchschmarutzen!'

62 *The village mayor*: the term is 'Schulze', not to be confused with anything so grand as a 'Bürgermeister'. Kniehase is no more than a chosen spokesman of the village in its dealings with the lord of the manor, Vitzewitz, and, in reverse direction, the agent through whom the lord of the manor communicates his wishes to the village. He enjoys the respect of both parties, or he would not be the *Schulze*, but he has no independent authority beyond that which this respect procures him. Vitzewitz 'sends for' Kniehase, and he comes; and he always addresses Vitzewitz with the respectful title of 'gnädige Herr', the normal mode of address of servants to masters. On the other hand, the relationship between the two is definitely not feudal: Kniehase is a 'free peasant farmer' and the owner of a large property (as are the other peasant farmers who drink and talk at Scharwenka's inn), and Vitzewitz cannot compel him to do anything he does not wish to do (he has to try to persuade him). Above all, there exists no machinery by means of which Vitzewitz could 'punish' Kniehase for an act of which he disapproved other than the sanctions of ordinary human relations. This relationship is

repeated, with some modifications, in the relationship between Vitzewitz and *his* superiors.

64   *the Peace of Hubertusburg*: concluded 15 February 1763 between Austria, Saxony and Prussia.

69   *Marie*: the seed from which the character Marie blossomed was the daughter of a travelling acrobat who was left behind in Letschin and taken in by the local schoolteacher; Fontane also appropriated the schoolteacher's name, Pachaly, for the night-watchman of *Before the Storm*.

72   *Flora*: the Roman goddess of flowers.

75   *the 'Lübeck Dance of Death'*: one of the many representations of this theme which decorated church walls; this example, executed in 1463, was in the Marienkirche in Lübeck until destroyed in the Second World War.

76   *Seidentopf*: this uncommon name was possessed by one of the teachers at the Gymnasium at Neuruppin when Fontane was a pupil there.

78   *Bekmann's History . . . Brandenburg*: Johann Christoph Bekmann's *Historische Beschreibung der Chur und Mark Brandenburg* was one of Fontane's source-books for the historical details employed in the *Wanderungen durch die Mark Brandenburg*.

camera archaeologica . . . camera theologica: archaeological room; theological room.

arcus triumphalis: triumphal arch.

79   *Germanic as surely as Teut himself had been a German*: an ironic commentary on the state of Seidentopf's historical knowledge: 'Teut' was an imaginary invention of the eighteenth century, to attempt to account for the origin of the word 'Teuton'.

'Ultima ratio Semnonum': 'final argument for the Semnones'; deriving from *ultima ratio regis*, the final argument of kings (i.e. cannon).

80   *'Imp. Caes. Trajano Optimo'*: 'Of the Emperor and Caesar Trajan the Good'.

Lutitian: the Lutitians were a nation within the Wendish civilization.

Justizrat: the equivalent of the English barrister-at-law; when I have not left it in German, however, the term 'magistrate' has seemed to me the one most suited to indicate Turgany's social position and function in the novel.

Göttingen: university town in Lower Saxony.

'*German Oak-tree*' . . . *Klopstock* . . . *Hermann and Thusnelda*: Friedrich Gottlieb Klopstock (1729–1803), a powerful and elevated poet, directed the youth of his day to the half-forgotten poetry and prowess of their remoter ancestors. The 'German Oak-tree' alludes to a circle of nationalist-minded poets inspired by Klopstock. Hermann (17 BC–AD 21), the hero of the victory over the Romans in the Teutoburg forest (AD 9), and his wife Thusnelda are the principal characters in Klopstock's dramatic trilogy *Hermanns Schlacht* (1769), *Hermann und die Fürsten* (1784) and *Hermanns Tod* (1787).

85 *Konrektor Othegraven*: a 'Konrektor' was the senior assistant master of a grammar school; but as Othegraven is hoping soon to take holy orders, he is sometimes regarded by the other characters as practically a clergyman: where I have not left the word in the original German I have translated it 'schoolmaster'.

87 *Holstein*: province in north Germany, at the base of the Danish peninsula.

Wandsbeck Messenger: the *Wandsbecker Bote*, a magazine appearing four times a week that attained celebrity during the years 1771 to 1775 under the editorship of Matthias Claudius (1740–1815).

Claus Harms . . . *Dithmarschen*: Harms (1778–1855), an evangelical theologian, held a living in Norderdithmarschen, a county of Holstein on the North Sea coast, between 1806 and 1816.

89 *Reppen and Drossen*: the artefact Turgany has given Seidentopf was in fact found at Drossen, on the east bank of the Oder, though not until 1848; according to a letter of Fontane's of 26 March 1866, it occupied the place of honour at the Zieten Museum at Neuruppin.

90 *Priegnitz*: two counties—West and East—occupying the northwest corner of Brandenburg.

Vineta . . . *Rethra* . . . *Oregunga*: Vineta is the legendary city of the Wends, supposedly sunk into the ground; Rethra and Oregunga were sites of Wendish temples.

Julin: another name for Vineta.

91 *Obotritan*: the Obotritans were a Wendish tribe occupying present-day Mecklenburg.

Pribislav or Mistivoi: names of Obotritan princes.

94 *tree-cake*: a confection shaped like a Christmas tree, with layers of 'branches' one on top of the other.

95   *Astrakhan*: city on the delta of the Volga noted for the production of caviar.

96   *The 29th communiqué*: See Introduction, p. xviii above.

    'On dit': 'They say'.

100 *Pastor Schmidt of Werneuchen . . . Ludwig Tieck*: a pairing of unequals, as though one should speak of the schools of McGonagall and Burns. Friedrich Wilhelm August Schmidt (1764–1838), known to his contemporaries as 'Schmidt of Werneuchen' after the Brandenburg village of which he was pastor, was the author of the kind of verse represented in English by the 'parlour poetry' of the Victorians. In his confounding of the simple with the prosaic he recalls the aged Wordsworth, and, like him, was the object of much derision. Tieck (1773–1853), on the other hand, was one of the leading and most innovative spirits of the Romantic movement; successful in most of the available genres, he created for himself a permanent place in German literature through his participation in the translation of Shakespeare (begun by August Wilhelm Schlegel, who translated seventeen plays between 1797 and 1810, and completed by Tieck, in collaboration with his daughter Dorothea and Wolf Count Baudissin, between 1825 and 1840). He also produced a German version of *Don Quixote*.

    Ziebingen: an estate near Frankfurt-on-Oder.

    Schmidt's Muses' Almanac: *Kalender der Musen und Grazien*, published by Schmidt. *Zerbino*: published in Tieck's *Romantische Dichtungen* in 1799. *Phantasus*: collection of tales, the first volume of which, published in 1812, includes 'Leben und Tod des kleinen Rotkäppchens' (Red Riding Hood) and 'Der gestiefelte Kater' (Puss in Boots).

101 *So many a night . . . .*: Schmidt's poem 'An den Mond', published in 1797; Fontane 'improves' it slightly. Set to music by J. F. Reichardt.

    spotless royal palfrey . . .: from the prologue to Tieck's comedy *Kaiser Octavianus* (1804): a passage that became famous separately from the play as a statement of the Romantic theory of poetry. Again Fontane quotes with slight alterations.

102 *Spanish writings*: the early German Romantics drew inspiration from Calderón and admired the Spanish drama second only to the English.

    'enchanted, moon-illumined night': from the prologue to *Kaiser*

Octavianus: 'Mondbeglänzte Zaubernacht,/Die den Sinn gefangenhält', etc: the definition of the Romantic sensibility.

Yon little golden star . . . : from Tieck's poem 'Nacht'.

104 *Pastor Schultze of Döbritz*: Christian Heinrich Schultze, the pastor of Döbritz, in the Havel-land.

Nomen et omen: Name and omen.

the rebuke it received from Weimar: Schmidt's *Kalender der Musen und Grazien* for 1796 was subjected to ridicule by Goethe in a poem, 'Musen und Grazien in der Mark'.

105 *'the golden stars . . . vault of heaven'*: from the very popular ballad, 'Lenore', by Gottfried August Bürger (1747–94).

107 *'Shepherd sweet . . .'*: by Zinzendorf.

110 *Schildhorn saga*: narrated by Fontane in the first volume of the *Wanderungen durch die Mark Brandenburg*: the Wendish prince, Jaczko, in flight from the Germans, plunged with his horse into the Havel river opposite present-day Schildhorn and attempted to gain the far bank; on the point of going under, he renounced the gods of the Wends, who appeared to have failed him, and called on the Christian god for help, whereupon he was lifted out of the river and borne to the other side. Jaczko then became a Christian. The event is set in 1155, but the 'saga' is, apparently, a much later invention.

113 *amende honorable retardée*: delayed apology.

'moutarde après le dîner': mustard after the meal.

114 *Montesquieu*: Charles-Louis de Montesquieu (1689–1755), French philosopher, his *De l'esprit des lois* being especially influential. *Rousseau*: Jean-Jacques Rousseau (1712–78), among the most influential philosophers of his or any other time.

'vaine fumée . . . le néant': 'vain vapours [which] the vulgar call glory and greatness, but which the wise know to be nothingness'.

115 *On renonce . . . son goût*: It is easier to give up one's principles than one's tastes (La Rochefoucauld).

116 *à la Reine Hortense*: Queen Hortense was the wife of Louis Bonaparte and the mother of Napoleon III.

117 *the Spree*: the river on which Berlin stands.

Kastalia: i.e. the Castalian spring, a fountain of Parnassus sacred to the muses, which bestowed the gift of poetry on those who drank from it. The fictional literary circle, Kastalia, of the novel is modelled in some respects on the actual Berlin literary circle called the 'Tunnel über der Spree', of which Fontane was a member.

BOOK TWO

123 *Schloss Guse*: the château and the estate that surrounds it are modelled on Schloss Gusow, which lies at the western edge of the Oderbruch, and has as its neighbour Schloss Friedersdorf, the estate of von der Marwitz (both châteaux are described in the *Wanderungen*). In so far as Berndt von Vitzewitz is modelled on Marwitz, Fontane has transported him from one side of the Bruch to the other, so that when the family at Hohen-Vietz visit Schloss Guse they have to travel across the Bruch. In addition to other considerations, this has the effect of distancing the world of Hohen-Vietz from that of Guse also in a physical sense, with obvious advantages for the structure of the novel.

Lestwitz and Prittwitz: Hans Georg von Lestwitz (1718–88), major-general in the Prussian Army, led the attack which decided the issue of the Battle of Torgau on 3 November 1760. Joachim Bernhard von Prittwitz (1727–93), cavalry general, saved the life and liberty of Friedrich the Great at the Battle of Kunersdorf by rescuing him after his horse had been killed under him and he was in immediate danger of capture by Austrian troops.

'Prittwitz a sauvé . . . sauvé l'état': 'Prittwitz saved the King, Lestwitz saved the country.'

124 *'Here without . . . a province'*: these, or words of similar import, are traditionally attributed to Friedrich on his viewing the completed draining of the Bruch and the beginning of its agricultural development.

'Seelower Höhe': the highest point of the Bruch, near the village of Seelow.

Georg von Derfflinger: (1606–95); he entered the service of Brandenburg in 1654 and became the principal military adviser to the Great Elector.

Battle of Fehrbellin: fought in June 1675.

the Pomeranian and East Prussian campaign: between 1676 and 1679.

125 *Count Baudissin*: Wolf Heinrich von Baudissin (1579–1646), field marshal and diplomat.

126   *Friedrich von Derfflinger*: (1662–1724), lieutenant-general in the Prussian Army but nothing of the 'warlord' his father had been.

   one of the most ferocious wars of all time: the War of the Spanish Succession, 1701–14.

   Turin: Battle of Turin fought on 7 September 1706, defeat of the French.

   the Berlin of the age of Schlüter: i.e. the end of the seventeenth and beginning of the eighteenth centuries. Andreas Schlüter (1660–1714), the Danzig architect and sculptor, was employed by the first Prussian king to design new buildings for his new capital; among them were the New Palace in 'Prussian baroque' and, outside the city gates, a palace for the queen, Charlottenburg.

   'agere aut pati fortiora': 'act or patiently submit to the stronger'.

   Count von Pudagla: the name derives from that of a forest estate at Swinemünde, on the island of Usedom in the Baltic (now Polish under the name Swinoujscie).

127   *Aunt Amelie*: modelled on Countess Karoline Amalie La Roche-Aymon (1770–1859), a figure at the Rheinsberg court of Prince Heinrich and described by Fontane in his account of the court in the *Wanderungen*.

   Henriade . . . Messiade: See Introduction, p. xvii above.

   the Battle of Leuthen: 5 December 1757: Austria defeated by Prussia.

128   *'frondeurs'*: the politically disaffected (from the 'Fronde', the seventeenth-century conspiracy against the French monarchy).

   'au fond du cœur': 'at the bottom of his heart'.

   paterna rura: paternal acres.

129   *défendu*: 'out of bounds'.

130   *Voltaire's conception of Joan of Arc*: in his satirical epic *La Pucelle d'Orléans* (1755).

   the Battle of Prague: fought on 6 May 1757; the Itzenplitz Regiment under Prince Heinrich were decisive in gaining the victory for Friedrich the Great.

   Hradshin Castle: fortress in Prague and the city's symbol.

   'Schwerin with the banner': Kurt Christoph Count von Schwerin fell at the Battle of Prague, banner in hand, at the head of the Prussian left flank; probably through the fact of his death he was accorded the glory of having been chiefly responsible for the victory.

130 *'bêtise'*: act of stupidity.

131 *the new regime*: that of Friedrich the Great's successor, Friedrich Wilhelm II (reigned 1786–97).

petticoat government . . . Madame Rietz: alludes to the mistresses with whom Friedrich Wilhelm entertained himself and who were supposed to have exercised more influence over his decisions than they ought to have done; Countess Lichtenau, Madame Rietz (1752–1820) was among them.

132 *'Je la déteste . . . jamais aux femmes'*: 'I loathe her to the bottom of my heart; as you know well enough, I am attentive to ladies, but never to women.'

133 *falconets*: light cannon.

134 *declamatoria . . . hombre*: the former are evenings of miscellaneous songs, recitations and musical numbers, the latter is a card game popular in the eighteenth century.

Count Drosselstein: adapted from the name of Count Finkenstein, a friend and political collaborator of Marwitz's. (*Fink* = finch, *Drossel* = thrush.)

Hohen-Ziesar: modelled on the estate of Hohen-Jesar, in the Oderbruch.

superintendent: a rank in the Lutheran Church equivalent to that of a bishop.

135 *'Tous les gens . . . l'ennuyeux'*: 'Everybody is good except the tedious.'

136 *Chairman von Krach*: in the original 'Präsident': in this instance the chairman of a court or a presiding judge.

Bamme: the name is that of a family from West Havel-land—a county on the western edge of Brandenburg—but the character is modelled on Emil Count von Zieten (1765–1854), the son of the founder of the Zieten Hussars, described by Fontane in the *Wanderungen*.

Königsberg: the then capital of the province of East Prussia.

137 *Potsdam*: town to the south-west of Berlin, the political and cultural centre of Friedrich the Great's Prussia.

138 *Rigi*: mountain near Lake Lucerne.

Altorf or Küssnacht: Swiss villages familiar in Germany from Schiller's *Wilhelm Tell*.

143 *'L'immoralité . . . contre l'hypocrisie'*: 'Public immorality is the only sure protection against hypocrisy' (La Rochefoucauld.)

144 *Cedo majori*: I give way to the greater.

146 *a descriptive account of the Oderbruch*: Walter Christiani's *Das Oderbruch* (1855), employed by Fontane for the *Wanderungen*.

150 *'Soyez les bien-venus'*: 'Be welcome.'

causeuse: sofa for two people.

151 *ça dit tout*: that says everything.

Bêtise allemande: German stupidity.

C'est étonnant: It is astonishing.

par un caprice du sort: by a caprice of fate.

Dieu m'en garde!: God save me from it.

A quoi bon?: To what purpose?

152 *et voilà ce qui me fâche*: and that is what annoys me.

je n'aime pas à marchander les mots: I do not like to haggle over words.

Oh cet air . . . ne se perdra-t-il jamais?: Oh, will there never be an end to this bourgeois manner?

Je ne le comprends pas: I do not understand it.

je les respecte . . . caricature: I respect them, but I despise distortions of them.

154 *Banquet of the Gods*: by Raphael. The Farnesina is a Renaissance building in Rome.

oh je me le rappelle très bien: oh, I remember very well.

155 *Count Haugwitz*: (1752–1832), Prussian chief minister in 1805–6.

'Eh bien . . . c'est très bien': Well, what is that supposed to mean?' 'Sire, this is how they handed dispatches to Louis XVI.' 'Ah, that is well done.'

156 *the White Room*: the grand hall at the palace at Berlin.

Abbé Sieyès: (1748–1836): played a leading role in many of the events of the revolutionary and Napoleonic periods, including voting as a member of the National Assembly for the execution of Louis XVI, when he decreed *'La mort sans phrase'* ('No quibbling: death').

Soult: Marshal Soult (1769–1851), Napoleonic general.

Davoust: Marshal Davoust (1770–1823), Napoleonic general.

King Murat: Joachim Murat (1771–1815), the son of an innkeeper, acquired in succession the titles of Napoleon's adjutant (1795) and brother-in-law (1800), Marshal of France (1804), Grand-Duke of Berg (1804), King of Naples and King Joachim I Napoleon of Both Sicilies (1808); one of the most flamboyant figures of the Napoleonic era.

157 *he rode . . . into the sand*: alludes to Murat's role in the Battle of the Pyramids (1798).

  Zietenscher: i.e. a member, or former member, of the Zieten Hussars.

  King Friedrich Wilhelm I: King of Prussia from 1713 to 1740, the father of Friedrich the Great; the acquisition of Berg had been one of his objectives (hence 'ruled not only Berg').

158 *the young man of Nain . . . celebrated female equivalent*: both raised from the dead by Jesus: see Luke 7: 11–15, and 8:41–6 (the latter is the daughter of Jairus).

159 *the elder daughter's son*: After their escape from the blazing Sodom, Lot and his two daughters took refuge in a cave, where, in anxiety for the survival of their race in the absence of men, the daughters seduced their father and became pregnant. The elder of the two bore a son, whom she named Moab; and the heirs of Moab became implacable foes of the Israelites. The local pastor leaves Bamme alone hereafter because Bamme has told him he is a Moabite.

161 *Nullum . . . hungaricum*: Hungarian is your only wine.

162 *Liebfrauenmilch . . . Hessians*: Liebfrauenmilch—now called more briefly Liebfraumilch—is wine from Rheinhessen. Traditionally supposed to have been at first the product of the vineyard around the Liebfrauenkirche—the Church of Our Lady—at Worms, it has long since been a generic name without legal standing.

163 *the cowhorns . . . filled with terror*: alludes to the Swiss victories of the fifteenth century over the Burgundians.

  Gustavus Adolphus: King of Sweden from 1611 to 1632 and a leading figure in the Thirty Years War.

164 *Suum cuique*: To each his own: the motto of the Prussian Order of the Black Eagle.

165 *the minister*: Karl August von Hardenberg (1750–1822). The details of Berndt's interview with the minister are derived from Marwitz's interview with Hardenberg at Christmas 1812. See also the note to page 23 (*Berndt von Vitzewitz*).

167 *il faut en convenir*: one has to agree with him.

ça se désapprend: that is something you unlearn.

il affronte nos préjugés: he defies our prejudices.

Louis Quatorze: Louis XIV, King of France from 1643 to 1715.

Ce n'est pas ça: Not at all.

et ce Louis . . . idole: and that Louis himself, he is not my idol.

Le bon roi Henri: The good King Henri: Henry IV, King of France from 1589 to 1610.

168   *'J'ai vu . . . Sa Majesté'*: 'I have seen the King, but not His Majesty.'

'Que s'il n'avait . . . été pendu': 'That if he had not been king he would have been hanged.'

the fair Gabriele: Gabrielle d'Estrées (1571–99), mistress of Henri IV.

169   *'Non, je ne veux pas . . . fâcherait trop'*: 'No, I don't want to go in; it would upset her too much.'

'Souvent femme . . . ': 'Women are very changeable, and he is a fool who trusts them.'

'Celui-ci est . . . notre bon Henri': 'This is the grandson of our good Henri.'

170   *Count Tauentzien*: Emanuel Count Tauentzien (1760–1824), a favoured courtier at Rheinsberg. His portrait is among those hanging at Schloss Guse. The introduction of his name moves the conversation from France to Germany, where it swiftly becomes more acrimonious: 'the prince' in the following sentence is Prince Heinrich of Prussia, brother of Friedrich the Great; 'the King' in the sentence after that is Friedrich.

'Le prince . . . de fautes': 'The prince is the only one who never made a mistake'; supposedly said of Prince Heinrich by Friedrich in allusion to the campaigns of the Seven Years War.

surprised at Hochkirch: the Battle of Hochkirch, 14 October 1758, at which a night attack by the Austrians decided the battle in their favour.

won at Leuthen: the Battle of Leuthen, 5 December 1757, at which Friedrich won a victory over a vastly superior Austrian force.

de temps à temps: from time to time.

171   *Princess Amalie*: Anna Amalie, Princess of Prussia (1723–87).

172   *Chez soi*: At home.

properly asleep: in the original the sentence continues: 'und es war eine Feinheit unserer Sprache, das richtig drapierte Grossbett ohne weiteres zum Himmelbett zu erheben', an observation which would lose its point in English.

176 *Tout va bien!*: All goes well.

le style c'est l'homme: the style is the person.

et comme j'espère: and, as I hope.

de la Harpe: Jean François de la Harpe (1739–1803), French dramatist and literary historian.

Lemierre: Antoine Martin Lemierre (1723–93), French dramatist; his *Guillaume Tell* was staged in 1766.

justement parce qu'il . . . maturité: precisely because it does not possess this maturity.

s'accommoder au goût . . . notre temps: To accommodate oneself to the general taste is what our age commands.

et encore plus la surprise: and then in addition the surprise.

cher Docteur . . . à bonté: dear Doctor, and that is why I am relying on your goodness.

J'en suis sûre: I am certain of it.

N'oubliez pas . . . votre affectionnée A.P.: Do not forget I am expecting you on the 30th. I am, with the very greatest respect, your devoted A.P.

178 *Crown Prince Friedrich*: i.e. the later Friedrich the Great; for his 'desertion' see the note to page 633 (*Katte*).

the same year as the English bombarded the city: i.e. 1807.

182 *when the Lichtenau soap-bubble burst*: with the death of Friedrich Wilhelm II in 1797.

Genoveva: Tieck's tragedy *Leben und Tod der heiligen Genoveva* appeared in the second volume of his *Romantische Dichtungen* in 1800.

184 *Arnold von Winkelried*: according to tradition, Winkelried secured the victory of the Swiss in the Battle of Sempach on 9 July 1386 by voluntarily sacrificing his life.

185 *Kleist*: Ewald von Kleist (1715–59), major, died of wounds received at Kunersdorf; he was also a poet and the memorial to him in Frankfurt is visited by Berndt and others during the 'reconnoitring visit' to the city.

186 *the Bug and the Vistula*: The Vistula flows from the Carpathian mountains through Poland to the Baltic at Gdansk. Its tributary

the Bug now forms the boundary between Poland and the Ukraine.

in medias res: in the middle of the thing.

'In manus tuas . . . spiritum meum': 'Father, into thy hands I commend my spirit'—the last words of Christ on the Cross.

190   *the two Schlegels*: August Wilhelm (1767–1845) and Friedrich (1772–1824), leading figures of the Romantic movement in Germany.

Wackenroder: Wilhelm Heinrich Wackenroder (1773–98), a pioneer of the Romantic movement.

191   *Roma locuta est*: Rome has spoken.

Novalis: Friedrich von Hardenberg (1772–1801), who wrote under the name Novalis, is by general agreement the finest lyrical talent among the early Romantics. His family were Herrnhuters.

his novel: *Heinrich von Ofterdingen* (published posthumously in 1802); the 'Hymn of the Crusaders' and the 'Miner's Song' are contained in this novel, to which Tubal's acquaintanceship with Novalis hence seems to be limited.

Hymns to the Night: published in 1800: some are in prose.

192   *Amid the people . . .* : From No. 5 of the *Hymns to the Night*; but again Fontane has not quoted literally.

de tout mon cœur: with all my heart.

193   *Sacred Songs*: published posthumously in 1802.

When all become unfaithful . . . : 'Wenn alle untreu werden', the first two stanzas of the sixth (not the first, as Faulstich says) of the *Sacred Songs*.

Paul Gerhardt: (1607–76), Protestant hymn-writer. 'O sacred head sore wounded' is the English version of 'O Haupt voll Blut und Wunden', referred to again on page 504. See also the note to page 654.

206   *Kyritz*: the events here described took place on 8 April 1807; Fontane derived his knowledge of them from a brochure published in 1845, from which Berndt's speech quotes almost literally.

209   *Hofer*: Andreas Hofer (1767–1810), the national hero of Tyrol, led the Tyrolese against Napoleon.

Franz'l: the Emperor Franz I of Austria.

215   *the last encounter . . . Kosciuszko*: Tadeusz Kosciuszko (1746–1817) led the Polish resistance to the Russian invasion from 1792 until he was taken prisoner at Maciejowice on 11 October 1794—the 'last encounter' referred to.

241   *tell me about the Greenlanders*: Aunt Schorlemmer's recollections of Greenland are drawn from the *Historie von Grönland* by the Herrnhut missionary David Cranz.

265   *Que Dieu . . . sa garde*: May God keep you, you and my letter, in his protection.

266   *Melpomene*: the muse of tragedy. *Clio:* the muse of history. *Polyhymnia*: the muse of lyric poetry.

       Racine: Jean de Racine (1639–99), the great tragic dramatist; reference to the house of Atreus, Electra and Clytemnestra alludes to the classical provenance of the plots of Racine's tragedies.

267   *Mon cœur aux dames*: My heart belongs to the ladies.

269   *Demoiselle Alceste*: modelled on the Aurora Bursay mentioned in the following sentence and on the popular actress Élise Rachel (1820–58), who enjoyed great success in Racine. The theatrical presentation at Guse is modelled on those that took place at the Rheinsberg court.

       Phaedra . . . coronation of Louis XVI: Racine's tragedy; Louis XVI crowned in 1774.

270   *'Je suis charmée . . . couronne de Pologne'*: 'I am delighted to see you . . . Madame la Comtesse, your dear aunt, has told me a great deal about you. You are Polish. Ah, I have a great love for the Poles. They are absolutely the French of the North. You no doubt know that Prince Heinrich very nearly accepted the crown of Poland.'

271   *'Mais quelle bêtise . . . roi de Prusse'*: 'But how stupid of me; I am altogether Polish yet now I am prepared to work for the King of Prussia.' The last phrase, *'travailler pour le roi de Prusse'*, also meant to labour without gaining anything.

272   *à tout prix*: at any price.

       lettre-de-cachet: arrest warrant signed by the King and executed without any legal formality.

273   *'Vous ferez tout cela'*: 'You will do all that.'

275   *Théâtre du Château de Guse . . . a Kirch-Goeritz*: Theatre of the Château de Guse. Thursday 31 December 1812. The perform-

ance will begin at nine o'clock. 1. Overture performed under the direction of M. Nippler, cantor of Guse, by 3 violins, 1 flute and 1 double-bass. 2. Prologue (Melpomene). 3. Début of Mademoiselle Alceste Bonnivant. Various scenes selected from William Tell. Tragedy in five acts by Lemierre. a. Cléofé, Tell's wife, addressing her husband: Why then are you keeping secrets from me, and hiding from me as though I were a stranger? b. Cléofé, addressing Gesler's [sic] guards: I want to see my husband, you detain me in vain, etc. c. Cléofé, addressing Gesler: What, Gesler, if I should fetch one of my sons here before you, etc. d. Cléofé, addressing Walther Fürst: That was the moment to raise up Switzerland in revolt. You have let it go by! 4. Finale composed for 2 violins and 1 flute by M. Nippler. The Assistant Director: Dr Faulstich. Printed by P. Nottebohm, bookbinder, bookseller and publisher in Kirch-Goeritz.

the 'bass's fundamental force': from the scene in Auerbach's cellar in Goethe's *Faust* I.

276   *'I have no second if the first should fail'*: a line from Schiller's *Wilhelm Tell* (Tell, meditating shooting the provincial governor, reflects that he has only one arrow).

278   *'The tyrant's dead! . . . is liberty!'*: Lemierre's French is reproduced in a free translation by Fontane; the present version is a translation of Fontane's German.

279   *Charles Douze: Histoire de Charles XII* (of Sweden), by Voltaire (1731).

281   *no cash, no Swiss . . . no Swiss, no cash*: this *bon mot* was, in its original form, 'Kein Kreuzer, kein Schweizer'—'No Kreuzers, no Swiss'—in allusion to the availability of Swiss troops only in exchange for cash.

        Lemierre, n'est qu'un auteur de second rang: Lemierre is an author only of the second rank.

        the Wilhelm Tell *of Herr Schiller*: *Wilhelm Tell* had been produced at Weimar on 17 March 1804 and published in the following October. 'Herr' is disparaging in the case of so famous an author. Schiller had died in 1805, but was none the less still a contemporary writer whose themes were in fact even more immediately relevant to the time of *Before the Storm* than they had been to his own. That of *Wilhelm Tell*, his last completed play, is of course the very theme of the moment. Like Berndt von Vitzewitz, Fontane's first readers would be familiar with it and ignorant of Lemierre's version of the Tell story; but from the scenes from

Lemierre presented at Schloss Guse and the nature of Aunt Amelie's objections to Schiller it is easy to see why the former is preferred to the latter: it is a preference for French Classicism over German Romanticism, regardless of the quality of the example by which each is represented. In the context of Fontane's novel, however, such a preference is reactionary; and Berndt, the advocate of Schiller, becomes, paradoxically in view of his social position and conservative disposition, the representative of the wave of the future. (I take the reproduction of the theatre programme in French to be, not a foible of the author's, but part of his representation of the 'freethinking' Schloss Guse as being in fact a fossil of the eighteenth century; just as the apparently unchanging Hohen-Vietz, with its church and parsonage and feudal-seeming social structure, in fact contains the seeds of the nineteenth.)

like Max Piccolomini: in Schiller's *Wallensteins Tod* (1799).

282   *ennobled him*: Schiller was 'ennobled' in 1802.

283   *Corneille*: Pierre Corneille (1606–84), French dramatist.

'Monsieur le baron . . . la meilleure politique': 'Monsieur le baron, you are right, and I am happy to make the acquaintanceship of a true nobleman. I have a great love of France, but I love even more good-hearted men wherever I may find them. . . . A thousand apologies, Madame la comtesse, but you no doubt recall the favourite maxim of our dear prince: the best policy is the truth.'

BOOK THREE

289   *Johanniter Palace*; 'Johanniter' is the German form of the Knights of St John of Jerusalem; Prince Ferdinand, whose residence is the Johanniter Palace, is the Grand Master of the Prussian branch of the order.

King of Portugal . . . Green Tree: the former an inn much patronized by the nobility; the latter is the inn in the Klosterstrasse obliquely opposite Frau Hulen's out of which Krist drove in the opening sentences of the novel.

290   *The heroic death of his eldest son*: already seized on, earlier in the novel, as the fact with which Prince Ferdinand is commonly identified; his son, Prince Louis (1772–1806), died at Saalfeld on 10 October 1806 after a career which had made of him a popular hero.

291   *Graff*: Anton Graff (1736–1813), German portrait painter.

Jupiter tonans: Jupiter the Thunderer.

293 *my great-nephew . . . the count, his first minister*: Friedrich Wilhelm III (King of Prussia from 1797 to 1840) and Count von Hardenberg; Hardenberg had already been chief minister at the time of the alliance with Napoleon and the resultant resignation of the three hundred officers (see Introduction, page xix above).

abolished with a stroke of the pen: by an edict of 30 October 1810 the original Brandenburg Province of the Johanniterorden was abolished; it was reconstituted as the Royal Prussian Johanniterorden in 1812.

commanderies: subdivisions of a province in the structure of a knightly order.

296 *Aide-toi . . . t'aidera*: Help yourself and Heaven will help you.

297 *Windmühlenberg*: i.e. Windmill Hill, a height outside the city opposite the Schönhauser Tor.

299 *Cottbus*: town on the Spree, about sixty miles south-south-east of Berlin.

301 *Masuren*: district of East Prussia.

302 *Saldern*: Friedrich Christoph Saldern (1719–85), Prussian general.

Möllendorf: Heinrich Count von Möllendorf (1724–1816), Prussian field marshal.

Ännchen von Tharau . . . O Schill, thy sabre doth hurt: except for the first and second—which are by Herder and Schiller respectively—these are popular ballads of the time.

'*Await, Bonaparte . . .*': by Fontane, in the style of a popular ballad.

303 *Austerlitz*: the Battle of Austerlitz, 2 December 1805; Napoleon welcomed the rising sun breaking through the fog on the morning of the battle as an omen of victory.

305 *Like Mack at Ulm*: the surrender of the Austrian general to the French at Ulm in 1805.

308 *Spoon Guards*: this expression is explained on pages 330–1 below.

309 *Giulio Romano*: Giulio Pippi (1499–1546), a pupil of Raphael's.

310 *the Moniteur*: at the time Ladalinski reads it the official organ of the French government.

311 *the accession of King Friedrich Wilhelm II*: in 1786.

von Bischofswerder: Johann Rudolf von Bischoffswerder (1741–1803), general and the King's chief minister.

312   *the campaign against Ivan the Terrible*: 1578–82.

       the Battle of Tannenberg: 15 July 1410.

       fell before Vienna: 12 September 1683, fighting the Turks.

314   *Szczekociny*: on 6 June 1794, Russian victory over the Poles.

315   *Praga*: suburb of Warsaw, entered by the Russians on 4 November 1794.

       Suvorov: Alexander Suvorov (1729–1800), Russian general.

       Reformed Church: tending towards Calvinism, and more Protestant in the modern sense than the Lutheran Church.

317   *et en effet . . . enchantée*: and they did indeed enchant me.

       avec un teint de lys et de rose: with a complexion of lilies and roses.

       Vous savez . . . nos volontés: You have known all this for a long time. But things are not ordered according to our desires.

       qui ne l'aurait pas?: as who has not?

318   *Et l'un est aussi . . . l'autre*: And the one is as bad as the other.

       mon cher beau-frère: my dear brother-in-law.

       comme je souhaite sincèrement: as I sincerely hope.

       Et je suis du même avis: And I am of the same opinion.

       Je faisais mention de la France: I mentioned France.

       Il organise tout le monde: He organizes everybody.

       'call to arms' . . . can appear only tragi-comic: the phrase translated 'call to arms' is in the original 'Letztes Aufgebot'; 'Aufgebot' means general summons, levy, conscription, and the like, but 'last summons' is equivalent to the 'last time of asking', the third and last calling of wedding banns: hence Aunt Amelie's amusement.

       C'est son métier: It is his profession.

       Marshal Ney: (1769–1815), French general.

       Quant à moi: So far as I am concerned.

       Car le ridicule . . . de pitié: For the ridiculous never evokes pity.

       J'en suis convaincu: I am convinced of it.

318   *le centre . . . Amélie P*: the centre of European civilization. I desire it in the general interest and in our own. May God take you into His holy protection, my dear Ladalinski. Wholly yours, your good friend Amélie P.

319   *'Like an eternal . . .'*: Ladalinski is interrupted at the beginning of a

quotation from Goethe's *Faust* I: 'Es erben sich Gesetz und Rechte...': in Albert Latham's translation: 'Like an eternal, rank contagion,/Statutes and laws are inherited./They drag from generation on to generation,/And stealthily from place to place they spread.'

320 *Die Räuber*: Schiller's first play, published 1781, performed 13 January 1783 in Mannheim.

322 *Queen Luise*: (1776–1810), the wife of Friedrich Wilhelm III.

328 *The* 'Schweizerfamilie': song by Joseph Weigl (1776–1846). *'Bei Männern . . .'*: from Mozart's *The Magic Flute*.

332 *the Rheinsberg memorial*: an obelisk erected at Rheinsberg in memory of the fallen in the Seven Years War and solemnly dedicated on 4 July 1791.

333 *Justitia fundamentum imperii*: Justice is the foundation of empire.

the mill at Sanssouci: according to a pious but, it appears, fictional tradition, Friedrich the Great wished to close down a mill operating close to the palace of Sanssouci at Potsdam on account of the noise it made but was prevented from doing so by the Court of Appeal when the miller applied to it for protection.

the trial of Arnold the miller: Johann Arnold, another miller, worsted in a court action, appealed to Friedrich the Great to reverse the court's decision; convinced (wrongly, it seems) that Arnold had not had justice, Friedrich instructed the court to find in his favour; the court refused to do so; Friedrich took the matter to a higher court, but with no better result; he had officials dismissed or arrested, he moved from one instance to another, but still he found himself defied, and for no other reason than that what he was demanding was illegal; finally he was obliged to settle the issue with a Cabinet Order, that is to say with a legal but, in the circumstances, wholly discreditable assertion of his personal will (the order was reversed after his death). These two stories, one a fiction, the other fact, were repeated as a demonstration that Friedrich's subjects were by no means blind hero-worshippers who fancied the King could do no wrong, and that, beyond respect for the monarchy and the army, the Prussian state reposed on a respect for the law.

'there are still judges in Berlin': a proverbial saying derived from a line in Jean Andrieux's verse tale *Le Meunier de Sanssouci* (1797).

335 *it was Major von Lestwitz*: this is the Lestwitz who *'a sauvé l'état'* (see page 123).

336 *'Where the Alpine roses clamber . . .'*: the original of these stanzas is by August von Kotzebue (1761–1819), who translated the operetta for performance at Berlin.

342 dame d'atour *to the Queen Mother*: lady-in-waiting to the widow of Friedrich Wilhelm II, the predecessor of the reigning Friedrich Wilhelm III.

343 *Herr Valentin von Massow . . . Herr Fleck*: all these personages were active in the Berlin of the time, except for Herr Fleck, who had died in 1801; the anachronism was pointed out to Fontane long after the novel had appeared but he was unable to correct it.

344 *Hauptmann*: captain of infantry. *Rittmeister*: captain of cavalry.

346 *Tres faciunt collegium*: Three make a quorum.

conspectus: watching.

347 *Goecking Hussars*: later name of the Zieten Hussars.

348 *York has capitulated*: See Introduction, p. xx above.

Eh bien!: And so?

351 *the equestrian statue of the Great Elector*: by Andreas Schlüter; now stands at Charlottenburg.

Bernauer: blowing from the north-east, the direction of Bernau.

352 *'Graue Kloster'*: an ancient and famous grammar school.

353 *Be consoled . . .*: poem by Fontane, dating from 1876.

354 *Savigny*: 1779–1861, professor of law. *Thaer*: 1752–1828, agriculturalist. *Fichte*: 1762–1814, philosopher.

355 *Percy's* Reliques: Bishop Percy's *Reliques of Ancient English Poetry* (1765), influential in the creation of the German Romantic sensibility and one of Fontane's favourite books.

357 *Schinkel's renovations*: the residence of Count von Redern (1802–83) was renovated, in a way not to Fontane's taste, in 1832 by Karl Friedrich Schinkel.

Kleist: Field Marshal Friedrich Heinrich Kleist (1762–1823).

358 *'Sans doute . . . comme toujours'*: 'Without doubt, today as always.'

359 *Substantia*: food.

362 *Kalkreuth*: 1790–1873.

de la Motte Fouqué: 1777–1843, a prominent writer and man of letters of the period.

'The Sabbath': Himmerlich's poem is 'The Poet's Sabbath' by John Prince (1808–66), freely translated into German. Prince was

one of a number of English working-class poets in whom
Fontane's interest was aroused in the 1840s and whom he
translated with the idea of publishing a selection of them. I have
given Prince's original reproduced in the annotations to the
above-mentioned edition of *Vor dem Sturm*.

363   '*Beneficent is* . . . ': couplet from Schiller's *Das Lied von der Glocke*.

366   *Tasso* . . . *Ariosto*: Torquato Tasso (1544–95) and Lodovico
Ariosto (1474–1533), Italian poets.

367   *Seydlitz* . . . *Calcar*: Friedrich Wilhelm von Seydlitz (1721–73),
Prussian general, born at Calcar (or Kalkar) in Cleves. Hansen-
Grell's poem is one of three written by Fontane in celebration of
Seydlitz. *Calcar* is Latin for 'spur'.

capitatio benevolentiae: begging of a favour.

370   *Recollections* . . . *at Plaa*: the following 'recollections' were drawn
by Fontane from a volume published in Berlin in 1863: *Erin-
nerungen an Eugen und Moritz von Hirschfeld aus Deutschland und
Spanien*. The Captain von Hirschfeldt of the novel is modelled
on General Moritz von Hirschfeld, who saw service in Spain in
the campaign against Napoleon between 1809 and 1815.

the Duke of Brunswick . . . *for England*: the Duke (1771–1815)
raised a militia in Bohemia in 1809, fought the French across
Europe, and made his way to England, where he offered his
services and was dispatched to the Peninsular War. (He continued fighting Napoleon until his death at Quatrebras.)

384   *Zelter*: Karl Friedrich Zelter (1758–1832), musician and composer; Mendelssohn's teacher and a friend of Goethe's (his
correspondence with Goethe, for which he is now chiefly
remembered, consists of 840 letters written over a period of
more than thirty years).

Rungenhagen: Karl Friedrich Rungenhagen (1778–1851), musician and composer.

385   *Herder's* Völkerstimmen: Johann Gottfried Herder (1744–1803),
who is credited with having coined the word 'Volkslied',
published his *Volkslieder* in 1778–9 as an attempt to do for
German popular poetry what Percy's *Reliques* had done for
English, but also including versions of poems from a large
number of other nations and by known authors. When Johannes
von Müller produced a new edition in 1807 he gave it the title
Stimmen der Völker in Liedern.

There was a big fire last night: Renate's account of the fire at the manor house is based on Marwitz's account of a fire at Schloss Friedersdorf in May 1806. Marwitz blamed 'the gypsies'. The incident involving Hoppenmarieken also comes from the same source, where Marwitz narrates it of 'an old man' (*Aus dem Nachlasse Friedrich August Ludwigs von der Marwitz*, Berlin 1852).

391   *Tintoretto*: Jacopo Robusti (1512–94), the Venetian master.

     Joshua Reynolds: (1723–92), the English portraitist.

     the 'Great Boot': the story of the Great Boot has been lifted into the novel from the *Wanderungen*, where it is represented as having actually occurred. The officers of the Gensdarmes Regiment had a reputation for wildness of behaviour and for what Fontane calls, in English, 'practical jokes'.

     Pepinière: the military medical school.

392   *coûte que coûte*: at whatever cost.

     Ruppin: county in north-west Brandenburg, between Ost-Priegnitz and the Havel-land.

394   *Counts Brandt and Struensee*: alludes to a political and sex scandal of the 1770s. Struensee, the personal physician of the mentally unsound King Christian VII of Denmark, profited from his position to form an alliance with Queen Caroline Mathilde, and together they ruled the country in all but form. Struensee's political and personal enemies found their hour had struck when, in 1771, the Queen gave birth to a daughter; the father, they maintained, could only be Struensee, who had thus committed, among other things, high treason; Struensee was arrested and, on 28 April 1772, beheaded. Brandt was a favoured friend of the fallen physician and suffered the same fate.

397   *A la bonne heure*: That I like.

400   *Borodino*: the Battle of Borodino was fought on 7 September 1812 between the Grande Armée on its way to Moscow and the defending Russians under Kutuzov. 75,000 men died. Fontane appears to have had no single source for Meerheimb's account; but as a war reporter in the years 1864–71 he had had much experience in piecing together the reports of witnesses, and here he has applied the technique he then acquired to a historical battle.

402   *Junot*: Andoche Junot (1771–1813), French general.

     the Viceroy: Eugene Beauharnais (1781–1824), Viceroy of Italy, the son of Josephine Beauharnais, Napoleon's wife.

Poniatowski: Joseph Anton Prince Poniatowski (1762–1813), commander of the Polish forces in the Russian campaign.

Prince Vorontsov: (1782–1856), general of the Russian Army.

404   *'Sir de Lorges'* . . . *'glove out of the lion-pit'*: allusions to Schiller's ballad 'Der Handschuh', in which the Ritter Delorges performs this act.

General von Thielmann: (1756–1824), led a cavalry brigade at Borodino.

409   *'Je payerai . . . ma patrie'*: 'I shall carry the can back, but I am sacrificing myself for the good of my country.'

410   *the* Vestale: opera by Spontini (1807).

415   *'Vous venez . . . de la Russie'*: 'You come . . . from Russia.'

416   *'Entendez-vous?'* . . . *'Ce sont . . . français!'*: 'Do you hear?' . . . 'Those are French trumpets!'

General Augereau: Charles Augereau (1757–1816), French marshal and duc de Castiglione.

418   *'Eh bien, hâtons-nous!'*: 'Very well, let us hurry.'

421   *Marwitz*: this is presumably Alexander von der Marwitz, the younger brother of Ludwig; he was a student of law in Berlin from 1811, and died in 1814 at the age of twenty-seven.

Turkish Pavilion: restaurant in Charlottenburg.

423   *Breslau*: city in Silesia about 300 miles south-east of Berlin (now Polish under the name Wroclaw).

428   *'Revelation 2:10'*: 'be thou faithful unto death, and I will give thee a crown of life.'

the ring of Polycrates: Polycrates, tyrant of Samos, threw his ring into the sea to ward off bad luck; a fisherman brought him a fish as a present; inside the fish they found the ring; Polycrates knew he was doomed. The 'ballad on it' is by Schiller.

six-le-va: a high stake at the game of faro.

429   *Puttkamers*: the noble family of which Bismarck's wife was a member.

431   *Lehnin . . . abbot's house*: Lehnin abbey, in the Havel-land.

433   *'All things . . . love God'*: from Romans 8:28.

'And if they . . . alive today': corresponds to the English 'And they lived happily ever after.'

the prophecy: the Lehnin Prophecy is an obscure and gloomy poem in Latin foretelling the fate of the March. Its author was one Martin Friedrich Seidel (died 1693).

436 *Heinrich von Kleist*: 1771–1811, dramatist and writer of fiction, a member of the Prussian military family and himself an army officer. He was born in Frankfurt-on-Oder. In 1811 he committed suicide, together with Henriette Vogel, on the edge of the Wannsee, the lake the party are now passing. His historical drama, *Das Käthchen von Heilbronn*, was first performed on 17 March 1810 in Vienna.

437 *communs*: buildings 'pour les communs'—i.e. the servants—next to the New Palace (new in 1769).

the Havel: river, rising west of Potsdam, flows north-west through the Havel-land until it joins the Elbe.

438 *Claude Lorrain*: Claude Gellée (1600–82), French painter.

439 *Anhaltians*: rulers of the territory of Anhalt, in central Germany; originally employing the name of the Ascanians, the various lines afterwards adopted their titles from the name Anhalt.

The Old Dessauer . . . Lustgarten . . . military march: Prince Leopold I von Anhalt-Dessau (1676–1747), called the 'Old Dessauer', field marshal of the Prussian Army. His statue stood in a former pleasure garden in Berlin transformed in 1716 into an army parade-ground, and the 'Dessauer March' is named after him.

Heinrich the Lion: 1129–80, Duke of Saxony and of Bavaria; he was a member of the Welf house and gained his honorific through his relentless contention with the Hohenstaufen Friedrich Barbarossa. As they were contemporaries, he and Albrecht the Bear inevitably came into conflict. The fair Matushka is, of course, merely recalling odds and scraps from her history lessons.

440 *the murder . . . of Lehnin*: Abbot Siebold, done to death in 1190: the story is told in the *Wanderungen*.

442 *Frater Hermannus*: according to Fontane, the true title of the so-called Lehnin Prophecy is: 'Prophecy of the late Brother Hermann, sometime monk at Lehnin, who lived and flourished in the year 1300'.

445 *Vivat Borussia! . . . Pereat Bonaparte!*: Long live Prussia! . . . Down with Bonaparte!

455 *the Hohenzollerns*: the ruling house of Brandenburg and then of Prussia. Johann Cicero was Elector from 1486 to 1499, Joachim Nestor, his son, from 1499 to 1535.

Director Bellermann: Johann Joachim Bellermann was director of the Graue Kloster from 1804.

459 *Hölderlin*: Friedrich Hölderlin (1770–1843); though his reputation now stands as high as it possibly could, in 1813 he was hardly known. 'In younger days' was written in 1798.

460 *'Lenore . . . at dawn'*: the opening line of Bürger's *'Lenore'*. The 'Wild Huntsman' is also by Bürger; Fontane produced a German version of the English ballad 'Chevy Chase'.

'Toujours perdrix': 'Always partridge'. The priestly confessor of Henri IV of France would not cease from upbraiding him for his numerous infidelities; the King had him served partridge every day for dinner; 'Always partridge,' the priest complained.

461 *Swabian Hyperion*: Hölderlin came from Swabia; *Hyperion* (1797–9) is the title of his one novel.

'One summer . . .': Hölderlin's poem 'An die Parzen', written in 1798.

465 *He had braid . . . tassel too thereon*: Lewin, apparently associating the *maréchal de logis* with Goliath, recalls a couplet from Matthias Claudius's poem 'The Story of Goliath and David'.

466 *'On the nameday . . . '*: Lewin remembers his rhyme in a slightly different form.

467 *'warm wind' . . . that is my role'*: a recollection of a line and the characters in Bürger's ballad 'Das Lied vom braven Manne'.

BOOK FOUR

480 *'Look down from Thy throne . . .'*: 'Schau von deinem Thron', hymn by Zinzendorf.

490 *Porst's hymn-book*: the hymnal edited by Johannes Porst (1668–1728).

501 *'All they . . . the sword'*: Matthew 26:52.

504 *'L'éloge . . . en mourant'*: 'Praise or blame no longer touch him who reposes in eternity. Hope beautified my life and attended me in death.'

507 *'Art thou . . . Vollgraf go!'*: an unsubtle pun on the name Füllgraf: 'Vollgraf' can be made to mean 'fully a count', i.e. a leader.

the 'Hohe Kavalier': a high bastion on the fortifications at Küstrin.

512 *Blücher*: Gebhard von Blücher (1742–1819), Prussian field marshal.

515 *Pirmasens*: Battle of Pirmasens, 14 September 1793, Prussian victory over the French.

518 *'Oft hast Thou . . .'*: from Gerhardt's hymn 'O Haupt voll Blut und Wunden'.

519 *the Fire of Moscow*: panoramic painting by Karl Friedrich Schinkel.

521 *Diderot*: Denis Diderot (1713–84), leading spirit of the Enlightenment.

527 *those gentlemen from Nuremberg . . . 'the Hohenzollerns versus Quitzow and Company'*: the Hohenzollern family originally came from Bavaria, where they were burgraves of Nuremberg; the old-established Brandenburg families affected to regard them as newcomers and upstarts.

531 *Pregelwater*: the Pregel is a river in East Prussia.

Junker von Otterstädt: as recorded in the *Wanderungen*, a certain Otterstädt inscribed a threatening verse on the door of the room occupied at Schloss Köpenick by the Elector Joachim II (1505–71).

532 *Manus manum lavat*: one hand washes the other.

533 *Bacchus*: god of wine. *Momus*: god of ridicule. *Pomona*: goddess of fruits and fruit-trees.

540 *the Proclamation*: see Introduction, page xx above.

542 *Tettenborn*: Friedrich Karl von Tettenborn (1778–1845), subsequently a cavalry general, was in 1812–13 in the Russian service at the head of a cavalry unit.

550 *ad vocem*: à propos.

551 *Dohna or Schön or Auerswald*: contemporary Prussian statesmen.

Chernichev: (1779–1857), commander of the Russian advance guard in the pursuit of the Grande Armée, subsequently a general.

554 *Peter Goldschmidt's* Höllischer Morpheus: published in 1698; an account of ghosts and poltergeists.

Rentsch's Brandenburgischer Zederhain: published about 1670; an account of the ruling house of Brandenburg.

556 *mais enfin, still une dame blanche*: but at any rate, still a woman in white.

tout-à-fait: wholly.

557 *'Ce maudit château'*: 'this accursed castle'; among the Woman in

White's appearances referred to by Bamme had been two at the château at Bayreuth while Napoleon was there.

ad latus: at the side of.

561 *Le jeu vaut la chandelle*: The game is worth the stake.

Hippel: Theodor Gottlieb von Hippel (1775–1843), the author of the Proclamation of 17 March 1813.

pur sang: of pure blood.

565 *'My very dear people . . .'*: the sermon that follows is adapted from one given under similar circumstances by Friedrich Schleiermacher, the leading Protestant theologian of the day.

574 *soutiens*: reserves.

576 *Carpe diem*: seize the day (Horace).

578 *Prince Eugen*: i.e. Prince Eugene of Savoy (1663–1736), celebrated general.

Montecuculi: i.e. Raimund Count of Montecuccoli (1609–80), general of the period of the Thirty Years War.

Alea jacta est: the die is cast (Caesar's words as he crossed the Rubicon).

579 *memorial to Duke Leopold*: he drowned in the Oder on 27 April 1785; according to tradition he was assisting in the rescue of people threatened by a flood.

582 *The Last Farthing*: Der letzte Heller was in fact the name of an inn in Alt-Berlin.

583 *the Karoline*: a billiard game played with five balls.

593 *the old rhyme*: it asserts that in Saxony pretty girls grow on trees.

597 *Battle of Budapest*: 17 August 1686.

horn of Uri: alluded to in Schiller's *Wilhelm Tell*.

604 *The attack*: the minuteness of detail with which the ensuing events are described notwithstanding, the attack on the garrison at Frankfurt is unhistorical and an invention of Fontane's. It appears from the memoirs of Marwitz already referred to that Marwitz proposed such an attack to Tettenborn but the latter already had in mind an attack on Berlin and declined to be diverted from it; whereupon Marwitz abandoned the idea. The burning of the bridge over the Oder was also envisaged by Marwitz, though this too failed to be put into effect (except by the French themselves later in the month as a means of covering their retreat). It was from these brief references that Fontane developed the action of the following chapters.

611   *Petit crevé*: Little scoundrel.

616   *'pour combler le malheur'*: 'to complete the misfortune'.

633   *the execution of Katte*: the father–son conflict between Friedrich Wilhelm I and the later Friedrich II produced at least one fatality: Hans von Katte, a lieutenant in the Gensdarmes Regiment, and one of the close friends of Friedrich's youth. Katte accompanied Friedrich in a decampment which the King decided to regard as an attempt at desertion; both young men were tried by court-martial and Katte was sentenced to death; the sentence was carried out with the sword at Küstrin on 6 November 1730, Friedrich being compelled to witness it.

635   *chasseur à pied*: foot-soldier.

644   *oratio pro domo*: speech in his own cause.

650   *patience or mariage*: card games, with of course a quibble on their usual meaning.

651   *'trocata'* . . . *'simplex'*: strong/weak sedative.

652   *Cita mors ruit*: Death is coming quickly.

654   *'When I must be departing . . .'*: a stanza from 'O Haupt voll Blut und Wunden'.

655   *'Salve caput cruentatum . . .'*: 'Hail, head sore wounded/Crowned all with thorns/Abused, injured/With face spat upon . . .' Medieval hymn of disputed authorship, the basis of Paul Gerhardt's 'O Haupt voll Blut und Wunden'.

667   *in corpore*: in a body.

669   *sub rosa*: concealed.

679   *Kloster Lindow*: in the county of Ruppin, north-west of Berlin, on the Gudelacksee.